BY ALISON WEIR

FICTION

A Dangerous Inheritance: A Novel of Tudor Rivals
and the Secret of the Tower

Captive Queen: A Novel of Eleanor of Aquitaine

The Lady Elizabeth: A Novel

Innocent Traitor: A Novel of Lady Jane Grey

NONFICTION

Mary Boleyn: The Mistress of Kings

The Lady in the Tower: The Fall of Anne Boleyn

Mistress of the Monarchy:
The Life of Katherine Swynford, Duchess of Lancaster

Queen Isabella: Treachery, Adultery, and
Murder in Medieval England

Mary, Queen of Scots, and the Murder of Lord Darnley

Henry VIII: The King and His Court

Eleanor of Aquitaine: A Life

The Life of Elizabeth I

The Children of Henry VIII

The Wars of the Roses

The Princes in the Tower

The Six Wives of Henry VIII

A DANGEROUS INHERITANCE

A Dangerous Inheritance

*A Novel of Tudor Rivals and
the Secret of the Tower*

ALISON WEIR

DOUBLEDAY CANADA

Doubleday Canada and colophon are registered trademarks

A Dangerous Inheritance is a work of historical fiction. Apart from the well-known actual people, events, and locales that figure in the narrative, all names, characters, places, and incidents are the products of the author's imagination or are used fictitiously. Any resemblance to current events or locales, or to living persons, is entirely coincidental.

Library and Archives Canada Cataloguing in Publication

Weir, Alison
A dangerous inheritance / Alison Weir.

Issued also in an electronic format.
ISBN 978-0-385-66710-4

I. Title.

PR6123.E36D36 2012   823'.92   C2012-902366-3

Originally published by Hutchinson, a division of Random House Group Limited, London.

Book design by Dana Leigh Blanchette
Title-page image: © iStockphoto
Jacket design: Victoria Allen
Jacket photograph: Jeff Cottenden

Printed and bound in the USA

Published in Canada by Doubleday Canada,
a division of Random House of Canada Limited

www.randomhouse.ca

10 9 8 7 6 5 4 3 2 1

To Rezia Jane Marston and
Persephone Gipps-Williams,
with lots of love

As circles five by art compressed show but one ring to sight,
So trust uniteth faithful minds, with knot of secret might,
Whose force to break (but greedy Death) no wight possesseth
    power,
As time and sequels well shall prove.
My ring can say no more.

—Lines engraved on
Katherine Grey's wedding ring

Love is a torment of the mind, A tempest everlasting . . .

—Samuel Daniel,
"Hymen's Triumph"

Love is blind.

—William Shakespeare,
The Two Gentlemen of Verona

Contents

The Royal House of Tudor

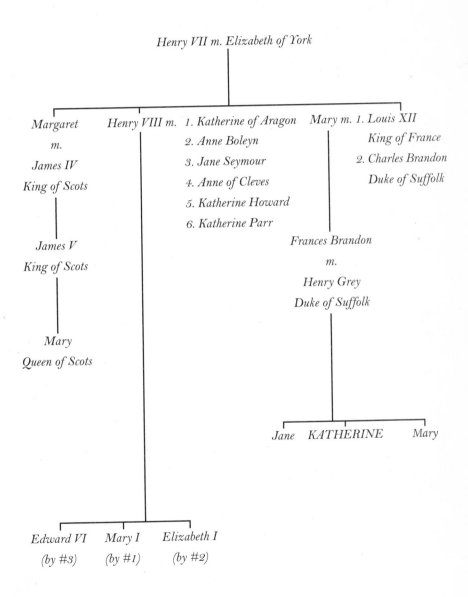

Henry VII m. Elizabeth of York

Margaret   Henry VIII m.   1. Katherine of Aragon   Mary m. 1. Louis XII
m.   2. Anne Boleyn   King of France
James IV   3. Jane Seymour   2. Charles Brandon
King of Scots   4. Anne of Cleves   Duke of Suffolk
                           5. Katherine Howard
James V   6. Katherine Parr
King of Scots   Frances Brandon
                                      m.
Mary   Henry Grey
Queen of Scots   Duke of Suffolk

Jane   KATHERINE   Mary

Edward VI   Mary I   Elizabeth I
(by #3)   (by #1)   (by #2)

The Royal Houses of Lancaster and York

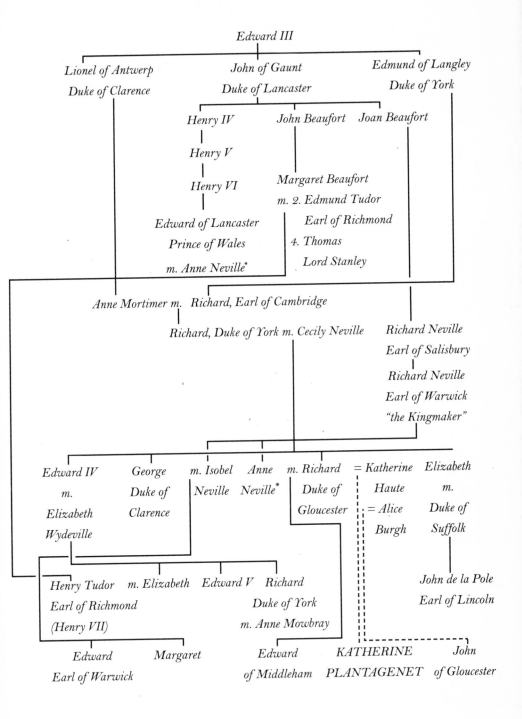

The Herbert Family

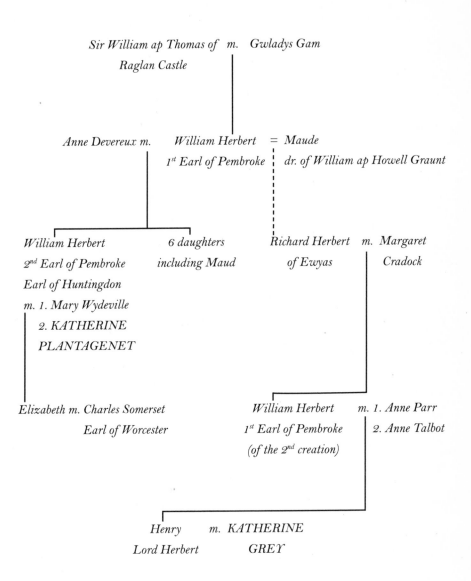

Sir William ap Thomas of m. Gwladys Gam
Raglan Castle

Anne Devereux m.   William Herbert   =   Maude
       1st Earl of Pembroke   dr. of William ap Howell Graunt

William Herbert   6 daughters   Richard Herbert   m.   Margaret
2nd Earl of Pembroke   including Maud   of Ewyas   Cradock
Earl of Huntingdon
m. 1. Mary Wydeville
   2. KATHERINE
   PLANTAGENET

Elizabeth m. Charles Somerset   William Herbert   m. 1. Anne Parr
     Earl of Worcester   1st Earl of Pembroke   2. Anne Talbot
                     (of the 2nd creation)

Henry   m. KATHERINE
Lord Herbert   GREY

The Seymour Family

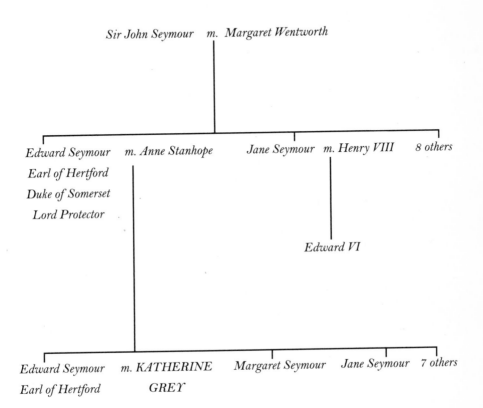

Sir John Seymour   m.   Margaret Wentworth

Edward Seymour   m. Anne Stanhope   Jane Seymour   m. Henry VIII   8 others
Earl of Hertford
Duke of Somerset
Lord Protector

Edward VI

Edward Seymour   m. KATHERINE   Margaret Seymour   Jane Seymour   7 others
Earl of Hertford   GREY

1568

I can never forget the day they brought me the news that my sister's head had been cut off. I was not yet thirteen, too young fully to understand why she had to die, but old enough to imagine the horrific scene at the end. They said she had committed treason, the foulest of all crimes, but it didn't make any sense to me, for Jane had only done what she was forced to do. And by that reasoning, I too had been an innocent traitor, just as she was.

We had none of us girls been born to inherit a crown, and yet it has overshadowed us all our lives—and blighted them. I thought once that it would be a wonderful thing to be a queen, to wield power and wear the coveted diadem—but I know differently now. Tangling with princes rarely brought anyone anything but ill-fortune and grief. I have learned that lesson too, in the hardest of ways. I am no longer the innocent, placid child who struggled with shyness and lessons, and was happiest running free in the spacious wilds of Charnwood Forest or playing with my dogs, my birds, and my monkeys.

If, in the future, there is to be any remnant of that kind of happiness for me in this world, it remains in the gift of Almighty God alone, for I can hope for little from my earthly sovereign.

In the meantime, I must languish here, in this fine house that is really my prison, having little to distract me from my trials but the routines of everyday life and the stilted exchange of pleasantries with my unwilling hosts. The only pleasures—if that is the right word—that are left to me are writing daily in this journal that I began so many years ago, and gazing yearningly from my window across the flat green parkland and skeletal trees to the forbidden distance, beyond which lives the man I love more than life itself.

Part One

Acts of Usurpation

KATHERINE

May 25, 1553; Durham House, London

Today is our wedding day. My sister Jane and I are to be married; all has been arranged so that the one ceremony will serve for both the daughters of my lord the Duke of Suffolk and my lady the duchess. It has come upon us so quickly that I have scarce had time to catch my breath, and am somewhat stunned to find myself standing in this royally appointed bedchamber being decked out in my bridal robes.

Below the latticed windows the River Thames, busy with craft and the shouts of boatmen, glides swiftly past London toward the distant sea. There is the usual whiff of fish, mud, and rotting stuff in the warm air, but the light breeze that stirs the heavy damask curtains and caresses my skin is pleasant, and faintly redolent of the flowers in the formal gardens that cluster below around Durham House.

We stand like statues as our nurse, Mrs. Ellen, and our tirewoman, Bridget, fuss around us, pins in their mouths, hands fiddling with points and laces, dressing us in such finery as I have never possessed, while our mother looks on, hawklike, screeching orders.

"Stand still, Jane! And try to look happy. His Majesty has been most generous in his provision for you, and in finding you such bridegrooms. You would not wish word to get back to him that you are ungrateful, I am sure."

Jane looks mutinous as the heavy gown of gold and silver brocade is lowered over her head.

"He knows that I did not want this marriage," she says defiantly. "And it is my lord of Northumberland whom I have to thank for it. King Edward might rule England, but my lord rules the King."

My mother would like to strike her, I am sure, but even she would not send a daughter to her wedding with bruises on her flesh. Instead she contents herself with tugging Jane's wedding gown none too gently into place over her kirtle, and arranging the heavy skirts and train, which are exquisitely embroidered with diamonds and pearls.

"You will keep your opinions to yourself, my little madam, and remember your duty to the King, to me and your father, *and* to the Duke of Northumberland, who is to become your father-in-law this day. Rest assured, you would not be getting wed if the King did not wish it. Now, let me look at you."

Jane stands awkwardly as our mother inspects her. She told me last night, not for the first time, that she despises outward finery; as a virtuous Protestant maiden, she insists on wearing sober, modest garments of black and white, which infuriates our mother, who is given to lavish attire. I can see that Jane is uncomfortable in more ways than one in her rich gold and silver brocade, with its low square neckline that reveals the slight swell of her small breasts.

I would give much to go forth to my wedding in such a dress, but I am the younger sister, and therefore not as important. Never mind that, unlike the spirited Jane, I am obedient, biddable, and—so my mother says—the beauty of the family, *and* (which she never says) clearly her favorite, I must always come second. I am second now, my marriage less important than Jane's, my gown of silver tissue banded with crimson velvet and pearls less costly; but as I catch sight of myself in the mirror, with my long strawberry-gold hair falling in glossy ripples down my back, my cheeks pinkly flushed, my blue eyes shining, and the tight cut of the pointed bodice outlining my slender figure, I know that I do not need more lavish finery to compete with my sister.

We are close, as sisters should be, but there has always been a healthy rivalry between us. Jane, my elder by four years, is the naughty, intransigent child, and I am the meek and dutiful one. Not for me the nips, slaps, and pinches that Jane frequently has to endure for this or that supposed misdemeanor, or for not doing what she was told as perfectly as God made the world. She could never please our parents. Everything she did or said laid her open to their criticism. Poor Jane; I have often seen her run weeping to our beloved tutor, gentle Master

Aylmer, for some respite from their harshness. Yet for me, the less clever but prettier daughter, there have been but mild reproofs and even occasional praise.

I was a quiet child, happy to bask in my brilliant sister's light, and it suited me to behave well, because I was timid and shy, and wanted as easy a life as possible. If doing so earned me the kindness of my fearsome mother, and spared me the rigor she showed to my unsatisfactory sister, then I was content. But as I grew older, it began to dawn on me that our mother was unnecessarily unkind to Jane, and did not love her, and I grew more protective toward my older sibling.

So I am sorry to see her looking so miserable, standing there in her unwanted finery, a frown on her plain, freckled face, as Mrs. Ellen combs her long red hair. Mrs. Ellen is dear and kind; she loves Jane much more than our mother does, and has stood up for her on many occasions, but my mother rarely takes any notice of anything that Mrs. Ellen says. She is a servant, beneath her notice.

Jane should be rejoicing that being married will enable her to escape, for she should be mistress of her own household very soon, although matters have proceeded so fast that nothing has been said of that yet. But she says she is merely changing one form of bondage for another. To me, it seems a wondrous thing to be married—and I hope she will find it so, although I fear she is resolved not to. I shall miss her, my dearest sister; what will her life be like without me there to comfort her?

Jane was supposed to be a boy, the son and heir who would inherit our parents' titles and estates, and their ambitions. For royal blood runs in my mother's veins, and she and my father have ever had the crown within their sights; indeed, my mother is next in line to the throne after the King's half sisters, the Lady Mary and the Lady Elizabeth, although—with them likely being in good health and to marry—the prospect of her ever succeeding is remote. It took me a long time to understand that my mother's unkindness toward Jane was born of disappointment in her being the wrong sex. After that, nothing she ever did was right.

Once, there had been an ambitious plan to marry her to King Ed-

ward and make her Queen. I know little of how it was to work out—
only that not very long ago our parents suddenly abandoned the idea
and agreed to these new marriages.

Poor Jane. She did not want to marry Lord Guilford Dudley; in fact,
she had railed bitterly against it. All in vain. Our furious mother beat
her into submission, shrieking that the marriage was highly advantageous for our family, while our father looked on, steely-eyed. "How
could an alliance with the Dudleys ever be advantageous?" Jane cried,
cowering under the blows.

"You will find out!" spat my lady. "Just do—as—you—are—told!"
Each word was accompanied by a snap of the whip.

It was different for me. Last month my lord and lady summoned me to
the great chamber at our house at Sheen, where I found my mother
seated by the hearth and my father standing with his back to the fire, his
hunting dogs at his feet. They smiled at me as I rose from my curtsey
and stood respectfully before them.

"Katherine, you will be pleased to know that your father has arranged a marriage for you," my mother said, her sharp features wearing a benign expression as she fixed her gaze on her lord. Her deference
to him is a sop to his vanity and the conventions, for it is no secret that
he is quite content to be ruled by her, his royal wife, in all things.

The news was a complete surprise to me. At twelve, I had not expected to be wed for some years yet, and was rendered quite speech-
less, which my parents mercifully took for obedient consent.

"You are young, it is true, to be a wife," my father said, "but you are
of age, and this match pleases us well. Above all, it will be of great
benefit to the realm."

Benefit to the realm? What was he talking about? Surely I, unimportant little Lady Katherine Grey, had no place in the high affairs of
the kingdom?

"Why, the child is struck dumb!" my mother laughed. "Are you so
overcome by your good fortune, Katherine?"

"I thank you, sir, madam," I stammered.

My mother turned to my father, crowing, "You see, Henry? I told
you she would be more biddable by far than Jane."

"I am relieved to see it," he replied with feeling. He loathes disruption, and having lost patience with Jane for making so much trouble over her betrothal, he had been difficult to live with for days.

"Well, Katherine, I expect you are waiting to hear the name of the fortunate young man who is to be your husband," he was saying.

"Yes, sir, I am."

My father put his hand into his doublet and pulled out a small, delicate oval object rimmed in bright gold.

"Behold!" he said, and gave it to me. It was a miniature portrait of a young man wearing russet clothing; he had brown curls, merry eyes, and a pleasant, open face. The gold letters on the blue background proclaimed, in Latin, that he was in his sixteenth year.

I am innocent of life, yet old enough to have looked blushingly on a handsome youth with interest; and when I gazed upon the comely features of my future betrothed, something stirred within me, and I was suddenly suffused with happiness. I had been taught that my duty would be to love the husband chosen for me, but this was a face I could love with no thought of duty.

I looked up at my waiting parents and found my voice.

"Sir, madam, I could not have asked for a more handsome gentleman for a husband. Thank you, oh, thank you!"

They beamed at me.

"Don't you want to know who he is?" my father chuckled.

"Yes, sir, please . . . Who is he?"

"Henry, Lord Herbert, son and heir to the Earl of Pembroke. The Herberts are an old and noble family. One day you will be my lady the Countess of Pembroke. It's an excellent match."

"It is indeed," added my mother, "and I am gratified to see that you are suitably grateful. You're a good girl, Katherine."

"May I ask a question?" I ventured.

"You may," said my father.

"Sir, I understand why you are pleased to be marrying me to Lord Herbert, for he is a fine gentleman and will make me a countess. But you said earlier that this match would be of great benefit to the realm. I do not understand."

"This marriage pleases my lord of Northumberland, and binds us to his affinity. Pembroke is a great and influential nobleman, and an alliance with him is much to our advantage."

"And I am certain that he sees it as being much to his advantage too, to be allied with our royal blood," my mother added dryly. "Katherine, you may rest content that your marriage will please many people, including the King himself."

"It is to take place as soon as possible," my lord informed me. "We are planning a double wedding with Jane and Guilford. But first you must meet your bridegroom."

It was arranged that my lord of Pembroke and his son should visit us in our new house, the former priory of the Charterhouse, at Sheen, which was granted to my father by the King earlier this year. Its splendid redbrick buildings and courts are dominated by a solid square tower with battlements, and it nestles close beside the River Thames amid the gentle wooded hills of Surrey.

When King Edward succeeded and England was proclaimed a Protestant kingdom, my parents ardently embraced the new faith. My father had profited well from King Harry's break with Rome and the closure of the monasteries: he got not only Sheen, and before that the Minories in London, but also Bradgate in Charnwood Forest, where he built us a grand house on the ruins of an abbey.

My parents keep great state at Sheen, which is arrayed with the very best in tapestries, Turkish carpets, displays of gold and silver plate, and gilded furniture, such as would impress even the King himself. And on the day when the Herberts were due to arrive, my mother decreed that I should be nobly decked out too, just as Jane had been when my lord of Northumberland had brought his son Guilford on a similar occasion.

That had not gone well. Jane did not trouble to hide her aversion to Guilford, whom I thought a handsome but stupid youth. He too clearly had no inclination for the marriage. That was the first occasion on which I met John Dudley, Duke of Northumberland, the man who rules England as Lord President of the Council while my cousin King Edward is a minor, and I was overawed by the cold and arrogant manner of this great lord. His very bearing exudes power; and yet, young as I might be, I sensed that there lurked a ruthless spirit beneath the urbane courtier.

He is not liked. My father is much in Northumberland's confidence, and active in the government of the kingdom, but I've heard my parents call the duke an upstart, a greedy and grasping knave, and scorn him as the son of an executed traitor—but only when they were not aware that I was listening. Since breaking the news of Jane's betrothal, they have loudly praised his virtues as a husband and father, his statecraft, his courtesy, and his exploits in the tiltyard.

But outward appearances are not always what they seem, especially among great folk. The very attitude of my parents toward Northumberland has shown me that a man or woman may say fair words outwardly, yet utter something quite different in private. I suspect that my father might merely be feigning friendship with Northumberland while using him for his own ends, for sure it is that an alliance with the duke is the fastest way to advancement in this kingdom.

I instantly disliked the man. I was almost beneath his notice, thank goodness: he was too puffed up with his own importance even to acknowledge me beyond a courtesy bow, and he was plainly simmering with anger at Jane's sullen reception of his son. My parents were all false gaiety and bonhomie, but later, when the guests had gone, they bared their teeth and snarled at my sister, who was sent to bed without supper for her discourtesy.

But today would be different, I was sure, for I was very happy to be betrothed to the fine young man in the miniature, and most eager to meet him. I could barely stand still for impatience as Mrs. Ellen laced me into my yellow velvet gown with its neckline edged with delicate gold filigree beads and cutwork embroidery, its full skirts spread gracefully over a wide farthingale and a kirtle of crimson silk. She reproved me for fidgeting as she adjusted my oversleeves, clasped the chain of my scented pomander around my waist, and brushed my hair till it shone.

"No hood today," she decreed. "You must wear your hair loose, as becomes a maiden."

The effect in the mirror she held up was very pleasing, and I was thrilled that Lord Herbert—I could not yet think of him as Henry— would see me looking so fine on our first meeting.

———

The day being warm, we had thrown open the parlor windows to let in the light, fresh breeze from the river. The long oak table had been spread with a crisp white cloth and laid with silver candlesticks and an array of gold plate laden with cold meats and raised pies, tarts both savory and sweet, and tall pyramids of fruit, with great ewers of Venetian glass full of good wine. There were bowls of sweet-smelling flower petals on the side table, and fragrant herbs scattered along the tablecloth.

My mother bustled about in her silken gown, hectoring the servants to ensure that no small detail should be overlooked. My father, who had gone out hunting at dawn, had been sent upstairs to change into his noblest apparel, and was now sprawling elegantly in his chair, reading a book. For all his inclination to sport and pleasure, he does love learning and is exceptionally well read.

Jane was reading too, huddled on the window seat. She was, as usual, in disgrace, having made her appearance in a black gown unadorned with any jewelry. It was only after some sharp words from our mother that she donned more festive-looking clothing, but that did not go far toward sweetening either of them.

Our younger sister, Mary, was not to be present. I have not spoken so far of Mary, because she rarely has a part to play in my story. My parents hardly mention her, and on the day of my betrothal they announced that, at eight years old, she was too young to join the gathering. Even so, she is not too young to be advantageously betrothed to the aging and battle-scarred Lord Grey de Wilton, a friend of Northumberland. The truth is that my parents do not want poor Mary seen in public at all, with her poor little humped back and her stunted stature. They fear that people will point a finger and say that God is so displeased with the Duke and Duchess of Suffolk that he has not only withheld the blessing of a son, but has also cursed them with a misshapen daughter; or they will say that a twisted character must lurk in a twisted body, like that wicked crookback King Richard III, who had the poor Princes in the Tower foully murdered all those years ago.

But there is nothing twisted or wicked about Mary. She is a gentle soul who strives to be as normal as Jane and I in order to please our parents. I have seen her holding herself as straight as possible, hiding her poor humped back under a shawl, oblivious to the pain it causes her. But my lord and lady mostly leave her to the care of Mrs. Ellen and the other nursery attendants. Anyone can see that, given the choice, they would prefer never to set eyes on poor Mary. But I am very fond of my little sister. I worry about her, knowing that I must soon leave her to go to my husband's house. Yet I know that Mrs. Ellen will go on caring for her as lovingly as she always has. She is a sweet, thoughtful lady, very fair and very feeling, and sometimes—God forgive me—I find myself wishing that I had her for a mother. But to think such thoughts is sinful, for I know I owe my love and duty to the mother who brought me into the world.

The truth is that I was so overwhelmed by the prospect of coming face-to-face with Lord Herbert that I gave my little sister barely a second thought.

At midday, craning my neck out of the open window, I glimpsed the Earl of Pembroke's barge, ornate and majestic, gliding slowly up the River Thames toward our landing stage.

"Hurry! We must make haste!" my mother hissed.

Needing no second bidding, I flew to the door, but then I felt a hand grip my shoulder and heard my lady's voice again, saying, "Slowly! It does not do for a bride to be too eager. It is unseemly. And you do not want to look like a hoyden, running down to the barge with your clothing flying in disarray. What would the earl think?"

I subsided into obedience, as I had done countless times before, and walked down to the jetty as sedately as a lady should, my hands folded over my stomacher, my eyes downcast, looking at the grass—although I was desperate to behold the face of my intended and assure myself that he was indeed as handsome as his picture.

"You are fortunate, sister," murmured Jane beside me, looking directly at our guests as we came to a demure standstill behind our parents. And it was then that I dared to raise my eyes.

The Earl of Pembroke, a soldierly, black-bearded figure garbed in fashionable attire that was no less lavish than our own, was making his vigorous way along the gangway between the raised oars of his boatmen, and leaping onto the landing stage. Behind him came a stately woman in a stiff brocade gown, who could only be his wife, the countess. And then—there he was, my bridegroom, a slim young man with brown curls, wearing silver and blue silk, and his face was recognizably the face in my miniature. I caught my breath.

But the painter, whoever he was, had lied. His brush had not been equal to its task. It had not captured the cornflower blue of Lord Herbert's wide, dancing eyes, or the manly contours of his face, with its straight nose, broad cheekbones, and full red lips. It had not delineated his graceful figure or his long, muscular legs encased in white hose and soft leather shoes.

There were introductions, I am sure, but I remember little of them except this glorious young man gazing down with sincere admiration into my eyes as he raised my hand to his lips and gently kissed it, warmly declaring himself well content with his beautiful bride. His father the earl was in a jovial mood, clapping him on the shoulder and saying how fortunate he was, and kissing my lips, saying I was even fairer than he had been told; then my father and mother welcomed their "son Herbert," and everyone was congratulating us as we turned and walked back toward the priory for the betrothal ceremony, the toasts, and the cold meats.

The day seemed more than sunny now: it had taken on a special radiance, its colors and hues brighter and sharper than I had imagined; it was as if the world was revealing itself anew because I was seeing it through the eyes of another. All through the afternoon, Lord Herbert and I observed all the courtesies of which our parents had told us to be mindful, but our eyes were saying much more. Our elders made very clear their belief that betrothed couples should be closely supervised, but later my debonair young lord contrived to speak to me in a quiet corner, saying that he fancied himself already in love, and could hardly endure the prospect of the empty days that must pass before we could be married. My cheeks burned at that, but my heart, my ardent, childish heart, was soaring.

It was late, and my candle had burned down almost to the wick, but I could not sleep. I lay abed, reliving the events of that happy, merry day, recalling the converse I'd had with my Harry—as he had asked me to call him, saying it was how he was known in the family—and thinking of Jane, who had smiled upon me and wished me every joy in my betrothal. "For you are meant for marriage, Kat," she told me. "You have a sunny, giving nature. I know you are going to be happy. Whereas I should like to be wedded to my books!"

Poor Jane! I do believe she meant it.

I had not eaten much of the feast provided by my parents. My head had been in too great a spin after looking into Harry's eyes as we made our betrothal vows and swore to be true and faithful to each other forever.

"I thank God it will be but a short time until we are wed, my fair Katherine," he had whispered just before we said our farewells. "I long to make you mine!" His words, and the way he squeezed my hand as he said them, promised so much. I had been brought up with horses, pet monkeys, and dogs, so I was not ignorant of physical things, but in that instant I began to realize that there was much more to human love than I could ever have dreamed. I blushed and just smiled; I had been brought up to be modest and discreet, and to regard all mention of such matters as proper only for the marriage bed. There was no way I could have conveyed to Harry how much I longed for him too.

After that, I could not expect to sleep, for I had much to dream about while awake. And presently I realized that I was hungry, having eaten so little, and took to wondering if there were any of the leftover cold meats, or anything else, in the court cupboard in the great hall.

I rose from my bed, donned my new nightgown—an expensive one with puffed sleeves and a high buttoned neck—and carried my candle down the curving stair that led to the hall. To my right the door to the parlor was slightly ajar, and I could hear voices. It was my parents, sitting up late as they often did, enjoying a drink by the fireside. I was about to go in, but stopped short when I heard something that disturbed me. I should have gone away then, I know, but I was ever a curious child, and did not pause to remember that eavesdroppers rarely hear any good of anything, especially themselves.

"I hope Pembroke doesn't waver." It was my mother's voice that had stopped me in my tracks. Waver? Why should the earl want to waver? Was it my marriage they were talking about? I held my breath.

"He, waver? Not a chance," my father said. "He's bound himself now, and cannot get out of it."

"Oh, but he can. This agreement about the marriage not being consummated immediately. I don't like it." My heart began beating fast at that, and it would be pounding heavily before I was finished listening.

My lady was strident. "I told you, you should have insisted on their bedding together on the wedding night, but instead you go and agree to the earl's condition."

"But Katherine is young—she's just twelve. He said he was being purely considerate of her age, which I rather liked him for." My father sounded defensive.

"Words! Fair, empty words! She's old enough for wedding *and* bedding," my mother snorted, as I shrank at her coarseness. "It's clear to me that Pembroke doesn't entirely trust Northumberland, and that he is sitting on the fence to see if my lord duke can hang on to power after the King dies. It's well known that Catholic Mary has no love for Northumberland. She'd as soon hang him, given the chance. I wouldn't give a groat for his prospects with her sitting on the throne."

The King—dying? He was but fifteen years old. I had heard he'd been ill, with measles or smallpox, but that he had recovered. He could not be dying, surely? It was too much to take in. As for the consummation of my marriage, I knew what that meant, but why shouldn't it be allowed? Surely Pembroke would want to bind himself to us, who are, after all, of higher rank than the Herberts, and of royal blood to boot? Modest as I am, I have been brought up to consider myself and my sister Jane great prizes in the marriage market.

"Northumberland will hold on, never fear." My lord's tone was confident. "The country was glad to turn Protestant under Edward. People will rally to the duke. It's too late to go back to the old ways. Mary must understand that."

"I doubt it!" my mother interrupted, tart. "She's spent most of his reign fighting for the right to have her Mass."

"But she has no support. Of course, the Catholics in the North will cleave to her, yet I doubt she'll command much of a following elsewhere. It may be that His Majesty and Northumberland have some other plan in mind."

There was a pause, and once more I held my breath, in case my parents should discover that I was listening outside.

"Do you know something that I don't?" my lady asked at length.

"I know nothing," my father replied, not entirely convincingly.

"But he is plotting something. If it affects us, I have a right to know. I am, after all, the King's cousin, and in line for the throne myself after his sisters."

My father never could withstand my mother's iron will, but what he said to her next I could not hear, only the sibilant hiss of a whisper.

"For me?" I heard my mother exclaim.

"Shhh! Walls have ears," my father muttered, with more truth than he knew. "I know for a fact that one of our servants is in the pay of Pembroke, and have no doubt that the earl is aware that something momentous is afoot. He has Northumberland's confidence."

"But is it to be me?" my lady persisted. Her tone was urgent.

"In truth, I do not know what the duke is planning," my lord murmured, so low that I had to strain to hear. "Only that he means to set her aside."

"But her right is enshrined in law . . ."

"Acts of Parliament can be repealed."

"And you think Pembroke knows of this? That explains everything. It's as I feared. He is pleased to ally himself to us, and thereby to Northumberland, but only for as long as the duke holds power. Pembroke means to hunt with the hare and the hounds, and if the hounds should by any chance win, he will have all the pretext he needs for breaking this marriage."

"That may be so," said my father, "yet I think you are fretting in vain. Northumberland is strong, and he has the nobility and the country behind him."

"I do hope so, my lord. I do hope you are right. It's a good match for Katherine. The child was much taken with Pembroke's boy. I don't want to see it broken."

I heard a rustling of silks as my mother rose from her chair, and I tiptoed back up the stairs, all thought of food abandoned. I could not have touched a morsel anyway, for my mind was in turmoil. Was my marriage in some way uncertain? Would it not even be a true marriage? I did not sleep at all that night.

But now it is my wedding day, and as I stand here in my bridal finery, waiting for Mrs. Ellen to make the final adjustments to Jane's train, and for my mother to clasp around our necks the priceless jeweled necklaces sent as wedding gifts by the King, I am still in torment. Whenever I think of my Harry's handsome face, his loving countenance, and all the promise in his fair words, I dread to think that I might lose him, or that they will forbid us to become man and wife in the truest sense.

But there is no more time to brood on this, for the trumpets are sounding and my lord my father, dazzling in white and gold, is waiting to escort us down the grand processional stair to the splendidly arrayed state apartments, through which we must pass toward the chapel. Durham House, where we have come to be married, is a palatial residence surrounded on the Strand side by a high wall buttressed by marble pillars. The guest chambers that have been allocated to us give onto the river, and the great hall and chapel overlook a wide courtyard. This is an old building, not much used these days, but I've heard that King Harry VIII's queens once lived here. It is now the property of His Majesty's sister, the Lady Elizabeth, who has graciously allowed us to use it for the celebration of our joint wedding. I have never met the Lady Elizabeth, but I know of her by repute as a great lady, and very learned. Jane was brought up with her for some years in Queen Katherine Parr's household, and although they were never close—being two very clever girls, they were too competitive for that—Jane did come to admire Elizabeth; indeed, she speaks often of her wit and erudition.

Sadly, the King cannot be here today. He has sent his regrets, and has generously commanded his Master of the Wardrobe to have the house refurbished in royal style, and to supply us with sumptuous wedding attire. These rich clothes that we are wearing, the cloth of gold and silver tissue, the damasks, the silks and velvets, the exquisite embroideries, are all the King's gifts. And as I walk in procession, my hand resting on my father's left arm, with Jane on his other side, through the great chambers of Durham House, I marvel at the magnificent display of King Edward's great bounty: the exquisitely woven tapestries, some of them shimmering with gold thread, the Turkish carpets on floors and tables, the brand new hangings of crimson taffeta. The vast chapel, smelling of old, hallowed stone, is royally adorned too, and I am overawed by the rich jewel colors of the tall, stained-glass windows and the altar furnishings—but even more so by the sight of my smiling but pale bridegroom, who is waiting for me in a shaft of rainbow sunlight.

I stare at Harry in alarm. He does not look like the robust young man who came to court me at Sheen. He looks ill, in truth, and thinner than I remember him.

The binding words are spoken over us; we make our responses, and I swear to be true and loyal all my days, and to be obedient and amiable in bed and at board; and now the blessed moment comes: we are pronounced man and wife, and kneel together for the Bishop's blessing. I have eyes only for Harry, whose hand is squeezing mine so meaningfully. But I cannot but notice his drawn face, and Jane's visible unhappiness as she is bound to Guilford Dudley.

But now here are our parents and guests, clapping and congratulating us, kissing me and Jane, and jocularly slapping our new spouses on the back. The Bishop beams as Harry ventures a chaste kiss on my lips, and I feel a great lightening of the spirits. Harry and I are wed now; surely no one can prevent us from becoming one flesh, as Holy Scripture enjoins.

It is only at this moment—for I have been utterly enrapt by the ceremony—that I become aware of so many great lords among the company.

"The entire Privy Council is here!" my mother breathes. "Are you not honored?"

"Yes, indeed," I stammer, overwhelmed that I should be thought so important, and hastily curtseying to the fine gentlemen. "I thank you all for coming, good my lords." Their presence, not to mention the splendid display put on for the wedding, is making me feel dizzy with conceit. These marriages must indeed be important to warrant such honors. But why?

The Duke of Northumberland bows.

"This day I have gained a daughter," he says, addressing Jane. "I hope you will be happy in your new husband, my dear."

Jane murmurs a reply. He cannot fail to see the resentment and misery in her eyes.

The Earl of Pembroke, my new father-in-law, is more effusive.

"You are heartily welcome to the family, my Lady Katherine," he declares, lifting my hand and kissing it. His wife, the Countess Anne, my husband's stepmother, hugs me warmly. She is a large lady, and no beauty, but she displays a good and loving heart.

The earl turns to his son. "I trust you are feeling better now, Harry. You will not know, Katherine, that he has been confined to his bed with a fever these three weeks, but he is happily amended now."

"Do not worry," Harry protests. "I feel much better than I did, really I do!" And he smiles broadly.

The trumpets are sounding again, and it is time for the wedding feast. Northumberland departs bowing, pleading urgent business with the King—much to my comfort, for I find the man intimidating—and a jubilant Harry takes my hand as, with Jane and Guilford, we lead the merry procession to the great hall. Here the tables are lavishly spread with dishes of every description, all artfully arranged on gold and silver platters, and an impressive array of plate is displayed on a tall, ornate buffet for all to admire. As we seat ourselves at the high table above the great gold salts, the servitors come running with napkins, ewers, and small manchet loaves, grace is said, and the feasting begins. Reassured about Harry's recovery, I begin to enjoy myself immensely.

On my right, Jane waves away roast peacock dressed in its plumage and a hot salad, on which Guilford pounces ravenously, then she turns to me and murmurs, "Do you not think it strange that every lord on the council has deemed it proper to come? And all this lavish display. Our parents did not merit as much when they married. I have heard them speak of it. It was a quiet ceremony, overshadowed by Queen Anne Boleyn's coronation. So why all the pomp?"

I lay down my knife and sip my wine. Her words reawaken my suspicion that there is more to our marriages than we have been given to understand; and suddenly I am no longer so confident about the future.

"This is disgusting," Guilford says, pushing away the salad and reaching once more for his goblet, which has already been refilled several times. Jane ignores him.

"Think on it," she whispers to me, toying with a venison pasty for which she clearly has no appetite. "For all their fair words to Northumberland, our parents hate him, and six months ago they would never have condescended to our marrying into a family tainted by treason and not long ennobled."

"But it is a good alliance," I argue, in my twelve-year-old wisdom. "He is a powerful man. It is important to be friends with him."

"Maybe." She does not sound convinced. Then she whispers: "I just wish I were anywhere else! Tell me, Kat, do you fear your wedding night?"

I can feel the heat suffusing my cheeks. "A little. But in truth I do long for it."

"You long for it?" Jane looks shocked. "I tell you, I dread it. I hate Guilford. I don't want him touching me." Her tone becomes vehement.

Our mother is leaning forward slightly, frowning down the table at us. We have been taught that it is rude to whisper in company, so I turn and smile at Harry, who has been holding my hand while engaging in a lively discussion with my lady about hunting. He has managed to eat a goodly dinner.

"Sweet Katherine," he says. "I shall never forget how beautiful you look this day."

"You are not looking so badly yourself, my lord!" I answer, pert. He laughs, and I am enchanted. The more I come to know of Harry, the more delighted I am in him. Unlike poor Jane, I am not dreading my wedding night.

Perhaps Harry knows why the councillors are all here.

"It's out of friendship for Northumberland," he tells me, and I feel greatly cheered by that. Of course, it must be. These lords all work closely with him, governing the realm, and many must be related to him. And when Harry leans forward and kisses me again on the lips, more slowly this time, I forget all about them, blushing at the whoops and knowing remarks of those who have observed us. By now everyone is rosy with wine, all but Guilford, who wears a petulant face; he doesn't just appear drunk, he looks green. Well, it serves him right for being so greedy!

After the feast, two masques are performed for our entertainment. One is outrageously bawdy, and I don't understand much of it, but the guests are guffawing and rocking with mirth, so I join in. Only Jane sits there stony-faced as the dancers in their indecent diaphanous costumes weave in and out, singing risqué songs to the very suggestive young man playing Hymenaios, the Greek god of weddings, and his youthful acolytes, the Erotes, gods of love.

Afterward, laughing and chattering, we go out into the sunlight, making our way in procession to the tiltyard by the river, where we take our places in the stands for the jousts that are to do honor to the marriages. Harry is one of the gallant contestants, and looks very splendid indeed in finely chased tilting armor, seated on his charger. When he bows in the saddle before me, lowering his lance for me to tie on my favor as his chosen lady, my heart feels fit to burst with happiness.

As the crowd roars, hooves thunder across the earth, spears splinter, and armored knights crash to the ground. Harry gives a good account of himself, even though he wins none of the prizes. But I am inordinately proud of him for his efforts. He is but fifteen, much of an age with Guilford, who is now too drunk even to sit straight on his horse and retires early from the tourney. His mother watches him go with a fixed smile. I sense her embarrassment, and I don't miss the angry looks exchanged by my parents, or Jane's barely concealed grimace of disgust. Poor, poor Jane, I think, yet again. Her obvious misery makes me feel guilty for being such a joyous bride.

As we walk back to Durham House, in a less orderly fashion than before, she catches up with me as I stroll arm in arm with Harry.

"Guilford has been sick," she mutters. "Our mother is worried that people will think we have poisoned him. I told her I didn't care if we did." Harry chuckles, but I am not laughing.

"What did she say to that?" I ask.

"She pinched me hard for my lack of duty to my husband, and told me that I had better start making the best of things and put a smile on my face."

Guilford is behind us, white-faced and leaning on his mother for support, as my lady makes solicitous noises and promises all manner of vengeance on the cook, who must, she insists, have put the wrong leaves in the salad.

It is now evening, and many of the guests take their leave, some of them a touch unsteady on their feet as they wobble onto their waiting barges. I see their early departure as ominous, for usually at weddings the company stays to see the bride and groom put to bed, but Harry seems unbothered and I push the thought aside. And anyway, the festivities are continuing, as my parents invite their new kinsfolk to a private banquet. Harry squeezes my hand as he leads me to the table; already there is a sense of togetherness between us. I am in no doubt that he likes me as much as I like him.

Guilford is looking a little better now—well enough to guzzle the delicious sweetmeats provided—and the Duchess of Northumberland is disposed to be gracious about the shortcomings of our cook. My lady the Countess of Pembroke is full of smiles for me, her new daughter-in-law, and talks of dogs and horses and the happy life I will lead with my new family at Wilton Abbey, the Herberts' country residence in Wiltshire; and the earl adds a kind word here and there, telling me how comfortable and welcome I will be there.

"But tonight you will lodge with us at our town house, Baynard's Castle," he says. "I hear that the Lady Jane is to return home to Suffolk House with your parents."

That sounds a little strange. Jane is to return home, while I am to go to my husband's house?

"What of Lord Guilford, sir?" I ask.

"He too is to return to his parents."

"I see," I say, but in truth I do not. And I am not much enlightened later, when I meet Jane coming out of the stool chamber.

"I am so glad to see you, Kat," she says, looking a lot happier than she had been earlier. "I have such good news. I am not to bed with

Guilford for the present. I can go back home to my studies, at least for a while!"

"But why?" I ask. This news may have pleased her, but it dismays me.

"I do not know, and I do not care. They are just using us. They made these marriages for their own benefit and profit, not ours. Are you to come home too?"

"No!" I say, more sharply than I had intended. "The earl says I am to go to Baynard's Castle with them."

Jane smiles and embraces me. "Well then, I wish you joy of your marriage bed, sister. I can see you are eager for it."

After hugging and kissing Jane and kneeling with Harry to receive my parents' blessing, I climb onto the Herberts' gilded barge and seat myself in the cushioned cabin for the short journey to Baynard's Castle. I have passed it often, that massive white stone building with tall towers that rises majestically from the river; and as we glide past the gardens of the Temple, Bridewell Palace, and the mouth of the Fleet River, it lies before us, with the tower of the church of St. Andrew by the Wardrobe behind it. But tonight, when I see Baynard's Castle, I feel an odd frisson of unease: eerily pale in the moonlight, it has something unearthly about it, as if it has taken on a different aspect with the coming of night. What secrets do its walls contain? I wonder. Who has lived here, laughed here, loved, suffered, and died here in the hundreds of years it has stood?

The impression of strangeness is fleeting, the result of too much wine, no doubt. I am with Harry, and this is his home, and it is one of the greatest houses in London. And now it is to be my home too. I should count myself fortunate!

Imposing stone stairs ascend from the lapping water to a first-floor doorway, and torches burn brightly to light our ascent. As the barge draws alongside, Harry takes my hand; we follow his parents up the steps, cross the balustraded bridge, and pass under the lintel on which is proudly displayed, carved in stone and painted, the arms of Pembroke, three lions on a red and blue ground. I feel the grasp of Harry's hand on mine and catch his sweet, loving looks in the moonlight glimmering on the river below us. The night seems magical, filled with promise.

Servants wearing the green dragon badge of Pembroke hasten to take our cloaks, unload my gear from the barge, and attend us to our chambers, and then Harry leads me through room after room appointed with lavish splendor. Yet the fine furnishings, the costly carpets, the brilliant tapestries, are as nothing compared to the young man at my side. Soon we will be alone together. The thought of that makes me catch my breath.

"This is a very old house, but you will grow to love it," Harry tells me, squeezing my hand again. His eyes are merry, warm, and inviting.

"The first building on this site was built in the time of William the Conqueror, for defending the City of London," the earl adds, "but later it was sold to our former neighbor, the Black Friars' monastery. This house was built early in the last century, on land reclaimed from the river. It was the London residence of the royal House of York."

"It was a fine mansion then, by all accounts," the Countess Anne continues, "and parts of it still remain today—I will show you tomorrow, if you wish—but much was remodeled by King Henry VII, who converted it into a royal palace."

"Indeed, many illustrious royal persons have lived here," the earl says with pride as we pass into a vast, opulent chamber graced with tapestries threaded with gold that glitters in the torchlight. "It was in this hall"—he waves an expansive hand at the cavernous timbered space—"that Edward of York was acknowledged as King Edward IV after his victory over the House of Lancaster. And it was here too, regrettably, that his brother, that villainous crookback Richard of Gloucester, was later offered the crown."

"You mean Richard III?" I ask.

"Yes, Katherine. He had no right to it, of course, but nevertheless he accepted it. He had meant to have it all along. He stood in that gallery up there, pretending reluctance." I look up, suddenly chilled.

I have heard this tale from several people over the years: how, seventy years ago, Edward IV, dying long before his time, had appointed his hitherto loyal brother, Richard of Gloucester, as Lord Protector of

England during the minority of his twelve-year-old heir, Edward V. Our tutor, Master Aylmer, told us the story, for there was some talk of these events in my childhood, after King Edward VI succeeded to the throne at just nine years old, and the kingdom again came under the rule of a protector. That was the late Edward Seymour, Duke of Somerset, brother to Queen Jane Seymour, and therefore uncle to King Edward, my cousin: the "Good Duke," the people had called him. I'm not sure just how good a duke he was, for there were those who resented his rule. Overthrown by Northumberland, he met his end on the block last year.

Richard of Gloucester had fared rather better in his struggle for power—at least to begin with. According to Master Aylmer, he was an ambitious man, a tyrant even, twisted in body and soul, and Aylmer held him up as one of the worst moral examples in history. Having ruthlessly eliminated all opposition, Richard had deposed the young Edward V and usurped the throne himself. By then the poor little King and his brother had been imprisoned in the Tower of London, and soon afterward they were secretly murdered, although even to this day no one knows for certain how. Because of this, their fate has never ceased to fascinate me. Certain it is that King Richard ordered their deaths, and Aylmer told us that, in the end, his ill fame was such that his supporters deserted him and switched their allegiance to the rightful Lancastrian heir, Henry Tudor. And everyone knows what happened at the Battle of Bosworth . . .

I gaze about me, awestruck, suppressing a shudder. This was where the usurper had stood, reading a prayer book to boast his piety, as his henchman, the Duke of Buckingham, recited his virtues and his right to the crown to the leading citizens of London. And here—their pockets no doubt lined with bribes—the city fathers had been persuaded to press Richard to accept what they were so humbly offering.

There is someone in the gallery looking down on us: a man in dark clothing, I think, although he is in shadow. It's a servant, no doubt, standing still and silent, awaiting his master's pleasure or—more likely—sneaking a peek at me, his future mistress. His scrutiny makes me uncomfortable, although the earl, the countess, and Harry ignore him. My mother would have reprimanded him for staring at us so insolently, and told him to lower his eyes when his betters passed. But maybe not all masters and mistresses are as particular as my mother.

Tonight, there is little time to stand and admire this magnificent hall where history was made. It grows late, and Pembroke is leading us onward, as his servants pull open the great double doors and light us through. We enter an antechamber; beyond, he tells me, are the private apartments of the family. There too, of course, will be the bedchamber we are to share, my young lord and I.

"I have something of import to say to you, my children," the earl says, turning to face us and regarding us intently. "Now heed me well . . ."

KATE

April–June, 1483. Middleham Castle, Yorkshire;
the City of London; Crosby Hall, London

Katherine Plantagenet—known to all as Kate—looked up in surprise as a mud-spattered courier, smelling of horse sweat, ran into the great hall at Middleham, threw himself onto his knees, and presented her father the duke with a letter. It bore the seal of Lord Hastings, whom she knew was a trusted friend of her uncle, King Edward. Kate and her father were seated at the table, where they had been enjoying a game of chess. Her half brother, Edward of Middleham, was kneeling by the hearth, playing with his model soldiers, watched by her stepmother, the duchess, who was born Lady Anne Neville, daughter of the Earl of Warwick, the famous "Kingmaker" who had turned traitor to King Edward and perished on Barnet field. Kate's brother John was out in the bailey, practicing swordplay with one of the sergeants. It was a peaceful Sunday afternoon, a rare opportunity for the Duke of Gloucester to spend time with his family, away from public affairs.

Kate watched as her father took the letter and broke the seal. She saw his expression change as he read it, saw him lay it down and close his eyes as if he were in unbearable pain.

"My lord?" The duchess half rose to her feet, her voice sharp.

Richard of Gloucester turned to her, his face bleak and ravaged. "My brother the King is dead," he rasped, almost choking with emotion.

"Dead? Oh sweet Mary! No, he cannot be. He is but forty-one and in good health." Anne was utterly shocked, and Kate could feel tears welling in her own eyes. She had met her uncle only twice, for he ruled England from Westminster or Windsor, but she had been impressed and charmed by the big, genial, pleasure-loving monarch who had kissed her most fondly on greeting, brought her thoughtful gifts—a wooden doll attired in cloth of gold, a ruby pendant, and even a dear little puppy—and taken time out from his important conferences with her father to talk to her and tell her jokes; and at dinner he had even passed her the choicest sweetmeats from his own dishes. He had little girls of his own, he'd told her: Elizabeth, Cecily, Anne, Katherine, and Bridget—lovely girls, the lot of them, and Elizabeth, the oldest and the most beautiful, was going to be Queen of France one day: it was all arranged. He'd spoken too of his pride in his sons, Edward, Prince of Wales, the heir to the throne, who was residing at Ludlow Castle on the border of his principality, being tutored in the art of ruling kingdoms; and Richard, Duke of York, a merry scamp if ever there was one, another like his father, if the King wasn't mistaken. Kate had quickly warmed to her uncle, and often regretted that she did not see more of him. And now she would never see him again, that larger-than-life, vital man with the twinkling eyes, sensual lips, and ready wit. Her tears spilled over.

"He became ill when he went fishing in the damp cold," Richard said. "He is buried already." His voice was bitter with anger as well as grief. "They did not wait. He was my brother and I loved him. I should have been there!"

Anne looked at him, understanding how deeply that had hurt him. "It was the Queen's doing, no doubt, and her Wydeville kin," she commented, tart.

Kate watched through her tears as her father's brows furrowed.

"They hate me," he muttered. "Nay, they fear me too—and they will have cause! What's worse, they have allowed me no time to grieve. Lord Hastings writes that I must act now, or the Wydevilles will seize power. You see now why they sent no messenger to tell me of Edward's death. They were playing for time, damn them. My brother's son is a child, and they are bent on ruling in his name. But according to this letter, Edward, on his deathbed, named me Lord Protector of England. *Me*, not the Queen and her party."

The duchess had turned pale. Her thin hands were unconsciously pleating the ribbed fabric of her skirts. She was a slender slip of a woman, twenty-seven years old, with fair hair pulled back severely beneath her embroidered cap, light blue eyes, and a finely boned face. She was delicate, like her son, and the rich blues and scarlet hues of her gorgeous high-waisted gown served only to enhance her pallor.

"What will you do?" she asked.

The ·duke began pacing agitatedly. "I will see that my brother's wishes are respected. Hastings advises me to gather a strong force and hasten to London, to avenge the insult done me by my enemies. He says I may easily obtain my revenge if, on the way, I take the young King under my protection and authority."

"But he is in Ludlow."

"Not now. He is being brought to London by his uncle, Lord Rivers, and his half brother, Sir Richard Grey—Wydevilles both!—with a small escort. My lord writes that the Queen wanted to send an army, but he warned her that it might court bloodshed, and threatened to abandon her cause if she persisted. She backed down, but I doubt it has made relations any the sweeter between them. After all, he and my brother shared—well, we have all heard of Mistress Shore and the others."

A look passed between the duke and duchess. Kate was aware that there were things about King Edward that her father did not want to discuss in front of his children. But for all his care, even she knew that Mistress Shore had been her uncle's whore. You could not stop servants gossiping.

"I will not speak ill of the dead," Richard was saying, "or this good lord who has warned me of the danger in which I stand. For, as he writes, he has put himself in peril by sending this letter: he says that the hatred of his old enemies has been aggravated by his showing friendship for me."

Anne rose, walked over to her husband, and encircled him in her embrace. "My poor Dickon," she murmured. "I am so sorry."

His eyes met hers. "How can I mourn Edward decently?" he asked, bitter. "My very life may be in danger. Remember my brother Clarence—dead through the malice of the Wydevilles! My lady, I must make ready." And he put her from him, bent to kiss his son's head, and briefly hugged Kate. "May God be with us all," he said, and strode to the doorway that led to the stairs.

There he stopped. He had his back to them, his slightly bowed back, for although he was strong enough to wield a sword with dexterity, he was a small man, so subtly misshapen that few were aware of it. It was a moment before they realized he was weeping, that great tearing sobs were racking his frame.

"Oh, God, oh, God," he cried. "I loved him. God, how I loved him!"

"I must go to him," the duchess said, rising, recovering herself after Richard had staggered out. At that moment John ran into the hall.

"What's going on?" he asked, seeing the downcast faces of his sister and stepmother.

"Will you tell him?" Anne asked Kate.

"Of course, my lady," Kate said. "You go to my father."

Anne hugged her and went. She had great affection for her husband's bastards. One had been conceived and born before her marriage to Richard of Gloucester, and one after, yet she had welcomed them into her household at Middleham Castle, her kindly heart aware that they were not to blame for their birth. The younger, John of Gloucester, was a strapping lad of nine with dark, unruly hair and refined features. Promising to be tall and broad, where his father was short and slight, he had inherited Richard's dogged determination and tenacity, not to mention his ambition.

His half sister, Kate, was four years older, and very beautiful. Her sweet round face and big, wide-set blue eyes were framed by a wealth of dark wavy hair that fell like a cape around her shoulders. She was small in build and slender, with tiny, childlike hands and feet. She had a winning smile, a spirited nature, and a ready wit. To all who knew her, and to her father especially, she was enchanting. There must be nothing but the best for his Kate, the duke had vowed. Bastard she might be, but he would marry her well when the time came, and make sure that the disadvantage of her birth was turned to advantage, for both of them.

There was no one like her father. He was her hero, the person she loved best.

Kate watched the duke ride away southward, somber in deepest black and attended by three hundred gentlemen of the North, all similarly attired. She felt cold with fear. He was riding into danger, into the teeth of his enemies, and she could only pray with all her might that he would stay safe and come back to them unscathed, his rights vindicated.

The long, anxious days stretched ahead, with no hope of news for some time. It took a fast messenger four days to reach Middleham from London, and it would surely be a week or more before they heard anything of real moment. In the meantime they could only fret about what the Queen and her kinsmen might do before the duke reached the capital. He had been planning to rendezvous on the way with his friend the Duke of Buckingham—himself no lover of the Wydevilles—so that might cause some delay. As it happened, they heard from him within a couple of days. He had not forgotten his duty to his brother: he had gone first to York, where he summoned all the nobility in those parts to attend a solemn funeral Mass in the Minster. He had wept all through it, he confessed, but had recovered himself sufficiently to bind the local lords by oaths of fealty to his nephew, the new King, Edward V.

Kate had never met the younger Edward, for he had spent most of his twelve years either at court or at Ludlow. But she grieved for this cousin who had lost his father so early in life, and prayed earnestly for him. It could not be easy to be a king, even when you were grown up.

"Another minority," the duchess said as they sat at dinner in the hall. "I fear very much for the future."

"But if my father is there to guide the King, all will be well, surely?" Kate asked, laying down her knife and wiping her fingers on her napkin.

The castle chaplain leaned forward. "There is an old prophecy, Dame Katherine: 'Woe to thee, O land, when thy king is a child.' This kingdom has not had a happy experience of royal minorities. They breed dissension and rivalry among the nobles of the realm. The late King Henry VI succeeded when he was a babe in arms, and factions ruled, and for want of firm government all law and order was undermined. Now the threat is from the Queen and her blood."

"My father will deal with it!" Kate insisted. "He is in the right."

"Alas, my child, we have seen too many instances of might prevailing over right in this unhappy land in recent years. But we must take heart: your father is powerful and respected. He is of the old royal stock; these Wydevilles are mere upstarts."

"Aye, but they have the King in their clutches, and you may make no doubt they have poisoned his young mind against my lord," the duchess countered. She had eaten very little.

"With my lords Hastings and Buckingham on his side, my father must prevail!" Kate persisted. She would not—could not—entertain the possibility of any alternative outcome. In her mind, the duke was invincible. Had he not taken Berwick from the Scots?

"Your admiration and zeal for your father is touching," smiled the chaplain. "We must pray for good news soon."

Kate prayed. She spent many an hour in the chapel, kneeling beside the duchess and beseeching God to preserve and keep the duke. Without his reassuring presence she felt bereft, and it was clear that the Duchess Anne did too. Both loved him truly: Kate with the innocent devotion of a daughter for a loving father, and Anne with a grateful passion for the knight who had rescued her. Anne was fond of telling the children the story, and on the third night of Richard's absence, when young Edward of Middleham demanded that she recount it again, she smiled at her fair, delicate son, felt the usual pang of fear for his health, and agreed. She could never gainsay him.

"He wanted to marry me," she said as they clustered around her by the fire. "We had known each other as children, for my lord was brought up in my father's household. We played together: I called him Dickon, and he was pleased, in time, to call me his sweetheart. He was the youngest of a large family, and not very big or strong, but he worked exceptionally hard to prove himself in his military exercises and his swordsmanship. I admired that in him. Then he went away to court, and we did not see each other for some years."

"Tell us about being rescued!" piped up Edward. Kate smiled and ruffled his wispy curls, as his mother went on with her story.

"When my father was killed in battle at Barnet, he left my sister Isabel and me a rich inheritance that was to be divided between us. Isabel was married to your father's older brother, the Duke of Clarence. He wasn't a nice man; he was overambitious and very greedy. Isabel's share of our fortune went to him, because she was his wife, but he was determined to have mine too. I was then living in his household, under his protection, but when he heard that Dickon wanted to marry me, he carried me off and hid me in this big house in London, and there I was forced to work as a kitchen maid. My lord of Clarence warned me that things would go very ill for me if I complained or revealed who I was, and as he had already threatened to send me to a nunnery for the rest of my days, I kept my mouth shut and endured."

"It must have been awful for you," Kate said.

"It was. I had no idea how to scrub pans or chop vegetables. I had had a gentle upbringing in a castle. The cook was constantly scolding me. He didn't know who I was, of course. But then"—and now her fair complexion glowed—"Dickon found me. Someone in Clarence's household talked; I think he bribed them. And he stormed into that house with a vengeance, and demanded that I be delivered into his care. Well, he was the King's brother, and he was dreadfully angry; they dared not oppose him. I cannot tell you how relieved I was to see him."

"Did he whisk you away and marry you?" asked John.

"Not immediately. He had to obtain the King's permission for the marriage. So, like a perfect, gentle knight, he escorted me to the sanctuary at St. Martin's and placed me in the care of the Archbishop of York while everything was sorted out. And then we did get married. It was a quiet ceremony at Westminster." A wistful look crept into Anne's eyes.

"And then did the King chop Clarence's head off?" asked Edward. At seven, he enjoyed gory details.

"No, my son, that was later, when he was discovered plotting against King Edward."

"Or is it true that he was drowned in a butt of Malmsey wine?"

Watching Anne blanch, Kate suspected that it was true. "Where did you hear that?" the duchess asked sharply.

Edward looked at her in surprise. "John told me." John had the grace to look guilty. Anne frowned at him.

"You shouldn't go telling him things like that," she reproved.

"But it's true, isn't it?" he asked, his black eyes holding hers.

"True or not, he's too young to hear such stories."

"I am not!" protested Edward. But his mother merely sent them both to bed, silencing their protests with a raised hand.

"Bad boys!" Kate murmured.

"Exhausting," the duchess sighed, gazing fondly at her beautiful dark-haired stepdaughter, for there was much affection between them. "But you are a good girl. I am blessed in having you for company. It often seems to me that you could be my own daughter."

"You have been more than kind to me, madam," Kate replied, touched. "I am deeply grateful for all that you do for me. I owe you so much." And it was true: as a bastard, she could not have wanted for more. She had been brought up as befit a legitimate daughter of a duke and duchess, learning manners, embroidery, and everything else needful for a nobly born girl who was expected to make a good marriage. And she'd had the great good fortune not to be sent to another lordly household or a convent, as many girls were, but to live with her father, the most tender and admirable of fathers, way beyond the common sort, some of whom hardly even noticed their daughters until the time came for them to make a profit by marrying them off advantageously. And in place of a mother, she had the Duchess Anne, who loved her well.

Yes, she was lucky, Kate often told herself.

Her mother, after whom she had been named, was alive and well. She was the wife of the Queen's cousin, James Haute. But Kate had no memories of the woman who had borne her because she had been fostered by a wet nurse immediately after her birth, and brought to

Middleham when she was two. Her earliest memories were of Middleham, with its strong walls, its mighty towers, and its sumptuous private apartments where her father and his family lived in great splendor. She had grown up to love the very air of Wensleydale, its high fells sprinkled with purple heather, its riverside meadows, green valleys, rushing streams, and ancient woodlands.

Kate was aware that her father sometimes dealt in business with James Haute's brother Richard; and she assumed he had met Katherine Haute and her husband socially through Richard Haute. Kate had never liked to ask her father about her mother because it was too delicate a matter, and it was obvious that he was uncomfortable talking about it.

She had not known until she was six that the Duchess Anne was not her mother. When the duchess bore her son that year, she suffered a terrible confinement, and as her screams echoed throughout the castle, Kate had been terrified that Anne would die.

After the screaming stopped, one of the exhausted damsels found her huddled, weeping uncontrollably, at the top of the spiral stairs.

"I don't want my mother to die!" she was wailing, over and over again.

"She's not going to die," said the damsel briskly. She had reasons of her own for resenting the bastards that had been forced upon her mistress; she felt that the duchess had been slighted, and that it showed scant respect on the duke's part. She knew of the grief that Anne had suffered over John of Gloucester and that strumpet Alice Burgh. Even now . . . Well, it stood to reason that it was still going on, didn't it, with that woman's sister appointed wet nurse to the duchess's baby? And yet the duchess still loved her lord, in spite of it all. But what would happen now, when the physicians had said that another child could kill her? Men were men, and they had needs, and solace was near at hand. It was her awareness of this bitter truth that loosened Cecily Clopton's normally guarded tongue.

"Listen, she's not going to die!" the damsel repeated. "And she's *not* your mother!"

The world had rocked. Kate stared up at her tormentor in horror, then fled past her to the safety of the nursery, where Agnes, her nurse, sprang up, surprised, and dropped the small bodice she was stitching. On the floor beside her, John of Gloucester, a sturdy two-year-old, had ceased playing with his puppy and turned up a troubled face.

"It's not true! It's not true!" Kate had cried, burying her face in the capacious apron covering Agnes's soft bosom. "It can't be true!"

"What's not true?" the nurse asked, kneeling down and holding the quivering child firmly by the shoulders. She was shocked at this display of uncontrolled emotion, which was so out of character, for Kate was normally a happy, plucky, biddable child. Agnes was also alarmed, but for a different reason. "Look at me. Tell me! Is the child born? Is Her Grace happily delivered?"

"I think so, but Cecily said the duchess isn't my mother," Kate wept. "I hate her! It's not true!"

There was a pause—a fatal pause—and then Agnes cleared her throat and hugged Kate tighter.

"Calm yourself, child. It's time you knew the truth. No, the duchess isn't your real mother, but she has been a mother to you in every other way, which is as good as being your mother in very truth."

Kate, still sniffing, took a moment to think about this. "Then who is my mother?" she asked tremulously.

"Sweeting, I do not know," the nurse replied, pulling her charge onto her ample lap. "But there is something else I should probably tell you, now that you know this. When a man and a woman marry, their children are trueborn and their lawful heirs. But your father was never married to your mother, and thus you are baseborn and can never inherit anything from him."

Baseborn. Kate didn't like the sound of that. It made her feel second best.

"But," Agnes was saying soothingly, "the duchess loves you as much as the duke does, everyone can see that, and I have no doubt that they will see you well provided for."

A thought occurred to Kate.

"What about John?" She nodded at the toddler, who had lost interest in their talk and was now rolling on the rushes with the puppy. "Is he baseborn too?"

"Aye," Agnes answered, although her mouth had that buttoned-up look that Kate knew so well, which usually meant that she disapproved of something and would not discuss it. "But the duchess loves him too. She is a great lady in more ways than one. You are both fortunate children."

"This new baby . . ." Kate began slowly.

"Heavens, child, what are we doing chattering here when we don't even know how the duchess is—or if the babe is healthy? We must hasten and find out." Putting Kate from her, Agnes pulled herself to her feet, scooped up John in her arms, and ushered her charges through the deserted rooms that led to the ducal bedchamber. Here, all was subdued bustle, with damsels and maids moving quietly hither and thither with stained towels, smelly basins covered with cloths, soiled bed linen, and empty goblets. The midwife was packing her bag in the antechamber.

At the sight of Agnes, come to claim her new charge, the ranks of serving women and noble ladies parted, and the midwife straightened.

"A boy," she announced. "Poor lady, she has had a terrible time of it, but she's sleeping now." The duchess could be glimpsed, a pale-faced figure lying in her great curtained bed, through the open door. Kate was relieved to see her there, and mightily intrigued as to the contents of the fine oak cradle beside her. Two rockers were gently tilting it, crooning to what lay within.

"Is all well with Her Grace?" the nurse asked.

The midwife hesitated. "The child is small, but he will grow. I've sent for the wet nurse." There was a pause, while her eyes met those of Agnes. "The doctors say the duchess will recover, but there will be no more children, so thank God it's a son and heir for the duke."

"Has the duke been sent for?" Agnes asked.

"Been and gone. He could see the duchess was exhausted, so he said he wouldn't tire her."

"How did he take it—about there being no more children?"

"I don't know. The doctors went into the great chamber with him. They spoke in private."

"Well, we must give thanks that my lord and lady have a son," Agnes said resolutely. "Shall we go and take a peep at him, Kate? John can come too."

The duchess slept on as they gazed on the tiny mite in the cradle. He was so little and looked so fragile.

"He favors his mother," said Agnes uneasily; she could think of nothing else to say. If this little scrap lived, she would be surprised.

"He's so sweet," Kate observed. "Can I rock him?" One of the young rockers moved aside to make room for her. Kate found it hard to imagine that this weakly mewling infant would grow up to be a great lord like her father. She did not voice her new fear that this true-born child would displace her in her father's affections, and that the Duchess Anne, for all her kindness, would cleave to her own blood far more closely than she had to the baseborn children she had adopted.

But soon Kate would find that her fears proved groundless. Anne loved her son with all her heart, and he was her favorite, of course, but neither Kate nor John would ever have guessed it, so fairly and lovingly did she treat all three of them. And it was the same with Duke Richard: proud as he was of his legitimate heir, he was equally affectionate to his natural children, and had grand ambitions for them all.

Edward of Middleham did live. He survived all the perils of early childhood, grew stronger, and thrived—although he would never be the most robust of children. He had even been created an earl by his uncle, King Edward: he was now my lord the Earl of Salisbury, and proudly bore the title that had belonged to his mighty Neville forebears. One day, with God's good grace, he would be Duke of Gloucester, like his father before him. But not yet, not for a long, long time, Kate prayed.

For all his exalted rank, young Edward was a boy like any other, and grew up to worship his older half sister and brother. He tried to emulate them in all they did, and learned quickly so as to keep up with them. The three children could often be seen building castles out of toy bricks, or playing make-believe games of knights and dragons, in which Kate was always the princess in distress, John was always St. George, and Edward insisted on being the dragon, ranting around and pretending to breathe fire. Fine weather found them running wild in the gentle dales around Middleham, with their attendants lazing on the grass in the distance. Kate and John always kept a protective watch on Edward, for while he was lively and full of mischief, he tired more easily than they did, and was younger and much smaller in build.

Life was good. From his great castle of Middleham, their father ruled the whole of the North, almost like another king. He kept great state in his household, a lavish table, and a vast train of retainers who wore his badge of the white boar. His family resided in luxurious apartments, furnished with the best that money could buy, and everything was carved and gilded by master craftsmen, or draped and hung with the costliest fabrics.

The best tutors were appointed to teach the children; the duke even insisted that Kate be taught lessons with the boys, saying a well-born girl should know how to read and write. Those skills would bring her pleasure, he promised, and gave her the run of his library, where she spent happy hours poring over exquisite illuminated manuscripts and some of the new printed books made by Master Caxton on his recently established press at Westminster.

She would also, Richard added, find that a good education would help her in other ways.

"One day," he said to her, when she was ten, "you will be the mistress of a great household, for I intend to find a wealthy husband for you." He had said this before, and meant well, but Kate hated to hear him talking about her marriage, because marrying would mean leaving her home, her close kin, and all she held dear, and perhaps living very far away. Her fear was all the greater because the years were passing by and she was well aware that girls of her rank were often married off at fourteen or fifteen, or even younger. But she never said anything for she knew that her father only wanted the best for her. He had often told her that too.

This time, though, he said more. It was growing late; the duchess and the two boys had retired to bed, and Kate was just about to follow them, wishing that the duke had not brought up the subject of her marriage. But he stayed her, and bade her sit opposite him by the hearth, in the duchess's chair.

"There is something I must tell you, my Kate," he said, his strong, lean face with its prominent nose and chin looking slightly tense. "You are old enough now. You must never doubt my love for you, child; you know I would do anything for you. But the truth is . . . that you were born out of wedlock. You are aware of this, I know: I charged Agnes to tell you as soon as you were of an age to understand."

"Yes, sir." She was amazed that he should speak to her of this. In the four years she had known she was baseborn, she had never dared mention it, for she knew that such matters were unseemly, and she could never have summoned up the words to voice her questions to her father. In fact, she had never voiced them to anyone. She feared to upset the duchess, and had no wish to draw attention to the divide between her and John and their half brother Edward. It was enough to know that she had been lucky, for to be baseborn was not a desirable state; and there was a worse word for it too—she had overheard the waspish Cecily saying it behind her back: *bastard, little bastard.* That had hurt. Fortunately, Cecily had since married and moved away, and was no longer there to torment her.

"I did not love your mother," her father said, "and she did not love me, but she was very beautiful, just like you."

Kate did not like to meet his furrowed gaze—it did not seem fitting—so she stared at the crackling flames instead. The duke, taking quick sips of his wine, continued his tale.

"I was her knight, paying my addresses to my chosen lady. But my chosen lady was married, and matters went too far. She told me she was with child. She had to tell her husband too, and he forbade her ever to see me again. Give him his due; he arranged for her to go away to a nunnery to be delivered, and although he forgave her, he would not bring up another man's child as his own, and so you came to me, as was only meet. I had done a dishonorable thing, but I did all I could to remedy it. I paid for your mother to stay at the priory, I arranged for you to go to a wet nurse, and then I brought you here. And I have been rewarded a thousandfold." His visage creased into one of his rare smiles. "I can only excuse myself by saying that I was young and ardent, and that I forgot myself and my knightly oath."

"What was my mother's name, sir?" Kate ventured.

"Katherine. You are named for her." And then he told her all he thought she needed to know about her mother: the few bare facts of her name, her station in life, and where she lived. He did not tell Kate what she burned to know. Did Katherine Haute think often of the daughter she had been forced to relinquish? Had it torn her apart to give her child away, or had her shame made her anxious to get rid of it? Had she ever felt love for her baby? Did she wonder what Kate was doing, and if she thought about the woman who had brought her into the world?

"What did she look like, my mother?" Kate asked, thinking this a safe question.

"She was brown-haired like you," her father said, "with blue eyes and a pretty mouth. She dressed well, as I remember. But in truth, Kate, I knew her for such a short time that my memory of her has faded. Suffice it to say she was a charming lady with a ready laugh and high spirits. And she was quick-witted, I remember. In fact, she was much like you."

Kate could not help herself. "Will I ever meet her?" she implored. "I would love to know her, even just a little."

The duke shifted in his chair and frowned. "No, Kate. I fear it is out of the question. I gave my word that I would never try to see her again. I did it for the sake of her marriage and her future happiness. I cannot go back on it. I am sorry."

"No matter," she mumbled. And in a way, when she thought about it in bed that night, it didn't matter, not too much. She was loved. She had a father, and to all good purposes a mother, and two brothers. Her real mother was a stranger. With sudden grown-up insight, she realized that Mistress Haute might not wish to be confronted with the living evidence of her sin, and that it might have disastrous consequences for her, given that her husband sounded a stern, vengeful man. And Kate was bound to honor her father's promise, as he did. So she tried very much to lay her inner yearnings aside and forget about her mother. But that did not stop her from wondering about her, and spinning fantasies about meeting her unexpectedly, or Katherine sending for her, or even secretly contriving to see her.

Being bastards both, John and Kate shared a common bond. When she judged him old enough, they would whisper together about their mothers, and speculate about them. John was an easygoing, unimaginative boy, though, and did not display the same lively curiosity as Kate did—and maybe it was just as well. For John was the fruit of adultery: he had been born not two years after their father's marriage. No one had ever spoken openly of this, and Kate sensed that it would not be wise to inquire about his mother. She thought it showed exceptional kindness on the part of the duchess to have taken him in and cared for him as tenderly as she did, for the news of his birth must have caused her great pain, and he was a constant living reminder of her lord's infidelity.

And yet, Anne loved the duke. That was as plain as day to anyone. They seemed as happy as any noble couple should be, with their shared interests and their great wealth, much of which had come to the duke by their marriage. He showed his wife every respect and courtesy; he deferred to her wishes; he looked to her comfort. In fact, he did all the things you might expect a good husband to do. But did he love Anne? As Kate grew older, she began to wonder.

She had overheard the damsels whispering one night in the maidens' dorter, which she shared with them after she became too old to sleep in the same chamber as the boys. They must have thought she had fallen into slumber, and in truth she nearly had, but what she heard made her prick up her ears.

"My aunt at court says it is no true marriage." That was Joan Tankerville, recently returned from visiting her kinsfolk near London.

"Really?" Thomasine Vaux sounded shocked.

"It's no secret, apparently. The duke did not seek a dispensation. They are close cousins, you know, and they should have had one before they wed."

The duke? Kate was bewildered. Were they talking about the duke her father?

"But why did he not get one?"

"Aunt Lucy said it was in case she bore him no heir, then he could get an annulment and marry someone else."

"But she brought him great lands, which he would stand to lose if he divorced her."

"Great lords like Gloucester don't easily let go of what is in their grasp. He would find a way, make no mistake about it! Force her into a nunnery probably, or shut her up, like he did her mother."

"What did you say?" Thomasine nearly squealed.

"The old Countess of Warwick. My aunt said he seized all her lands and lured her out of sanctuary at Beaulieu. Then he had her brought here, and locked her up in a tower. He had Parliament pass an Act declaring her legally dead, so that he could keep her lands."

Kate was outraged. How dare they speak of her father so! She reared up in her bed and took pleasure in seeing their faces aghast in the candlelight.

"If I reported you, you could be whipped for what you have just said, or worse!" she warned, her voice icy. "The duke my father loves his wife. I should know, and I will hear no more! And my grandmother is not locked up: she wanders in her mind, and is cared for by a servant, *and* she goes out sometimes. So get your facts right before you spread evil gossip! Now can we get some sleep?" And with these words, she turned over and presented her back to them.

Yes, her father loved his wife. Of course he did. She had been wrong to doubt it. And all this talk of dispensations was nonsense, for the duchess had borne him an heir, and even if she hadn't, it would surely never have occurred to him to put her away.

But how could she really know the truth of it? Kate wondered. No one could be privy to all the secrets between husband and wife. And she was no longer as naïve as she had once been. She knew that her father had not always been faithful: John was the living proof. And she remembered that there had been some dark mystery, and muttered innuendos, about Isabel Burgh, who had lodged in the household for two years as Edward's wet nurse and now lived over Knaresborough way. Was Isabel John's mother? She had never believed it. Isabel had been as correct in her conduct as any servant could be, and Kate had never once seen her lift her eyes to the duke or show any interest in him. And she was not the kind of woman one could imagine inspiring lust: in fact, as Kate recalled, she was rather plain.

But she'd heard that Isabel Burgh had a sister, Alice, who had once worked as a chamberer to the Duchess Anne until, suddenly, she left. Later, she had been appointed wet nurse to the son of the Duchess of Clarence. Over the years, Kate had become aware that voices became even more hushed and secretive whenever Alice Burgh's name was mentioned; there had been gossip—quickly but belatedly silenced when Kate appeared—about the duke awarding the woman a pension, and she had deduced that Alice Burgh left her employment some months before John was born. Could it be that Alice was his mother? That would explain many things.

If so, she reasoned, John must have been the result of a passing fancy on her father's part. Had it been more, matters between the duke and duchess would hardly have mended to the point where they could appear so contented together. And Kate had seen her father grip Anne's hand and look at her with dark passion in his eyes as she stood at his stirrup in the courtyard at Middleham and bade him farewell.

No, there was nothing wrong with their marriage, and the duke's brief fall from grace had meant little. He was a sinner, like everyone else, and no one had the right to throw stones. His lapse made no difference to Kate's feelings for him. He was her father, and she could not have loved and revered him more.

As for her grandmother, that sad, feebleminded figure who lived in the southeast tower and rarely ventured out of it, the duke had given her a refuge. She could not manage her estates, he had explained, so it was better that he had charge of them. And it was clear that he had provided well for the old countess, for she was housed in good comfort, and provided with a servant and an allowance for her small pleasures, and sometimes Kate and the boys would visit her. But they never stayed long because she often forgot who or where she was, or would rant and rage against their father, who had been such a succor to her.

"She is losing her mind," he had said sadly, after they told him of one especially vitriolic outburst. "Pay her no heed. She imagines herself at odds with the world, and with me in particular. Alas, she has had a sad life; it must be hard to be so reduced in circumstances when she was once the wife of great Warwick. Small wonder her mind is gone."

And small wonder too that silly girls made up silly stories about an old lady locked up in a tower!

The news that filtered piecemeal through to Middleham was relentlessly disturbing.

In London, the duke wrote, the Wydevilles were busy trying to consolidate their power in the face of strong opposition from Lord Hastings and other powerful barons, and the hatred of the commons, who had always reviled the Queen and her faction as upstarts.

My Lord Hastings has proposed to the council that I should govern, the duke informed them.

"And he is right to do so," said the duchess, looking up from the letter, "because King Edward, in his will, directed that the government of the realm ought to devolve on my lord until the King attains his majority."

"When will that be?" Kate asked.

"When he is fourteen or fifteen, perhaps. Kings are often declared of age long before ordinary mortals. It's not a very long way ahead, but it's long enough for your father to make a difference, and to wean His Grace away from the influence of his mother's blood. I fear he is entirely their creature."

"Then he probably hates my father," Kate said.

"That is a very shrewd observation." The duchess smiled, although the fact that the smile did not reach her eyes betrayed her anxiety. "It is what my lord greatly fears, and why the boy must be removed from their care."

Kate felt a pang of sadness for her cousin, who might be the King, and hostile, but who was also a boy of twelve about to be deprived of his mother and the kinsmen who had brought him up.

"But will my father succeed in becoming Lord Protector? Has it been agreed?" She was twisting her embroidery in agitation.

"When he wrote this letter they were still arguing about it, and for all we know, they still are." Anne sighed, leaning her weary head against the chair back. She essayed a weak smile. "Mind that altar cloth, Kate, you are ruining it!"

The next news was better. Gloucester had been assured he now had many supporters, with more people declaring for him each day. But still the Wydevilles were asserting their power and refusing to agree to his being named Lord Protector.

"But why?" young John had asked.

Anne laid a gentle hand on his curly head. "Because they know he considers them upstarts, and that he will remove the King from their clutches. And without the King, they are nothing."

Then events had begun to move ahead dramatically. Gloucester met up with the Duke of Buckingham at Northampton, and they had ridden south together, their combined strength at their heels. In the meantime, the little King, escorted by his uncle, Earl Rivers, and his half brother, Sir Richard Grey, was making for London, where he was to be crowned.

My plans are complete, the duke wrote.

There had then been a few agonizing days without news. Kate was painfully aware of the possibility that her father could be lying dead somewhere, killed in battle, for all they knew. The duchess was brooding about that too, going about with a drawn face and spending many hours on her knees in the castle chapel, praying for her lord's safety and gazing heavenward through the soaring tracery windows in near despair. Sometimes Kate would join her before the altar, and they would beseech God together to spare the man they loved.

The news, when at last it came, was sensational. Gloucester and Buckingham had intercepted the King's party at Stony Stratford; they had been forced, for safety's sake, to arrest Rivers and Grey, and had taken the boy Edward into custody. They were now on their way with him to London.

Not a single drop of blood was shed, the duke assured them, in a letter written at an inn late one night. *Yet you may be sure that, after expressing to the King our grief and condolences at the death of his sire, my late brother, of happy memory, we took care to impute his early demise to wicked ministers who had corrupted his morals and ruined his health. We referred, of course, to the Queen's blood.*

That sounded like her father! He might have fallen from grace in his youth, but he was now the most moral of men, upright and God-fearing, and quick to condemn those who fell short of his high standards.

Anne continued reading: "He goes on to say that, lest these same ministers should play their old game with the son, he has removed them from the King's side, because he, being a child, would be incapable of governing so great a realm by means of such puny men. I like the way he puts it." She smiled, but then her face clouded. "He also writes that the Wydevilles were conspiring his death. They had prepared ambushes on the road, and in London. Oh, dear God, I wish I could know that he is safe!"

"They would not dare, surely?" Kate cried in alarm.

"He says the ambushes were revealed to him by their accomplices, so we may hope that the threat has been dealt with. The King stood up for his kinsfolk, as one might expect, but your father told him that he did not know everything that had been going on, and that he himself could better discharge the duties of government, and assured him he would neglect nothing of the duty of a loyal subject and diligent Lord Protector. The King defied him, saying he had great confidence in his mother the Queen and her blood, but my lord of Buckingham answered that it was not the business of women to govern kingdoms, and His Grace should place all his hope in his barons, or those who excel in power and nobility. And so King Edward has perforce surrendered himself into the care of the duke your father."

"It was a wise decision," Kate declared. "He will not regret it."

Anne was reading farther down the page. Her face paled. "There is more. You should read it," she said. "You are old enough to know what is going on."

She sank distractedly into her chair as Kate read what her father had written.

> *I have separated the King's Grace from his household, and ordered all his servants to go to their homes. Many are saying that it is more just and beneficial for the King to be with his father's brother than with his Wydeville kin. The news from London is that the Queen, hearing that we have gained charge of His Grace, has taken sanctuary in Westminster Abbey with the Duke of York and the princesses, as if she needed protection from me. Lord Hastings writes that she believes we are all laboring to destroy her and her blood. Yet she has nothing to fear from me if she ceases her meddling. I have ordered a watch to be made on all who visit her in sanctuary. In London, the citizens are arming, thinking that there will be fighting, but I will do all in my power to prevent*

*any bloodshed. Whatever rumors you hear, pay them no heed, for they
are saying in London that I have brought my nephew the King into my
power rather than my care, so as to gain the crown for myself. You will
be gratified to hear that my Lord Hastings has assured the King's council that I am fast and faithful to my prince, and that I had arrested his
kinsmen only out of fear for my own safety. He himself told the councillors of the plot to murder me.*

Her father, her dear father, could so nearly have died, slain at the
hands of the unscrupulous Wydevilles! Small wonder the duchess was
looking so anxious. But the final lines of the letter brought comfort.
The councillors had praised the duke for his dutifulness toward his
nephew and his intention to punish his—and the King's—enemies.
Rivers and Grey and their associates had been sent north to be held
securely at Pontefract Castle. Her father had also commanded that the
Great Seal of England be given into the safekeeping of the Archbishop
of Canterbury. Now he was on his way to London, and would write
further as soon as he could.

The next messenger brought a summons to London. The duchess was
to join the duke and bring Kate and John with her. A date had been set
for the young King's coronation: it would be on June 24, the feast day
of St. John the Baptist. The duke wanted them present at the great
solemnities that were to take place in Westminster Abbey. But they
could not look forward to it as they should. The coronation might be
the end of everything.

"I have to tell you, Kate: I am in fear for your father," the duchess
confessed, with tears brimming in her light blue eyes. They had set out
on their journey and were seated in a private parlor of a priory guest
house near Stamford, with several tempting dishes laid out on the table
before them. But Anne was merely toying with her food. Another letter lay folded by her plate. "He has informed me that his office of Lord
Protector lapses with the coronation. He expects—nay, he hopes—that
he will be chosen to head the regency council that will govern thereafter in the King's name, but he is aware that the sympathies of several
councillors are with the Queen and her party, so nothing is assured. Yet

even if he is chosen, how long could he expect to be in control? The King could declare himself of age in two or three years' time—and then what?" She buried her face in her hands. "Kate, again I should not be burdening you with this—you are barely thirteen, my poor child—but I know you would want to be told the truth."

Kate embraced her stepmother. Disarmed by this, Anne began weeping uncontrollably, and Kate felt a pang of desperate longing for the tranquil, ordered life they had been leading until the King's death set these disturbing events in motion. Certainly it would be a long time—months, years, if ever—before the duke could return home to Middleham and take up the reins of that old life once more. By then, Kate thought, she might be married and living far away, and the happy years at Middleham would be but a memory for her. And even if she escaped the snare of wedlock, would the new King ever repose such trust in his uncle as his father had? Edward IV had relied on Gloucester heavily, but his son had been brought up under the influence of the Wydevilles, the duke's mortal enemies. Nothing was certain anymore.

Anne's halting words echoed her own thoughts. "The King's loyalties are to his mother and her blood. Dickon writes that young Edward is resentful and hostile. He feels his mother has been slighted. He demands that Rivers and Grey be freed from prison. He loves his uncle Rivers especially: Rivers brought him up at Ludlow. You cannot blame the boy!"

"Certainly he will seek to restore them and the Queen to power," Kate said, realizing what that would mean for her father.

"Aye, and their first thought will be to exact vengeance on my lord. And the King, I fear, will not lift a finger to stop them. The duke can expect no favors from him, nor mercy at the hands of the Queen. My lord makes no secret of his fear of the Wydevilles; and yet he is only fulfilling his brother's dying wishes in taking up the reins of government during this minority."

Anne paused and raised frightened blue eyes to Kate. "Your father's letters betray some agitation of mind, yet all might yet be well. He writes that he has acted as an avenger of treason, and that the Londoners applaud him for it. He says he is popular in the City, for which I thank God. He also states that, if the need arose, he could command troops from the North, which were ever faithful to him. He has already taken the precaution of removing the navy from the control of the Wydevilles. He has summoned Parliament, in the King's name, to assemble after the coronation, and he constantly urges that his protectorate be extended. He is doing all he can, it seems, to ensure his future security. Yet it is plain as day that he anticipates some conflict."

"My lords Hastings and Buckingham are loyal to him," Kate said. "They will insist upon the term of his office being lengthened."

"I think they will," Anne answered thoughtfully. "Especially Buckingham. My lord has rewarded him handsomely for his support. The duke praises him highly, and writes that Buckingham is always ready at hand to assist him with his advice and his great wealth and influence."

"What of Lord Hastings?" Kate asked. It seemed to her that Buckingham was getting the lion's share of the rewards. "Surely his help has been as invaluable? After all, it was Hastings who first warned my father that the Wydevilles were plotting to seize power. If it were not for Hastings, he might not have been in time to take the King."

Anne looked slightly disquieted. "Your father has confirmed that Hastings shall continue to serve as Lord Chamberlain of England and he has put him in charge of the mint."

"Is that all?" Kate was surprised.

"In truth, I think it a little strange," Anne confessed. "Your father says he loves Hastings well, and yet he has been far more lavish with favors to Buckingham."

"Maybe he has something else in mind for Hastings," Kate said.

A messenger caught up with them near Royston. The duke was now Lord Protector: the council had formally invested him, and had entrusted him not only with the governance of the realm but also with the tutelage and upbringing of the King.

It was done with the consent and goodwill of the lords, he had written, *and I have sovereign power to order and forbid in every matter, just like another king. Lord Hastings cannot sufficiently express his joy at such a happy outcome, and we all thank God that it has been achieved without any blood being spilt.*

But it might yet be. The duke had pressed for the condemnation of

Rivers and Grey and two of their associates, but the council had refused to convict them. *They say there is no certain evidence,* he fumed, *and they remind me that, at the time of the alleged attempt on my life, I was not Lord Protector, so cannot press a charge of treason. Some even think those men innocent! They condemn me instead for imprisoning them without judgment or justice.*

"But if he lets them go, they will seek his death," the duchess protested, her voice shaking, her face drawn with fear. "If he has gone too far in the matter, it was because he had no choice. He was right to imprison them, for they were powerful men and would certainly have risen against him, with the backing of the Queen and the rest of her faction. But seizing their estates too? I'm not sure he should have done that, for they have not been attainted by Parliament."

"Not yet," Kate said confidently. "They will be. They must be! Cannot the council see that they are men of blood who would do my father a mischief, given the chance? What else could he have done?" Her little face was unusually flushed with anger. It was rare for her to become so heated.

Kate never forgot her first sight of London. Approaching from the northern heights, after the long journey south from Wensleydale, she suddenly saw before her the fabled city nestling in its broad valley: a marvelous, teeming panorama of rooftops and church spires, dominated by the massive presence of St. Paul's Cathedral, and ringed by strong walls. And as the noble cavalcade progressed slowly downhill from the village of Highgate, she saw fine houses set in spacious gardens and orchards, which presently gave place to more populous and prosperous suburbs.

They were to have gone to Baynard's Castle, the palatial riverside residence of her grandmother, the Duchess of York, but the duke had sent ahead to say that he had removed from there to Crosby Hall, a great mansion he had rented in the City of London, and would await them there. Kate had felt a pang of disappointment about that, because she had been looking forward to seeing her grandmother, but no doubt they would visit her during their stay.

They entered the City through Aldersgate, their route taking them past the great priory of St. Martin-le-Grand, then east into Cheapside and Cornhill, and so to Bishopsgate; and suddenly Kate found herself in a maze of bustling thoroughfares crammed with overhanging timbered buildings and hordes of people. There were stately merchants, rowdy apprentices, sober tradesmen and craftsmen, elegant dames attended by servants, and beggars crying for alms, all jostling each other, eyeing the myriad wondrous wares on display in the shops, and getting in the way of the drays and carts that plied their business. The cacophony of noise was deafening, and the smell was awful. All manner of rubbish, offal, and ordure was strewn across the street, and the mass of unwashed, sweating bodies only added to the stench. Kate pressed a handkerchief to her nose, though before long she would find that she no longer needed it, because you soon got used to living with the London stink. But it was a world away from peaceful Middleham and the spacious dales and moors of Yorkshire.

"Make way! Make way for my lady the Duchess of Gloucester!" cried the captain at the head of their escort, as the townsfolk—some very fine and puffed up in their velvets and gold chains—stepped unwillingly out of the path of the horses. A few doffed their hats and bowed; others peered curiously at the occupants of the horse litter.

The Londoners knew of the Duchess Anne mostly by repute, for she had spent most of her life at her father's castle of Middleham in Yorkshire, now the property of her husband and his favorite seat. From there he had ruled the North like another king, and ruled it well. He was not well known in the capital, but the people cheered Anne as she passed, for they had loved her father, the Kingmaker, and it was said that she was a good and loyal wife, a kindly lady who performed many acts of charity, and most pious and devout. A loving mother too, by all accounts. A shame that she had borne just the one son and heir, after eleven years of marriage.

Many assumed that the robust boy sitting next to the duchess was Edward of Middleham. But, to her sorrow, Anne had to leave him behind in Yorkshire, for he had not been strong enough to travel. Neither had she, in truth, but Richard needed her in London, and to London she had come as fast as she could, ready to stand beside her lord.

Kate, looking avidly beyond the looped-back curtains of the litter, and waving back to some of the friendlier bystanders, had quickly perceived that London was in a ferment of anticipation. Overheard snatches of conversation, meaningful looks thrown in their direction by a cluster of merchants engaged in heated debate, the catcalls of street boys, and the nervous demeanor of the duchess all gave her to understand that they were riding unprepared into the midst of a city split by unrest.

As the litter clattered and juddered along Bishopsgate, Kate felt a deep sense of foreboding. It was clear that her father's authority was by no means fully established. Judging by the mood of the citizens, many were still anticipating that another civil war might break out. She saw men wearing hauberks, brigandine, padded jackets, and even armor; most carried daggers, and some had swords. There were more people than normal on the streets, Anne said anxiously.

The mood of the people was wary, turbulent. "Gloucester wants the crown himself, I tell you!" one man could be heard insisting, while another was loudly proclaiming his opinion that the duke was planning to cancel the coronation.

"How can they speak so of my father?" Kate spoke into the duchess's ear.

Anne's face was taut. "They are ignorant fools!" she hissed, with unaccustomed vehemence. "What did he say to them when he rode with the King into London? He cried repeatedly, 'Behold your prince and sovereign lord!' And he kept deferring to the boy very reverently. The people could have seen his loyalty with their own eyes. It is the Wydevilles and their kin who stir up trouble."

"Ask your lord about the weapons, lady!" yelled a red-faced man in a butcher's apron. Anne blanched and looked away.

"What is he talking about?" John asked her. "What weapons?"

"I wish I understood," she replied. "All I know is that your father wrote to say that, when he entered London with the King, he sent ahead four wagons loaded with weapons bearing Wydeville devices, and had the criers announce that these arms had been collected by his enemies to use against him."

"Where's the Queen?" a woman shrieked suddenly, jabbing a gnarled finger at the litter.

"I shall ignore that," Anne muttered, tight-lipped. "They must know she is in sanctuary. It was a cunning move to gain sympathy and discredit the duke—acting the poor widow, in fear of what he might do to her and her children."

Kate knew all too well that the Queen's continued sojourn in sanctuary was doing her father no good. It must embarrass him greatly, for it looked at best as if he had not taken fitting care for her protection, and at worst as if he meant ill to her and her children. After the seizing of Rivers and Grey, people might easily believe that—as some in this crowd plainly did. Yet Richard had written that he'd been trying to persuade Elizabeth Wydeville to leave sanctuary. *But she refuses, and keeps on refusing!* he had complained. *How does that make me look to the world? By her refusal, she proclaims me a danger to her!*

"She must know he was loyal and devoted to King Edward," Anne said. "How could she think he would harm Edward's wife and children? My lord does not make war on women and infants!"

"No, he does not; and he is taking good care of the King," Kate responded indignantly. He had summoned the lords and citizens to swear fealty to young Edward, and ensured that all due honors were paid to the boy. He had ordered coins to be minted in his sovereign's name. Then the council, at the Duke of Buckingham's suggestion, had arranged for the King to take up residence in the royal palace in the Tower of London, which had been one of his late father King Edward's favorite residences, and surely held many happy memories for his son. Kate had never seen the royal apartments there, but her father had told her that they overlooked the river and were sumptuous, with a great banqueting hall and richly appointed chambers with exquisite stained-glass windows. The walls were painted with angels and birds in gold and vermilion, and there were floor tiles emblazoned with heraldic badges. Kate thought that her cousin the King was very lucky to be living in such a beautiful palace, and she had no doubt that her father had thought of everything needful for his comfort.

———

They were approaching a fine stone mansion, so tall that it dominated the Bishopsgate skyline and dwarfed the other houses.

"Crosby Hall—at last!" the duchess said thankfully. "I could not have borne to be jolted about on these cobbles for much longer."

The litter trundled through a wide archway into a spacious courtyard, and drew to a halt outside an imposing outdoor stone staircase. Kate looked up in awe at the arcades of tall traceried windows on the upper story of the building that towered above her, and the fine stonework of its walls, turrets, and parapets. Crosby Hall was one of the grandest houses she had ever seen.

The courtyard was a hive of noisy activity, as servants hurried in and out of the house unloading carts and sumpter mules. The duke, they soon learned, had taken up residence here only that morning, and his stuff was still being brought into the house. Kate climbed down behind Anne, leaving John to bring up the rear, and they ascended the stairs. And there, at the top, flanked by his chief household officers, Richard himself appeared, waiting to greet them.

Kate's joy at seeing her father was slightly marred by the sight of his tense, drawn, unsmiling face. She watched as he raised the duchess from her curtsey, took her in his arms, and kissed her full on the mouth.

"My lady, it does me good to see you," he said. "And my children! It has been too long." So saying, he beckoned Kate and John forward and embraced them in turn as they rose from their obseisances. Yet it was a formal embrace, Kate noted, as if her father, conscious of his new office, was standing on ceremony. He seemed unusually distant—he, who had normally been so warm to his children. Poor man, he must have a lot on his mind, she told herself.

"Come within!" the duke invited. "You shall see that I have found us a fine house. You might even say it is fit for a king!"

Kate could only agree when she walked into the soaring hall and looked up at the red-and-gold-timbered ceiling arching far above her head. It was a magnificent room, lit by a tall, elegant oriel and a row of high clerestory windows, and its white walls were hung with the most intricate tapestries shot with gold. She saw that Anne and John too were impressed by the splendor of their new residence.

"Is this one of the King's houses?" John asked.

"No, my son, it was built by an Italian merchant, and enlarged by Sir John Crosby, from whom I lease it," the duke explained. "There is no finer residence in the City, apart from Baynard's Castle." By all accounts that too was a palatial building, so Kate wondered why he had removed here.

Richard indicated that Anne should seat herself in one of the carved chairs set on either side of the vast stone fireplace. Stools had been set for Kate and John, and a groom was sent to command wine and comfits from the kitchens. "I know you like them," the duke smiled, sounding more like his old self. "I have ordered a feast for tonight, to celebrate your arrival. My lady, how is our son?"

"He was well when last I heard, thanks be to God," Anne said. "But my lord, I am more concerned about you. You are looking tired."

"The last weeks have been especially challenging," the duke replied. "You know most of what has been going on, but there is more. Tell me, what was the mood of the people when you traveled through London?"

"I did detect hostility, but there was also some cheering," Anne recalled.

"Good," the duke said briskly. "Generally I am popular in the City. These merchants and men of business foresaw only instability with the government in the hands of a child and the grasping Wydevilles."

"We saw men in armor," John piped up.

Their father frowned. "These are uncertain times. Some fear that these tensions might lead to war. The Queen's supporters have the ear of some of the councillors. My motives have been questioned." His expression was grim.

"Your motives? I don't understand." Anne was bewildered.

The duke's eyes met hers. "They say I have meant all along to take the throne myself."

Kate's gasp was audible. John stared at his father incredulously. The duchess had gone very pale.

"But you have never given them cause to think that!" she protested. "What of all the things you have done to ensure the King's peaceful succession? Your care and deference for him, your nurturing of him for kingship?"

"That all counts for little beside the gossip," the duke retorted bitterly. "Which assuredly you will hear, I warn you. That is why I have prepared you."

"Have you spoken out in your defense?" The sharpness in Anne's voice betrayed her distress.

"I have indeed." He got up and started pacing up and down the marble floor. "Why do you think I have based myself here in the City? Every day I have been wooing the chief citizens of London with fair words and gifts, and assuring them that rumor speaks false—and I do believe that I am beginning to calm the fears of some who suspected from the beginning what mark I shot at!"

Kate saw that her father was very angry. He was gnawing his lip, and that was always a sure sign.

"But I have yet to convince the council," Richard was saying. "There are those who wish to prevent me from extending my power beyond the coronation. Well, I know what I must do. A house divided is bound to fall. I will divide the council. I have summoned those councillors who support me to meet with me here, in private. The rest can amuse themselves planning the coronation, which should keep them out of mischief. The real business of the realm will be carried on here."

"My lord, take care, I beg of you!" Anne urged. The Duke ceased his pacing.

"Rest assured I will, my lady."

But Anne still looked troubled. "I heard . . . on the way here . . . things that disturbed me. One man asked where the Queen was; it was like an accusation."

"I have invited her back to court. I have sent messages assuring her of my good intentions toward her and her children. I encourage people to visit her without hindrance, to demonstrate that I intend her no harm."

"While you keep her brother and her son in prison, she will never believe that," Anne warned.

"And if I release them, having justly imprisoned them, accused them of treason, and seized their estates, they will surely exact vengeance on me."

"There was something else," Anne said. "A man shouted at me to ask you about the weapons. What could he have meant?"

"He must have been referring to the cartloads of arms that I commanded to be sent before us when I entered the City with the King," Richard said. "Some allege I faked evidence of a plot against me. In this climate, people will say and believe anything. You must give such calumnies no credence."

He made a visible effort to relax. "But enough of this kingdom's woes. I have thought of nothing else these past weeks. Right now, I want you all to cease worrying and enjoy your stay in London. There is nothing I cannot deal with, and we have a coronation to look forward to. No doubt you ladies have been discussing your attire. I have sent for the best mercers and goldsmiths in Cheapside to attend upon you. And now we must to dinner!"

KATHERINE

May 1553; Baynard's Castle, London

The earl has waved all the servants away, and as a door closes behind them and their footsteps fade away into the distance, he looks intently at us.

"For now, you must curb your feelings for each other, my children," he announces. "It has been agreed that you shall not lie together just yet."

"No!" Harry's response is quick and furious. "No! Father, we are man and wife, and we are both old enough to become one flesh, as Scripture enjoins us."

I cannot speak for shock and disappointment.

"It grieves me to forbid you, my son, but I assure you that all has been decided for the best," the earl says kindly.

"But why?" demands Harry. "If I am to be kept from my wife, I have a right to know why!"

The countess, slightly flushed, steps forward and places a hand on his arm. "My son, there are things—great matters—that you know nothing of. If our plans come to fruition—"

"Hush, woman!" Pembroke interrupts.

"I but sought to assure these young people that if matters go our way, all will be well," she protests, then comes over and embraces me. "Do not look so unhappy, child. It will only be for a short time, I am sure."

"Katherine is my wife! I have a right to lie with her," Harry insists, his temper rising. "You shall not stop me!"

"Don't you understand, you ignorant young cub?" his father barks, jabbing a forefinger at him. "We are doing our best to protect the interests of you, your lady wife here, and our two families. More than that I cannot say, but you must accept my judgment—and you owe me obedience!"

Harry's mother says gently, "You may keep each other company at will, and enjoy life together—all we ask is that you postpone the consummation of your marriage until such time as it may be accomplished in perfect harmony and peace."

Harry looks defeated. Maybe the finality of his father's tone has silenced him.

The countess takes my arm. "Dear daughter, I myself will show you to your bedchamber. Bid good night to your husband and attend me."

Harry embraces me, kisses me hard on the lips, and whispers in my ear, "Don't lock your door." I thrill to his words. We will defy them all, my love and I: we *will* be together, in spite of what they say! My heart is racing as I meekly follow the countess without a backward look. They think they have won—but we will be the victors!

My room is beautiful, lavish! The tester bed is carved, gilded, and built on a dais. The curtains are of rich red damask looped with gold tassels, the counterpane of costly cloth of gold, with lozenges embroidered with the lions of Pembroke on a background of red and blue velvet. Over a chair is draped the most exquisite nightgown of crimson satin edged with pearls. A bowl of dried petals gives off a fragrant scent.

My maid is waiting. She detaches my oversleeves, unlaces the heavy wedding gown, and lets it fall onto the rich carpet so that I can step out of it; then she attires me in a lawn smock and brushes my hair—twenty, forty, sixty strokes. I am ready for bed now, and she turns back the covers, helps me in, douses all the candles but the one on the table, curtsies, and silently closes the door behind her.

I feel very alone, lying in this strange bed. I had not expected my wedding night to be like this, and suddenly I experience an unexpected pang of homesickness, which I'm sure I would not be feeling if Harry was with me. Trying not to weep, I fix my gaze on the pictures on the walls: a curious painting narrating the terrible story of Jephthah's daughter, and a portrait labeled ANNE PARR, who was the earl's late wife, Harry's mother, and sister to Queen Katherine. On my night-stand is a dish of figs, a rare delicacy, and a goblet of sweet wine. I am cosseted in luxury. I lack for nothing but my husband.

Will he come? I lie waiting for what seems like hours. Of course, he must wait until the house has settled down for the night. Dare he come? Or has he thought better of his rash defiance? Lord, please let him come!

What was that? The sweep of a night owl's wings as it swooped to its prey? Nay, it was a footfall. And another, stealthy, only audible to one who is awaiting it. And suddenly the door opens and there is my Harry in his black nightgown, his eyes alight with love, and desire in his pale face. My heart is fit to burst with joy!

Silently, slowly, he closes the door, then pads on bare feet toward me. I hold out my arms and he comes into them and kisses my lips. Then he pulls down my smock and bends to nuzzle my budding breasts.

"Harry!" I whisper, blushing.

"Sweeting!" he murmurs, and makes to remove his nightgown.

"What is the meaning of this?" barks a sharp voice from the door-way. "I thought I had made myself clear!" It is the earl, standing there like an avenging angel, hands aggressively on hips, black brows knit in a frown.

Harry jumps up startled, gathering his nightgown about him, while I hastily pull up the sheet, my cheeks flaming.

"Get you hence, my son!" the earl commands. "And do not think to disobey me again. It's fortunate that I was awake listening for you. I know you, my boy. Adventurous like me. Well, I can't blame you, but you will not defy me again. Say good night to your young lady and go back to your room, and we will say no more of the matter."

"And if I refuse?" Harry challenges.

"Then I will call my men and have you thrown out." Pembroke's shoulders suddenly sag. "Look, it's late, and I'm tired. I don't intend to stand here arguing. I am sorry, but you must be patient for a while longer. Now get back to your chamber, my son. And you, my lady, go to sleep. Good night." He holds open the door.

Harry is vanquished. He stoops and kisses me briefly, then sullenly walks out of the room, his father following. This time, the key does turn, leaving me a prisoner. I am a wife, yet not a wife: a virgin still, and I fear I will remain so for God knows how long. It is enough to make anyone weep. And I do.

KATE

June 1483, Crosby Place and the City of London

There was a great stir and commotion in London. People were busy making ready for the young King's coronation. Whenever Kate, accompanied by the new maid her father had appointed, ventured out of the house to browse in the enticing shops in Cheapside, she saw queues of liveried servants at the goldsmiths' and the mercers,' collecting jewels and fabrics ordered by their noble masters and mistresses.

London, to Kate, was still an intimidating, if exciting, place. That air of menace she had sensed when she first arrived still pervaded the streets, and many citizens continued to parade about in their armor, clearly fearing trouble. She was aware of the tension within Crosby Place, where the King's councillors had been gathering for private meetings. She had seen them from her window, dismounting in the courtyard and being ushered into the house. Her father often sat up late at night in conference with them; she had glimpsed the candle flames flickering through the diamond panes of the council chamber.

One morning there had been a stranger at breakfast, a handsome, smooth-tongued lawyer whom the duke introduced as Sir William Catesby. He was clearly liked and trusted by her father, but Kate took an instinctive aversion to him. He seemed sly and crafty, and he spoke with scant respect of his master, Lord Hastings. Kate had always imagined Lord Hastings to be a kindly, upright man, and she knew he had rendered a timely service to her father, so she felt indignant that Sir William Catesby seemed to regard him with derision. And her indignation rose higher, as her father walked with him to the porch to say farewell, when she overheard their muttered exchange.

"Fear not Lord Hastings, good my lord." That was Catesby. "He is content that the council should be divided. The fool thinks I am reporting all our proceedings here to him and the rest."

"As long as he thinks you loyal to his interests, we need not concern ourselves with him," the duke replied. "And so fare you well, Sir William. I will proceed with our other matter. And I am ready to offer you good lordship at any time."

That did not sound very charitable toward Lord Hastings either, Kate thought. What could his lordship have done to offend her father and his lawyer?

There came an evening when the Duke of Buckingham, a grand, lordly northerner with a bluff manner, came to dine. He was good company at table: even her father—so taciturn and brooding these days, and often as somber as the mourning he was wearing for his brother—fell to laughing at his jests.

Buckingham made much of the Duchess Anne, showing her every courtesy and deferring to her opinions as if they were pearls of wisdom dropping from her lips. He means to flatter and cozen my father, Kate thought. For Gloucester had many privileges within his gift: he was king in all but name. That was what it meant to be Lord Protector.

Buckingham praised John highly. "Ye have a fine boy there," he observed. "What will ye be, young man? A knight?"

"If my father so wishes, sir," John answered. He had been well schooled in courtesy and obedience.

"I see no reason why not." The duke smiled, but he looked so tired, Kate thought. John was happy, though. To win his knighthood was all he asked of life.

"And this fair damsel, is she to be wed soon?" asked Buckingham, helping himself to another chicken leg and beaming at Kate.

"She is but thirteen," Anne said. "There's plenty of time to think of marriage."

"Aye, Duchess, but your good lord here could find a husband to warm her bed *and* prove useful as an ally," Buckingham said. "Two birds with one stone, eh?"

"All in good time, Harry," Gloucester intervened. "I would keep my fair Kate with me a little longer yet. More wine?" The subject—to Kate's relief—was closed.

They sat late at the table. The wine pitcher, refilled twice, was nearly empty again, and the candles were burning low. John had been sent to bed, and Kate had withdrawn to the fireside with her sewing. At the far end of the hall a lone minstrel plucked a lute. Kate recognized the tune: *"Mon souverain desir,"* an old French chanson, and found herself humming along with it.

"What of the Queen?" Buckingham asked suddenly.

Gloucester gave a snort of exasperation. "She is adamant she will not leave sanctuary. In fact, she's been so obstructive that the councillors are refusing to visit her anymore."

"Someone ought to persuade her that she has nothing to fear from you, my lord," the duchess put in.

"Ah, but do I have anything to fear from her?"

"Maybe it's better she stays in sanctuary," Buckingham said. "At least we know where she is and what she's about. But there remains the problem of what to do about the Duke of York."

"He must leave sanctuary as soon as possible," Gloucester said. "It does not do for a boy of his age to be cooped up in confinement with his mother and sisters. And his presence is needed at the coronation." He got up and began pacing. He had imbibed several goblets of Rhenish, and his gait was a touch ungainly. It was one of those times when it became noticeable that he had one shoulder slightly higher than the other. "I will have the boy out of there, whatever that woman says," he vowed darkly. "How will it look if he is absent from his brother's crowning?"

"Bad," replied Buckingham. "A political embarrassment."

"Go gently with the Queen, my lords," Anne urged. Her face in the firelight was drawn; she too was feeling the strain of these difficult days.

Kate's fingers were working automatically with her needle, but her mind was wholly focused on the conversation going on behind her. "The Duke of York is but nine years old," the duchess was saying.

"You have a soft heart, Anne," Richard said. "But a boy of nine should not be governed by women."

"In a couple of years he'll be of an age to go into battle," Buckingham declared. Anne said nothing: she was rarely one to confront the decrees of men. But Kate could imagine what she was thinking, and that her thoughts had turned to her own fragile little boy, who would probably never be strong enough to fight in the field.

"Aye, well, ye'll just have to insist that the Queen gives up the lad," Buckingham was saying. "Tell her his brother needs company of his own age in the Tower."

"Indeed he does," Gloucester agreed.

A chair scraped the floor. "Forgive me, my lords, I am going to retire," Anne said, and the two dukes stood up. It was the signal for Kate to leave too, and having gathered up her sewing things, said her goodnights, and followed her stepmother out of the hall, she heard her father say, "Now, what of Hastings? Will you sound him out?"

"I have done that already," Buckingham replied. "It was useless."

The City was still abuzz with rumors. Whenever she went abroad, Kate was aghast to hear common folk pronouncing freely on the deeds and motives of their betters, and she quickly learned not to open her mouth, because the Londoners seemed to regard all northerners as savages, and as far as some were concerned, her father was one of them.

It was horrible, horrible! But worst of all was the venom of a friar preaching to a crowd on Bishopsgate.

"Where is this leading but to treason of the worst sort?" he cried, his red, well-fed face a mask of outrage. "The King in the Tower, in the power of the Duke of Gloucester. The Queen and her children in sanctuary, afraid to come out. The Queen's kinsmen either unlawfully imprisoned or fled overseas. And now talk of a new enmity between Gloucester and Lord Hastings."

"Hastings is loyal to the King!" shouted a bystander.

"Aye, but he has no reason to be loyal to Gloucester," the friar retorted.

Kate could not help herself. "Gloucester is loyal to the King too!" she cried out. "He is a good man!" To her dismay, her words were greeted with jeers and hoots of derision.

"Loyal my foot!" trumpeted a stout woman beside her. "He's after the crown, the crafty bugger. That's what he wants!"

"And Hastings knows it, mark my words," chimed in a man whose bloody apron proclaimed him a butcher. "With luck, he'll be the ruin of Gloucester."

"Hark at her!" shrieked a fishwife, pointing at Kate. "It's clear where she hails from. You got a tail under that fine gown, love?"

"No!" Kate squealed, then fled in terror, pushing her way through the astonished mob, leaving Mattie, her little maid, struggling to stay with her. People called after her, but she was running, running, hastening back to the ordered world of Crosby Place.

Her father caught her in his arms as she raced into the hall.

"Those dreadful people!" she panted. "Sir, they say that Lord Hastings will be your ruin. It cannot be true, surely?"

Gloucester looked her straight in the face, still grasping her arms.

"It may be true," he said. He was deadly serious, and it terrified her. "But never fear, daughter. I am on my guard, and every precaution is being taken."

"But Hastings helped you," Kate protested.

"My enemies have poisoned his mind, telling him that I covet my nephew's throne. They are clever and plausible, and so he plots my downfall."

"Be watchful!" Kate begged, pressing her damp face into the seamed velvet of his doublet. Behind her Anne looked at him with pain in her eyes.

"I did not ask for this," Richard said.

Her father looked ill. He dragged himself around the house, as if in pain. He barely touched his food, took hardly a sip of wine, and complained that he could not sleep and was suffering from a strange, inexplicable malaise. Anne was sufficiently distraught to summon his mother, the Duchess of York, from Baynard's Castle. The duchess had just arrived in London to attend the coronation of her grandson.

She came, the venerable Cecily, looking the very image of a devout widow in her black, nunlike garments, a snowy wimple framing her haughty, aristocratic face. She had the high cheekbones and strong features of most of the Neville race.

"You must take care of yourself, my son," she admonished the duke as he knelt for her blessing. "You look sick and haggard. For the love of God, go to bed and rest."

"There is too much to do, madam my mother," he protested, rising to his feet. "I have one especially urgent matter to attend to."

"Can it not wait?" the Duchess Cecily barked.

"I fear not, madam," he replied.

"Is it concerning that hussy who calls herself Queen?" His mother was visibly bristling. "Has she not caused enough harm?"

"Yes, it is the Queen and her following," the duke said testily. "I will tell you presently. Pray be seated, my lady." The duchess unthinkingly took the chair that was usually his—the most imposing one in the room. Anne came and knelt before her, receiving a loving look— the duchess approved heartily of her daughter-in-law and great-niece. And then it was the turn of John of Gloucester, and finally of Kate.

"You have bred a little beauty, my son," Cecily pronounced, tipping Kate's chin upward to see her better. "A modest decorum too. Most edifying." She nodded, well pleased.

"So, Richard," she went on, "tell me about the Wydevilles. God knows I curse the day when that woman married your brother."

"She and her kin loathe me," the duke said. "I am convinced they mean to utterly destroy me, my cousin Buckingham, and all the old royal blood of this realm."

Cecily grimaced, but looked skeptical. "How can this be, my son? The woman is in sanctuary, her kinsmen imprisoned or fled."

"She is allowed visitors. I cannot be seen to be keeping her a prisoner. She is free to leave sanctuary if she pleases. But Shore's wife, for one, sees her frequently."

Kate noticed a look of distaste shadow her grandmother's face.

"That slut!"

"She acts as an agent for her lover Hastings, plotting against me with the Queen," Gloucester growled. "I tell you, madam, it is openly known, for they do not trouble to hide it. Oh, they think they are subtle, but certain it is they are conspiring the destruction and disinheriting of me and many others, all good men of this realm!" His voice shook with anger.

"Summon the men of the North," his mother counseled. "The city of York is loyal to you and will send soldiers to your aid. Do not tarry on this, my son."

Gloucester lifted her hand and kissed it.

"I will do it!" he said. "I could ever rely on your counsel."

"Is help not nearer at hand?" Anne interrupted. "If the situation is as bad as you say . . ."

"If?" Richard shouted, to Anne's evident dismay. "Of course it is as bad as I say. I am in peril of my life—and all because I have been loyal to my king. Naturally I intend to summon aid from elsewhere. Even as we speak, summons are being prepared for the Earl of Northumberland, Lord Neville, and their affinities. My councillor, Richard Ratcliffe, is waiting to depart."

Anne was struggling to control her tears. She was unused to being silenced so severely.

"Shore's wife should be apprehended," the duchess warned. "The woman is a menace."

"I will deal with her anon," Richard muttered. "But there are more serious threats to be neutralized first. I mean the Queen's brother, Earl Rivers, and her son, Sir Richard Grey, whom I sent as prisoners to Pontefract."

"Surely they can do no harm to you there?" Duchess Cecily sniffed. "That castle is all but impregnable."

"So the King's Council tells me," the duke muttered. "But those two will ever be a danger! What happens when the King comes of age and frees them? They have already treasonously conspired to kill me."

"Are you now king, then?" asked his mother. "My son, it is not treason to conspire the death of the Lord Protector, heinous crime though that be."

"It's an arguable point," he responded testily.

"Have they been proven guilty?" the duchess persisted. There was a silence. Kate realized they had all forgotten she was there. She felt that she wanted to curl up and die. It was bad enough that her father was being so grievously threatened by his enemies, so why was her grandmother treating him as if he were somehow in the wrong?

"I asked if they have been tried or attainted by Parliament?" Cecily said reasonably. "My son, if you do what I suspect you are planning to do, then you lay yourself open to charges of tyranny."

"But if I have those men tried, my enemies will acquit them, and they will be free to do their worst!" protested the duke. "I am in an impossible position. Whatever I do, I cannot win. Madam, do you not see that I cannot afford to let them live?"

"The King will never forgive you if you kill his kinsmen without trial." Anne spoke out at last. "My lord," she went on tremulously, laying a gentle hand on his sleeve, "I fear for you, I truly do. I fear for us all."

Kate could bear to listen no more. Excusing herself, she escaped up the stairs to her bedchamber, and there she too gave way to tears.

The next morning, she learned from the Duchess Anne that her father had gone after Mass to the Tower of London for an important council meeting, about which he had remained tight-lipped. His going there filled Kate with a sense of dread; there was something about the Tower that repelled and unnerved her. She could not for the life of her say why. She only knew she had gone there one day to see the menagerie but was unable to bring herself to set foot in the vast, forbidding fortress.

"I have received a letter from Edward's tutor," Anne was saying.

"My little lord is doing well at his lessons, and is in good health." She sighed. "I miss him. I ache to see him. The distance between us seems so great." Her blue eyes held a faraway look. "If it were not for my lord, who needs me, I would go home."

"Oh, so would I!" cried Kate.

"Well, after the coronation, we will think about it," Anne said. "But we cannot miss that. And the tailor is making you a splendid gown." He was indeed. Just thinking about it made Kate feel a little better. It was in indigo-blue damask with raised flowers of yellow and gold, and it was to be trimmed with miniver at the bodice and cuffs. The court train was longer than any she had ever worn, so long that she would have to carefully practice walking with it.

But today she had donned a plain dove-gray gown of soft wool because she did not desire to look too conspicuous. She was planning to go again to Cheapside, which had become one of her favorite haunts in the City. A master jeweler there had a beautiful pendant displayed among his wares and, having persuaded him to set it aside for her, she had prevailed on her father to give her the money for it. Richard had ever been generous toward his children, and never stinted on their allowances, but last night he had seemed distracted as he agreed without demur to her request, even though the pendant was expensive. He had not been listening when she told him it would go with her coronation gown.

She took her maid Mattie with her, a plump and comely Londoner with a lively nature and a spirit of adventure that chimed with her own. Despite the difference in their status, they were fast becoming friends. Kate enjoyed having a girl near her own age as a merry companion, and she had been delighted to discover that she and Mattie were kindred souls in many ways.

Mattie was fourteen, a year her senior. Happily, just as the duke had decided his daughter was of an age to need a maid, Mattie's father, a member of the Vintners' Guild, which supplied the duke's household with wine, had inquired if there might be a place for his daughter at Crosby Hall, anticipating that service in the Gloucester household might lead to an opening at court and preferment, and secure Mattie a prosperous husband one day. But Mattie was unconcerned about that: let an apprentice lad whistle at her, and she was smitten. Plain-spoken like most Londoners, she had an earthy appreciation of the opposite sex, and did not bother to mince words about it. She was also full of the lore of the city that had nurtured her, loved pretty clothes, good food, singing, and dancing, and laughed out loud at merry or bawdy jests. She and Kate were doing very well together, and Kate was firmly of the opinion that her father could not have chosen a better maid for her.

With Mattie at her heels, she sped along Cornhill, weaving through the London crowds who thronged the narrow thoroughfares, and so into Poultry and Cheapside, where Master Hayes had his shop. He greeted her obsequiously, for she had told him whose daughter she was to impress on him that she was not wasting his time. But there was a faint edge to his manner. It seemed that he too was infected with the prevailing hostility toward her father. She stiffened and, putting on a manner so regal it would have done the Duchess Cecily proud, asked for the jewel to be brought.

It lay on a bed of black silk, a diamond-shaped gold pendant set with a brilliant sapphire stone. On its obverse the goldsmith had masterfully engraved a tableau of the Trinity with the crucified Christ at the center, and surrounded it with a border of burnished gold. On the reverse, when she turned it over, Kate found a finely delineated nativity scene.

She counted out her gold coins and handed them over.

"See, it is hinged here," Master Hayes pointed out. "You can open it and use it as a reliquary. There is space inside for a small relic."

"My father the duke owns several relics. I will ask him for one. Thank you."

Master Hayes stiffened. "I will have it wrapped for you, my lady," he said abruptly.

Kate's delight in acquiring the pendant was muted by the goldmith's barely veiled animosity. As she and Mattie walked back along Cheapside, Mattie chattering away and steering her toward a stall selling gingerbread and lavender cakes, she was asking herself why her father should have so many enemies.

He was at the Tower even now, for that important council meeting, and she still had the feeling that something evil was afoot. Suddenly, she knew what she must do: she must set aside her silly fears of the place, go to the Tower, and wait for her father to emerge from the council chamber. Then she would be the first to hear any important news he had to impart.

She swung left into Gracechurch Street. "Let's walk down to the Tower," she said.

"Yes, my lady." Mattie, who had demolished the gingerbread, bought two apples from a fruit seller to stay them until dinner, and they walked along Eastcheap crunching them. It was a beautiful, mild spring day, and presently they saw before them the mighty walls and white masonry of the Tower, massive and stately against the blue sky.

As they walked down Tower Hill, they passed a raised wooden platform surrounded by a fence.

"What's that?" Kate asked.

"It's the public scaffold, my lady. It's where traitors are beheaded or gutted. The executions here always draw a goodly crowd."

Kate shuddered. Men had died here, horribly, bloodily. And the unwelcome thought came unbidden that her own beloved father was in danger of meeting such an end. It would take only one twist of fate . . .

She recovered herself. "Have you ever been to an execution?" she asked.

"No, there haven't been any here for years," Mattie replied.

"Then I pray God there will not be for many more." Kate made herself walk forward to the Tower.

KATHERINE

June 1553; Baynard's Castle, London

My lord of Pembroke cannot do enough for me. It is as if he feels he must make up for depriving me of the private joys of marriage. My days are spent in glorious idleness, in rooms and halls of the brightest splendor, or in gardens sweeping down to the river, gay with flowers and heavy with fruit.

My every whim—but one—is gratified. Do I but express a wish for a bunch of cherries or a cup of cordial, it is there, in my hand, within minutes. My wardrobe is stuffed with gorgeous gowns of every hue, rich furs, embroidered kirtles, and costly velvet hoods—for now that I am a wife, even though I am still a virgin, I must bind up and cover my hair. That crowning glory is now for my husband alone, or it would be were he allowed to be with me when I take my hood off. The Herberts did not have to provide me with such attire, for I brought a fitting trousseau with me when I married, but they dismiss such largesse as the least they can do for a daughter-in-law in whom they are well satisfied.

Daily I feast on the choicest foods served on gold and silver-gilt plate; I drink from glasses of the best Venetian crystal. I attend divine service in a lofty chapel plainly appointed, as befits the house of a good Protestant, but hung with arras and paintings of scenes from the life of Our Lord. Musicians while away my evenings on lutes and virginals, as I beat my lord at chess and tables, or read my book.

It seems strange not to have my days governed by the strict round of lessons that my parents decreed for us. At home, even before we were old enough to put away childish things like the baby dolls dressed in crimson satin and white velvet, we had to get up at six and eat our breakfast before we visited my lord and lady for their daily blessing. Then, when our proper tutoring began, we had lessons in Latin and Greek, which lasted all morning. I struggled, God help me I did, for I was nowhere near as good at mastering those ancient tongues as Jane. She even learned Hebrew, at her own request.

After dinner we would be drilled in French and Italian, and then we had to read from the Bible or the classics. I think I read the Bible three times over. Even then we were not free, for after supper we were expected to practice our music, dancing, and needlework before being banished to our beds at nine o'clock. There was hardly any time for our own favored pursuits. Even on holidays, when the merry maypole was set up and the Morris dancers made sport on our lawn, we were kept to our daily tasks and not allowed to take part. So I find it difficult to live in idleness. I do not know how to fill the long, spacious hours.

"What shall I do?" is my constant question. My lady the countess kindly takes time to instruct me in the ordering and running of the household, which will be my responsibility one day, but not for ages yet, God willing. She finds me books to read, or tapestry to stitch, although I am not very good at it. I cannot, whatever I do, make the stitches small enough. My mother-in-law is endlessly patient. I believe she feels sorry for me, but does not like to say so for loyalty to her husband.

With Harry, it is difficult. It is hard to be together, knowing we are man and wife, yet not free to love each other. Yes, we kiss and we embrace, but only furtively or self-consciously, for we are never left alone together: there is always at least one servant within sight or earshot. And at night my door is locked. My lord earl will not risk his will being thwarted a second time. It would be easier if I could understand why we are being kept apart, but it still makes no sense to me. If I venture to ask, I am told—not unkindly—that I am too young to understand.

But Harry has of late been taken a little into his father's confidence. When I suggest, only half jesting, that he attempt to steal the key and come to me at night, he tells me no, it cannot be, for fear of Northumberland.

"Northumberland?" I echo. "What has our marriage got to do with him?"

Harry looks unhappy. There is no one within earshot in the courtyard, only a gardener deadheading the flowers in the stone urns, but still he bids me lower my voice.

"Northumberland urged our marriages, ours and that of your sister to his son," he mutters. "Maybe he feels being allied to royal blood enhances his power."

There is something that does not make sense. "In that case," I say, "it would make better sense to let us consummate our marriage."

Harry looks at me admiringly. "It would indeed! It would bind our families irrevocably to him. By God, I have it! Maybe Northumberland and our parents don't want to be committed for good."

"That makes sense, given what I overheard my father and mother saying," I say.

Harry shakes his head. "But why would they not want to be bound? Why agree to the marriages in the first place?"

"I cannot think," I say. "You could ask your father."

"He would not tell me," he answers glumly.

Nevertheless, that evening, at the supper table, Harry makes so bold as to bring up the matter.

"Sir," he ventures, "why do you and my lord of Northumberland not wish our families to be bound for good by our marriage?"

The earl appears disconcerted, but recovers himself at once and lays down his knife on his plate. "Who said that we do not?" he asks.

"We worked it out for ourselves, sir," Harry says. "We know that Northumberland suggested these marriages, and that, in some way that you will not reveal, they are advantageous to him. But maybe there are disadvantages too."

There is silence for a moment, and then the earl roars with laughter. "You're a statesman, Harry, by God! And you have a good grasp of politics. But rest assured, your mother and I would not bind you in a disadvantageous match. The Lady Katherine here is the King's own cousin, of royal lineage, and herself in the line of succession. Who could be more suitable? Nay, lad, curb your passions and let wiser heads rule you. You will not be stayed from your wife for long. Be patient, I counsel you." And with that, the earl changes the subject and speaks of hunting. It is an end to the matter. But am I the only one who noticed that, when he laughed, his eyes remained cold?

Harry and I are bored. We have played chess in the garden, read our favorite poems aloud to each other, raided the kitchens for marchpane and comfits, and played hide-and-seek in the great state rooms, always with the inevitable servant keeping a safe distance.

We are getting to know each other. His face, so utterly dear to me, is now as familiar as my own. I try to stop myself wishing that his body could be too, for in every other respect we are becoming closer in our minds and hearts, united in our shared sense of injustice against the world, Northumberland, and our parents. It has bound us faster than I could ever have imagined.

I am finding Harry to be not just a loving husband, but a young man of letters and culture. He has been well tutored, which is no surprise, since his mother—dead these two years now, and much mourned by her son—was very learned. After this early grounding, the earl sent Harry to live with a tutor at the university at Cambridge, yet he is no bookish dullard: he likes a good play too, is passionate about racing horses, and collects books and manuscripts on heraldry.

He snatches every opportunity to touch me, to kiss and caress me, but he always ends up on fire for me, and finds it very frustrating to have to hold himself back. In the beginning I would ask myself if I truly loved him, as is my duty as a wife. Now I no longer need to ask myself that question. It is my duty—but also my greatest joy and pleasure. I am a changed person because of Harry. I feel myself opening outward, blossoming like a flower, as I reveal myself to him bit by bit—my inner nature, my hopes and fears, my very soul—knowing that everything about me is precious in his eyes. And he is no less dear in mine. I cannot have enough of him.

So here we are, this hot June day, weary after so much running about, wondering what to do next to fill the empty hours, when we are both tense with the knowledge that we could be spending them in bed, were we allowed to. Wandering through the vast house, we enter the old wing, the only part that escaped the attentions of my great-grandfather, Henry VII. Here, the chambers are smaller, wainscotted and paneled, with stone fireplaces and mullioned windows grimed with dirt. Dust motes dance in the musty air; there is a faint smell of damp, and something nasty, probably a dead mouse, behind the wainscot. Wrinkling my nose I walk on into the next room, where I pause before a portrait of an old lady dressed as a nun, in a long wimple and chin barbe. She looks very severe and forbidding. There is a date painted above her shoulder: *1490.*

"I know her," I say. "I've seen her likeness before. That's the Lady Margaret Beaufort, the mother of Henry VII, and my great-great-grandmother."

"Wrong!" cries Harry. "It's the old Duchess of York, Cecily Neville. She was the mother of Edward IV and Richard III, and your great-great-great-something-grandmother! She lived here in the last century—ran the household like a nunnery, for she was very religious. But that wasn't always the case!"

"I heard tell that she was a very venerable lady," I say.

"Not always. It was quite openly said that she betrayed her husband with an archer, and that Edward IV was the archer's son."

"I can't imagine her betraying her husband with anyone, looking at her picture!" I giggle.

Harry laughs. "I can't even imagine her having a husband," he says.

"Do you think it's true, what people said?" I ask, staring at the portrait and trying in vain to imagine the Duchess Cecily as she would have looked in her younger days.

"Who can say? My tutor told me that two of her sons, no less, made the accusation. Richard III was one of them."

"Oh, well, in that case it can't be true," I retort. "Richard III was a deceiver and a murderer. How could he have said that about his own mother?"

"Indeed, especially if it wasn't true."

"I'll wager he just made it up."

"No, *he* didn't," Harry tells me. "Apparently his older brother, the Duke of Clarence, had said it first, many years before, when he wanted to impugn Edward's title so he could get the crown for himself. He was a villain too, by all accounts. He was executed by drowning in a butt of Malmsey." I had heard that old tale many times.

"They were all villains, by the sound of it," I laugh.

We wander on, through several more interconnecting rooms, most of them bare of furniture and very dusty. It is obvious that even the servants rarely come here. The few old pictures that still hang on the walls are cracked or buckled. There is one that strikes me particularly. It is very finely done, a half length of a young girl, a very pretty girl with a sweet round face, serene dark wide-set eyes, and thick, wavy chestnut hair bound only by a filet. She wears a rich blue gown figured in gold with an embroidered border around the neckline, and an exquisite diamond-shaped pendant. Her beauty and grace are arresting, and the colors look as fresh as if the picture had been painted yesterday.

"Who is that?" I ask Harry.

"I have no idea," he replies. "It's probably been here for years. It's not anyone I recognize."

I peer closer. "There is no clue, no coat of arms or date or age. But she must have been someone important to have had her likeness painted."

The girl seems to stare back at me: her face is skillfully painted and uncannily lifelike. I feel I know her from somewhere, but that cannot be, as the style of her dress is years out of date; and yet I am drawn to her. It's not just that it's a beautiful portrait. There is something more, something about the eyes. The limner has caught them so craftily: they seem to be looking directly into mine, holding mine, appealing . . . He must have been a master of illusion, I think, as I drag myself away, breaking the spell.

Harry slides his arm around my waist, and just at that moment there is a muffled footfall not far behind us. We are being watched again. It's a horrible feeling because the watcher is keeping himself just out of sight in the next room. But Harry seems unaware. He is looking at the painting.

"Those clothes are very fine, but very old-fashioned. This must have been done years ago, possibly back in the Duchess Cecily's time."

"Maybe it's a princess," I venture.

"Aye, one of the daughters of Edward IV perhaps. They were Duchess Cecily's granddaughters, and what is more natural than for her to have a picture of one of them? I wonder if there is anything on the back." He lifts the painting off its hook, scattering enough dust to make us cough, and turns it around. There is nothing to see but the date *1484* inked in spiky faded script.

"Well, I was right!" he declares. "It does date from the Duchess Cecily's time. She died in 1495, I recall. Possibly it's Elizabeth of York."

I know it cannot be. We have a portrait of my great-grandmother, Henry VII's queen, at home at Bradgate, and she looks nothing like this girl. She had fair, reddish hair.

Harry slides the picture back onto its hook, and I take one last, wistful look at it before following him into the next chamber. I am much taken with the young girl in the portrait. If only I could discover who she was.

There is little of interest to me in the rooms beyond, although Harry is intrigued by a rusted sword that rests suspended on hooks above a fireplace, and stops to examine it.

"This was a fine weapon once," he murmurs. But I am not inter-

ested in swords. I walk ahead, into a narrow windowless passage leading only to a spiral stairway. It is dark here, but from above a bright
shaft of sunlight illumines the stairwell. I stop, my blood running cold.
For there appears before me, in the pool of light reflected on the wall,
what seems like the black shadow of a moving hand, its index finger
extended, beckoning me up the stairs.

I start trembling. Is there someone up there, playing a trick on me?
A ghost? Surely not, I pray: it is broad daylight, and ghosts are creatures
of the night, or so I have always been told. But there is something horribly sinister about the summoning shadow, and although it is a hot
day, the passage has suddenly turned freezing cold. With the chill fingers of fear creeping up my neck, I stand shaking, unable to move but
compelled to watch.

Then suddenly the beckoning hand disappears, and Harry is behind
me. The spell is broken and I turn to look at him, relieved beyond measure to have him near me.

"By God, what's the matter, sweetheart? You look as if you've
seen—"

"I have! A ghost! There was a shadow—a hand beckoning me upstairs. There, on the wall. It's gone now. It was there, and then it just
wasn't there anymore." I realize that it is considerably warmer now.

Harry's face darkens. "So help me, if anyone has played a cruel
prank and affrighted you, they will answer to me and my father for it!"
he assures me. "Wait here. I will go up and investigate."

"No, don't leave me!" I plead.

"You are not alone," Harry says comfortingly. "Sanders is not far
behind us. Aren't you, Sanders?" His voice rises on the last words.

His father's groom—our unwanted shadow—immediately appears
in the doorway. "Aye, my lord."

"Stay here with my lady," Harry commands. "No doubt you overheard all that. I won't be a moment."

The sight of Sanders, solid, dour, and for once strangely welcome,
has steadied me. I am happy for him to guard our rear.

"I'm coming with you," I say to Harry. "Let Sanders keep watch
down here."

"Very well," says Harry. "I'll go first."

"My orders are to attend on you both at all times, my lord," Sanders protests.

Harry looks furious. "We will not be gone long; we'll only be up the stairs. And I have reason to believe that there is someone up there who is bent on making mischief. If I need you, I will call you, or send my lady down to you. Someone has to stay here to make sure that the culprit has no possible means of escape." He speaks with an authority he has never before asserted in my presence, and although Sanders looks unhappy, he nods and acquiesces.

Harry grips my hand and leads me up the twisting stair. We climb higher and higher, me bunching up my skirts so as not to trip, and emerge at last in a circular turret room lit only by a narrow window overlooking the broad width of the busy Thames. There is no exit—and no one here. The room is empty, apart from an old iron-bound chest below the window.

"You must have imagined it, my love," says Harry, and then in one swift movement he gathers me in his arms, kisses me hard on the mouth, and pushes me against the cold, whitewashed wall before I can catch my breath. He is breathing heavily, grappling with my skirts and whispering hotly in my ear, "We must be quick, dear heart! It's not the way I wanted it to be, but I must have you . . ."

He is panting so hard I cannot make out the words, and soon I no longer care, for I am swept along by his sense of urgency. We are clinging to each other as if we can never let go, opening up to each other, striving to become one, and hastily disarranging our clothing—and then there is a cough from below, and footsteps coming up the stairs. Quickly I smooth down my skirts and my hair, while Harry, breathless, . ties the points of his codpiece—and just in time, for Sanders appears a moment later, looking at us suspiciously. I feel my cheeks flaming and turn to the window. I have to admire Harry's composure. He is superb.

"No one was up here," he tells the groom, as calmly as if he had not been in the throes of desire only seconds before. "My lady must have imagined what she saw. There is nothing of note here, just that old chest. We checked inside, to see if someone was hiding in there, but there are only a few old papers. Does that satisfy you?"

"I am just obeying my orders, Lord Herbert," the groom says resentfully. "I don't enjoy it any more than you do, sir."

"No, I don't suppose you do," Harry says, more kindly. "The view from here is splendid," he adds. "We have been admiring it. You can see the heights of Highgate and Islington." He winks at me and I try not to giggle.

Sanders grunts, and says we should go down, and Harry, squeezing my hand and mouthing "I love you," follows him, preceding me on the stairs. If only our spy had not appeared! Up in that turret room, my love awakened a need in me; I wish, how I wish, I could recapture the moment.

"We must be getting back," Harry urges. "We have got ourselves all mucky in here, and Heaven only knows what my lady mother will say if we appear at the supper table looking like two vagrants, eh, Katherine!"

We retrace our steps through the old wing, emerging thankfully into the gilded splendor of the modern part of the house and summoning our personal servants to attend us. It is only when I am back in my bedchamber, seated at my mirror, that I start shuddering again at the memory of that beckoning hand.

My maid comes and unlaces my gown. It is damp with sweat and dusty.

"That'll need sponging, my lady," she decrees, hanging it up on a peg. Then, as I stand there at the mirror in my petticoat, dabbing my armpits with rosewater, I catch her reflection: she is looking at my skirts.

"I see your courses have come, my lady," she says. "I'll fetch some cloths for you."

When she has disappeared into the inner closet, I sit down and reprimand myself. What if Harry and I had gone so far . . . ? In the heat of the moment, I had not given a thought to the possible consequences.

But I *must* think of them. What if I had proved with child? Of course, I should be delighted to have a child, but it would plunge us both into awful trouble. I should have been more prudent; I should have stopped Harry from getting carried away; and yet I cannot but regret that we did not love each other properly. I understand now why men and women risk much for passion, and why they get into terrible tangles simply for a few brief, ecstatic moments of it. But that matter is not the only cause of my disquiet. The chilling memory of what I saw on those stairs still disturbs me. There is something that escapes me about the matter, some connection to be made.

Elegantly garbed and bejeweled, I make my way to the great parlor, where supper is to be served, and stand behind my chair as the family gathers and grace is said. I dare not meet Harry's eyes for fear of blushing and giving myself away, and yet I can feel his admiring gaze upon me.

We sit down. The earl lays his napkin over his shoulder, carves some meat from the serving platter and serves us, then breaks his bread. "I hear you two young people were exploring the York wing today," he says. Clearly Sanders has made his report.

"Katherine wanted to see it," Harry replies easily. "We enjoyed looking at the old pictures, didn't we, sweetheart?"

"Never go there myself," says Pembroke. "One day I hope to refurbish or rebuild it, but I have extended my credit on this side of the house. I hear there was a little upset." He looks at me inquiringly.

"I thought I saw a shadow on the stairs," I say, embarrassed in case they think me a fool. "It was a trick of the light or the eye, I'm sure, but it did give me a fright."

"We went to investigate," said Harry, "but there was no one up in the turret room. The only thing we saw was an old chest. There was no intruder hiding in it!"

"They would have found it difficult, for that chest contains all the old records and papers from Raglan," his father commented. "I had it stored up there, out of the way. Anyway, my dear, I trust you are over your fright now."

"Yes, sir, I thank you," I say.

"You may have heard of Raglan Castle, Katherine," the earl continues, signaling to the servants to fill the goblets. "It is—or was—our ancient family seat on the Welsh Marches. It was the greatest fortress of its time, and my grandfather, the first earl, built it."

"It's a mighty castle still," Harry says. "If only we still owned it!"

"What happened?" I ask, hoping I am not being too forward in asking.

"My grandfather, whom men called Black William, was a staunch Yorkist," the earl explained. "He was created Earl of Pembroke by Edward IV, and given custody of the little boy who would one day grow up to be King Henry VII. He brought him up at Raglan Castle. But during the wars between York and Lancaster, my grandfather was defeated while fighting for the King at the Battle of Edgecote, and beheaded."

"I'm very sorry to hear that, my lord," I say, looking, I hope, suitably mournful.

"Oh, you must not fret, my dear," the earl says kindly. "It happened more than eighty years ago. I never knew him, and my own father died when I was four. Ancient history, as they say."

"Black William's son married twice, but left only a daughter, Elizabeth," the countess chimes in. "When she married the Earl of Worcester, Raglan Castle formed part of her inheritance; and so it went out of the family."

"But why didn't it pass to you, my lord, as the heir?" I ask, puzzled.

The earl chuckles. "Because I was not the heir then. I wasn't even born. Truth to tell, my dear, my grandfather left several bastard sons, and my father was one of them. I had to make my own way in the world. It's good service to your monarch that does that—and being a stout fighting man. I prospered under King Harry, and his son made me Earl of Pembroke, not two years since. As I was saying, my dear, that chest of papers came from Raglan Castle. I should go through it one day; one's family history is always fascinating."

In my lonely bed I dream vividly of the girl in the picture, and in my dream she is beckoning me, giving me that intense, appealing look again, yet this time her face is shadowed by sadness. Even in the dream I have that sense of recognition, as if I know her from somewhere. But I can never have seen her before.

After sleeping only fitfully through the night, I am resolved. I dare not venture up there alone, but I ask Harry to accompany me to that turret room and open the chest—and he agrees. This time there will be no snatched moments, for Sanders insists on accompanying us. No doubt he told the earl how we gave him the slip yesterday.

I approach the dark passageway with trepidation, scarcely daring to look ahead of me at the wall of the stairwell, and reminding myself that I have two strong men with me. But today there is nothing there. We mount the stairs, and then Harry and I sink to our knees by the chest, while Sanders perches on the top stair, balancing an account book on his knees, seemingly absorbed in checking his columns of figures.

Harry snatches a kiss behind his back, runs his fingers up my arm, and allows them to stray for a moment to my breast, then grins mischievously at me as he unlocks the chest. The old lid creaks as he raises it, and the dry, musty smell of long-forgotten documents is released. There are piles and bundles of them to be gone through: deeds, grants, warrants, formal letters, a treatise on hunting ("I'll keep that," Harry says), a crumbling missal with faded pages, broken seals, a long scroll bearing a family tree, plans of Raglan Castle on brittle parchment, a tattered heraldic banner, a marriage contract bearing the date 1484, and a thick bundle of yellowing papers tied up with frayed satin ribbon. We spend ages sorting everything, but it soon becomes clear that the chest's contents are very old and mostly of little interest. There is nothing recent here, nothing that could possibly concern me. Nothing for which some supernatural entity might beckon me up the stairs. I *must* have imagined it.

But wait a minute!

"Let me see that marriage contract," I say, and Harry passes it to me. "It was dated 1484?"

"Yes, sweetheart."

"The same date as the portrait downstairs, the one of the girl in blue. I wonder if this is her marriage contract." I read the tortuous legal script. "'William Herbert, Earl of Huntingdon, covenants with King Richard III to take the King's daughter, Dame Katherine Plantagenet, to wife before Michaelmas of that year.' There is more, about the marriage settlement. Harry, it must be her, the girl in the picture! That could be her marriage portrait."

"It's possible, my love, but we can't know for certain."

"She *is* richly dressed, and that pendant must have been costly—fit for a king's daughter. I think it's her."

"Well, it may be . . ."

"She was your ancestress."

"I don't think so. My father is the Earl of Huntingdon's nephew. Huntingdon left only a daughter. I'm sure my father would be delighted to tell you more of the family history if you ask him. He's inordinately proud of it."

We are nearly finished now. Harry is poring over the family tree, absorbed in the lineage of his ancestors, so I carefully untie the rotten ribbon and begin looking at the yellowing papers, which are all written in the same faint hand. They are very thin and very fragile, and prone to tearing along the creases.

"Look at this!" Harry says suddenly. He is dangling something bright and shiny, a diamond-shaped pendant on a chain. Old-fashioned as it is, it is of gold, and cunningly wrought. A great sapphire winks as he rubs the jewel on his sleeve.

"I recognize it!" I cry. "It's the pendant the girl is wearing—the girl in the portrait. The very same."

"Really?" And before I can say anything, Harry leaps up and bounds down the stairs. "Yes, you're right, my sweetheart," he says as he returns, a little breathless. "It is the same pendant."

Now that I know it was hers, I want it for my own. I cannot explain why I am drawn to the girl in the portrait, but I know I felt that sense of recognition when I saw her likeness. And she came to me in my dream, smiling sadly, pleadingly . . . as if she wanted something of me. Can she be haunting me? That shadow beckoning on the stairs—was it her? Might she have been guiding me to the chest, to the pendant . . . maybe she wants me to have it. After all, I am another young Herbert wife like her, and so she thinks it should be rightfully mine. Maybe she loved her husband as much as I love Harry . . .

Harry leans forward and clasps the pendant around my neck. "There, it suits you!"

Then suddenly, inexplicably, I am filled with a sense of despair so powerful that I feel I might faint. I rip off the pendant, fearing it must be bewitched.

"I cannot wear this, Harry," I gabble. "It—It would be seen as Papist idolatry, with those images. My parents would have a fit! As for Jane— she would never speak to me again. But it is lovely." And it is too, lying there in my palm, as innocent-looking as anything. As soon as I took it off, the feeling of despair dissipated, and now it is hard to believe I did not imagine it.

"I suppose my parents would disapprove of it too," he concurs, "even though it was made long ago. You may keep it all the same."

Reluctantly, I put the pendant in my pocket. But I am deeply troubled by the effect it had on me. That beckoning hand, my strange affinity with the girl in blue, the dream, and that dreadful feeling of despair . . . What could they all mean? Are they somehow connected? Or am I just imagining things?

Resolutely, I turn back to the papers.

The old-fashioned script is hard to read, and although I persevere, it is not easy to decipher the words. But suddenly it becomes clear that these are no mere letters, as I read something that strikes a strange chill into me, even on this beautiful sunny morning. And now it occurs to me that I was beckoned into the tower chamber to find much more than a pendant.

KATE

June 13, 1483; Tower of London
and Crosby Hall, London

The guards at the entrance gateway to the Tower whistled apprecia-tively at the two girls. Nothing out of the ordinary seemed to be happening; in fact, the place was quiet. Kate approached one of the sentries.

"My father is the Duke of Gloucester," she told him, as he eyed her skeptically. "Is he within?"

"And my father's the King of England!" the man retorted.

"Very well, I shall wait over there until the duke comes, and then you shall believe me," Kate said with dignity.

"Show him the pendant," Mattie whispered.

Kate drew the package from her velvet purse and unwrapped it.

The large sapphire glinted in the sunlight. "Now do you believe me?" she challenged.

The man was dumbfounded. "I crave your pardon, lady. We get all sorts of nutters here. Yes, the duke is in council in Caesar's Tower—the big white keep yonder. I was on duty when he arrived. He came out for an hour or so, with his henchmen—but then he returned. He didn't look too happy."

"Oh, no!" Kate said. Something was amiss, as she had feared.

"Go on in, my lady. The public are allowed into the Tower. We're just here to keep out troublemakers."

The sentry waved the girls through the gateway, and they found themselves in the outer bailey, walking past the great barred water gate where the Thames lapped at the steps. Mattie knew her way around the Tower well.

"I've been here before, my lady," she revealed. "My uncle brought me to see the lions and other beasts in the menagerie; he's one of the warders here. We've had supper at his house a few times."

To their left was one of the inner towers, a tall, ancient edifice. Kate looked up at it and glimpsed a face staring through one of the upper windows. It was the face of a young woman. The window was barred.

"There's someone up there," she said to Mattie. "Is she a prisoner?"

"I can't see anyone," Mattie said. Kate was puzzled. The girl was still there. But Mattie was walking on, leading her through an archway, then along a narrow passageway. In front of them was a massive gateway, next to what was obviously Caesar's Tower, built of white stone; to the right was a high wall with buildings behind it.

"That's the royal palace," Mattie said. "We're not allowed to go in there. That big gatehouse ahead—that's the entrance, the Coldharbour Gate."

"The King is in there somewhere," Kate said. Poor boy, she thought, spending his days in regal isolation, surrounded by a court of adults, and required not only to do his lessons but also to learn about the heavy business of governing his subjects. He was expected to attend council meetings, her father had told her, but had been excused of late because he was suffering from some malady of the jaw that his physician could not alleviate.

Things would be better for him when he had his brother for company. Her father's determination to bring the Duke of York here was a wise resolve, and showed how much he had his nephews' welfare at heart.

Kate and Mattie emerged from the passageway onto Tower Green, a wide-open grassy space in the Tower's inner bailey. Great towers and wall walks surrounded it, and leafy trees shaded the enclosure. Mattie pointed out the Lieutenant's Lodging, a fine house on the left, and the Chapel of St. Peter ad Vincula ahead, where the Tower garrison worshipped. Beyond that was a broad arena where, Kate learned, tournaments were sometimes held.

There were few people about. Some men-at-arms were sitting dicing on a bench. A couple of their fellows stood guard nearby at the Coldharbour Gate. On Tower Green, in front of the chapel, some workmen were sawing wood. There was no one else in sight, although Kate could hear horses neighing and snorting nearby.

Then suddenly there were shouts from the other side of the Coldharbour Gate.

"Make way for my Lord Hastings!"

The sentries looked at each other, shrugged, and opened the gate. Immediately, a small band of angry men burst through it. One, an official in a black gown with a rod of office, was dragging a well-dressed nobleman who was putting up some spirited resistance, although his face was twisted in what looked like terror. Behind followed a furious priest.

"In the name of God, stop!" he was bellowing. "This is outrageous! You have allowed this poor wretch no time for any long confession or any space for remembering his sins."

"Spare me! Oh, my God, spare me!" the nobleman was pleading.

Kate did not wait to hear more. She grabbed Mattie by the hand and ran back to the passage, where they could hide behind the wall. She prayed no one had noticed them.

They stood there for a moment, looking at each other helplessly.

"What's happening?" Mattie cried. "What are they going to do to that poor man?"

"Shhhh! I don't know," Kate whispered. "I wonder which one is Lord Hastings. Surely he will not allow anything bad to happen."

"Where have you been all these years?" Mattie hissed. "That poor nobleman *is* Lord Hastings!"

"Oh, sweet Holy Mother," Kate breathed. "I think they are going to kill him. Oh, what can we do?"

Gathering every ounce of her courage, she peered around the wall. The men were now on Tower Green, in front of the chapel. They had set up a stock of wood from the astonished workmen's pile and were forcing Lord Hastings to his knees in front of it. He was praying aloud, and although she could not hear what he was saying, she could detect the desperation in his voice. His tormentors were arguing, and a man-at-arms was waving his hands and protesting angrily about something. Then another was summoned, one of the soldiers from the bench. A man in a rich gown turned and she suddenly recognized the Duke of Buckingham, who seemed to be in charge; he barked an order and the second man-at-arms drew his sword. At this, Hastings's prayers grew frantic. The furious priest was on his knees beside him.

Kate drew back behind the shelter of the wall, shuddering. It was horrifyingly clear what was to happen next, and she shrank from witnessing it. Behind her, Mattie was sobbing silently, hugging herself in distress, and Kate put her arms around her, as much to comfort herself as Mattie, wondering how people could treat an execution as a public spectacle, a holiday even, as it seemed they did in this alien city—and no doubt elsewhere.

There was a sickening thud, then a short silence, broken by Buckingham's hoarse shout: "Behold the head of a traitor!" This was greeted by desultory cheers, and sounds that the gathering was breaking up.

"They might come this way and see us!" Mattie whispered, quivering. Kate feared she might be right, and guessed that those wicked men would not have wanted witnesses to their dreadful deed. There had been something furtive and underhanded about it. What had the priest said? That poor Lord Hastings had been allowed no time to make a proper confession. The cleric had been indignant, and rightly so.

But how had this happened—and why? These questions struck her as she grabbed Mattie's hand and hurried back with her through the winding passage. There was no one about but the sentries on the gate. The two girls fled past them, ignoring their cheery farewells.

"Don't bother to say good-bye!" one sentry called after them.

Why? Kate kept asking herself as she half ran through the streets of London, and then again as she hastened up the stone stairs to the door of Crosby Hall, where she dismissed Mattie and went alone to her chamber. *Why?* It was a question she could not, would not, pose to her faithful maid, because it concerned her father.

No one else had such compelling cause to wish Hastings dead. Hastings had disloyally suspected her father of scheming to seize the throne from the lawful King. He had treacherously plotted against Gloucester, even allying with his enemies the Wydevilles. Her father believed they had been compassing his death. And he had gone this day to that council meeting at the Tower.

She sat down in the window embrasure. The stones behind her back were painted with bright trefoils and borders, and the glass panes between the mullions were stained in jewel colors, blue, yellow, red . . . rich red, the color of blood. She could not help thinking of Lord Hastings kneeling in terror on Tower Green, and of what she had shrunk from seeing. There would have been blood . . . rivers of it.

She was twisting her russet curls tightly around her finger, unaware that she was doing it. She was imagining her father—her beloved, kindly father—sending Lord Hastings to his death. For who else could have done it? Her father was the Lord Protector; it would not have happened without his sanction or order. And the Duke of Buckingham, who had been in charge of the beheading, was his staunchest ally.

It was all beyond her comprehension and her competence. She could not deal with it herself. She hoped that all would become clear when the duke returned home.

There was shouting outside in the street. Agitated male voices were crying, "Treason! Treason!"

"Oh, dear Holy Mother!" Kate whispered, as it dawned on her suddenly why Hastings might have been executed. "No! Not my father!"

She flew out of her chamber, and in the great hall collided with the Duchess Anne, pale and flustered, making her way to the outside stairs. Kate's frightened eyes met hers—but, of course, the duchess knew nothing of the fate of Hastings, or the terrible possibility that the duke had been assassinated, so her concern was nowhere near as acute as her stepdaughter's. They hastened, with John of Gloucester and members of their household following, down the stairs to the courtyard and out into Bishopsgate, where they saw an angry, heaving mob of retainers sporting the duke's white boar badge fighting their way through the crowd. Others were taking up the cry of "Treason!" while some reached for daggers and swords, and there was an air of panic throughout.

The Duchess Anne was a gentle soul, but fear made her bold. Without hesitation, she headed into the throng and grabbed the arm of one of the liveried retainers.

"A word, please!" she cried in his ear. He was about to race on, but realized that it was his liege lord's wife who had accosted him, and paused, with obvious reluctance.

"What is the meaning of this? Why are you shouting 'Treason'?" Anne demanded. She spoke with an authority worthy of the King-maker's daughter, and people stopped to heed her. Her father had been popular with the Londoners in his day, and they were ready to listen to his daughter.

The retainer, realizing that many expectant faces were turned in his direction, and that a hush was descending, cleared his throat.

"My lady, good citizens, you should know that an ambush had been prepared for my Lord Protector when he went to the Tower today. His enemies, led by Lord Hastings, had plotted his destruction." Kate went cold at that; bracing herself to hear the worst, she saw Anne blanch and sway a little, but she also heard a swell of angry murmurs in the crowd, and voices raised in denial. The duke's man ignored it. "The traitor Hastings," he shouted above the increasing roar of protest, "had plotted with several lords of the council, and with the Queen and Mistress Shore, against the Lord Protector's lawful authority—and his very life!" He paused for dramatic effect. "But mercifully His Grace discovered this treason in time, and knew that his adversaries had hid-

den their arms in the council chamber, ready to attack him. Thus fore-
warned, he summoned his guards, and Hastings and the rest were
taken, resisting violently. Hastings has now suffered the full penalty
that the law demands, and my lord duke, God be thanked, is preserved
from the malice of his enemies."

Anne looked shocked, and the mood of the mob turned angry.
Some were weeping openly for Hastings and crying out against his
death. Behind Kate, a man remarked to his neighbor that Hastings had
been the only hope of King Edward's children, while another growled,
"Well, if anyone wants proof that Gloucester has his sights on the
throne, this is it." Kate glared at him.

Mattie was at her elbow. "The people loved Lord Hastings," she
explained. "It is hard for them to believe him guilty of such wickedness."

Kate rounded on her. "You think my father is making it up?" she
challenged. "He was in danger of his life!"

"Oh, no, my lady, a thousand apologies! I meant nothing like that.
I was merely trying to explain why the citizens are so perplexed. I am
sure the duke would not have condemned him without proof of his
treason."

"Of course he would not," Kate snapped, edging her way toward
the duchess, who was making her way back into Crosby Place. They
left behind them a restive crowd, and they had not been indoors long
when they heard more shouts. It was the duke returning home, and
plainly his reception was hostile.

Anne and Kate stood at the top of the stairs with the chamberlain
to welcome him, and watched his slight figure dismount from his
horse and ascend the stairs. He looked energized, triumphant almost—
and better than he had for a long while.

"My lord." Anne sank into a curtsey, as Kate dipped behind her. The
duke raised them both and kissed them. "Come, we shall dine!" he said.
"We have much to celebrate. God be praised, the traitors are routed."

"So we have heard, my lord," Anne said, her voice a touch strained.
"There have been crowds in the street here, bruiting it about. I mislike
their mood."

"They have been fed persuasive lies," the duke said, leading his womenfolk into the hall. He called for wine and the best feast that could be mustered, and within minutes they were seated at the high table on the dais, drinking a fervent toast to his deliverance from his enemies. Kate could not believe that her father was here in their midst, alive and well, when only an hour before she had feared him dead. Involuntarily, she plucked the velvet of his sleeve, just to make sure he was real. He smiled at her.

"Truly, Kate, we have much for which to thank God," he said.

He was expansive about the events that had taken place that morning in the Tower. "I asked the traitor Hastings what men deserved for plotting the destruction of one who is so near to the King in blood, and the Protector of his royal person and realm." And he said—he actually said—"that if they had done thus heinously, they were worthy of heinous punishment. 'If?' I asked him. 'Do not serve me with ifs!' I told him they had done it, and that I would make good upon his body."

John was agog. The duchess sat still and remote, her face inscrutable.

"It was then that I accused him of plotting with the other traitors on the council against my office and my life," the duke continued. "And I told them I knew they were in league with the Queen and that strumpet Mistress Shore. The traitors did not deny it! I challenged them, saying they had laid an ambush for me, and then Buckingham brought the guards. As you have heard, the culprits were apprehended and taken into custody in the Tower. To them, I mean to be merciful. But Hastings was the architect of this treason. Him I could not spare. He had to be made an example to others." His thin lips were set; the prominent jaw jutted defiantly.

There was a brief silence.

"What of the Queen and Mistress Shore?" Anne asked.

"The Queen remains in sanctuary; we know now why she will not come out. I will deal with Mistress Shore presently."

An usher entered the hall and announced the arrival of the Lord Mayor.

"Good," said Gloucester. "I summoned him here with all haste."

Perspiring in his furred red robes and chain of office, the mayor swept into the hall, bowing several times at the august company.

The duke rose and extended his hand across the table to be kissed.

"Madam," he addressed his wife, "may I present Sir Edmund Shaa. Sir Edmund, the Lady Anne, my duchess. And my children, the Lord John of Gloucester and the Lady Katherine Plantagenet."

The Lord Mayor bowed gallantly.

"A plate for my Lord Mayor!" the duke called, inviting his guest to the board. Much honored, Sir Edmund bustled into the proffered seat.

"You will have heard how the traitor Hastings had planned to murder myself and my lord of Buckingham at this morning's council meeting," the duke said, "and that I acted just in time to save our lives. After we have dined, my Lord Mayor, I want you to ride through the City, if you will, telling the people of this foul plot against me." And he recounted again the grim events of the day, with Sir Edmund munching away and frowning ever more concernedly as the tale unfolded. Gladly he went on his way after dinner, to acquaint the citizens with the truth of the matter. And to back him up, the duke sent his own herald to calm the mood of the populace by proclaiming Hastings's execution, reading out a long account of his treason, and bidding the people be assured.

That evening, Kate noticed that Anne was quiet during the private supper they shared with the duke in the great chamber. And he noted it too.

"This day has been a great strain on you," he said to his wife, covering her hand with his. "No matter; the immediate danger has been averted."

Anne looked up at him. Her expression was somber, questioning.

"Three things puzzle me, my lord, and I pray you to put my mind at rest, for it will not be stilled," she said, swallowing.

The duke frowned. "What troubles you, Anne?"

The duchess laid down her fork. She had barely touched her food.

"You have not said how you learned of Hastings's treason," she began.

"I have my spies," he stated. "I have been aware for some time that he was working against me. Evidence was brought to me—evidence I could not ignore." His tone was defensive; Kate could see he did not like being called to account by his wife for his actions. And she did not blame him. Anne had been cool toward him all day. The relief she had obviously felt to begin with at his lucky escape had not been much in evidence later on. It was as if she was angry with him. Kate could not understand it.

The duchess spoke again, as if with an effort. "You accused Hastings of treason. But against whom?"

"You have been paying too much heed to my mother." Richard was clearly upset. "I am the Lord Protector, Anne. I am appointed to rule during my nephew's minority, by the council and by the will of my late brother. Any crime against me is a crime against the King and all the realm—and that is treason."

"Then my lady your mother had it wrong when she said that the law of treason does not extend to the Lord Protector?"

"Yes!" Richard was really riled now; his face wore a belligerent, injured look. "What is this, Anne? An interrogation? Who has committed a crime? Not I. It was my life that was in danger. I do not deserve this. Ask yourself what would have happened to the kingdom if those traitors had succeeded. It would have descended into faction fighting and civil war, as it did when my father justly contested the crown all those years ago. I am the only man who can hold it together and contain the troublemakers. Are you satisfied now?"

Anne nodded uncertainly. "I have only one more question," she persisted. "When I was out in the street today, I heard people saying that Hastings was executed suddenly, without judgment. One man told me he was put to death within minutes of his arrest. My lord, forgive my ignorance, but I thought that even the poorest subject of the King was entitled to justice and a fair trial?"

Kate shrank from her father's expression. It was thunderous.

"Yes, madam, you are ignorant," he said scathingly. "Poor men are put on trial. Great lords can be tried by their peers or attainted by Parliament. And Acts of Attainder can be passed retrospectively. It seems to me, my lady, that you think me the villain of this piece, not Hastings. You seem to be insinuating that I executed a man without trial, on unsound grounds, and with no good evidence. Well," he concluded, rising to his feet, "I am touched by your faith in me. I know not what I have done to deserve this. It is bad enough to be deserted by a man I thought my friend—but to be thought ill of by my wife, who should be supporting me, is intolerable!"

He stalked from the table toward the stairs.

Anne fell to her knees. "My lord, forgive me! I beg your pardon. The news of the execution was shocking. I did not fully understand the circumstances." She was pleading with him. He looked at her impassively.

"I wish you both good night," he said, and was gone.

Kate could not sleep. She lay fidgeting, her mind in turmoil, remembering that stark tableau on Tower Green. And when she did finally drift off, her dreams were of a soldier with a drawn sword, the final terror of a dying man, and dark blood soaking into the grass.

KATHERINE

July 1553. Baynard's Castle, London;
Syon House, Middlesex

It has been unbearably hot and thundery. Two nights ago there was a terrible storm, with raging thunder and hailstones red as clotted blood raining down. Harry and I, like most of the household, were unable to sleep, and as we moved from window to window, watching the tempest, we could hear our fearful servants warning that it was an omen.

The air has been thick with rumors. It's even being bruited on the streets—and indeed, in the nether regions of Baynard's Castle—that the King is dying, or even dead. It's true, he has hardly been seen in public for weeks, but my father-in-law Pembroke was sanguine when Harry asked outright if His Majesty was ill.

"No, he is recovering," he said. "He is able to walk in his galleries and gardens at Greenwich."

But that's not what Annie our cook says. I'm fond of Annie. I am often in the kitchens and larders with my lady, learning how to govern this household that will one day be mine, and Annie enjoys a familiarity and freedom of speech with the earl and countess that comes from long years of service and skill at her craft. She's a dumpy, homely soul with a short temper and a sharp tongue, but beneath it all, she has a warm and true heart.

Not long after my exchange with the earl, Annie went to visit her aging mother in Deptford one Sunday, but got caught up in a crowd of Londoners converging on Greenwich Palace, whither—concerned by the prayers for the King's recovery posted on church doors that morning—they had made their way, bent on demanding to see him.

"Well, this gentleman came out and spoke to us," Annie recounts, surveying with evident satisfaction her avid circle of listeners in the great kitchen. I'd come to find something sweet to eat, and she had given me a piece of marchpane and bidden me stay to hear her tale. "He said we was to go home, because the air was too chill for His Grace to come out and greet us. But we stood our ground, and some folks spoke up and said we weren't leaving until we had seen him. He went away, saying he'd see what he could do, and we waited and waited, and then suddenly the King appeared at a window above us."

She pauses for effect. Her audience is riveted, and she is savoring keeping them in suspense. Such dramas do not often enliven the daily lives of servants.

"Well," she says, "I was that shocked. We all were. I mean, he was so thin and wasted. He had two attendants with him. I swear they were holding him up. You should have seen the change that come over that crowd. When the King waved and bowed to us, there were a few cheers, but you could tell most people was thinking the same thing. And when he'd gone, men were saying he was doomed. Well, you could see it, plain as day. Poor little King." She dabs her eyes with her apron.

I hasten away to tell Harry.

"I thought there was something badly amiss," he says, taking my hand as we stroll in the brilliantly blooming gardens with Sanders keeping a respectful distance. "His Majesty has not set foot outside his palace for ages."

"But he is so young—not much older than I am," I comment sadly.

"Death strikes young and old alike," Harry observes. "We should live our lives to the full, and dread God. Heavens, I am beginning to sound like my parents!" But his smile touches his lips only. "What worries me is what will happen when the King dies," he says, lowering his voice—there are gardeners scything grass nearby. "The next in line for the throne is the Lady Mary. She is a staunch Papist."

I know this. I have often heard my parents deploring the Lady Mary's fervent Catholicism. But I have also felt sorry for her. Declared a bastard after King Harry's divorce from her mother, Katherine of Aragon, she has clung stubbornly to the faith of her childhood, even after it was outlawed when King Edward embraced the true Protestant religion. Since then she has lived quietly in the country, rarely visiting the court, a sad spinster who spends her barren days telling her beads and praying to her idolatrous images—or so my mother told me.

I do not need Harry to explain to me what will happen if Mary becomes Queen. Any fool could foresee that the whole country will be forced to turn Catholic again, and where will that leave Northumberland and those who have supported him, not to mention the reforms of the past six years? What of his ally Pembroke? Indeed, what of my own father and mother, stout Protestants both? And it dawns on me that we are all—even the little, unimportant people like myself and Harry, Jane, and Guilford Dudley—enmeshed in this web of loyalties and convictions.

On this balmy summer evening the sky has a golden tinge and the setting sun is reflected in the rippling water as the earl's gilded barge glides upstream on the Thames. Everything looks tranquil and peaceful. Would that my mind could be too.

My lord of Pembroke has told us only that we are going to join the court at Syon House, and ordered us all to wear black. Has the King died? Surely, then, we would be going to Greenwich, in the other direction?

Seated in the plush cabin, doleful in our mourning garb—so at variance with the golden beauty of the day—Harry and I exchange glances. My lady the countess speaks of pleasantries only; even if she is aware of the purpose of our outing, she gives no clue, for she obeys her husband unquestioningly. Pembroke grunts in answer to her prattle; he is much preoccupied with his secret thoughts.

At Syon, we leave the barge at the landing stage and walk up to the former nunnery, passing between the service wings to the steps that ascend to the magnificent Italianate mansion built by Protector Somerset on the site of the abbey church. Here, an usher is waiting to conduct us through a great chamber hung with tapestries to the presence chamber, which is crowded with lords and ladies, all in black. Their ranks part as Pembroke leads us to the farther end of the room, where a throne is set up on a dais beneath a cloth of estate bearing the royal arms of England. The King must be coming! He must be better, praise be to God. Perhaps he will announce the death of Northumberland and declare himself of an age to rule unaided. Oh, I pray it will be so! Then we will not have to worry about the Lady Mary ascending the throne—and maybe Harry and I can now be allowed to live properly as husband and wife.

People bow as we pass, and some stare or nod in our direction and murmur to their neighbors. Then I espy my parents waiting for us near the dais. I have not seen them since my wedding, nearly two months ago, and kneel to receive their blessing. They raise and kiss me, more affectionately than they ever have, and exchange warm but muted greetings with the earl and countess.

Then my father and Pembroke excuse themselves, saying they must join the other privy councillors in the great hall. They will be waiting to attend on the King when he arrives.

Lord Guilford Dudley joins us. As he greets us haughtily, I am struck by his arrogance. But where is Jane?

"My sister—is she well?" I ask.

"Much amended after a fever," he replies, but I cannot probe further as there is a sudden fanfare of trumpets, and the courtiers hasten to arrange themselves in order of rank, the greatest standing beside us, nearest the dais. As a respectful hush descends, a small procession approaches through the throng. I crane my neck to glimpse the King, and see the privy councillors processing into the chamber and taking their places near us at the front; but behind them, instead of His Majesty,

Northumberland comes into view, escorting—goodness gracious, he is escorting my sister Jane! She looks confused, alarmed even, a tiny, slender figure in her high-necked black gown, her red hair blazing loose about her shoulders. Beside me, I can sense my mother puffing up with pride. Guilford is staring speculatively at Jane, but she is oblivious. I see the bewilderment in Harry's face—it must mirror my own.

But where is the King? Why all this pomp and ceremony if he is not here?

Northumberland steers Jane toward the dais. The privy councillors bow as she passes, and suddenly everyone in the room is making an obeisance to her. I am so clean amazed that I forget to follow suit until my mother gives me a sharp pinch.

Jane's white face registers fright. She trembles and shudders as the duke hands her up the step to the dais, where she stands, awkwardly self-conscious, looking as if she would rather be anywhere else. She seems not to be aware of any of us.

What is the matter with her? Were all these lords and ladies to bow to me, I should revel in it!

Northumberland turns to face us. His face is solemn.

"As Lord President of the Council," he says gravely, "I do now declare to you the death of his most blessed and gracious Majesty, King Edward VI, whom God has now called unto Himself."

He pauses so that we can digest this heavy news. I find that I too am shaking, for fear of what might happen now that the Lady Mary is Queen, and I look back toward the door, expecting her to enter. But why has Jane been brought here?

The duke tells us that King Edward, in his wisdom, took great care to defend his kingdom from the Popish faith—and to deliver it from the rule of his evil sisters.

I gawk at that. Surely it is rash of the duke to provoke the Lady Mary by such treasonous words. But there is more . . .

"His Majesty intended to pass an Act of Parliament," Northumberland continues in ringing, even challenging, tones. "He was resolved that whoever acknowledges the Lady Mary and the Lady Elizabeth as heirs of the crown should be accounted traitors, for the Lady Mary was disobedient to him in regard to the true religion. Wherefore in no manner did His Grace wish that they should be his heirs, he being able in every way to disinherit them."

There is a shocked hush. People glance at each other, stunned. Only the councillors look complacent; they, of course, must have known about this for some time. I hardly dare look at Jane, but when I do, I notice her shivering again, and now the duke turns to address her. "His Majesty hath named Your Grace as heir to the crown of England. If you die without issue, your sisters will succeed you and Lord Guilford."

Jane—our Queen? I cannot believe it! It is the best and most marvelous news I have ever heard. And her sisters next in line to the throne? That means *me,* and Mary, of course, poor hunchbacked Mary, who rarely sets foot outside the house. But this is impossible. It cannot be true, surely? But it is, it is!

Jane looks as dazed and uncomprehending as I feel; she too is clearly stupefied. But me—I am bursting with excitement and finding it very hard to stand as still as becomes the solemnity of the occasion. No wonder our mother is preening! She knew about this, no doubt, and probably schemed for it—she has ever been ambitious to a fault for her blood. And my father is looking highly satisfied with himself, like a tomcat that has caught a mouse. Father to the Queen! That will suit his vanity.

Jane has still said nothing. Northumberland, with a touch of exasperation in his voice, informs her that her title has been approved by the privy councillors, the peers, and all the judges of the land. "There is nothing wanting but Your Grace's grateful acceptance!" He adds that she could never sufficiently thank God, the disposer of crowns and scepters, for so great a mercy, and should cheerfully take upon her the name, title, and estate of Queen. Then he falls heavily to his knees and offers her his allegiance, whereupon we all kneel and do her reverence, I still unable to believe that this is happening.

Jane suddenly keels over in a faint, crumpling in a heap on the dais. I expect people to rush to her aid, but no one moves. I want to go to her but am paralyzed with uncertainty, for if she is Queen, her person is sacred, and it would be presumption to touch her. The duke stands looking down on her. I watch her face, willing her to come to her senses. To my relief, her eyes open and she blinks. Lying on the floor, she starts crying bitterly, making no effort to get up. What on earth is she *crying* for? She should be rejoicing and praising God to the skies for her great good fortune!

Everyone is silent, waiting for her to compose herself. For several minutes the only sound in the room is Jane's muffled sobbing—and then my mother's audible, impatient sigh.

"She weeps for the King," murmurs the Countess of Pembroke.

Jane stops crying. She gets awkwardly to her feet. Her eyes are red and her shoulders shaking, but she faces the duke with determination.

"The crown is not my right," she declares, her voice surprisingly firm. "It pleases me not. The Lady Mary is the rightful heir."

My gasp is audible in the shocked silence. Northumberland loses patience with Jane. "Your Grace does wrong to yourself and to your house!" he fumes, as our father and mother step forward angrily.

"Remember your duty to us, your parents!" my lady snarls. "And to my lord duke here, your father-in-law, and to the King's will, and to those who are now your subjects!"

"No," Jane says defiantly, just as if she is sparring with our mother over her apparel, as of old.

My mother flares in anger. "You owe me obedience, daughter, and you will do as you are told!"

The courtiers are watching, agog.

"No," Jane says again. Northumberland is clearly finding it hard to conceal his fury.

Now Guilford steps forward and bows very low. Rising, he lifts his finger to caress Jane's tearstained face and stroke her arm, but she shakes him off.

"Do as the noble lord my father asks, I pray you," he urges. "Much good can come of it. We need a new defender for our faith."

"Leave me be!" Jane cries, and falls to her knees, lifting her joined hands. "Give me a sign, Lord!" she beseeches. "Tell me what I must do."

She remains there praying, while the court fidgets with impatience. "She'll have to give in," Pembroke mutters. Harry bends to my ear. "In truth, I am sorry for your sister. But Guilford is right: she must accept, for the whole realm stands to benefit. Otherwise it will suffer under the Lady Mary."

"Of course she should accept it!" I whisper, and my mother nods.

"She will," she mutters.

Jane is on her feet once more. "God in His mercy has not vouchsafed me a sign," she says miserably, "so I can only conclude that He wishes me to obey the will of my parents, as is laid down in Scripture." As my mother huffs in exasperated agreement, Jane bends her head. "I accept the crown. I pray that I may govern to God's glory and service, and to the advantage of the realm."

There is an air of palpable relief in the chamber as she seats herself on the throne, and Northumberland, expansive with triumph, kisses her hand and swears allegiance even to death, with all the lords following in his wake.

She is calmer after that, and when it is my turn to kiss her hand, she embraces me and whispers in my ear that I should rejoice, for the true faith will now be preserved in this kingdom, and that I must come and serve her as soon as it can be arranged. And now I am overwhelmed with excitement and jubilation, for my sister has accepted the crown and is acknowledged the true Queen of England—and I am now, as her recognized heir, the second lady in the land. One day I too might be a queen!

KATE

June 15, 1483; St. Paul's Cathedral
and Crosby Place, London

The press of people outside St. Paul's was solid, and Kate and Mattie congratulated themselves on slipping out after early Mass and securing a place near the front of the crowd. They were not supposed to be here, and Kate had concocted a tale to explain their absence, telling her father that they were going out to walk along the Strand to see the great houses that lined it. The duke had looked at her fondly.

"How grown-up and beautiful you are becoming," he reflected. "I will soon have to find you a husband. But not just yet. I would keep you with me awhile longer to enjoy your company." It was some time since he had spoken to her so tenderly, and she was filled with the familiar rush of love for him. He *was* just the same as ever; there was no need to worry. He had not changed: he was just preoccupied with the heavy cares of his office, and the plotting of the men and women who coveted his power. His eyes were sad, troubled. Impulsively, Kate hugged him. "We will be back in time for dinner," she said.

It was he himself who had let out the news that Mistress Shore was to be punished as a strumpet and sorceress, and that this morning she would do public penance at St. Paul's Cathedral. Both Kate and Mattie were agog to see this immoral witch who had cast a spell on the duke and fornicated with the late King and Lord Hastings, but they knew instinctively that any request to watch the woman doing penance would meet with disapproval. Well-brought-up young ladies were not supposed to take an interest in such things.

They made their way through the bustling London streets, wearing plain unadorned gowns so as not to draw attention to themselves, and waited impatiently outside the cathedral. Soon there was a shout. "She's coming!" A small procession came into view, escorted by guards marching before and behind the sheriff and his prisoner, and as the people caught sight of that unfortunate woman, a hubbub broke out. For Mistress Shore was barefoot and dressed only in a thin sheet that she was clutching tightly around her voluptuous body, while in her other hand she carried a lighted taper, a symbol of her penitence. People were pointing and catcalling, and most of the men were whistling and making lewd remarks.

"Drop your sheet, love!" bawled a coarse individual in homespun standing at Kate's left.

"Now we can all see what King Edward saw in her!" his companion observed.

Indeed, as Mistress Shore passed, Kate could see that she was beautiful, with long honey-colored hair and flawless skin. She had dainty hands and feet, and plump white shoulders, while the rest of her shapely body was clearly delineated by the thin fabric of the sheet. "Made for bed sports," Homespun was saying.

"She doesn't look like a witch, does she?" Mattie said in Kate's ear. Kate giggled.

"What did you expect? A haggard crone with a black cat and a broomstick? No, she's very pretty. Looking at her, I find it hard to believe she has it in her to cast malicious spells, but my father the duke would not have accused her falsely."

Mistress Shore looked embarrassed as she struggled to hold the lighted taper upright and preserve her modesty. There was misery in her eyes.

"What will happen to her?" Mattie wondered.

"The duke said she would go to prison," Kate told her. "But it will not be for long. It's just to make an example of her."

The shameful procession moved on into the cathedral. It would not emerge for some time.

"We'd better not wait," Kate said. "We should get to the Strand, so that we can speak of what we have seen." Pushing their way through the crowd, they set off down Ludgate Hill and into Fleet Street.

They arrived back at Crosby Place late for dinner and flustered. The duke and duchess were already seated at the high table in the hall, and the food platters were being borne in when Kate, excusing herself, hurried to her place. The duchess smiled, and the duke raised an eyebrow.

"So the Strand was interesting? You've been gone a long while," he said.

"We stopped to pray in St. Clement Danes," Kate said.

"Very fitting. I am pleased to see you are growing up to be pious." Her father smiled. He himself was very devout, an example to them all. Kate felt guilty that she had lied to him.

Gloucester turned to his wife.

"I've had a letter from my solicitor, Lynom," he said. Anne inclined her head. Her manner was slightly distant.

"The fool wants to marry Mistress Shore," the duke told her.

"Will you allow it?" she asked.

"I don't see why not. I'll let that harlot cool her heels in prison for a week or so, then let her go. Master Lynom can vouch for her, and keep an eye on her."

"She will have performed her penance by now," Anne said.

"Aye, and I hear that a lot of the good men of London were most appreciative of the spectacle," Gloucester stated wryly. Kate said nothing, but kept her eyes on her plate. She hoped her father might not guess the reason for her being late.

She was saved from any speculation on his part by the arrival of a burly man in the duke's livery.

"Pardon me, my lord, but there is news. The Marquess of Dorset has fled the sanctuary at Westminster." The marquess was the Queen's elder son by her first marriage; it was his brother, Sir Richard Grey, whom her father had imprisoned at Pontefract.

The duke leapt to his feet. "Where has he gone?"

"No one seems to know, my lord. Your man Pickering thinks he might be in hiding near Westminster."

"Surround the area with troops, take the dogs, and carry out a thorough search!"

"Yes, my lord."

The man hastened away and Gloucester sat down, his face taut.

"Dorset must be found," he declared. "He is as much of a danger to me as Hastings."

"Doubtless he has fled because he heard of what happened to Lord Hastings," Anne said quietly. "If you find him, what will you do to him?"

"That will depend on what he has to say for himself." The duke's tone was clipped. He sat there brooding, toying with his goblet but never raising it to his lips. "I must tighten security at the Tower," he said at length. "Who knows what Dorset is plotting? He may attempt to seize the King."

"But he would have to rely on the help of the King's servants, and you chose them yourself," Anne pointed out. "Surely they are loyal to you?"

"Are they?" he retorted. "I can trust no one these days. Who knows, those servants may have been corrupted already by my enemies. There is danger from every side, madam. The King's attendants must be removed forthwith."

Anne looked distressed. "He must have someone to wait upon him. If you deprive him of his attendants, he will be lonely."

Richard's mouth was set, his eyes steely. "I will appoint new servants, and I have resolved to send his brother York to keep him company."

"Think you the Queen will let him leave sanctuary?"

"If the council ordains it, she must."

"But no one can force someone to leave sanctuary; once that right is claimed, it is sacrosanct," Anne protested.

The duke gave her a sharp look. "York must join his brother. I have reason to believe he is being detained against his will by his mother. If that is the case, he should be liberated. Sanctuary was founded by my ancestors as a place of refuge, not of detention, and the boy wants to be with his brother."

Anne said nothing.

"I will lay the matter before the council on Monday," the duke said.

KATHERINE

July 10, 1553, Tower of London

It's another glorious hot day. This morning the royal heralds proclaimed Jane Queen throughout the City of London, and from Baynard's Castle there were fanfares of trumpets. This afternoon she will go in state to the Tower of London, where, by custom, she must lodge before her coronation. We must all look our best, and my mother has commanded Mrs. Ellen to bring me my wedding gown.

At noon Pembroke summons his barge to convey us to the Tower. At the Court Gate we are received by the lieutenant, Sir John Bridges, and conducted in procession to Caesar's Tower. Never before have I been treated with such deference and ceremony, and it really brings home to me the exciting reality of being the Queen's sister.

We ascend in great state to the council chamber, which has been fitted out as a presence chamber with a chair and canopy of estate. Here the entire Privy Council is waiting, with a great company of peers. They bow deeply, and I am so overcome with the import of it all that I begin to tremble. But Harry is beside me, holding my hand tightly and looking exceptionally handsome in his short coat and doublet of crimson damask banded in black velvet.

Jane enters, preceded by the Marquess of Winchester and escorted by Guilford, her hand resting lightly on his. She is followed by our mother, who is acting as her train bearer—our proud mother, attendant on her own daughter, if you please, and looking very much like a queen herself in her rich cloth of gold.

At Jane's entrance, we all sink in deep obeisances, and Guilford bows very low to her as she seats herself in the chair of estate beneath the richly embroidered canopy blazoned with the arms of England. I rejoice for her, yea, and for England too—and I envy her, I do confess it, for I would give much to be in her place. How I should love to be a queen, above anything else!

More wonders! Our father and Northumberland fall to their knees before Queen Jane, bidding her officially welcome to the Tower, and to her kingdom. There too is proud, petulant Guilford, bowing again, almost to the ground, every time she addresses him. What it is to have such power over the great ones of the land! Then Jane leads us in procession up the ancient stairs of the keep to the old chapel of St. John the Evangelist for a service of thanksgiving, and I offer the Almighty my fervent, heartfelt gratitude for our great good fortune. Afterward we return in solemn fashion to the council chamber.

And now the Marquess of Winchester brings the crown jewels for the new Queen's inspection. I cannot take my eyes off the glittering array of golden regalia studded by diamonds and other gemstones that wink and flash in the sun's rays streaming through the narrow windows. I have never seen anything so glorious in my life. I notice my mother eyeing the crown jewels greedily. They are what she has wanted for Jane all along.

"It will be my honor to place the crown on your head, madam," says the courtly marquess, lifting high that most precious diadem.

"No!" Jane says sharply. "I refuse to wear it."

"More silliness," my lady growls. I can only agree with her—what is wrong with Jane, that she cannot thankfully accept this great blessing that has been bestowed on her?

"Forgive me, Your Grace, I but wished to see how well it will become you," the marquess protests, much abashed.

"No, I will not wear it," Jane repeats.

"Your Grace may do so without fear," he persists.

"Very well," she demurs, with bad grace, and he places it on her head. She does indeed look becoming, very queenly with her quiet, solemn dignity, and again I cannot help wishing that I were in her place, wearing that beautiful crown. Around me everyone is breaking into applause. The deed is done, and there can be no turning back; Jane is Queen and, God be praised, we are safe from the Catholic threat.

Evening has descended, and we are all guests at a great feast served in Caesar's Tower in honor of Jane's accession. The tables are liberally laden with choice dishes and the wine is flowing. Minstrels play; there will be dancing later when the board has been cleared. The chatter is deafening, and the chamber stuffy from people sweating in their velvets and silks. I have almost had my head turned by courtiers paying me compliments and outdoing each other to win my favor. I can hardly believe that it is I whom they court—I, who never considered myself very important. But I am the Queen's sister now, and I cannot help thinking that, if Jane were to lay down her crown, I would be Queen. I wish no ill to Jane, of course I do not, yet I cannot but feel that the crown is wasted on her, who does not want it, and I can't help myself thinking that, had I been the one set upon a throne today, I should have presented a much happier—indeed an ecstatic—face to the world.

Harry is at my side, a little drunk; his hand keeps straying to my breast or my knee, and to my astonishment, Pembroke is looking on benevolently. I feel myself blush under his interested scrutiny.

Harry whispers in my ear. "I have great news, my Katherine. I am allowed to come to you tonight. My father is at last content that we should consummate our marriage."

My heart sings.

"Are you content?" he asks eagerly.

I giggle. "Of course I am content. I am in Heaven!" He kisses me again, more boldly this time. I am thinking that I have one blessing that Jane does not, for all that she is Queen: a husband who loves me, and whom I am able to love in return. And as Harry smiles broadly at me with love in his eyes, it occurs to me what a handsome, noble king he would make—unlike that oaf Guilford.

Suddenly a hush descends on the company. A man has come into the hall. He wears green and white, the royal livery of the Tudors. He strides boldly up to the high table and bows.

"My lords and ladies, I am Thomas Hungate, come with a letter from Queen Mary!" he announces. "You shall hear what Her Grace has to say!"

There is a stunned silence as he produces the letter from his pouch.

"Where is the Lady Mary?" Northumberland barks.

"At Kenninghall in Norfolk, where she has been proclaimed Queen," Hungate informs him. "She has addressed her letter to the Privy Council. She greets every man well, and reminds you all of the will of her father, King Henry VIII, and the Act of Succession passed in his reign, whereby she is the lawful heiress to the crown, as all the world knows, and of which no true subject can pretend ignorance. She writes that God will aid and strengthen her in her right."

The duke's face is suffused with fury; his hands are gripping the arms of his chair.

Keeping his gaze on Northumberland, Master Hungate continues: "Her Grace finds it strange that she has received from the council no word of the King's death, especially since the matter is so weighty. Yet, knowing you for wise and prudent men, she has great hope and trust in your loyalty and service." He bows to the lords again.

"Nevertheless," he goes on, "Her Grace is not ignorant of your consultations, and can only conclude that political considerations have moved you; she cannot believe you have any evil intent. So doubt not, my lords, that she takes your deeds in gracious part, and is ready to pardon them fully and freely, to avoid bloodshed and violence, and she trusts you will take this grace and virtue in good part. Wherefore she requires and charges you, for the allegiance you owe to God and to Her Grace, that, for your honor and the surety of your persons, you will cause her right and title to the throne to be proclaimed in Her Grace's City of London and other places, not failing in this, as her very trust is in you."

The messenger's words are greeted by an appalled silence that is broken only by the Duchess of Northumberland's anguished wail. "My lord, I thought you had sent men after the Lady Mary to seize her?"

"By God, my lord duke, you've let her slip through your fingers!" my mother cries.

"The Lady Mary has no forces to back up her bold words," Northumberland says, striving for urbanity, but he seems to be trying to convince himself.

"Not so, my lord. She has gathered a company of loyal gentlemen, and has sent out letters of summons to towns throughout her realm," Hungate informs him. "Furthermore, she has let it be known that she will maintain the religion of England as established by her brother, and make no rigorous changes."

"Give me the letter and get out," says Northumberland, and Hungate departs, smirking at my lord's discomfiture.

"She has pulled the carpet from under the duke's feet," Pembroke mutters, his face tense, as Harry nods grimly. "Her declaration of tolerance will appeal to many. They will no longer see her as the enemy of the true faith, but as one who embraces all faiths."

"Don't be deceived," my mother says savagely. "I know her. She is a fanatic. She will not be as tolerant once the crown is on her head."

Jane has said nothing. I truly believe that being Queen is unimportant to her, and that she is hardly concerned at all about this latest development.

"I assure Your Majesty that the Lady Mary, a woman alone without friends or influence, poses no threat to your throne," the duke reassures her, and several councillors say aye. She inclines her head but does not reply.

Northumberland turns and beckons a warder. "Arrest the man Hungate and throw him into a dungeon for his insolence," he orders.

I feel like crying. The banquet has been ruined by Hungate's intrusion, and the air of celebration has evaporated. Clearly the festivities are at an end, for the duke rises and summons the councillors to attend him. "We must draw up a document repudiating the Lady Mary's claims," he tells them. There is a scraping of chairs and benches as the lords depart to the council chamber. I have no doubt at all that they will deal with this threat with the briskness it deserves.

They are gone a long time. Harry and I sit with the Countess of Pembroke, sipping the spiced hippocras wine that has been brought for those left at table.

Jane retires to bed. Before she departs to the Queen's lodgings, she makes her way past the bowing and scraping courtiers, and embraces and kisses me.

"Good night, sweet sister," she says in a low voice, holding me upright when I would have curtsied. "Remember, my crown is a matter of indifference to me, and it shall never come between us. Pray for me, please. They want me to make Guilford King, but I will never consent to it. So ask God to give me the strength to resist them."

"I will," I promise, thinking that, if I were Queen, I would not deny Harry a crown. He would be Harry IX! It has a certain ring to it . . .

After Jane has gone, the atmosphere in the hall is dispirited. Jubilation has turned to fear. "What if the Lady Mary *does* press her claim?" I say to Harry and his mother. "Surely the country will not rise for her?"

"We must pray it will not," Harry says. "Do not fret, darling. We have much to look forward to—especially tonight." I am reassured by his words. I am young and in love, and nothing shall stand in the way of my happiness.

The councillors return at last, and Pembroke joins us, unsmiling.

"I must lodge here at the Tower tonight," he says. "There is a furious row going on in the Queen's apartments. Jane is refusing to name Guilford King, and his mother is doing battle with her. In truth, I would rather be anywhere else. But you should all be getting back to Baynard's Castle."

The countess summons her maid for her cloak.

The room is emptying and the courtiers are leaving; there is nothing now to stay for. The earl escorts us out to the Court Gate, where our barge awaits us. On the way, I am suddenly struck by a frisson of fear and the strong urge to run. I cannot explain it, for the fear is formless, and seems not to be connected with the momentous events of the past days. Is it a reaction to them—or is it a portent? I shiver. Fortunately, the feeling is fleeting. I put it down to my having drunk too much wine.

As the barge approaches the steps, Pembroke mutters, "Hearken, all of you. I do not like the situation in which we find ourselves. Mary has always been popular. Katherine, your sister is not known to the people, and her reception today was cool. They think she is the tool of Northumberland, and he is hated. This letter from the Lady Mary has divided opinion. During the council meeting I sensed a certain cooling off on the part of several lords, and there were even those who were openly suspicious of Northumberland's determination that Guilford should be King. As I left the council chamber, the Earl of Arundel took me aside and said he feared that the duke's arrogance will be infinitely greater as father-in-law to the Queen than as Lord President of the Council. Then Winchester confided to me that he is only supporting Northumberland to preserve his own skin. Clearly, some lords are waiting on events."

"And you, sir—where do you stand?" Harry asks, his face troubled.

His father frowns. "I do not think it wise to be bound irrevocably to Northumberland," he murmurs. "If necessary, I will break with him. But not yet. I too think it best to wait to see who emerges triumphant."

I say nothing. It is plain that Pembroke owes no true allegiance to either Northumberland or Mary, and certainly not to Jane; he is thinking only of himself and his future influence and prosperity. And that becomes even more brutally clear with his next words.

"Harry," he says, as we prepare to make our farewells. "You must forget what I said earlier, because everything has changed. I absolutely forbid you to consummate your marriage. We may not wish to be allied to the House of Suffolk if events go against Northumberland."

I am horrified to hear him say that; horrified and outraged. Does he not care one jot for my feelings? How dare he disparage my family!

And is he not being overpessimistic? Mary has no support to speak of, and Northumberland has sent men after her, so she may soon be his prisoner, and Jane will be the undisputed Queen—and then, yes then, I will remind my lord Earl of Pembroke how he insulted her sister. But for now I am devastated, fighting to stem the tears. I will not look at Pembroke; I will not give him the satisfaction of seeing how he has wounded me.

Harry's eyes flash. I thrill to hear him argue in a sibilant whisper, "Katherine is my wife and I love her! You cannot keep us apart like this, sir. We are married!"

"Marriages like ours are made for policy, boy," the earl says evenly. "Love is not a consideration. If we need to extricate ourselves from this tangle, you will thank me that I did not commit you to this alliance. If the marriage is not consummated, it can easily be annulled."

I am weeping bitterly now, not caring who sees.

"I don't want it annulled!" Harry shouts, and the oarsmen in the barge look up at us, startled. "I want Katherine for my wife, and no other. Even if I did not love her, I could not make a better match. Remember who she is!"

"And remember that she might soon be accounted the daughter and sister of traitors, you young fool," his father mutters.

I find my voice. I will not have my family's honor impugned thus. "No traitors, my lord," I hiss through my tears, "but people zealous for the faith that you profess! My sister does not desire the crown. She has only accepted it because she believes it to be God's will, and that she may preserve true religion in this land."

Pembroke looks as if a mouse has just roared at him. But my blood is up, the blood of kings and princes, of King Harry and King Edward, and all the great monarchs back to William the Conqueror and Alfred. I will *not* be treated as a nonentity! My parents would be proud of me if they were here, and as offended as I at the earl's attitude.

"God's will in the matter has yet to be revealed," Pembroke growls, "and until then, daughter-in-law, you would do well to hold your peace and pray for a happy outcome. In the meantime, do not defy my order. You may have to wait only a few days longer."

Harry looks as if he is about to cry too, from anger and frustration;

he is struggling to control himself. Without a word, he hands his mother and me into the barge and flings himself down on the cushions in the cabin. The boat rocks alarmingly, bumping against the steps.

"Have patience, my children," the countess counsels. But we've been patient long enough. Harry sits there stony-faced, and I cannot stop crying as the barge plies its short course along the moonlit Thames.

KATE

June 16, 1483. Crosby Place, City of London;
Baynard's Castle

"Your father has returned from the Tower," the duchess told Kate, as they sat in the courtyard garden, working at their embroidery and enjoying the sunshine. A clatter of hooves, shouts in the street, and scurrying grooms confirmed her words.

Gloucester rode into the courtyard and dismounted. "Bring wine!" he called. "And keep White Surrey saddled but give her some water." Servants sprang to action. The duke walked across to Kate and Anne, a dark figure with the sun at his back and the breeze stirring his long hair.

"I cannot stay, ladies," he said. "I came only to tell you that York is to be removed from sanctuary."

Anne eyed him warily. "The council meeting went well?"

"It did," he told her. "I laid the matter of York before the councillors, and insisted it was bad for him and the King to be apart, and to have no one of their own age to play with."

"And did they agree?"

"They did. So I proposed sending Cardinal Bourchier to the Queen, to command her to release her son. I reasoned that the Archbishop of Canterbury's persuasions would carry much weight with her."

"That was well done, my lord," Anne said. "But has the Cardinal agreed to it? Will she receive him?"

"It was Buckingham who saved the day," Gloucester related. "He told the Cardinal that the Queen's stubbornness was prompted not by fear but by womanly contrariness. He said he had never heard of sanctuary children, and that a child of York's age has no need of sanctuary, and therefore no right to it. That carried great weight with the Cardinal and the council, and they sanctioned the boy's removal. So I must go to Westminster. Lord Howard is commandeering boats and assembling soldiers."

"Soldiers?" echoed the duchess.

"In case the Queen proves obdurate," the duke said. "Never fear, it will only be a show of force."

That afternoon, the duchess summoned Kate. "Make haste, and get your maid to pack your gear," she commanded. "Your father has sent to tell me he has taken up residence in the Tower until the King is crowned. He has given orders that we are to move to Baynard's Castle to lodge with your grandmother the duchess."

Kate's heart sank. She hated the idea of her father being away from them at this time, when his life might be in peril. Of course, the Tower would be the safest place for him, but for her it was indelibly associated with the horrible end of Lord Hastings, and would forever be a sinister place.

That evening, as dusk was falling, the Duchess Cecily received them graciously, greeting them at the top of the imposing stairs that led up from the jetty. But as Kate stepped onto those stairs, she experienced a moment of blind panic and despair; so strong was the impression that she caught her breath. The horrible sensation persisted until she was inside the house, and only then did she feel like her normal self again. She wondered what it was that had made her feel so desperately sad and terrified, but she put it down to anxiety over her father, and the moment passed.

The duchess led them through a series of vast, splendid chambers, each more exquisitely appointed than the last, with tiled floors, stained-glass windows, vaulted ceilings, and traceried windows. But there was little furniture, just the odd bench or chest.

"I rarely use these rooms now," the duchess told them. "I observe a conventual regime, and normally confine myself to my chamber and the chapel." Later, Kate got to see her grandmother's chamber, a stuffy, dark room with a simple bed and a portable altar. In fact, the whole mansion was dark, hung with rich, gloomy tapestries that obscured much of the light and gave the lofty rooms a sad, oppressive air.

"Three years ago, child, I decided to dedicate myself to God and take the Benedictine habit," Cecily explained, as Kate knelt at her feet by the fireside. "My life is now ruled by prayer." Looking at her, upright and frail, seated in her high-backed chair, her once-beautiful features framed by a nun's wimple and veil, and her only adornment and concession to her rank the enameled cross at her breast, Kate had an impression of strength and piety. She wished she could unburden her fears to this old lady, who was clearly very wise and could see beyond the preoccupations and vanities of the world.

The following evening, as they sat in the solarium after supper, she listened avidly as the Duchess Cecily told her stories of the old days, of the civil wars between the houses of Lancaster and York, and of an even earlier time, when Cecily had been young and renowned for her pride and her exquisite aristocratic looks.

"They called me the Rose of Raby," she reminisced, "and that wasn't all! The other name they used was Proud Cis, and I deserved it, I tell you. I had a very high opinion of myself in those days."

York—she always referred to her long-dead husband as York, although Kate knew her grandfather's name had been Richard Plantagenet—had adored her. "Fourteen children I bore him. Your father was the last but one. Nine of them are with God." Her face clouded; Kate thought she was thinking of Edmund, Earl of Rutland, dead in battle at seventeen, and George, Duke of Clarence, drowned in Malmsey wine in the Tower by order of his brother, King Edward. How terrible it must have been for the duchess to have had one son killed by order of another.

Kate did not like to say anything; indeed, did not know what to say.

"They put a paper crown on his head," the old lady went on, toying absentmindedly with her rosary beads. Kate was nonplussed, but the Duchess Anne had warned her that her grandmother's mind was apt to wander in strange directions. "He was their rightful king, yet they slaughtered him in battle," Cecily continued, "and, not content with that, they cut off his head and crowned it with that paper crown, then they set it on the Micklegate Bar at York. They mocked him! Our Lord enjoins us to forgive, but I cannot."

Kate realized that the Duchess Cecily was talking about her husband, York, who had been slain at the Battle of Wakefield more than twenty years earlier.

"It was a terrible thing to do, my lady," she said gently. The elderly duchess patted her head.

"You're a good girl, Kate," she said, "and I fancy you have a look of him about you. Your grandsire, I mean. Your father is more like him than any of my other children." Her eyes were wistful. Then abruptly she turned to Anne and changed the subject.

"The duke my son sent word that young York has joined his brother in the Tower," she said.

"I know," Anne replied.

"Strange about Dorset disappearing," Cecily observed. "But he will have heard what happened after the Battle of Tewkesbury, when Richard had the Lancastrian leaders dragged out of the abbey to summary execution, saying it was his right as Constable of England."

If her father had said he had the right, then he must have had. Yet her stepmother was looking uneasy, and her grandmother's face was grim.

Anne broke the silence. "My lord has commanded me to take care of Clarence's son, young Warwick. He will be a playmate for John."

"My grandson Warwick is a backward child, as you will see," Cecily said sadly. "It is as well that his poor father's attainder prevents him from ever inheriting the crown, for he would be next in line to the throne after the King and young York. But if anyone wished them harm, they might try to use Warwick for their own ends. Attainders can easily be reversed."

Kate was beginning to feel very edgy about all this. It was fast becoming clear to her that being of royal blood and close to the throne was not just about honor, power, and obligation; as her father's anxieties over the past weeks had shown, it was also about going in fear of your life, and in danger of the intrigues of others.

"It is only ten days to the coronation," Anne was saying. "Then Parliament must decide whether my lord continues in office. We must pray that Dorset does not show his hand." She was pale with fear.

Kate and Mattie were walking through London when they suddenly encountered a procession led by none other than the Duke of Gloucester, astride White Surrey. Kate was astounded, not only to meet her father riding abroad, but also to see that he had put off his black mourning clothes and was wearing a sumptuous purple robe. Behind him followed a huge contingent of his liveried retainers, all wearing his white boar badge.

"There must be a thousand of them, as sure as I live!" Mattie muttered. Realizing instinctively that it might be better to preserve their anonymity, the two girls moved quickly to the back of the crowd, such as it was, for few were bothering to line the street, and even fewer to doff their bonnets. But the duke did not see his daughter and her maid: he was bowing from left to right, intent on gaining the goodwill of the people, although he was enjoying little success, judging by the mood of the Londoners.

"Look at him, acting like a king!" one said. "I'll be damned if he don't seize the crown."

"I'd curse him with a fate worthy of his crimes," spat another. Kate was just about to round on the speaker, but Mattie grabbed her hand and pulled her away, diving down a side street. "Best not to say anything," she said when they came to a breathless halt at the other end. Kate was angry with the man for his unjust words, and with Mattie for depriving her of the chance to challenge him, but when she calmed down, she realized that her maid had been wiser than she. Nothing she said now could disabuse people like that of their fixed opinions. Only her father could retrieve his reputation—and retrieve it he would, given time, she knew it.

London was becoming very crowded, its population swelled by an influx of great lords and their retinues, come for the coronation, along with many other visitors up from the country. Inns were full, cookshops busy, and thieves were doing good business: whenever they went out, Kate and Mattie saw the sheriffs' men chasing after pilferers, followed by an outraged merchant or gentleman complaining indignantly of his loss. All was bustle and expectancy—and then, out of the blue, came the proclamation: the coronation was to be postponed. No reason or new date was given, and suddenly London was abuzz with speculation. Yet it was not long before it became common knowledge that preparations were still going on apace at Westminster, and everybody relaxed: there *would* still be a coronation—the only question was when.

"I wonder why it has been postponed," Kate mused, fingering the gorgeous blue damask gown that was now finished and hanging from its peg in her chamber, and wondering when she would get the chance to wear it.

"I have no idea," the duchess said. "My lord writes that the King's coronation robes are ready, and that some dishes have already been prepared for the banquet in Westminster Hall, so probably this is just a minor delay."

"I hope so," Kate said fervently. She did not want her father's detractors to be given any more cause to think ill of him.

KATHERINE

July 1553. Baynard's Castle, London;
Sheen Priory, Surrey

Against all the odds, it seems, the Lady Mary has eluded capture. In many shires men are arming in her favor, not only Catholics but also Protestants, loyal to King Harry's daughter. The only heartening piece of news is of a rising against her in Cambridge, yet we hear no more of that.

"Northumberland must act now if victory is to be ours," Harry says.

But Northumberland remains in London.

"He dare not leave yet," says Pembroke grimly, on one of his rare visits home. "He does not have enough men, and is doing his utmost to recruit them. He has drafted a letter for Queen Jane to send to the lord lieutenants of the counties, commanding them to do all in their power to defend her just title." His tone is slightly ironic, as if to imply that her title might be anything but just.

I turn my head away. I have nothing to say to my father-in-law. I hate him. But in a few days, God willing, he may have to come craving my forgiveness. I am looking forward to that moment.

In the meantime I need distractions to take my mind off my anxieties. One morning—much encouraged by the news that Northumberland has mustered an army at least two thousand strong—I open the little silver casket in which I keep jewels, letters, poems, and the bundle of papers I found in the turret room. First, I take out the gold pendant. Even though it is of a style long out of fashion, and frowned on these days, I would that I could wear it. It is so beautifully wrought, and the sapphire is a heavenly blue. As I hold it in my hand, it feels alive, vibrant! Guiltily, I hang it around my neck—and immediately am swamped by that awful sense of despair that I had before. It is a terrible feeling—as if all hope has gone and only death remains. Clawing at the chain, I struggle to extricate myself, and my breath is coming in short gasps when I finally succeed in tearing off the pendant. Surely it *is* bewitched! I must never put it on again. And yet—it is so beautiful, and seemingly harmless when I look at it lying on the table. I stare at it for a bit, then make up my mind. Wrapping it in a scrap of taffeta from my needlework basket, I thrust it to the bottom of my casket, resolving that there it shall stay.

I wonder if *she* experienced those feelings—that girl in the blue dress. I still dream about her sometimes, dream of her reaching out to me, as if she wants something. But I never discover what it is; I always wake up. I have her painting in my bedchamber now—Harry asked the earl if I could. I am convinced that she is Katherine Plantagenet, Richard III's daughter. I hope that horrible sensation of despair has nothing to do with her. Who knows how many people have worn that pendant since?

I turn to the bundle of papers. I have been meaning to read them properly, but events have overtaken me. I need time and concentration, for they are written in an ill hand, very cramped and hard to decipher. Because of what I saw on the stairs to that tower room where I found the papers, I have come to believe that someone wants them to be read.

The first few lines are in bigger, clearer script. I can read them easily; I have, indeed, done so several times, and memorized them, for they are startling, and of some import. I read them again, wondering.

These lines I write for posterity. It is said that King Richard murdered
his nephews in the Tower of London, so that he could usurp the throne.
But that is surely a calumny, put about by his enemies, which in these
days may not be denied.

There is more, but the handwriting suddenly becomes minuscule, almost illegible. Given the preamble, I suspect that what I have before me was once highly controversial, even dangerous, and probably kept hidden by its author.

I am sitting at the table in the parlor trying to make out the next line when Harry comes in and flops down beside me.

"Phew! Archery practice is hard work in this heat," he grumbles, mopping his brow with his sleeve. "What's that you have there, Katherine? Oh, it's those papers from the chest. May I see?"

I show him the first page. "What do you make of that?"

He reads, exhales, and raises his eyebrows.

"It's about Richard III. Look, there's a date—1487. But he was killed at Bosworth in 1485."

I peer closer. Yes, there is the date 1487 right at the foot of the page—and I can just make out the words "appreh" and "Raglan Castle." Most of the bottom lines have faded away.

"It must have been written by one of my ancestors," Harry says.

"Would they have known something about the fate of the Princes in the Tower?"

"Who knows? What is there to know? King Richard murdered them."

"Whoever wrote this didn't think so."

Harry shrugs. "But we don't know who wrote it, or why, so how can we judge it? And Richard was a wicked, evil man. We may thank God that Henry Tudor vanquished the bloody tyrant at Bosworth."

"I suppose anyone claiming in 1487 that Richard was innocent would not have been popular."

"They'd have been laughed at, or worse!" Harry sniffs. "It would have been rash, even perilous, to write such nonsense. Yet my forebears of the time were staunch Yorkists, loyal to Richard's house. They evidently found something to admire in him, and maybe they didn't believe the rumors that the princes had been murdered. My great-uncle was married to Richard's daughter; he was also in the service of Richard's son; and he got word to Richard that Henry Tudor had landed."

"I don't suppose he was very popular with Henry Tudor afterward."

"He made his peace with the new King," Harry tells me. "You see, he was rather like my father. He did not fight at Bosworth. He was said to have turned up late, but I suspect he waited to see which way the wind blew before committing himself. It is a regrettable family trait, I fear." He gives me a rueful look. "But it was as well, because King Henry craftily dated his reign from the day of Bosworth, so that all who fought for Richard were traitors. My great-uncle kept his earldom. He was a canny man."

I look at the papers again. "So he could not have written this."

"He *would* not have written it!" Harry is adamant. "Henry Tudor was suspicious of all those who had been close to Richard. William would have had to go out of his way to prove his loyalty to the Tudor dynasty. Anyway, I think this was written by a woman. A man would not have tied these papers up with a ribbon." He dangles the tawdry, fraying thing.

"I have it!" I say, but am silenced when the countess enters the parlor, obviously bursting with news.

"My lord has sent word. Northumberland is to ride to Norfolk at the head of the army, to take the Lady Mary. He has said that Jane and Guilford shall be crowned in Westminster Abbey within this fortnight."

"Hurrah!" cheers Harry, and my heart leaps! The duke must be sure of victory if he is planning a coronation. I can start to think about a new gown—and, which is far more precious, bedding openly with Harry!

"Good news at last," I breathe. "But did not the Queen refuse to have Guilford crowned?"

"That might be the price of the duke's support," my lady says shrewdly. "Now, Katherine, I should like you to come to the still room to help me make some honey. I've got some lovely lavender in, and if we've time, we can mix some balms and salves too. And, Harry, I have word from the stables that your new courser has arrived. You had best go and check that you are satisfied with him."

My husband disappears in an eager hurry, and I tie up the little bundle of papers and put them back in their casket before hastening after my lady's retreating back.

I am not allowed to go out. My lady is adamant. There are rumors of a mutiny in Yarmouth against Northumberland, and armed men prowl the streets of London.

"They are deserters from the duke's army," she says. "The mood of the people is ugly. They suspect these deserters of being spies, sent by him to seek out dissidents."

"The soldiers are deserting?" I ask in alarm. How swiftly the wheel of fortune turns.

"Yes." She is tight-lipped. I know she feels sorry for me, but her first loyalty is to her lord. "They complain they have not been paid. Our steward heard some of them spouting forth in a tavern. And he heard something else, my dear—something I think you should know."

We are alone in the quiet of the still room, making scent with the rest of the lavender—a scent I shall never want to smell again.

"What is it?" I ask, sharper than I had intended because of my fears.

"He heard people saying that the Lady Mary is marching on London with a force of thirty thousand men, and that most towns have declared for her and proclaimed her Queen." The countess looks unhappy. We might all be casualties of Northumberland's ambition.

We sit late after supper that evening, going over and over the latest news and its possible consequences, as the candles burn down and, beyond the open latticed windows, the sun disappears, leaving a soft, velvety sky studded with stars. It grows late, but none of us are ready to sleep. In fact, I doubt I could sleep. I keep dwelling on Jane, shut up for her own safety in the Tower. Has she heard these disturbing reports? Does she realize that, if Mary wins, she might be branded a usurper and traitor? She, who never wanted her crown! Does Northumberland realize what he has done? And our parents? Did it ever occur to them, when they abetted him in this grand scheme, that they might be putting their daughter in danger—and themselves? And that there might be evil consequences for me too?

"I do fear for my sister," I blurt out.

Harry reaches for my hand. His eyes are kind and full of compassion. "Do not worry, sweetheart. All is not lost yet."

"The Lady Mary is known to be a merciful princess," the countess says. "She will understand that Jane is young—and that she did not want to accept the crown."

Her words strike a chill down my spine. It is as if she believes it is a foregone conclusion that Mary will triumph.

The door opens and the earl walks in. He looks haggard and weary, and sinks into his great chair at the head of the table.

"Greetings to you all," he says flatly. "Is there any wine left?"

My lady picks up the ewer and pours. Her husband downs his goblet in one go. "More. I need it." The countess pours again.

"What has happened?" Harry asks.

"Northumberland is facing ruin," his father replies grimly. "He is finished, and it is only a matter of time before he is taken."

I start to shake. Harry grasps my hand tighter.

"But all may not be lost," the earl is saying. "Most of us on the council are ready to declare for Mary. We have seen how the tide is turning." He looks at me. "Your father, my dear, has been doing his best to prevent us from leaving the Tower. Fortunately, the Master of the Mint managed to escape with all the gold from the Queen's privy purse, which he was taking to Mary's supporters in London."

"And you have escaped too, my lord, thank God!" the countess cries fervently.

"Aye, by the skin of my teeth. When my lord of Suffolk heard how great an army was poised to march on London, he had his daughter proclaimed all over again, then ordered the gates of the Tower to be locked—not to keep Mary's forces out, you understand, but to keep us privy councillors in! He trusts none of us. But if Mary wins, we stand to be accused of high treason. You all know the penalty for that."

There is a chilling silence. I hardly dare breathe.

The earl continues: "Yet I cannot think that Queen Mary will arraign and execute almost her entire Privy Council, especially if we now declare for her. Who else is there to help her rule? She is a woman: she will need advice and support. So yes, my dear, I made my escape before they locked the Tower."

You might have made your escape, I think bitterly, but you have left my poor, defenseless sister to face the consequences of your actions. I rise, sketch the briefest of curtseys, and murmur a frosty good night. I must get to my bedchamber before I say too much and disgrace myself.

I am making my way to my lonely bed, in great torment, when there is a resounding banging at the door to the water stairs. Hastening in alarm to the hall, I hear men's voices commanding, "Open, in the name of the Queen!"

The earl arrives at the same time, with Harry and the countess behind him, and nods to the porter to open the door. There are soldiers with pikes outside.

"What is the meaning of this?" Pembroke thunders.

"Sir, we are sent by the Queen," the captain says.

"Which queen?" Pembroke barks.

"Why, Queen Jane, of course," the man responds angrily. "We are sent to escort you back to the Tower, where you are to attend upon her."

"And if I refuse?"

"My lord, we would not wish to use force, but our orders are to see that you obey the Queen's command."

"Very well. My cloak." He turns to a servant, ignoring the frightened faces of his household, which has clustered around, alarmed by the banging and shouting. The cloak is brought and the earl steps out into the night.

Two anxious days later he is back.

"It is finished," he tells us, as my heart plummets wildly. "Northumberland sent news of reports that the Lady Mary was advancing with an army forty thousand strong. His men were deserting like rats, and he urged us to send reinforcements—but there are none, even if we were so inclined. The usurper Jane—or rather her father, Suffolk—ordered the guards around the Tower to be doubled, but there was no point, for the guards were refusing to force people to stay. I, and several others, walked out unchallenged. In fact, Jane gave us permission to leave; I told her we were going to ask the French ambassador for aid for Northumberland. Suffolk wanted to come with us—he's no fool—but it would be dangerous to be associated with him now, so we told him we would have him executed if he abandoned the Queen his daughter at this time."

"He meant to abandon her, his own child?" The countess is shocked.

"He looks to his own skin." Suddenly, the earl notices I am here listening, and remembers that it is my father of whom they speak. His face softens a little.

"Katherine, I am aware this is distressing for you," he tells me, "but you have to know the truth."

"What will happen to Jane?" I ask, my voice tremulous. "Is all now lost?" I still cannot believe it.

"I fear it is," he says. "Only three members of the council remain with her in the Tower. The rest will declare for Mary, mark my word. They are on their way here now. I'm afraid I do not know what will happen to the Lady Jane. No doubt Mary will deal leniently with her; this was not her doing."

"No, it was not," I say, a touch defiantly. But Pembroke ignores me, and it is left to Harry, all care and concern, to attempt to comfort me. I look long at him, drinking in his fine, honest face, his fresh good looks, his kind eyes, and his soft curly hair—as if I might never see them again.

The councillors have assembled in the great chamber with the door firmly closed. The countess gives orders for dinner to be served as normal, and we seat ourselves at table in the parlor. I know I will not be able to touch a morsel. In fact, the smell of the good roast beef and pigeon pie is making me nauseous.

Then the earl comes in.

"Forgive me, my lady, I am not staying," he says. "I am for St. Paul's. We have decided, all of us, to abandon Northumberland and declare for Mary. The duke is deemed guilty of treason against his lawful sovereign, and we have summoned him back to London to account for his actions, and offered a reward to anyone apprehending him. For now, I go with the other privy councillors to give thanks for this realm's deliverance from treachery; and to proclaim our loyalty to Queen Mary, we are having Mass celebrated in the cathedral."

"What of my poor sister?" I cry.

"Your sister remains in the Tower," Pembroke replies curtly, and turns on his heel.

I spend much of the afternoon on my knees in the chapel. I am distraught, on my own account and Jane's. Will I be accounted a traitor too? And what of my marriage? Will Pembroke really have it annulled? God aid me, I feel so helpless!

Yet my peril is as nothing to Jane's. Repeatedly I beseech the Almighty to be merciful, and to make Queen Mary merciful too. And when I have prayed until I can pray no more, and cried myself out, I wander through the deserted state rooms distractedly, not knowing what to do with myself.

I find myself in the great hall with its fine gallery. Here, seventy years ago this summer, they offered the crown to Richard III; like Jane, he was a usurper; unlike her, he had plotted and schemed—and killed—to be King. I saw a portrait of him once, a thin-lipped man with cruel, wary eyes and a humped back. For he had been evil in appearance, just as he was evil inside: it often falls out—so I have been told—that the two go together. Crookback, they had called him; and he was crooked through and through. But Jane is not evil like Richard. Why should she suffer because of the treacherous schemes of others?

It is late afternoon, still sunny outside, but the cavernous hall is cool and dim, the gallery in shadow, too high to benefit from the jewel-colored light coming from the tall, narrow stained-glass windows.

Again that dark-garbed fellow is up there, watching as before, on the night I first came here. Has he nothing better to do, no duties to attend to? He is standing stock-still, his shadowed face looking down over the vast chamber. Is he staring at me? I cannot be certain, but that unwavering scrutiny is making me feel mightily ill at ease.

I stare back boldly, trying to make him aware of his rudeness and to discern his features, but it is dark up there, and the sunlight through the window dazzles me. Only gradually do I realize that behind the varlet there are three more dark figures. One seems to be a woman in an outlandish headdress, the second is veiled like a nun, and the third appears to be a young girl with long hair. There is a disturbing stillness about all four of the people in that little tableau.

"Who's there?" I cry. The answering silence is unnerving. The figures stand motionless—and then suddenly they are not there anymore. Did I blink? Did they see me and make themselves scarce as I did so? Truly, there was something uncanny about them. And why am I shivering on this warm July day? Suddenly frightened, I pick up my skirts and hasten to the door, fleeing as if from a pack of devils, and wondering if there is some evil at work in this house.

I must find something to distract me or I will go out of my mind with fear. Returning to my bedchamber, I take out the old bundle of papers and make another serious effort to decipher them.

I have a good idea who might have written them. Harry said it could not have been the William Herbert who was Earl of Huntingdon— but it could have been his wife, who had been King Richard's daughter. If anyone would have wanted to believe the best of Richard, it would have been her—Katherine. We share a name.

I read over those short lines again. *But that is surely a calumny . . .* The use of the word "surely" suggests that whoever wrote it wanted to believe in Richard's innocence. It must have been his daughter.

I peer at the jumble of faded script below, my eyes scanning the text. A few words stand out. *The ru . . . s that are damaging to the King . . . mayhap Bokenham knew ye truth . . . he is dead. My lord Bishop of L . . . says they live yet . . . mayhap Mancini knew more than he told Pietro . . . Tyrell was at the Tower . . . 1487 . . . appreh . . . Raglan.*

I try to make some sense of it. I spend so long poring over this page that there is no time to attempt any more. I try to recall my history lessons and the books that once captivated me. I'm sure it was Richard III who was damaged by rumors, so that part makes sense. And Bokenham must surely mean Buckingham. I seem to remember reading of a Duke of Buckingham who supported Richard but later rebelled against him. As for the Bishop of L, that will need a more learned mind than mine. And who were Mancini and Pietro? Italians by the sound of it. How could Italians know anything of the secret affairs of England?

They live yet. The princes? In 1487? They had been murdered in King Richard's reign.

But what if they had not?

I remember Master Aylmer telling us about the pretenders who threatened Henry VII's throne, and how many people believed they were the true heirs of York. Master Aylmer could not sufficiently stress how perilous it is to tangle with princes: "For look what happened to those pretenders. Both were exposed as frauds. Henry VII was merciful to Lambert Simnel, and put him to work in his kitchens, but Perkin Warbeck tried the King's patience too long, and ended up hanged. Henry VII never rested easy in his bed all those years."

My tutor's words come back to me now. Why, if the pretenders were only pretenders, had Henry not rested easy? Was it because he did not know for certain that the princes were dead? Did he fear that they "lived yet"?

When Harry, with Sanders in tow, comes to tell me that the earl is back and commanding us to supper, I try to delay the evil moment I feel sure is coming. Gabbling a little, I ask Harry what he makes of all this, but he is skeptical. "I imagine the King did not rest easy because he was worried that people would accept the pretenders as the true heirs to the throne."

"Then why did he not just execute them?"

"He had to catch them first."

As I tie up the notes and put them back in my casket, my hands shaking, the reference to the Tower leaps out at me. "Have you heard of someone called Tyrell, Harry?" I ask. The name sounds familiar.

"I think a man called Tyrell was beheaded by Henry VII, but I can't remember why. Now come, sweetheart. My lord and lady do not like to be kept waiting."

At supper Pembroke announces that Queen Mary is to be proclaimed in London on the morrow. "There will be much rejoicing when the news breaks." But I am not rejoicing. The glorious days are done, all too soon. My sister is no longer Queen, and the dread shadow of treason lies over us all.

In the morning, the earl is for the Guildhall with the Privy Council, to wait upon the Lord Mayor and aldermen of the City and witness the proclamation.

"You must all stay indoors," he says. "It would not do for the usurper's sister to be seen in public, especially with my son." I open my mouth to protest, but he has gone.

"Try not to worry," Harry says, hugging me, although his voice betrays his own anxiety. I am too frightened to speak. Pleading a headache, I go to my chamber and lie down, falling into troubled dreams in which the girl in the blue gown is running from some nameless horror, and I have to stand by, unable to help her.

After dinner, Pembroke is back, bringing the mayor and all his brethren with him. There is a lot of commotion in the house, with people coming and going and doors opening and closing. Through my window I recognize some of the visitors as lords of the council. Then silence falls, and I assume they have all left.

The rest of the afternoon is quiet. Beyond the open windows, I can hear the usual traffic and shouts from the river. It is a hot day, but a gentle breeze is stirring the damask curtains. I wish I could sleep again, and escape this misery and uncertainty. I should be with Harry, making the most of what might be my last hours with him, for I fear now that my marriage is doomed. At the thought of losing my love, I fall to weeping. I would with all my heart that I could give myself to him just once.

Inspiration comes out of the blue. If we tell the earl that we are husband and wife in very truth, he cannot part us! It would be a lie, but we would be safe. For on what other grounds could he have our marriage annulled?

My heart is pounding. I flop back on the bed, thinking it through, and decide that this ruse could work. I must tell Harry. But when I go to find him, Sanders tells me that he has ridden to Cheapside to hear the new Queen proclaimed. He has defied his father's orders yet again! How glad I am to know that he is in such a bullish frame of mind, for no doubt he will be ready to defy my lord further.

I return to my chamber and sit at my table beneath the window. I refresh my face with some lavender water, pick up my comb, and tidy my tangled hair. Setting the French hood atop it, and easing the band under my chin, I peer into the mirror and see myself, all white skin and great blue eyes shadowed by anxiety. I look ill. I pinch my cheeks to redden them and bite my lips. I must look fetching for Harry when he returns.

The clock strikes five. There is a great shout from the street, followed by yelling and cheering, and the sound of running footsteps. "God save Queen Mary!" someone calls, and there are hurrahs and whistles. Then the bells begin their joyful pealing, as each parish church takes its lead from the next, and suddenly it seems that the whole world is rejoicing and ringing out the good news. Except me.

I race through the house to the landward side and look out of a window. Moments later the countess joins me. We watch, in silence, people running hither and thither with excitement, crying out the news and throwing their bonnets in the air, neighbor clasping the hand of neighbor, folk lighting bonfires and dragging tables into the street, setting them with food and liberal quantities of ale and wine.

"I cannot remember ever seeing such celebrations," my lady says at length, as the sound of singing rises to us. "Look at them—they are even throwing coins out of windows. I'll wager they'll be carousing all night."

I open the window and lean out. "Look!"

There in the street below me are normally dignified aldermen and merchants, worthy, respected men of substance, casting off their gowns and leaping and jigging with the common folk. And here returns the Earl of Pembroke, to much cheering. I see him smiling expansively, as if he personally has conferred this great blessing on the people who now crowd around him. We watch as he takes off his cap, fills it with gold angels, and tosses it to the crowd.

"Make you merry!" he cries. "God bless Queen Mary, our rightful queen!" The citizens roar their approval and scramble for the earl's bounty. Then he holds his hand up to gain their attention, and declares in ringing tones: "Good people, I would have you know that my son's marriage to the Lady Katherine Grey, made against my will by Northumberland, is to be annulled forthwith. The Herberts do not ally with traitors!" This is greeted with more cheers, but I hardly hear them, for I am faint and the countess has to help me to a chair.

"No! No!" I wail. "It cannot be!"

"Hush!" she admonishes, as the servants come running to see what is amiss. "You do yourself no good by such displays, child. Look, here is Harry. He knows it is best to obey his father's will in this matter."

Harry's face is grim. He kneels beside the chair and clasps me to him.

"No one shall separate us!" he declares.

I grasp his hand tightly. I never want to let it go.

"We have to tell them!" I urge.

"Tell them what?" It is the earl.

"Tell your father, Harry, why he cannot have our marriage annulled," I cry to Harry, who looks nonplussed.

Pembroke frowns. "Indeed I can!" he declares.

"On what grounds?" Harry asks, defiant now.

"That it has not been consummated. You know that, boy."

"Then you cannot proceed—because it has," I declare, feeling myself grow hot with embarrassment, but determined to be staunch in my resolve to save my marriage. Harry regards me with admiration: he has caught my drift.

Pembroke laughs humorlessly. "Hah! That horse won't run."

Harry defies him. "I assure you, sir, that Katherine is my wife in every sense. We have lain together in secret. To annul our marriage now would be to flout God's law."

"It is true," I say. "I swear it."

"Spare me your oaths," Pembroke snarls. "How can it be true? Sanders has kept watch on you throughout, on my orders."

"Then ask him," Harry says. "Ask him if he accompanied us to the tower room where first we looked at the old records."

"Pah!" the earl snorts. "I will not believe it. You think to turn me with vain lies."

"I do not lie!" insists Harry.

"Or I, sir," I echo, crossing my fingers in the folds of my skirt. "It is the truth." I am determined to stand my ground.

"This is all nonsense," declares the earl, "and I will not listen to any more of it. You will leave my house tonight, Katherine. You will take with you only those things that you brought with you. And if you attempt to repeat your lies in order to subvert the annulment, it will go worse for your sister."

"No!" I scream, and cling to Harry as to a life raft, begging an unheeding God not to let us be parted. Harry, unmanned, starts weeping too, holding me tightly and swearing great oaths at his father, but the earl is unrelenting.

"I have spoken. That is an end to the matter." And he stalks out of the room, leaving me half fainting with misery in Harry's arms.

"Go now, my Katherine," he enjoins me, harshly, as if he is tearing the words out of himself. "I will fight for you, I vow it." He releases me, his eyes intense, insistent. Their promise gives me the courage to do his bidding and let go of him.

"Farewell for now," he says, holding my gaze, and lifting a gentle finger to brush away my tears. "Remember how much I love you, sweet wife."

"And I you, my dear lord," I whisper. Then, feeling as if my heart is utterly broken and can never be made whole again, I turn away and walk out of the room. I do not trust myself to look back.

The earl has wasted no time in summoning his barge for me, with instructions to the boatmaster to deliver me to the house of my parents at Sheen, like an unwanted parcel. He has provided no attendant or escort, just the crew of the boat. I am not even permitted to take the maid he appointed.

His chamberlain briskly ushers me out of the house and down the stairs to the jetty, servants following behind with my hastily packed belongings. I am distraught, with tears streaming down my face, but no one appears to notice. My tragedy is not their concern.

I know that Harry meant what he said, that he will move heaven and earth to get me back. Yet Harry is his father's son, and the earl, as has been proved to me tonight, is a formidable opponent. I have to accept the worst now: I am henceforth no more than the sister of the usurper. No one will want to know me or associate with me, let alone marry me. At almost thirteen, this is a terrible thought. My life is over before it has barely begun.

The priory is in darkness, the grounds drenched in shadows that loom in the moonlight. The barge master does his bidding and no more, and after he has deposited me and my gear on the jetty, he jumps back into the barge and gives the order to depart. The dim lights of the boat recede downstream and disappear into the night, and I am alone, with only the cold moon to light my way up to the dark bulk of the shuttered house.

"It's me, Lady Katherine!" I cry, banging hard on the gatehouse door, but the only response is the eerie hooting of an owl. I rattle the big iron handles, but the portal is securely locked. The blackness of the night, the rustling of the tall trees silhouetted against a starless sky, and the black mass of the gatehouse looming up above me are terrifying. Crying noisily now, I sink to my knees. Soon, I am screaming, "Help me! Help me! For the love of God, help me!" Nothing in my short, sheltered life has prepared me for this.

"Who's there?"

God be praised, is that my mother's voice? And can that be footsteps approaching the door? "Who's making that racket?" calls the voice. It *is* my mother! Oh, thank God, thank God! Now I know that prayers are answered.

A light appears at the window above me.

"Get down here, you fool!" I can hear my lady saying testily to the porter, who has somewhat belatedly risen to do his duty. "Someone's screaming fit to wake the dead!"

The great key turns in the lock, and there she is, my lady, staring down at me with a horrified expression on her face. She looks tired and drawn, and her brocade gown is mud-spattered at the hem.

"What are you doing here, child?" she asks, astonished.

"The earl turned me out of his house," I tell her.

"He did what?" But I am beyond speech. I break down again, and am amazed to find her arms about me, she who has never been a demonstrative parent.

"You shall tell me everything later," she says as she raises me to my feet and supports me as she walks me to the house. I am staggered to hear a tremor in the voice of my strong, formidable mother.

My lord is nowhere to be seen.

"Your father and I have not long arrived," my lady says as we enter the hall, where their baggage is piled in a heap on the floor. "I will send the steward to rouse the staff. There is no food in the house and the beds are unaired. But of course, they did not expect us."

She sits down with me on the settle.

"Tell me what happened," she commands, and in a halting voice I obey. It is only when I reach the part where I am forced to say farewell to Harry that I break down again. For once, my mother does not reprove such weakness. She is plainly furious, but not with me.

"Pembroke ordered his barge master to abandon you here like that?" she cries. "That is outrageous!"

"There is more," I venture, knowing that my next words might earn me a beating or worse, but I must pursue my only hope. "Harry and I—we . . . we told his father we did lie together. The earl had forbidden it, and had a man watch us, but we said we had given him the slip."

My lady does not erupt in rage, but stares at me intently. "You spoke truth?"

"No. I don't think the earl believed us anyway. He called us liars, and nothing we said could move him."

"It would not have, even if your marriage had been consummated," my mother says stonily. "He has to break from us to win the favor of Queen Mary. You do know, I suppose, what has happened this day?"

"Yes, madam, I saw the celebrations in London for the new Queen. But what of poor Jane? Is she not here with you?"

"You may well ask!" she replies. "We had to leave Jane in the Tower, and for all I know she is now a prisoner."

"You *had* to leave her?" I have never presumed to question my mother, but the circumstances are like no other.

"Good God, girl!" she snaps. "Don't you understand? In accepting the crown that was rightfully Mary's, Jane has committed treason, and far be it from me, or your father, to attempt to remove her from the Tower. It is for Queen Mary to decide her fate."

"But Jane did not want the crown!" I protest, stunned by the injustice of it all.

"We must pray that the Queen takes that into consideration," my lady mutters.

"She must!" I cry. "They are saying she is a merciful princess."

"She is indeed merciful. I know her of old. I am placing all my hopes in her." The stern façade is crumbling: my mother suddenly looks as if she might collapse. It seems like the end of the world.

"How is Jane taking this?" I ask her.

"I did not see her. Your father broke it to her that she was no longer Queen, and himself tore down the canopy of estate from above her head. She took it well, saying she put off her royal robes far more willingly than she had put them on—and then she asked if she could come home. At that, knowing he had to do all he could to preserve our lives and fortunes, your father left her, and went to Tower Hill, where he proclaimed Queen Mary. Then we made all speed to return here."

They had escaped and left Jane behind. They *had* abandoned her to her fate. That made two of us they had used for their own ends and ruined. Suddenly I am no longer a child, unquestioningly accepting the wisdom of my elders; suddenly I have become aware that they have feet of clay.

My lady is pacing up and down now, her muddied train swishing behind her.

"Where is my father?" I ask.

"He has gone into hiding," she tells me. "It is better for you that you do not know where. If the Queen's men question you, you can say with truth that you have no idea where he is. But it will not come to that."

"Why?" I ask.

"Because I am going to the Queen! I am going to plead for Jane and for your father, and convince her that they were forced by Northumberland to act against their wishes. Northumberland is finished. His capture is only a matter of time. Nothing I say now can make any difference to his fate."

"But what of me and Harry?" I cry. "Will you not plead for us, my lady?"

"You must have patience. There are matters far more pressing, and you are not the only one to be abandoned. Your sister Mary has been repudiated by Lord Grey."

"That is no loss to her! Harry and I love each other, and it is a fit match. We are wed in the sight of God!"

My mother's eyes narrow. "Sometimes one has to achieve what one wants by subtle means. If I can persuade the Queen to pardon your father, and she takes him into favor, as I pray she will, then Pembroke will know it, and your marriage may be mended."

My heart feels instantly lighter. There is, after all, hope, something I abandoned forever earlier when I left Baynard's Castle. How strangely that wheel of fortune revolves. All may not yet be lost! My mother is still my mother, fierce, omnipotent, and capable. Once again she is in control, and the world may right itself—and my sweet Harry and I may be reunited.

KATE

June 22–26, 1483; Baynard's Castle, London

"Never, in all my days, did I think to hear that vile calumny again!" the Duchess Cecily stormed, her habitual calm shattered. She had burst into the solarium like an outraged black crow. "Conceived in adultery, eh? How could he do this to me? It is Clarence all over again. Was ever a mother so betrayed by her sons?"

Anne hastened to comfort the old lady, who crumpled in her arms as Kate looked on helplessly. Cecily was breathing heavily, and Kate feared she might collapse or die.

"Now, my lady," Anne said, "pray tell us what has happened."

"My chamberlain has just returned from Paul's Cross, where he goes every week to hear the Sunday sermons," the duchess related, less agitated now, but still angry. "Today, it was the mayor's brother, Dr. Shaa, who mounted the pulpit. And do you know what he took as his text? *'The multiplying brood of the ungodly shall not thrive, nor take deep rooting from bastard slips.'*" The duchess was shaking. "He has corrupted that preacher, who did not blush to say, in the face of all decency, that the sons of King Edward should be instantly eradicated, for neither could be a legitimate king, nor could King Edward's issue ever be so."

Anne's hand flew to her mouth.

"Who has corrupted Dr. Shaa?" she cried.

"My son—your husband," the old lady said contemptuously. "That I should live to see yet another day when my own blood should so shamelessly slander me!"

"Oh, sweet Jesus!" exclaimed Anne. "Tell me what exactly was said, I beg of you. Do not spare me the details."

The duchess snorted. "That priest had the effrontery to claim that my son, King Edward, was the fruit of my adultery—and was in every way unlike my husband York. Then he said that Richard, who altogether resembles his father, should come to the throne as the legitimate successor. It was then that Richard—I will not call him my son anymore, for he is no son of mine—it was then that he made an appearance with Buckingham, but they had miscalculated the mood of the crowd, who booed and jeered at them, and yelled at Shaa that he was a traitor. How can I ever show my face in public again, after Richard has publicly insulted and slandered me?"

Anne knelt beside her. She spoke gently. "You can, because nothing can rob you of your good fame and virtue, dear madam. You can hold your head high because everyone will know you have been unjustly slandered."

"It is not to be borne!" Cecily raged.

"You should lie down. This has been too much for you. Let me assist you to your bed."

"Lie down?" the duchess retorted. "Nay, I am going to the Tower to see Richard and demand an explanation, and then I am going to complain to all the noblemen who will hear me of the great injury that he has done me. Nay, do not think to prevent me. I will have my chariot made ready now."

"Are you sure this is the best course, my lady?" Anne asked.

"It is the only course," the duchess answered emphatically. "Richard owes me filial obedience and honor, and I will remind him of that!"

Anne exchanged glances with Kate, whose mind was in turmoil. This could not be happening. The duchess's chamberlain must surely have made a dreadful mistake.

Her grandmother stalked out of the room, an outraged and determined figure in black. When she had gone, Anne said nothing; she just went over to the window and gazed out at the Thames.

"This slander is no new thing," she said. "Your uncle of Clarence and my father Warwick dreamed it up many years ago when they were plotting to overthrow King Edward. You see, they hated the Queen and the Wydevilles. My father thought that he, the greatest nobleman in the realm, should be the King's chief counselor, and he resented the Wydevilles bitterly, as did many other lords. So there was a rebellion, and King Edward was deposed and fled abroad. When he came back, there was a big battle at Barnet." Her voice trailed away. "My father was killed. Of course, no one believed the slander about your grandmother. My father and Clarence had claimed that she'd betrayed York with a common archer called Blaybourne, but it was mere propaganda; there was no truth in it. What made it doubly shocking was that it was her son Clarence who put this tale about. And now, it seems, another son has repeated the slander."

"But why? Why would my father do that to his own mother?"

"Because," Anne said, sighing, "he wants to be King. I have long suspected it."

Kate sat stony-faced, listening, unwilling to believe what she was hearing.

"There was something that did not ring true about those weapons that my lord claimed the Queen's party were plotting to use against him," Anne went on. "Some say they had been placed at the ready before the King's death, for use against the Scots. And then there was poor Lord Hastings, who was hurried to his death barely shriven, and without trial. What is that, Kate, but tyranny?"

"But it is my father of whom you speak," Kate protested.

"And my husband, who has become as a stranger to me!" Anne cried, showing rare passion. "I have loved him, as God is my witness, and I have been a good and true wife to him, but I do not know him anymore."

Truly her father had changed: he was no longer the gentle and loving lord of Middleham, but Kate loved him still and would defend him to the last. She could not believe all this of him, even though Anne—trustworthy, honest Anne—was saying it.

"He is weighed down with the cares of his office," she insisted to her stepmother. "His very life is in danger. I'm sure he truly believed that those weapons would be used against him. And maybe—maybe—he believes too that there is truth in the slander against my granddam. Wicked people may have persuaded him . . ."

"He is no fool," Anne declared. "He can make up his own mind and not be swayed by persuasion. If he believes it, it is because he wants to believe it."

"How can you say such a thing of my father?" Kate retaliated, weeping. "He is a good man, and you should know! And maybe it *is* true about my granddam and that archer!" And she hurried from the solarium to the sanctuary of her chamber.

Kate did not see her grandmother until dinner the following day, and then Cecily did not refer to her meeting with the duke; she just ate her sparse meal silently, listening to her chaplain, who always read aloud from devotional books during mealtimes. Anne sat beside Kate, toying with her food as usual, although none of them had much appetite. Kate would not look her way. She was still very upset at what her stepmother had said the previous day. When dinner was over, and Cecily had retreated to her chapel, Kate got up and left too, sketching the briefest of curtseys to the Duchess Anne before going out into the garden, where she sat brooding under a tree.

The mood in the house did not lighten that week. The Duchess Cecily would not be drawn out on what had happened in the Tower—"That is between the duke and me," she said reprovingly—and Anne kept her distance. Kate sensed that Anne was somehow disappointed in her when, really, it should have been the other way around. But she would not, could not, believe any ill of her father.

There had still been no word about the coronation. London seethed, packed with restless, suspicious citizens, and lords and gentlemen, up from the country, complained about the delay and the ruinous cost of staying indefinitely in the capital. When Kate and Mattie gave their elders the slip, and slunk past the gateward to go to the market at Smithfield, even though they had been warned it was not safe to go out, they became aware that the City was alive with rumors and gossip. The latest word was that the Duke of Buckingham had gone to the Guildhall to address the mayor, and many Londoners were making their way there to find out what was going on. Kate and Mattie went along with them, and were among the crowds who watched Buckingham emerge and go his way. Then the mayor and his aldermen and sheriffs came out, and were immediately besieged by the mob, demanding to know what the duke had said. But Kate hung back. She was afraid of being crushed in the press—and of what she might hear.

Mattie had no such qualms. She pushed her way nearly to the front, and because she was so pretty, most of the men let her through, one or two pinching her bottom as she sidled past. Kate's last view of her maid was of the girl giving a saucy grin to an apprentice. But when Mattie came back, she was no longer grinning.

"Let's go somewhere quiet, my lady," she urged. "There are things you should know." Something in her face made Kate catch her breath; she guessed that what Mattie had to tell her would not be easy to hear.

They escaped into the quietness of the nearby church of St. Lawrence Jewry. There was no one there except for an old woman on her knees near the altar, so they sat on a bench at the back and Mattie talked in hushed tones.

"The Lord Mayor said Buckingham had come to tell them that my lord of Gloucester should be their rightful king."

Kate clapped her hand to her mouth to stifle a gasp, and Mattie laid a kindly hand on hers. "There's more, my lady. The mayor said my lord of Buckingham had spoken so well that all who heard him marveled, and that he said that he wasn't going to say anything about the

bastardy of King Edward, since the Lord Protector bore a filial reverence toward his mother. Then he said that King Edward had been secretly precontracted to another lady when he wed the Queen, so that
the marriage to the Queen was no lawful marriage, and their children
are bastards, so the poor little King in the Tower has no right to the
crown. You can imagine the uproar when the crowd heard that."

Kate could not take this in. "Who was the lady to whom King Edward had been precontracted?"

"Lady Eleanor somebody," Mattie supplied. "I couldn't hear properly, as people were muttering all around, some saying it couldn't be
true."

It couldn't be, could it? But surely her father would not have made
this public without knowing it to be an indisputable fact?

They hastened back to Baynard's Castle. Kate was coming to terms
with what she had learned, and she could also feel a rising sense of
excitement, even relief. For at thirteen it was a fine prospect to be the
daughter of a king, and bastard though she was, she would still be a
very important young lady. At last all had been made clear: the reason
for her father's long absence in the Tower, when he had surely been
investigating these matters; the worrying rumors she had heard, which
she now knew to be based on ignorant people's mistaken assumptions;
and the reason why the duke's enemies had feared him. It was no wonder, for they had had much to hide! He had uncovered a dreadful scandal, but his ascension of the throne would put everything to rights,
restoring the legitimate heir and retrieving the honor of the House of
York.

She had been right not to doubt her father.

That evening the Duke of Gloucester came to Baynard's Castle to dine
with his family. He was once again wearing sober black garments, although they were of the most sumptuous velvet and damask. He
looked tense, but was clearly making an effort to be good company.
Toward the Duchess Cecily, he was more than courteous and considerate, as if to make amends for the injury he had done her, but the duchess remained frosty. Anne allowed him to embrace and kiss her when

he had raised her from her curtsey, yet she too stayed aloof, her manner remote and cool.

No sooner had dinner been served than the Duchess Cecily broke the ice. "Do the people believe this precontract story?" she asked suddenly.

"They must believe it, for it is the truth," the duke said.

"That does not answer my question. A king must be accepted by his people. If they question his title, how is he to command their obedience?"

The duke was visibly riled by that. "You think I am seeking a crown," he said. "I assure you, I know it is no child's office. I do not want it, but I will accept it if the people press me to it."

"Buckingham urged them to do so—at your bidding. He even got his men to throw their caps in the air and shout 'King Richard!' "

"Buckingham is convinced of my right to it." The duke was tight-lipped.

"And what *of* your right to it, my son?" His mother turned to face him, her expression cold. "Suddenly we are hearing of this precontract, of which I never heard before. Obviously the people did not believe that calumny about me, so another pretext had to be thought up."

"Believe it or not, the precontract existed," Richard replied tautly, drumming his fingers on the polished wood of the table. "Bishop Stillington came to the council two weeks ago and said he had some important information to disclose. I saw him in private, and he told me that my brother King Edward had been much enamored of Eleanor, Lady Butler, the Earl of Shrewsbury's daughter, and had promised her marriage if he might lie with her. She consented, and the Bishop has deposed that he married them afterward, without witnesses. But there had been an earlier promise to marry that *was* witnessed, and constituted a precontract and a barrier to marriage with anyone else. Stillington showed me the relevant passages in canon law, as well as legal instruments and the depositions of witnesses."

"But why was the Lady Eleanor not made Queen?" Anne asked.

"The King knew the marriage to be invalid, and wished the precontract to be kept secret, fearing a scandal, for he had tired of the lady; and the Bishop, knowing his good fortune depended on the King, persuaded her to keep quiet. Thus it remained a secret. I believe there was a son, whose birth was also kept secret."

"And Bishop Stillington is asking you to believe that, when King Edward married Elizabeth Wydeville, the Lady Eleanor was prepared to keep quiet about the fact that he was already precontracted to her?" Anne's tone was sharp. "What of her family? The Talbots are ancient, noble stock. They would surely have protested on her behalf."

"Apparently they persuaded the Bishop to come to me with the truth," the duke explained. Kate saw that he was weary of all these questions. He must have gone over it all many times with the lords and councillors.

"But it is inconceivable that they did not speak out when the marriage to Elizabeth Wydeville was made public! God knows, that marriage was so unpopular that they would not have lacked for supporters."

"Anne, do you suspect me of making this up?" Richard flared. "I assure you, I have agonized for days over it. The implications were alarming. I said nothing for a time after the Bishop disclosed it to me, knowing that once this was made public, the disinheriting of my brother's children would be a certainty. For the proofs Stillington brought are beyond dispute."

His mother drained her goblet. "Proofs can be forged, my son. And do not forget that the good Bishop fell foul of King Edward five years ago and ended up in prison for a time. Maybe he had thoughts of revenge in his heart, and the hope of regaining royal favor from a new and grateful king—you."

"If he looks for that, he shall look in vain," the duke said. "I do not like the man, even though I believe his story. Those were no forgeries that he showed me."

His wife and his mother fell silent.

"The lords and commons gathered at Westminster today accepted the fact of the precontract," he said defensively. "The council summoned them, and Buckingham presented them with an address on a roll of parchment. The address was a supplication to me to accept the crown, and therein it was set forth that the sons of King Edward are baseborn, on the ground that he had contracted marriage with Eleanor Butler before his marriage to Queen Elizabeth. Thus it was shown to the lords and commons that King Edward and Elizabeth lived together sinfully in adultery against the laws of God, and that all their children are bastards and unable to inherit."

Gloucester downed his wine. "The question of Warwick succeeding was raised, only to be rejected," he went on. "He is disbarred from the succession by my brother Clarence's attainder; and anyway, he is too young and feeble to rule a kingdom. Therefore, as Buckingham explained to the lords and commons at Westminster today, there is at the present time no certain and incorrupt descendant of my father York but myself, who am his undoubted son and heir." Cecily pursed her lips at that, but held her tongue.

"Buckingham told them I had no wish to take up the burden of the crown," the duke continued, "but that I might be persuaded if they signed the supplication. And so he left it with them, and we shall know tomorrow how many have signed it."

"They may remember the fate of Lord Hastings and feel it is politic to sign," the Duchess Cecily observed. Anne shuddered visibly.

"Hastings was a traitor!" the duke snapped. "He had to be removed. And while we are on the subject of traitors, you ought to know that Rivers and Grey were executed this day at Pontefract."

There was a shocked silence. Kate felt sick and pushed her plate away.

"I trust that *they* were afforded the boon of a fair trial," the Duchess Cecily said.

"Whose side are you on, madam?" the duke exploded. "They had plotted my death. The Earl of Northumberland acted as chief judge."

"But Lord Rivers had the right to be tried by his peers in Parliament," his mother persisted.

"He *was* tried by his peers," Gloucester said. "Let that be an end to it." He got up and walked to the door. "I am going to bed," he said. "Tomorrow will be a testing day. My lady?" He held out his hand, and the Duchess Anne arose, her face set.

"We bid you good night, ladies." The duke bowed and led her out of the room.

"The lords are here!" Mattie announced, bursting into Kate's chamber the following morning. "They are waiting in the great hall."

Kate had dressed herself carefully, anticipating that she should be looking her best on a day that promised to be momentous. The forest-green gown swirled in graceful lines from the black sash under her breasts, and its deep collar and cuffs were of a contrasting pale green damask. Her thick dark hair was loose, as became a maiden, and she was wearing her new gold pendant, which looked most becoming with the gown. She was ready, outwardly if not inwardly, for the previous night's revelations had disturbed her. She had been left with the distinct impression that her father had lost a battle of words with her grandmother, and she could not understand why, for she had not the wit or the knowledge of Cecily. Clearly, Cecily saw aspects to these events of which she herself could divine nothing, and it bothered her.

Kate and Mattie arrived in the antechamber to the minstrels' gallery above the hall at the same time as the Duchess Anne and her chief ladies. Anne looked regal in pale blue silk and her customary gauzy white butterfly headdress, which crowned a caul of cloth of silver.

"Attend me please, Kate," she said. Then the Duchess Cecily arrived, and they all three passed into the gallery and stood waiting, just inside the door.

Below, crammed between the dais and the screens passage, were gathered most of the peers of England, their robes a riot of all the colors of the rainbow, their heavy collars and bejeweled bonnets winking in the sunlight that was streaming through the tall stained-glass windows. There too, attended by the aldermen and sheriffs, was the Lord Mayor, while toward the back, below the gallery, were crowded many knights and citizens. Kate had a strong sense that what was about to take place here would be of far-reaching importance. This was the place where her uncle, the late King Edward, had been offered the crown after the defeat of the House of Lancaster. Was this lofty, magnificent hall now to witness the accession of another king of the House of York? The prospect sent shivers down her spine.

At the sight of the Duchesses Anne and Cecily, the lords had uncovered their heads and bowed low, Anne responding with a graceful curtsey. The whole august company was expectant, waiting. And now the duke appeared at the other end of the gallery; he was clad somberly in black, and attended by his chaplain. He nodded briefly to his women-folk.

"My good lords, may I ask the meaning of this deputation?" he asked, gazing down at the assembly. The lords bowed again, and then the Duke of Buckingham leapt forward onto the dais.

"Your Grace, we come to present our petition, beseeching you, of your lordly goodness, to accept the crown and royal estate of this realm, so that the kingdom might escape the dangers of a disputed succession and a minority, and enjoy the blessings of peace through firm and stable government."

Richard said nothing, but looked doubtful and troubled.

"My good lord," Buckingham went on boldly, "we see you are reluctant to accede to our petition, but the people are adamant: they will not have the sons of King Edward to reign over them. If you refuse our reasonable and legitimate request, then we will have no alternative but to choose another to reign over us."

There was a silence. The two duchesses were standing still as statues, their faces impassive, and Kate was so overawed by the momentousness of the occasion that she felt herself also frozen into immobility.

Just then she glimpsed a young girl among the throng, a fair-haired maid who was staring up at her curiously. Her eye was drawn to the girl's outlandish attire, the high ruffle around her neck and the sleeves puffed at the shoulders. Their eyes met, and in that brief instant there was an odd frisson between them, and she thought she had seen that face before somewhere. Then some men were jostled forward by newcomers cramming into the hall, and the girl disappeared from view. It was strange, Kate thought, to see a girl among all these important men. Mayhap some lord had brought his young wife or daughter with him. But her attention was distracted, for her father was addressing the assembly.

"Good my lords, my Lord Mayor and citizens, you are most welcome," he said, his mien humble. "I fear you have caught me all unawares, and I must confess that I am most perturbed at the prospect of giving up my status as a private person for the throne. It is not my wish or my desire to occupy it. I had hoped to spend my days serving my brother's son."

"Alas," chimed in Buckingham, "if you will not heed our earnest petition, to whom shall we turn? Your Grace is the right and natural heir to your late father of blessed memory, the Duke of York. There is no one more fitted by birth, lineage, and aptitude to rule us, is that not so, my lords?" There were loud acclamations from the crowd. Gloucester bowed his head; he appeared to be praying for guidance. Then he looked up resolutely. Kate caught her breath.

"My lords and commons, since His Grace of Buckingham here has so eloquently entreated me on behalf of you all, and since you acknowledge my just title, I do consent to occupy the throne."

The hall exploded in a roar of cheers and shouts. "God save King Richard!" the people cried. "Long live King Richard the Third!"

KATHERINE

Late July 1553; Sheen Priory, Surrey

My lady has returned. I can hear the commotion in the courtyard, and race to the window of my chamber. I have languished here fretting for ages, it seems, although truth to tell it is little more than a week since my mother departed to seek out the Queen. And the time has dragged because I cannot bear to go out and face the world, for when I ventured last Friday into the nearby town of Kingston, neighbors, and those I once called friend, ignored me or moved away at my approach. No one wants to be tainted by associating with the daughter and sister of traitors.

Praying that the news will be good, I speed downstairs to the hall, where my mother is drawing off her riding gloves, and make the sketchiest of curtsies.

"Be at peace, child. There is nothing to fear," she says, sinking wearily into her chair by the fire. Her master of horse, handsome Mr. Stokes, follows her into the room with a cup of wine and relieves her of her whip. She thanks him warmly, and for a moment their eyes meet, his keen, hers speculative. In the absence of my father, who seems to have disappeared from the face of the earth, Stokes has shown himself to be a devoted support to my mother, insisting on escorting her on her journey and calming the servants, who are naturally fearful about their future.

When Stokes has gone, my lady invites me to sit on the stool at her feet, and sips her wine.

"I caught up with Queen Mary at New Hall, on her triumphal progress to London," she relates. "I must say she is indeed a most gentle and kind princess, for she granted me an audience and did not keep me waiting, despite the fact that people were flocking and clamoring to see her." She sighs. "I threw myself on her mercy. I humbled myself. On my knees, I begged her to spare your father's life and Jane's. I insisted that we were under threat from Northumberland and much afraid of him. God forgive me, I lied to save us: I said I knew on good authority that he meant to poison your father if we did not do his bidding. Her Grace asked if I had proof of this, so I told her about Northumberland poisoning the King . . ."

"He poisoned the King?" I am shaken to my heart.

"He did, yes," my lady laments, "although it was not to end Edward's life, but to prolong it, so that the duke could bring his plans to fruition. He secretly called in this cunning woman who knew much of poisons, and so it was done. Your father was privy to it, yet he would have stopped it if he could, for the arsenic caused the King terrible suffering. But the duke was adamant it was necessary."

I am dumbstruck. Truly, Northumberland deserves whatever fate the Queen has in store for him, which will no doubt be the block and the axe.

"I'm not sure that the Queen believed me," my mother continues, "but by then I was so agitated that she raised and kissed me, and reassured me that she would not harm either your father or Jane. Jane, she told me, has been moved to the house of the Gentleman Jailer in the Tower, where she is being well looked after and is permitted to continue with her studies. Her Grace said she knew that Jane was innocent of any treasonous intent, and that when things have quieted down, she will release her."

The relief is tremendous. I cannot describe how worried I have been about my dear sister. My heart is filled with grateful thanks to God.

"As for your father," my mother says, "he is here, hiding in one of the monks' cells in the old wing. He has been here all the time. I now have to tell him that he must give himself up when the Queen's men come for him, as they assuredly will within the next few days, and that he must go with them to the Tower; but he will be pardoned and freed as soon as the Queen arrives in London. I have Her Grace's word on it." She rests her head wearily on the high back of the chair. "I can only thank God we are all safe," she concludes.

Yes—and I too must thank God a thousand times. But will the Queen receive my parents back into favor? And what of my marriage?

"Are you to go to the court?" I ask hopefully.

My lady frowns. "No, child. Not yet. The Queen commanded us all to stay here at Sheen until she sends for us."

"But when will that be?" I cannot hide my disappointment, and my tears are welling.

"When things have quieted down, I assume," she replies flatly. "Katherine, don't look so discouraged. We are lucky to have escaped with our lives and wealth, and they are more important than any marriage. The best advice I can give you is to forget Harry. It may take some time to gain the Queen's favor, and Pembroke will not wait so long. I imagine he is still eager to end the marriage and his association with us. You must accept that Harry may be lost to you now."

KATE

July 6, 1483; Westminster Abbey

The day of the coronation came, and at last Kate was able to put on her beautiful blue gown. She was to attend the Duchess Anne—Queen Anne, as she must now get used to calling her—to Westminster Abbey as one of her maids of honor. The day before, King Richard and Queen Anne, with their vast trains of lords, officers, and attendants, had gone in procession through the City of London, from the Tower to Westminster. The King, swathed in a gown of blue cloth of gold and a vast mantle of purple velvet trimmed heavily with ermine, had gone on horseback, but Anne, who had lost weight through the past anxious weeks, and whose white mantle and gown of cloth of gold hung loosely upon her, had followed in a litter, with Kate and the other ladies jolted along behind in chariots. The entire nobility rode in the procession, the end of which was brought up by four thousand of Richard's northern retainers, all proudly sporting his white boar badge.

His soldiers, wearing that same badge, were stationed along the streets, keeping the sullen and hostile bystanders under surveillance. Clearly the King feared that the mood of the people might provoke rioting or worse. Kate had been nervous as she rode past the crowds. She could see her father on White Surrey, some way ahead, nodding his bared head right and left, greeting his people. But while a few shouted out their acclaim, most remained silent and resentful.

Now the coronation procession was forming in the White Hall at Westminster, and Anne, Kate, and all the waiting lords and ladies made deep obeisances as King Richard appeared, splendid in robes of scarlet.

Kate's eyes alighted appreciatively on a handsome young lord who was standing near the King, carrying the orb. Tall and impressively dressed in the robes of a belted earl, he cut a dashing figure. His dramatic dark locks tumbled nearly to his shoulders, framing a face that could have been chiseled from the finest alabaster, with a strong nose and sensual lips. They were introduced: he was John de la Pole, Earl of Lincoln, the King's nephew and her cousin. She supposed he must be about twenty years of age.

She could not draw her gaze away from him, he was so comely. And he, sensing it, met her eyes and held them. His intense regard took Kate's breath away.

Another man was also watching her, the lord who had the honor of carrying the Queen's scepter. He was older than Lincoln by several years, of middle height and stringy build, and nowhere near as handsome; in fact, his face reminded her of a ferret, and it was framed by black hair cut straight at jaw level. She looked away. She did not want him staring at her.

It was time. Richard and Anne made their way to Westminster Hall, the lords and clergy following, and sat enthroned as the great procession began wending its slow way to Westminster Abbey. Then, hand in hand, the King and Queen went forth, walking barefoot along a carpet of striped cloth to the holiest sanctuary of the abbey: the shrine of St. Edward the Confessor, England's canonized King. Kate walked decorously behind the Queen with the other ladies, following Margaret Beaufort, Lady Stanley, who had the high honor of carrying Anne's train.

Kate had not warmed to Lady Stanley, a stern, austere woman with a severe face and a prickly manner. A Lancastrian by birth and allegiance, she had ancient royal blood in her veins, for she was descended from Edward III's son, John of Gaunt, Duke of Lancaster, and the mistress he'd later married, Katherine Swynford. Henry Tudor, Lady Stanley's son by her first husband, the Earl of Richmond, was in exile in Brittany, but was still viewed by a few malcontents as the Lancastrian pretender to the throne, and the King had judged it wise to treat Lady Stanley with the respect her rank deserved but to keep her under his eye at court.

There was only one notable absentee from the coronation, and that was the Duchess Cecily, who had made it clear that she had not forgiven her son's outrageous allegations, and that she did not believe the tale of the precontract.

For Kate, the long, slow ceremonial passed in a blur of pageantry, prayer, and stolen glances at John de la Pole. But she would never forget the moment when Cardinal Bourchier placed the crown on her father's head. Her heart soared as the voices of the monks rose to the vaulted roof in the *Te Deum* that followed, and she too rejoiced, for the solemnity of the occasion must surely wipe out all doubt about the justness of her father's title. She was thrilled to see the peers come up, each in his degree, to kneel and swear fealty to King Richard, and her eyes lingered on the debonair figure of the Earl of Lincoln as he took his turn.

The coronation banquet in Westminster Hall lasted five hours. At the start, the King's champion came riding in on his horse to challenge Richard's royal title, as was customary. None disputed it, and the celebrations continued, with wine flowing abundantly, and dish after dish of flesh and fowl and wondrous sugar subtleties borne to the high table. Kate was seated some way along the board from Lincoln, but several times he leaned forward to catch her eye, and by the end of the fourth course there was a silent, unspoken conversation going on between them. When the salt cellars were removed and the cloth was raised, Kate knew she had her glorious lord in the palm of her little hand.

They were bringing in the hippocras and wafers when, swiftly, he moved through the throng of courtiers and prelates and was suddenly there beside her. Already she knew her power over him, knew herself beautiful in the gorgeous blue gown and golden pendant, knew that she was alluring with her great blue eyes and wealth of dark hair. Both of them were a little flushed with wine.

Lincoln took her hand and raised it to his lips.

"Allow me to pay my respects, my lady," he said. His voice was deep, assured. "Or are you a goddess who has bewitched me? In truth, I have had eyes for no other since I first saw you. But I think you were not aware of me until today."

"How could I have been?" Kate laughed lightly, but the expression in her eyes belied her levity. "I never saw you before, my lord!"

Lincoln, chuckling, took a goblet from a servant and handed it to her before accepting one for himself. "Pray call me John, kind goddess. Your heavenly face reminds me of old Chaucer's 'flowers white and red.'"

"You are a poet?" she asked.

"I love his verse," he answered. "Indeed, he was my ancestor, but it is not of Chaucer that I would speak. I would tell you how lovely you are, but you disdain to listen."

"I am listening now!" She was discovering how easy it was to flirt. It seemed the most natural thing to do, and her handsome admirer was making it very easy for her.

"Then I shall recite you a poem," he said. "I came across it some days after I first set eyes on you in the court. I had been watching you from afar." And as he recited the lines, they seemed to speak to Kate's heart.

"I shall say what inordinate love is:
The furiosity and frenzy of mind,
An inextinguishable burning, faulting bliss,
A great hunger, insatiable to find,
A dulcet ill, an evil sweetness blind,
A right wonderful, sugared, sweet error,
Labor without rest, contrary to kind,
And without quiet to have great labor."

There was a pause as John's eyes met hers. Kate could not quite believe this was happening. He had spoken of love, her young knight, and yet they were hardly acquainted. But still, it seemed they knew each other, had known each other forever.

"It's a beautiful poem," she said at last. "Yet I cannot believe I have cast you into such a frenzy, as you put it!"

"Oh, you are cruel, my sweet lady!" His grimace, though, was feigned. He was bantering with her.

"Am I no more then than a sweet error?" she countered mischievously.

"Ah, maybe, but you are too, as I said, right wonderful and the disturber of my rest!" He cocked his head to one side and looked meaningfully at her. She felt her cheeks flush.

"I think we must postpone this singular pleasure," John murmured. Kate looked around and saw that the King was preparing to retire. Queen Anne looked to be all but fainting on her feet, yet still she stood there valiantly with her lord, graciously accepting the congratulations of one dignitary after another. At last there was a great fanfare of trumpets, and the royal party could depart to their beds. Reluctantly, Kate dragged herself away from the handsome earl, who bowed extravagantly and wished her good-night so boldly that she blushed again.

It had been the most exciting, exhilarating day, but as Kate's spinning head hit the pillow, her thoughts still on John, she realized that there had been someone missing from the great ceremony. In the rush of preparations, she had spared little thought for the boy whose crowning this was to have been. How had he felt, left in the Tower with his brother, knowing that it had taken place without him? What was it like to be dispossessed of your crown and what you had thought to be your birthright, and relegated to bastardy?

She was a bastard herself, and yet she had never been made to feel the pinch of it. Her brother, John of Gloucester, was a bastard too, and yet he had been present at the coronation, and knighted by their father. It did not seem quite right that her disinherited cousins in the Tower, and their unfortunate sisters in sanctuary, should have been forgotten on this great occasion. So before she finally fell asleep, she offered up a silent prayer for them all.

KATHERINE

August–October 1553; Sheen Priory, Whitehall Palace, and Westminster Abbey

Queen Mary has entered London to unprecedented rejoicing. She kept her word, for my father was freed, after only three days in the Tower. Northumberland, having cravenly converted at the last to the Catholic faith in order to save his neck, died on the block.

Soon afterward we hear talk of a marriage for the Queen.

"She must wed," my mother says. "A woman cannot rule alone."

"You could, my dear," my father observes wryly. He is listless these days, and knows not how to occupy himself while waiting in vain for a summons to court. It rankles bitterly that Mary has forgiven the entire Privy Council for supporting Jane—except him.

"She must get an heir to succeed her," my mother says, "although I doubt she will find it easy at thirty-seven."

My sister Mary is playing with her kittens on the carpet. I have one on my lap, and it is ripping my embroidery apart. I chide it severely and lift it down to the floor, where Mary grabs it. "Gently!" I admonish her.

She is a plain child, which is unfortunate, as some pretension to beauty would compensate for her poor humped back and small stature, yet her mind is lively and questioning.

"What would happen if the Queen doesn't get an heir?" she pipes up.

"Then we would have the Lady Elizabeth to rule over us," my lady says.

Mary and I have never met the Lady Elizabeth, but we both know that, although she is only the bastardized daughter of King Harry by Anne Boleyn, she is second in line for the throne under that Act of Succession that had been subverted so Jane could be Queen. We know too that Elizabeth is a very learned and clever young lady, and much loved by the people. We heard there were great cheers for her when she rode into London beside the Queen, when Mary took possession of her capital.

"I doubt that would please Her Majesty," my lord declares, "for Elizabeth is a Protestant, although I dare say she will turn her coat now that the Mass has been restored."

"Ah, but the Queen has said she would not compel or constrain any man's conscience," my mother reminds him.

"True, true, which is as well, because mark ye, I will never embrace the Catholic faith. Never! But can you see Mary remaining so tolerant if she marries Prince Philip of Spain?"

My lady shrugs. "I doubt she will achieve that unless it be at the cost of her popularity. A Spaniard for king? And a fanatical Catholic at that, one who has been a champion of the Inquisition? Nay, she would do better to look closer to home for a husband!"

"And invite faction fights at court?"

"Then who *can* she marry?" my mother asks, tart.

I leave them to their wrangling and wander out into the gardens. This talk of marriage makes me sad. The fresh breeze on my face feels like a bitter caress, reminding me of what I have lost. I have had no word or token from Harry, and my heart is heavy.

I trail my fingers in the clear water of the fountain and peer into its depths. My distorted reflection stares back at me, a slender, tragic-faced girl in a yellow gown, with her fair hair straggling about her shoulders and her blue eyes watery with tears. Oh, my Harry, where are you? What are you doing right now? Are you thinking of me with as much grief as I think of you? Are you thinking of me at all?

Not knowing is torture. Not being able to do anything to change the situation is even worse. If only I could be given some sign, some hint even, that he still loves me, I would abandon the rest and die content. What have I done to deserve this misery, except be born with royal blood in my veins?

I walk along the lime alley, nursing my sorrow, and then I see, riding toward me, a messenger in the Tudor livery. He salutes me and rides on. Suddenly I feel the stirrings of excitement. What can his arrival mean?

I am summoned to court, appointed to the exalted office of Lady of the Privy Chamber to the Queen! I cannot believe my good fortune, for—next to the privileged post of Lady of the Bedchamber—it is the highest court office that can be bestowed upon a woman. And there is more, for Her Majesty has been not just merciful, but bountiful too, and generously forgiving, and has sent to say that she will also receive my parents back at court. We are to present ourselves there as soon as is convenient, and are also commanded to attend her coronation, which is set for October.

The news is cause for a great celebration, and I recall joyfully what my mother said to me that night I returned to Sheen. If I am seen to be in royal favor, Pembroke may think again about annulling my marriage to Harry.

My mother, much restored in spirits, displays her usual energy and ambition in preparing me for my debut at court. The dress I am to wear for the coronation is scarlet velvet, by the Queen's command and gift, so I am swathed in yards of the stuff, stuck with pins, and prodded and tugged about by the dressmaker. When the gown is finished, the effect is stunning, and I marvel at the tight, pointed square-necked bodice, the rich folds of the skirt with its long court train, the gold-embroidered chemise and neck ruff, the brilliant cloth-of-gold oversleeves, and the rich matching kirtle. There are ten other new gowns also, of forest green, white, tawny, scarlet, yellow, mustard, black and silver, nut brown, pink, and cream, their velvets and damasks sewn with the requisite number of pearls, or embellished with embroideries and black-work, and all are in the latest fashion, and very flattering. I pray that Harry will see me in them!

To match them, there are kirtles, sleeves, petticoats, French hoods, cauls, snoods, shoes of soft leather, jeweled girdles, and an assortment of precious pendants, brooches, and rings. Small wonder my father grumbles about the exorbitant cost of kitting me out for court, but my mother insists I go there royally attired, as befits my rank.

Amid all the bustle, I stifle pangs of guilt over Jane, who should be coming to court with me but languishes still in the Tower. Not, I think sadly, that she would think much of these fine clothes. But if she could be restored to us, my happiness would be complete. I still pray for that daily.

For the first time in months, though, my heart is lighter. I will repay the Queen's kindness by serving her to the utmost of my ability; I will set myself to earn her favor; and then—newly confident in my gorgeous attire—I swear I will win back my bridegroom and my sister!

I depart for the court tomorrow. Today I must pack those personal possessions that I wish to take with me. My mother says I will be assigned a small chamber of my own off the maidens' dorter, where the Queen's female attendants sleep—those who are under the supervision of the Mother of the Maids, although as a Lady of the Privy Chamber, I will not come under her jurisdiction. Yet my bedchamber is certain to be small, so I must take only essential items. Into the ironbound wooden traveling chests go my beribboned lute, some books, a manuscript of poems, my sewing basket and embroidery, a vial of rosewater, my toilet set, brushes, and silver mirror. I am just about to stow away the casket in which I keep my jewels and letters when I remember that it contains the Herbert pendant and the bundle of papers that were probably written by Katherine Plantagenet—whose portrait I was not, of course, allowed to bring with me from Baynard's Castle. I have not dreamed about her since I left that house.

I take out the pendant and the ribbon-wrapped bundle and stare at them, engulfed in a great wave of pain. They are cruel reminders of that other life that I have lost, and I can hardly bear to look at them. The last time I did that, Harry was with me. Suddenly, my interest in Katherine Plantagenet and the mystery surrounding those illegible papers seems tainted by the ruthlessness and brutality of Pembroke. They are too poignant a reminder of that time, and I thrust them to the bottom of the casket, beneath all the other papers and jewels. I know I will not be able to look at them again for a long time.

"Oh, Harry, Harry!" I whisper. "I seem as far from you as if I were on the moon." My puppies jump up on the bed and nuzzle at me as I sit weeping alone. They are a recent gift from my father, whose bitch whelped a few weeks ago: a pair of fluffy, leggy scamps named Arthur and Guinevere. My lord expressed the gruff wish, when he gave them to me, that they would help to distract me from my sorrow. It is a comfort to know that ladies are allowed to bring their lapdogs to court. At least I will have someone there to love.

At last the waiting time is over, and we arrive at Whitehall. Now all that remains is to say farewell to my parents before I depart for the Queen's lodgings. As I kneel before them to receive their blessing, my father beams at me proudly and my mother's smile is warm; all their hopes are now in me.

"Rise, Lady Katherine." To my surprise, the Queen has a deep voice like a man's. Daring to raise my eyes, I see before me a prematurely aged lady of small, spare stature in a heavy plum-colored velvet dress with a cloth-of-gold kirtle and a wide stand-up collar lined with exquisite embroidery. Around her waist is a bejeweled girdle, and on her breast is a large cross set with gems. Her hands are loaded with rings, and her French hood is trimmed with pearls and goldsmith's work. The whole effect is dazzling, yet it cannot mask the sad fact that the wearer has no claim to youth or beauty, with her heavy brow, watchful eyes, snub nose, pinched lips, and determined jaw. All this I see in an instant, and in that moment I begin to feel sorry for the Queen, for all the sadness of her life is reflected in her features.

Yet suddenly she smiles, extending her hand to be kissed, and my fears are allayed.

"You are most welcome to Whitehall, little cousin," she says. "It is time you took your proper place here. Be assured I do not hold you responsible for events that are better left in the past. You are very young, and your sister too. I assure you, I intend her no harm, and she is being well cared for. You will see her again one day soon. I trust that my lady your mother is well?"

"Very well, Your Majesty. She is here at court. She sends her love and duty to Your Majesty, and awaits your pleasure, and my lord my father too."

The Queen inclines her head graciously. "I am sorry for the breaking of your marriage. It must have been hard for you."

"Very hard, Your Majesty," I agree fervently; then, inspired by her kindness, I fall to my knees and raise my clenched hands in supplication. "Please, madam, is there anything that can be done to mend it? Harry—Lord Herbert and I—we love each other, and our separation is painful to us both."

The Queen frowns, then gently pulls me to my feet again. "Hush, child! I feel for you, indeed I do. But you must understand that my lord of Pembroke has his reasons for seeking an annulment, and that this is a private matter in which I cannot intervene. I am very sorry."

Even I, innocent as I am of the world, know that the Queen could command Pembroke in this matter if she were so inclined; but clearly she is not. She too considers me an unfit, nay, a dangerous bride for his son, for I am a Protestant with royal blood and a sister in the Tower. My hopes wilt and die.

"Do not look so crestfallen, little cousin," Mary counsels me. "You are young yet, and one day, God willing, you will be found a more suitable husband. In the meantime, you will be joining the other ladies in my Privy Chamber. I trust it pleases you to serve me there."

"It is an honor that pleases me more than I can say, Your Majesty," I say humbly, not wanting her to think me in any way unmindful of her kindness.

As a member of the Queen's privy chamber, elevated and favored by her, I can hold my head up again and face the world. It is less than I asked for, but far more than I could have expected. Better still, my new status gives me cause to hope that when Pembroke sees me high in favor, the chosen servant of the Queen, and in a position of honor, he will decide after all that I am a fit bride for his son.

I have not been at court two days before I hear from the other ladies how the Lady Elizabeth, the Queen's young half sister, is proving obstreperous in regard to religion. Susan Clarencieux, who is closer to Her Majesty than most, tells me that our good mistress was deeply touched when Elizabeth had ridden to offer her allegiance at the time of her accession—"although not until she heard for certain that the Queen would be victorious," remarks Clarencieux tartly—and had welcomed her warmly to court.

"They hadn't seen each other for years, and it always saddened the Queen to know that Elizabeth had embraced the Protestant faith. So she told her that it would make her very happy if she would accompany her to Mass. And that's when the little madam began to play up, turning up late, or pleading a headache or a stomachache. She even got one of her ladies to rub her belly for her as she neared the chapel!" Clarencieux laughs at the memory, but her smile quickly fades. "It grieves the Queen," she says, shaking her head. It is obvious that she loves her mistress dearly, but has little affection for the Lady Elizabeth.

"In the end she had no choice but to go to Mass," adds Anne Wotton, "and Her Majesty was overjoyed. But then the Lady Elizabeth absented herself again, and the Queen was forced to summon her and demand an explanation."

"Oh, she dissembled cleverly!" Clarencieux snorts. "She's a minx, that one, just like her mother, and look what happened to her. No wonder the Queen doubts her sincerity, and quite rightly too, if you ask me. She fears that if she does not marry and bear a child, the throne will go to Elizabeth, and all her cherished hopes of restoring the faith will come to naught."

"But surely the Queen plans to wed?" I ask. I have heard much gossip that the choice is now between Prince Philip of Spain and Lord Edward Courtenay, a descendant of the House of York, although no one seems very keen on the prospect of either as King.

"Yes, Lady Katherine, but nothing is certain yet," Clarencieux tells me.

I rise to go—I have many errands to run, and the gardens are beckoning. They are beautiful, and I want to make the most of the last warm days of the year.

The privy garden, with its symmetrical beds of flowers and herbs, railed and decorated with figures of heraldic beasts on gaily striped poles, is a tranquil place, enclosed by the long gallery on the river side and the Queen's apartments on the other. Here, members of the Privy Chamber are free to walk and enjoy the sweet-scented air, untroubled by the courtiers who throng the Great Gardens farther north.

Today there are only a few ladies seated on stone benches, conversing quietly, and a gardener unobtrusively deadheading the late roses. I have with me my puppies, Arthur and Guinevere, who gambol at my feet, reveling in their freedom, for in the royal apartments they are expected to be as sedate as the ladies, and I have much trouble controlling and cleaning up after them.

It is in the privy garden, fragrant with those roses, that I encounter His Excellency, Monsieur Simon Renard, the Imperial ambassador. I am already aware that he is a highly important dignitary and one of the chief advisers to the Queen: naturally she favors him as the representative of her cousin, the Emperor; of course her inclination is toward Spain, of which the Emperor is also King, because her mother, Katherine of Aragon, whose memory she reveres and cherishes, was Spanish.

To my astonishment—it is a week of wonders—Renard sweeps a courtly bow, introduces himself, pays his addresses to me in an uncommonly friendly manner, and offers me his arm, indicating that he would walk with me.

"Her Majesty speaks especially highly of you, Lady Katherine," he tells me as we stroll along the paths, admiring the blooms, the puppies trotting happily beside us. Renard's strong, handsome features are infused with warmth and admiration, and it occurs to me that his wife—whom he tells me he has perforce had to leave behind in Brussels—is a very lucky lady; he speaks of her several times, confiding how much he misses her. Yet he is not averse to paying compliments to another. "Rumor does not lie as to your beauty," he says, raising my hand to his lips and kissing it chivalrously. "May I speak frankly, my lady?"

Rumors of my beauty? People are talking about me? I suppose, as Jane's sister, I must be an object of interest at court. But I am taken unawares by this. It makes me realize that I am an innocent among wolves here.

The ambassador does not miss my recoil. "Fear not, Lady Katherine, Her Majesty has asked me to approach you," he murmurs, "which is why we must be private, by your leave." And he steers me away from the chattering ladies, whistling for the pups to follow us.

"I am told that Her Majesty's father, King Henry, conducted much of his confidential state business in his gardens, where he could be certain that no one was able to eavesdrop," Renard says, leading me to a stone seat at the end of a path. "Naturally, the Queen will marry," he goes on, "yet all prudent monarchs must decide who should succeed them in the event of their dying childless. Her Majesty, as you know, is no longer young, and childbirth may not be easy for her. We all of course pray that she bears Prince Philip many fine sons."

I am startled to hear him speaking of the proposed marriage as a foregone conclusion, for according to court gossip, it is by no means settled.

"Amen to that," I say dutifully.

"But who is next in line if Her Majesty—God forfend!—dies without leaving an heir of her body?" Renard asks. "It is the Lady Elizabeth—yet Her Majesty would be loath to leave her crown and royal estate to such a one, for she knows Elizabeth to be a heretic through and through. Nor is she trueborn, for her mother was punished as a public strumpet, and her paternity is not beyond question." Inwardly, I doubt this, for anyone who has seen portraits of the Lady Elizabeth and her father, King Harry, might easily see that she is his own daughter. Yet I have heard the Queen openly questioning it, and so it has become the fashion to do so—although behind hands and closed doors.

Renard is now speaking about King Harry's Act of Succession, of which I have heard much this tumultuous year. "The next heir is the Lady Jane, your sister, but she languishes in the Tower, and is of the same religious persuasion as the Lady Elizabeth. The next in line, my lady, is yourself."

I am struck dumb, yet at the same time filled with elation! Suddenly I recall the whole court bowing, the glorious crown lifted onto that young head . . . To be named heir to the Queen, and with her approval! It is beyond anything I could have imagined.

"There is another claimant," Renard is saying. "Mary, Queen of Scots, the Dauphine of France, and she, of course, is a Catholic. That carries much weight with Her Majesty, but the Scottish Queen has no rights under the Act of Succession—King Harry passed over that line— and she is a stranger born out of this realm, which many believe disbars her. The French are naturally supporting her claim to be heir, but France is the great enemy of Spain, so my master, the Emperor, and his son, Prince Philip, are eager to see you, Lady Katherine, named as the Queen's successor."

He looks into my eyes. "I see the prospect pleases you, my lady. And you will be heartened to know that the Venetian ambassador is also for you. But above all, it is the Queen's will that you be named heir presumptive."

"It is more than I could ever have deserved or looked for," I breathe, feeling a little light-headed and struggling to find the appropriate words. "I am Her Majesty's loyal subject, and will humbly bend to her will in this. Yet although it pleases me greatly, I pray that God vouchsafes the Queen many strong sons for the continuance of her line."

Renard smiles approvingly, and I know I have said the right thing. "There is just one thing, madam," he says. "The Queen knows that you have been brought up in the Protestant faith, but Her Majesty is hopeful that you, being young, would be willing to be guided by wiser minds in the matter of religion. It would make her the happiest woman alive to know that her preferred successor will carry on her good work."

I hesitate. I can imagine my parents' reaction to this, and Jane's. They are all staunch Protestants and hot for their faith.

"You will think seriously on this?" Renard asks. "I need not remind you how much is at stake."

"Oh, certainly, sir," I tell him warmly, not wanting to risk compromising my chances of being acknowledged the Queen's lawful heir by hesitating—and yet not wanting Her Majesty to think I take matters of faith lightly. "I will think on it most earnestly."

As I go about my tasks in the Queen's privy chamber, I can think of little else. Above all things, I desire to be Queen one day. It is my greatest dream, and now it could well become reality, with only one ailing woman's life standing between me and the crown of England.

Yet my ambitions are not entirely selfish. I think of all the good I could do as Queen, how magnificently I could advance my family, and—most important of all—that Harry and I could be reunited and I could make him my consort. How I should love to discountenance Pembroke thus, and see him humbled and chastened, bowing the knee before me!

I vow to do all in my power to live up to Her Majesty's expectations. I hope never to give my kind mistress any grief over religion. Yes, I have been brought up in the reformed faith, yet it seems to me a mark of gratitude to do the Queen's pleasure in this crucial matter. I confess I am not as fervent in religion as Jane or my parents, and thus I am the more easily tempted to bow to Her Majesty's wisdom. If I do not, I fear I will do myself and my family no favors; and if I do, there are many benefits to be gained—maybe even in Heaven itself.

I wonder how staunch in their faith my parents would prove if they knew that my conversion is the price of my becoming Queen. I suspect that their ambition is every bit as great as their love for the reformed faith, if not greater, and that they might consider the price worth paying. But Jane, I know, would never compromise her beliefs, and I fear she might never speak to me again if I become a Catholic. Yet even she might come to see the wisdom of it if it brought her the benefits of freedom and a life devoted to study, which is what she desires above all else.

Should I discuss the matter with my parents? I must think awhile before I do that. To be plain, I am nervous of their reaction. But in my heart I know that the decision is already made.

The September weather is mild, and I am always glad of the chance to take my leisure in the privy garden. Today I have my puppies and my embroidery with me, and am just placing my basket on an unoccupied bench when I see a tall young lady a little older than myself coming my way, with two attendants walking demurely behind her. She is striking-looking, with long red hair that falls below her waist, and wears a modest cream damask gown with very little in the way of jewelry. She is not beautiful—no one with that thin face and hooked nose could be called beautiful—yet she has presence, and a certain charm, which is evident in the gracious smile she bestows on me, and the graceful carriage of her slender figure. I know instinctively who she is, and rise to my feet and curtsey, aware that she towers over me.

"You are new at court," she says; it is a statement, not a question. "I have not seen you here before."

"I arrived only a few days ago, my Lady Elizabeth," I tell her.

"And you are?"

"Lady Katherine Grey," I tell her. I nearly add "your cousin," but think better of it. I am not sure how to take her. Is she friendly, just curious, or even hostile? I cannot tell.

If she is surprised, she does not show it. "Welcome to court, little cousin. I had looked to see you here."

"I am come to serve the Queen, Your Grace, and to attend the coronation."

Elizabeth moves toward the bench and I hurriedly remove the basket and place it on the ground. She sits down and stoops to pat my two dogs. At her nod, her attendants walk on and wait for her a little way off.

"I knew your sister, the Lady Jane," she says. "We were together in Queen Katherine's household, God rest that good lady. I am sorry for your sister's trouble." I notice that when Elizabeth is talking, she has a habit of moving her slender, long-fingered hands into affected but attractive poses against the fine fabric of her gown.

"I thank Your Grace. Her Majesty assures me that Jane is well and in comfort."

"And she has you here, under her eye, so that you may not get up to like mischief all unwitting!" Elizabeth smiles, watching my face intently with those sharp, hooded eyes. "Did that not occur to you, little cousin? That the Queen has brought you to court because she fears some fool might seek to use you as Jane was used by Northumberland? Jane is out of reach—but you are another matter."

"I would never do anything to hurt Her Majesty!" I protest.

"Nay, you would not; I'll wager there is no malice in you. But you do not have to do anything; others might do it on your behalf. It is not what you do that worries my sister, but what you are."

"Her Majesty has never expressed any concern about that." I decide to keep silent about the Queen's wish to name me her heir.

Elizabeth sighs. "We have learned in a hard school, you and I, but you do not seem to fully understand the lesson. Listen." She leans toward me, and I can smell the spicy scent of her perfume, see the flawless clarity of her fair skin against her fiery hair. There is a gleam of malice in her eyes. "You think yourself in a place of honor, little cousin. In truth, it is a place of surveillance." But that I cannot believe, especially in view of what Renard told me. I fear Elizabeth is just seeking to discountenance one who might be a rival at court—or for the succession itself.

"We share a common bond in many ways," she continues. "We should help each other."

"If I can do any service to Your Grace, I am ready," I say uncertainly, hoping she will never ask me to do anything that conflicts with my loyalty to the Queen or jeopardizes my hopes for the future.

"I see you are already a courtier!" She laughs shortly. "But listen, little cousin. We are bound together by our close kinship to the Queen. If she bears no heir, I am to succeed her. Then comes your mother, who has waived her claim once and might again; then Jane, who is in the Tower; and, after her, you, Lady Katherine. That is the law, as ordered by my father, King Henry. It is no treason to say it. But because of what happened with your sister, the Queen is suspicious of all those with a claim to the throne. She wants us out of the reach of would-be traitors. That is why she keeps us at court, under her eye."

I wonder if the Lady Elizabeth has heard any talk of the plan to exclude her from the succession in favor of me. Maybe not, but I imagine she can be a clever dissembler. Is she baiting me, or fishing for information? Or is she genuinely in ignorance, believing her position inviolable? Well, I will not be giving anything away, so I decide to say nothing.

"You pine for your husband," she says suddenly. I stare at her in astonishment.

"How does Your Grace know that?"

"The Queen told me. She said she grieved for you, but she could not allow the marriage to stand, and will not interfere with its dissolution. You should forget him." Her eyes are hard. I cannot imagine her ever allowing her heart to rule her head.

A tear trickles down my cheek; I cannot help it. I do not want to hear such brutal advice. My hopes have been dashed for good, it seems. Even if Pembroke changes his mind about annulling my marriage, the Queen herself now stands in the way. I am sobbing openly now, mortified at losing control in front of my tormentor.

Suddenly Elizabeth's mood softens and she rests one of those delicate hands on mine. "You poor little fool. She said you asked for her intercession. Do you not realize that she does not intend for either of us to marry? Because, little cousin, if you or I take a husband, we become an even more dangerous threat to her. We were both brought up in the reformed faith, which is cause enough for suspicion. And any man that you or I marry might press a claim to the throne. A foreign prince might come with an army at his back; an English lord might foment a court conspiracy. God knows, we do not even have to marry! Anyone could use us, the Protestant heiresses, as the focus for his treasonable ambitions. Wake up! You have the example of your sister before you! What is more, if either of us bears a son, the clamor for a masculine succession will be deafening. People will always prefer a crested prince to a cloven one!" Her tone is bitter.

Her reasoning is clear, horribly clear. It is like a death sentence, being told that I might never be permitted to wed—and that Harry is forever barred to me. There is a lump in my throat, choking me.

"You understand now why the Queen can never trust you, however loyal you may be?" Elizabeth asks me. "It is the same for me."

"But if she marries and bears a son?" I counter, clutching at my last hope.

"Then things may be different. But there are those who would readily plot to overthrow a Catholic queen, especially if she marries Philip of Spain. Not I, of course, or any of her true subjects. Yet I do fear that if Her Majesty insists on this marriage, she will forfeit the love of many of her people."

"Your Grace, may I ask why you are telling me all this?"

Elizabeth raises her eyebrows. "Is it not obvious? We share common bonds, of blood—and other things." She does not elaborate, but I suspect she is referring to religion. She is too clever to say it, though. She has daily to pretend that she is willing and eager to embrace the Catholic faith, and is playing a perilous game. Many doubt her sincerity, but she dare not give herself away; she must convince the Queen that her conversion is genuine, and somehow leave the Protestants with room to hope that she has converted against her will.

Is she trying to enlist my support?

"I am Your Grace's servant," I say, for want of anything else. I know I am out of my depth here.

"If you hear anything said of me, pray tell me," she says lightly. I believe she thinks that I will now be ready and willing to show solidarity with her, two Protestant heiresses united in a common cause and supporting each other. I might be a lamb among wolves, but I am aware she is trying to cozen me into acting as her spy in the Queen's chamber.

I dare not refuse her outright. I sense that she might make a formidable enemy.

"I thank Your Grace for your kindness," I say. "Pray excuse me now, as I am needed to help Her Majesty robe for the evening." And I curtsey, pick up my basket, and hurry off, Arthur and Guinevere yapping at my heels, leaving Elizabeth sitting there with an unreadable look on her face. She is going to be very disappointed when she sees me going freely to Mass every Sunday and realizes I am keeping my counsel about what I overhear in the privacy of the royal apartments.

Elizabeth is distinctly cooler toward me when we meet on the morning of the coronation, as the great procession is forming in Westminster Hall. She has been a distant figure during the past two days of celebrations: the triumphal progress along the river to the Tower, where it is customary for monarchs to lodge before being crowned; and the magnificent progress through a London decked with tapes-

tries, flowers, and pageants to Westminster, our ears resounding with
the salutes of trumpets and cannon. She is not present when we
deck the Queen in her purple and ermine on her coronation morning,
but she is waiting in Westminster Hall to take her place in the procession, and in the seconds before she executes a dramatic curtsey that
shows off the wide white-and-silver skirts beneath her sweeping scarlet mantle, she catches sight of me and gives me a faintly malevolent
glance. I am stung by it: it is as if, by sending no word since she asked
me to report anything said of her—and she surely must guess there
would have been something to divulge by now—I have betrayed her.
But she is not stupid: she must know I am in the most invidious position.

Resolving to ignore her, I refuse to meet her eyes as she takes her
place next after the Queen and lifts up her train. Behind her, the Lady
Anne of Cleves, King Harry's divorced wife—a very merry lady, and
no wonder—moves into position, and then it is my part, as a princess
of the blood, to occupy the third place of honor. Mayhap this evidence
of the Queen's favor will serve to stop people avoiding me, as many
have done since I arrived at court. For what else could be so plain a
token that Her Majesty thinks kindly on me?

The fanfares sound, then the lords start processing out of the hall
in stately fashion, and in a little space we three ladies follow, walking in
line behind the Queen's Majesty along the bright blue carpet that has
been laid along the path to the abbey, and through the abbey itself. I
am overwhelmed by the sights and sounds of this day: the bells ringing
out joyfully, the choir bursting into song, the awe-inspiring majesty of
the organ, and the Queen, that small, thin figure weighed down by her
heavy robes, dedicating herself with shining sincerity to the service of
her country and people. And one other thing I will always remember:
Harry's face, among the lords, glimpsed as I pass on my way out of the
abbey in the wake of my crowned sovereign. I turn my head—how
could I not?—and our eyes meet for a heartbeat. It is three months
since I last saw my love. I smile—but he, like so many other people
have done, looks away.

Part Two

Innocent Blood

KATE

July 1483, Windsor Castle

Kate thought her father looked magnificent in his royal mantle, seated on White Surrey at the head of his vast retinue, as he led the great procession through the lower ward and out the gates of Windsor Castle. He was bound for London, and then Oxford, on the first stages of a great royal progress through his kingdom, the purpose of which was to greet his new subjects, and to court and win their loyalty.

She had stood by the mounting block as Queen Anne offered the stirrup cup and the King bade them a formal farewell and went on his way. She watched as his slight, erect figure on its magnificent destrier passed through the gates of Windsor, then searched desperately for a last sight of John de la Pole, who rode with the lords who followed their King; elegant in his black and gold doublet and a black bonnet with a curling feather, he waved to her gaily and blew a kiss. With a bereft heart, she stood looking after him until he had long disappeared from sight.

It was frustrating being left behind, but it would not be for long. The Queen had been slightly indisposed—a summer fever, the doctors had said—and did not feel up to traveling at the moment. It had been arranged that she and Kate would miss the first stops on the progress and travel directly to Warwick Castle to join the King there. And then—oh, joy, Kate thought, her heart soaring—she would be reunited with John! The days could not pass quickly enough.

"It will be good to be in Warwick again," Anne said, as Kate joined her in the Queen's chamber, a spacious apartment hung with gorgeous painted and gilded fabric, and graced with a fair stone fireplace and tall lattice windows. "I was brought up there."

"Will we be going to Middleham?" Kate asked. She was still nostalgic for her old life, but these days she could think of little but John. They had met several times in the dean's cloister garden behind the new chapel that was being built and would be dedicated to St. George. The first time, John had given her a pink rose; he said it matched her cheeks. He was always paying her poetic compliments, calling her his "flower of beauty, excellent above all others, lovely, good, and wise . . ." He'd told her of his family, of his irascible sire, his lovable mother— her father's sister, Elizabeth—and of the great houses he called home: Wingfield in Suffolk and Ewelme in Oxfordshire. He made her feel so important and special. She knew now, beyond any doubt, that she was in love with him.

The long days of their separation seemed to stretch endlessly ahead. She did not know how she would bear them. How inconvenient of the Queen to be ill at this time! She caught herself up at that. Anne was not strong, never had been. How could she think so unkindly of her?

Anne was watching her. "Where have you been?" she chided. "I said I long to go to Middleham, to see my little boy."

Kate started. "I beg your pardon, madam, I was thinking about the progress."

"And a certain young man." The Queen smiled, but the smile did not reach her eyes.

"I—you know?" Kate asked, floundering. But she had done nothing wrong, nothing of which she was ashamed. John had never even attempted to kiss her.

"There are no secrets in courts," Anne said. "You have been seen together, more than once; my ladies like to gossip. Dear child, I must caution you to be careful. I understand what it is to be young and smitten, and my lord of Lincoln is a very handsome young man with a persuasive way about him. Yet he is eight years older than you, and the game of love he plays is common at court. He knows he can never have you, so for him it is purely chivalrous dalliance."

"It is no game!" Kate cried. "We love each other, I swear it. And he is unwed, and so am I, so why can he never have me?"

"For a start, you are first cousins; you could not marry without the Pope's dispensation, and that might prove expensive, given the close kinship. And forgive me, Kate, but you are baseborn. He is the Earl of Lincoln. He is destined to succeed his father as Duke of Suffolk, and should—God forfend!—anything befall my son the prince, he may be in line for the throne itself."

"We can overcome all!" Kate cried. "I may be baseborn, but I am the daughter of the King, and he has often spoken of arranging a great marriage for me. And John loves me! He will not quibble at seeking a dispensation."

"Has he spoken of marriage?"

"Not yet. But we have only known each other a short time. He has spoken much of love, though, so I have no doubt his intentions are honorable."

"Oh, my sweet Kate, how innocent you are!" Anne exclaimed. "When men speak of love, they are not always thinking of marriage. And when they speak of marriage, they are thinking of rich dowries and lands."

"Surely my father will give me a rich dowry?"

"Indeed he will. He has said so. But it is he who will choose the man you marry."

Kate was beginning to feel desperate. "Then I will tell him I want to marry John."

"Might it not be best to wait and find out if John has marriage in mind? Or if his father has chosen a bride for him already?"

"John is not betrothed. He told me so." She could remember the moment: they had been standing in a window embrasure late one evening, looking out at a starry sky. It was one of those moments she felt she wanted to hold on to forever. John had asked her if she was pledged to anyone, and squeezed her hand when she told him she was not, and then he had said he was not pledged either. At the time, it had felt like a promise. She had been certain he was hinting that he desired to wed her, and her heart had soared again.

Anne was silent. "You run ahead with yourself, Kate. Listen, child: this must go no further until I have spoken to your father about it. We must find out his wishes in the matter."

"Will you speak for us?" Kate's spirits were suddenly uplifted.

"I will ask him if he approves," Anne corrected her, and would not be drawn out further.

KATHERINE

November–December 1553, Whitehall Palace

Jane and Guilford are to be tried on the fourteenth of November. Although the Queen has assured me that the trial is merely a formality, and that a pardon will follow when the time is right, the announcement strikes dread into my heart. It reminds me how perilously close Jane has been brought to her utter ruin. May God grant that the Queen stays firm in her resolve to show mercy.

I wish I could see Jane and comfort her, and tell her that all will be well, that Her Majesty is warmly disposed toward our family and bears her no malice. But I have not seen her for four months, and she is allowed no visitors.

I am in great fear lest this trial prejudice my own future. I told Renard that I, for my part, would be content to embrace the Catholic faith, but that, in all duty, I had to discuss the matter first with my parents, and I was sure he would understand that I needed to choose my moment. He warned that I must not say a word to my lord and lady about the possibility of my being named the Queen's heir, which of course leaves me in a dilemma, because how else do I justify to them my sudden conversion?

Renard was deferential, yet he did not court me as before. Mayhap I have taken too long in making up my mind. Perchance he is not as warm in my cause as he was in September. And maybe this coming trial is too vivid a reminder that my close kin were traitors to the Queen only a few short months ago.

My life is a continual tempest. I am tormented by my need for Harry, and the devastation I feel in the wake of his snubbing me at the coronation, but somehow our paths never cross at court. I am sure he is avoiding me. Then there are new rumors that I and my sisters are to be declared bastards, on the grounds that my father was already wed when he married my mother. It's nonsense, but rumormongers care naught for the truth! I suspect that the tale originated with the French ambassador, who probably knows by now that Spain and the Empire are putting their weight behind me in regard to the succession. It is all too much, and I find myself continually on the verge of tears, with only Arthur and Guinevere to comfort me.

My mother seeks me out one rainy day as I am taking some exercise in the long gallery with my dogs, brooding upon my woes.

"I have to talk to you," she says, and leads me to the lodging she shares with my father; it is deserted just now, for he is at the cockpit, watching prize birds tear each other to pieces.

My mother seats herself in her chair. "I will not waste words," she says. "They are putting pressure on us, your father and me, to convert to the Roman faith. I think you know something about this. They said you are willing."

"Monsieur Renard did approach me about it," I say carefully. "He told me it was the Queen's wish. I said I would consider it, but that I wanted to discuss it with you." It is not quite the truth, but it is near enough.

"Indeed. It was the Privy Council that approached us," she tells me. "We told them it was out of the question, but they tried to bribe us, saying that great benefits would follow."

"And they will!" I blurt out.

My lady stares at me in astonishment. "What do you mean? Out with it, girl, and tell me the truth!"

"The Queen wishes it, I know that," I say, aware that I must dissemble well if I am to deceive my hawklike mother. "She has said so, therefore it must follow that she will be generous to those who do her will. I can think of nothing that would please her so much as the conversion of her close kin."

My lady gives me a long, penetrating look, then relaxes a little. "I did discuss with your father the possibility of our converting back to the Roman faith. I said it would go better for Jane, with her trial looming, if we complied with the Queen's will. But he is unshakable."

A week later, though, I learn that, bullied by my mother, my father has at last agreed to be received once more into the faith of his youth. It is all over the court that they have both recanted the Protestant religion; it is a feather in the cap of the Catholics.

Jane and Guilford have been tried and condemned to death.

"Rest assured, Lady Katherine, I am resolved to be merciful," the Queen told me kindly when she broke the news in the privacy of her closet. "However, the formalities had to be observed. My councillors demanded it. I promise you it was a fair trial, and the witnesses were allowed to speak freely. I warned my judges that I would have no intimidation, and that it was my pleasure that whatever could be produced in your sister's favor should be heard."

"I thank Your Majesty for your great mercy," I said, and falling on my knees, kissed her hand fervently. Tears were spilling down my cheeks.

"Do not distress yourself, child," the Queen said, lifting me up. "In a short space, I will order the Lady Jane's release. When I have a son." Her eyes took on that dreamy look we are all coming to know so well, as she turned away to gaze for the thousandth time at Master Titian's splendid portrait of Prince Philip, to whom she is now betrothed.

"It will not be long until he is here," she breathed, sounding like a girl in love.

"Oh, I do wish for Your Majesty's happiness!" I cried.

"Bless you, dear child," she smiled.

Not everyone likes the idea of this marriage. Go out into London, and you will hear outraged protests about it. The people do not want "Jack Spaniard" in England. They say openly that they would rather die than have the Spanish rule here; that Philip will be a harsh master, and bring in the Inquisition to torture and burn Protestants; and that this marriage will make England just another province of the mighty Habsburg empire. At court there are lewd jokes about the prince's debauchery and whispers about his thieving nature. The Queen does not hear them—or chooses not to acknowledge them. Her mind is made up, and she fancies herself in love; she will not hear of any opposition to her marriage.

Personally, I think Prince Philip looks an attractive man, with his full lips and proper features; I can see why the Queen is so smitten with his portrait. I pray that he will be kind to her, for she is eleven years his senior, and looks it—and she is so full of maidenly modesty that it was some while before she could even bring herself to say the word "marriage" in the presence of her councillors. She told us that herself, blushing furiously. I cannot imagine her bedding with a man!

The Lady Elizabeth is much discountenanced by the news of the Queen's marriage. Her long hooked nose is much out of joint, for she is her sister's legal heir, and if Her Majesty bears a son, she—like me—will never succeed to the throne, which I am sure is what Elizabeth desires fiercely.

Maybe she should not have made so much fuss about going to Mass, for if she had put herself out to please the Queen, Her Majesty would trust her far more, and would look more kindly on her as her successor. But Elizabeth has dissembled once too often, and now she sulks about the court, intriguing with the French ambassador, or urging Queen Mary to let her go to Hatfield or Ashridge, or another of the many houses she owns. But always the Queen refuses. She remains suspicious of her sister, and understands the necessity for keeping her where she can be watched.

There has been little love lost between Elizabeth and me since my actions made it clear to her that I was not going to spy for her or support her stand on religion. When we meet, she is polite, even talkative, but never warm. Yet today, when I am standing all forlorn in the deserted maidens' dorter, having fled here to try to calm down after receiving the news of my sister, she seeks me out.

"I heard about the Lady Jane's condemnation," she tells me. Her voice is gruff; she seems unusually moved.

"The Queen herself told me the news, Your Grace," I say, trembling. "Even though she has promised mercy, it is a terrible thing to hear. Burned alive or beheaded, at Her Majesty's pleasure . . ."

"I hear Jane took it well. They say she was calm when she walked from the Guildhall with the axe turned toward her. The crowds were silent when they saw she had been condemned." Elizabeth shudders; of course, her mother, Anne Boleyn, was beheaded for treason and other shocking crimes when Elizabeth was very young. How terrible it must be to live with that knowledge. No wonder she is so affected by today's news.

"Jane is innocent," I say. "The Queen knows it."

"How many are called traitor who are innocent?" Elizabeth asks, unnerving me.

"Dear God, how did we come to be in this situation?" I wail, breaking down in tears.

"Because of your Tudor blood," Elizabeth says. "It is a curse as well as a blessing. And since you are a woman, men seek to use you to satisfy their own ambitions, as Northumberland did with Jane. They sought to use me too, but I was cannier—and luckier. We poor creatures are but pawns on a chessboard. Even the Queen—if she marries—will be at the mercy of her husband."

"*If* she marries? It is certain that she will."

Elizabeth flushed. "A slip of the tongue. Of course she will. But she will be no better off than any country wife. God's blood, I will never marry. I'll have no man rule me."

I am sorry for her cynicism, and that she accounts love so lightly. Unlike me, she has not known the happiness of marriage. And yet maybe she is wiser than I, for those who fly high with happiness set themselves up to be dashed down with sorrow. I still relive that terrible moment in Westminster Abbey when Harry looked away.

Forgetting in whose presence I am, I sink down onto a bed, crying hopelessly, emitting great tearing sobs. Despite the Queen's assurances, the full horror of Jane's sentence keeps overwhelming me, and I cannot get it out of my mind. Burning is such a dreadful death. When I was very young, I saw a woman burned at the stake in London. Mrs. Ellen hid my eyes, so I only watched for a few awful seconds, but I have never forgotten it, or the screams of the condemned. Not Jane! Please God, not Jane!

Elizabeth rests a hand on my shoulder.

"I am sorry you have fresh occasion for sorrow," she says, more kindly than I have ever heard her speak. "You must have faith. Be obedient to Him whose strokes are unavoidable. He will not test you, or your sister, beyond your endurance."

It is comforting to realize that Elizabeth has a more sensitive side. I cease crying and struggle to my feet, reaching in my pocket for my kerchief.

"I am sorry, I forgot my manners to Your Grace," I sniff. "I thank you for your kind advice, and I will take comfort in God."

The moment of closeness has passed. Elizabeth regards me coolly; her mood, ever mercurial, has changed again. "It is said you will convert to the old religion," she says. "Is that from conviction, or because Spain wants it?"

How does she know that? The French ambassador, of course!

"If I convert, Your Grace, it will be because I am persuaded it is the right thing to do," I say, righteous with indignation. But her barb has hit home. I *would* be changing my religion primarily to further my own ambitions—and she has made me feel bad about that.

"Well, go and pray to your God—whoever He is," she says, reverting to her usual acerbity. She cannot but regard my conversion as anything other than apostasy.

"I thank you for your kindness, Your Grace," I say, suppressing my resentment. "I will do as you enjoin me."

"It will only be efficacious if you follow the true path," she says coldly, and disappears through the door with a swish of her green silk skirts.

I am beginning to suspect that Elizabeth hates me; I think I have always known it. What else can there be between us but rivalry? We are both too close to the throne for comfort; and she may have more than a suspicion that there is a move afoot to supplant her in the succession.

If her parting thrust made me feel guilty, her behavior in the days and weeks that follow compounds it. I am, after all, the daughter of parents who were hot for the cause of church reform in King Harry's reign, and came out as Protestants under King Edward, so I was mostly brought up in the new religion. Jane, of course, is one of its most passionate exponents, and had she been let to rule over us, I have no doubt but that England would have stayed firmly Protestant. But instead we have Catholic Mary, who has brought back the Mass and the holy images that were once deemed idolatrous, and made England's peace with Rome. It has been a marvel to see so many hitherto ardent reformers suddenly confessing that they have secretly been Papists all along, so what choice do I have, if I want to survive at court—and if I want to be Queen?

Elizabeth has seen through me, and makes it clear she despises me for my pragmatism. She shuns me at every opportunity, and utters bitchy remarks in my presence about people who are too craven to follow their conscience. Oh, she is clever: she speaks in reference to herself returning to the faith of her childhood with a whole heart—but I know where her darts are aimed. She thinks to occupy the moral high ground; yet this is the lady who complained that her belly hurt when it was time to go to Mass, or that she didn't understand this or that finer point of Catholic theology. Her, with her brains and acute intellect!

To be honest, never having been much of a scholar, and having come under Queen Mary's patient influence, I cannot now comprehend why being a Catholic is so wrong. Indeed, I have discovered that there is much about it that appeals to me. I love the sweet statues of the smiling Virgin and her Babe that the Queen has set up in her chapels, the silvery tinkling of bells at the altar, the spicy waft of incense, and the comfort of knowing that the saints are praying for me in Heaven. Indeed, to my good cheer, I have learned that there is a whole panoply of them, of whom I might beseech a timely intercession with the Lord God, each having a special patronage. And I must confess myself glad to be spared the interminable sermons of the Protestant preachers, having never been able to sit still and suppress my yawns in Sunday services, much to my mother's annoyance. How she would prod me sharply in the arm, to make me pay attention! It is a relief to have all that behind me.

But Elizabeth is cut of a different cloth. She will stand there, demure and maidenly in her unadorned black-and-white Protestant garb that she affects because she knows it riles Queen Mary, and with her long red hair loose over her shoulders in token of her virgin youthfulness—another way of showing herself in a more favorable light than the aging Queen—and look disapprovingly down that sharp, hooked nose at the jeweled crucifix I have taken to wearing on my breast; and she will give me that hurtful, withering glance that brands me a hypocrite.

Her dislike is palpable, and, of course, there are other reasons for it. When we do meet, she takes pleasure in telling me that my skin is too pale, my hair too fine and too light in color, or my figure too thin, twisting her own luxuriant red locks in her fingers as she speaks, or smoothing her cheeks, or spanning her slim waist with her hands. She cannot bear to think that anyone might be more beautiful or attractive to men than herself.

I suspect that what lies at the root of her dislike is fear. She knows full well that I am next in line to the throne after her; and therefore, whatever attributes I might have to recommend me—and she makes it plain that, in her opinion, they are not up to much—I am her rival.

I know I must be wary of her; she is her father's daughter.

Jane Dormer, who serves alongside me in the Privy Chamber, is one of Her Majesty's maids of honor and closest friends, and a young lady more sweet, pious, or learned you could not hope to meet. When the Queen herself sends her to me, it becomes apparent that my position in regard to religion is of the highest importance to Her Majesty.

Mistress Dormer bids me follow her into Her Majesty's oratory, a closet richly decked out with blue and gold hangings, with an altar on which stands a bejeweled crucifix and a painted statuette of the Virgin and Child, and a prayer stool covered with a costly Turkish rug.

"We can be private here," Dormer says, smiling kindly. "Do not look so anxious, Lady Katherine. There is nothing to fear. Now—Monsieur Renard has approached you in regard to the succession to the throne." It is a statement, not a question. My heart starts thumping with excitement. This is the moment I have waited for.

"You can imagine how important—nay crucial—your conversion to the Catholic faith is to the Queen," Jane says. "And that of your lord and lady too. However, I am charged to tell you that your father has this day recanted, which has caused Her Majesty great distress, for he has changed his coat twice now, and clearly cannot be relied upon."

Her words strike ice into my heart. "I am deeply sorry to hear of my father's offense," I stress. "I would not wish his fault to be imputed to me."

"Nor is it," she assures me. "But Her Majesty is hoping to hear that you have now come to a decision over your own faith. I believe you have had some weeks to think about it. If you have any questions or doubts, I am here to assist and advise you."

"I thank you, Mistress Dormer, but I have made my decision," I say, feeling I am on the brink of something momentous. "Please tell Her Majesty that I will willingly and gladly convert to the Catholic faith."

KATE

August 1483, Warwick Castle

When Queen Anne's party finally arrived at Warwick, riding through the mighty new Tower House gate after what seemed an endless journey in sweltering weather, they found the court buzzing with talk of a conspiracy to set the deposed Edward V back on the throne. King Richard greeted them affectionately, but later, when they supped together privately in the solarium, he dismissed the servitors as soon as the first course had been brought in, and unburdened his troubled mind.

"My throne is not as secure as I thought," he said darkly, clenching his fist as it lay on the table. "Never mind my just title, or that magnificent coronation, or my efforts to court the favor of my subjects: they hate me. They do not cheer when I pass, or return my greetings. Instead, they mutter or call out against usurping northerners, whom they hate as a matter of principle, ignorant fools."

"There will always be distrust between southerners and northerners," the Queen said.

"Madam, I cannot discount the half of my kingdom," Richard answered. "I am King of the South as well, and it is in the South and West that these conspiracies originated. Confederacies were formed, assemblies gathered unlawfully, their purpose to free my nephews from the Tower. Some were plotting to divert the jailers with a blaze."

"Jailers? Are the princes now prisoners?" Anne's shock was evident.

Richard frowned. "Madam, in the circumstances, I have had to order a close guard to be kept on the 'Lord Bastards.'" His emphasis reproved her for calling them princes. "But they are safe and well cared for. You need not trouble yourself about them."

"They are children! They cannot lead their lives in captivity."

"Nor will they," Richard assured her. "As soon as I am safely established on my throne, they will be set free, and provided for honorably."

Kate was relieved to hear that, and she could see her stepmother visibly relaxing. Cheered, she helped herself to another slice of lark pie. Her father smiled at her.

"In truth, it does me good to see you both again," he declared. "My lady, you have brought young Warwick with you, as I commanded?"

"I have, my lord," Anne said, and Kate had an uncomfortable memory of her futile attempts to make conversation with the awkward lad on the journey.

"I need Warwick under my eye, for his own safety," her father said. "Who knows what these traitors will do next? Fortunately, the late conspiracies were uncovered in time and dealt with, but there may be others." He got up and began pacing up and down the room. "Why cannot people accept that none of my brothers' children are his rightful heirs? The Wydevilles never cease plotting against me. Even Buckingham has abandoned me, I fear."

"Buckingham?" gasped Anne. "I cannot believe it!"

The King sat down, shaking his head. He looked pale. "We quarreled at Gloucester. He accused me of not keeping my promise to grant him the Bohun lands; he has been claiming they are his for a long time. He took umbrage and departed for his estates at Brecon, saying he had pressing business there."

"But he owes all his wealth and power to you! Without you, he is nothing."

"You forget I owe my throne to him, my lady. He was most eloquent at persuading people that I should be King." He sighed. "Do not worry about Buckingham. I will deal with him."

"What of the other lords? Norfolk, Northumberland, Stanley, and the rest?" Anne asked worriedly.

"Loyal, as far as I can tell. Stanley will always be suspect because of his Beaufort wife, but so far he has kept her ambitions in check."

"Her ambitions?"

"The woman is obsessed with her son, Henry Tudor. Those two like to keep up the fiction that he is the Lancastrian claimant to the throne. Can you believe that? The Cousins' Wars between Lancaster and York were over and done with twelve years ago. Someone should tell them!"

"But how can Henry Tudor be the Lancastrian heir?" Kate asked.

"He cannot," her father said. "He is of bastard stock. John of Gaunt's Beaufort bastards were the children of his mistress, Dame Katherine Swynford, born before their marriage. They have no right to inherit the crown."

"What of his father?"

"He was Edmund Tudor, the son of some unknown Welshman—and Henry Tudor, as far as I am concerned, is another unknown Welshman, and not worth bothering about. Lady Stanley is welcome to her fantasies, but that's all they can ever be. No, my Kate, the true heir is your brother, Prince Edward. And Anne, I mind, when we are at York, to have him brought there from Middleham so that I can invest him as Prince of Wales."

"Oh, that is good news!" Anne exclaimed. "I have missed Edward so much. I long to embrace him." Richard laid his hand over hers; such gestures of tenderness were rare between them these days.

"That is not the only piece of good news I have for you." He smiled. "This day, there arrived at my court ambassadors from King Ferdinand and Queen Isabella of Spain, come to negotiate a marriage for our little prince with a Spanish infanta. Edward will have a fit mate to match his royal status as England's heir."

"A Spanish infanta?" Anne echoed, delighted. "Any daughter of the Spanish sovereigns will be an excellent match for Edward." She paused. "Speaking of marriage, there is something I must ask you, my lord."

Kate's spirits wavered. This was the moment she had been dreading. At least her father was in a better mood, beaming at the thought of those proud little infantas. She reached for the ewer and refilled his goblet, hoping to mellow him further.

"It concerns Kate's marriage," the Queen said.

"Indeed?" the King asked, his grin fading. "Has someone asked for her hand?"

"No, but your nephew Lincoln has been paying her his addresses." Kate quailed as her father looked piercingly at her.

"He has done nothing wrong, sire!" she hastened to say. "He just pays court to me, reads me poems, and tells me I am beautiful."

Richard raised his eyebrows. "As indeed you are, my Kate." He reflected for a moment. "In truth, I had not thought to see any man come courting you so soon, but now I perceive that I have been thinking of you only as a child. I see I must come to terms with your growing up. How long has this been going on?"

"Since the day of the coronation."

"Indeed. Has my nephew spoken of marriage?"

"No, sire—only of love." Kate blushed. "But we have not known each other very long. And I have not seen him since you left Windsor."

Her father appeared to consider the matter, as Anne sat silent and Kate waited in trepidation. Never before had it been made so plain to her that her future happiness lay in the hands of one man, who had absolute power over her fate.

"Lincoln is a fine young lord, the best servant a king could have," Richard said at length. "However, you are not the first damsel to whom he has paid court like this, although I have never heard that his behavior has ever been dishonorable. We must wait to see if he intends marriage."

"And if he does?" Kate breathed.

"I will consider it. The idea does not displease me, but there is no haste. You are not yet fourteen, and I would keep you with me for a while longer."

"Then I may go and find him?" she asked excitedly.

"I will not forbid it, so long as, for now, you think of him only as your cousin and conduct yourself accordingly. There is to be no more talk of love, still less of marriage. Such decisions are best left to those who are older, wiser, and not blinded by their passions to all good sense. So, yes, you may enjoy my lord of Lincoln's company, but never alone. Do you heed me?"

"Yes, sire," Kate replied, a little crestfallen.

Her father smiled. "I am not so old that I cannot remember what it was like to be young. Youth needs the friendship and company of its own kind. Long before your stepmother and I were betrothed, we spent every moment we could together at Middleham and Warwick— not that her father knew about it." He smiled at Anne. "But we never overstepped the bounds of friendship, and that is as far as it can go with your cousin of Lincoln, Kate. I am trusting you to behave virtuously and with decorum."

As soon as supper was over, Kate made her curtsies and sped down- stairs to the great hall, which was packed with the King's nobles and liveried retainers, carousing and singing. There was no sign of John among them, so she hurried out into the bailey and looked for him there. To her delight, she spotted him in a little garden at the foot of a grassy mound in the far corner, lounging on the sward with two other men. They were deep in conversation, and she hesitated to intrude, but when one of John's companions—whom she recognized as the sly lawyer, Sir William Catesby, now her father's Chancellor of the Exchequer—espied her and rose quickly to his feet, the rest followed suit. John's face broke into a radiant smile when he beheld her, and he made a courtly bow and kissed her hand. The other man, she saw, was Lord Stanley. He was much older than the first two, with long, straggly graying hair and creased brows that made him look permanently trou- bled. "My lady," he said, and bowed too.

"Come join us, Kate," John invited, and she sank down onto the grass, her mustard-colored skirts spread out about her. "We were just enjoying the evening air—it's hot and noisy in the hall." He offered her some marchpane. "We were saying how concerned we are about the late conspiracies," he said.

"My father the King has just been telling us about them," she said. "I cannot believe that the Duke of Buckingham has abandoned him."

"Strange business, that," said Stanley. "No rhyme or reason to it."

"It's possible, of course, that he was bound up in the conspiracies," Catesby said. "Before he went off to Brecon, he told us they'd tried to involve him in one of the plots, so I suppose he could have been playing a double game. But he did inform the King of the approach that had been made to him, and that information certainly led to some of the conspirators being caught. So we might wonder just why he turned on the King, after being one of his staunchest supporters."

"What could the conspirators offer him beyond what the King has given him?" John asked.

"They quarreled over the Bohun estates," Stanley said. "The Duke accused King Richard of not keeping his promise to grant them to him."

"That's strange too," Catesby mused. "The King made him a provisional grant of them last month."

"Maybe Buckingham didn't like the fact it was provisional," John suggested. "Although he must have known he'd get them in the end."

"The fact remains that he may now make mischief for our liege lord," Stanley pointed out.

"While the sons of King Edward remain in the Tower, King Richard can never be secure on his throne," Catesby said. "The late conspiracies proved that."

"But the Tower is a safe place," John chimed in. "They cannot leave, nor can would-be traitors get at them. They are well guarded by our trusty Constable of the Tower. No one could get past Brackenbury." That was comforting. Kate had known the kindly, popular Robert Brackenbury when he served in her father's household at Middleham, and knew him to be devoted to his master. He would be a gentle jailer for the two princes.

"But it's not just a question of keeping the boys under guard," Catesby was saying, his voice lowered. "Even though the Lord Bastard is innocent of any involvement in those conspiracies to put him back on the throne, he is a danger to King Richard—and his brother too. Some still persist in regarding them as the rightful heirs of York."

It was a warm evening, but Kate suddenly felt chilly.

"What is your thrust, William?" John asked. "How should my uncle deal with that threat?"

Catesby shrugged. His expression was unreadable.

Stanley spoke with some vehemence. "Ask yourselves what happened to other deposed monarchs. What became of Edward II and Richard II? Why it is that the princes have not been seen since before the coronation? They were out shooting at the butts in the lieutenant's garden several times before that. But since then, to my knowledge, no one has seen them." Kate noticed, to her dismay, that Stanley was weeping.

"Good my lord, take comfort from the fact that my uncle the King would never harm his nephews," John said.

"No, he would not!" Kate cried. "He was loyal to King Edward. He will be a protector to his sons."

"I am not the only one to voice fears for their safety," Stanley muttered. "Listen about the court; hearken in the streets. Men are asking what has become of them. I do not accuse the King of any crime, or of bearing ill will toward his nephews. I just wonder why they have been withdrawn from men's sight. Surely His Grace has heard the rumors? He has but to show the boys to the people and they will be quelled!"

"Rest assured I will speak to him about it," John said.

"I thank you, my lord," Stanley replied, rising to his feet. "And my Lady Katherine, forgive an old man for worrying too much, and for spoiling this beautiful evening. It was intended for dalliance, not for politics."

"Yes, my lord, of course." Kate nodded, but she was still reeling from the enormity of what Stanley had implied.

"I must go too," Catesby said. "Good evening, Lady Katherine."

John turned to Kate and placed his arm about her shoulders. "Do not heed malicious gossip," he advised her. "I'll wager Stanley's wife has been pouring poison in his ear."

"He *was* very upset," Kate observed. "And it seemed that Sir William was trying to insinuate something."

"He's a cold fish, and I could easily believe that he would urge the necessity of doing away with the princes," John said, frowning. "But that the King would sanction it—that I cannot, and will not, believe."

He moved closer to her. "Forget all this, Kate, my sweeting. Let us talk of more pleasant things. I have been saving a poem for you."

But Kate's mind was in a turmoil. Her mind retained that shocking image of Lord Stanley weeping; his distress had not been feigned.

"I can't bear the thought of people thinking such dreadful things about my father," she said.

"Sweetheart, I make no doubt that, once I have spoken to the King about those rumors, he will ensure that they do not. Now, be at peace, and listen to this." He began to recite, but Kate was not listening. She could not forget what Lord Stanley had said. Her father must refute those rumors. He must!

KATHERINE

January 1554, Whitehall Palace

The palace is in an uproar. It is terrifying! Some of the women are saying we shall all be murdered in our beds, and the Queen too! There have been rumbles of discontent for weeks—since the Queen's forthcoming marriage was announced, in fact—but now a Kentish gentleman with a grievance, the hotheaded Sir Thomas Wyatt, is advancing on London at the head of a great army of rebels, in protest against the Spanish match. Only days ago he raised his standard at Maidstone, and the people flocked to him. Now word has come that they have taken Rochester Bridge and the royal fleet moored in the Medway and are marching this way. There is much panic among the ladies of the court— and indeed in London itself. Who knows what the rebels intend?

There have been concerns expressed about the Lady Elizabeth, who was finally allowed to leave court last month after bringing much pressure to bear on her sister. Relations between the Lady Elizabeth and Queen Mary had become uncomfortably strained, and no doubt Her Majesty was glad to see the back of her. Yet now people think it strange that she departed the court not long before the rebellion.

The Queen, unlike most of the rest of us, is calm. Not for nothing is she a Tudor. I wish I could be like her, for the same blood runs in my veins, but I am of poor courage, wanting to run as far away from here as I can. Yet I must stay where I am, where I can be seen to be loyal to my sovereign. I am spending much of my time at prayer, fearfully imploring God for a speedy deliverance from these traitors.

The most terrible news has come. There have been further uprisings in Devon and the Midlands, both linked to Wyatt's rebellion, and orchestrated by the same traitors. Fortunately they have proved abortive, but the worst news—for me—is that the revolt in Leicestershire was led by my father. He even went so far as to declare for Jane, proclaiming her Queen once more. I am mortified when the Queen herself breaks these tidings to me, and she can see how covered with shame I am, for she speaks kindly to me and assures me she knows I am loyal and true to her, even if my father is not.

Words fail me when I think of the duke my lord. Even though I have been brought up to respect and honor him, and never to question his word, I have to acknowledge that he has acted with great stupidity and lack of judgment. Did he not think how his rash and treasonable acts could rebound on us all, especially on poor Jane, innocently biding her time in the Tower, waiting to be freed? Everyone knows she had nothing to do with this.

As I do my best to look invisible, the Queen commands the Lady Elizabeth to return to court. Back comes the reply: Her Grace has a cold and a headache, and is too ill to travel. The Queen frowns as she puts down the letter. "I do not believe it," she says. "She is intriguing with the French; I have proof of it. She is no sister of mine!" She rises and angrily raps out an order that the Lady Elizabeth's portrait be taken down from the gallery.

My mother, in the foulest of tempers, seeks me out at court on the day that my father and other rebel leaders are publicly proclaimed traitors.

"Well, I did warn him!" my lady says when we are alone together. "Of course, the fool would not listen, and now I wouldn't be surprised if he brings us all down with him. There'll be no reprieve this time. The Queen is no longer so disposed to mercy."

She speaks truth, and certainly there are no grounds for pleading for my father.

"What will happen to him?" I ask, heavyhearted.

"What happens to all traitors," she answers gruffly, betraying no emotion but anger. "You had best face up to it. He knew what he was risking."

The rebels are at Gravesend. The gates of London are now under heavy guard, and the drawbridge on London Bridge has been raised.

I am among the ladies waiting on the Queen when she receives a deputation of the Commons, who beg her to reconsider her decision to wed Prince Philip.

"I cannot do that," she tells them, "for my word is given, and this alliance will bring the kingdom great benefits. I consider myself His Highness's wife. I will never take another husband; I would rather lose my crown and my life. Yet I assure you, my loyal Commons, that this marriage will never interfere with your liberties."

Her spirit remains firm. Ignoring the chorus of protest from her ministers and her ladies, she is resolved upon a personal appeal to the Londoners, and in the afternoon we nervously follow her to the Guildhall. Up to the last minute, she adamantly rejected all her councillors' pleas to consider her safety and not venture forth into the City.

She is fearless. We stand behind her as she faces the Lord Mayor and a vast crowd of people. Her speech is long and masterful. I listen, marveling, as she reminds them that she is their Queen, and tells them she loves them as naturally as a mother loves her child. She assures them she would abstain from this marriage if it did not appear to be for the high benefit of the realm.

"I am minded to live and die with you!" she cries in her deep, manlike voice, reminding them that all they hold dear is under threat. "And now, good subjects, pluck up your hearts, and like true men face up to these rebels, and fear them not—for I assure you I fear them nothing at all!"

The response is tremendous. Caps are thrown into the air and tears are shed as there is a resounding ovation. We depart to the roar of cheering, heartened by the knowledge that Queen Mary, by her courage, now has London in the palm of her hand.

The Londoners have destroyed London Bridge, so that Wyatt and his hordes may not cross the river from the Surrey shore. There are frightening reports that he has sacked the old priory of St. Mary Overie in Southwark and Winchester Palace nearby. In the City there is much noise and tumult as men shut up their shops, put on their armor, and obey the Lord Mayor's command to guard their front doors.

In the palace, it is as if we are under siege. The Queen's presence chamber is thronged with armed guards. In her privy chamber, we ladies huddle together, many of us weeping and lamenting our perilous position; I confess I am among the most tremulous. My mother, though, sits tight-lipped and straight-backed. She will not give way to fear.

The waiting is intolerable. When will the violence begin?

The Queen remains calm and steadfast. "You must place your trust in God," she exhorts us. "He will deliver us from this present danger."

She refuses to allow the Tower guns to be fired across the Thames at the rebel army.

"My innocent subjects in Southwark might be killed," she protests. But Wyatt clearly underestimates the Queen's compassion. To avoid being bombarded, he leads his army upriver to Kingston, and crosses the Thames. There is near panic at Whitehall. Women can be heard shrieking and wailing; doors slam as people race about trying to find hiding places for themselves and their valuables; and many of the servants have fled. I push Arthur and Guinevere under my bed and wag my finger severely, commanding them to stay there.

The Queen is urged by her advisers to escape by river, a suggestion she rejects with derision. "I will tarry to the uttermost," she declares. "I only wish I were not a weak woman and could take to the field in person."

Arms are hastily issued to every member of the royal household. I'll even wield a pistol myself if necessary.

It is my father-in-law, the martial Earl of Pembroke, who checks

Wyatt's advance. News comes that his cavalry has forced the rebels to halt at St. James's Park, a stone's throw from Whitehall. So close had we come to disaster! Then we hear gunfire, which sets all the courtiers panicking again. "Fall to prayer!" the Queen exhorts us. Yet soon comes the news: Wyatt has been taken at Charing Cross, and is on his way to the Tower! The rebellion is over. We are safe.

Of my father, still no word.

"God has worked a miracle," the Queen declares. "Now I will strike terror into all who are disposed to do evil."

The leaders of the revolt are to be executed, as an example to other would-be traitors. My father, when he is caught—and that can only be a matter of time—will surely suffer the same fate. Suddenly people are avoiding my mother and me. The prospect of the crown now seems a very distant one. But I am more distressed about my father.

"He brought it on his own head," my lady repeats dully, as if the fight has gone out of her. She seems resigned to his death. Yet it seems a very terrible punishment to me, even though he has fully deserved it. And I find it hard to accept that the father I have known—and looked up to until these last days—is soon to die.

KATE

August 1483; Pontefract Castle, Yorkshire

Coventry. Leicester. Nottingham. Doncaster. It was a long progress, and the Queen was finding it exhausting. What kept her going was the prospect of seeing her son, and when the court at last arrived at the great stronghold of Pontefract, there was the most joyful of reunions. The fair, delicate little boy was restored to his mother's arms, and his proud father lifted him high and announced to everyone that Edward of Middleham was to be invested as Prince of Wales as soon as the progress reached York. There were cheers from the assembled lords;

this was a much warmer reception than in most other places, for King Richard was now in the heartlands of his affinity, and many northern lords had ridden over eagerly to pay their loyal respects.

Kate became aware that someone was watching her, and among the officers of the prince's retinue she saw him again: Ferret Face, the black-haired man who had stared at her on coronation day. She gave him a disdainful glance and then forgot about him.

A few days later Kate followed among a bevy of noble ladies as the King and Queen, holding the little prince by both hands, walked with him into York Minster for his solemn investiture. The child won all hearts, as he lisped his way through the great ceremony and sat patiently while all the great lords, one by one, paid him homage and swore oaths to him as his father's heir; but at the feast afterward he became restive and wanted to go off and play ball, and was only with difficulty constrained to stay in his high seat. King Richard looked happier and more relaxed than he had in weeks, and Queen Anne was all smiles, doting on her son.

If there had been rumors about the princes, there was no echo of them here. There was nothing but praise for the new King, and fervent expressions of loyalty. With the realm so quiet, Kate had no doubt that her father would keep his word and release the princes very soon.

Her feelings for John were growing. They would try to slip away from the revelry at court or their respective duties and seek each other out in deserted gardens or shadowed arbors. It was in the garden at Nottingham Castle, that mighty fortress built on a rock, that he first kissed her, on a bright afternoon with a fragrant hint of autumn in the air. Without warning he'd bent forward and gently brushed her lips with his. And then they were in each other's arms, kissing as if the world was about to end, and not caring who saw.

"Sweet lady," John gasped, "no one has ever held such mastery over my heart as you. I am in torment!"

"Torment?" Kate echoed.

"I would serve you all the days of my life, so I were allowed," he breathed. "I love you, Kate. Without you, all joy must be at an end. It is that which torments me, for there can be no remedy."

He loved her! Her heart sang.

"There *can* be a remedy," she told him. "Why do you think I would not permit you to serve me?"

"It is not what *you* would not permit," he answered. "It is not you who can heal my malady."

"Then who?" She felt a twinge of fear. Had her father said something to John?

"Let us not speak of it. I want nothing to sully our precious time together."

"It is sullied already," she said, near to tears. Something or someone was standing in the way of their love: she knew it.

"We will defy them all!" he said fiercely.

"Defy who?" Her rare temper, born of fear, was rising. John pushed his fingers through her luxuriant dark hair and took her face firmly in his hands.

"The whole world, if need be!"

"I cannot fight an unknown enemy," she told him, her voice cold.

"Believe me, little love—let well enough alone for now. All may right itself in time. Leave it to me."

"I am not a child!" she cried, and walked off, leaving him to keep his secrets to himself.

He sought her out again, of course. He came and sat quietly beside her in chapel when she was at her devotions, but she refused to acknowledge that he was there. It seemed more than coincidence that she kept running into him in halls, courtyards, and other public places, and had repeatedly to force herself to ignore him. Her heart was breaking, but she kept her head high.

"You will slay me unless you soften your hard heart," he muttered, waylaying her by the door to the Queen's lodgings.

"The remedy is in your hands!" she said, but that hard heart of hers was fluttering like a trapped bird's wings.

"Very well, have it your way. But you will not like what I shall say to you."

"I would prefer honesty, sir!"

"It is my father. He has chosen a bride for me, and is already negotiating the marriage contract. I have told him I would wed you instead—and he said that if you were the King's lawful daughter he might consider it, but that we are too near in blood anyway."

It was the first time her bastardy had hit her like a slap in the face. She had been made to look of scant consequence in the eyes of the man she loved. Seeing her distress, John took her hand and squeezed it.

"I paid him no heed, Kate. He is a bully and a blusterer, but I am used to him. I told him I would always love you whatever your birth, and that you are a lady worthy of the highest honor. I said I could never love another."

"And what did he reply?"

John frowned. "No matter. I will wear him down. It won't be the first time. And if he thinks he can stop me from paying my addresses to you, he can think again."

"He has forbidden it?"

"I will not let him come between us. It is you I want, Kate. Your beauty, your gentleness—all the wondrous things that make you what you are. If I cannot love you, I should be dead! Say I may remain your servant, I beseech you."

She said it; of course she did.

KATHERINE

February 7, 1554; Whitehall Palace

It is rare to be alone in a court, and in Her Majesty's privy chamber there are always servants about. The Queen is never alone, even when sleeping or performing her most intimate functions. Thus, when my mother suddenly appears, grim-faced, and drags me into an anteroom, brusquely dismissing two grooms and saying we need some privacy, I know that the matter is serious. Yet just how serious I could not have dreamed.

"I have just come from the Queen," she blurts out, and to my horror I see that her eyes, normally so sharp and piercing, are brimming with tears. I have never seen my mother weep before—ever. "Katherine, there is no easy way to say this. Jane and Guilford are to be put to death." Her voice breaks.

Words fail me. I am looking into an abyss. My world is coming to an end.

I sway on my feet, and my mother steadies me, her hands on my shoulders, tenderer than I have ever known them.

"But the Queen gave her royal word!" I wail. "We trusted in that. How can she go back on it?"

"Things are different now." She sits me down on a stool and half collapses into a chair, trembling. "I don't know what I can do. I feel so helpless. Your father—I can live with that. But Jane! She is a child. She has done nothing but what she was bid. Oh, God forgive me, that I ever consented to Northumberland's stupid, stupid plans!" Suddenly we are both sobbing helplessly in each other's arms, devastated by this tragedy that is overtaking us.

When my tears finally subside, I find myself beached on a strange shore, where nothing makes sense anymore.

"Jane is innocent," I declare. "She *cannot* die for that."

"The Queen knows that," my lady says, dabbing her eyes. She is now recovering her composure and striving to be the controlled, practical mother I have always known.

"Her Majesty has capitulated, for her councillors will not hear of her exercising clemency in the wake of the rebellion," she says, bitter. "She has signed the death warrants. She said the least she could do was to break the news to me face-to-face. She wept, and assured me that this is the last course she ever wanted to take, but that she has no choice. But she has promised to do all she can to bring about a reprieve. Tomorrow she is sending the Abbot of Westminster to the Tower, to persuade Jane to convert to the Catholic faith. If she consents, her life will be spared."

I remember the staunchness of my sister's faith, her scathing comments about the Pope and his cardinals, her contempt for those who compromise their religion for worldly considerations. Dear God, let her not be so dogmatic now!

"Oh, my lady, do you think she will?"

"I pray for it. But she was ever a froward, difficult girl. I just pray that God guides her to make the right decision."

God has indeed so guided her: but it was the right decision for Jane, not for the rest of us. That she—a young woman of seventeen, young and comely, and with her life ahead of her and so much to live for— could willingly embrace death for the sake of the finer points of a creed is to me beyond comprehension. Does she care at all about us, her loved ones, who are suffering the tortures of the damned on her account? One word, one little word—and her life would be given back to her. Why can she not say it? Why?

A letter from Jane arrives. It is the first I have had from her since those short days of her reign—a lifetime ago now, it seems—and it will probably be the last. I seize it, hoping to read that she has changed her mind; but instead, she reminds me sternly that the New Testament is worth more than precious stones and will win me more than our woeful father's lands, which we will surely lose when he is attainted for treason. She speaks of our being God's elect, and set on the path of righteousness, even to the point of martyrdom. I am in misery, knowing she will die thinking me perfect in the new religion, when in fact I have betrayed it—and the ideals in which she firmly believes, and for which she is prepared to pay the ultimate price.

Reading on, I realize that she is already gone from us.

Live to die. Trust not that the tenderness of your age shall lengthen your life, for, as soon as God will, go the young and the old. Labor always and learn to die. Deny the world, deny the devil, and despise the flesh. Take up your Cross. As touching my death, rejoice, as I do, that I shall be delivered from corruption and put on incorruption. Farewell, dear sister. Put your only trust in God, who only must uphold you.

   Your loving sister, Jane Dudley

The letter falls to the floor. I see two little girls, dabbling their feet in the stream that runs through the gardens at Bradgate, playing hide-

and-seek amid the oak trees in Charnwood Forest, practicing their dance steps, and huddling together in the face of parental wrath. I see Jane as she was when I last saw her, slender and earnest, her red hair long and luxuriant, her skin creamy, apart from the freckles that have been the bane of her life. *Her life,* which will soon be at an end, when the living, breathing entity that is Jane Grey, with all its hopes, fears, beliefs, and everything that matters to it, will be no more.

I remember I should be attending on the Queen. I am late. I look in the mirror to make sure I am tidy. I hardly recognize myself, I look so wasted. My eyes are ravaged with crying, my face drawn, my hair dull and lifeless under my hood. I smooth it ineffectually and splash water from the basin onto my face, then try to rearrange my features into some semblance of composure.

When I enter the Queen's chamber, she is alone save for an elderly priest.

"Lady Katherine, this is Abbot Feckenham," she tells me. "I have brought him here because he has been with your sister. I pray he can give you some comfort."

I find myself looking into the kindliest pair of eyes I have ever seen.

"How is my sister, Father Abbot?" I ask.

"Firm in her resolve and her faith, I regret to say." The old man looks deeply saddened. "I did all I could to turn her mind, but she would not deny her God. Certainly He is a tower of strength to her. She declared she would not suffer me to tempt her beyond her power, yet when put to the test, she stood staunchly by her faith. Her steadfastness is an example to us all, even if it is misguided."

"*She* does not believe that," I say. The Queen glances at me sharply.

"No," the abbot agrees, his thin voice hoarse with emotion. "She said it was not her desire to prolong her days, and that she does not despise death and willingly undergoes it since it is the Queen's pleasure." He pauses, and gazes on me with boundless compassion. "She told me these times have been so odious to her that she longs for nothing so much as death."

The Queen looks so anguished, I can find it in me to feel sorry for her. "Katherine," she says without ceremony, "there is something I must explain to you." Her eyes are troubled as she takes my hands in hers most kindly; it is as if we are no longer Queen and subject, but two women bound by tragedy.

"I do not seek your sister's death," she says, her eyes filling with tears. "I am constrained to it by my council and by Spain. They will not let King Philip marry me until the land has been purged of traitors. I know full well that Jane is no true traitor, but nevertheless she accepted the crown that was rightfully mine, and the late rebellion, which was partly led by your father, was raised in her name. It nearly cost me my throne, as my councillors constantly remind me. I have no choice! But I want you to know that I have done everything in my power to save your sister."

She squeezes my hands and swallows nervously. "I sent my beloved Abbot Feckenham to Jane to persuade her to convert to the true faith. I have arranged to have her examined tomorrow by a panel of matrons, to determine if she is with child, when, again, I could spare her life. But that, I fear, is a vain hope. She and Lord Guilford have not been alone together for months. So I have no choice, God help me! But I tell you now, Katherine, that her death is something I shall regret to the end of my days. She is my flesh and blood too—and she is so young."

I turn away, forgetting the courtesy due to my sovereign. I feel as if a torrent is building up within me, that I might scream and cry and never cease. But I struggle to control myself.

"Madam . . ." I falter. Until now I have not dared to ask this question. "When—When is it to be?"

"Tomorrow morning," the Queen says. Her cheeks are wet. "Your lady mother knows."

"I have promised your sister I will attend her to the scaffold," Abbot Feckenham says. "It is the least I can do for her, and she wants me there, even though she fears we will never meet in Heaven."

This is all too much for me. Forgetting that I am in the presence of my sovereign, I collapse into the abbot's arms, howling my heart out.

"I will be there, child, never fear," he soothes. "I will be with her to the very end."

KATE

September 1483, York

York had been a triumph, but it had worn the little prince out. Everyone agreed that the healthy air of Middleham, to which he was used, was the best thing for him.

Kate had a lump in her throat as she stood with her stepmother, waving him off. She knew how keenly Anne felt the parting, but there was more to it than that. The duchess always looked pale and tired these days, and she had developed a slight but persistent cough. Kate feared for her.

She was sadly aware too that since Anne had cast doubts on the King's claim to the throne, the old familiar closeness between stepmother and stepdaughter had diminished. Kate still loved Anne, and deeply respected her, but she was aware that Anne had distanced herself from Richard, and that relations between them were becoming increasingly strained. She knew that the Queen was thinking of taking up permanent residence at Middleham, as far as that fitted in with her state duties. That would mean that she, Kate, would have to live there too, for an unwed girl could not remain in a court of men.

She fretted constantly about the prospect of being parted indefinitely from John. If only they could be married! That would be the ideal solution. She must make it happen! Driven by the need for action, she confided in Mattie. Not that Mattie could be of much help, but at least she was willing to listen, and when it came to affairs of love, she showed herself to be Kate's champion.

"My life would be empty without John," Kate declared. "I cannot bear the thought of being so far away from him. I will *make* my father the King consent to our marriage. I will warn him about the earl's possible betrothal, and beg him to speak to the Duke of Suffolk. But first, I *must* see my dear lord."

In the end they agreed that Mattie would take a sealed message to John to tell him that Kate needed to meet with him urgently.

"What did he say?" Kate asked eagerly when Mattie returned later that day.

"Nothing. He wasn't there. I left the note with his valet."

Kate hoped that the valet was discreet.

"Don't look so worried, my lady," Mattie reassured her. "He thinks 'tis me in whom my lord earl has an interest—I gave him to believe that."

Kate watched the hourglass marking the passage of time. She prayed that John would send word to her, or even contrive to seek her out himself. The waiting was pure torture.

He came at ten o'clock, cloaked and hooded, so that none would have recognized him. As Mattie closed the door on them, he held Kate strongly and tightly, and kissed her passionately. With that, the world receded and she was lost.

It seemed the most natural thing to lie down together on her bed, with the curtains drawn, and to kiss and caress each other with increasing ardor. It seemed so right for John to stroke her breasts through the thick velvet of her bodice, and to press his searching lips to the inviting cleft that disappeared into the neckline of her gown. When he ran his fingers over her hips and thighs, she made no protest. Nothing else mattered except the dizzying sensations that were consuming her and banishing all reason. And indeed, she would have let him do more, save for the fact that John himself, breathless and tousled, drew back, forcing himself away from her and grimacing as if he were actually in pain.

"No, my darling, we must not! I honor you too greatly," he breathed in her ear. For answer, she clung to him more tightly until he groaned and pried her eager fingers away.

"Let be, sweetheart," he cried, "or I will not be able to trust myself. Oh, my Kate, my sweet lady, I do worship you! It has seemed an eternity being apart from you."

She was so rapt in wonder that she could not speak. He smiled down at her.

"We must be married!" he declared. "I will speak to my father and make my position plain, and then I shall go to the King—if you will have me, of course." He looked at her pleadingly.

"Did you need to ask?" she teased him. "Of course I will have you. And please speak to my father soon, or I might be banished to Middleham."

"That I will not allow." John stood up, straightening his clothes. "I will see my father in the morning." Then, with a radiant smile, he executed a courteous bow and left her sitting on the bed, unable to believe how easy it had been.

KATHERINE

1554–55, the Court

In this bitter spring that has followed hard upon the tragedies, the world seems dead to me, and the budding blooms and glorious flowering of Dame Nature are no more than cruel mockery. My soul is consumed by loss: husband, sister, father, all taken brutally from me. There can be nothing good for me in this life now, and I sometimes wish that the grave would swallow me too.

My dreams are of blood-spattered axes and the mutilated corpses of the beloved dead, or of Harry and me in those brief, bittersweet weeks we had together; Harry, my love, who is gone from me as surely as if Death had done his work upon him too. How dare the flowers open out their beauty to the heavens; how dare the lambs gambol in the fields; how dare the gentle warmth of the breeze caress my face like a lover, when all is lost to me?

The Queen has been uncommonly kind to me, my mother, and my poor sister Mary. She has done everything she can to support my lady in her grief, and has even restored to her some of the lands and manors confiscated by the Act of Attainder that condemned my father. Of course, there is between the Queen's Grace and my lady a wary courtesy, for how could it be otherwise, when the one has sent the other's husband and child to their deaths?

Her Majesty's bounty has extended to me too, for she has bestowed on me the most generous pension of eighty pounds a year, which has made me financially independent. And, because my mother is much preoccupied with settling her own affairs, and consumed with sorrow as well, the Queen has charged her loyal friend, the Duchess of Somerset, to keep a watchful eye over Mary and me. Her Majesty, seeing the poor, downcast case in which we languish, has judged it neither fair nor fitting to keep us with her at court. For my part, I can no longer abide the poisonous atmosphere of that hateful place, where all has turned to tragedy and others rejoice in the fall of my house. And so I and my sister Mary go to lodge with the Duchess of Somerset's family at Shelford Priory, near Nottingham. I go willingly, thankfully.

The duchess, who was born Anne Stanhope, is the widow of Edward Seymour, the late Lord Protector, who was brother to Queen Jane. Her Grace is a strident woman, a high-nosed snob with the pride of Lucifer, and ceaselessly ambitious for her children, of whom she has nine yet living. Still, she is a kindly guardian, and content to leave Mary and me to our own devices, so long as we do not disturb her peace. The duchess herself was a prisoner in the Tower for two years following her husband's execution, and was liberated only last year by Queen Mary, so she relishes her freedom, and cannot bear any constraint upon it.

Summer comes with heartening news: my mother is appointed Lady of the Privy Chamber to the Queen, and soon afterward Mary and I are commanded to put off our mourning and join her there, to serve Her Majesty once more. I go reluctantly. I am still grieving for Jane, still yearning for Harry, still mourning my lost hopes of a crown. The way I am feeling, it matters not where I am or what I do. I struggle to perform my duties, but my mother tells me it will do me good to concentrate on something other than my grief, so I do my best to give satisfaction to the Queen, hard though it is for me.

The Lady Elizabeth is in the Tower. It is a great scandal. The talk is that she was secretly involved in Wyatt's rebellion, and will shortly be accused of treason and sent to the block, going the way of her mother. That rouses me a little, but I am in no mood to gloat over an enemy brought low: I can only feel for her. Yet the investigation drags on and on, and still the council does not proceed against Elizabeth. Next we hear, she has left the Tower and been moved under house arrest to Woodstock, where the Queen—who has no love for her sister these days—means to keep her out of mischief.

Gradually, as I reaccustom myself to the routine of Her Majesty's daily round and my duties, I begin to take pleasure in small things once more. My dogs, for example—they have been my one comfort through all this. And there are others. Sometimes, when there are festivities at court, we are allowed to leave off our regulation black or tawny gowns and borrow finery from Her Majesty's own wardrobe. It is while trying on a selection of elegant beaded or beribboned dresses with some giggling maids of honor that I learn to smile again, and begin once more to enjoy the camaraderie that exists in the privy chamber and the maidens' dorter: the merriment, the music, the sweetmeats, and the endless games of cards and dice.

In July, feeling in slightly better spirits, I am present with my mother and sister in Winchester Cathedral when Queen Mary marries Philip of Spain amid magnificent celebrations. I watch Her Majesty vow herself, enraptured, to the fair but cold-eyed prince, and observe them together at the great feast in Wolvesey Palace that follows. She looks ecstatic, he reserved and correct, and plainly disdainful of English customs. I notice his eye alight with interest on statuesque Magdalen Dacre, one of Her Majesty's ladies, and then flicker away again, with fleeting distaste, to his royal wife. I feel sorry for my mistress, for she has expected so much from this marriage. But she sits there in her purple cloth-of-gold gown, a look of bliss on her face, seemingly unaware of anything amiss.

I see Harry among the laughing, jesting guests, and want to weep because he does not seem to notice me. I've heard he has been appointed to serve the new King. He is on his way up, I think bitterly, unhampered by an unsuitable marriage. I could even feel envy for Queen Mary, but when I look at that stiff young man who is now her husband, I wonder how he will deal with his aging wife's innocent devotion. And when, later, I hear the cruel gossip about the wedding night, I can feel only indignation on behalf of my kind mistress.

———

My true restoration to life and happiness is down to Lady Jane Seymour, the Duchess of Somerset's daughter. Jane and her sister Margaret are both maids of honor to Queen Mary, and I first met them when I joined the Queen's household. The elder, Margaret, is haughty like her mother, and I could never take to her; but Jane is a fair, ethereal-looking, and merry maiden of thirteen, a year younger than I. After ten minutes in her company, I felt I had known her all my life. She is gentle and warm with me, and enfolds my poor lost soul in kindness. Before long, I realize I have made a true friend.

Soon, I find myself spending most of my free time with Jane Seymour. She is one of only two unmarried daughters left in her family, and disgruntled because of it. She fears she will never escape her mother's clutches, for she is delicate in frame and in health, and deemed too frail for the duties of matrimony. And yet matrimony is all that she thinks of.

"Ah, but I do dream that one day some great lord will ask for me and persuade my mother to give her consent," she sighs, as we kneel in our nightgowns, gossiping on her bed. "In truth, I long to bed with a man!" And she collapses into giggles. I am touched that she deems me worthy of her trust and friendship, and glad to have someone to confide in, although there are some things of which it is painful to speak.

"It is my constant desire to be reunited with my husband," I confess haltingly.

"I'm sure the Queen will permit it, in time," says Jane, her smile kind. "Cheer up, do! We shall be very merry now that we are gossips, my good Kate!" Then her face falls. "Forgive me—I did not think. In my pleasure at having you here in the privy chamber, I had forgotten that you have so much to be sad about. How very insensitive of me. Do say you forgive me."

She is irrepressible, like a puppy, and seems mature for her years, for she has been well-educated and has even had her Latin poetry published in Paris—I am much impressed by that. Intrepid Jane must always be the leader, always the one who makes the suggestions. "We shall go riding today!" she tells me, or "We shall practice our dance steps—I will teach you how to do a very stately pavane!" And I, by dint of having been a younger sister always in the shadow of an elder, and not much minding what I do, am content to follow, sadly wishing myself with another Jane in another time. Alas, it can never be, and sometimes the sense of loss is unbearable.

"Do not overtire yourself, Lady Jane," my mother often admonishes. "The duchess would not wish it." But Jane ignores her. She is a strong character and very willful. "I am perfectly *well*," she mutters under her breath, but then she will pant heavily as we climb the endless palace stairs, or sink onto a bench after racing through the gardens. I know not what is wrong with her, and do not like to ask. Apparently she has always been delicate, right from birth. "I was not expected to live," she told me once, "but look at me now!" And she twirled before me, her wide skirts flaring out from her too-thin waist. Then she began coughing. "I'm all right, really I am," she choked.

As the weeks pass, and the dark days of tragedy recede into the distance, and I learn that life goes on and that the human spirit can still find much to enjoy in it, I come to value Jane's friendship. At last there is someone who understands me, for the Seymours too have known tragedy.

Jane is a true daughter of her house. She and her family burn to restore the Seymour family to greatness, and all have big ambitions. Jane speaks often of her eldest brother, Lord Edward, who was once betrothed to my sister Jane. She sounds as ambitious for him as she is for herself. She longs to see their father's titles and honors restored to him.

"It is a pity our families were not allied by marriage," she says. "I would have rejoiced to have you as a sister."

"But we are more than sisters," I tell her. "You are my heart's friend, and it shall ever be so!"

I receive astonishing news. My mother has remarried, at the advanced age of thirty-eight. Many think it quite shocking that she has condescended to wed her Master of Horse, Mr. Stokes, but I suspect he has long been her lover. It has caused a stir, of course, for he is far below her in rank.

But I've always liked Mr. Stokes. Although he's not wealthy, and has debatable dress sense, he's amiable and loyal, and he has ever been kind to me and my sisters, so for these reasons alone I have no objection to the marriage. At least my mother now has someone to comfort her and distract her mind from her terrible losses. (Would that I had the same!) And the Queen, bless her, has received them both at court, confounding the gossips and those who audibly whispered "Traitor!" whenever my mother showed her face. In time the scandal will die down, as all scandals do, and I think Mr. Stokes will prove himself an admirable stepfather.

I am promoted! I am advanced to be Lady of the Bedchamber, and my sister Mary also. That ranks us both among Her Majesty's closest and most trusted attendants. I am with her when she triumphantly announces her pregnancy; when she grows ever heavier with child, and euphoric with anticipation; and, at the eleventh month, when she is finally told, to her grief, that there is to be no babe after all. I see the cold-eyed Spaniard shake his head in exasperation and abandon her to fight his interminable wars. I am there too when the old heresy laws are revived and the burnings of Protestants begin. Shuddering, I hear terrible tales of the heroism of men and women chained to the stake to die a cruel death; and I observe with concern the Queen's increasing fanaticism, and her deafness to those who care how rapidly this persecution is destroying what is left of her popularity.

Like many in this kingdom, I am horrified by the burnings. Sometimes I find it difficult to reconcile the kindly mistress who has been so warm and generous to my family, who loves babies and is godmother to so many, and is loved by all who know her well, with the driven crusader who demands this persecution. Queen Mary insists she does it in hope of saving the souls of heretics by giving them a taste of eternal hellfire. It is a kindness to them, she says. She is sincere in her convictions.

My enemy, the Lady Elizabeth, comes back to court much humbled and subdued after her year's imprisonment in the Tower and at Woodstock. Whether she ever was involved in Wyatt's rebellion, neither I nor anybody else could ever say, and certainly not the Queen's

Council, for she was perhaps shrewd enough to cover her tracks. In the end they could prove nothing against her, and King Philip sued for her to be received once more into favor. It's said she practiced her wiles on the King, and I can well believe it. And so she was reconciled with the Queen, to all appearances, but I know for certain that Mary will never trust her again. Her Majesty has accorded my mother and my cousin, the Countess of Lennox, precedence before her sister, and I can well imagine what the Lady Elizabeth thinks of that!

Elizabeth's prevarication and insincerity cannot but contrast most unfavorably with my new zeal for the old faith, which continues to delight Queen Mary. This is reason enough for Elizabeth to hate me; I know she regards me as a traitor to the new religion. It must gall her to see the Queen showing me favor—me, the Catholic heir.

KATE

October 1483, Lincoln

The court was lodged at Lincoln Castle, on its way south, when there came the shocking news that the Duke of Buckingham had openly repented of supporting King Richard—"the usurper," he had called him—and was rallying under his banner all those with a grievance against their sovereign. There had already been an uprising in Kent, quickly suppressed by the Duke of Norfolk, but Henry Tudor was said to be in league with Buckingham and gathering an invasion fleet in Brittany.

There was no question now of Kate staying with the court. The King was adamant that his wife and family go to Middleham, which was strongly fortified. With Buckingham on the Welsh Marches, and reports that the Wydeville exiles were arming and the South was in ferment, he insisted they would be safer there.

"I myself will travel back to London with the court, to deal with the rebels," he said, his voice harsh. "Just let me get my hands on that traitor Buckingham!"

John, somber-faced, sought Kate out. He was to remain with the King, of course, for his sword might be called upon in the coming conflict.

"My father the duke is immovable as a rock," he said. "He is set on this other betrothal. I told him I'd never consent to it, but he would not listen. Don't look so crestfallen, sweet Kate. All is not lost, believe me. I will never cease to oppose him, and they cannot make me say the words that bind me to another."

For a moment Kate knew despair, and she clung to him, but a quick kiss was all they had time for, since she had to help the Queen's ladies to pack. As she ran back to the royal lodgings, she was oppressed by the thought of the arid weeks of separation from John stretching ahead drearily, endlessly . . . Who knew when they would meet again—and if he would prevail over his father?

The court was tense, waiting for Buckingham to strike, and Kate sensed hostility mounting against her father the King. Every time she espied him, he looked more troubled, his brows permanently furrowed. His face was marked with cares, tense and haunted. She had put it all down to anxiety over Buckingham's treachery, but then she began overhearing the gossip.

That was nothing unusual in a court, but this was different. It was pernicious, damning, and nothing less than treason.

She first became aware of what was being said when, descending some stairs, she overheard two guards talking below.

"Some say those poor princes have died a violent death," a voice said, sounding as if it reveled in the imparting of such terrible news.

"How?" asked another.

"It's the common fame that they were silenced so as to make Old Dick safe on his throne."

"He ordered it, then?"

"That's what people are saying."

Choking back tears, Kate fled back up the stairs, locked herself in her room, and flung herself on the bed, weeping as if she could never stop. But there was worse to come. Later, as she was smoothing down her skirts and washing her heated face, she heard voices in the outer chamber. She recognized them as belonging to two of the Queen's ladies, Alice Skelton and Elizabeth Bapthorpe.

"I despair for those poor innocents," Alice was saying. "And there's many in the court—and the town—that are shedding tears over them. I've even seen grown men crying when their murder is spoken of." Kate had a sudden, disturbing vision of Lord Stanley weeping.

"It's an atrocious crime," Elizabeth replied, "and the King should be brought to account for it."

"If he intended to court popularity on this progress, he should have thought twice before doing away with his nephews," Alice said. "Mark me, we'll see many desert him when Buckingham makes his move."

"The whole world is talking about these rumors," Elizabeth observed, "so you're not going to tell me the King hasn't heard them. And if they're not true, why doesn't he do something to stop the gossip? He must know it can't be doing him any good."

"How would he do that?" Alice wondered. "I'll wager he can't produce those boys alive. Come, let's hasten with this mantle. The Queen is waiting."

"Surely she's heard the rumors too?" said Elizabeth.

"She must have. But she keeps her own counsel. You never know what she is thinking."

"She's a loyal wife."

"Yes, but not a happy one, I think . . ."

Their chatter faded away, and soon Kate realized she was alone. She was hugging herself in her distress, unable to fully assimilate the implications of what she was hearing, and with a hundred questions teeming in her head. What was worse was that, for the first time, she found herself doubting her father, and that felt like the worst kind of treachery.

She felt the need to unburden herself to John. He was close to the King and knew something of state affairs.

He was delighted to see her, and walked with her into the bailey, where they braved a stiff autumn breeze to sit on a low stone wall. Fortunately, the weather had kept most people indoors, so they were alone for a time.

"What is wrong, my darling?" he asked at once, taking her hand.

"I have heard terrible rumors . . ." She could not bring herself to say more. It was as if giving voice to them would make them true.

John's fine features grew serious. "There are many rumors. Buckingham and his friends have seen to that. But I would not give them any credence."

"These rumors are about my father . . . and the princes that are in the Tower."

John was silent for a moment. Then he said, "You must not believe them for a moment. They are wicked lies, put about by Buckingham and his fellow traitors to bring down the King. The princes live yet, I would stake my honor on it. Your noble father is incapable of doing them ill, whatever some may say."

"I pray he will refute these rumors."

"I dare say he will."

"He should show the princes to the people," she persisted.

"Would that be wise?" John wondered. "In the wake of the late conspiracies to free them, the King might have had them moved secretly elsewhere, and it would not do for Buckingham's supporters to find out where."

"I had not thought of that. So you think I should not worry about the rumors?"

"No, my sweet Kate, you should not." And he leaned forward and kissed her lips. "I will miss you desperately when you are gone," he murmured. Feeling much happier, Kate forgot who might be watching, and for a few moments they were oblivious to anything but each other, until the approach of distant voices made them spring apart, giggling.

"It does my heart good to see you smiling again, my fair maiden," John said.

"You have given me reason to smile," Kate told him. "You have banished my doubts and fears."

Only rarely did the King have time to dine privately with his family these days, and even though his wife and children were to depart on the morrow, and this would be their last night together for some time, he insisted on their joining him at the high table in Lincoln Castle's

great hall, with its timbered roof, tiled floor, high windows orna-
mented with stone lions, and brightly painted armorial cloth hanging
behind the dais. The entire court rose as the royal party entered, then
after grace there was a scraping of stools and benches as everyone was
seated. Kate was next to the Queen, and after the servitors had presented napkins, manchet bread, and ewers of fine wine, she soon realized that this was to be no convivial farewell dinner, for her father
could speak of nothing else but Buckingham's treachery.

"There's much more to this treason than I at first thought," he said,
his face haggard. "That traitor is uniting the malcontents, and he
means business. I have no doubt that Lady Stanley and her friends have
their fingers in the pie, aiming to further the ambitions of Henry
Tudor. And my spies tell me that the Wydevilles are up to their necks
in this. They say Buckingham would be another Kingmaker, like Warwick."

Anne frowned. "This beggars belief," she said. "Buckingham put
everything into making you King, and now he is working against you.
I am at a loss to understand it."

"He misliked the deaths of Hastings, Rivers, and Grey," the King
said, "and he was not satisfied with his rewards. He is the kind of man
who always wants more."

"And Henry Tudor can give it to him?" Anne sniffed.

"If Buckingham believes that, he's a fool."

"What will you do about Buckingham, sire?" Kate asked.

"Raise an army and march against him and his allies. Thanks to
Norfolk, I have learned of this rebellion in good time to deal with it.
There are many measures in place already, thanks be to God. And two
can play at character assassination." He smiled waspishly. So he *had*
heard the rumors, and was ready to counteract them. That was just
what Kate wanted to hear.

"We will break the duke, one way or another!" Richard declared,
his mouth set in a grim line.

Part Three

Knots of Secret Might

KATHERINE

Last year, Her Majesty, God comfort her, suffered yet another false pregnancy. Her grief was terrible to witness, but what was even worse was the anguished outburst that followed when King Philip let it be known that he was leaving England. When our poor mistress went to wave him off at Greenwich, she was in a state of near collapse, and nothing anyone could say or do could cheer her. And when the disgraceful news came that Calais, England's last possession in France, had been lost in Philip's useless wars, she became weak and ill, and retired into virtual seclusion.

Jane Seymour, never robust, has been unwell too, with an evil cough. Thanks to the concern of our good Queen, she is to leave court to rest at her mother's house at Hanworth, near Hounslow, and I have been given permission to accompany her. My mother, who is herself not in the best of health these days, and spends much of her time at Sheen, will come with us, and is gladdened to be visiting her old gossip, the Duchess of Somerset; it will make a pleasant change for her.

"Go with my blessing," Queen Mary says, her face dull with melancholy. "It will be good for you to get away into the country. My court is no place for bright young girls like you. I pray that the Lady Jane will soon be much restored. Give her our good wishes."

I suspect that Jane is in a worse case than she would have us believe, yet her natural high spirits are not so easily suppressed. Riding beside her litter, I listen to her gay chatter and could believe that she is in high good health; God send it will be so soon.

———

It is at Hanworth that I meet once more the young man who is to be my joy—and my downfall, although I have no inkling of that to begin with, of course. Indeed, I have long thought on him purely as one to whom my sister Jane was once betrothed, and the brother of my friend. He has no place in my thoughts as we ride up the driveway and grooms come hurrying to take the horses, while the Duchess of Somerset's chamberlain descends the porch steps to welcome us all.

The sumptuous palace of Hanworth was recently granted by Her Majesty to my guardian, the Duchess of Somerset. It is a great house, built by King Harry for Anne Boleyn, and looks like an English castle, yet it is adorned with terra-cotta roundels of Italian work chiseled with goddesses of classical mythology. Indoors, it is a feast for the senses, with fine tapestries, gilded furniture, and wonderful paintings of legendary heroes adorning the lofty ceilings of the principal rooms and staircase; and in the great hall, brilliant lights from the stained-glass windows reflect in myriad colors of sunlight on the marble floor. Everywhere there is the sweet scent of fresh rushes and dried flowers.

Jane is embraced and clucked over by her mother the duchess, then carried off by an army of female servants and put to bed. The two dowagers, my mother and the Duchess Anne, well matched in strident character and choleric temperament, enjoy a lively reunion, which turns into an exhausting round of condolences, backbiting, and competitive reminiscing. I escape into the fresh air.

The sadnesses and strains of the past months seem distant in this beautiful place, with its exquisite formal gardens, its broad green vistas across the hunting park, and the hot sun sparkling in the waters of the moat that encloses the imposing Renaissance house. But now, walking along an avenue lined with yew trees, I see an even more captivating vision.

Striding toward me is a slender young man of middle height with a hound bounding along by his side. The man is dark-haired, and better looking than I have ever realized, with an angular face, a strong aquiline nose, deep-set eyes, and a firm jaw, and he is wearing hunting clothes of good-quality cloth. His face is, of course, familiar: I have seen him often at court, and he used to visit my father's house when my sister Jane was alive. This is the duchess's eldest son, Lord Edward

Seymour, he who was once betrothed to poor Jane. How different her life and mine would have been had she married him. She would be living today.

"Ho, sirrah!" Lord Edward cries to his hound, as we draw nigh, and the ungainly beast comes reluctantly to heel before it can bother my little lapdogs. The young lord's beautiful heavy-lidded eyes—a startling blue against his dark hair—twinkle at me as he makes a brief bow.

"To which fair lady do I have the pleasure of addressing myself?" He smiles, his voice seductive and melodious. I had thought Harry handsome, but the effect that this vision of robust masculinity is having upon me is startling.

"Do you not remember who I am?" I ask him, a little teasing.

"Yes, of course. You are the Lady Katherine. I remember you well. My mother told me you had arrived when I came down from London today, and I was hoping to see you. You have fine weather for your visit."

His eyes are saying far more than his lips. I read in them admiration and undisguised interest.

"It is a pleasure to see you again, my lord," I say formally.

"A pleasure for me too, indeed," he responds, his smile as dazzling as the sunlight. "Shall we take a turn around the gardens? If you are not too warm, that is."

I assent readily, and as we traverse the neat graveled paths, his dog bounding joyously around us on the leash, and my silky darlings nestling in my arms, we make the kind of conversation expected in polite circles. Later, Lord Edward escorts me back to the house to visit his sister. We find Jane fully dressed and much amended.

"I am joining you all for supper this evening!" she informs us. "Just try and stop me!"

A week has passed since then, and Jane is almost her old self again. We have fallen to our usual laughing and giggling, and she takes great pleasure in showing me over the house and its many nooks and crannies.

Edward—or Ned, as Jane calls him—is displaying more than a brotherly interest in me. There comes a hot August day when, walking to the gardens with my dogs and my lute, I see someone ahead, waiting for me. It is Ned, standing there in a fine lawn shirt and slashed and padded buff-colored breeches, holding his bow and arrows; he has been practicing at the butts. His shirt is open at the neck, and the sight of a faint dusting of black hairs and the sheen of sweat on his tanned chest excites me. It is years now since I stopped mourning the loss of Harry, stopped longing for him and wanting him. I have learned perforce to live a chaste life, troubled only by naughty dreams that leave me restless and unfulfilled. But of late it has been Ned who has started to feature in those dreams.

"Shall we walk down to the lake?" he asks, offering me his arm. We converse lightly of songs we both know, and mutual acquaintances, but there is something more subtle going on as well. Amid the mulberry trees, the heady scent of the rosebushes, and the beds bright with gillyflowers drowsing in the golden afternoon sun, we manage to convey, by smiles that promise much, the touch of our hands as he guides me down a pretty flight of marble steps, and the language of our eyes, that we like each other very much.

Seated on a stone bench by the rippling, sparkling water, we tell each other our life stories. Ned already knows something of mine, and I am touched by his sensitivity in skirting over the tragedies that have blighted my family. He says nothing of his broken betrothal to Jane, or what came after. But he does ask about my marriage.

"You were wed to Lord Herbert," he says. It is a statement, not a question.

"Yes," I say, remembering Harry's sweet smile and the curly hair through which I once loved to run my eager fingers, and marveling yet again that conjuring up these images no longer causes me a pang, even though they are reminders of what is missing from my life. "But our marriage was dissolved."

"So I heard. Did you love him?"

The question is unexpected; but I am aware that it matters to Ned.

"Yes, very much," I say. "But that was a long time ago." Even now, I feel disloyal saying those words.

Ned looks at me with compassion. "That must have been a terrible time for you," he says gently.

"It was. I had lost my sister and my father, and then I lost the husband I loved. I was thirteen, and did not know how to cope. Truly, I thought I might drown in grief." Suddenly tears are welling in my eyes, and I bend my head so that he shall not see.

Ned's hand—tanned and lean-fingered, with delicate dark hairs— closes over mine.

"I understand perfectly," he answers, his own voice a little unsteady. "My father died on the block. It's not just losing them that grieves you, but the manner of their deaths, and I still have nightmares about that."

"I too," I chime in with feeling, turning my hand to clasp his, as I perceive the pain in his eyes.

"It's the loss of family standing that follows," he goes on. "Feeling as if you are somehow unclean because your father was branded a traitor. Being shunned by the court and society, as if you too are tainted with the same dishonor. My family had ascended to greatness by the time I was born. I was tutored with King Edward himself, and considered noble enough to marry your sister, a princess with royal blood. When my father was attainted by Parliament, they passed an Act, prompted by pure malice, to limit my inheritance. I was restored in blood only when Queen Mary came to the throne, and even then I was barred from bearing my father's titles."

"I was a wife but no wife," I add bitterly. "I was kept from the husband I loved. I paid a heavy price for the crimes of others."

Ned stands up. "We should not be so mournful, Katherine. Come! Let me show you something cheerful." He pulls me to my feet and leads me back through the trees to a pretty knot garden enclosed by fragrant hedges of lavender, hyssop, marjoram, and thyme.

"Isn't it a little paradise?" he asks as we stroll arm in arm between the beds of marigolds and violets, as naturally as if we had known each other all our lives. "It is my favorite place on earth. I spend a lot of time here." We stop to admire the riot of glorious colors and sniff the fragrant scents of Dame Nature at her most bountiful. Our dogs—they are friends now—gambol in the sun.

"Forgive me if I have said too much," I say, feeling as if I have overstepped all kinds of bounds. "It's just that we share a sad history, and you understand how I feel, and have been so kind to listen."

"And will be kinder still, if I am let," Ned murmurs, his beautiful eyes holding mine. He stoops, plucks a marigold, and presents it to me with a courtly bow. His gaze becomes more intent.

"You are so very beautiful," he breathes. "You looked to me like a heavenly vision coming toward me along the yew walk that day. They told me you had grown into a charming young lady, and they did not lie. But you are so much more than that, my dear Katherine—if I may . . ."

My heart has begun to beat very fast. I want him—not in the desperate and naïve way I wanted Harry, but as an older and wiser young woman who knows that this man is the one. And so it seems the most natural thing in the world to go into his arms in the healing peace of his magical garden.

It seems that our idyll will last forever. My sweet Ned cannot do enough for me. Safe and happy at last in this beautiful place, and far from the court with its tainted air, I find that I can love again. In Ned's arms, I am healed.

Thrown together by circumstance, we snatch every opportunity to enjoy our freedom. With Jane often in tow, we spend long hours riding around the estate and the deer park where once King Harry hunted buck and hare with Anne Boleyn. We wander laughing through the orchard and along the hedgerows, filling our baskets with ripe fruit or cramming it in our mouths, giggling as the juice runs down our chins. We visit the aviary and try to teach the birds to talk. We throw stones in the moat, seeing who can make the biggest splash. We are young and silly, yet it matters not. The only people we have to please are ourselves.

We might be running wild, Ned and I, but we are well behaved, tempted though we might be to be otherwise. We frolic shrieking in *our* garden, as it has become, or in the long grass, Ned tickling me and I fighting him off, yet we cannot ignore the needs of our bodies, and tickling often turns to cuddling and kissing. Such sweet caresses we share as we lie together under God's great blue Heaven! Whenever we are alone, which we contrive often, we slowly savor the delights of fingertips on skin, tongue on tongue, cheek on cheek, and Ned's urgent hands wandering adventurously over my bodice and skirts. As we cling to each other, I can feel his hardness against me, even through the stiff material of his codpiece and my petticoats. Yet that is as far as it goes. Always one or both of us will pull back; for it seems that our spacious days at Hanworth must go on forever, and that we have all the leisure in the world to enjoy each other.

There are, of course, other reasons for our caution. I am reluctant to abuse the hospitality and kindness of Ned's mother, knowing it would reflect badly on her, my good guardian, if I was discovered to have fallen from virtue under her roof. And Ned respects me too much to tumble me like a lewd dairymaid, even though he is mad for me.

Jane encourages us. I have seen her watching me approvingly as I frolic with her brother. And one day, as we are out walking, and he is striding ahead with his bow, she sidles up to me and whispers, "Ned has asked me to break with you the subject of marriage."

I stare at her. It would suit her ambition—and that of her mother—to have him marry one who is close in blood to the throne, for the Seymours have had a taste of royalty and are hungry for more. And yet I cannot suspect her of mere calculation, for her warmth toward me is unquestionably genuine, as is her love for her brother. Were he to wed one in whom ambition and affection were combined, she—who lives through him, forbidden her own marriage—would be the happiest lady alive. Apart from me, that is!

"Well," I say, "I would he would break it himself."

"I *told* him that it was not the office of a sister to play Cupid!" She giggles. "But you would not be averse?"

"I will think on it," I say, and race ahead to catch up with Ned.

There comes a day of glorious weather when Jane is picking blackberries some way off, and Ned and I are sitting at the edge of the lake, with our dogs lazing beside us. I marvel once again how far I am removed from the sad girl I was four years ago. That girl was miserable and defeated, thinking there was nothing left for her in life. But not now. Oh, not now! This girl is in love.

My bare feet are splashing in the water, my skirts pulled up over my knees, exposing my sun-browned legs. Ned has his fishing rod, but has not caught anything yet.

"Katherine," he says, "I must return to court soon."

I am shocked. This idyll cannot be allowed to end, nor the world to intrude upon it. "For long?" I ask plaintively.

"I must take my rightful place there," he replies, not looking at me. "This summer has been the best of my life, but I cannot remain here in idleness when there are honors to be won."

"I would you did not have to go," I whisper.

"I must make my way in the world, Katherine," he tells me. "And maybe I have more need now to store up treasure for the future." He looks at me meaningfully, and I realize what he means. "When I go to court, sweetheart, I want to take with me your promise that you will become my wife."

I can see the longing burning in his eyes. How could I ever resist him? He is my Adonis, and so fine and comely in every way. To be his wife will be a foretaste of Paradise; indeed, who would need Paradise, having the love of such a one on Earth?

I cannot speak. Ned takes my hand and raises it to his lips. "Say you will, Katherine!" he urges.

All other considerations fly away on the summer breeze: the Queen's wishes, my mother's, my royal status, the succession . . .

"How could I not?" I whisper, and then I am in his arms, lying on my back on the lush grass, his mouth devouring mine with kisses. He is perfection, I think, melting with happiness, as I clasp him ever tighter and surrender to the pleasure of being close to him. And there the duchess finds us, as she strides across the park with her dogs.

She does not berate us, or beat us with her cane, as I fear for a moment she will, as we scramble to our feet and stand there flushed, aware of our disheveled state. Instead she bids us put on our shoes and follow her back to the house immediately, then goes striding ahead.

"Fear not, sweetheart," Ned says. "We have done no wrong. We will be married, I swear it. My mother will agree, I have no doubt, and when I get to court, I will obtain the Queen's permission. Be strong! All will be well, you'll see."

———

We stand before the duchess in the great hall. She sits regal in her high-backed chair, like a queen sitting in judgment, with a keen-eyed Jane standing behind her—and she comes to the point straightaway.

"Tell me, Ned, what are your intentions toward Katherine?"

"I love her, my lady," he tells her, taking my hand, and I thrill to hear the pride in his voice. "We have reached an understanding. We wish to marry, when it shall please you and the Queen."

"So, my son would have another Grey bride. It might please me, but it may not please Her Majesty," the duchess says. "You might be wise to forget all about it." I tremble at that, yet I sense she would be delighted if this marriage came to pass.

"You know that you risk angering the Queen by this entanglement? And that she might be angry that it has gone so far without her sanction? She has no child of her body to succeed her, and many look to Katherine as her heir. But Katherine is a Catholic, and Mary is unlikely to countenance her marrying a Protestant, for a wife must be subject to her husband, and the Queen's chief concern is to preserve the Catholic faith in England. So it is not a good time to be thinking of marriage. The answer would be no, however kindly Her Majesty might look on both of you."

"I will wait for as long as I must to make Katherine my wife," Ned vows, and turns to me. "It will be worth it, my lady, will it not?"

"I would wait forever for you, my lord," I declare.

Soon, it seems that we might indeed wait forever. Ned goes off to court, leaving me to mope at Hanworth without him, driving poor Jane crazy with my need to speak ceaselessly of my beloved—although mostly she encourages it. The days turn into weeks, and still I languish bereft, surviving from letter to letter. I have those letters under my pillow; they are creased from constant reading and the kisses I cover them with. Ned writes so lovingly, so ardently; I can hear his voice murmuring the tender words.

There is no point in remaining in the country anymore. I cannot bear being at Hanworth without Ned. Jane is better, and we have prolonged our excuses for too long. And so we return to court. Here, Ned and I see each other only infrequently, for neither of us wants to be thought in any way disloyal to Queen Mary. We have to be content with furtive embraces snatched in secluded corners. And, more often than not, someone is coming.

KATE

November 1483; Middleham Castle, Yorkshire

It was a hard winter, and the wind whistled around Middleham like a vengeful boggart, but that was the least of their troubles. Daily, the Queen and Kate looked for news from the South. It was frustrating, and frightening, being immured here in Yorkshire, not knowing what was happening.

There had been messengers, riding lathered and weary up to the castle from time to time. They brought news that Henry Tudor's fleet had sailed but was driven back toward Brittany by a great storm. On that day, Kate had gone to the chapel with Queen Anne and her brothers, and they all thanked God on their knees for His mercy and grace.

Next they heard, the King had proclaimed Buckingham a traitor and a rebel, but that had not deterred the treacherous duke from raising his standard and marching south toward the River Severn, clearly aiming to meet up with other traitors in the West and South. But the King had put a price of a thousand pounds on his head now, and advanced from Leicester at the head of a great army.

Kate was desperate to know what was happening, but Anne had withdrawn into herself. The cold weather, the constant damp, and the drafts had made her cough worse, and she looked pale and weary. She was at her happiest when helping Edward with his lessons or telling him stories by the fire. Then she became much more animated. But at other times, she would not discuss the present situation. True daughter of the Kingmaker that she was, she said she would face with courage whatever came. But her anxiety was graven in new lines on her pale face for all to see.

For ten days, gales swept vengefully over the troubled kingdom, then the weather settled and a wintry sun came out, bringing in its wake another messenger sporting the white boar badge. There had been no battle, he said; there was no need for one. The gales had done the King's work for him. Buckingham's men had deserted, and the duke had sought refuge in the Forest of Dean, where one of his tenants betrayed him. After that his rebellion collapsed.

"He was taken to the King at Salisbury, madam," the messenger told the Queen. "Henry Tudor had again attempted a landing at Plymouth, but once he heard of Buckingham's capture he fled back to Brittany as fast as he could."

"And Buckingham?" Anne asked.

"The King came to Salisbury with his army, and the duke was tried and sentenced to death. He begged an audience with King Richard, but it was denied him, for there were fears that he might try to assassinate His Grace. Then the duke suffered execution in the marketplace."

Anne and Kate crossed themselves.

"God be praised that the King my lord is safe," Anne said. "Are any other traitors to be put to death?"

"Six, I believe, madam," the messenger answered. "But the word is that many will be attainted when Parliament meets after Christmas. Madam, the King requests that you now repair to London with the Lord John and the Lady Katherine."

Anne was quiet on the journey south; once more she had torn herself away from Prince Edward, who was to remain in the North as his father's nominal representative. Yet as they passed through the towns and villages of Yorkshire, the Queen put on a brave smile, and nodded and waved graciously to the people who flocked to see her, cheering heartily. But when the little procession moved farther south and approached London, the people came more often to stare sullenly, or to call out against King Richard and ask what had become of the sons of King Edward.

KATHERINE

November 1558–January 1559; Sheen Priory, Westminster,
and Whitehall Palace

The Queen, overburdened by her tragedies, is in a decline, God save her, and has little need of my services now, wanting to be tended only by her oldest and most faithful servants. She has given Mary and me leave, with her blessing, to visit our mother, which is why we are now at Sheen, lodging with my lady and our stepfather, Mr. Stokes.

My mother has always been an indomitable woman, but her health is not good these days, and I grieve to see her strong constitution failing. It is hard to see mortality encroach on one's parent, and to find that the roles are reversing, with her now leaning on me, instead of the other way around. It is against Nature, this tragic reversal, yet I am glad to be a strong arm and support for my lady, for she has softened in these last years—and her life has not been easy.

My lady often likes to reminisce. It is one of the few pleasures left to her, and I indulge her by listening. She invariably harks back to the days of her youth and my grandmother, King Harry's sister. "They called her a paradise, and she was. You have seen her portraits, so you'll know what I mean. You have her sweet nature as well as her pretty face, and I daresay you will break a few hearts in your time."

I have sat here for so long and I can be silent no longer: I have to break it to my lady about Ned and me. Arch-intriguer and ambitious as she has been, her teeth are now drawn, and this time, I know, caution will be her watchword.

"Ho-ho, my girl, what is this?" she cries with her old asperity. "Looking to wed, are ye? You have been previous!" But I can tell she is delighted all the same, for she does not reprove me further for proceeding so far without her sanction. Nor did I fear she would, for she was once content enough to have Ned betrothed to Jane, and she has long been fond of him. Her father was his godfather; and even after

Jane was wed to Guilford, my lady continued to call Ned "son" whenever they met.

"Madam my mother," I urge, "this marriage is so precious to me that I beg it be handled carefully. I would not wish to prejudice a happy outcome. You see, I am in good hope that very soon our cherished dreams will be fulfilled, and in the happiest of ways."

"Wherefore spring these hopes?" my lady presses.

"Ned writes that the Venetian ambassador says openly that when the time comes, I will be able to claim the crown unopposed, for Queen Mary—who distrusts and hates the Lady Elizabeth—favors my succession. My lady, will you help us?"

"Aye, Katherine. I owe it to you, after all that has happened. But now I must rest. We will speak further about this later."

It is a frosty November morning. My lady is still abed—she sleeps in late these days—and Mary and I, warmly cloaked and pink-cheeked, are for the stables to feed titbits to our mares and see them cozily blanketed in their stalls. Beyond the courtyard wall we hear the trundling of carts making their way to the City of London, and the clip-clop of hooves. Then another sound breaks the peace of this early hour—the distant toll of church bells.

I look at Mary. "What's that?"

She claps a hand to her mouth as the chimes ring nearer and louder, and are taken up by other bells nearby; they will have been ringing already across the City and in outlying parishes, and soon they will be tolling out their heavy news throughout the land of England.

My hour, I believe, has come.

We go back into the house and change our clothes, putting on black out of respect for Her Majesty. I kneel with my mother and all our household in the chapel, praying for the repose of the soul of our beloved Queen Mary; and I shed tears for that kind lady. Yet all the while I am bursting inside with excitement and the pressing urge to hasten to court and claim what is rightfully mine. For now I am Queen at last, and all the power and glory that were so quickly and cruelly snatched from Jane are to be mine. And Ned will be mine too! There is no one to forbid it. And Elizabeth, and Pembroke, must bend the knee to me. I cannot wait for my reign to begin.

Yet the decent formalities must be observed, both here at Sheen and at St. James's Palace, where Her Majesty lay at the time of her death. The council must be allowed a space to convene. The events and processes leading to my proclamation will unfold in God's good time. I steel myself to wait patiently for the lords to attend upon me, or for a summons to court.

By midmorning I am in a frenzy of anxiety. Surely I should have been sent for by now? I cannot keep still, but keep pacing up and down my chamber, wringing my hands. I must know what is going on.

In recent weeks I have heard talk that the courtiers were abandoning the dying Queen and making for Hatfield to wait upon the Lady Elizabeth, anticipating that she would soon succeed. Well, they will soon learn that they have miscalculated; and if Elizabeth thinks to profit by their support and deny me my rightful title, she must think again. Yet I will be merciful to all, even her. My reign will begin not with accusations and ill will, but in a blaze of glory and acclaim. And I will find her some good husband to keep her under control.

In the end I can bear the waiting no more. Wrapping myself again in my cloak, I tell my mother I am for St. James's Palace, and order the barge to be made ready for me, summoning my maids and urging the boatmaster to make haste.

When we alight at last at Westminster, I see that huge crowds of people have gathered there. Surely I should have received a summons earlier, or some word from the Privy Council? But maybe they did not know where to find me. I push my way through the press of people, desperate to get to St. James's; and then I espy a herald stepping up on a mounting block and unraveling a scroll of parchment.

Surely it is strange to proclaim a monarch before that monarch has even been informed of her own accession?

"Hear ye, hear ye, good people!" the herald cries. "Elizabeth, by the grace of God Queen of England, France, and Ireland, Defender of the Faith, sends greetings to her beloved subjects and bids me read you Her Majesty's most excellent proclamation."

Elizabeth, by the grace of God? How can this be? It should be I, Katherine, by the grace of God—as Queen Mary intended. This is wrong, all wrong—there has been some grave mistake! Someone should tell the herald!

But no, he is reading from the scroll, crying aloud: "Because it hath pleased Almighty God to call to His mercy out of this mortal life, to our great grief, our dearest sister of noble memory, Mary, late Queen of England—on whose soul God have mercy—and to bestow upon us, as the only right heir by blood and lawful succession, the crown of the kingdom of England, we do, by this our proclamation to all our natural subjects, notify to them that they be discharged of all bonds and duties of subjection toward our sister, and be from this day in nature and law bound only to us as to their only sovereign lady and Queen; promising on our part our love and care toward their preservation, and not doubting on their part but they will observe the duty which belongs to natural, good, and true loving subjects."

There is more, but I do not hear it. The crowd has erupted in such a roar of joy and approbation that the herald's final words are drowned, and all around me there is cheering and praise for Elizabeth, "Great Harry's daughter," as at least one reveler calls her.

"God be praised, that's an end to the burnings!" a fat goodwife next to me cries. "The dread days of Queen Mary are over, and we'll have a world of blessings with good Queen Elizabeth!"

"There'll be bonfires and merrymaking aplenty tonight!" someone else calls. And suddenly, above the deafening hubbub, all the church bells of London are pealing out in celebration, and everywhere around me people are hugging and kissing each other, and even weeping for gladness. I am jostled and pushed by unheeding, ignorant citizens. This is not what Queen Mary intended! Even before she is cold, she is betrayed. How did Elizabeth bring this to pass?

The fat woman turns sharply to me. "If I were you, dearie, I'd get rid of those black weeds and that miserable face. You should be giving thanks for our new Queen."

"I feel a little faint," I lie, desperate to be gone from here.

"Oh, sorry, love, I didn't realize. Do you need a helping hand?"

"No, I'll be all right," I manage to say, and blindly retrace my steps to the waiting barge. It is too late for me: Elizabeth has proved too clever an adversary, and she has the love of the people on her side. And I am not too stupid to realize that, given the rapturous reception that news of her accession has prompted, few are ever likely to support me as a rival for her crown.

Our horses are draped in black caparisons down to the ground. Our mourning clothes are sumptuous but somber, as are my thoughts as I ride in procession behind Queen Mary's hearse toward Westminster Abbey, where she will be laid to her rest, and take part in the lavish obsequies ordered by Queen Elizabeth. Listening to the soaring requiem Mass—a service soon to be outlawed—and sitting beside my sister Mary as the funeral meats are served at the banquet that follows, my heart simmers with resentment.

For already Elizabeth has made plain her dislike—nay, her hatred. Barely had the ink dried on her accession proclamation than she made her position very clear, and suddenly there was a cold draft blowing in my direction from the throne.

Elizabeth is twenty-five and has never married, so has no child to succeed her; and she has already declared that she means to live and die a virgin. Most people at court think it a bluff, or just maidenly modesty asserting itself. They little know her, for she can be as coarse and foulmouthed as any sailor. But the fact remains that she is as yet unwed, with no heir of her body. And therefore she plainly sees me as a rival.

Queen Mary never went so far as to change the Act of Succession in my favor, which is why Elizabeth was indisputably her lawful successor. Under that same Act, I, by law, am still Elizabeth's heir—and thereby a threat.

We both know why Elizabeth does not feel secure on her throne. It is well known that Catholic Europe regards her as a bastard, a heretic, and a usurper, and wants her set aside for a Catholic queen. That in itself is enough to keep her awake at night, but she is extraordinarily sensitive on the subject of her marriage too.

She is disposed to flirt politically with this prince and that, as well as with her courtiers, and in particular Lord Robert Dudley; but she is in no hurry to wed and give up her freedom. "I will have but one mistress here and no master!" she is fond of saying. Nor is she eager to have children. I myself watched her flare up when Mistress Astley, her Chief Lady of the Bedchamber, suggested—as none else has dared—that having a child of her body to succeed her would bring her great joy.

"God's teeth!" Elizabeth cried. "Do you think I could love my own winding-sheet?" And in her eyes, for that one unguarded moment, I could see fear. I suspect the matter goes very deep with her.

Yes, she is reluctant to wed and bear heirs to continue her line, but she must still name a successor, for what would happen if she were to die suddenly? By law, I should succeed Elizabeth, as I am next in blood, but has she acknowledged me? Nay, she would as soon turn Catholic.

It is my right; yet for all my desire to become Queen, I would not intrigue for her throne, on my word of honor, not though many are fawning upon me and paying me flattering addresses. I have seen too much of what happens to traitors.

How do I know she hates me? It has been made plain to me in so many ways. Not being named heir is bad enough, but when Elizabeth added insult to injury, she put me in the most difficult and embarrassing position. Under Queen Mary, despite my youth and inexperience, I was a Lady of the Privy Chamber, later promoted to the bedchamber, and as such one of Her Majesty's most honored and intimate servants, as befit my rank and royal status. And by a further act of that Queen's kindness, my poor misshapen sister Mary was similarly elevated.

But our gracious Queen Elizabeth has now seen fit to deprive us both of that honor. It is humiliating beyond words, and of course I cannot speak of it to anyone at court, but must go about with my head held high, and my pride in the dust. For my sister, it is worse, for people do not now disdain to call her "Crouchback Mary," even to her face.

Of course, Elizabeth cannot banish me from her presence—even *she* has to have some regard for the proprieties—so she has made me one of the ladies of her presence chamber—a lesser honor, one that does not rank me as a princess of the blood, denies me the precedence that is my due, and keeps me at a distance from her.

"Lady of the Presence Chamber, if you please! You are her heir!"

my mother exploded when she heard the news. Yet, shocked as she was, she was the voice of reason, telling me that I must not take it personally. But I did, and I still do. Elizabeth is resolved to eclipse me utterly. I have to put up with catty remarks about my lack of religious principle—which I dare not answer as I would, because she is the Queen—or about my pale, blond looks, which Elizabeth is now pleased to openly compare unfavorably with her own red curls, now done up in the most fantastical styles, and made-up face. Where my skin is fair, hers is sallow, even swarthy, so she sees fit to mask it with a paste made up especially for her, the recipe of which she will confide to barely a soul. Indeed, she likes to pretend she shows to the world her natural complexion!

She has hated me all along. She has dealt me a very public insult—and it hurts, as she fully intended. It has certainly diminished my standing at court. I know what people have been saying: they are not so eager to pay their addresses now, or so nice as to lower their voices when giving their opinion that this demotion means Elizabeth is determined to name someone else in my stead—Mary, Queen of Scots, perhaps—or marry and get a child of her own, although there's no sign of that happening, and privately I doubt it ever will. One reason, of course, is not far to seek, in the person of that son and grandson of traitors, Guilford's brother, Lord Robert Dudley, whom she loves inordinately. Lord Robert, who would be a king, so the gossips say. He has a wife living, so it cannot be, but that does not silence the rumors.

Yet not everyone is as demoralized as I about my prospects. Since returning to court, I have renewed my old friendship with Jane Dormer, who is now being courted by the Spanish ambassador, the Count of Feria. He assures me that his master, King Philip, is ready to put all his weight behind my claim to the succession.

"For your ladyship is the hope of Christendom," the count effuses, "the hope of Catholics everywhere."

This makes me feel slightly guilty. My conversion to the Catholic faith was to a degree a pragmatic one, made when I was very young to please Queen Mary and further my chances of being named her heir. Truly there are aspects of Catholicism that appeal to me—as they appeal, I feel sure, to Queen Elizabeth, who favors the high ritual and ceremonial of her childhood, and insists on keeping jeweled cruci-fixes—which some Protestants regard as graven idols—on the altars in her chapels. Thus, converting was not difficult for me, and outwardly I have practiced the old religion ever since. But inwardly I remain in-clined toward the Protestant beliefs instilled in me by my parents, and recently, now that it is safe to do so, I have been on the brink of recant-ing my Catholicism. But if King Philip, with all the might of Spain behind him, is ready to put pressure on Elizabeth to name me her heir, then I must show his ambassador that I remain staunch in the faith and am the most suitable Catholic claimant.

Playing this role is not as dangerous as it might seem, for the Queen has said she will not make windows into men's souls, and that she will tolerate Catholics so long as they make no trouble for her. She is un-likely to object to my going to Mass and wearing a rosary on my girdle, as long as I draw no overt attention to myself.

"The French are backing the Queen of Scots, of course," the Count of Feria tells me. "She is married to the Dauphin, and her father-in-law King Henri relishes the prospect of England coming under French rule. He has already quartered the arms of England with those of France on her armorial bearings. Thus it is unlikely that your Queen will ever countenance the Scottish Queen's succession, and besides, Mary was not born in England, which I gather is a legal prerequisite for succeeding to the throne."

"And that leaves you, Lady Katherine, as the strongest claimant," Jane Dormer chimes in.

"That has long been my understanding," I say. "But I fear it will be hard to bring Her Majesty to acknowledge me as her successor."

"King Philip will know how to persuade her. He wants to marry her, isn't that so, Gomez?" Jane confides, fluttering a flirtatious glance at the elegant, handsome count.

"He is seriously considering it," the count reveals. "And you will be his security in case she does not bear him a child."

So the rumors are true: as soon as one sister is dead, Philip begins pursuing the other. It has long been whispered at court that Elizabeth worked her wiles on him from the first, and that he was mad for her all the time he was wed to Queen Mary. Now, as ruler of a great and mighty kingdom, he must surely have much influence with her. It may be that the Fates are working in my favor.

There is another who clearly believes my prospects of a throne are high. To my astonishment, my lord of Pembroke appears before me one day, bows his black head, and says he would speak to me in private. I invite him into my lodgings, and send my maids away. Then I seat myself in my gilded chair and keep him standing, savoring the turning of the tables between us. He is come as a supplicant, I do not doubt.

"I am aware that you do not think well of me, Lady Katherine," he begins, his face inscrutable, "but I am sure that you understand the realities of politics. I may tell you that my wife and I were delighted to have you as our daughter-in-law, and deeply sorry when circumstances dictated that your marriage should be declared null."

"I too was very sorry, my lord, when I was cruelly parted from my husband, then deposited at night, and abandoned in the dark, at my father's house," I say. I have wanted to call Pembroke to account for that for more than five years. "My lady mother was shocked."

He looks uncomfortable. He was expecting to treat with the meek little bride he had known, not a young woman conscious of her royal status. "I apologize if my boatmaster was overzealous in interpreting my orders," he says stiffly. "But my lady, I would make it all up to you. That is why I am here. My son Harry remains unwed. I am come to reunite you both. With your consent, you shall be wedded again, and bedded this time. You have my word on it."

I had not expected this. I try to recall the happiness I shared with Harry, and the agony our parting caused me. Then I remember how Harry shunned me afterward, and feel only indignation. And I think of Ned, dear, beloved Ned, and the love that is between us, and feel a sense of irony. Once I would have given all to be reunited with Harry, but now that he can be mine for the taking, I do not want him; while Ned, whom I want as much as life itself, and more than any crown, is all but forbidden me, because the Queen almost certainly would not consent to our marrying. Life is not fair!

Pembroke's dark brows furrow. He sees my hesitation.

"I pray you, Lady Katherine, think on this carefully. Much hangs upon it. The Spanish ambassador approves the match, and he has his finger on the pulse of affairs. Spain may do much for you, you know."

"And you, my lord, have your sights once more on a crown for your son, and a dynasty of Herberts sitting on the throne!" I cannot resist saying.

He bristles. "I do not deny it! What man would not? But this would be to your advantage too, remember."

"The Queen may marry and bear children," I remind him. "That would put paid to my chances of ever succeeding her. And when I am no longer of use to you, will you have my marriage annulled again?"

"I understand your anger," he says, glowering. "Verily, you have every reason to speak thus. But what good can it do us both? This match would be an advantageous one from all points of view."

"And what of Harry? What does he say? He has spent the past five years avoiding me."

"On my orders," Pembroke barks, losing patience a little. "He is a dutiful son and he does my bidding. But I have put this to him and he is eager for the marriage."

"Then I will think on it," I say, knowing what my answer must be.

Under cover of darkness I seek out Ned. Our meetings these days are few and furtive. We dare not be seen too much together, and have taken to sending each other messages through the good offices of his sister Jane, who is now also serving Queen Elizabeth. Ned does not lodge at Whitehall, but at Hertford House, his stately London residence nearby in Cannon Row, Westminster. I have visited him there twice now, in secret, with Jane. But tonight we are hiding in an alleyway at the end of the Stone Gallery. It is freezing, and Ned has wrapped his thick cloak around us both. He senses at once that something is amiss.

"What is it, sweetheart?" he asks, seeking my lips.

I kiss him, then the tears start. "Pembroke came to see me today. He wants me and Harry to remarry."

"God's blood!" Ned explodes. "Well, you don't have to say yes, so why the distress?"

"It's not as simple as that," I sob. "The Spanish ambassador approves, and Spain is backing my right to be named Elizabeth's successor. Pembroke has much influence too, and he will throw all his weight behind me if I marry his son. Sweet Ned, I do not want this marriage, but I think it may be the price of the succession."

Ned releases me, his face shadowed under his hood, but I do not need to see it to know that he is hurt and angry.

"Dear Ned, it is you I love!" I cry, desperate. "I cannot bear the thought of going back to Harry now. Once, I would have rejoiced to do so, but those days are long gone. I want to marry *you!*"

He clasps me to him again and covers my face with hungry kisses. "Listen! You don't have to marry Harry. Just dissemble and pretend to be considering the proposal seriously. While they are in hope of a favorable answer, they will do all the more for you. It's called politics, my sweet innocent!"

I stop weeping. This is sensible advice, and I shall take it.

"In the meantime," Ned says, "here is something to cheer you. Jane has come up with a plan. She thinks that we should get your lady mother and mine to go with us to the Queen and urge her to let us marry."

"That *is* a good idea!" I breathe excitedly. Both duchesses are formidable women, and if anyone can persuade Elizabeth to give her consent, it is they. "Do you think they will agree?"

"We can but ask them," Ned says. "But Katherine, I must know: what is more important to you? Me—or the succession?"

"You, of course!" I tell him. "Did you really need to ask?"

When next I see Jane Dormer and the Count of Feria, at a court banquet, the count draws us into a window embrasure away from the other courtiers, and speaks of Pembroke's proposal.

"This marriage would please my master, King Philip, for the earl is a powerful man and can do much to advance your cause," he says.

"I am not averse to remarrying Lord Herbert," I lie, "but I must think carefully on the matter. What happened before, you understand, was . . . most distressing. I have to know I can trust the earl." That was a masterpiece of diplomacy, I think to myself.

"Of course, dear lady, of course. But if you will take a little well-meant counsel, as from a father, you will put your trust in the judgment of others wiser than yourself, and weigh well the advantages this marriage will bring. And Lord Herbert is an admirable young man. I have heard that you were happy with him once."

I curse myself for confiding in Jane Dormer. "It is five years ago, sir, and we were very young. We have both grown up since then, and that too I must take into account."

"Alas, my lady, I fear that personal considerations must give way to high policy when marriages such as this are put to making," Feria says. I am beginning to be irritated by his assumption that a woman has not the brains to think these things through for herself.

The count senses my impatience. "Do not think I am unsympathetic, or insensible of your reduced circumstances at court," he says gently.

"I am much grieved by it," I tell him. "Our new Queen bears me no goodwill."

Dormer nudges me. "Change the subject!" she mutters. I look across to where the Queen sits beneath her canopy of estate, with Lord Robert Dudley leaning proprietorially on the back of her throne. She is watching me, and her expression is hostile. I have been making it too obvious that I am speaking of serious matters, and with the Spanish ambassador at that.

"May I have the pleasure, my lady?" asks Feria, and leads me out to where the gentlemen and ladies are tripping across the floor in a *basse* dance. But the Queen's cold eyes are still upon me.

In the weeks before Christmas, I encounter several lords and councillors eager to compliment and court me. Feria is doing his work well; or it may be that Pembroke has put it about that my chances of being named heir are better than people have been led to believe.

Mindful of the Queen's hostility, I take care not to be seen too much with Feria. When we meet, our exchanges are hurried and confined to pleasantries and his reassurances that he is doing everything he can on my behalf. Then one day he comes upon me as I am walking along the cloister that surrounds the Preaching Place, my arms full of evergreens collected in the marshy wilderness of St. James's Park.

"Greetings, my lady! May I have a word?" He bows with a flourish. "There is no one here to listen."

"Even so, I must be careful," I tell him. "But pray speak, sir."

"I have been waiting to hear from you on the matter of your marriage," he says. "I would not want to put pressure on you, but the matter is important."

"I appreciate that," I say, "but I have to be sure in my mind that I am making the right decision."

"Of course. All I ask is that you do not marry without first seeking my advice."

"I will not," I promise, knowing I may not be able to keep my word.

"The most important aspect of your position, as I am sure you are aware, is not your marriage but your religion. You are the hope of Catholics everywhere, particularly in England, where they fear they will find it increasingly difficult to practice their faith. I know it cannot be easy for you, maintaining this stance in Queen Elizabeth's household, but I beg you also, do not think of changing your religion without my consent. Believe me, King Philip understands your predicament, and the temptation to take the easier course and convert to the reformed faith."

I agree to that also, then bid him a hasty farewell, saying I will be missed if I don't return soon.

He believes me sincere. He little realizes that I cling only to the pretense of Catholicism now in order to retain the support of his master.

I ponder on what might happen if I did declare myself a Protestant. King Philip would abandon me, and Feria, that is certain. But not Pembroke. And indeed, several lords on the council would surely favor a Protestant heiress. But the Queen has made it clear that she would regard any heir, Protestant or Catholic, even a child of her body, as her rival. Therefore, for the time being I lose nothing by staying a Catholic.

I am wondering if word of all this plotting of my marriage has reached the Queen, because out of the blue comes a blunt order, personally conveyed to me by Sir William Cecil, her Secretary of State, and the man who has her ear and mind more than any other.

"My lady," he says, his long, thin face impassive, his all-seeing eyes hooded and guarded. "I am commanded by Her Majesty specifically to remind you that, considering who you are, you must not marry without her consent, on pain of the most severe penalties."

It is a heavy blow, considering what is afoot with Ned and me, and it leaves me utterly dismayed. I have been hoping—as we both have, stupidly, it seems—that Elizabeth will look kindly on our proposed marriage if it is put before her by our mothers in a persuasive and diplomatic manner. But now I begin to fear that might be a vain hope. Have Ned and I come under suspicion? But how? We have been so careful . . .

"I am Her Majesty's to command," I stammer. "I have no thought of marrying." I could wish the lie unsaid, but it is too late. The words are out. And now it occurs to me that the Queen might never permit me to marry anyone. It is a horrible prospect, and I need reassurance that I am not to be condemned to a life of chastity.

"Has Her Majesty any match in mind for me?" I ask.

"No, madam, she has not," Sir William replies in a rather final tone, and, sketching a bow, departs before I can ask any more questions. After he has gone, I fall to bitter weeping. My heart is Ned's, and Ned's alone. He is my hero, my life and joy. I do not want marriage for its own sake—I just want him.

But wait! There must be a very real prospect of my gaining the throne one day. Only Elizabeth stands in the way, and there are many who do not regard her as the rightful Queen, because she is baseborn and a Protestant. Her crown has been insecure from the first. Then again, she might die young, or marry and succumb to the perils of childbirth—if, indeed, she ever marries. I do not wish her any harm, that is God's truth, but the prospect of becoming Queen still excites me greatly, and it has come to seem like natural justice, after what happened to Jane. I only ask for what is mine by right. I acknowledge that Elizabeth has the prior claim, by law. I speak no treason.

All the same, the Queen's disfavor is evident, even now, at her coronation. Instead of being in a place of high honor, as I was at Queen Mary's, I am relegated to the shadows, and might be a commoner for all the notice that is taken of my royal status. Clad in the same red velvet I wore five years ago, I find myself seated among a bevy of ladies in a chariot that follows far behind the Queen's litter. Ahead of me, mark you, ride dozens of ladies of the court on horses with red velvet saddles—and by rights, I should be at the head of them! Once in the abbey, wearing my coronet and a long train, I walk two by two with my fellow attendants as we process in the distant wake of the Queen. Oh, the insult!

KATE

January–February 1484, Palace of Westminster

The Yuletide revels at Westminster had barely come to their merry end on Twelfth Night before news arrived from France that Henry Tudor had gone to Rennes Cathedral on Christmas Day and made a solemn vow to take the crown of England and marry Edward IV's eldest daughter, Elizabeth of York, and so unite the Houses of York and Lancaster. His supporters, many of them Yorkist defectors, had then sworn allegiance to him and paid homage as if he were King already, vowing to return to England and overthrow the man they were pleased to call "the tyrant Richard."

The King invariably made light of Henry Tudor's pretensions, but he went about with a stormy countenance after hearing this news. And for Kate, it was cataclysmic.

She went running to find John.

"What ails you, darling?" he asked, when she found him in the King's library. He lifted her hands to his lips. "Tell me."

"You will have heard of Henry Tudor's vow to wed my cousin the Princess Elizabeth?"

"The whole court is talking of it," John said, "although I fear that, since she and her brothers and sisters were declared baseborn, she is a princess no more."

"Not in Henry Tudor's eyes! John, don't you see? If he wants to marry Elizabeth and so make good his claim to the throne, he must regard her as the legitimate heir of the House of York. And that can mean only one thing—that he knows her brothers are dead!"

John stared at her. "Not necessarily," he said. "It would suit Henry Tudor to believe the vile rumors and slanders that were put about by Buckingham and other of the King's enemies."

"Then what will he do when he has made himself King and married Elizabeth, and her brothers turn out to be alive?" Kate cried. "Even Henry Tudor cannot be such a fool as to risk that. He *must* know they are dead. Maybe Buckingham knew. It's possible Lady Stanley passed on that information from him."

"Kate!" John said, gentling her. "You must not believe those stories about the princes being done away with. Mark me, you'll see Henry Tudor proved to have been a fool."

"Then you still believe the princes are alive?" she asked hopefully.

"Of course I do. The time is not yet ripe for them to be released. What do you think would happen if the Wydevilles or the Tudor got their hands on them?"

Kate felt somewhat reassured.

The Palace of Westminster was a sprawling complex of buildings, bustling with courtiers, clerics, officials, lawyers, servants, and hangers-on. Kate knew her way around it now, and recognized the faces of many of those who served her father.

One courtier whom she particularly liked was the ebullient Pietro Carmeliano, an Italian who had gained patronage and prominence as a court scholar. He was a clever, witty fellow with graying curls and a grizzly beard, and seemed quite old to Kate, although he was younger than her father. He had won great praise for his work, and after he lauded King Richard in prose, the King had kept him on to edit a series of letters on statecraft.

This warm and wise little man always showed himself pleased to see her, and one day, early in February, she was whiling away an afternoon with him in the royal library, looking through his folio of papers, when she came across a poem entitled "On Spring." It was dedicated at the top to Edward, Prince of Wales.

"Oh, you have written something for my brother!" she exclaimed.

"No, Madonna, it was not for him," the Italian said, and turned back to the letter he was translating.

"Then you must have written it for King Edward's son," she stated. "It is a beautiful piece."

"Yes, Madonna. It was written as an Easter gift, two years ago."

"So much has happened since then," Kate said sadly. "My poor cousin was heir to the throne; now he languishes in the Tower."

Pietro looked up at her sharply. "It is not wise to speak of such things," he muttered.

"Yet he *is* there, whatever rumor says," she declared, challenging him to deny it.

But she saw doubt in his eyes, and fear too.

"You are the King's daughter, Madonna. I am but a poor poet. I cannot speak of such things to you."

"You know something, I can tell it," she insisted. "I beg of you, Master Pietro, to tell me everything. I would never betray your confidence. Please! It is torture to me, hearing those dreadful rumors. It is my *father* whom people slander."

The Italian considered for a moment. "You ask me to tell you everything, Madonna. Well, I cannot do that, so I may not be able to put your mind at rest. But I will tell you what I know."

KATHERINE

March 1559, Hanworth and Sheen

Dusk has fallen, and when I arrive at Sheen, my lady mother is already in her bedchamber, waiting to be put to bed. Kneeling beside my lady's chair for her blessing, and seeing her sitting there immobile, looking old and somehow defeated by life, I find myself on the verge of breaking down—for when one is under such strain as I am, the tears are ever ready. Forgetting all considerations of my lady's health, I start railing against the Queen's unkindness. For Elizabeth herself, echoing Cecil's words, told me only today, before I left court—and in no uncertain terms—that I was not even to think of matrimony until she raised the subject herself. And that, her cold black eyes suggested, would be never.

"She dare not permit you to marry," the stiff figure in the chair croaks, "and I will tell you why. If you marry and bear a son, you will create a focus for dissension and rebellion, just like Jane. A beautiful young queen-in-waiting with a hearty boy in her arms—who could resist? But beware, daughter, for when that boy grows not so much older, you will find that the eyes and hopes of men focus on him, not you—and good-bye Queen Katherine!"

She snorts impatiently. "She *should* have named you her successor by now. It is your right, and Stokes tells me there is a powerful lobby at court urging it. But Elizabeth only sees that you have set yourself up as a Catholic rival—and that you pose a threat just by existing. And, daughter, there is another pertinent reason why she sees you as a rival, trivial as it seems, but not trivial to her, who was ever vain of her looks, right from childhood. It is because you are beautiful and she is not!" My lady's tone is tart. "That increases your appeal, not only for men—and I warn you, she cannot abide a rival in that way—but for those who question her title to the throne, and they are many."

"The Catholics," I say.

"Yes, and those who will never believe that King Henry was legally married to her mother, that strumpet Anne Boleyn."

It is as well that the women have left us alone and closed the door, for now that Elizabeth is Queen, such talk about Anne Boleyn would be considered seditious, even treasonable.

My lady eyes me speculatively. "You are truly a Catholic still?"

"I must be practical. I have subtly let it be known that I am ready to champion the cause of the Catholics, and so win their support. King Philip is the most powerful prince in the world, and the strongest in Europe. He is backing me."

My lady smiles. "So he will put pressure on Elizabeth to name you her heir. She is in no position to refuse. She needs his support. Remember, her throne is insecure: in the eyes of much of Christendom, she is a baseborn heretic with no right to the crown. You, Katherine, are of unquestioned legitimacy." She has lowered her voice, for her words are nothing less than high treason, and she could lose her head for them. Unbidden, I get up and go to the door, peering out to see if anyone is listening, but the women have gone. With relief, I espy them all through the window, walking in the garden on this unseasonably mild day.

"I have done my best to attract King Philip's support," I say. "I go to Mass openly on Sundays. I wear a crucifix and carry a rosary, especially where the Spanish ambassador can see me."

"I see you have used your head, my girl!"

"I try to be circumspect. I do take care to make public displays of my faith, yet not, I think, so overtly as to incur the suspicions of the Queen."

"You have done well, Katherine, and I am pleased to see you are learning the game of politics," my lady beams. Such praise, coming from her, is rare.

"What news of my son Seymour?" she asks.

"Good news! Queen Elizabeth has restored to him the earldom of Hertford, which was held by his father; surely, my lady, that would make him a fit mate for me in Her Majesty's eyes?"

She regards me skeptically. "Do not expect her to see any man as a fit mate for you. In truth, I do not see how this marriage you desire can be accomplished."

Looking at my poor mother, slumped in her chair, I realize with a jolt that I should make haste to avail myself of the weight she carries with the Queen.

"We need your help, my lady," I blurt out. "That is why I have come. Ned waits without. He has ridden over from Hampton Court. He—We—have something we must ask you. He wants to do things properly. Please hear what he has to say. We think you can help us."

My mother sighs. "You had better summon Stokes." And she raises herself with an effort, and sits resting her hand regally on her cane.

"What of Ned?" I ask.

"He can wait awhile."

Master Stokes arrives and fusses over my mother, settling her more comfortably in her chair, which she bears with grim fortitude.

"Husband," she says, "there is much goodwill between yon belted earl waiting without and my daughter. They wish to wed, and in my opinion, he is a very fit husband for her. It remains for the Queen to give her consent to their marriage."

"A fitting match indeed, my dear. But will Her Majesty agree?" he asks doubtfully, clearly used to being governed and guided by his wife.

"She will make difficulties, of that you can be sure. Yet I have long had some influence with Elizabeth, and I am willing to attempt to persuade her."

"Then shall we see the earl, my dear?"

My mother indicates the door with her beringed hand, and Stokes ushers Ned in. He bows elegantly before her, and she invites him to kneel for her blessing.

"Welcome, Son Seymour," she says, with just a hint of amusement. "You may kiss me." And she smiles as he rises and bends his head to her. "You have something to ask me, I think."

"Yes, madam." Ned's voice betrays nervousness. "I have called upon Your Grace formally to ask for the Lady Katherine's hand in marriage."

"Then I gladly give my consent." She smiles. "I have long wanted you for a son-in-law, and I should like to see Katherine happily settled before I depart this life."

Ned, standing beside me, grips my hand discreetly in a fold of my skirt and exhales with relief. He looks so handsome standing there, his cheeks slightly flushed, his eyes alight with triumph.

"Well, daughter," my lady barks. "I have provided a husband for you, if you can like well of it, and if you are willing to frame your fancy and goodwill that way."

"I am very willing to love my lord of Hertford," I declare avidly.

"Then it is settled. Now, Stokes, we must compass the best way of approaching Her Majesty. Confronted by myself in person, she may instantly refuse; but a letter explaining the benefits of the marriage, and reaffirming our loyalty, may be read again and digested at leisure, leaving space for consideration."

My stepfather claps Ned on the back. "Her Grace will write a letter for your lordship to the Queen's Majesty."

"Nay, we will write one together, husband," my lady decides. "I pray you, devise a rough letter for me to copy, so that I may add my persuasions to yours, and thereby hopefully obtain the Queen's good-will and consent. But before I do that—a word in private, Katherine."

The men bow and withdraw from the room.

"Tell me again, girl—is this marriage what you really want?" My mother pierces me with those hawklike eyes that have lost none of their fierceness.

"Yes, my lady!" I cry. "I long to marry Lord Hertford!"

"Then I shall do all in my power to see that you do. I failed one daughter, but I shall not fail another. I needed to make sure that you have enough fight in you for what may lie ahead. Now, I must write that letter, and then we shall celebrate!"

I am bursting with excitement, and when we are alone, Ned picks me up and whirls me around in delight, then kisses me heartily until I am near to swooning with pleasure. Soon—very soon—we might be man and wife, and all this torturous longing will be behind us. My mind racing ahead, I see us happily married, seated at our hearth, our children at our feet; or being fêted at court as society's golden couple, and even Queen Elizabeth, assured once and for all that we are no threat to her, smiling benevolently on us. I even envisage a time fur-ther ahead, and two people seated on thrones, queen and king to-gether . . .

This happy reverie is interrupted by Stokes calling for us. They have finished writing the letter. It is brief and to the point, the best thing to start with, my lady explains, shifting uncomfortably in her chair. I take it and read the words that appear after the elaborate salutation re-quired by courtesy:

> *The Earl of Hertford does bear goodwill to my daughter, the Lady Katherine, and I do humbly require the Queen's Highness to be a good and gracious lady unto her, and that it may please Her Majesty to as-sent to her marriage to the said earl.*

Is that all? Does my mother think such a letter sufficient appeal on my behalf? I pass it to Ned, and he reads it, frowning.

"With respect, Your Grace, we had hoped for more persuasions."

"Trust me," my lady says, grimacing. "It must not look as if we anticipate Her Majesty's refusal. This is just a beginning. I shall send the letter, and then, the ground being laid, I shall bestir myself to go to court and obtain Her Majesty's favor. I do not think she will refuse her old gossip. And now, I must go to my bed. I have had enough excitement for one day, and am feeling weary to my bones."

She makes to rise, and both Stokes and Ned move to assist her. But as she walks heavily away, leaning on my stepfather's arm, I see to my horror bright blood pooled upon her chair and staining the back of her gown. I know it cannot be her monthly flux, for her courses ceased three years ago.

I look at Ned and see him staring at the chair, then our eyes meet. I am beyond embarrassment, even though I know whence this blood must have come; instead, I am in dread, confronted with this terrible evidence that my majestic mother, the rock and mainstay of my life, and the hope of my future, is but mortal.

My mother has a humor of the womb, Dr. Allen says. Rest should help, and infusions of geranium and rose. There must be no question of her leaving the house—and therefore no question of her going to court.

And because of that—oh, my sweet Ned, how can I bear it?—her letter cannot yet be sent to the Queen.

KATE

February 1484, Palace of Westminster

"Madonna, last summer there was an Italian visitor to court, Dominic Mancini," Pietro Carmeliano said in hushed tones, although he and Kate were quite alone in the royal library. "He was my friend. He was in the train of the French ambassador, and his task was to send home reports of affairs in England. Thus he made it his business to know what was going on."

"What was he like, this Dominic Mancini?" Kate asked.

"He was a monk, a very devout and compassionate man, and wise too. He wrote an account of the rise of your father the King to the throne, but I never saw it completed, for it was unfinished when he left England last summer." Pietro hesitated.

"Please speak freely!" Kate urged. "Whatever the truth, I would rather hear it."

"Very well, Madonna. I will tell you everything." And he did.

"Dominic got his information from several people at court, including Dr. Argentine, who was physician to your cousin, King Edward. Forgive me, Madonna, but Brother Dominic was suspicious of your father's intentions from the start. He thought him ambitious and cunning. He knew Edward had been well served by Earl Rivers and Sir Richard Grey, and was shocked when my lord of Gloucester had them executed."

"But they were a danger to my father," she protested.

"Yes, Madonna, Brother Dominic knew that; he knew too that your father hated the Wydevilles and blamed them for his brother Clarence's death. He found much to praise in Gloucester for governing the North well, for his renown in war, and for his exemplary private life. But even though Brother Dominic was appalled at the power wielded by the Wydevilles, he was impressed by the young King Edward, and praised him to the skies."

Again Pietro hesitated. "Knowing that Gloucester hated and feared the Wydevilles, my friend came to believe that, from the moment he heard of King Edward's death, the duke determined to take the throne for himself."

"No, that was much later," Kate insisted, "when Edward V was proved to be illegitimate."

"Forgive me, Madonna. You asked me to tell you what I know, and I am only repeating what Dominic Mancini showed me in his book. And that was just his opinion, based on what he learned at court. I do not—how you say—comment on the truth of it."

"I am sorry, Pietro," Kate apologized. "Please go on."

The Italian continued with Mancini's account of the events following King Edward's death, most of which was familiar to her. But she was disturbed to hear Mancini's view of her father.

"Brother Dominic was convinced that the duke was in haste to remove all the obstacles that stood in the way of his plans. He believed he was driven by ambition and lust for power, and that he had set his thoughts on eliminating everyone who stood in the way of his mastering the throne."

"Everyone who was a threat to him, you mean!" Kate interrupted. "He was trying to do things honorably, as he made plain at the time, but he was beset by enemies."

"That, I fear, was not Brother Dominic's view. Would you prefer me not to go on?" Pietro was regarding her unhappily.

"Nay, I will hear it all, even if it is hateful to me," she replied. "Only then can I weigh it wisely. You see, I know my father. He is a good, upright man. Why did Brother Dominic slander him so?"

"You tell me," Pietro said. "He had no involvement in your English politics. He was just an observer, and an impartial one too."

"But the information fed him may not have been impartial."

"Forgive me, Madonna, but I think he had wit enough to judge of that."

"And others might have judged it differently!" Kate was angry. It seemed that, whatever she said to counteract Dominic Mancini's view of her father, Pietro had a rational argument against it. But this Mancini might well have been fed a distorted and hostile view of events. It stood to reason.

"Go on," she commanded, a trifle coolly.

"As you wish, Madonna," Pietro said. "It seemed to Brother Dominic that Gloucester felt his future was not sufficiently secure without the removal of those who were faithful to his brother's offspring. Hastings was killed on a false pretext of treason, not by the enemies he had feared, but—it must be said—by a friend he had never doubted. After that, Gloucester put up the hue and cry for Lord Dorset, but he had prudently escaped abroad. Then something ominous occurred."

"What?" Kate's tone was sharp.

"After Hastings was removed, all the attendants who had waited on the King in the Tower were dismissed and debarred access to him."

"My father said he could not trust them," she argued. "He feared that Dorset had suborned them. How did Brother Dominic know that, anyway?"

"Dr. Argentine told him."

"Was Dr. Argentine dismissed too?"

"No, Madonna. He was treating the young King for a swelling of the jaw. The King was in much pain with his teeth and gums. The duke could hardly dismiss his doctor. But the boy was now effectively a prisoner. Dr. Argentine confided to Brother Dominic that Edward believed death was facing him and, like a victim prepared for sacrifice, sought remission of his sins daily. He was without all hope, and sunk in despair."

"No, I will not believe it!" Kate cried out. "My father would never have countenanced him suffering thus. He kept on the doctor! Was that not a kindness? And the King was ill and in pain. Probably he feared he would die of his malady, not by violence."

"But Madonna, Dr. Argentine seems also to have feared violence." The little Italian looked unhappy. "And it was just after that that the duke surrounded the sanctuary with soldiers and forced the Queen to surrender the Duke of York into his keeping. For well he knew that York would be King if anything happened to Edward V."

"But my father feared the Wydevilles! That was at the root of it all. A child cannot seek sanctuary. It was not right to keep him there. And in the Queen's hands, York was a threat to my father. But she would not give him up, and so he had to make her."

"Well, Madonna, you may put your own interpretation on these events. But Brother Dominic told me that soon after York was sent to join his brother, the two princes were withdrawn into the inner apartments of the Tower, and day by day began to be seen more rarely behind the bars and windows. Occasionally people could see them shooting at the butts in the lieutenant's garden."

Kate thought of Caesar's Tower, that massive white keep: that was where they were being held, no doubt. It was said to be so strong and secure that no one could possibly escape, or attempt a rescue, so it made sense that her father had confined his nephews there. Given the plots to rescue Edward V, it had been a wise decision.

"Gloucester then began acting like a king, putting off his mourning robes and wearing purple," Pietro was saying, and Kate recalled her father riding triumphantly through London in that great purple man-

tle. "He had the sons of King Edward declared bastards. He had corrupted preachers to proclaim them as such, putting forward some false
tale about a precontract."

"It was not false!" Kate averred.

"Brother Dominic thought it was."

"Brother Dominic was clearly not a reliable witness," she countered.

"That is as may be, Madonna. I but relate what he wrote. And he
said that the lords in London, seeing the alliance of Gloucester and
Buckingham, and perceiving that the dukes' power was supported by
a multitude of troops, became fearful for their own safety. They had
heard of the fates of Lord Hastings, Rivers, and Grey, and decided it
would be hazardous to resist Buckingham's calls for Gloucester to be
acknowledged King. And so they consented, and Gloucester occupied
the kingdom. Brother Dominic left England after the coronation. It
was just before he departed that he told me he had heard that the
princes had ceased to appear at the windows of the Tower. He said he
had seen many grown men burst into tears and lamentations when
mention was made of them after their removal from men's sight; already there was a suspicion they had been done away with. That was
long before the rumors of which you speak."

"But it was only a suspicion," Kate insisted, clutching at the loop-
hole in the argument, although again the uncomfortable memory of
Lord Stanley weeping came to her unbidden. "Was there any proof?"

"There was no proof, Madonna. Brother Dominic wrote that, as to
whether the princes had been done away with, and in what manner, he
could not say."

"So his account is based on speculation," Kate said firmly. "Others
might place another construction on these events."

"Indeed they might, Madonna. As I said, I but repeat what I heard.
I trust you will not hold that against me." The little man looked nervous: he must know that much of what he had said might be construed as treason.

"Of course not," Kate replied, but already she was aware that there
would be no more afternoons spent in the library with Master Pietro
Carmeliano. In her mind, he would forever be associated with this sor-

did fantasy of a tale. True, she had pressed him to recount it, and he had been reluctant; but its unfolding was more disturbing and distasteful than she could ever have anticipated. And yet, despite that, she still believed in her father's integrity, for Pietro's allegations rode so ill with what she knew of him. It was all malicious invention, she told herself.

She did not linger after that—she just wanted to get away. And when she did, she asked discreetly around the court as to whether anyone had seen Dr. Argentine. She wanted desperately to speak to him, for he, of all people, would perhaps know if the princes still lived, and in what conditions. But no one could answer her. She met with blank looks and shaking heads.

Eventually, unwillingly, she returned to the library. Pietro must know the doctor's whereabouts, surely. He was still there, scratching away with his quill pen.

"I forgot to ask," she said. "Where can I find Dr. Argentine?"

Was it fear she glimpsed fleetingly in Pietro's eyes?

"Why do you seek him, Madonna?" he asked.

"To find out more about my cousins, since you cannot tell me the latest news of them."

"Alas, I cannot. You are months too late. Dr. Argentine also left England after the coronation, and where he is now I could not say."

"He was made to leave?"

"No, Madonna—he fled."

KATHERINE

August–September 1559; Eltham Palace,
Nonsuch Palace, Whitehall Palace

July brought news that the King of France was dead, killed by a lance piercing his eye during a tournament. His son, Francis II, being married to the Scottish Queen Mary, my cousin, now saw fit to use the royal arms of England in her right. It was a deadly insult to Queen

Elizabeth, for it proclaimed her a usurper, unfit by stain of bastardy to wear her crown. And verily, from that moment, I am sure, she began to hate the Queen of Scots.

But something has come to light to convince Elizabeth that I am even more of a danger to her than Mary.

I knew nothing of it, I swear it. Kindly, supportive Feria had gone home and been replaced as ambassador by Bishop de Quadra, and although the Bishop has been lavish in his courtesy and compliments, I have never had any cause to trust him—rather the opposite. And now it has been discovered that the Spaniards were plotting my abduction to Spain, where I was to be wed to King Philip's son, Don Carlos, and be proclaimed heiress presumptive to the English throne. It is bad enough that Don Carlos is a deformed sadist with a penchant for torturing servants and animals, but worse still that Philip, de Quadra, and all the others involved in the plot assumed that my consent was a foregone conclusion.

"You have only yourself to blame," scolded Kat Astley, Chief Lady of the Bedchamber, when I came begging an audience with the Queen to protest my innocence. "You have shown yourself discontented and complained you are held in poor regard by Her Majesty."

"But I did nothing to encourage the Spaniards," I wailed, seeing that the door to the privy chamber was still firmly closed to me.

"Your discontent was enough," I was told tartly. "Aye, and your Romish faith. No wonder the Queen cannot abide you!"

I fled in tears to the safety of my chamber, and there flung myself on my bed and wept my heart out for very despair. And thus I have continued to this day, beset on every side by dread and fear: of what the Queen might do to me, if she chooses to believe that I was involved in that dastardly plan; of what others might yet be plotting on my behalf; and of how this might impact on Ned and me, and our hopes of marriage. In vain have I written to my ailing mother, begging her to send her letter to the Queen, or to come herself, if she can, to plead our cause; but there has been no reply. This I see as ominous: either she is too ill, or—I fear—she has forsaken me, thinking our matter too difficult.

———

At last I have news of my lady, and it is encouraging: she writes that she is feeling a little better. And Ned is here! When the Queen began her summer progress, he himself was unwell, and sent word to say he was sorry he could not be present, but now he has returned to court, and the summer days suddenly seem sunnier and more golden. We seize every moment to be together.

"There is great love between you two, I wis!" young Lady Anne Russell trills. I look at her in alarm. I had not thought we had been so transparent. "Oh, yes, the whole world is talking about you!" she declares, to my dismay.

Three days later, in the maidens' dorter, Douglas Howard, another of the Queen's ladies, seeks me out.

"I hear you are like turtle doves with Lord Hertford," she mutters, "and everyone is saying that nothing can come of it, for he is using you to further his own interests, and means you no good."

"What do you know of it?" I seethe. "You and all the others? You have no idea! I'll thank you to keep your opinions to yourself!" And I go to bed in a temper.

But Ned is true, I'd swear on that. Daily he gives me proof of his love. At Nonsuch, the most exquisite little jewel of a palace ever built, my uncle, the Earl of Arundel, lays on great entertainments for the delight of the Queen, and Ned and I have plenty of opportunities to meet at the lavish banquet, the ornate masque, the hunt in the park, and the play performed by the choristers of St. Paul's. The revelry goes on until three o'clock in the morning, and then Ned and I escape to walk in the groves and kiss by the marble fountains. Such snatched moments are bliss to me.

Yet this idyll cannot last, and not long after our return to Whitehall, Ned comes to me with a long face.

"It is not good news," he blurts out. "I have sounded out several on the council now, and the answer is always the same. It is not the right time to consider our marriage."

"But why?"

"Prince Erik of Sweden is here to pay court to the Queen. Until the outcome of that is known, we are advised to wait. In the meantime, I will do my best to win favor with Prince Erik. I hear he enjoys tennis."

"In that case, he must approve of you. He could not have a better opponent. But it is hard to have to wait. I would I were a private person and could marry where I pleased!"

"Come, you would not like that, Katherine!" Ned snorts. "And nor would I. Just be patient awhile longer—and then, God willing, we can have it all!"

KATE

February 1484, Palace of Westminster

Kate fretted about Dr. Argentine's flight. Might he have known more than was good for him about the fate of the princes? Had he meddled too far in matters that did not concern him, or had he simply been an incompetent doctor?

The thought struck her that her cousin Edward might have died of natural causes, or at the hands of the doctor who was trying to cure him. She had heard of many cases where the remedy had proved more fatal than the disease. That would have been reason enough for Dr. Argentine to have fled. And it was easy, in this present climate, to see why her father would never have announced the death of his nephew, for people would surely have laid the blame for it at his door. They had been quick to call him murderer as it was!

It was all a tangled puzzle, and she found it hard to think straight. How could she make sense of the many loose ends? Could she keep on believing that her beloved father had done no wrong? Truly, she did not know anymore.

When Kate sat down at the chessboard in the King's privy chamber on the evening after her talk with Pietro, she found herself looking at her father afresh.

"You are not paying attention, Kate," he chided. "I said, watch your knight. What ails you?"

She summoned her courage. "Sire, I have been much disquieted by foul rumors about my cousins in the Tower."

Richard's eyes narrowed. "You should not pay attention to pernicious rumors," he reproved.

"Then my cousins are well?"

"Why should they not be?" His tone was defensive and sharp. Queen Anne, seated by the crackling fire, looked up from her sewing. She shook her head almost imperceptibly at Kate.

"No reason at all, sire," Kate said quickly. Her father frowned and said no more.

The next morning, after Mass, Kate stayed on her knees in the empty chapel, trying to make sense of everything. But it was all too much for her, and she found herself weeping uncontrollably. And that was how the Lord Chancellor, the Bishop of Lincoln, found her when he entered the chapel a few minutes later.

"Why, my dear child, what is wrong?" he asked in his mellow, cultivated voice. Kate lifted a tearstained face in which her misery was written clear. She was relieved to see Bishop Russell standing beside her. She knew him for a just man of great learning and piety, a man of integrity who had sometimes been a guest at her father's table. The sight of his strong, serene face calmed her.

She stood up, wiping her eyes. "I have done my father the King an injury," she sniffed. "But I would not have hurt him for all the world."

"I am sure that a young lady like yourself could not have done anything that was so very bad," the Bishop said kindly. "Would you like to tell me about it?"

Kate realized that she would, very much. She needed reassurance about the dark matters that had been gnawing at her for weeks, and her talk with Pietro had only added to her torment. She was painfully torn: she could not bear to have those horrible things said about her father—and yet she was tortured by the possibility that there might be some truth in them. Every time she had tried to talk to John about her fears, he'd offered some comforting explanation; yet she suspected he was biased, immovably her father's man. And then she would feel guilty about being so disloyal herself. But these terrible suspicions would not be stilled!

Bishop Russell was an experienced politician, well acquainted with the workings of the court, the council, and Parliament, and an honest man at the center of affairs. If anyone knew the truth, it was he.

She sank down in the royal pew and His Grace seated himself comfortably beside her.

"Now," he said, "there is no one to hear, and you may speak freely. Do not think that anything you say can shock me, for in my calling I have heard the whole panoply of the human condition; and this will be between ourselves only." He paused and waited, contemplating his episcopal ring.

"There have been dreadful rumors these past weeks," Kate began, then faltered. Even now, she hated to give voice to them. "They accuse my father of murdering his nephews." There—it was said.

The Bishop was silent at first. He appeared to be considering. Kate was holding her breath in trepidation.

"The King was ambitious, there can be no doubt of that," he said at length. "He wanted the throne, although when he first conceived that desire I cannot say. And he removed those who stood in his way. I know for a fact that Lord Hastings never conspired against him. So yes, he displayed a certain—shall we say—pragmatism. He may well have believed there had been a conspiracy. But innocent blood was shed."

"Innocent blood?" Kate whispered.

"I meant Lord Hastings—and Rivers and Grey," the Bishop replied, then fell silent.

"And the princes?" She could hardly speak.

"When the Duke of York was taken from sanctuary, his mother was assured that Gloucester intended no harm toward him," the Bishop recalled. "With that guarantee, she assented to the boy's going. But from that day, the duke openly revealed his plans. It was clear he was aiming for the throne itself. My dear child, you must forgive me for speaking too freely, but I am telling you the truth. Never think I am disloyal to my King. I serve him faithfully, and think no ill of him. Our Savior teaches us that we must not judge our fellow men."

"I know that, Father," Kate assured him.

"Sometimes, in matters of state, the end justifies the means," the Bishop said.

"The precontract between King Edward and Lady Eleanor Butler—did it ever exist?" Kate ventured.

Bishop Russell sighed. "No, my daughter, it was a false tale put forward by Bishop Stillington, which the duke chose to believe. It gave him the pretext he needed to take the throne."

"Then the princes are truly legitimate?"

"Some would say so."

And they might also say that her father had usurped the throne and had no right to be King, she realized. But surely he had believed the precontract to be lawful?

"But my father *is* the rightful King?" she asked.

"Indeed he is. He was recognized as such by the estates of this realm at his coronation, and Parliament has just passed an Act, *Titulus Regius,* confirming his title."

That was some comfort. But she needed more.

"It is said that the princes were killed before the coronation," she ventured.

"That is untrue," the Bishop said. "At that time they were living in the Tower under special guard, and I know they were still there when the Prince of Wales was invested at York."

That gave the lie to Brother Dominic's hints and suspicions.

"But what happened to them after the investiture?" she persisted.

The Bishop's gaze rested on the great jeweled crucifix on the altar.

"I cannot say," he said. "They may still be in the Tower now. I promise you I have not heard otherwise." He stood up, somewhat abruptly. "I hope I have given you some consolation, my daughter. Now I must leave you. I am due in the council chamber shortly." And he placed his hand on her head in blessing before departing.

Walking back to her lodging on the Queen's side, Kate considered what the Bishop had said. Certainly his account of events was at variance with Dominic Mancini's, and that alone cast doubt on Mancini's sources of information. Malicious persons, to be sure, she said to herself, resolving never to doubt her father again. Whatever means he had used to come by the throne, he must have believed them legitimate. And the princes were still in the Tower: Bishop Russell himself thought it.

It was only later, when she was lying wakeful in bed, staring unseeing at the firelight flickering on the walls, that she recalled the Bishop's answer when she'd asked what had become of the princes after the investiture. "I cannot say," he had replied. Had that meant he could not say because he did not know—or because it was politic—and safer—not to say? And then another terrible notion came to her: if the princes *had* been murdered in the Tower, they—or rather, their bodies—*would* still be there, and of course Bishop Russell would not have heard otherwise.

John, meanwhile, had been busy putting pressure on his father to permit him and Kate to wed.

"He is thinking about it, that's all he will say," he fumed when next they met. "God's blood, why is it that older people forget what it is like to be in love? They think they can push us into this betrothal or that to suit their own advantage, but they have no idea what it is like when your blood is racing through your veins and you have eyes only for one special person. And for me it is you, my Kate!" And he swept her up and twirled her around, her green skirts and long hair flying.

"John! People will see!" Her eyes scanned the frost-rimed garden anxiously. Lincoln set her down and followed her as she walked to the riverbank. Below them the Thames glowered dark and sullen in the February gloom. It matched her mood. She had been utterly miserable since her talks with Pietro and Bishop Russell.

"What is wrong with you these days, sweetheart?" John asked, looking at her anxiously. "Tell me honestly—are you tiring of me?"

"God, no!" she cried, shocked that he should think it, and that she had become so self-absorbed as to not notice his concern. "I love you, John! I always will. I long for you to be my husband. No—you have nothing to do with my melancholy; rather, you are the one thing that lifts it."

"I am not doing very well today, then." He smiled ruefully.

"In truth, I do not know how to help myself," she confessed.

"Just tell me what is wrong, or I shall go mad with worry."

"It is my father . . . the rumors about the princes . . ." She shook her head helplessly.

"Not that again!" John sighed. "Just forget it. You are chasing demons that don't exist. The princes are in the Tower, alive and well."

"You know that for certain?"

"I am sure of it. And the good news today is that the Queen and her
daughters have agreed to leave sanctuary. The King has sworn an oath
to protect and care for our cousins. Queen Elizabeth would hardly entrust them to a man who had murdered her sons. Think about it,
sweetheart."

"But he had her other son, Grey, executed without trial," Kate had
to say.

"There was justification for that, as you know. Queen Elizabeth
must know it too. And the King has offered a pardon to her eldest son,
Dorset, if he will abandon Henry Tudor and return to England. So you
see, my Kate, there is no cause for melancholy, I promise you." He
bent and kissed her long and hard, his cheek rough and cold in the
freezing air. It was the most passionate kiss he had ever given her, and
when he broke away, she was gasping.

"I trust you feel better now," John said, and winked at her.

She thought she did, as she hastened back into the palace, her thick
cloak pulled about her, her hands blue with cold. And then she was accosted by a fresh-faced page in the King's livery.

"I've been looking for you everywhere, my lady," the boy said. "The
King is asking for you. He desires that you attend him in his privy
chamber."

"Of course," she said, and hurried on her way, unsuspecting.

KATHERINE

October 1559, Whitehall Palace

God, Fortune, or the Fates—call it what you will—have not been kind
to us, my love and I. To my grief, my lady mother has grown weaker

and taken to her bed, and there she has remained ever since, her condition steadily deteriorating. Once more, our hopes of her intercession with the Queen have been cruelly dashed.

Today, stiff in my tight-waisted embroidered damask gown with the high, ruffled neck and wide, pearl-encrusted sleeves, and bursting with resentment, it is my turn to wait upon Her Majesty. I am aware of the covert, hostile glances of my fellow Ladies of the Bedchamber, the bristling disapproval of Mistress Astley, and the icy demeanor of my royal mistress. Elizabeth could be angry with me for any number of reasons—but why does she not speak her displeasure, or even tell me what my punishment is to be?

I burn with the unfairness of it all. I have done nothing—*nothing*—to deserve this!

Anger boils inside me. So when the Queen slaps me for dropping her glove, I explode like a cannon.

"Your Majesty is most unkind!" I cry. "It is not my fault that others have plotted in my name, entirely unbeknownst to me, and yet you have blamed me for it. That is unwarranted, and most unbecoming in one who is supposed to be the fount of all justice!"

As soon as I have uttered the words, I wish my tongue had been cut out of my mouth. One look at the astonishment and fury in Elizabeth's face, and I know I am irrevocably lost, and bound for the Tower, at the very least. With a few ill-chosen words let fly in wrath, I have wrecked all my hopes of the succession, yea, and of marriage and all that is precious to me.

"Well, Lady Katherine, you have made yourself very clear," the Queen says acidly. "Even if there was none of your malice in that evil conspiracy, you have made it plain now."

"But madam," I keen, falling to my knees, "I but pleaded my case. I meant no offense, truly." The women are looking down on me with unconcealed contempt.

"Have I accused you of aught, that you should have any case to plead?" Elizabeth barks.

"No, madam, but you have never shown kindness to me, and it is clear that I am now held in derision by everyone in this court, they following your lead, for you have made it plain you think me a guilty party, when I am not. But I have been sorely tried, especially considering I have not been named as your successor, as is my right—"

"Enough!" the Queen bawls. "Get ye hence, girl, and do not show your face here again until I command it, on pain of my severe displeasure. Go!"

I rise to my feet and, dropping the scantiest of curtsies, flee from her presence. And then I wait . . . and wait . . . and wait. What will my fate be? How many laws have I broken in speaking thus to my sovereign? Was it treason, or bordering on it? Yes, I was right in what I said— but I wish now, oh, I wish that I had borne that slap patiently and never opened my mouth.

I have ruined everything. I have irrevocably offended the Queen's Majesty, and will surely suffer for it. Was there ever such a wretch as I? Yes, of course there was, I realize with horror: my poor sister Jane. Memories of her awful fate haunt me. Will I be next?

Bishop de Quadra seeks me out as I walk with my dogs, alone and shunned by the courtiers, in St. James's Park. But before he can speak, I challenge him.

"By God, Bishop, what is this I hear about you trying to kidnap me?"

He looks disconcerted but quickly recovers himself.

"That is a strong word, my lady. You have clearly been misinformed. Rest assured that Spain would never do anything without your consent."

"But I am assured that there was a conspiracy to marry me to the Infante Don Carlos."

"Such a match was mooted," he admits. "His Majesty has only ever sought to make a good and beneficial marriage between your ladyship and a great Catholic prince. It has now been suggested that his nephew, the Archduke Ferdinand, would be more worthy of your consideration. Don Carlos will be King of Spain one day, and must remain in that kingdom. Your ladyship, once Queen of England, must live here. The Archduke has no ties, and can remain at your side. His Majesty remembers the difficulties that arose when he was married to Queen Mary, and wishes them to be avoided in the future." He pauses. "Am I right in thinking that you are unhappy at court and would leave willingly? His Majesty would provide a remedy and a refuge."

"I will think on this," I murmur, mollified, but uneasily aware that this conversation might be treasonous. And although I can see the political sense in what the Bishop is offering, and am flattered at the prospect of such a great match, my heart is Ned's, and can be Ned's alone.

"I am sorry to see you looking so downcast, Lady Katherine," de Quadra says. "I have heard about your quarrel with the Queen. You were brave to speak out—yet a little rash, if I may say so. But the Queen's wrath never lasts long, I am told."

"I wish I could believe that," I tell him. "She has always hated me."

"She hates you because she fears you, my lady, and with good reason. In my master's view, you would make a more desirable queen than she."

"You must not say that to me," I reprimand him. "It is treason, no less." But my heart is leaping. My friends in Spain, who have caused me so much trouble, may yet find a way to champion my cause.

Bishop de Quadra looks consideringly at me. "If any disaster were to befall the Queen, my master would support your claim, by force of arms, if need be."

I stare at him. I had not imagined that Spain felt so strongly about my succession. And for the first time in weeks, my spirits begin to soar.

KATE

February 1484, Palace of Westminster

King Richard was reading in his carved box chair when Kate arrived in the privy chamber and made her curtsey. Queen Anne was present too, in her usual place by the fire, swathed in furs.

Her father smiled, laid down his book, and held out his arms, and Kate went into them, hating herself for ever having doubted him.

"I have very good news for you, Kate," he announced. "You are to be married!"

Her heart pounding, she clapped her hand to her mouth. "I thank Your Grace!" she cried. "It is what I have longed for." There were tears in her eyes.

Richard looked at her uncomprehendingly for a moment, then his smile faded.

"Ah, daughter, you think it is my lord of Lincoln, but I am afraid he is not the lucky man. No, you are to be wed to the Earl of Huntingdon."

"No!" She could not stop herself. She had been schooled to obedience since birth, and taught that her father's word was law, and her father was also her King, so she owed him a double duty—but she was ready to defy him in this. Forsake John for a stranger? She would rather die!

The King took her hands. "No?" he said gently. "That is not the reaction I expected from my dutiful daughter when I have provided carefully for her future." It was a reproof, but a kindly one.

"It is not your place to question your father's decision, Kate," Anne added.

Kate was trembling. "Sire, you knew I wished to wed my cousin of Lincoln." Tears were streaming down her cheeks.

Her father looked pained. "I thought I had warned you not to think of marriage with him. You are my daughter, and your marriage must be made for policy. This match with the Earl of Huntingdon is a brilliant one for you, and much to my advantage—and yours. You will be a countess, a great lady—it is a union I would have sought for my true-born daughter, if I had one."

"But I love John!" Kate burst out. "I can never love the Earl of Huntingdon!"

Her father's face darkened, but Anne came over and took her hand.

"Listen, Kate," she enjoined. "It is the duty of a wife to love her lord, once she is married. You must try as hard as you can. No good can come of falling in love where you will; you must see that now. My lord of Lincoln is a charming young man, but you are too close in blood."

The King spoke. "Knowing that there was goodwill between you and my nephew, I did sound out his father on the matter of a marriage between you. He said he would not forbid it if I wanted it, but he was unhappy about the consanguinity, and he does have another bride in mind for his son."

Of course, she had known that, but she knew too that the duke had a deeper reservation, one he would never have dared voice to her father. Her distress was unbearable; she was now weeping so copiously that Richard and Anne were quite concerned about her.

"Kate, he is not for you," Anne said gently, putting an arm around her heaving shoulders and proffering her own kerchief.

"Nay, because I am baseborn!" Kate cried. "That is the real reason why his father does not want the marriage!"

Richard looked stricken. "That cannot be so," he protested. "It is an honor for any man to marry the daughter of the King, baseborn or not. And the Earl of Huntingdon is sensible of it. He has long admired you from afar. My lord of Suffolk has good cause to object to the match—but that is not my only consideration. Far more important are the benefits that this marriage with Huntingdon will bring. Will you let me explain?"

Kate's nod was barely perceptible. She dabbed her eyes but could not stop shuddering. Then the King began speaking.

William Herbert, he said, was twenty-eight years old. (Old, she thought, too old!) His father and namesake had been one of the most powerful supporters of the House of York, for which he had fought valiantly during the late wars. After his accession, Edward IV had given the older Herbert high offices in south Wales, made him a baron, and granted him Pembroke Castle and many other strongholds and manors.

Lord Herbert had vanquished the Welsh Tudors, who had fought for the House of Lancaster, and soon he was given their earldom of Pembroke. After that, the King related, he was the effective ruler of all Wales. His friend, King Edward, had entrusted him with the wardship of young Henry Tudor, who had spent his early years in Herbert's care at Raglan Castle, the family's chief seat.

"This Earl of Pembroke had started out as a humble squire," Richard said, "but within a decade he had become one of the greatest lords in the kingdom. And it was well deserved, for he had rendered loyal and excellent service to our house."

Kate could not see what the career of this paragon had to do with her marriage, but she ventured no comment and sat there silently grappling with her misery, and trying to focus on what her father was saying.

"Your future husband grew up during these years. He was knighted at the age of eleven, created Baron Dunster, and married to the Queen's sister, Mary Wydeville."

Kate could tell by her father's tone that he had not approved. But what stirred her interest slightly was that Huntingdon had been married before.

"What was she like, this Mary Wydeville?" she asked.

Her father looked at her hopefully. He was thinking that she was coming around to the idea of this marriage. But she was merely curious.

"In faith, I do not know," he said. "There were so many Wydeville sisters. She cannot have been at court long before she was taken as a bride to Raglan."

As I shall be, Kate thought desperately. God, where is Raglan? In some Welsh mountain fastness? No! Never!

"Lady Huntingdon has been dead for two years. She left one daughter, Elizabeth, who is the earl's sole heir."

And no doubt he seeks a brood mare to provide him with sons! Kate could not contain her bitterness. Well, he can look elsewhere. I will never wed him.

"That has not been the only sadness in Huntingdon's life," Richard was saying. "Alas, in 1469, his gallant father, Pembroke, was captured by the Lancastrians at Edgecote Moor. They beheaded him at Northampton. His son, your future betrothed, then tried to establish his authority in Wales, but he was very young, and without the experience of his father. His rule was not effective, and the Herbert influence declined. He was unable to prevent Henry Tudor's uncle, Jasper, from seizing the boy from Raglan Castle and escaping with him to France."

None of this sounded much like a recommendation. William Herbert had suffered tragedy, yes, but he was clearly not the man his father had been.

"The young earl served King Edward loyally, both in Wales and during the war with France," Richard continued. "Five years ago he agreed to surrender his earldom of Pembroke to the King in exchange for the earldom of Huntingdon; King Edward wanted the Pembroke lands to come under the authority of his son, the Prince of Wales, and his Council of the Marches. He desired to build up the authority of the prince in those parts. It was a judicious plan."

It sounded, thought Kate, a fair exchange, and William Herbert's readiness to agree to it proclaimed his loyalty. But that could not make her love him! She could never love anyone other than John; and at the thought of him, the tears welled again. She fought to hold them back.

"It is in recent months that my lord of Huntingdon has proved his worth," Richard told her. "He served as my Chief Justice and Commissioner of Array in south Wales during Buckingham's rebellion, and he held the area for the crown against the rebels. For that, I have handsomely rewarded him, as he deserves, with high offices in Wales and made him my chief lieutenant there in Buckingham's place. My daughter, your new husband is a virtual king in that country; he is my deputy, and as such enjoys much power and influence."

"I am sure the earl is a worthy man," she said dully.

"He is indeed. If he were not, I would not have made him secretary and chamberlain to your brother the prince. And his marriage to you will cement his loyalty. That is of prime importance, for I have need of men like him at this time. I will bestow you with a rich dowry and make a generous settlement on you both. Above all, Kate, you have an eager bridegroom! All that is wanting is your consent."

He regarded her with raised eyebrows. He was her father. He thought he had provided well for her. How could she refuse him?

Anne knelt beside her. "It is an excellent match for you, Kate. You should be grateful to your father. It would be kind of you to show it."

"I am grateful for your care for me," Kate said tearfully. "Do not think me ungrateful. But, oh sire, this is not the husband I wanted!"

"Now you see what happens when young folks are let to follow their foolish hearts," the King muttered to Anne. "It is good-bye to God, good order, and all. I was a fool myself to permit her to associate with Lincoln. I did warn her of the difficulties, and they are well-nigh insurmountable. I had no idea, Kate, that there was such goodwill between you both; and when Huntingdon showed himself willing, I thought you would be pleased."

When Huntingdon showed himself willing? Her father must have broached the marriage himself, must have offered her as security for the earl's loyalty, for it would be a testing job holding Buckingham's disaffected heartlands. And that generous dowry and settlement— well, it would have to be generous, wouldn't it, to compensate for her bastard status? Because whatever the King said, his baseborn daughter was no great prize in the marriage market. The reaction of John's father had shown her that. Come to think of it, she had never heard of any other royal bastards making a brilliant match. John was forever forbidden to her, and Huntingdon had been bribed to take her. The realization was like a leaden weight in her heart.

"Some fathers would have beaten you for defying them," Anne chided, taking her sullen silence for mutiny. "Be grateful yours is a kindly one. But kind or not, you must obey him. And think, Kate: you will be mistress of a great household. Raglan Castle is a fine and famous residence, I hear, built in a lavish style."

"But it is in Wales!" Kate sobbed, breaking down again. "It is far from you and my father and from—everything I hold dear. I would never see you . . ."

The King spoke gently. "Kate, at some stage, every child must leave its father and mother and cleave to the spouse God has chosen for it. That is what Holy Scripture teaches us. You will have a husband to compensate, and children too, I pray. They will be your life. And you shall visit us at court, and mayhap my journeyings will take me into Wales. In the meantime, we can write to each other. Now, I ask for your consent to this marriage. Will you freely give it?"

She knew herself trapped. If she was to retain her father's love and goodwill, she must obey him and take this man he had chosen for her.

To refuse would only arouse his ire, and anyway, she had no choice. A
· father's word was law—as was the King's.

"I will," she whispered, and again burst into tears.

How she kept her composure as she curtsied and left the privy chamber she did not know, but once she had reached her own chamber she
found herself shaking, her knees weak, her breast heaving. Resting her
hot cheek against the cool stone of the window embrasure, she
thought about what she had just agreed to, and realized she could
never go through with it. Let the whole world condemn her for an
undutiful daughter, but she would not marry Huntingdon! She *could*
not. Nothing must be allowed to come between her and her beloved.

Her blood—the blood of kings and princes—was up. She knew
what she must do. She would enlist John's help, and they would run
away and marry in secret. She would give up everything. It was her
only chance of avoiding the tragedy that would be her marriage. She
must speak to him as soon as possible. He would agree, she had no
doubt of it; he had said they were meant to be together. And once they
were wedded and bedded, no one, not even the King, could part them!

Mattie came in. Mattie would help her.

"Why, mistress, whatever ails you?" her maid exclaimed, seeing her
ravaged face.

"I will tell you, but first, pray seek out my lord of Lincoln for me,
and bid him wait for me at the fountain in New Palace Yard, for our
happiness depends on it!" When Mattie hesitated, Kate cried, "Go!"

Left alone, she splashed cool water on her flushed face, brushed her
hair, smoothed down her blue gown, and clasped about her neck a
three-stranded gold necklace hung with pearls—a coronation gift from
her father. Then she paused to admire her reflection in the mirror, re-
gretting that no amount of artifice could hide her reddened eyes. John
would see at once that she had been crying, but no matter—that might
be to her advantage, and would hopefully make him all the more willing to agree to her plan.

She flung on her cloak, then sped down the stairs and through the
palace, emerging at last into New Palace Yard. And there was John,

already waiting by the canopied fountain. He appeared so tall and debonair in his great velvet cloak, his long locks framing his chiseled features, that it was painful to her to look at him.

"I came at once," he said. "What has happened?"

"The King my father wishes me to marry the Earl of Huntingdon,"
she told him, and burst into weeping afresh. After a pause, he took her
in his arms, not caring who saw them, and held her until she quieted.

"Tell me," he said. And she did, pouring it out in a torrent as they
sat together on the octagonal stone rim of the fountain, John watching
her gravely, shaking his head.

"In faith, I know not what we can do." He sounded despairing.
"Your father is the King: you must obey him."

"Could you get your father to speak for us?" she urged. "If he were
to ask for me as your bride, I know the King would consider it well."

John looked down at his feet. "I have done all in my power to persuade my father to let me marry you. I have begged, cajoled, even lost
my temper . . ." He fell silent.

"There is a way we can be together," she said. "We could elope and
marry in secret! With the help of my maid, it could be done!"

John gaped at her. "Are you mad?" he gasped. "Have you thought of
what that would mean? We are not just any village Jack and Jill, but
public persons of high estate: you are the King's daughter, I his nephew.
I am Earl of Lincoln and will be Duke of Suffolk in the fullness of time.
And you, by the King's decree, are the promised bride of the Earl of
Huntingdon. Royal blood runs in our veins. Were we to run away together, the hue and cry would be after us within minutes, with all the
hounds of hell on our heels. And even if we did escape that, and found
a priest willing to defy the King and marry us, what then? Disgrace!
Dispossession, if not worse, for me. Infamy for you. We would have
nothing to live on. We could not survive. I would not do that to you."

She stared at him. She felt as if the whole world was crumbling
about her. What John was saying made sense, but it was a rational response: his heart was not in it. And it sounded as if he thought more
of disgrace and disinheritance than of her—while she, God help her,
was ready to defy the world for him and risk all.

She did not think she could ever feel any worse than she did at this moment.

She looked at John bleakly. "Then there is no more to say. I am sorry if I asked too much of you."

"Kate . . ." he began, but already she was walking away.

At the end of the month, Richard summoned his daughter and his future son-in-law to the White Hall, where the court had gathered for the betrothal festivities. Queen Anne gave Kate a new gown of dark red silk with a deep black falling collar and high cummerbund. Already the tailors and seamstresses had been set to work on her trousseau, and each day saw fresh bolts of luxurious fabrics delivered by London merchants.

Kate wore no adornment save for her diamond-shaped sapphire pendant. Her hair hung loose down her back, as became a virgin. When the Queen escorted her into the crowded chamber, she was shaking so much that she thought her legs would give way. She saw the King seated on his throne beneath the rich gold canopy of estate; ranged around him were the chief lords of his kingdom, and among them she saw a white-faced Lincoln. She looked away, aware of him watching her. But here was her father, descending from the dais and taking her hand, smiling. She cast her eyes down modestly, but not before she glimpsed a man stepping forward, gorgeously clad in a low-belted gown of green velvet edged with fur. A pair of tan-booted feet presented themselves before her; a hand reached for hers. She looked up into the eyes of the man with the ferret face.

How she recovered from her initial shock and revulsion she never knew, but she allowed him to lead her after the King and Queen into an antechamber where the betrothal contract had been set out on a table. John Russell, Bishop of Lincoln, waited behind it. He bowed courteously and raised his hand in a blessing. Kate tried to catch his eye, for he had shown himself her friend before, but he gave no sign of recognition or sympathy. Instead, once the King and Queen were seated, he went over the terms of the contract.

"My lord, His Grace here provides that he will give with his daughter lands and lordships from the confiscated estates of the late Duke of Buckingham worth a thousand marks annually, and that these are to be settled on you and Dame Katherine here, and on the heirs of your bodies." Kate suppressed a shudder at that, and tried not to think about the getting of those heirs; if she did, she knew, she would be in tears again. It should be the heirs of her body and John's who would inherit her father's bounty; if it had been, she would be rejoicing this day, not in misery. But John had abandoned her without a fight. She felt choked.

The Bishop was droning on, listing all the financial benefits of the marriage: it registered that her jointure was to be lands worth two hundred pounds a year. The King had been more than generous. And there was more. "His Grace will bear the whole cost of the marriage," Russell announced. "In return, you, my lord, are to take Dame Katherine to wife before Michaelmas." The earl nodded his head in agreement, and bowed to the King. Richard smiled.

Michaelmas. The twenty-ninth of September. She might have seven months of freedom left. Anything could happen in that time. She consoled herself with that thought as they proceeded to St. Stephen's Chapel for the betrothal ceremony. Much of it passed her by. She would not listen to the words that bound her to the man beside her. She could hardly bring herself to look up at his pointed nose and wide-set slanting eyes, or to stand too near to him, for there was about him a whiff of stale sweat, as if his fine gown had been worn too often and too long ago. His shock of black hair seemed like an insult; it looked as if someone had put a basin on his head and snipped around it. It was a style years out of date, yet his rich robes marked him as having some pretensions to fashion. He was looking at her slyly, a gleam of possessiveness in his eyes. She could not bear to think that she was bound to this man, with his ferret face and his malodorous body, for life.

KATHERINE

November–December 1559; Whitehall, Sheen,
Westminster Abbey

My mother is dead, God rest her. She breathed her last at Sheen, with me, Mary, and the devoted Stokes at her side. Although she had been poorly for months, her final decline came suddenly, and there was barely time to summon us from court.

I weep for my mother, and I weep even more bitterly for my dashed hopes—for her letter, that crucial letter, was never sent.

Three days later the Queen herself summons me. It is with some relief that I escape from the black-draped house and my mother lying in her coffin on a bier in the chapel, covered with rich palls of damask and cloth of gold.

I find Elizabeth dressed in deepest black, against which the whiteness of her unnatural complexion makes her look like a ghost. It is the first time I have been in her presence since that dreadful day I lost my temper with her. Although her manner is cool and watchful as ever, I can sense she is upset.

"I weep with you in your sad loss, Lady Katherine," she says. "Your mother was my beloved cousin and gossip."

"I thank Your Majesty for your kindness, which I confess I do not deserve," I reply meekly, lowering my gaze.

"We will not speak of that now," she says, her black eyes cold as ever. "I brought you here to tell you that I have arranged for your lady mother to be buried in Westminster Abbey, as befits a princess of the blood, and that I will defray the expenses of the funeral." I am sensible of this being a high privilege, and that the Queen is being uncharacteristically generous. Already she has a reputation for parsimony. She does not spend money unless she has to. So she must have thought very well of my mother to do this for her.

I fall to my knees. "I thank Your Majesty for your magnanimity."

"You will have much to do, so you may depart the court now," Elizabeth says, dismissing me. "You have our leave to return to Sheen."

I hasten away and look for Ned, only to learn from one of his friends that he has already left the court, bound for Sheen too, with the Queen's blessing. Despite myself, I am touched, for Elizabeth knows that my lady regarded him almost as a son. Maybe there is in her some spark of kindness, that she has sent him to succor me and Mary in these dark days of bereavement.

Ned caught the tide; I did not, so he is waiting for me at Sheen when I finally arrive there. Stokes greets me mournfully, weeping at my news, and Ned takes me openly in his arms, not caring that the duchess his mother and all the household officers and servants are standing by to see.

"I came at once, sweetheart," he murmurs. "You will not endure this alone."

My mother, being a staunch Protestant, would not have approved of prayers for the dead, so I fall wordlessly to my knees before her coffin. I cannot believe she is in there, that strong, tempestuous woman who has dominated my life; nor did I expect to feel so bereft at her loss. I comfort myself by imagining her being reunited with Jane and my father in eternal joy and peace, and weep afresh with the emotion of it all, burying my face in my hands.

When I sit up, dabbing my eyes with my kerchief, Ned is sitting quietly beside me. He waits until I have composed myself, and gently escorts me from the chapel.

We speak of my mother, the coming obsequies, and the Queen's generosity, and then his face looks pained.

"I heard of your confrontation with the Queen," he says.

"Everyone has, it seems. In truth, I could not help myself. I wish I had kept my mouth shut."

"So do I," he mutters. "Not that what you said was untrue, but it can have done us no good."

"She was kind to us both this morning, after her fashion."

"She is a great dissembler! Nothing she does is without calculation.

But even if she has relented toward you, you should beware of courting her wrath further at this time."

"You may depend upon that," I assure him grimly.

As soon as I get a moment to myself, I go up to my mother's chamber
and, trying not to look at the empty, stripped bed, search in the chest
where she kept her private papers. And there I find the letter, as I had
expected, written in a shaky hand. It is addressed to the Queen, and
below the lines I had read already, my lady had written: *This marriage
is the only thing I desire before my death, and it will be an occasion for me to
die quietly.* There is no more, and no signature. She died before she
could finish or send it.

Ned, the duchess, and Stokes are grouped by the fire when I enter;
it is a cold evening, we are all huddled in furs, and Arthur and Guinevere are stretched out so close to the hearth that they are in danger of
being singed by sparks.

I show them all the letter. "Read this, I pray you. You will see that it
was my lady's dying wish that Ned and I be married. Should we not
send this now to the Queen? She can hardly refuse, in the circumstances."

"Elizabeth is not well disposed toward you at present, Katherine,"
the duchess says bluntly. "You spoke unwisely to her, I hear. That was
foolish in the extreme, and it betrays a want of prudence. One should
never say such things to queens, only tell them what they want to be
told. My advice is to wait a while until tempers have cooled."

"But the Queen spoke kindly to me this morning, and I gave her an
apology," I protest.

"The Queen has a long memory," the duchess says. "I counsel you
to wait."

"Mr. Stokes, what do you think?" I ask. Stokes was zealous in my
cause: he will not abandon me now, and others value his wisdom.

But for once he seems to be at a loss for words. "I cannot advise
you, Katherine, until I know my lord's mind in the matter," he says
finally. Bewildered, I turn to Ned, but his eyes are fixed on my stepfather.

"What do you want to do about the letter, my lord?" Stokes asks.

Ned does not look at me. "I will meddle no further in the matter," he declares. "Burn the letter. In view of the late Spanish conspiracy and the Queen's anger with Katherine, it could destroy us all." And Stokes takes it from me before I can gainsay him and throws it into the fire.

"But why?" I wail, seeing my hopes char and curl up and burst into flame, gone from me forever.

"Because, my sweetheart, I will not risk either your neck or mine at this present time. We must be patient and endure this waiting a while longer, until Elizabeth's wrath is truly abated. Our moment will come, I promise you."

"When? I cannot bear this uncertainty any longer!"

"You can and you must bear it," the duchess hectors me. "Make your move now, and all will be lost. Is that what you want? Besides, there are other considerations to remember."

"What do you mean?" I ask.

"Ned has his way to make in the world; he desires to restore his house to the greatness that was once ours. He cannot do that if he has offended the Queen by marrying, without her consent, one whom she fears because she is the rightful heiress to the throne."

I look at Ned, who is staring at his boots. I know that his mother speaks sense. Reluctantly I am coming to see that it *would* be a bad move to approach the Queen now, and with a leaden heart I steel myself for another seemingly endless wait before my real life can begin.

As chief mourner, I follow my mother's coffin to the high altar of Westminster Abbey. In deepest black, my face obscured by a voluminous hood, I strive to focus my thoughts on her whom I have lost, yet I cannot help reflecting, with some bewilderment, on the latest, unexpected favor bestowed on me and my sister at the Queen's hands. I do believe that Her Majesty genuinely sympathizes with us, for she has been uncommonly kind. For these royal obsequies, she had been pleased to command that Mary and I be accorded the dignity of princesses of the blood. Considering how rudely I had spoken to her, this was magnanimity indeed. And thus, as tokens of my new status, my mourning train is carried by a Lady of the Queen's Bedchamber, and I find myself and my sister kneeling on velvet cushions on the steps of the chancel, as the service begins amid a forest of banners and escutcheons—the whole panoply of a state funeral.

One of the heralds—Clarenceux King of Arms—commences with a ringing proclamation: "Laud and praise be given to Almighty God that it hath pleased Him to call out of this transitory life unto His eternal glory the most noble and excellent princess, the Lady Frances, late Duchess of Suffolk, daughter to . . ."

I cannot concentrate. My mind is a turmoil of emotions and hopes. My grief for my mother overrides all on this dismal day, but beneath it there stirs new hope that this elevation of my status is a prelude to my being formally acknowledged as heiress presumptive.

KATE

April–May 1484, Nottingham Castle

All that season, the land was quiet, save for the persistent rumors that rumbled like distant thunder. But Kate was so sunk in despair that she paid little heed to them, or to anything else—until something happened that jolted her back to reality.

The court was at Nottingham Castle, a massive stronghold perched spectacularly on a great rock overlooking the ancient town below, and Kate was lodged in the palatial apartments built by King Edward. Her betrothed had returned to his duties at Middleham, but John was still with the court; he kept well away from her now, although once or twice she glimpsed him watching her. He was suffering too: she could see that. Maybe he had been right to take a realistic view of her madcap plan to run away, yet still she could not face him. She was barely holding herself together as it was.

The King, however, was in a merry, satisfied frame of mind. He had overcome his enemies, he had given the lie to the rumormongers—or so he believed—and he was on his way back to the North, where he was popular. And the Queen's spirits had lifted because soon they would be at Middleham, where she would be reunited with her son.

Easter came and went with its usual solemnities and celebrations. Then, two days later, a messenger came seeking the King.

The prince was dead. That fair, delicate child had fallen violently ill with pains in his belly, and had suffered an unhappy death—eleven days ago. Eleven days! He had breathed his last, the poor, frail boy, as the court made its unwieldy way northward, and had been lying cold in his winding-sheet at Middleham as his parents feasted on Easter Day.

Kate could not stop crying, and her grief was not all for her half brother. Some of it was for herself, and his death had created an outlet for it. The remembrance of her sad situation and her approaching marriage made her weep all the more; it was as if there was a fount within her that would never run dry.

As for her father and stepmother, their grief almost bordered on madness. The shock had been terrible, and nothing could console them for their loss. They would see no one, but remained shut off from the court in their private apartments. Kate could only hope that they were managing to console each other in their shared agony. She longed to go to them, but the remembrance of her father's anguished face when he told her the news, and his terrible cry of pain when he doubled up and howled at her to go from him quickly, was enough to deter her.

She spent long hours on her knees in the chapel, praying to a God who seemed cruel and vengeful rather than kind and loving. One day, she knelt sobbing for an hour and more. Suddenly, there was someone there beside her. A hand came to rest on her heaving shoulder. It was John.

"I am so very sorry," he said quietly. It was more than a conventional expression of grief, she knew. "Is there anything I can do?"

"Oh, John," she wept, and fell into his ready arms. He held her while the torrent of weeping passed. "I have cried so much these past weeks that it is a wonder I have any tears left to flow. He was their only child. And you are my only love, and I have lost you too."

"He was your father's heir too, the assurance of his dynasty. And your stepmother is not a strong woman. Maybe she will bear another child, with God's grace, yet I fear she may not."

"She loved Edward so much." Kate wept. John was still holding her, as tightly as if he could never let her go. Sad as she was, she was savoring this moment of closeness, knowing that it might have to last her for a long time.

"When are you to be married?" he asked, his voice hoarse.

"By Michaelmas. The date has not been set yet. I hope it never will be!"

"Would to God you could escape it," he breathed, crushing her to him. "But there is small hope of that. With the contract signed, and Huntingdon fattened with lands and offices, with more to come, I hear, the King will not renege on his word."

"I cannot bear the thought," Kate whispered. "I want only you. John—will you do something for me? Just this one thing, and then I will ask no more of you."

"If it is in my power, I will do it, you may be assured of that, my love." He looked at her uncertainly. "What is it?"

"My heart, soon I must go to my marriage bed. I dread the thought. But I could bear it if I went to it knowing what true love really is." A faint blush tinged her pale cheeks. She knew she was taking a perilous risk that might rebound on her in various ways; and she feared that John might think her wanton. But that hardly mattered now.

"You are asking me to take your maidenhead? To steal it from your husband?" John's face was a battlefield of warring emotions.

"Yes. At least we would have that, a memory we could treasure all our lives."

"And if you should be with child as a result?"

"In law, it would be my husband's, if we lie together at the right time. He would never know. We are cousins, so any likeness could be explained."

The aristocratic dynast in John was plainly at loggerheads with the lover. "But sweetheart, much as I want you, a man should be able to count on his heir as his own, not a cuckoo in the nest."

"Do you think I care about that? Huntingdon means nothing to me! And what better heir than the offspring of royal blood, yours and mine? He will never know, John. But if you have such qualms, then I am sorry I asked."

He hesitated. For a moment she thought he would weigh the dangers more heavily than the joys, as he had before. Then his arms tightened around her again. "How could I refuse you?" he whispered, and sought her lips.

Emerging from the seclusion of their mourning, the King and Queen were tragic specters of their former selves. Richard's face was hard-set and careworn, Anne's white and ghastly. It did not help that some had chosen to see the hand of God in the prince's death. Preparing to leave the chapel one morning, Kate had overheard Bishop Russell talking to Lord Stanley in a closet that led off it, where they had probably thought themselves private.

"Now we have fully seen how vain are the thoughts of a man who desires to establish his interests without the aid of God," the Bishop was saying, his voice low but loud enough to carry. "Some are saying this is a judgment on him—an eye for an eye, so to speak." His words made Kate's blood turn to ice.

"Without an heir, his position is even less secure," Stanley muttered. "I'll wager this will drive many into the arms of my stepson."

She could not bear to hear more. It was cruel, vile, that this tragedy of the prince's death should be interpreted this way—and it was disloyal. What hope was there for her father when even his chancellor was faithless?

Calumny was not confined to the court. As Kate and Mattie wandered through the market in Nottingham one morning, they heard people openly giving their opinion that, in taking to Himself the usurper's son, God had heeded the cries of the anguished Queen Elizabeth; others were shamelessly asserting that the princes had been rid out of this world, and a particularly vociferous few brazenly claimed that it was the King who'd had those innocents put to death.

"Murdered between two feather beds!" said a stout stallholder, shaking his head sagely. "And it was Sir James Tyrell that was sent to do it!"

That was news to Kate. She vaguely knew Sir James Tyrell; he had been in her father's service for some years, and she had seen him about the court occasionally. Why people should think he had murdered the princes was a mystery to her, and sounded far-fetched. What pressed on her more heavily was a growing awareness that the King had lost the hearts of his subjects—if he had ever won them in the first place. She was even conscious of a growing hostility toward him at court, where some had reacted with only muted sympathy to the loss of his heir.

"I'd rather have the French to rule us than be under that hog's subjection!" a butcher in a filthy apron opined. The crowd laughed.

"Forget the white boar—it should be the bloody boar!" someone cackled.

"Richard won't last long," a merchant in a furred gown declared. "From what I hear, he can only keep people loyal by intimidation or bribing them with gifts." Kate winced at that.

"He must know that people murmur and grudge against him," said an innkeeper.

"He has the remedy in his own hands," the merchant declared. "All he has to do is produce the princes alive. That would still the rumors and confound his enemies."

"But can he do that?" the stallholder asked. "I don't think so!" Heads began shaking, and there were boos and catcalls of derision. Kate tried to shut her ears.

At last Mattie came back with her purchases.

"We must go," Kate muttered, and steered her away.

"John, what do you know of Sir James Tyrell?" she asked suddenly, late that night in the chapel. It was past midnight and most souls were abed. She had made her way by stealth through the silent castle and flung herself into John's embrace as soon as the chapel door was closed behind her. Now they were sitting in the choir stalls.

"He's one of your father's retainers, from the North," John replied, stroking her hair. "He serves now as a Knight of the Body, guarding the King at night, and performs many labors for him. Why do you ask?"

Kate told him what people had been saying in Nottingham. He frowned.

"They are ignorant fools and know nothing."

"But why should they mention Tyrell?"

"I have no idea. Those peasants will seize on any gossip and make much of it. I'll wager Sir James would be mortified if he knew. Just forget it, my love. We have better things to do than discuss Tyrell." He nuzzled her ear and drew her to him. "When will you be mine? I am aching for you."

"When I am to be married. It is the only safe time, if I am not to risk the shame of having a high belly before the wedding. Dear heart, I long for it, even though I dread what must follow."

Lying in bed later that night, hugging to herself fond thoughts of her stolen hour with Lincoln, Kate recalled what he had said about Tyrell, and wondered if Mattie knew of the man. She was a veritable font of knowledge concerning what went on in the court.

"Mattie, are you asleep?" she whispered loudly.

"Nay," came back a cheerful voice from the pallet bed on the floor. "I can't stop thinking about Guy." Guy Freeman was one of the grooms, a big, easygoing, handsome lad, and he was always flirting with Mattie.

"He likes you."

"Aye—I think he does. He told me I'd make a bonny wife!"

"He might ask for your hand." Delighted as she felt for her maid, Kate was envious. People of Mattie's station in life never had to worry about marrying for policy—they could wed where they chose, and for love too.

"It's just a matter of time!" Mattie giggled. "What did you want, mistress?"

"Do you know anything about a courtier called Sir James Tyrell?"

"Er, um . . . yes," Mattie muttered, her tone changing. "I was hoping you wouldn't find out."

"What?" Kate was puzzled.

"I don't just know *of* him—I knew him very well, the bastard."

"You mean, you—he . . ."

"Yes," Mattie confessed. "It was last year, on the progress. I'm really sorry, mistress—I shouldn't have done it, and you have every right to tell me off, but he cozened me with sweet words and cheap trinkets, and then I let him. I wish to God I hadn't."

"But I knew nothing of this. What happened?" Kate was stunned. She had suspected nothing—and the coincidence was astonishing.

"He went off south to London. Had to get stuff from the Royal Wardrobe for the poor prince's investiture in York. When he came back, he didn't want to know. He's one of those rats who lose interest once they've got what they wanted."

"I'm so sorry for you, Mattie. It's lucky he didn't leave you with child."

"I thank our Holy Mother for that. She must have had me under her protection that night. Oh, Lord, I was a fool." She sighed. "Can I go to sleep now, mistress? I'm that tired."

"Of course," Kate said. "Good night."

The next day she and Mattie looked for Sir James in the court. He noticed them staring at him and turned his head away. He was a handsome wight, Kate had to admit, but he looked vain with it, and too assured of his place in the world. She decided to ruffle his peacock feathers.

She did a daring and impulsive thing. She sent Mattie off on an errand, then went over to where Tyrell was standing. He leered at her.

"My Lady Katherine," he said, bowing extravagantly.

"I heard something rather disturbing yesterday, Sir James," she said. "It was about you."

"My lady?" His expression was shifty now.

"Yes. It seems you took advantage of my maid and then abandoned her." Kate was surprised at her own boldness, but reminded herself that she had every right, as Mattie's mistress, to make a complaint.

"Who said that, my lady?"

"She told me herself when I asked about you."

"Oh?" He looked nonplussed.

"Someone had mentioned you in connection with a different matter." She paused; let that confound him! "I do confess, sir, that I was disappointed to hear of such dishonorable conduct."

"She was willing enough," Tyrell said sourly.

"I daresay she was. But she was very young, and you, sir, are a knight, and a man of years and experience. It did not become you to use her so."

He was angry now.

Kate continued: "Unless you wish to be reported to the King my father, I would suggest you do not treat any other ladies in the same way. You know how strict he is where morality is concerned."

"Are you threatening me, my lady?"

"Only if you conduct yourself dishonorably in the future. I must respect the example my father sets. I'm sure you can appreciate that." She smiled sweetly.

"What is all this about?" Sir James puffed. "You say you've heard about me in connection with another matter. Why did you ask Mattie about me?"

Kate lowered her voice. "I heard your name mentioned in the marketplace yesterday. Someone said—and I only repeat it—that you were sent by the King to the Tower to murder his nephews."

Tyrell gave nothing away. His face did not change. If there was a tightening around his lips, it could have been put down to indignation that people could accuse him of such things.

"You should not pay heed to gossip, my lady," he growled.

"I did not say I heeded it, sir," she sparred.

Tyrell gave her a hard look, as if he guessed she was testing his reactions. "Well, thank you, my lady," he said grudgingly. Then he nodded his head in the briefest of bows and stalked off.

With the prince dead and buried, and having no need now to remain at Middleham, the Earl of Huntingdon—Kate could not yet think of him as William—rode south to attend upon the King. Having established himself and his retinue at court, he took to calling upon Kate every day, often with gifts. He never stayed long, for her manner was courteous but cold. She could not overcome the revulsion she felt. There was nothing between them, no affection or even liking. They remained two strangers. How would they ever make a marriage?

As she lay wakeful in bed one night, after a stolen hour with John on the battlements, Kate made a disturbing connection. She remembered Mattie saying that Tyrell had gone south to London to get stuff for the investiture in York. That would have been on the King's orders, surely. The investiture had been in September, and soon afterward rumors of the murder of the princes had begun to circulate, followed speedily by Buckingham's rebellion. Had there been any connection between Tyrell's trip to London and the princes' disappearance? Had he had another, more sinister purpose than just fetching necessary stuff for the investiture?

After a sleepless night, she questioned Mattie after Mass, as they broke their fast over bread and ale.

"I reprimanded Sir James Tyrell for his treatment of you," she said. "But I wondered . . . Did he say anything to you about that journey he made to London?"

"He just said he had to go to the Tower to collect stuff from the Royal Wardrobe. I can't recall him saying anything else—oh, he said it would be a fast ride: four days each way. I remember that because I was counting them on my fingers."

The Tower. He had been to the Tower. The realization sent shivers of ice down Kate's spine. But again—where else would he have gone, with instructions to collect things from the Royal Wardrobe, which just happened to be housed in the Tower? His presence there did not mean that he had murdered the princes.

This is becoming an obsession, Kate thought. Yet still there were so many unanswered questions, not the least of which was why her father had not shown the princes to the people and given the lie to the rumors that were destroying his reputation.

Again she told herself that there would be an honest reason for his not having done so. What if the boys had died natural deaths? Disease was rife in London, especially in the hot summer months, and the elder prince had not been well. Given the widespread rumors, if her father announced now that one or both princes had died through illness, no one would believe him.

She was going round and round in circles with her arguments. Was she imagining a mystery where none existed? Did the princes still live in the Tower, as John had insisted? She wanted desperately to believe it.

Fetching writing materials, she stayed in her chamber setting down everything she knew in note form. She wrote of the rumors that were damaging to the King; the likelihood that Buckingham had known the truth about the fate of the princes, although he was dead and could not talk; that Bishop Russell had more or less said they lived yet; that Tyrell had been at the Tower, and more . . .

She recorded how both Brother Dominic and Bishop Russell believed that her father had been determined to seize the throne from the first, although neither of them had actually accused him of murdering his nephews. She noted how the Bishop dismissed the precontract story, yet said her father had chosen to believe it. But that did not make him a child killer. And apart from the rumors, which could have been started by any of his enemies, and the fact that no one had seen the princes since July, ten months ago, there was no evidence at all that he had destroyed his brother's sons.

She had to know the truth about the precontract. Gathering her papers together, she tied them up with a length of hair ribbon and locked them in her chest, where they would be secure. It would not do to leave such contentious writings lying around, for she could not bear the thought of her father finding out what she was doing. She had already overstepped the mark with her questions as it was.

Locking her door behind her, just to be on the safe side, she made her way around the vast warren of the castle, hoping to find Bishop Stillington, the man who had laid evidence of the precontract before her father. She knew him by sight, a plump, aging, high-nosed cleric who seemed to be always hovering in the King's wake. By great good fortune, she ran into him in the chapel.

"God's blessing on you, Lady Katherine," he said unctuously. "You are a little late for Mass, I fear."

She curtsied. "No, Father, I heard Mass earlier. It is you I seek."

"I?" He smiled. "If I can be of any service to such a charming young lady . . ." She found his manner ingratiating.

"Yes, Father. Something troubles me," she said. "Something I overheard."

"Tell me, child," Stillington said, ushering her to a pew. "Tell me all about it."

Kate assumed an air of innocence. "Father, I know well that my father became King because the young King Edward and his brother were found to be illegitimate. There was something about a precontract . . ."

The little Bishop's smile had slipped somewhat. He looked uneasy. "Yes, my child, there was, and your father's title has now been confirmed in Parliament. What can possibly be troubling you?"

"I overheard two men—I know not who, they had their backs to me—saying there was no precontract and that it was a false tale used as a pretext for my father to take the throne. In faith, I was very upset to hear such talk." She was making, she felt, a good job of playing the damsel in distress.

Bishop Stillington appeared discomposed for a moment, then collected himself with an effort, assuming again his urbane manner of moments before. "That is a foul calumny, my lady!" he declared. "I wish you had marked the men who said it, then they should have been dealt with as they deserved. Even so, they were only repeating idle gossip."

Kate tried to look relieved. "I am glad to hear you say that," she said. "I thank you for your words of comfort. That lady—Dame Eleanor Butler, was it?—what happened to her?"

"She died long ago," the Bishop said firmly. "And now, if you will excuse me, I must attend on the King your father." And he sketched the sign of the cross over her and departed. She sat there awhile, thinking that he was not a man she would trust; certainly he had not wanted to talk about Eleanor Butler.

When she looked up, William, her betrothed, was standing in the doorway, watching her in that disconcerting way he had. "Good day, my lady," he said stiffly, bowing. "I have been looking for you. We are summoned to wait upon the King's Grace."

———

Richard was seated in his closet, clad in deepest black, his only jewel the ruby and jet brooch with the drop pearl that he customarily wore on his hat. He looked shrunken, diminished by grief, his face a mask of sorrow; his voice was hoarse and his manner distant. Yet he welcomed them kindly enough, and embraced and kissed Kate.

"I have some good news for you both, which shall be a comfort to us all," he said. "I have decided that you are to be wed before I leave this, my castle of care."

Married now! Kate knew her distress must be visible in her face. She had thought it would not be for months yet. Desperately, she tried to compose herself, aware that everyone—her betrothed, her father, and his courtiers—was looking at her.

"Bishop Stillington has consented to perform the ceremony in the castle chapel," the King was saying. "Given the circumstances"—his voice faltered slightly—"it will be a small wedding. But never fear, Kate, we will feast you as becomes a bride, and make merry, eh?" He gave her a weak smile, which she tried to return. She thought: In his grief, he has forgotten that I love another, and that this news of my wedding can only grieve me.

"Afterward, you will ride with the court to Durham, and thence to York," the King informed them. "I should like to keep Kate with me for just a little longer." He looked at her wistfully, and it was all she could do to keep from crying. "But then you must go into Wales, and guard it for me, William; guard it loyally. The Tudor skulks in Brittany, and who knows what mischief he is plotting!"

"I am Your Grace's man unto death," William declared, bowing.

"You will be well rewarded, I promise it. Kate, my child, the Queen is waiting to assist you with your wedding attire. Go to her now."

Kate dipped in another curtsey. William was giving her that look again, and there was a hint of lust in his eyes that had not been there before.

Emerging from the Queen's lodgings, weary of trying to look pleased with the fine fabrics that had been displayed before her, and of standing still while the tailors pinned them on her, Kate turned urgently to Mattie.

"Go seek out my lord of Lincoln," she directed her. "Bid him be in the chapel at midnight, as you love me."

Mattie looked at her, comprehension dawning. "So that's how it is," she said. "You are to be wed, yet you are still seeing your young lord. Have a care, mistress!"

"I love him!" Kate said brokenly. "This will be the last time, I vow it. After that, I will belong to my husband and my life will be over. But I swear he will never have any pleasure of me!"

KATHERINE

September 1560, Whitehall Palace

The court is an in uproar, and no wonder! Lord Robert Dudley's uncherished wife has been found dead, her neck broken, at the foot of a flight of stairs at Cumnor Place, near Oxford. Such a scandal has not erupted in a long time. It is all over the court, and no doubt will soon be all over Christendom too; and the word on everyone's lips is "murder." Tongues wag ceaselessly, and suspicion centers on Lord Robert, but fingers point secretly—and sometimes not so secretly—at Queen Elizabeth. The Dudley scandal is so sensational that it seems she may never recover from it. There is even talk that King Philip is urging her to wed Lord Robert in order to discredit her, so that he will then be able to press my claim to the throne.

But he does not know Elizabeth! I would wager a fortune on her never having allowed Robert Dudley to pass beyond caresses; and I saw for myself how dismayed she was, not only at Amy Dudley's death, but at the realization that Lord Robert was now a free man. Him she loves: I do not doubt that; but she will never surrender her body or her autonomy as Queen.

Yet there remains talk of my marrying the Archduke Ferdinand or—horrors—even Don Carlos. Bishop de Quadra returns to that theme whenever we meet, and I smile and profess myself flattered, yet remain noncommittal, telling him that he must seek my sovereign's permission for my marriage. Maybe he knows I am stalling—and goodness knows, I have good reason to do so! Because at last, at long last, there is hope for my sweet Ned and me.

Only yesterday Sir William Cecil approached Ned and informed him it had been noticed that he sought me out whenever he came to Whitehall. Ned was much alarmed, for he feared Mr. Secretary was about to forbid him to see me again. But no! He asked Ned if there was goodwill between us—but Ned was so afraid of our being parted that he said there was no such thing.

Cecil told him he knew of the Spanish plot to marry me to the Archduke or Don Carlos. Ned could not hide his astonishment when Sir William said he would like to forestall that plot by arranging my marriage to a loyal Englishman. But, he added, as he saw now that there was nothing between us, he would forbear to pursue the matter further. "And good day to you, sir," he had ended.

Ned did not know what to do. He feared a trap, that Cecil's words were a lure to ensnare him into admitting that there has been talk of a marriage between us, against the Queen's express wish. So he detained Cecil and told him that he had long admired me from afar and should be honored to marry me, if it were the Queen's pleasure. And Cecil said he would be our friend and speak with Her Majesty! We could not have a better or more influential advocate! At last I can dare to hope that our long wait will soon be over.

Days, then weeks, have passed—and nothing, no word, no sign from Mr. Secretary. When I saw him this morning, he merely nodded courteously and hurried on, his arms full of scrolls. I am going mad with frustration, desperate to know if he is still our friend, and if he has spoken to the Queen on our behalf.

And now there are fresh rumors, that the Scots want me as a bride for the Earl of Arran, another imbecile who is Queen Mary's heir, unless she bears a son. Perchance the lords of Scotland see this marriage as a means of uniting the two kingdoms, in the event of both Mary and Elizabeth dying childless. They say de Quadra has bet a hundred crowns that it will come to pass. Well, they can negotiate all they like, but I will not have the lunatic earl, nay, not even if the Queen herself commands it—which she will not, I am certain.

There is talk too—will it never cease?—of another Spanish bid to entice me away to Spain, by means of some loyal Catholic English gentleman acting for King Philip. What especially vexes me about these continual plots to marry or carry me off is that I, the person most concerned, am never consulted! It's true: my royal blood is a curse.

But now some good news! Against all expectations—although some say it is because she is at present vexed with my rival, the Queen of Scots—Her Majesty has suddenly decreed that I be restored to the post of Lady of the Privy Chamber that I had held under Queen Mary. And she has received me there today, right graciously, in the presence of Bishop de Quadra.

"I look upon the Lady Katherine as a daughter," she tells him, raising me from my curtsey and embracing and kissing me. For an instant the Bishop looks as amazed as I, but we both recover ourselves quickly.

"Now that she is an orphan, I am considering formally adopting her," the Queen continues, smiling at me—although her eyes remain cold. I can barely express my thanks. What game is she playing at now?

I am not surprised when, later, after I am dismissed from my new duties, which are little more than to bear the Queen company when she wants it—which I suspect will not be often—de Quadra is waiting for me.

"Any feeling between Her Majesty and yourself, Lady Katherine, can hardly be that of mother and child!" he observes with a smile. "Methinks she is making much of you in order to keep you from intriguing with the likes of me and the Scots."

"Do you think it might presage my being acknowledged heir?" I ask, unable to restrain my exhilaration at the prospect.

"Who can say?" The Bishop shakes his head. "Knowing this Queen, it could mean anything. I will make some inquiries."

———

Two days later de Quadra is waiting for me again.

"I have spoken with Sir William Cecil," he tells me. "I asked him if the favor shown you by the Queen heralds any particular announcement. He took my meaning immediately. The answer is no. Her Majesty, he said, is of the opinion that Henry Hastings, the Earl of Huntingdon, who is descended from the old royal blood of this realm, has a greater claim than yourself. I asked him if Her Majesty would consider naming you as her successor, but he said by no means, because the English always run after the heir to the crown rather than the wearer of it."

It seems I must settle for a compromise: marriage, rather than the throne. For me, the choice is an easy one. I would rather have my sweet Ned than be the greatest Queen crowned.

KATE

May 1484, Nottingham Castle

John was waiting for her in the chapel. She could see him in the shadows beyond the dim light cast by the single lamp on the altar, signifying the eternal presence of God. He came and clasped her hands, gazing into her eyes without speaking, then his arms went around her.

"You are sure about this?" he breathed in her ear, threading his fingers through her hair.

"Never more," she whispered. "But we cannot be together here."

"No, but I have found us a place." He smiled at her: she loved his smile; it was open and boyish, and it always made her melt. He took her hand and kissed it. "Before we go there, my love, there is something I want to do, something important."

He led her to the altar, with its golden crucifix and the statue of the Virgin with her Babe, and stood there beside her, still holding her hand and looking into her eyes.

"Hear me, Kate. I will give you my promise. I, John, take thee,

Katherine, to be my true lady before God, and I vow I will love you always, until death and beyond." She looked at him wonderingly, tears starting in her eyes, for she was overcome by the awe of the moment.

"Now you, sweetheart," he said. "Your turn . . ."

"I, Katherine," she swore, "take thee, John, to be my true lord in the sight of God, and hereto I pledge thee my love, until death and beyond." The words came strong and clear, impelled by the conviction that whatever was to come, this was her proper wedding, even without any witnesses to make it valid.

And then, hand in hand still, they crept out of the chapel, through the sleeping castle and along a dark stone passageway lit only with one dying torch in a wall bracket. At the end of it, John unlocked a door and led Kate into a small chamber sparsely furnished with a tester bed hung with green curtains. And it was in that bed, presently, that they lay together; and it was as if God had sent His angels down to smile upon them and hallow their union.

KATHERINE

October 1560, Whitehall

My bosom companion, Jane Seymour, has been at court with me through all the late tortuous shifts of fortune, solidly supporting me and Ned, and going back and forth between us, passing messages, notes, and love tokens, and helping to arrange snatched meetings, which are few and far apart, for we know now that we have been watched by Mr. Secretary Cecil.

But Jane is not well. Her cheeks, once rosebud pale, are now flushed with an unhealthy hue; her gowns hang loosely upon her; and there is blood on her kerchief when she coughs. She gets out of breath easily these days, and suffers terrible sweats at night.

Jane loves Ned more than any other human soul; and it is her dearest wish to see him well and happily married.

"There could be no better wife for him than you, my dear Katherine," she tells me, hugging me fondly. "I will do all I can to help you two achieve the happiness you deserve. God knows, you have waited long enough for it!"

"The time is now right, at last," I say. "There was never a better moment to press for Her Majesty's consent."

Ned frowns. "Will there ever be a right moment? I fear she will never give that consent. We have to be realistic. Look at the way she keeps her many suitors dangling—this waiting could go on for years!"

Jane is thoughtful. "Why not present the Queen with a fait accompli?" she suggests. "Marry in secret now, then throw yourselves upon her mercy. If the thing is done, she must relent."

"Of course!" I agree excitedly. "When the Queen realizes that it is purely a love match, and that we intend no threat to her, she will surely forgive us. And we have Sir William Cecil on our side, remember. He will support us, you may count on it!"

Ned shakes his head. "I think not. I met him by chance today. He asked me how I did, the usual pleasantries, and then he said he was still hearing rumors that I was in love with you and hoping to wed. He advised me to cool my ardor, and walked on."

"But he was in favor of our marriage," I say helplessly.

"Sir William must know that this marriage makes sense," Jane says. "He ought to be on your side, Ned," she adds. "It was our father who first gave him a post at court and set him on the road to the greatness he enjoys today."

Ned looks dejected. "That counts for little now. But Lord Robert might help us. Now that the coroner has cleared him of the murder of his wife, he is again influential with the Queen. And, Katherine, his brother was once married to your sister. But wedding without the Queen's permission? The thing is fraught with dangers, and might be construed as treason."

"How can it be?" I flare. "I am not recognized as heiress presumptive. If I were, then it might be treason, but I remain a private person. The Queen cannot have it both ways!"

"You have been restored to the status of princess of the blood," he reminds me. "Therefore your marriage is a matter of public concern. Usurp the Queen's privilege, and you may yet be accused of treason."

"There is no law that says I would be guilty of it!"

"Have you forgotten that the Queen herself warned you not to wed without her consent?"

"Things have changed since then," Jane puts in. "The Queen and her council must know that a far more deadly threat than your marriage comes from Spain or Scotland. Do it, brother! Do not sacrifice all you hold dear for the want of a little courage."

"I will think on it," Ned says reluctantly. "If I seem unenthusiastic, it is because I do not wish to bring down the Queen's wrath on us both. Katherine is too dear to me for that." And he stoops and brushes my lips with his own.

KATE

May 1484, Nottingham Castle

Kate stood before the altar with William, barely hearing the words of the nuptial Mass. This travesty of a ceremony was a perversion of everything that marriage should be, yet she stood there meekly, every inch the King's daughter in her sumptuous gown and train of black-figured cloth of gold, with tight scarlet velvet sleeves and a surcoat of white silk. Over her shoulders flowed her luxuriant hair, loose in token of her supposedly virgin state. If only they all knew!

She made her vows to William without a tremor. They meant nothing.

She knew John was behind her somewhere. He had said he would be. "Think of me when you are at the altar," he said as they had lain together in the blissful peace that followed rapturous lovemaking. "I will be thinking of you, and of our true vows."

She had given him her word, and she kept it. She was his, and no one could take that from her, not even her new-made husband standing by her side.

———

Not for Kate and William a small bedchamber with an old bed hung
with dusty green curtains; instead, they were assigned two spacious
rooms overlooking the town below. In the larger of the two stood a
red-draped bed with a carved table beside it, upon which had been left
a silver tray bearing a glass ewer with a silver stopper and jeweled wine
goblets. In front of the fireplace stood a long carved cushioned settle,
and from the beamed ceiling hung a gilded chandelier, its candles flickering in the breeze from the open window. No detail, no comfort, had
been overlooked.

But there was small comfort in the thought of what lay ahead. *At
least,* Kate thought, *I do not have to face being deflowered by this stranger.*
It had been painful enough with John, yet he was gentle with her, and
the hurt had soon been replaced by a wondrous new sensation of pleasure. She could not bear to think about that now; her sense of loss was
too acute.

When Mattie had gone, having turned down the sheets, plumped
the bolster, unlaced and laid away the beautiful wedding gown, and
brushed her mistress's tresses until they shone, Kate climbed into bed
in her chemise and sat there waiting, her heart pounding. She thanked
God for one small mercy: that, because the court was in mourning for
the prince, there was to be no public bedding ceremony.

Soon William appeared, clad in a silk robe. "Well, here we are,
wife," he said, pausing to pour them some wine. "I hope you are not
afraid of me." He handed her a goblet.

"No, my lord," she answered, but gulped down the wine gratefully,
averting her eyes as her husband shed his robe and climbed naked into
bed. She had a glimpse of sinewy limbs, white flanks, and thick thatches
of black hair over his chest and between his legs.

"A toast to our marriage," said William, and they clinked goblets.
When he had drained his, he laid hold of her. Before she had time to
catch her breath, he was raking up her shift, clambering on top of her,
and forcing an entry. She gasped a little, for his thrusting was painful
after all and there was no need to fake any discomfort. When he was
done, he slumped beside her, panting, and she lay there, her head turned
away, her heart empty. What had been so exalting last night meant

nothing at all today. Was this how it was to be for always and always? And was William not going to speak even one word of love to her?

She made an effort. She had to do something to make her marriage bearable. "Do I please you, my lord?" she whispered. There was no answer. Instead, William began snoring.

KATHERINE

November 1560, Hampton Court Palace

One morning, as I am walking my dogs through the gardens overlooking the Thames at Hampton Court, I espy my beloved, kissing—for all to see—the hand of Frances Mewtas, a Gentlewoman of the Chamber to the Queen. Unaware of my presence, they talk privily, those two, and she giggles, then Ned bows and goes on his way, leaving her flushed and smiling to herself.

How *could* he? It is not to be borne! Have I waited these long years for Ned, only—with marriage at last in our sights—for him to forsake me for that trollop Mewtas?

Grief and rage burning within me, I race back into the palace, forgetting all decorum and not caring who sees me looking flustered and dismayed, and hasten in search of Jane Seymour. She will know how to deal with her faithless brother! She wants this marriage as much as I do.

I find her in her closet off the maidens' dorter, and Ned with her. They both stare at me, so wild I appear.

"How dare you?" I rail at him. "I *saw* you making advances to Mistress Mewtas just now. Don't try to deny it! I suppose this is why you will not commit to marrying me."

Ned looks horrified. Covering the distance between us in two paces, he grasps my shoulders and looks fiercely into my eyes.

"What are you saying?" he asks. "I have never held that lady in any esteem, or anyone else for that matter. I thought that if people saw me flirting with her, aye, and with others too, they would cease conjecturing that there is anything between you and me. But, as God is my judge, I have never, ever betrayed you. I adore you, Katherine! And so let's be done with all this waiting, for I will marry you out of hand, as soon as we can find a convenient time."

"Oh, Ned!" I cannot speak further for very joy and relief, and Jane is clapping her hands in delight.

"When will that be?" she asks.

"When the Queen's Majesty returns to London," Ned says, and kisses me passionately, not caring that Jane is looking on.

KATE

May 1484; Augustinian Friary, York

Kate looked out of her window at the muddy waters of the River Ouse, which flowed past the friary guest house where the royal party was lodged. Farther along, to her right, lay the Guildhall, where they were to be entertained to a feast tonight, and to the south was Clifford's Tower and the ancient castle. Beyond, in the meadows across the river, was the Micklegate Bar, the royal entrance to York, through which they had come in procession a few days ago, to be welcomed by the mayor and the city fathers. The King had led his company to the great Minster, to give hearty thanks for being safely returned to the North. It was obvious that his heart lay here, in the bracing air of Yorkshire, although Kate knew that part of it had been sealed forever in that sad little tomb at Sheriff Hutton. He and Anne had gone there, alone, two days before. Their faces had been stricken when they emerged from the church and rejoined their waiting entourage.

She sighed. Tomorrow, she and William would say farewell to the King and Queen and depart for Raglan. She was dreading that moment, hating to leave her father and stepmother, especially when their grief was still so raw. And her lost lover, John: she would be saying a silent good-bye to him too, for a long, long while. She had seen him about the court often since her marriage, but they'd had no converse.

It was what they had agreed when they parted after their one blissful night together. Kate had to live with William, after all. Even so, she sometimes thought she would die of yearning for John.

After a fortnight of marriage she knew William little better than she had before. He observed the courtesies by day, lay with her every night, and was at her side whenever convention demanded it. No one could have faulted him. Yet he hardly talked to her, and there was no spark of any sort between them. She bore his attentions patiently, but they were joyless, and left her weeping silently into her pillow every time. This had nothing to do with love! This was mere duty, and she had begun to see married life as a long, dreary, barren road stretching out endlessly ahead of her.

She had tried; oh, yes, she had tried. She had started conversations, made little jests, or asked questions calculated to prompt some discourse. William always answered politely, but he never engaged with her beyond that. She knew he did not love her, and was grateful for it. Yet why did he not cooperate in making things easier and more pleasant for them both? He seemed to look upon her as one of his chattels, no more, and to assume that she was happy being left to gossip with Mattie over their embroidery. He made no attempt to restrict her in any manner, he was generous in his way, but he was simply indifferent to her. Let her bring him her good dowry and bear him heirs, and he would require no more of her. She wished she had not bled John's seed away days after her wedding.

It was time to make ready for the banquet. She summoned Mattie.

"My, you do look a glump!" the girl said cheerfully. She had spent the afternoon with Guy, her sweetheart. William had agreed to take him on, and the happy couple was to be married when they reached Raglan. "Missing Lord Lincoln, are ye?"

"Horribly," Kate said. "I do not know how I bear it. But Mattie, *never* mention his name once we leave here. My lord does not care much for me, but he would care very much if his good name were sullied."

"I promise, my lady," Mattie vowed. "Now, it's the crimson tonight, isn't it?" And she helped Kate into a figure-skimming velvet gown with tight sleeves that belled out at the wrist, a low neck edged with a border of gold damask, a skirt that trailed in rippling folds on the floor, and a silk hip belt from which jangled gold ornaments. Then she drew her mistress's hair back into a tight plait and pinned it coiled to the back of her head. Over this she fixed a tub-shaped hennin covered in damask that matched the border of the gown, and atop it pinned the winged butterfly headdress of stiffened gauze. Once the unwieldy thing—now the height of fashion—was in place, Kate found she must keep her head level and not move it for fear of sending the whole contraption tumbling to the ground. Wearing a head covering, even one so elegant, was another of the things she hated about being married. She wondered how Queen Anne and the other great ladies of the court managed to move so serenely and effortlessly. Oh, how she longed to go about with her hair flowing freely again!

The feast was lavish, the city burghers puffed out in their furred robes anxious to attend to their King's every comfort. There were cheers for Richard when he entered the Guildhall, and for once his careworn face lightened. There had been no whisper of a rumor up here, Kate reflected, and felt heartened.

In the morning, she and William rose early, heard Mass, and ate breakfast. Then they attended on the King, who greeted them warmly and announced that he was bestowing on them, jointly, fifteen manors in Somerset, Devon, and Cornwall. It seemed he could not shower them with sufficient bounty. He had made them rich enough to keep great estate, and he had done it for her, and to keep William loyal. She doubted he had needed to. William did not have the imagination to plot treason. Loyalty to the House of York was rooted in his family anyway.

Her father told William he had confirmed him in his earldom, and William stolidly expressed his gratitude.

"Now, son Herbert," the King said, "these honors, and the gift of my daughter, are not for nothing. In return, you will hold south Wales for me against the Tudor, for there is no doubt that he will make another attempt on England sometime soon. In the meantime, I will look to the North." His face suddenly twisted with pain. The prince, of course, was to have been his representative there.

He pulled himself together with an effort. "I mind to set up the King's Household in the North, which will be established at Sandal Castle under the rule of my nephew Lincoln, who is now to represent me in these parts. He will also have charge of Sheriff Hutton Castle, where I intend to house the heirs of the House of York in safety. Warwick will be sent there, his sister Margaret, and, because it will benefit him, my bastard, John of Gloucester."

He paused. "I will tell you something, both of you, that is as yet a great secret, but will be made known when I think it politic. Warwick is next in line, but cannot succeed me. He is a fair lad, but his wits are not up to the demands of kingship. God knows, I fear my own wits are not always up to it either! Therefore, I intend to name Lincoln my heir."

Kate started at that. She barely heard her father rehearsing all the compelling reasons why Lincoln would make a good King. She could only think that, had Fate arranged things differently, she might have been Queen of England, seated beside John on his future throne. John II, he would be; given the example of the first King John, it was not the most auspicious of styles—yet her John would cause the name to ring with renown, she had no doubt of it.

"A wise choice, sire," her husband said. "The noble Lincoln has the mettle for it."

"Aye, indeed," the King agreed, watching Kate speculatively for a moment. She caught his eye and lowered her gaze. "And now you must make haste," he said. "You have a long journey ahead of you." His voice sounded strained. He was feeling this parting as keenly as she was.

The Queen came, wine was brought, and they all drank a toast to a bright future for Kate and William, and the confounding of the King's enemies. Then Kate summoned a page to bring in the parting gift she had commissioned for her father: a framed portrait of herself, very fine and like, wearing the beautiful blue gown she had worn for his coronation and her diamond-shaped pendant. He gazed at it in admiration, then a sad smile creased his face.

"You could not have given me anything better," he told her. "Now I shall have a daily reminder of you to take wherever I go. Thank you." He kissed her lightly on the forehead.

At last, with the goblets drained, and Kate grateful for the warming wine running through her veins and dulling the pain, it was time to say good-bye. She and William knelt for the blessings of her father and stepmother, and then were raised and embraced.

"God go with you, my daughter," Anne said, smiling at her sadly. It was the warmest she had shown herself in months.

Richard folded Kate tightly in his arms. "You are most precious to me," he murmured. "I pray Our Lady to have you in her special keeping." She felt him tremble as he said it, and when he broke away from her, she could see he was near to weeping.

"Love my daughter well, son Herbert!" he commanded briskly.

"Your Grace may be assured of that," William declared, taking Kate's hand and kissing it. As he led her from the chamber, she felt choked, and could not bear to look back at those two forlorn figures in black, standing bereft before their chairs of estate, surrounded by all the empty trappings of majesty.

KATHERINE

November 1560, Greenwich Palace and Whitehall Palace

When the court moved to Greenwich, Ned returned to Hertford House in Westminster, and there he fell ill of a fever. He wrote in anxious vein to Jane. To my dismay, his courage appeared to have deserted him. He was wavering again, fretting about how our wedding might be accomplished.

"It is his sickness that speaks," Jane said, looking sick herself. "Do not let it upset you." But I did. These past days have been a nightmare, for I have thought of nothing but what I might do if Ned forsakes me. I could not live. It is as simple as that.

Yet now comes another letter.

"He asks me to further his suit!" cries Jane. "He says that, although your marriage must be secret, he intends to do all properly, according to custom. Thus he will propose himself formally to you, and you will be betrothed; and your wedding will then take place. All this he insists upon, so that your children shall be of undisputed legitimacy. He asks if you are content to agree. Oh, Katherine, it really is going to happen!" And she embraces me heartily.

"Content? I am the happiest woman alive! Pray tell my dear love that I am well inclined to whatever arrangements he desires to make, and that I shall give him my resolute answer in person when the court returns to Whitehall next week."

And it is at Whitehall, in Jane's closet, that I next embrace my beloved, who looks a shade pale, for he is not fully recovered from his malady, yet handsome and ardent for all that. And when, finally, we draw apart, breathless, Ned goes down on one knee before me and takes my hand.

"Katherine," he says, "I have borne you goodwill for a long time, and I am content, if you will, to marry you."

I smile down upon him. "I like both you and your offer, my Ned, and *I* am content to marry with *you,* be the consequences what they may."

"When?" he asks eagerly, rising to his feet.

"As soon as possible!" I laugh. "Next time the Queen's Majesty leaves the palace!"

"Then it shall be done," he agrees, embracing and kissing me. "And now we must be formally betrothed." He summons his sister, and when we three are together, he takes my hand in his and puts a ring on my finger. It is set with a pointed diamond, a glittering stone of unfathomable depths, which represents power and protection, its greenish hue the color of life, beauty, and constant love. Now, we join hands, and Ned vows to take me, Katherine, as his wife. It is done. We are promised.

We agree that as soon as the Queen leaves for the good hunting to be had at Greenwich or Eltham, either Jane or I will get word of it to Ned, and then we shall come to Hertford House. We cannot have long to wait, as Her Majesty has already said she means to depart within the week, and I am almost trembling with anticipation, knowing that the consummation of all my hopes is near at hand.

"I will seek out a minister to marry you," Jane undertakes. Her zeal for us is touching; of course having her brother married to one who might be Queen will be the answer to her family's prayers. Yet I know she loves me for myself.

"The minister must be a Protestant," Ned insists, looking questioningly at me.

"Of course," I say. I have now decided where my spiritual allegiance truly and properly lies.

"And I myself will stand witness," Jane adds.

"There must be two, I am certain," Ned says.

"Who can we trust?" I ponder.

"One of your maids?"

"I suppose it will have to be. Mistress Coffin is a chatterbox, so not her. Mistress Leigh is discreet, and she is loyal. I will ask her, although not until the day itself."

"Good. And as soon as I hear from you, I will send my servants out of the house," Ned promises.

"I cannot believe this is happening, and that we are to be wed at last," I say, suffused with happiness, which is all the more precious for having been so hard won.

"It is an answer to all my prayers," Ned declares, and clasps me to him.

KATE

June 1484, Raglan Castle

It had been a weary, seemingly endless journey, and Kate lost track of the inns and monastic guesthouses in which they had stayed. Pontefract, Nottingham, Tamworth, Worcester, Gloucester, Monmouth, and countless other towns and villages had all passed in a blur. She'd been so sunk in misery and increasing homesickness that she had paid little account to the vast, spectacular landscapes, the cathedral spires, or the distant mountains of Wales that could now be seen more clearly in the distance. A man on a chain of fast horses could have covered the distance in less than six days, but because she and William had with them a train of retainers, and carts and packhorses loaded with their belongings, it had taken them almost twice as long, and William, despite his new riches, had grumbled at having to pay so much for accommodation along the route. He himself would gladly have slept under a hedgerow, wrapped in his cloak, he told her crossly, implying it was all her fault. And he barely ventured a word to her unless he had to.

He really was the most unattractive of men. Well, no matter! She had Mattie with her, and Mattie could talk for England!

But they had left England behind them now and crossed the mighty Severn into Wales, that strange, alien land she was now to inhabit. And it was a poor land, and an oppressed one—anyone could see that. The countryside was scattered with ruined buildings and slighted castles; the towns lay wasted and broken down, having clearly suffered devastation at some time in the past; the people looked ill-fed and resentful; and only a few thin cattle grazed in the empty fields.

"It was Owen Glendower's revolt that brought them to this," William said suddenly, bringing his horse up beside Kate's as they rode past a ruined monastery standing stark and blackened, its treasures plundered. "It was a brave bid for independence, but it brought the land to ruin, and after Henry IV crushed the rebels, every English king was resolved that never again should the Welsh have an opportunity of rising against their rule. They were determined to teach them a hard lesson, that rebellion brings only destruction and misery."

"But Glendower's revolt was long ago, wasn't it?" Kate asked, shocked at what she was seeing.

"Eighty years ago. But he united the Welsh behind him. They are a proud people, and refuse to be conquered. They hate us. But they have paid a bitter price for their resistance."

"How do they live?" Kate asked.

"Meanly. Do not try to extend charity to them when you are lady of Raglan. They will not thank you for it." William's mouth set grimly. "And never go beyond the castle precincts without my permission and an armed escort. The countryside is not safe. I dare not risk your being taken hostage: the King would never forgive me; and even if you are not abducted by those who would overthrow their lords and masters, there are gangs of dispossessed men roaming the moors and wastes who would not hesitate to commit rape and murder. So heed my warning, my lady!"

On the afternoon of the tenth day they at last caught sight of Raglan Castle in the distance. It was truly impressive: a massive, majestic fortress of reddish-gold stone that held a commanding view over the wide, undulating green countryside and distant hills.

"Look yonder!" William called, suddenly more animated than Kate had ever seen him. "Raglan lies ahead! Nearly there now." His men gave a little cheer.

Unusually talkative for once, he told her that the castle had been built fifty years before by his grandfather, an ambitious but loyal Welsh gentleman called William ap Thomas; his father, the great Earl of Pembroke, had converted it into a palatial mansion and made it impregnable. "He wanted a seat that would reflect his power," William explained. "As indeed it still does."

"How did your father come to be called Herbert?" she ventured, hoping to prolong the conversation by showing some interest.

"He chose the name himself," William said. "He felt an English name would do more for him than a Welsh one. After that, the Welsh called him Black William. It did not bother him. He was the King's man, through and through."

They were nearing the fortress now. The approach road led up through patches of woodland to an ornately battlemented gatehouse, and Kate could now see that what had looked from a distance in the late afternoon sun like reddish stone was in fact a blend of purples and browns. The castle was huge and formidable, surrounded by a mighty curtain wall intersected by six strong hexagonal towers, the whole dominated by a great keep. She would be safe here. She doubted that anyone could breach those defenses.

"That is the Yellow Tower," William said, following her line of vision and pointing to a lesser keep, tall and octagonal, that stood solidly outside the walls to their left, surrounded by a wide moat. "It was built for defense, but there are spacious chambers in there, which are kept for guests. And that range of lodgings to the left of the gatehouse, where you can see the shields carved in the stone, is where our apartments are. They are handsomely appointed."

They were. Raglan was like a palace inside. "It is the greatest castle of our age," William said proudly, and Kate had to agree. Even Middleham, luxurious as it was, was not so fine; and beside such modern splendor, Westminster Palace itself seemed old and outdated.

Her new home was built around two vast courtyards, with a great hall and chapel in the center, each boasting a wondrous fan-vaulted roof. William had mentioned guests, but Kate thought it unlikely that they would be entertaining often, with the countryside so hostile roundabouts. She wondered if there were local lords whose wives were disposed to be friendly.

The apartments she was to share with William were up a grand stair that led off the south court, where a fountain spouted jets of water. Their great chamber was magnificent, the parlor next to it small and intimate but sumptuous. Beyond it was a gallery hung with tapestries and armorial bearings. The Herbert lions on their blue and red ground, surmounted by the family crest of a green wyvern breathing fire, were prominent everywhere.

William was a different man on his home ground. He took pleasure in showing her the castle, and it was obvious that his household officers and servants admired him. Seeing this more expansive side of him, she found herself liking him more, although she was certain that she could never feel love or desire for him. There was not that in him to inspire it.

He presented her to the other women in his life. His mother, the Dowager Countess of Pembroke, the former Anne Devereux, was the sister of Lord Ferrers and a strong-willed old lady full of character, who clearly ruled the castle. She had taken holy orders in widowhood, like Kate's grandmother, the Duchess Cecily, and wore nunlike black robes and a wimple with a chin barbe. She greeted Kate warmly, promising to do all she could to assist her in her new duties as chatelaine, and assuring her that everything would be ordered for her comfort. "We shall make merry together!" she said, a twinkle in her eye. Not for

Anne Devereux the austere rigor of a conventual routine, as Duchess Cecily had imposed at Baynard's Castle; judging by the rings on her fingers and her plump figure, she enjoyed life's pleasures. And she evidently doted on her granddaughter.

Elizabeth Herbert was six years old. William had never mentioned his first wife, so Kate thought she must favor her, as she resembled him not at all. Elizabeth was fair, with more than a look of the Wydevilles; *We are cousins,* Kate realized, *through the Hautes.* She was prettily pale, with ash-blond hair, and dressed in a simple gown with a garland of daisies on her head. She curtsied formally at her father's bidding.

"This is your new mother," he said. It was a daunting prospect to Kate, having a stepdaughter thrust upon her when she herself was only fourteen, but she anticipated already that the Dowager Countess would continue to care for the child. That would be the best arrangement; and Kate would play the part of a big sister.

As she lay down exhausted in her soft, richly curtained bed that first night at Raglan, she reflected that life in this great castle might not be as terrible as she had imagined, although still it seemed to her a gilded prison, the symbol of her bondage, isolated as it was in this wild and dangerous land. There was Mattie's wedding to plan for, and a household to run; she had much to learn, she knew, and with the help of the Dowager Countess, she meant to make a success of it all; and in time, God willing, there might be children—already, William had started quizzing her as to whether his nightly labors had yet borne fruit. Her days would be busy and full of distractions, and for that she was grateful.

KATHERINE

December 1560; Whitehall and Hertford House, Westminster

I have barely been able to contain myself these past days. My betrothal ring, now hanging on a chain concealed beneath my clothing, is a con-

stant pressure on my heart. Yet at last comes the longed-for announcement that the Queen is departing on the morrow for Eltham, followed
by the command that we, her servants, are to make ready to accompany her.

Fate has been kind to me. Jane and I were going to plead illness as
an excuse to stay behind, but this very day, I have developed such a bad
toothache that my face has swollen up. I can with all conscience say to
the Queen that I am unwell. And Jane too is ailing, although sadly that
is no new thing, and it is now generally acknowledged within the privy
chamber that she is delicate and needs special consideration. She will
plead that she is not feeling well enough to travel.

We go together to the Queen, I with a kerchief tied around my
face, and ask to be excused from our attendance upon her on the morrow. She looks at us sharply, with those piercing black eyes, but there is
no denying that we both look poorly, I with my puffed-up cheek, and
Jane with her hectic visage.

"Very well," she says, probably relieved to be spared my company
for a space. "You have my permission to remain behind. We will not be
gone long, just a matter of days." Long enough! I think gleefully.

Back in her closet, Jane scribbles a note to Ned, telling him to expect us early the next morning. Now everything is set, and all we have
to do is wait.

After the Queen departs, in a great procession and amid much bustle,
I stay in her deserted apartments until all is quiet, my mind feverish
with agitation. What I am about to do is dangerous and probably rash;
but my love for Ned is stronger than my fear of Queen Elizabeth. Still,
I am filled with a sense of dread, fearful in case we should be discovered.

It is early, not far past seven o'clock, and I am being laced into what
will serve as my wedding dress: a square-necked black velvet gown that
shows off my breasts to advantage; it has a tight bodice and a wide,
round skirt, and sleeves slashed with white silk; an elaborate ruff is tied
around my neck.

I pick up my white French hood with the gold-and-gem braiding,
wondering whether to put it on: a bride should go loose-haired to her

wedding, as a sign of her virginity, but I dare not even hint to the world what my purpose is today, so I hand it to Mrs. Leigh and she places it on my head. I have decided that it would be wiser not to involve Mrs. Leigh in my wedding plans: the fewer that know of them, the better, and the minister can serve for a second witness. And so, when she is done, I dismiss her.

I am determined to dress as becomes a wife after the ceremony, even though I can only do so for the short time I am with Ned in private— that time of which I have dreamed these many years. Opening the little chest in which I keep my jewels, I draw out a coverchief, a triangular-shaped piece of linen that I have fashioned, hemmed, folded, and pinned to make a cap; this I will wear to show that I am a virtuous married woman. I put it in my pocket.

Jane arrives, looking pretty but too thin and pale in crimson velvet, and now the hour is upon us. Filled with a curious mixture of misgivings and anticipation, and giggling nervously, I slide my betrothal ring onto my finger and pull on my gloves with shaking hands. Then we wrap ourselves in our cloaks and pull our hoods down well over our faces.

I have visited Ned's London house several times with Jane, and usually we come by river, as the main entrance is through a water gate on the Thames, but this morning the tide is out. Speed is essential, for we dare not be missed, so we hurry along the privy gallery, patter down the stairs, and slip out of the palace into a small courtyard. There is hardly a soul about, just a couple of workmen repairing a window. It is freezing, and the wind is bitter.

It feels strange to be abroad unaccompanied. All my life, whenever I have ventured out into the world, I have been attended by a maid, at the very least, and I am sure that the same could be said of Jane. Yet here we are, two lone gentlewomen, out on our own and embarked upon the most daring and perilous adventure. No wonder my legs feel as if they are about to collapse under me.

We pass through a small door in the wall to the frost-rimed orchard, and so hurry southward to the riverbank, where at the edge of the sands there is a narrow pebbled path that leads to the river stairs of Hertford House. It is unlikely that anyone will spot us, because only a few servants remain to take care of Whitehall, yet still I look about me furtively, and in some terror, as we hasten on our way. Jane too is watchful and wary, ready to shield me if she sees anyone who might know us.

When we approach Hertford House, I look up; there is a movement at an upper window, and then I catch sight of my beloved looking anxiously out of another, over the gateway. As soon as he sees us, he waves and disappears. We are here! We have done it!

Suddenly a man emerges from the house and tries to push past us, but Jane is too quick for him.

"Barnaby!" she exclaims as I pull my hood close about my face. "Whither go you?"

"On some business of my lord," he replies sullenly, and hastens away.

"Learn some manners!" she calls after him. And quietly, to me: "Now where is the minister? He should be here."

As she watches for his approach, Ned himself opens the front doors, looking tense but splendid in a fine suit of cloth of silver and a jaunty cape of sage-green velvet. He smiles and opens his arms; and I run to him. We remain locked together for a long, breathless moment before he breaks away, embraces his sister, and closes the front door behind us. We are alone in the withdrawing chamber.

"You got rid of the servants," Jane says.

"Yes, I sent those I trust least on lengthy errands, and the rest have been told to take their leisure and remain belowstairs until after they have eaten their dinner. So we have a good three hours."

"We ran into Barnaby," his sister tells him.

"A graceless oaf," Ned smiles. "He is delivering a letter to my goldsmith in Cheapside. He will think nothing of your coming here."

"We have to be back at Whitehall for dinner at eleven, or the Lord Comptroller might become suspicious," Jane tells him. "Is the minister here?"

"No, he is not," Ned frets. "I've been looking out for him. Hopefully he will arrive soon. Come up and take some refreshment while we wait."

We ascend to his bedchamber, which overlooks the river. It was through its mullioned window that I had glimpsed him earlier. My eyes are drawn at once to the grand four-poster bed with carved posts, elaborate wooden reliefs, and a solid tester; it lies there waiting for us, made up with the finest linen, its rich counterpane folded back ready . . . Ned's eyes meet mine. He has seen me looking at it, and his gaze is warm.

I notice a book lying open on a chest by the bed.

"I was reading, or trying to," he says. "I've been up since six, making all ready. I could not settle to anything until I knew you were safely here. I even went for a walk, as I could not sit down. Katherine, Jane, help yourselves to some food."

He waves us to the laden sideboard, spread with platters of cold meats and cheeses, manchet rolls, bowls of almond comfits, and flagons of ale. Yet none of us can fancy a mouthful. Ned is distracted, pacing the floor between the sideboard and the window, looking again and again to see if the minister is in sight. I pour some ale and sip it, feeling increasingly dispirited. Where is the man?

Ned fumes. "He isn't coming."

"He promised," Jane says plaintively. "He seemed genuine."

"What shall we do?" I ask.

"We dare not wait any longer," Jane says. "Stay here, both of you, and I will go and find another minister to marry you."

We protest, fearing the danger of her being discovered, but she is adamant, and before we can deter her, she is gone, her black cloak flapping behind her. And so we are alone at last in Ned's bedchamber.

We stand awkwardly, unaccustomed to this new intimacy. Then Ned crosses the distance between us and draws me to him. I shiver.

"You are cold, sweetheart," he murmurs, holding me against his breast. Our two hearts are thumping so hard you can almost hear them.

"I am frightened," I say. "Frightened that Jane will be caught. Frightened that our marriage cannot take place . . ."

"Hush now," Ned gentles me. "You should not always think the worst."

"I have had good reason to all my life," I reflect. "Are you not afraid?"

"Of course," he confesses. "Many might call us mad even to contemplate what we are doing this day. But I want you, Katherine, and I am prepared to risk all to have you. I love you."

Instantly I am opening my mouth to his, running my hands over his back and shoulders, and feeling faint with longing. He is going to be mine, this glorious, wonderful man whom I have adored for so long, and once I am lawfully his, nothing, not even the Queen, can come between us.

Within half an hour a breathless Jane returns with a plump little cleric with fair, freckled skin, a red beard, and a long black gown furred with lambskin such as the Calvinists wear in Geneva; she'd found him in St. Margaret's Church by Westminster Abbey. Easily persuaded by the ten pounds offered by Ned, he professes himself willing to join together two young and eager lovers in holy wedlock. He asks no questions as to our identity, although he must realize from our surroundings and attire that we are nobly born—yet neither does he give us his own name, nor don any surplice.

Jane helps the minister to prepare for the ceremony, and he tells her she is as comely an acolyte as he's ever seen. It breaks the tension a little.

"Pray stand here, facing the window," he commands, opening his *Book of Common Prayer.* We take our places, side by side, with Jane standing behind us, and the nuptials begin.

Ned produces an elaborate gold ring and places it on my finger as we make our vows, then the minister pronounces us man and wife, and the service is over. We have done it! We are wed—at last!

Jane takes the minister downstairs, pays him his fee—since Ned does not have enough money—and shows him out of the house, and while she is gone I share another loving embrace with my husband and admire my ring. It is cunningly crafted with a spring that opens up five gold links engraved with a poesy Ned has composed specially for me. Delighted, I read the delicately engraved verse:

As circles five by art compressed show but one ring to sight,
So trust uniteth faithful minds with knot of secret might,

Whose force to break, but greedy Death, no wight possesseth power,
As time and sequels well shall prove, my ring can say no more.

Though disquieted a little by the mention of greedy Death, I thrill to read of the secret might of the knot we have just tied, and Ned's acknowledgment of the trust and fidelity that have bound us all these long years. This ring, like the one he gave me at our betrothal, is symbolic of the power of the marriage bond. It makes it all—this strange day, the anonymous minister, the furtive ceremony—seem real.

Jane returns and attempts a little celebration. She has brought wine and pours it into three goblets. "A toast to your bridal!" she says. "I have longed for this day, to see you both happily wed. May every happiness be yours!"

We clink goblets and drink, then Jane presses us to take some food.

"I could not eat a thing," I confess, having other, more pressing bodily needs on my mind. Ned stands silent beside me.

Jane smiles. "I perceive you are ready for bed. I will wait downstairs," she says, and leaves us alone.

Oh, the joy of lovers becoming one flesh! We consummate our marriage most heartily, and maybe more passionately than most, but first there is fumbling! I have brought no night gear with me, my lord's has not been laid out, and we have no attendants to help us take off our layers of winter clothing.

"I will be your tirewoman, sweetheart," Ned chuckles, tugging at the laces of my gown as I pull off my hood and hastily don my wifely coverchief. Soon it is all I am wearing, everything else having been cast on the floor—girdle, gown, kirtle, quilted petticoat, fine lawn smock— as my love and I, warmed by the wine singing in our veins, divest each other of all our clothes. Ned is undressed first, but I am not long after; he pulls me naked onto the bed where he has flung himself, and we fall into each other's arms, and I know at last what it is to lie skin to skin with my beloved between cool, crisp sheets.

We cannot have enough of each other, and take our pleasure again and again, rolling over and over on the feather mattress, so that sometimes I am on my back on one side of it, and then I am straddling Ned on the other! All the time we are murmuring the sweet words that lovers say when they are intimate. It is as far removed from those innocent fumblings with Harry as the sun from the moon. Had I ever dreamed there could be such joy in this world?

Never did two hours go so fast. Only once do we leave the bed, to get some wine, and then we hasten back, unwilling to waste time. Later, I look up, flushed and dewy with sweat, and see that the weak November sun is high in the sky.

"Oh, no, I must fly!" I wail, devastated, for I had not dared to dwell on the inevitable parting.

"Good God, the time!" Ned cries, leaping from the bed. "Let me help you, sweet wife." I rise and run unashamed to him, clinging to his body for one last embrace, and then we force ourselves apart and drag on our clothes, and Ned makes a very creditable job of assisting me into mine.

"There," he says, pulling on his doublet over his rumpled shirt and fiddling with the buttons. "You look very fine. No one would ever suspect what you have been doing!"

"For shame!" I chide, but despite my jesting I am dying inside and finding it hard to stem my tears. "When shall we meet again, my husband?"

"As soon as it can be arranged," Ned assures me. "Jane will help us, you may depend on it. Kiss me, my love."

We race downstairs, where, the tide being up, an anxious Jane has hailed a wherry. Ned kisses me one final time, then I tear myself away and climb into the boat. When I look around, Ned is at the top of the river stairs, waving farewell, his face wistful; then he turns and disappears back into the house. The boatman pulls out into the river and rows downstream to Whitehall. And at eleven o'clock precisely, neat and prim as a Lady of the Privy Chamber should be, I am seated at table with the Lord Comptroller.

KATE

1484, Raglan Castle

Life, for Kate, settled into a routine. Early Mass; household tasks; learning to supervise the servants under the kindly guidance of the Countess Anne; presiding with William at table, if he was at home, for his responsibilities often took him around the countryside, rallying support for the King; spending endless hours sewing and gossiping with the dowager, or listening to the castle minstrel singing the old bardic songs; and taking supper at the board before retiring to bed with her lord, who invariably claimed the marriage debt.

Rarely, as she had anticipated, were there guests. Just the occasional traveler begging a night's hospitality, and sometimes William's bastard half brother, Richard Herbert, come visiting from his home in Herefordshire. He was a bluff, hearty, feet-on-the-ground man with the dark Herbert looks, although his hair was graying because he was much older than William, having been the child of his father's misspent youth. Kate always looked forward to his dining with them, because he was a witty raconteur, and much livelier company than her husband.

William, though, was more communicative these days. Here at Raglan he was among his own people, people he had known all his life. When he rode out, they came running to see him and called down blessings on him, for he was a good lord to them; and because of that, they were polite to his English wife—if a little wary of her because of whose daughter she was. But Kate set herself to charm them with her winning ways and spirited chatter, and soon she was a familiar figure in the village that clustered behind the castle. She and Mattie—who was married now and sported her goodwife's coif with pride—would take a small escort of soldiers and go down to the weekly market that was held at the village cross. And sometimes they would go into the little church dedicated to St. Cadoc, a Welsh prince who had become an abbot and been canonized, far back in the mists of time, although local folk spoke of him familiarly, as if he were still living among them.

Kate thought the church pretty enough, and she was intrigued to find inside it the tombs of some ancient lords of Raglan. Pembroke, who had enlarged and beautified it, was not among them: his broken body had been laid to rest at Abergavenny, William had told her. She wondered if someday she herself would lie here, and the thought chilled her. She could not bear to think of spending the rest of her life in Raglan, or leaving her bones in Wales for all eternity.

The countess proved herself a staunch friend. When Kate miscarried, in blood and fear, her first child, early on in her pregnancy, it was Anne Devereux who calmed her and sat with her, holding her hand until the pains were over, herself wrapping in a cloth and taking away the tiny, unformed morsel of humanity that would have been her grandchild. After that, relations between the two women grew close, and they began to share confidences.

It was Anne who told Kate the truth about William's past. One autumn afternoon, as they sat together embroidering an altar cloth for the church, she began reminiscing about her departed lord, Pembroke.

"We loved each other well, more than most." She smiled wistfully. "When he knew he was to be executed, he could not bear to think of me in the arms of another man, so in his will he exhorted me to take the order of widowhood—and so here I am, my dear, not particularly devout as a nun should be, but consecrated to the memory of my true love."

"Were you content to do it?" Kate asked, thinking that it must be hard to give up all prospect of loving again, knowing that never more would you lie with a man's arms about you and his seed in your belly.

"Yes, I was content, and I am still," the dowager said. "No one ever could match Pembroke. He was strong and brave and respected, and he loved me well." She paused, remembering. "William is not his father," she observed sadly, then held up a hand to still Kate's ready, well-meant protest. "Nay, I am his mother, and I may speak the truth about him. He was very young when he had to take on his father's responsibilities and offices; too young. King Edward had a fondness for him and was ready to treat him as well as he had Pembroke, as long as he served him staunchly. But William wasn't up to it—he himself knew it, and he wasn't interested anyway. As a young man, he cared only for hunting and hawking. The family fortunes and influence began to decline; Henry Tudor was snatched from Raglan; better men were brought in to shoulder the burdens. King Edward gave William the odd commission, and took him to France when he went to war, but he knew he couldn't depend on him. Then the blow fell."

"The blow?" Kate's needle was poised in midair.

"The Queen and her party were behind it; we all thought that. She wanted her son, the Prince of Wales, to be influential in these parts. She wanted the rich lands of Pembroke for him. So she persuaded the King to dispossess William of his earldom. He wasn't deprived of it as such, but he was forced to surrender it in exchange for the much poorer earldom of Huntingdon. What could he do? He had no choice but to agree. And you could see the King's point of view. William hadn't been very successful at ruling in south Wales. I can still see what was written in the King's letter: he said the exchange was being made for the public weal, restful government, and the administration of justice in these parts. The message could not have been plainer."

"How did William take it?" Kate found she was feeling sorry for her husband. To have been deprived of that great inheritance, that proud earldom borne by his father, must have been so humiliating. She could see why her father had not told her the whole story, for he could not have done so without making some criticism of her future husband.

"He was bitter, as you may imagine," the countess told her. "But he has been more than compensated by King Richard, who has been good to him. He has given you to him, and that alone is a great blessing!" She smiled and patted Kate's hand. "And William is much more diligent these days, and effective at his duties too. He works hard in the King's service. Maturity has made a great difference to him." She leaned forward, and Kate could smell the faint scent of lavender. "You do not love him, do you?"

The question took Kate unawares, but Anne's expression was sympathetic.

"I try," she said. "I know it is my duty."

"Give it time," the countess said kindly. "I think you will do very well together."

"I hope so," Kate said, and half meant it. Her life here had not been as bad as she had anticipated. It had its good moments, especially in the company of the countess, Richard Herbert, and Mattie of course, and little Elizabeth was a delightful scamp. Even William had been unexpectedly kind after she lost the babe, ordering choice foods for her comfort and gruffly telling her not to worry, there would be another child soon. There were no horrible rumors about her father in Raglan, and she had almost lulled herself into accepting that there had never been any substance to them anyway; only a faint, nagging anxiety remained, and that she refused to dwell upon. Yes, life was tranquil, and even pleasant at times. Yet she spent her days feeling no more than half alive, an exile in a strange land—and knowing that the chief part of her heart lay somewhere in England, wherever John lived and breathed.

KATHERINE

December 1560–March 1561. Whitehall Palace;
Greenwich Palace; Hertford House, Westminster

There follows a strange time, when I live outwardly as a maid and privately, when it can be managed, as a wife. If it were not for Jane, Ned and I could never be together, but she is indefatigable. When her brother visits her at Whitehall or Greenwich, no one remarks on it, of course; but they do not know of the stolen hours we regularly spend making frantic love in Jane's little closet off the maidens' dorter, with her on watch in case anyone should come. And it is nothing unusual for me to accompany Jane on her visits to Cannon Row, where Ned and I tumble into our naked bed while she waits downstairs and keeps the servants at bay.

And the Queen suspects nothing, I am sure. She is as sharp with me as ever—no mother-daughter affection to be seen!—and yet I am still accorded the deference due to my royal status, and the court still buzzes with speculation that I might soon be elevated further, and the question of the succession thereby settled.

We have taken Mrs. Leigh into our confidence, Jane and I: she now knows the truth, and I am touched to find that she is glad for me, and never looked to see me so happily settled in wedlock. I am sure as can be that I can rely on her discretion, for she is a good woman who has given me faithful service.

Six days after our marriage, during one of our trysts at Whitehall, Ned gives me a hundred crowns for my keep, and a deed of land worth a thousand pounds, made over to his "dear and well-beloved wife." How I rejoice to see myself described thus.

He also gives me something very precious to him: a tiny book bound in red velvet that was owned by his father, Protector Somerset. There is a lump in my throat when I open it and find a faded inscription addressed to Ned: *The day before my death, from the Tower.* Choked, I add my own name, and lay it in the little silver casket in which I keep my personal papers and jewels.

I fear the unthinkable has happened. I have had only a light show of blood for the second month now. At first, never having been very regular in my courses, I thought it but the result of all the anxieties and joys I have swung between lately; but now I find my breasts are slightly swollen, and I am uncommonly tired. God help me, I think I may be with child.

Some might regard me as exceptionally naïve, enjoying carnal copulation and not anticipating its natural consequences. But I had thought that all would be resolved with Her Majesty before long; that, in a short space, Ned would have found powerful patrons to support us, and the need for secrecy would be over. Now I am not so sure, for we are too mired in fear to confess what we have done, and Ned has to go very carefully in this matter. One false move and we may be lost. We certainly will be lost if what I fear comes to pass, and someone does not help us soon.

When we three—Ned, myself, and Jane—are next alone together, in his bedchamber at Hertford House, Ned, who seems a little with-drawn tonight, asks if aught ails me.

"You look weary, sweetheart."

"I am worse than that!" I burst out. "I fear I might be with child!"

If ever I saw a man blanch with fear it was then.

"Are you sure?" An inane question, but one which, I have heard, is often asked by gentlemen at such times.

"Not yet," I tell him. "There are certain tokens, but I may be mis-taken. I pray that I am."

Jane is brisk. "If you are pregnant, there is no remedy but for us to make it known how the matter stands with you."

"I agree," Ned concurs. "We must trust to the Queen's mercy. We will have no choice."

We have to face it: Jane is fading away. The illness that has been con-suming her for years has finally extinguished even her ebullient spirit, and she has grown weaker by the day. When she finally takes to her bed, I obtain leave from the Queen to go to Hertford House to nurse her. She is deteriorating fast, and it agonizes me to see it. Jane and I are kindred spirits in so many ways, united in our love for Ned, so I take up my sickroom duties willingly, tenderly caring for her in her tragic de-cline, sitting with her while she dozes in the afternoons, or talking away the night hours when sleep deserts her.

Ned is often with me during these vigils. We welcome the chance to be so constantly together, but we both wish it were in happier cir-cumstances. Sometimes we seize the opportunity to bed together, but those stolen hours are short, because we are both aware that time is running out for Jane, and we want to be with her while we can.

I seem always to be fighting tears these days; and in my grief at the inevitable parting to come, I almost forget my fears about my condi-tion. The prospect of motherhood, with all its terrible consequences, has become a remote one. And if Ned now seems preoccupied, and not quite so loving, I put it down to his concern for his sister. And then I find out that it is due to something else entirely.

———

Entering our bedchamber one morning, I happen to glance at the table and see a document lying there. It bears the Queen's seal. Of course, I have to read further, and soon wish that I had not done so, for the paper is a safe conduct, signed by Elizabeth herself, requesting the King of France to let pass without hindrance her faithful servant, Edward Seymour, to Paris and other parts of the kingdom of France, as he goes about his lawful business in her service.

Paris? France? Lawful business? What is this about? In a fury of agitation, I race around the house looking for Ned, and find him in the courtyard, inspecting a new mare. He looks up startled as I dismiss the grooms, then his face falls as I thrust the safe conduct at him.

"What is this?" I cry, like a wounded animal.

"I had to apply for it. I had no choice. I was going to tell you, Katherine, but I could not face it, what with Jane being so ill and you being so worried about, well, you know . . ." He makes to embrace me, but I fend him off. "I did not wish to add to your burdens," he says desperately. "This mission has been thrust upon me. I did not seek it!"

"What mission?" My blood is up. I have no cause to be reasonable.

"I am to go to France on diplomatic business, which is a great honor and a sign of the Queen's favor, and may lead to further advancement, which can only benefit us, sweetheart. And I am also commanded to go to Paris as companion to Mr. Secretary's son, Thomas Cecil, while he completes his education. In truth, Katherine, I am as dismayed as you at the prospect of our being parted so soon, but I know—"

"While he completes his education? And how long will that be?" I rage, tears streaming down my cheeks.

"Hush, my love, do not weep so. I cannot bear it!" Ned blusters. "Listen, please: the date of my departure is not yet fixed; there are arrangements to be made. For all we know, Her Majesty may change her mind and I will not go at all. You know how changeable she is. So please, I beg of you, dry your tears. I would not leave you for the world, of my own choice. But if the Queen commands it, I *have* no choice. You *must* understand that."

I subside into his arms, unable to bear any bad feeling against him for long. I am weeping uncontrollably, desperate at the prospect of his being gone from me overseas for an indefinite time, for even the short days and weeks between our meetings are misery to me; and because it has occurred to me that he may secretly wish to be gone, away from the tangled mess that our lives have become. Then I regain control and administer a silent reprimand to myself for having such uncharitable thoughts about the man who is holding me tightly and murmuring his love into my ear. This is his career, and it is important. How could I be so unfair to him?

Jane is dying: we all know it. I watch helplessly as she slips from us, meekly and patiently, too weak even to mouth a farewell. I see Ned sobbing openly as he kisses her dead hand, holding it as if he can never let it go.

The Queen orders a magnificent funeral, and commands her ladies and chief household officers to attend. Clad in heavy black once again, and weeping in the privacy of my hood, I walk behind the stately bier with two hundred other mourners, up the long nave of Westminster Abbey, retracing the path I trod only fifteen months ago when my lady mother was buried here. And it is beside the tomb Stokes commissioned, with its serene sculpted image of her in her coronet and robes of estate, that Jane Seymour is laid to rest. My eye alights on the Latin inscription on my mother's monument, and soon I cannot see for tears, for it moves me immeasurably:

Nor grace, nor splendor, nor a royal name
Nor widespread heritage can aught avail;
All, all have vanished here. True worth alone
Survives the funeral pyre and silent tomb.

And I think of these two, my mother and my friend, and those others I have loved and lost, now dust in lonely graves.

Without Jane to look out for us, Ned and I have small hope of seeing each other. The interval allowed for mourning over, I am commanded back to the privy chamber, where my black gown draws little comment, as the Queen always insists her ladies wear black or white so as to appear insipid next to her own peacock finery. Meanwhile Ned tidies up Jane's small affairs and undertakes his duties elsewhere in the court.

Our need for each other is such that we cannot long bear to be apart. I beg Mrs. Leigh to replace Jane as our go-between. She consents with reluctance, if only because she is moved by my evident distress. Twice in the week after the funeral, Ned and I, a touch embarrassed, meet in Mrs. Leigh's chamber at Whitehall, she making it available, and herself scarce, looking to see there is no one watching, of course.

It adds spice to our coupling, this secrecy; we time our trysts for when the Queen's ladies are about their allotted duties and busy in the privy chamber. Our lovemaking is always hurried, and usually we dare not undress completely for fear we may be interrupted.

Then Mrs. Leigh comes to me. "If it please you, Lady Katherine, my mother is ill and I crave leave to go down to the country to be with her."

"Of course," I say, my heart sinking. "I pray you find her amended."

Mrs. Leigh thanks me most warmly and departs. I never see her again.

Our meetings now are few and far apart. When we do meet, anxiety mars our reunions, for I am still unsure whether I am with child or not, and I am loath to confide my fears to Ned. My courses are regular, but still scanty, and I could swear my stomach is rounder. Whether these signs betoken I am with child I cannot say, but they trouble me deeply. Yet I do not say anything, as I hate to spoil our brief times together.

Then comes the awful day when Ned breaks it to me that he is soon to depart for France.

"Tell me truly, Katherine," he urges, "are you with child?"

"In faith, I do not know," I sob, devastated at the imminence of our parting. "I bleed a little each month and I have put on weight, but I am so hungry and keep eating, so that is not surprising. I fear I am very ignorant of such things. I wish there was some wise woman I could ask, but I dare not." And I burst out crying again. I am afraid that if I go on this way, always distressed and weeping, Ned will be glad to leave me. And with the width of the English Channel between him and Queen Elizabeth's wrath, should she discover our secret, I am sure he will be very glad to be in France. But he surprises me.

"If you are with child," he says distractedly, "I will not leave you to face the Queen."

Mrs. Ellen, my old nurse, has come out of retirement to replace Mrs. Leigh, and seems very glad to be back in my service. Inevitably I soon find myself confiding in her. Without hesitation, she agrees to pass messages between Ned and me, and after a few days she tells me he wishes to meet me opposite his house, by the old canopied fountain in New Palace Yard, in front of Westminster Hall. I hasten there at once.

There is no one about as I approach the octagonal fountain. I am early, and Ned is nowhere to be seen. I make to sit down on the low stone rim, but without warning I find myself engulfed by the most terrible sensations of anguish and despair, similar to those I experienced on the water stairs at Baynard's Castle all those years ago, but far worse. I fear I am drowning, submerged by powerful waves of desperation and horror. I am going to faint . . .

"Katherine?" Ned is suddenly before me, steadying me as I sway.

"I must get away!" I gasp. "I cannot stay here! Help me!" He grabs my arm and drags me away, over to Westminster Hall, where I slump in the porch, trying to steady my breathing. Once the dreadful sensations have dissipated, I look fearfully over at the fountain.

"Now," Ned says, alarmed, "try to calm down, and tell me what all that was about. Are you ill, my love?"

"Nay, I was affrighted." I tell him about the horrors I have just experienced. "Truly," I say, "I did not imagine what I felt. That fountain is cursed; maybe something bad happened there once. Did you not feel *anything*?"

"Nothing at all. You *must* have imagined it, sweeting; you have been overburdened with troubles lately."

"I know I did not," I insist, "and I am never going near that fountain again."

Several lawyers are going in and out of Westminster Hall, where the courts sit, and some glance at us curiously. We are very exposed here.

Ned looks anxious. "We should not be seen together. Listen, I have received orders to go to France in two days. I know this news is as unwelcome to you as it is to me." He sounds formal and stiff, as if warding off another storm of weeping on my part. But I am frozen in misery, knowing myself powerless against the might of the Queen and her ministers.

Ned regards me with concern. "I will send letters to you by the common packet," he says. "I will entrust them to my servant Glynne, whom you may depend on. And I will leave money with you, in case you prove to be with child. If you tell me it is so, I will not depart the realm. But you are not certain yet?"

"I am not sure," I say dully, "but Mrs. Ellen says I could not be pregnant and still have my courses. I pray she is right."

"So do I," Ned agrees fervently. "Well—I must go then. But if it proves otherwise, my Katherine, send for me at once. I will not tarry abroad; I will defy the Queen and come home to support you."

"I cannot face you going from me," I mumble.

"It will be hard for us both." He shrugs with a helpless gesture. "I would we could lie together before I leave, but how could we manage it?"

"I do not think I could bear it," I tell him, "for then I could never let you go." I have felt like that every time we have bedded together: the pleasure has always been marred for me by the awareness that a parting inevitable as death must follow—and that was when we had some prospect of seeing each other again in a matter of days or weeks. But this parting will be worse, for we have no idea when we will be reunited. I am bowed down by it, burdened by a heavy sense of loss, and by the fear of pregnancy that yet nags at me. Was this what those terrible sensations at the fountain presaged?

"You are punishing me for leaving you," Ned protests. "That is unfair and cruel. Would you have me defy the Queen and face ruin?"

"Nay, nay," I say wearily. "Forgive me, my dear heart. I know you are not to blame."

Ned holds me close and our mouths meet. His body moves against me, and I can feel mine responding. Yet even at the height of desire, we are looking out for eavesdroppers. And with desire unsatisfied, we tear ourselves apart and go back to our separate lives, knowing it will be a long time ere we will behold each other again.

KATE

1484–55, Raglan Castle

News from court filtered through only slowly; often it was days old by the time the royal messengers reached Raglan. The King wrote that he had now designated Lincoln his heir, and Lincoln was now practicing for kingship, presiding over the Council of the North and the royal household at Sheriff Hutton. How she wished she could be there, with her brother John and her royal cousins—and her dear love!

As Christmas approached, Kate felt especially homesick. They would be preparing for the twelve days of revelry at Westminster—and she would not be there to enjoy them. Her father and stepmother would be facing their first Yuletide season without the prince, and that would go hard with them, she knew. And then came a letter that really upset her: Queen Anne was ill, her father wrote. The doctors were concerned. He would keep her informed.

In the early spring, Richard Herbert came visiting again. He had been to London, and William and Kate were eager to hear all about it. For her, it was a tenuous link with all that she held dear, and she hoped he might have tidings of the Queen. But the news he brought was not the news she wanted to hear.

"It was being said in the City, a few days after Epiphany, that Her Grace had fallen extremely sick," Richard reported. "I am sorry to be the bearer of sad tidings, my lady."

Kate felt near to tears. Anne was very ill, but no one had summoned her, not even her father, unless another letter was on its way. She longed to go to her stepmother, and even had the wild idea of taking a horse and riding full speed into England.

She found it impossible to make conversation and excused herself, leaving the men to their wine and their desultory talk. It being a cold night, a heavy curtain had been drawn across one end of the parlor, to conserve the heat from the fire, and after she had closed its folds behind her, she heard Richard speaking in a low voice.

"I didn't like to say too much in front of your wife, William, but there is more to this business of the Queen, and I think you should know it."

William grunted. "You'd better tell me, then." Kate stood very still in the darkness beyond the curtain, hardly daring to breathe.

"There's no chance of the Queen bearing another child. It's said the death of the prince broke her last year, poor woman, and that she's been in a decline ever since. But the King needs an heir, and it seems he would marry again."

"He has an heir, the Earl of Lincoln," William pointed out.

"Like all men, he wants an heir of his own body," Richard Herbert said. "And it seems he now lusts after his own niece, the late King's daughter Elizabeth. She and her sisters were at court for Christmas, and there's talk about her all over the City. It's said King Richard made her appear in the same apparel as Queen Anne, which set tongues abuzzing. Have you ever heard of such a thing?"

"It's disrespectful to the Queen, at the very least," William agreed.

"God knows what that poor lady made of it. I know what everyone else did. It's being widely bruited that the King anticipates her death and is bent on marrying Elizabeth. Some even speculate he will divorce the Queen in order to marry the girl. It's said he has sufficient grounds, because he never obtained a proper dispensation for his marriage, even though he and Anne Neville are close cousins."

Kate almost put her hands over her ears. She could not bear to hear more of this—this treason!

"But his own niece!" William was scathing. "That's disgraceful."

"He is said to be motivated by political concerns. Believe that if you will. But think of it in practical terms, brother. Over a year ago Henry Tudor vowed to wed Elizabeth of York to make good his weak claim to the throne. But if King Richard were to marry Elizabeth himself, that would scupper the Tudor's plans."

William chimed in: "The King had all his brother's issue declared illegitimate. How then can marrying Elizabeth make good anyone's claim? And even if she were trueborn, she cannot confer any title while her brothers live."

"If they live!" Richard interjected, and Kate began to tremble.

"Well, we've all heard the rumors," William murmured. "But there's no evidence that the King has had them killed."

"Is there not? Why has he not exhibited them alive? God knows, he has cause enough for doing so. And wanting to marry their sister—it's a tacit acknowledgment that that precontract story was a load of nonsense. He knows his title is unsound, so he seeks to bolster it by marrying the true heir—and in doing that, he effectively admits that her brothers are dead!"

Kate thought she might faint, hearing such cruel, hard-nosed logic. It had brought all her buried fears about her father crawling to the surface.

"There's more to this than politics, I hear," Richard Herbert continued. "The girl herself is said to be willing, and the King, according to the gossips, is pursuing her for her own sake. She *is* very beautiful. But when his determination reached the ears of the people, he was castigated for it. No one wants or approves of this marriage. It is condemned unanimously as unlawful and incestuous."

"Is it unlawful?"

"I'm no canon lawyer, brother, but I have heard of uncles marrying nieces before. No doubt if enough money changed hands, a dispensation might be obtained. But I tell you who *will* be put out by the news—Henry Tudor! He must be shitting his nether hose."

"This would all explain a letter my mother received from him a week ago," William ventured slowly.

"Your mother had a letter from Henry Tudor?" Richard was shocked.

"They correspond from time to time, purely on domestic matters. You'll remember, Dick, that she was as a mother to him when he lived at Raglan as a child, and he has an enduring fondness for her. His letters come via merchants, under a false name, but there is nothing treasonable about them, I assure you. I read them all."

"Even so, some might deem it treason, this correspondence," his brother muttered. "I'm surprised at you for allowing it."

"There are no royal spies here at Raglan," William said. "We're pretty isolated."

"You're married to the King's own daughter, man! Are you a fool?"

"She knows nothing of this. I do not involve her in my affairs, and my loyalty is not in question. But I have digressed. In his letter, Henry Tudor spoke again of marrying our sister Maud."

"Maud? But it was years ago that our father mooted that match."

"Aye, but the fact that Henry is reviving it now suggests he believes Elizabeth will marry the King and that he is casting around for an alternative bride. Maud might not be royal, but she would bring the Welsh rallying to his cause."

"We should avoid all dealings with this!" Richard snapped. "I trust your mother destroyed the letter."

"She burned it. But you know, she was a little torn. It was our father's dying wish that the betrothal be revived, and she was loath to go against his wishes. But fear not, I made it plain to her that meddling in Henry Tudor's marriage *would* be treason."

"Aye, it would. And so would any further communication with him at this time."

"I hear you. Will this marriage of the King's go ahead?"

"I know not, such is the outcry against it. But I'm told he is determined. He has shunned his wife's bed, for obvious reasons, and if you believe the London gossip, has abandoned her to waste away. It's said he complains of her barrenness, and voices his belief that she will die soon. Some say he can't rid himself of her quickly enough."

Kate found all this impossible to credit. In her mind was a picture of her father and Anne at Middleham, loving and happy together. Her husband and his brother could not be speaking of the same couple. She remembered there had been some coolness between the King and Queen, but even that rode ill with these new allegations. She could not imagine her father being so cruel or callous. He was not like that. It seemed that knaves and fools were, as ever, ready to believe the worst of him.

She could listen to no more. Tiptoeing away, she hastened up to bed, and wept into her pillow. When William came up soon afterward, he noticed that her cheeks were streaked with tears. But being a man of little imagination, he did not trouble himself to wonder what might have upset her.

KATHERINE

June–July 1561. Greenwich Palace; the Savoy Hospital, London; Wanstead and Beaulieu, Essex

May God help me. I know for certain now that I am with child, and probably have been for some time, for my courses have dried up entirely and my belly is swelling. Since soon after that sad day when I bade a piteous farewell to Ned and watched his tall, elegant figure disappear into the dawn mist, I have had to instruct Mrs. Ellen to lace my stomacher ever tighter.

"For pity's sake, Lady Katherine!" she cries as I urge her to pull harder. "This cannot be doing the babe any good."

"It has taken no harm," I declare, gritting my teeth and trying to breathe in even more. "I first felt it move a week ago, and it has not ceased since. In fact, it may have been moving before, but I thought I had wind."

"You cannot go on like this," she warns, shaking her head in despair. "Go to the Queen. Confess what you have done. She will not harm a pregnant woman."

"Ah, but what will happen once the child is born?" I am quaking with fear at the prospect. Women who plead their bellies still face execution after the birth.

"I do not know," Mrs. Ellen admits, looking troubled.

"I have no choice. I must conceal my condition for as long as possible, then feign illness so that I can leave court when I can hide it no more."

This is not my only pressing worry. There comes a day when I have an appointment with Mr. Secretary Cecil. It is of my seeking, for my allowance has not been paid. The matter is dealt with quickly and to my satisfaction, but I am aware all the time of Cecil's appraising glances, and when our business is concluded, he sits back in his chair, folds his hands on his belly, and regards me evenly.

"Lady Katherine," he says, "it has come to my notice—and that of others—that you have a certain fondness for my lord of Hertford."

"I am fond of him, sir, for he is brother to the Lady Jane Seymour, for whom I grieve yet. We were all good friends."

"'Friends' is not how I would describe what has been reported to me," he says. "I am advised that there is more between you than that. Indeed, your familiarity with the earl is increasingly the subject of comment, and I must warn you that it would be foolish to continue it without Her Majesty's consent. Do you still say there is nothing between you?"

"Nothing of which I should be ashamed!" I retort, wishing he had made himself as plain last year, and not tried to cozen us with false friendship.

"Then there is something." Cecil's eyes are kindly, inviting confidences. "My lady, if there is anything that you should confess to the Queen's Majesty, I urge you to do it now, and throw yourself on her mercy. I say this as a friend."

"I assure you, sir, there is nothing to confess," I persist.

"If there were, I should counsel you to avoid such familiarity in the future," Cecil says.

"There would be no need," I declare.

"Naturally, since Lord Hertford is in France," the Secretary says smoothly. "I assure you his mission there is a necessary one." And by that I know Ned has been sent there to get him away from me. Maybe the Queen knows everything, and it is all a plot to shame and discredit me.

"Of course, his sister did say something about it," I mumble.

Cecil gives me a long look, but says no more. When I take my leave, I am trembling.

I know there is gossip about me in the privy chamber. Conversations cease as I enter a room, and I catch the maids whispering and glancing in my direction. Then one day two of the ladies attendant on Her Majesty draw me aside.

"Lady Katherine, forgive me," says the gentle Lady Northampton, "but I have heard disturbing talk of great goodwill between you and the Earl of Hertford."

"Aye," says pretty Lady Clinton, "and that is not all that is said." Her eyes glance down briefly at my belly.

"There is nothing between us!" I flare. "Even Mr. Secretary has spoken to me of these rumors, but I have reassured him that they *are* just rumors! I don't know what all the fuss and ado is about."

"It is Mr. Secretary who has asked us to speak with you," Lady Northampton reveals. "He fears he was unhelpful in his approach to you, and thinks that we, as women, might put the matter better. But my dear, he is assured by reliable reports that you and my Lord Hertford are more than mere friends, and he urges you to make a clean breast of all to the Queen."

"There is nothing to tell her!" I protest, my voice sounding shrill. "Lord Hertford is a good friend of my family, no more. My mother regarded him as a son after he was betrothed to my sister Jane. His mother was my guardian, and I was bosom friends with his sister. How could I not be close to him? The rest is lies, and I am astonished that people should believe them!"

"Then forgive us," Lady Clinton soothes. "We have spoken out of turn, and Mr. Secretary is clearly mistaken. Yet he did say we should warn you to beware of keeping company with the earl, so we felt we should do so."

I accept her apology graciously, thank them for their concern for me, and go on my way, but my breath is coming fast and uneven, and the child in my belly is squirming in what must be discomfort. I cannot endure it here at court much longer. I must get myself away!

I have said nothing lately of my lord of Pembroke, but he has been hovering on the periphery of my vision for some months now, either paying me extravagant compliments or dropping heavy hints about how desirable a second marriage between myself and his son would be. In the wake of those threats of my being abducted by either Spain or Scotland, he thinks it would be seen by the Queen as a safe course.

Pembroke is quite open about his ambitions. He wants a royal bride for his son, a bride with a good claim to the throne. He foresees a royal dynasty of Herberts regenerating down the centuries. And now that Lord Hertford is out of the way, that royal bride might welcome his son's attentions once more. Harry, I must concede, has grown into a very personable young man; if I were not in love with Ned, or wed to him, I should welcome this match. But although it would once have been the answer to all my prayers, it is no longer.

Now Pembroke comes again, imploring me to accept his son's suit.

"I cannot," I tell him. "I must not marry unless the Queen approves it, and in truth I am not inclined to do so."

"May I remind you of something, my lady?" Pembroke asks smoothly. "When, all those years ago, I spoke of annulling your marriage to Harry—which was for political reasons only, I assure you— you both told me it had been consummated. Were that the case, the annulment would be worthless, and you would still be man and wife. Even the Queen could not dispute that."

I am chilled listening to his words. "It was not true," I say. "We made that up so that we could be allowed to stay together."

"You were vehement enough about it back then," he says, his eyes narrowing.

"We were desperate at the prospect of being parted. I assure you, my lord, it was a lie."

"There is gossip that you love the Earl of Hertford these days. Perchance that is coloring your remembrances."

"It is only gossip," I snap, "and I resent the implication, my lord."

"Then pray accept my apologies, my lady," he says, bowing, and takes his leave. Yet I suspect he will not go away.

The stomacher is tighter than ever. And, to my utter distress, although I have sent many letters addressed *To my loving husband,* I have had no word from Ned since he left England.

The Queen still shows a great misliking toward me. Her manner is even sharper and colder than before. She will undoubtedly have heard the gossip; and if Cecil heeds it, she must too. Worse still, being in daily contact with me, does she suspect I am with child?

Each morning finds me wan and weary. I do not sleep at night. I lie awake in terror lest Ned has abandoned me, praying that a message or letter from him will arrive soon. Does he love me still? Or have they ordered him not to communicate with me, or even intercepted his letters? I would not put anything past them. In truth, I have been such a mope that I could hardly blame Ned if he chose to abandon me.

I resolve at last to write to him about my condition. He promised he would not tarry in France if I found myself with child, and assured me I should not face the consequences alone. Whatever his feelings for me now, I must hold him to that. This is his child too, and I am his wife.

It is near midnight. I light my candle and find pen and paper. *I am quick with child,* I write, my handwriting straggly because I am trembling. *I pray you therefore to return and declare how the matter stands between us.*

In the morning, I seek out Master Glynne and beg him to forward my letter to his master without delay. He takes it and bows, touching his cap, and disappears down the stairs. Then, as more days pass, I wait, and wait—and wait. There is no reply from Ned.

Nor is that all. The latest talk is that my husband, having attended the coronation of the new French King, and seen all the sights, has tired of Paris, and is seeking new pleasures in Italy. It is said he has corrupted young Cecil with his idleness and dissipation, and that they have both been wallowing in filthy pleasures and spending like water the money provided by careful Cecil.

My world collapses in ruins. Hope shrivels and perishes. To die in childbed would be a blessing.

Weeping uncontrollably, I seek solace in the kind arms of Mrs. Ellen.

"Hush, child, you should not give credence to rumors," she counsels, stroking my damp hair back from my fevered brow. "And think: was your young lord ever given to fornication and the kind of life of which these rumors accuse him? Is it in character?"

I have to admit it is not. "I was ever one to fear the worst," I murmur.

"Then pay the gossipmongers no heed! Their calumnies may be spread deliberately to discountenance you and drive a wedge between you two."

A little heartened, but not really reassured, I retire to my lonely bed. Even if Ned is true, I reflect miserably, I have a more immediate problem to solve.

What am I to do? I am waxing ever greater with child, and time is running out. And if Ned really has forsaken me—for he has not replied to any of my letters—who can help me?

Then one day, on my way to the privy chamber, I come face-to-face, after so many years, with Harry, my former husband. He bows courteously—how different from when we knew each other in our youth—and when he rises and smiles at me, I see how tall and comely a man he has become. He cannot compare with Ned, of course, but Ned has betrayed me, I am sure.

I smile back, and we go our different ways. But later I fall to thinking. Desperate problems require desperate remedies. Pembroke, who has great influence with the Queen, wants me to marry Harry, and Harry, by the warmth in his smile today, is not averse to that. Were I to take him, I could have my revenge on Ned and find a father for my child.

Yes, there are difficulties. I am wed to Ned. But that is a secret; Jane Seymour, the only witness, is dead, and I have no means of tracing the minister, who is unlikely to come forward and confess he married us in the face of the Queen's displeasure. If I deny that the wedding ever took place, it would be only Ned's word against mine; and sadly, I think he will not dare to make any protest.

I make a decision, then change it. Then I make another, and waver about that too. I go round and round in circles, trying to anticipate how I would feel in every circumstance. Even if I can find the courage to repudiate Ned, dare I accept Harry's suit? I am too far along in pregnancy for him ever to think the babe might be his. I can feel it kicking lustily now, can even see the bumps of its tiny hands and feet when they press against my belly. Yet I know Harry to be kind and chivalrous. If I tell him about my terrible predicament, he might help me. It is asking a great deal, though, expecting a lord of high rank to father another man's child, yet I think Harry is rare among that breed, and that he would do it. The legal niceties could be sorted out, I am sure.

The decision is made. I have no choice, I tell myself. I write to Harry. I say I am ready and contented to renew our acquaintance and look favorably on his suit.

Back, by return, comes a joyful letter, accompanied by a miniature portrait of himself enclosed in a locket, and a ring set with a small sapphire, symbolizing fidelity. Harry writes that we must stand by our tale that our marriage was consummated, for there is the Queen's consent to be obtained; he adds that he looks forward to our being reunited as husband and wife.

The Queen's consent! But will she give it?

I am pondering my terrible dilemma when the order comes for me to attend Her Majesty on her annual summer progress; this year she is to visit her good subjects in Essex and Suffolk. Now I am trapped indeed. There is no good excuse that I can give, apart from feigning illness, and my courage deserts me even at the prospect of that, for the Queen has little patience with bodily weakness and is apt to lash out if she suspects one of us of malingering. And if she guesses the real cause of my "malingering" . . . well, I dare not think of it. Oh, dear God, what am I going to do?

That there is gossip about me at court, I can well imagine. Even I, seeing myself going about the court now, would be asking questions about my big belly. And yes, I have seen people looking covertly at me, murmuring together, and—increasingly of late—avoiding me.

Does the Queen herself suspect? Is that the cause of her displeasure? Surely not, or she would have taken me to task before now. I doubt she could have contained her wrath. No, I do not think she is aware of my condition, although she cannot be unaware of the gossip. Maybe she does not believe it, even of me. I may be safe for a little while longer.

Yet Harry's latest letter comes as a terrible shock, especially after the loving ones he has sent me, and all the thoughtful gifts. I tremble with mortification as I read it. Someone—God knows who—has obviously talked, and he is furious with me, aye, and indignant too, for leading him to believe I was chaste. He says I abused his trust to cover my whoredom and adultery, not to mention Ned's knavery. He demands I return his letters and his presents, and storms:

> *Do not think I will risk loss of honor to lead the rest of my life with a whore that almost every man talks of. Through the enticement of your whoredom, you sought to entrap me with some poisoned bait under the color of sugared friendship. I thank God I am not touched by the loss of a few tokens and gifts that were got out of my hands by cunning, to cover your abominations, and his likewise.*

If I ever knew desperation, it is now. I am in terror lest Harry report my offenses, and crushed and shamed by his cruel condemnation. God knows, I am no whore; I have never given myself to a man not my husband, so it is wicked and unjust to slander me so. As for loss of honor, he should look to himself, for no true gentleman would treat me so despicably!

I have to act soon. The Queen must not hear of my condition from Harry or his father. And clearly, others know of it now.

On the night before the progress begins, Sir William Cecil hosts a farewell dinner for the Queen in the great hall of the hospital of the Savoy in London. The revelry continues long into the night, but I am bruised and smarting because of Harry's letter, and so tired that I can barely keep my eyes open. The next day, we depart for the royal manor at Wanstead, and there, Ned's brother Henry brings me a packet. A letter from my husband at last! But all it contains is a pair of gold bracelets, a gift from Paris with a brief note of greetings from him, sent weeks ago. There is no letter. At that, I let fall the pretty jewels to the floor, tumbling myself into despair. Dear God, let me have just one word from him, in response to my urgent letters! One little word of love, or better still, a message to say he is coming home.

There are ladies in the court whom one could only describe as bitches. They are the ones who taunt me with gossip, or laugh snidely behind my back, encouraged by the Queen's evident disfavor. And now, when I go abroad bravely displaying my new bracelets, they seem to have some new cause for laughter, and take great pleasure in telling me that I am not the only recipient of love tokens from Lord Hertford.

"It seems he purchased a dozen of them!" they trill. And it is true, there are others sporting similar trinkets.

He has abandoned me, I know it at heart, and soon I will be shamed as a fool before the whole world.

At the palace of Beaulieu, I find a letter pushed under my chamber door, just as I am retiring to bed exhausted after another lavish feast. It is a second angry missive from Harry, who is clearly out to have his revenge on me. He was my friend, he writes, but he is now sorry for that. He demands I return the letters and gifts he has sent me, without delay. *Or else,* he threatens, *to be plain with you, I will make you and your whoredom known to the whole world.*

I do not summon Mrs. Ellen or anyone else. As I unlace my stays, weeping, and with difficulty, and see the mound of my poor constrained belly exposed, I know I have no choice anymore. I must go to the Queen.

KATE

Summer 1485, Raglan Castle

Weeks afterward, news reached the castle that Queen Anne had passed away at Westminster. Kate mourned her profoundly, wishing she'd had a chance to make things right between them. Anne had had her doubts about King Richard, and Kate thought that disloyal. Yet hadn't she had her own suspicions? She of all people knew how deeply those doubts had tormented Anne. And since overhearing Richard Herbert's revelations, those horrible uncertainties had resurfaced in her own mind, leaving her even more in turmoil than before.

Kate thought she might go mad if her doubts were not resolved, once and for all. They ate at her. She would go to her grave obsessing about them, she thought. She waited in trepidation for news of the King's marriage to Elizabeth of York; if that went ahead, she would have to believe that the rumors had been well founded. None came. Instead, her brother John—in one of his brief, rare letters—wrote from Sheriff Hutton that Elizabeth of York had joined the household there with her sisters. Clearly the marriage was not to take place—or not immediately.

William told her that the King had granted them yet another annuity. Later she wondered if it had been to ensure William's loyalty, because the next piece of news that reached Raglan was bad. Her father had good reason to send Elizabeth of York north to a secure place, for Henry Tudor's invasion was now expected at any time. William had received fresh orders to hold south Wales against the invader, and was now away much of the time ensuring that the local magnates stayed staunch to the King and that efficient defenses were in place. Richard himself had moved to Nottingham, where he was mustering the forces he had commanded his lords to array. The whole kingdom was, it seemed, up in arms.

But for whom? Kate was terrified for her father because there was no question that the rumors about the princes' disappearance had undermined his following. William himself, when he was fleetingly at home, expressed doubts about the loyalty of the great nobles, for some lords had already defected to Henry Tudor.

"The King relies heavily on Norfolk, Northumberland, and Stanley," he said, "but I would not trust Stanley. His wife is the traitor's mother."

"Norfolk is loyal, I am sure," Kate said. "But what of Northumberland?"

"Who can say? Let us hope they will all support the King when the time comes."

"Will there be a battle?" she asked fearfully.

"Assuredly, unless Henry Tudor is killed or taken by stealth first. I have the coast guarded; he cannot attempt a landing here in the south. But he must march through Wales or England to confront the King's forces—and who knows what might happen on the way?"

"I pray to God that some loyal subject puts an end to his evil designs," Kate cried. "I cannot bear this uncertainty much longer."

William rode away again, making it his business to keep watch over the territory under his command, ensuring that, as far as possible, all was safe and secure, and that the men he had cozened, arrayed, and instructed were prepared, and his captains vigilant. Kate rarely saw him. She and the countess were busily provisioning the castle for a siege, just in case Henry Tudor came this way. It might all be a waste of effort, she thought, as she went through another long list of foodstuffs with the steward, but they were taking no chances.

It was a hot August. The grass turned brown in the sun's rays, and streams dried up. It would not be easy for men wearing armor to fight in this weather, she realized uneasily, and prayed it would not come to that.

Another letter arrived from her brother John. He sounded excited, and with good cause, for he was bound for Calais, England's last outpost in France. Their father the King had appointed him Captain of Calais, and although he was too young at eleven to carry out his duties by himself, he was going to be taught them by those who were fulfilling them for him. *Imagine, dear sister,* he wrote, *your brother, Captain of Calais!*

William came home in a foul temper.

"I cannot stay long. Henry Tudor has landed at Milford Haven!" he announced. "Carmarthen and Brecon are safe for the King, but I fear some traitors have gone over to the Tudor. I've sent a fast rider to warn King Richard of the invasion."

Kate felt a deep tremor of fear. It had come at last, the conflict they had all been dreading.

"God help me, I failed to prevent those traitors from crossing the Pembroke River to join Henry Tudor," William fumed, crashing around the hall in frustration. "I was not far behind them too. At least I have blocked the southern route to England, but the bastard is marching north, so I must leave you again, and do my best to intercept him. I just need a few provisions to keep me and my men going, and the arrows in my store."

"Take care, my son," the countess enjoined. "I shall pray constantly that you come back to us safe with good news."

"God speed you, my lord," Kate added, with unusual warmth: it was her father whom William was going to defend.

KATHERINE

August 1561; Ipswich, Suffolk

Blessed be God—for it puts her in a sweet temper—the Queen has spent a most enjoyable day visiting the town of Ipswich and meeting the local dignitaries and the people; and she has now returned in a high good humor to the magnificent house of Sir Edmund Withipoll, where we are lodged. It is called Christchurch Mansion, and was a monastery before King Harry dissolved it, but there is little left from the monks' days here. Costly oak paneling clads the walls, the chambers are appointed with richly carved beds and chairs and tables, and we are served our supper on silver-gilt plates. Her Majesty is well pleased with the hospitality, and Sir Edmund expands visibly with pride at her praise. I pray God her good mood lasts until I have a chance to make a clean breast of my heavy matter.

I have eaten barely a morsel. My laces are unbearably tight and I know I cannot hope to conceal my condition any longer. I have no choice but to confess all and beg for the Queen's mercy.

As soon as my royal mistress has retired for the night, I hasten to the fine chamber assigned me, and take from my traveling chest the little silver casket that goes everywhere with me. I hunt through the contents, looking for the deed that Ned gave me a few days after we were wed; it is the proof of our marriage that I must show the Queen. To my horror, it is not there. I scrabble frantically through my papers again, but it is still missing. *What am I to do?* My heart is pounding: I am in terror.

I have thought much lately about what Ned said, weeks ago, about getting influential people on our side. I clutch at the idea as at a straw. In my present state of mind, I fear I am likely to make a mess of things.

Ned mentioned approaching Lord Robert Dudley, but I could not, for very shame, confess everything to a man. It must be a lady of my acquaintance, one who is friendly toward me, although of those there is precious little choice these days.

I opt for someone known to my family for many years: Mrs. Saintlow, a Lady of the Privy Chamber, a wealthy, forceful, strong-willed woman who carries much influence with the Queen—"a rock within the sea," as I've heard her called. Bess Saintlow—or Bess Hardwick, as she was—was once a lady-in-waiting and good friend of my mother, and I have known her since I was seven. She is sensible and reliable, even though at times, despite her evident goodwill, I find myself overwhelmed by her personality. Yet she has shown such regard for me as to make me godmother to her daughter Elizabeth, and to keep a motherly eye on me at the court.

Bess will help me, I am sure of it! Why did I not think of her before?

I wait until the household is quiet, then I tap at her door.

"Who goes there?" she cries in her strident voice.

"It is I, Katherine Grey," I reply, as low as I can.

"Pray come in," Bess calls.

The room is warm with candlelight. Bess is sitting up in bed in her night rail, an account book spread across her knees, her long red hair tumbling about her shoulders, and an embroidered nightcap tied under her chin.

"Lady Katherine!" she exclaims. "Whatever is wrong?" I realize I must look a sad sight, with my eyes red from weeping.

"Oh, dear Bess," I sob, and sink onto a stool. Out it all comes, my woeful story, blurted in fits and starts between much nose-blowing and dabbing of my eyes.

Bess hears me out in unnerving silence, then, to my amazement—for she is a strong, stiff-backed lady—bursts into furious tears.

"You rash little fool, why have you involved me in this treason? Do you want to get us both sent to the Tower? Think you I would risk my good credit with the Queen for this? God's blood, Lady Katherine, I am very sorry to hear that you have married without the consent of the Queen's Majesty and of your friends, and I would you had made Her Majesty privy to your trouble from the first, you foolish girl. Pray get yourself gone from my sight! Go to your bed, while I think what should be done with you, and hurry—my husband will be here soon!"

Thus chastised and castigated, with no chance given for argument, I creep back to my chamber, feeling as if the world is about to fall on me.

In the morning, Bess pointedly ignores me, and in church I am aware of certain courtiers whispering and nodding in my direction. I must act, now!

Lord Robert Dudley is my only hope. A year on, the scandal of his wife's end has died a slow death, and he is again close as can be to the Queen, although all talk of their marrying has been stilled. Some say he shares her bed at night, giving the lie to her oft-repeated declarations that she means to live and die a virgin. But I cannot believe, knowing her as I do, that she would allow even him that final intimacy.

Remembering that we are brother- and sister-in-law, his own long sojourn in the Tower in the wake of his father's fall, and his banishment from court last year, Lord Robert might help me. He, of all men, knows what it is to suffer the pains of royal displeasure. I summon my courage and resolve to seek him out.

There is no chance during the day, for we have to accompany Her Majesty to dine at the house of a leading citizen, Thomas More, on the high street, and afterward go to inspect the impressive high tower built by a wealthy merchant at Freston, outside the town—although I am in such a state of trepidation that I cannot pay much heed to this most curious building.

Later, after supper, I watch Lord Robert fawning upon the Queen, never straying from her side as the court enjoys an interlude acted by local players and then settles to gambling as usual. When the gathering breaks up near midnight, and I am near dead on my feet for weariness, I have not found a single opportunity to speak privily with my lord.

Retiring to my room, I am on a knife edge. I hardly know what I am doing. I cannot delay any longer. I *must* see Lord Robert—in my mind, he has become my lodestar, my rescuer and my savior, and so I wait until all are in bed, and then, taking my candle, go stealthily to his room, taking care to tread silently, because it is next to the Queen's own bedchamber.

I tiptoe the last few paces, terrified lest I should waken Her Majesty. I listen at Lord Robert's keyhole. What if I find them together within, in bed even? But all is quiet. There is no sound beyond the sturdy oak doors.

I tap lightly on Lord Robert's. No response. I tap again. Nothing. As carefully as possible, I try the door and, to my relief, find it unlocked. Summoning all my courage, I lift the latch and slip into the room. Moonlight streams through the open lattice windows; it is a warm, balmy night. A figure rears up in the bed.

"What the devil . . . ?"

"Please, Lord Robert, hush!" I whisper urgently. "It is Katherine Grey. I must speak with you. I need your help. I am desperate."

"What?" He sits up. I can see his form clearly in the moonlight. He is bare-chested and quite a feast for female eyes, with his hirsute muscular torso, dark good looks, tousled black hair, neat beard, and chiseled features. Not for nothing does the Queen call him her Gypsy. His face, however, is in shadow.

"What are you *doing* here, Lady Katherine?" he hisses, sounding none too pleased to see me. "The Queen lies only next door! Do you want to get us both into trouble? If she heard us and came in, there would be a lot of explaining to do!"

"My lord, I beg of you!" I cast myself down on my knees by the bed, weeping, unable to help myself. "A few minutes of your time is all I crave. Hear me out, please! I beg you to be a means to the Queen's Highness for me. My very life may depend on it."

He does not look surprised, although my distress seems to soften his heart a little.

"Very well," he whispers. "But be quick, and keep your voice down, for God's sake."

It takes more than a few minutes, of course, but he listens as my sorry tale unfolds, shaking his head at intervals and at one point burying his face in his hands and sighing, as if he cannot bear to hear more.

When I have finished, I remain kneeling there, looking at him beseechingly, but his voice comes low and disdainful.

"And you want me to intercede for you with the Queen, and tell her what you have done? Why should I do that? You have acted with the crassest folly. Did you never take warning from what happened to your sister and your father?"

"I have not committed treason!" I protest.

"Some would say you have, and that, in defying the Queen's express order not to marry without her consent, you are a rebel too. Are you mad, Lady Katherine? Do you not understand that you are near in blood to the throne, and the peril in which that places you?"

"I but married the man I love!" I weep.

"You little fool. You thought to defy the Queen and all good order and sense by taking a husband for love, rather than waiting for a suitable one to be found for you. In one of your estate, that is sheer insanity. By yielding to your lewd affections, you have defiled your royal blood by an unlawful union. And if this be not treason, then I might remind you that your intrigues with Spain may yet be viewed as such."

I am in full flood now, racked by silent sobs.

"Go now!" Dudley commands me coldly. "I can have no part in this. You have compromised me enough this night."

I rise, gathering the remnants of my dignity. "I am sorry to have troubled you, my lord," I whisper brokenly. "Good night."

After taking care to close the door quietly behind me, I hasten away from that hated chamber, stung by Lord Robert's cruel words. And yet, if I am honest with myself, I have to confess that there was truth in them. I have been a fool—a fool for love, indeed—but, as God is my witness, I never meant harm to any. What to do now? If Dudley will not speak for me, who else is there?

I lie down with a heart of lead, knowing that nothing can avert the tempest that must surely erupt in the morning.

KATE

August 1485, Raglan Castle

They waited anxiously for news, Countess Anne in the chapel, on her knees, and Kate in her chamber, watching the empty distance from her high window, hoping to see a messenger bringing glad tidings. Far below, in the fields, the peasants were gathering in the harvest. It was such a peaceful scene that it was hard to believe that somewhere to the east, men—her father and her husband even—might be dying violently in the field, while the future of the kingdom hung in the balance. She felt sick with worry.

It was toward the end of the month that William at last came home. She saw him approaching with his escort, and flew down to the courtyard to greet him, with the countess and the rest of the household not far behind her.

"My lord, what news?" she cried.

He looked down on her impassively from his great destrier, then his gaze moved to the people crowding behind her in the courtyard. He remained in his saddle and addressed them in ringing tones, not looking at his wife. "There has been a great battle in Leicestershire," he told them, "at a place called Bosworth. The usurper Richard has been killed and we have a new king—Henry VII, by the grace of God."

"No!" screamed Kate. "No!" She began trembling violently, and would have fallen, but the countess and Mattie were at her side at once, supporting her and trying to calm her. All around, folk were looking aghast at each other, dismay in their faces. Their lord had backed the losing side. What would this mean for them? Suddenly a great swell of lamentation burst forth.

"Hush, you fainthearted fools!" William cried. "There is no need for your howling. By a lucky chance, I did not get to Bosworth in time. I was delayed, rooting out so-called rebels. And when I did arrive, they were breaking up the camps and burying the fallen. Fortunately, King

Henry was still there, preparing to depart. I hastened to where he was sitting before his tent, wearing the royal circlet that had been Richard's, and made my submission on my knees, apologizing for my tardiness, and offering him my sword and my allegiance. And he was most gracious to say he accepted both, as tokens of my future loyalty." William's steely eyes raked the assembled company. "So if you value your skins, good people, you will remember that our loyalty has long lain with the Tudor, because we were persuaded thereto by the widespread fame that the late tyrant Richard had shed the innocent blood of his own nephews."

Kate stared at her husband in horror. She could not speak; this was too much for her to take in, and worse—far worse—than anything in her nightmares. People gawped at her as she stood there with wild, ravaged eyes and a countenance white as a corpse. In a few faces she detected compassion; in most a chilly distancing and an aversion born of fear. And that, she suddenly realized, was how it was going to be from now on. She was the tyrant's daughter—and she was alone in a hostile world.

As William raised his sword and a cheer for the new King, the countess and Mattie led a half-fainting Kate away from the courtyard and helped her up to her chamber, where they made her lie down. Mattie stayed with her, holding her hand, while she lay there in a shocked daze, trying to come to terms with what had happened. All she could think of was that her father was dead and those people—her own household officers and servants—had looked at her with hostility. She did not think she would ever want to leave this room again. She could not face the changed world outside.

Mattie sat silent, her sweet, pert face sad beneath the white coif, her hand warm on Kate's. It seemed like hours that they stayed there thus. At length the countess came back.

"Drink this," she commanded, offering Kate a goblet with steam rising from it. "It is wine infused with chamomile leaves and honey, to soothe you, my daughter." At her kindness, Kate began to cry again.

"There, there," Anne soothed, cradling her in motherly arms. "Let it go, sweeting, let it go." And she did. She cried as she had never cried before: for her father, dead in the field and lost to her forever; for John, her lost love; for Anne the Queen; and for a world that would never live again. And then she cried once more for her father, because his enemies would now rejoice in vilifying him, and that loving, careful prince she had known would be lost to history.

She cried herself to sleep, and Mattie gently laid a sheet over her and closed the shutters against the sunset. Hours later, when Kate awoke to the awful realization of her terrible loss, the countess was sitting beside her, reading her missal.

"You've had a sound sleep, child," she said, "and a good thing too."

"William—where is he?" Kate whispered. "I must ask him . . ."

"He is out, visiting our neighbors to tell them the news and ensure their silence," Anne told her. "If you want to ask anything, ask me. William and I talked late last night, and I now know nearly as much as he does."

"My father the King . . . what happened? I would rather know."

The countess took her hand. "Very well, then. It was a most savage battle, William said, although it lasted but two hours. Henry Tudor did not engage in the fighting but stood behind the lines beneath his standard. That wily knave Lord Stanley waited with his forces to see which way the battle was going. King Richard's army fought fiercely, but neither Stanley nor Northumberland came to his aid, although Norfolk was killed fighting for him. In the end, Richard made a desperate, furious charge, aiming to cut down Henry Tudor, and he would have succeeded, but at that moment Stanley and his men bore down on him. William said he fought like a noble soldier, and went down crying 'Treason!' dying manfully in the thick press of his enemies."

She crossed herself, and Kate did likewise. So he had died valiantly, fighting to the last. But what a dreadful death it must have been, with all those soldiers falling upon him. It did not bear thinking about. If she did, she would surely be sick.

"What happened to him . . . afterward?" she faltered.

"When William reached Bosworth, your father's body had been carried back to Leicester, on horseback, and he heard it was to lie exposed to the public for three days in the Grey Friars' church; after that, no doubt, it would have been buried by their charity." Anne was plainly picking her words with care, and Kate suspected that there was a lot more she was not telling her. After all, who would show respect to a vanquished king who had been branded a usurper and a tyrant? She did not want to hear any more: it might be more than she could take. It was bad enough that her father, the last Plantagenet King, and the end of a line of illustrious rulers that stretched back for more than three hundred years, should be accorded no royal tomb or solemn obsequies, as befit his rank.

"One day I will visit the place where he lies," she said. "In the meantime, I will pray for his soul. He was my father and I loved him." She bit her lip. "My lady, I must ask you: do you believe that he was the tyrant they are saying he was, and that he ordered the murder of the princes?"

The countess did not answer immediately. She seemed thrown by the question, and it appeared that, again, she was searching for the right words. "A tyrant is one who governs without recourse to the rule of law," she began. "I have heard that Richard carried out some questionable deeds when he was Lord Protector. I have heard it said he had the princes killed, and now, of course, it will be hard to find any that say otherwise. It is always the victors who write history. I honestly do not know the truth of it all, my daughter; and I hope I am just and wise enough to weigh fairly what I hear. It is possible, that's all I can say; but it is by no means certain."

Kate realized that was not very far removed from what she herself thought, although she had hoped and prayed all along that her father was innocent, and that she would find some proof of that. But where she would find it now was anyone's guess.

She could not stay secluded in her room forever. When her tears had dried, she felt only anger, and with that came indignation. Why should she hide, when she had done nothing wrong? She had nothing to be ashamed of. So she donned the same black gown she had worn out of respect for Queen Anne, washed her face, combed and plaited her hair, covered it with a black veil, and, gathering her courage, walked along the gallery to the parlor for supper.

The room was full of men, booted, spurred, and cloaked. They had come, she learned later, to show solidarity, for all had been steadfast to King Richard, and now they were falling over themselves to demonstrate their loyalty to the Tudor—she could not bring herself to think of him as King Henry. William was directing his page to offer them drinks. When he saw Kate, his face froze into a glare.

"What do you think you are doing coming here dressed like that?" he spat.

Anger flared in her. Her grief was too raw for her to care what she said. "I am in mourning for my father, the late King," she asserted. The men stared at her, embarrassed and looking not a little fearful. Of course, they would not want to be associated in any way with King Richard, or his daughter.

"Do you so far forget yourself as to mourn a tyrant?" William roared. "Get back to your chamber, woman, put on some brave attire, and then come back and join these gentlemen and me in a toast to our new King."

"My father was not a tyrant!" she flung at him. "And even if he was, he was a tyrant whom you were pleased to serve, and whose bounty to you was lavish!"

In two bounds William had crossed the floor, and, before she could put up a hand to protect herself, had slapped her cheek hard. "Are you mad?" he growled. "Don't you know it might mean death to express loyalty to your father now?"

"Your husband speaks truth," put in an elderly man standing by the fireplace. "King Henry has dated his reign from the day before Bosworth, so that all who fought for Richard are now deemed traitors. Some are already punished, some are fled; and who can blame them? I hear my lord of Lincoln is among those who will be called to account, when he can be found."

Her heart turned ice-cold at that. So John had fought for her father at Bosworth. He had been loyal to the end, unlike this craven oaf of a husband of hers. But where was John now? If they were looking for him, he must have gone to ground somewhere. Were some good folk succoring him in hiding, or had he managed to escape abroad? She sent up a silent prayer for his safety and comfort. God grant that there was good news of him soon!

"Even this new king must have a heart," she said bravely, her face smarting. "Surely even he would not deny a daughter the right to mourn her father? And if he were to appear here now, I would challenge him on that."

"I won't be allowing you within a mile of him," William vowed. "Do you think he'd even allow you into his presence, the bastard spawn of his enemy?" His brutal words stung, but Kate was not going to give him the satisfaction of knowing that.

"I will withdraw, my lord, but I will not be returning," she said. "Since the sight of me in mourning offends you, I will remain within my chamber. Good night, masters." And she swept out.

Back in her room, her composure deserted her, and all her grief and hurt and anger exploded in yet another outburst of heart-wrenching crying. This time she weathered it alone, weeping her heart out into her pillow, with no one to see or to comfort her. It was only later that Mattie came to her, at the usual hour; and then she found her in an exhausted sleep, the ravages of pain etched upon her young face.

KATHERINE

August 1561, Tower of London

The great forbidding fortress of the Tower of London looms into view, and within me my child stirs. He must sense my terror. Poor, unknowing little lamb—he can have little idea of the trouble his presence in my womb has caused. What has he ever done to deserve imprisonment? Nothing! He is an innocent.

I shift uncomfortably. The barge that has conveyed me to the City glides smoothly across the black water, but I am great with child now and cannot remain in one position for long. They have seated me on cushions, with brusque consideration for my condition, but they speak no kind word to me. I have offended Majesty, and therefore no longer merit normal, comforting, human discourse. And thus it has been since Lord Robert Dudley betrayed my crime to the Queen.

I did not see Elizabeth after that, but I can well imagine the explosion that followed Lord Robert's revelations. It was Mrs. Astley who came to inform me frigidly that I was banished from Her Majesty's presence and must keep to my chamber, which I did shrinking with dread. Less than an hour later there came a loud rapping on my door, and there stood one of the captains of the Queen's guard with a warrant for my arrest. He led me, all atremble, down to a waiting litter, and an armed escort bore me off to London. I do not like to think of that terrible journey, or the curt hostility of my warders. Colchester, Chelmsford, Brentwood . . . all passed in a blur of terror, and when we reached Tilbury, I knew very well where I was going.

The walls and towers of the great fortress are nearer now. I can see the cannon on the wharf, the court gate in the Byward Tower. We are making for St. Thomas's Tower beyond it, beneath which is the sinister water gate through which so many doomed wretches have passed and never emerged again.

I cannot enter the Tower, I cannot! It is a place of horror to me, and I would never voluntarily have come here to save my life. My dear sister Jane died here on the scaffold these seven years and six months since, butchered to death at just seventeen, and she innocent of any crime! But I—I have offended grievously, and I am horribly aware that I too might soon find myself standing before the block.

If only Ned would come home and explain everything, then maybe the Queen could be made to understand that we have never meant her any ill. But he has now been gone beyond seas for five months, and can have no idea of this ordeal I am suffering. My fervent hope is that he will hasten home soon and succor me. I have thought ill of him, I know, and all but abandoned him, yet I am very sorry for that now. In my extremity, beside which all other troubles seem trifling, I see clearly that that was but a fantasy, born of anxiety and unwarranted suspicion. In my dreadful predicament, I remember only the love Ned gave me, and his marrying me in defiance of the Queen's express order. I know in my bones he is still my sweet lord, my dearest true husband, and I dare not think of that now, or I will surely die of longing and grief.

My mind is filled with horrible imaginings: of my sister, my father—who also perished here during that dreadful winter—and of

Guilford Dudley. I recall how Guilford went weeping to the public scaffold on Tower Hill. I never liked him, but I was filled with pity when they told me. Three heads lost to the axe: a savage ending. And they were not the only ones who suffered in this place. Who has not heard of Queen Anne Boleyn and Queen Katherine Howard? They do not spare women the block in this kingdom. Will I be next? Oh, sweet Jesus, spare me that, I beseech Thee!

The solid walls are above us now, menacing and implacable; the barge passes under the gloomy arch below St. Thomas's Tower, and as it slows to a halt, it rocks, battered by the waves slapping at the steps of the water gate. I grip the boat's sides instinctively, but in truth I do not care if it sinks and drowns me. Better that than a worse fate.

In front of us the heavy oak gates, slatted in iron, grind open inch by inch, to reveal a tall, thin man with a soldierly bearing, wearing sober, well-cut clothes. He looks to be around fifty years old; he has thick graying hair, a drooping mustache, and high cheekbones in a craggy, lined, and rather sad face, and wears an unnervingly grave expression. He waits with a small detachment of yeomen warders. These men, I realize, with a sick feeling, are to be my jailers. I pray God they may not also be my executioners.

After the guards have helped me to my feet, I alight from the boat with trembling legs and dread in my heart. But as I make to mount the stairs, the tall gentleman descends hastily and offers his arm.

"Sir Edward Warner, at your service, my lady," he says. "I am the Lieutenant of the Tower, and you will be in my charge." I am relieved to find him so courteous and thoughtful, and his tone cordial, even a touch avuncular, although a treacherous little voice in my head is reminding me that a similar kindness was extended by the Tower officials of the day to my sister, and, so I have heard, to Anne Boleyn.

"Follow me," Sir Edward murmurs in a low voice, his expression pained as he sees the terror in my face. "There is nothing to fear." I take much courage from that, for I had expected yet more cold treatment from those appointed to have custody of me; even so, with my fate yet to be decided, no comfortable words can unravel the tight knot of fear in my breast.

"I understand how you must feel, my lady. I too have been a prisoner in this place," says the lieutenant as we ascend the stairs. "It was my punishment for supporting the claim of your sister, the Lady Jane. I was held here a year after Wyatt's rebellion, and then languished in disgrace until the accession of our blessed Queen Elizabeth, for which I daily give thanks."

I cannot myself feel so thankful, naturally, but I am heartened by Sir Edward's words, and especially cheered to learn that he had espoused the claim of my sister, for surely that will dispose him to look kindly upon me. I am almost content to follow him, although I am aware of the warders with their pikes at my back.

We turn into a cobbled lane, which looks vaguely familiar, and looking around me, I recognize the place where Harry and I boarded Pembroke's barge on that momentous night eight years ago, and remember the inexplicable terror that seized me in this very place, when I was suddenly desperate to get out. Was that some premonition of my present imprisonment? I am terrified now—but that was worse. God forbid it was a portent of what is coming to me . . .

The Tower seems vast, all high, forbidding walls and stern buildings, and I have no idea where I am being led. What I dread most is being immured in a dungeon—and coming upon the spot where my sister's lifeblood was spilled. That, I could not face.

"Where are we going, Sir Edward?" I inquire.

The lieutenant steers me through an archway. In front of me, to my left, there is a wall, with trees beyond. "Ahead is the inner ward," he tells me. "You are to be accommodated in the Bell Tower." He points upward. "The garden of my lodging is next to it, beyond the wall." If there is a garden next to my prison, it surely cannot be that grim. I hope I will be able to see it from my window.

The archway leads to a narrow passage, and it is here, near the exit at the far end, that I suddenly feel desperately cold, even though it is August, and warm. Sir Edward and his men remain oblivious, but for a space I am freezing, and enveloped in a sense of panic and horror that I know is not entirely connected with my circumstances. Then we turn left, and the feeling disappears as instantly as it came—only to be succeeded by something far worse. For as we emerge into a wide-open space, in front of me is the vast expanse of Tower Green, enclosed by more towers and walls, while to the right, the great white keep known as Caesar's Tower rises toward the sky, its gilded onion domes gleaming in the sunlight. But I barely notice them, because beyond the green is the chapel. I stop dead in my tracks.

The lieutenant has seen me staring ahead in horror. Briskly, he takes my arm and steers me toward a tall timbered house on the left, one of several fine residences in that corner of the bailey. It's an impressive building, with a high stone tower behind it, but I barely notice either because I am feeling sick to my stomach, knowing that my sister's butchered remains lie in that chapel, and that somewhere on Tower Green stood the scaffold on which she died. If the Queen had wanted to punish me, she could not have devised a better way.

Fighting down nausea, I turn my head away and stare fixedly ahead. We enter the Lieutenant's Lodging, a fine modern house with spacious paneled rooms and rich furnishings such as normally grace a knightly household. Sir Edward leads me along a passage, then through an anteroom furnished sparsely with benches, and so to the door of what he tells me is the Bell Tower.

"This is the only entrance," he explains, as if he anticipates that, heavy with child as I am, I will try to escape. "Her Majesty's orders, you understand. It is a secure place."

"I am no threat to Her Majesty," I cannot resist saying. "I am her loyal subject."

He frowns. "Come, my lady," he says.

The Bell Tower is very old. The lieutenant informs me—as if we were enjoying a tour of the place—that it was built by King Richard the Lionheart many centuries ago. I can well believe that. The downstairs chamber, octagonal in shape, has great thick, rough walls pierced by tall glazed windows. Today they admit shafts of sunlight, but even so, the place is cool and dank, and I know it will be freezing in winter. Please God, let them not force me to give birth to my child in here!

But the lieutenant is moving on, leading the way up a steep spiral stair.

"Sir Thomas More was imprisoned down there thirty years ago," he tells me, "and the cold was a martyrdom to him." So had his execution been, in many people's eyes, as I have read. He too defied his King, and paid the ultimate price. I shudder at the thought.

"You, my lady, will be more comfortable," Sir Edward assures me.

He opens a door, indicating I should enter, and I am relieved to see that the upper chamber, which is circular in shape, is much better appointed than the room below, with wooden shutters at the windows and clean rush matting on the floor. A threadbare tapestry hangs on the whitewashed wall, its colors so faded that I can only just make out a battle scene. There is a carved wooden tester bed made up, thankfully, with good bleached sheets, a battered-looking drawing table, two stools, and an empty iron brazier. But I will not be here when winter strikes, I promise myself, calmer now. By then I will have protested my innocence before God and the Queen's Council, and been vindicated. For surely it is the intent to do harm that counts. Alas, says a warning voice in my head, I should know better. I have the example of my sister before me. I can only pray, most fervently, that Queen Elizabeth is more merciful than Queen Mary.

I am not alone, for I am allowed the services of a maid, Honor, on account of my rank. My lady the Countess of Hertford—for so I am, whatever they may say—cannot go unattended, even in prison. So little Honor, who is just fourteen years old, will share my dreary, anxious days here and sleep in the serving maids' chamber in the Lieutenant's Lodging at nights.

The infant inside me kicks lustily. God grant it will be a son; that would please Ned, for all men want an heir to succeed to their titles and lands—if, of course, there are any, after this dreadful business is concluded. And suddenly I am fearful for the little one's sake as well as my own. For if my child is a son, then from his birth he will pose a greater threat to the Queen than my sisters and I ever could.

KATE

August 1485, Raglan Castle

The next morning, when Kate awoke, Mattie was bustling around, pouring water into a basin and laying out fresh body linen. The black dress Kate discarded the night before had been hung up and brushed, and was hanging on its peg. She struggled to regain her wits. Her head felt terrible, and her eyes were stinging.

"What time is it?" she muttered.

"Good morning," Mattie responded. "It is nigh eight o'clock. How are you today, my lady?"

"Wretched," she sighed. "My head aches and I feel sick. God knows I wept a storm last night—and I had cause. My lord was hateful to me, hateful! In faith, I do not know how I can bear to live with him anymore. And he doesn't want me now that my father is dead. I am an embarrassment to him, an obstacle in the way of his gaining favor with the Tudor. I tell you, Mattie, I shall go into a convent, and then he and I can be rid of each other."

"I'd hold your horses a bit if I were you," Mattie said, folding some clean linen. "When did you last bleed, my lady?"

Kate thought back. In the anxiety and turmoil of the past weeks, she had not taken much notice of her body's rhythms. But now it dawned on her that she had not seen her courses for some time. She looked at Mattie in dismay.

"I reckon it's seven weeks since I had to wash your clouts," Mattie said. "I think you're with child—and that makes two of us!"

"Mattie!" Realization was dawning. "Yes—it must be. I feel a little sick today, just like before. Dear God, what shall I do? My lord hates me. He will be angry to think I am pregnant with King Richard's grandchild."

"Him? No, like all men, he wants an heir. You tell him you're expecting and he'll perk up, see if I'm right."

"This is unreal," Kate said. "And you too, Mattie! Are you pleased?"

"Delighted, and Guy too. And I'm pleased for you, my lady. When God closes one door, He opens another. This will help to blunt the edge of your grief."

Kate thought that nothing could do that, but it was true that a baby would give her something else to think about. And whatever anyone else might say, she rejoiced in the knowledge that it was her father's grandchild she was carrying, and that something of him would live on, something she could cherish.

She rested in her chamber that morning, and Mattie gave out that she was indisposed. When the sick feeling had passed, she got up and had her maid dress her in her mourning gown, then she seated herself at the table. In her portable writing desk—a curiously wrought box with painted panels, a velvet lining, and secret compartments—lay her bundle of jottings about the princes. She sat there thinking about them, poring over them, trying to make sense of them. She wondered if she should try to write down her findings so far. She wanted to be able one day to tell her child the truth about his grandfather. But how could she do that when she did not know the truth herself?

Yet maybe—just maybe—her doubts would be resolved soon. Henry Tudor had sworn his intention of marrying Elizabeth of York, and no doubt he would make good that vow shortly. For he held his throne only by right of conquest, not through right of blood. There were others of Yorkist descent who had more right—Warwick and his sister, and John, of course. It was clear that Henry Tudor believed that the precontract story was nonsense; otherwise he would not have vowed to wed Elizabeth of York. Soon he must honor that vow, and it was possible that he would make some proclamation about the fate of the princes—although, Kate thought dismally, it was bound to be injurious to her father's memory, which could only be to the Tudor's advantage. Even if Henry had no proof that Richard had killed his nephews, he would find it politic to say he had.

She wondered again how Henry Tudor had been sure they were dead. He must have learned something from Buckingham, probably through his mother, Lady Stanley. She made herself face the possibility that Buckingham had learned that her father, alarmed by the plots in the boys' favor, was planning to do away with the princes. For those plots had been proof that a lot of people still held that the sons of Edward IV were the true heirs to the throne—and that they were still a threat to Richard.

They had been close, the King and the duke: her father might well have confided his intention to his friend. That was sufficient to explain Buckingham's disaffection. But did Buckingham, or Henry Tudor, ever find out that the princes were actually dead? Maybe Buckingham had known nothing of their fate after all.

She laid down her pen. She had written nothing. She supposed she would have to wait to see what transpired now, although she knew she might wait a long time for news to filter through to Raglan. For certain it was that her husband would not willingly enlighten her.

She tied the papers up again and was just about to put them away when the door opened and William walked in. Their eyes met: hers flashed with hurt and anger at the remembrance of his cruelty the night before; his alighted on her black dress.

"Your maid said you were indisposed," he said.

"I was. I am feeling better now." Kate's tone was cool. She was not going to make this easy for him. In fact she would not have cared if she never saw him again.

"I spoke harshly last night," he muttered. "But you must know that I am in a very difficult position. Married to King Richard's daughter, and thus bound to him in his lifetime, I fear I might find myself under surveillance on a suspicion of disloyalty. I have done what I can to forestall that, but—God, woman, were you insane, proclaiming your loyalty to your father by appearing publicly in mourning for him? People will talk! Those gentlemen that were here—everyone's running scared, fearing the Tudor's vengeance. They won't scruple to throw me to the wolves to save their own hides. I *had* to reprimand you."

"You didn't have to call me a bastard spawn!" Kate retorted with spirit. She wanted him to apologize.

"I had good reason. Drawing attention to your bastardy suggests I despise you for your father's sake. I need people to think I was coerced into this marriage."

Kate gaped at him, appalled. "Is that true?" she whispered. "Were you coerced?"

He would not meet her gaze. "I do not despise you yourself," he muttered, "but I would I had never consented to this match. I had my reservations, the stain of your birth being paramount, although that was compensated for by your father's generosity." His words stung. She felt the color flare in her cheeks. He was cruel, cruel!

"Hearing me berating you last night, no one could have doubted my loyalty to King Henry. We must needs distance ourselves from your father, and make it appear that we had abandoned him because of his wickedness."

"You make me feel like Judas," she said, bitter. "Just tell me you don't believe there is any truth in those allegations you made against King Richard, that he murdered his nephews."

"All part of the same strategy," William said.

"But do you believe it? That he had them killed?"

"What else is there to believe? No one has seen them alive in more than two years."

"There could be many explanations for that!"

"Then believe what you want to believe. But keep your mouth shut on that issue, d'you hear me? Because, mark me well, we will no doubt be told that he had them murdered."

They faced each other, all conversation run out. He had not apologized, and even if he had, forgiving him was another matter. For all his good reasons for uttering them, the things he said to her had injured their marriage irrevocably.

"I am sorry you regret taking me to wife," she ventured.

"I would not do so now," William replied bluntly. "But since we are wed, we must make the best of it."

"Last night, I thought of disappearing into a convent," she told him. He did not look too surprised, so perchance the idea had occurred to him too. A husband whose wife became a nun could be released from his marriage vows.

"That might be for the best," he said, his face lightening a little.

"Yes, it *would* have been, I'm sure," she said, tart. "But this morning

I had cause to think again. I had not realized it before, and it took Mattie to make all plain, but by sure and certain tokens I am with child."

William's face was a mask of warring emotions. She knew how desperately he wanted a son; and yet he would not want it to be the grandson of a defeated king.

"Is that so?" he said. "Then maybe God at least smiles upon our marriage. This pregnancy, coming at this time, must be a sign that I should not put you from me."

"You had considered it?"

"Yes. But this makes a difference." He sighed. "We must make the best of things now, for our son's sake."

"I pray God it will be a son."

"I need an heir. I do not want my line to end with Elizabeth, or my lands and title to go to the man she marries. But my son's mother should not be dressed in mourning for a vanquished tyrant, which is what people are calling Richard now. I am sorry for your loss: I know what it is to lose a father by violence. But your grieving must be inward; outwardly, you must show you are looking to the future. I will not permit you to draw attention to whose daughter you are."

INTERLUDE

August 1561; Ipswich, Suffolk

Queen Elizabeth paces up and down the council chamber, a volcano waiting to erupt. Her councillors look on apprehensively; they know what she can be like when she has a temper on her. They glance at each other, thinking that it might be less harrowing to do battle with the French than face the Queen when she is in a fury.

She is now nearly twenty-eight years old, a tall, slender woman with a thin face, hooked nose, and swarthy skin whitened with cosmetics. Her long, curly red hair is coiled up on her head beneath a jaunty crimson velvet cap adorned with black plumes. Everything about her is stylish, from the matching gown with its pointed stomacher that shows off her tiny waist to advantage to the pearls and jewels that drip from her ears, wrists, and bosom. She is by no means beautiful, but she has a commanding presence and great personal charm, while men find her desirable—and not only because she is powerful. It pleases her vanity to encourage them; she is very vain indeed.

But she is in no mood for flirtation or preening now. She is here to discuss this latest threat to her security as Queen, and to demand answers.

"I tell you, this is a conspiracy!" she snarls. "Why will you not believe me?"

"Because, madam, there is no evidence," Sir William Cecil replies calmly.

"Oh, my Spirit, I cannot believe you are so naïve!" Elizabeth flings at him, this man who is her closest, wisest, and most loyal adviser.

Cecil takes the reproof in his stride; he has been on the receiving end of far worse.

Elizabeth frowns. "But there must be many who were privy to this marriage, according to what I hear," she persists. "To me, my lords, that smells of a conspiracy!"

"So far our investigations have uncovered not a single person who knows anything about it," Cecil tells her, aware that his fellows are more than content for him to act as spokesman.

"What of the minister?" the Queen barks.

"Disappeared without trace, madam."

"And Mrs. Saintlow?"

"In the Tower. Madam, I would remind you that the Lady Katherine also sought out my Lord Robert here." He bows slightly in the direction of the man who is his rival for power.

Elizabeth glares at Cecil. "And he came immediately to me." Lord Robert ventures a smirk at Mr. Secretary. "Mrs. Saintlow did not think to tell me of her conversation with the Lady Katherine," the Queen continues. "I want her closely questioned. What of the Earl of Hertford?"

"He has been summoned home."

"I want him and the Lady Katherine *rigorously* examined by the Privy Council," Elizabeth demands. "So far, we have only heard her pathetic claim that she married for love. For love, mark you—and she a rival for my throne! God's wounds, she has shown herself ungrateful for the favor extended to her, and insolent, yea. Mr. Secretary, have Sir Edward Warner make inquiries to discover how many were privy to this marriage from the first!"

"It shall be done," Cecil says.

"Have it done now, before the official questioning," the Queen commands. She is still beside herself with anger. "By her disobedience and rashness, the Lady Katherine has managed to undermine my own careful policies," she hisses. "God knows, my lords, I spend my life playing off one royal suitor against another so they stay friendly toward this kingdom, and that I do without thought for my own inclinations. One day it may please me to wed, but I shall do so for the good of my realm, not to satisfy my lusts. Yet the Lady Katherine has contracted marriage without a thought for the consequences, and that, gentlemen, proves to me that she is unfit to be my heir. I want her removed from the succession, and the way to do that is to have her attainted, because this is treason, no less!"

Mr. Secretary clears his throat. "In that, madam, alas, you are mistaken. Under your father and brother, any man contracting an unauthorized marriage with a princess of the blood would have been guilty of treason, but King Edward repealed that statute. So legally, in marrying, neither Lord Hertford nor the Lady Katherine has committed treason, and they cannot therefore be attainted or put to death."

"She has gone against my express command not to marry without my consent," the Queen flares. "Is that not treason?"

"It's disputable, madam, insufficient as a basis for proceeding too harshly against her."

"Then what is to be done? Answer me!"

"Your Majesty might require the Lady Katherine to renounce her claim?" suggests the Earl of Sussex.

"Could she be trusted to keep her word?" Robert Dudley asks.

"Even if she did, there are those who would break it for her," Cecil says. "She has a goodly following both in England and abroad. No, we cannot go down that road. But there might be another way."

"What way?" the Queen asked sharply.

"We could have the alleged marriage declared invalid. There was only one witness, and she is now dead. We cannot trace the officiating minister, although the search is still going on. That leads me to believe there was no secret wedding, and that all Lady Katherine's protestations that there was are but a pretense to cover up her shame. She well knows that naughty conduct is reprehensible in one so near in blood to the throne." Cecil is aware that Elizabeth hates to be reminded that, under the Act of Succession, the Lady Katherine is in fact the next in line. He knows she has no love for her Grey cousins. He knows also that Elizabeth is jealous because Katherine, who bears a familial resemblance to her, is by far the more beautiful, and seven years younger, to boot.

"What of the marriage lines?" Sussex asks. "The Lady Katherine may produce those as proof that she is a good woman and a wedded wife."

"My lord, you are too shortsighted," Cecil reproves. "If there are any marriage lines, which I doubt, then we will deal with them as we think best. And when this pretended marriage is proved no marriage, which must be done with all dispatch, the Lady Katherine's child will be born a bastard, and can pose no threat to Her Majesty's security. And, as the world knows, any princess who bears a child out of wedlock must be entirely shamed and discredited, and none will ever again think of her as fit to succeed."

Elizabeth has been regarding her Secretary of State with keen eyes. "By God's blood, Spirit, you have the sow by the right ear, as my father used to say. By all means proceed along these lines, with our hearty consent." There is a chorus of ayes from along the council table.

"Madam, may I have a word in private?" Cecil asks later, after the other business of the day has been concluded. Only he, and the detestable Lord Robert Dudley, whom she favors inordinately, can speak candidly to the Queen, and what Cecil has to say is of a highly sensitive nature. Even Elizabeth's trusted privy councillors should not hear it.

Her Majesty dismisses the rest with a regal nod, and sinks back into her cushioned chair at the head of the long table. She is taut with agitation.

"Madam," Cecil begins, "may I remind you, again, that you are as yet unwed and without an heir?"

"You never cease reminding me, William," she retorts wryly. "I tell you, I am already married to a husband, and that is the kingdom of England."

"The kingdom of England is not going to give you an heir." Cecil smiles. They have had this conversation before—countless times. His smile, though, is fleeting. "It is my duty to remind you that, until you bear a child, the Lady Katherine is your rightful heir, according to the Act of Succession passed in your father's time." He himself would have championed Katherine's cause, had indeed tried to help her, but now things have gone too far, and he has had to abandon her, even though he knows she has the best claim. In truth, he likes not this business, and while he is doing what he knows the Queen expects of him, he is aware that the long-term consequences might be serious. Because all he wants is for this interminable problem of the succession to be settled—and he fears it is less likely than ever after this. Yet he dare not appear to be supporting the Lady Katherine now. Without her, though, who shall succeed the Queen?

"Never!" Elizabeth glares at him. "I will not have that strumpet follow me on the throne."

"I agree, it would be most unfitting, especially now that she has disgraced herself. Her illicit pregnancy is a sure sign that God does not approve of her succeeding. But the Act of Succession provides that if you, madam—Heaven forfend—die without issue, the crown must go to the heirs of your father's sister Mary, late Queen of France and Duchess of Suffolk. That means her granddaughters, Lady Katherine and Lady Mary Grey. Failing them, what is to be done about the succession?"

"*I* will name my heir, when I am good and ready!" Elizabeth snarls. "As I said, I may yet decide to wed and have an heir of my body." Cecil, that astute man, is aware of her biting her lip. He knows how overmuch she fears marriage and childbirth.

"No one will rejoice more at that than I," he replies smoothly, "but until that happy day, the Act remains in force."

"I'll not have Lady Katherine as my successor! I cannot abide the sight of her."

"Some would use the persuasive argument that she is a Protestant, born in this kingdom—unlike Mary, Queen of Scots."

"A Protestant? Bah!" Elizabeth bangs her fist on the table. "She trims her sails to the wind. She was a Catholic when it suited her, when she thought it would win her a crown. Her conversion in my sister's reign was purely self-seeking. Since then she has been all things to all men."

"Might I remind Your Majesty that you too had to make a pretense of conforming to the old faith?" ventures Cecil. "Those were dangerous times. And I have no doubt that the Lady Katherine had in mind the fate of her sister, who was the focus of Protestant ambitions. Standing so near to the throne, she really had no choice—not when Queen Mary was burning Protestants."

"That's as may be," Elizabeth mutters, not prepared to be mollified. "But she should have reverted to her faith when I came to the throne. There was no threat then. Instead, she began dallying with the Spaniards."

"Maybe she felt she was being unjustly treated," Cecil says bravely. "You had, after all, forbidden her to marry, and a Spanish match was in the offing."

"To court it without my blessing was nothing less than treason," the Queen fumes. "And now this misalliance with Hertford. God only knows how long that was going on. Mayhap that dalliance with Spain was a cover for it. I tell you, William, I will never name her my heir, especially now. And *you* would do well to consider where your loyalty should lie! Methinks you would be her advocate."

Cecil ignores the barb. "But Your Majesty must of necessity name someone, and soon. All this uncertainty does nothing to bolster your throne, which is, I need not remind you, less than secure, what with the Catholics all over Europe calling you a bastard, a heretic, and a usurper, God confound them. Some, may I remind you, would prefer the Queen of Scots."

Elizabeth looks at him sharply. "Over my dead body! A Catholic and a foreigner, who has already quartered my royal arms with her own and proclaimed herself Queen of England."

"I agree with Your Majesty entirely. She is the last person who should rule here. But if you repeal the Act, who else is there? The Earl of Huntingdon?" It is an old joke between them, for the earl, despite having a distant claim to the throne, is known to have no desire to occupy it, and could expect little support anyway. "So we are back to Lady Katherine. I must say I do not share your view that she has designs on your throne. She wants only to be named your heir presumptive."

"Pah! She has been a thorn in my side from the first. What of those Spanish plots to carry her off? I would remind you that Lady Katherine was going about my court flaunting herself as the Catholic heir, and then suddenly King Philip was plotting to abduct her so that he could wed her to his son and set them both on the English throne, as a means to restoring the old faith here. And good-bye, Elizabeth! She was involved, make no mistake. She went to the Count de Feria, by God, and told him she knew I did not want her to succeed me. It was tantamount to giving her consent to the abduction."

"If I may say so, Your Majesty—and you will remember that I expressed my views at the time—it was a mistake at the beginning to downgrade her to the presence chamber. She had held higher rank with honor in Queen Mary's time, and she had done nothing then to deserve such a slight. Some might think she had every right to make a fuss and air her grievance."

"Time has proved me right," says the Queen grimly, toying with the great jewel at her breast. "I have been nourishing a serpent in my bosom. Katherine is ambitious, no doubt about it. She wants my crown. She has never ceased to plot against me with the Spaniards. I've marked her toadying to Philip's ambassadors, cozening their support with her wiles. Then there was that talk of her marrying the Scottish pretender, Arran, and so uniting the thrones of England and Scotland. Again, good-bye Elizabeth! And now this marriage to Edward Seymour. I would not put it past those knaves beyond seas and north of the border to have engineered it to discountenance me."

"I hardly think so, madam. Indeed, that marriage has put paid to any intriguing with the Spaniards and the Scots," Cecil soothes. "Seymour has no claim to the throne, so you can set your mind at rest there."

"I still believe there is more to this," Elizabeth persists, gnawing her lip in anger. "If the Lady Katherine cannot have my throne one way, she means to have it by another. Once she bears a son, bastard or not, there will be a clamor for me to name her as my successor. And as that boy grows to manhood, there will be those who ask why England cannot have a king to rule it, instead of a weak and feeble woman, and there will be plots against me. No, don't look at me like that, my Spirit! I know you think it against Nature for a woman to wield dominion over men. It would not surprise me if you yourself were behind this!"

Cecil is shaken, but he has weathered more turbulent storms. "I confess I was of that opinion at one time, but Your Majesty's wisdom and greatness have proved me wrong. And I swear before God I never meddled to make this marriage. As for the child, the lords of England will never agree to a bastard succeeding: they have too much respect for the laws of inheritance. You may rest well assured on that point."

"Hmm. As I say, have the lieutenant question the Lady Katherine. Have him ask for her marriage lines. And have Mrs. Saintlow questioned soon; she was privy to this, I'll wager. Even if there is no conspiracy proved, we must take all possible steps to establish that there was no marriage. As you say, if the child is born a bastard, it cannot pose a threat. Destroy any evidence, if you must, even if it bears the signature of the Archbishop of Canterbury himself. And if there was a treasonable conspiracy . . ."

"I think Your Majesty will find that there was not," Cecil interposes.

"If there was," Elizabeth continues unheeding, "we will have to think carefully about what is to be done with my fine Lady Katherine."

KATE

October 1485, Westminster Palace

It seemed very strange to be back at Westminster, and for a moment at the water stairs Kate felt overcome by grief and loss, and had to steel herself to walk on. How often had she walked through these gardens, these magnificent halls, this labyrinth of a palace? It was hard to credit that another king ruled here now. Almost she could believe she would see her father seated on the dais in the White Hall, with Queen Anne beside him. But they were gone now, and Henry Tudor reigned. She was glad when she and William reached the lodging assigned them. She did not want to meet the man who now called himself King. She could not trust herself to be civil to him. But for him, her father would be alive now, and hastening to welcome them in honor.

It had been expected that William, one of the peers of the realm, would receive an invitation to attend the King's coronation. Wives, of course, were not invited. So far, Henry had shown no sign of making good his promise to marry Elizabeth of York; thus, with no queen, there would be no ladies at the coronation.

Kate, desperate for some pleasant diversion, had pleaded with William to take her up to London with him, but he had said no. Always it was the same excuse: she must not draw attention to herself. Since learning of her pregnancy, he had allowed her to go no farther than the village. At Raglan, she was inconspicuous, and in time people in the wider world might forget she existed. That seemed to be his hope.

But then had come the King's letter. William was commanded to bring with him to Westminster the Lady Katherine his wife. No reason was given. Henry Tudor wanted to meet her, it seemed.

That confounded William. Why did the King want to see Kate? How could she be of any importance to him? Or was it just sheer curiosity on the part of a man who wanted to meet the tyrant's daughter? He went on and on about it, fretting and fuming. He fussed too about her condition: was she up to traveling? It was a long way to London. Maybe they should offer her pregnancy as an excuse for her not to go? In the end he ordered a new horse litter, plumped out with cushions; and it was in that, with William riding beside her, and an escort afore and behind, that Kate made the journey—with the leather curtains closed, so that none should see her. And for her it was no hardship at all, because every mile took them farther into England. Even though so much had changed for the worse since she was last here, she was glad to be back in her native land.

She must keep to their lodgings, William insisted, and not go abroad. People might recognize her; it was best not to draw attention to herself. So she stayed, resentful, in the two rooms they had been allocated: fair chambers, well appointed, but by no means luxurious, and nothing like the apartments she had been used to occupying.

Two days after their arrival, the summons had come, and William and Kate were ushered into the King's presence. William had made her wear a subdued gown of green cammaca: good quality, but nothing that suggested royal pretensions, and the color was that of the Tudor livery.

Kate's first impression was that Henry Tudor looked more like a clerk than a king. He was in his study, standing behind a desk piled with parchments, papers, and scrolls, and rummaging through them with a frown on his face. He did not look up as they entered. They made their obeisances, Kate most unwillingly, and a thin voice said, "Rise." She found herself facing an unimpressive man in his late twenties. He was tall and lean, with wiry reddish hair that was already thinning, and his gray-blue eyes looked out suspiciously from an angular face with a sharp, prominent nose and thin lips. He smiled, revealing decaying teeth, and seated himself.

"Welcome to Westminster, my lord, my lady. I trust you had a good journey and that you are comfortably lodged."

"Yes, I thank Your Grace," William said. He had told Kate that he would do the talking. On no account was she to open her mouth unless the King spoke to her directly.

"I have summoned you today for two reasons," Henry said. "First, my lord, to confirm you in your earldom." William bowed again, expressing his gratitude profusely. Kate could sense his relief. He had fretted about that, as he fretted about everything else, fearing that the King would decide to confiscate his title after all.

"Second, there is a matter with which you might be able to help me, my lady," the King went on, and Kate was aware of William tensing beside her. She swallowed, being unsure how to respond, and worried that her hostility might be apparent. But William dived in.

"You must answer the King's Grace, my lady."

"Yes, sire," she said. Henry Tudor was looking at her speculatively, his eyes darting down to the barely perceptible mound of her stomach. He too would be aware of whose grandchild she carried. Her hatred of him hardened.

"This is a sensitive, secret matter," he said. "My lady, I want your word that it will go no further than this room."

"Yes, sire," she said again, trying to keep her voice dispassionate.

"You are with child," he said. "Pray be seated. This may take a while." He indicated that she should sit on the polished wooden settle before the fire, and sent a clearly unwilling William to wait without. Then he sat down beside her, keeping a respectable distance between them.

"My lady, you may be aware that gossip about the sons of King Edward has flared up again," he began. "It is bruited in London that they died a cruel death by order of the usurper." He regarded her sternly. "Madam, I must ask you: what have you learned privily of this matter?"

This was the last subject she would have expected the Tudor to raise with her. But she collected her wits, hoping she might learn something herself. "I know nothing, sire," she told him.

"Your late father, the usurper Richard, never spoke of the princes?"

She wanted to refer to her father as King Richard in her reply, but thought better of it. Suppressing her anger, she answered, "No, sire, never in that respect."

Henry regarded her suspiciously. "You were aware of the rumors of their deaths?"

"Yes, sire. But I always set little store by them, seeing that they were just rumors. I imagine I know no more than anyone else." She was surprised at her own boldness.

"You 'imagine.' But what *do* you know!"

"I heard that the princes were alive last year," she revealed, then wished she hadn't said it.

"From whom?" Henry barked.

"My lord of Lincoln told me they still lived."

"And how did he know that?"

"He said he believed it, sire. He was at the center of affairs and I assumed he was well informed."

Henry frowned. "I do not think so. Madam, I myself had it on good authority, two years ago, that the princes had been murdered. They are not in the Tower now, so I believe that to have been the truth."

He had given away too much! If they were not in the Tower now, and he was quizzing her like this, he did not know for certain that the princes were really dead. And he was looking for proof that they were, because without it, his hold on the throne must be tenuous indeed, and he could not rely on their sister being the true heir to the House of York. If the princes yet lived, they might rise up at any minute—from the dead, as it were—and claim his throne! And he, by vowing to marry their sister, would himself have endorsed their legitimacy. He did not know where they were. Oh, she saw his dilemma very clearly now! There was some justice in this world.

And there was something else too. *They are not in the Tower now.* Had she cause to hope that they had not been murdered?

"Has a search been made for their bodies, sire?" she ventured.

"Yes, and will be made again. Assuredly, they will be found. But I thought your father might perhaps have offered some explanation of their disappearance to you," Henry said.

"No, sire, he never spoke of it. And I never believed the rumors because I did not think my lord my father capable of such a deed. There *is* no proof of murder, is there, sire?"

Henry threw her a sharp look. "The shedding of infants' blood is a dreadful matter," he pronounced. "It is the foulest of crimes, and I will have the truth!"

"Sire, I would like to know the truth too," she said quietly.

He looked hard at her. His eyes were cold and calculating. "So you have nothing else to say to me?"

"No, sire. I am sorry."

He dismissed her, commanding her again to say nothing of their conversation to anyone, and she went away, her knees trembling. She knew she had made an enemy, but he had been one already, given who she was. She had revealed herself to Henry Tudor, much as he had given himself away to her, and no doubt he thought her defiant and provocative; well, she had been, deliberately: she would not let him drag her father's name in the mud by his hateful insinuations. She'd had to speak out. Yet she thought he had believed her when she said she could not help him.

KATHERINE

August 1561, Tower of London

I cannot complain about my treatment. I have been here but six hours, yet already Sir Edward Warner has given me permission to take the air in his garden, a privilege he tells me I am permitted to enjoy daily, for an hour in the afternoons. Of course, I must be attended by armed warders, as today, but it is a relief to know that I will not be shut up all the time. And so here I am, looking up not at prison walls but at God's glorious blue sky. The garden is so pleasant, with its flowers all in glorious bloom and its shady, rustling trees. For a space, just a little space, sitting in here on the stone bench, my heart feels a touch lighter.

But now I must return to my prison, and my spirits are once more crushed, and I am a very sorrowful woman for the Queen's displeasure, even though a good dinner is being laid before me. Certes, it would be small hardship to be a prisoner here, but for my terrible fears as to my likely fate.

The lieutenant comes to ask if all is to my liking and comfort. Am I mistaken, or is his manner a little stiffer than hitherto?

"Good Sir Edward," I blurt out, "what will they do to me?"

He pauses—ominously, I fear, for he seems to be searching for the right thing to say to me. "As far as I know, my lady, nothing has been decided. My orders are to keep you here, in such estate as beseems your rank, until I receive further instructions. I am told that the Privy Council will interview you, and I have some preliminary questions for you now. The Queen's Majesty has commanded me to say that you shall have no favor from her unless you tell me the truth about which lords, ladies, and gentlemen of the court were privy to your union with Lord Hertford. For it does appear to her that several persons have dealt in the matter. And if you do not declare all, I must warn you that it will increase the Queen's indignation against you."

That sets me shivering. "Sir, I do protest, there was no conspiracy, and only a few persons knew of my marriage."

"Who were they?" The lieutenant seats himself at the table, produces writing materials from his pouch, dips a pen in the inkwell, and waits.

"The minister."

"His name?"

"He did not tell it." *Scratch, scratch.* He writes this down.

"In which parish does he serve?"

"I know not, I fear."

"The witnesses?"

"Lady Jane Seymour, but she is dead."

"The other? There must be two for a marriage to be valid."

"There was no other." I falter. "We took the minister for a witness."

"Who else knew?"

"No one beforehand. Afterward, I took my maid, Mrs. Leigh, into my confidence." I am resolved not to mention dear Mrs. Ellen.

"What became of Mrs. Leigh?"

"She went to the country to nurse her sick mother. She did not return."

"Was there anyone else who knew of the marriage?"

"Mr. Glynne, Lord Hertford's man, who went beyond seas. And then I told Lord Robert Dudley and Mrs. Saintlow."

"And that is all."

"Yes."

"No other noblemen or ladies?"

"No, certainly not."

"Not even the Duchess of Somerset?"

"No. We did not tell her."

"You are sure? You would be prepared to swear an oath on that?"

"Yes, sir."

"Can you show me your marriage lines?"

I falter again. "I never had any."

Sir Edward raises his eyebrows. "Then have you any proof at all of your marriage?"

"I did! I had a deed of land granted me by my husband after our wedding. It was in that casket before you. But I lost it." The lieutenant frowns. "I assure you, sir, the Earl of Hertford did deliver such a deed to me! It was written on parchment, and he gave it to me six days after our marriage. But what with removing from place to place, it is lost, and I cannot tell you where it is." I am almost weeping with frustration. "Good Sir Edward, you have to believe me. I had that deed. And I will tell you all about my marriage and what came before." And I do, going right back to that first day at Hanworth, three years ago now.

It is a long tale, poured out with passion. The lieutenant takes it all down without comment. I wish I could tell what he is thinking, but he gives away nothing; indeed, he seems most uncomfortable in his task. When I am done, there is a long pause while he looks over what he has written.

"How would you describe the minister?" he asks.

I tell him as accurately as I can, aware that I may be bringing a heap of trouble on the priest's head. "He wore no surplice," I recall. "But sir, my husband gave me a wedding ring. Look!" I show him the elaborate band on my finger, and open the links so that he can read the inscription. He looks at it without comment.

"Are you sure you cannot recall the minister's name?"

"I never did hear it."

"Would you know him if you saw him again?"

I consider for a moment. I do not want the minister's punishment on my conscience. "I am not sure."

"Would Mrs. Leigh know where to find the deed of gift?"

"I do not know."

"Where is she now?"

"I know not."

"Tell me what you remember of the morning of your wedding."

I recount that hasty walk to Cannon Row and the events that followed. "And thereafter, in my heart, I thought of the earl as becomes a wife. So it was no small grief and trouble to me when I found his passport to France. I only saw it by chance. And after he had gone, I knew myself watched by the court, and feared people had discovered I was with child by him."

The lieutenant clears his throat. "Tell me of the love practices between you and the Earl of Hertford." I look at him, shocked and embarrassed. "Forgive me, I am instructed to ask," he says, a little shamefaced, for I can sense he is a decent man.

"I cannot, and will not," I declare. "Pray do not press me, for the answer will be the same."

"I will not press you, for shame," Sir Edward says. Sighing, he rises to his feet and gathers up his things. "Thank you, Lady Katherine," he says. "That will be all for now."

"Sir," I cry, a little wild. "Have you any word of my husband?"

"I am not at liberty to discuss him with you," the lieutenant says, as, bowing, he leaves me.

Again I rummage through my casket—as I have done several times before now. Ned's deed really is not there. I am distraught, realizing I have mislaid the only proof of my marriage.

My first night as a prisoner. I go to bed early, as I am exhausted. Honor helps me into my nightgown, then turns down the bed and departs, and I am left alone with my terrifying thoughts. I try not to think what it must be like to feel the steel of the axe slicing into one's neck. It is something I used to dwell on much, of course, but now the imaginings I try to ward off are beyond horrible.

Outside my window the glorious sunset has given way to a velvety blue night. I have lit my single candle now, having sat here without light for a long time as the dusk deepened, lost in my ceaseless fretting. Forcing myself not to think of worse things, I have been imagining myself arguing my case with the Queen. It galls me that I have had no chance to convince her of my innocence. Whatever has passed between her and Lord Robert Dudley, she must have some idea what it is like to be in love, and to be loved in return. So why does she not look more kindly on me? Is it because she is incapable of love? I could easily believe it.

Lying wakeful in this horrible place, far from my beloved, I cannot stop my teeming thoughts straying in his direction. Where is he now? Is he still beyond seas? Or have they summoned him home? He could even be here, in this very tower, not far away from me. The thought is at once comforting and alarming, for has he not committed treason in wedding me, a princess of the blood?

It has grown late, and chilly, and there are dark shadows beyond the bed where demons may well lurk, and night owls hooting in the trees outside. Their eerie cries send shivers of unease down my spine and make my skin crawl. If an owl were to land on the roof of this tower, it would be an omen of death. Suddenly, I am praying for the owls to fly away, but they keep up their unearthly din, and that seems ominous too.

I wonder how many other poor wretches have been shut up in this room, weighed down with fears as I am. How many of them left it only to go to their doom? Were any allowed to go free? And if not, have they really departed this place? Might it be that some unquiet souls yet linger, and that they walk at night? In the gloom, my imagination is alive with horrifying possibilities. In this dark watch of the night, I can easily convince myself that I may face the same fate as my sister—and that the ghosts of those who have gone before are about to materialize.

I am shaking, desperate for the warmth of human company, but it is late and everyone must surely be asleep by now. I call out: "Hello? Is anyone there?" but there is no answer. I rattle the door, which remains stubbornly locked, and call out louder, but no one heeds me. I stumble to the window and look out, expecting to find guards on duty below. I see no one but two girls walking below. One looks disturbingly familiar, but they are gone before I can get a proper look at her, and now it feels as if I am utterly alone in the middle of the Tower of London, a prey to my fears and the phantoms that must lurk in this place.

As the candle sputters and dies in a draft from the window, the room takes on a strange aspect. It looks different in the gloom; I cannot exactly lay my finger on how, but it is as if there has been a shift in atmosphere—as if, somehow, it is not of this time. Am I going mad? I fear so.

I must calm myself and try to think of my child. I do not want it to be affrighted by my terrors. Shivering in my chemise, and not entirely from cold, I climb into bed, ease my bulky body down between the sheets, and pull the heavy coverlet over my head, shutting out the menacing world. I lie tense, fending off frightening thoughts and feverishly reciting my prayers, but the words come haltingly.

And then I hear it, so softly at first that I think it might be the wind sighing in the trees, or some poor creature preyed upon by an owl. But no, there it is again—a child's voice, barely audible.

Help me.

It is pitiful and plaintive, and very well-bred.

Help us!

There it is again, stronger now! I lie rigid, not daring to move, and too terrified to come out from under the coverlet.

Help us, please!

The voice, higher in pitch, breaks on a sob. It seems to be disembodied, coming out of the night beyond my window. And now there are two voices. I am petrified. I could no more go and investigate than grow wings and fly.

"Who calls?" I whisper.

Silence.

"Is anybody there?" I cry, more boldly this time.

Nobody answers. I wonder if this is some kind of plot to frighten me to death. Was that what they did to the princes? It would not be difficult in my case, I fear, for I am eight months gone with child, by my reckoning, and it is well known that a fright can precipitate a woman's travail. And it would, of course, be most convenient for some I could mention if I died.

But there remains that strange atmosphere, that odd change in the aspect of the room, the ethereal quality of the children's voices. I begin to suspect that no human agency is at play here, and that what I have heard was not of this world. In the darkness, such things are all too believable.

I lie still, waiting, holding my breath, alert to every sound. There is nothing but the sighing of the leaves beyond the window and a distant shout from the direction of the river. It seems that there has been a shift back toward normality; and as the silence reasserts itself and I calm down, I start to wonder if I imagined it all. But I am chilled when I think whose voices I might have heard.

Master Aylmer schooled us well in history. I grew up to be familiar with the popular chronicles of Richard Fabyan and Edward Hall, and because my parents kept a good library, I had even read parts of Polydore Vergil's history of England. From these, Aylmer had drawn lessons in morality, with the varying fortunes of our kings and queens as examples. And one example he had held up was that of Richard III. All those old chroniclers said it was the common fame that King Richard had, within the Tower, secretly put to death the two sons of his brother, King Edward. They had condemned the deed as a foul murder, and I grew up accepting that story as fact, for no one I knew, least of all Aylmer, ever questioned it.

They suffered and died here, those poor princes. So if any ghosts haunt this place, it would be them. Was it their long-silenced, plaintive voices I heard? In the dark reaches of the night, it is all too believable.

In the morning, I decide that I must have dreamed it all. Soon after sunrise the door is unlocked and Honor appears, and being restored to human congress lends me a new perspective on things. My fears today are for the realities confronting me, not the imagined terrors of the night.

At nine o'clock Sir Edward Warner presents himself and inquires after my health and if I have slept well.

"No, Sir Edward, I had a nightmare that was too vivid for comfort," I tell him. "It is hardly surprising, given the desperate situation in which I find myself. But I took such a fright that I was fearful for my babe. I pray you, can you find me a midwife? I would be assured that all is well."

"I will do what I can, my lady," he assures me, and leaves the room.

Darkness falls, and I am no longer so certain that the voices of the night before were a dream. Alone, curled up beneath the covers, I try to pray, yet cannot concentrate, as my ears are attuned to any slight disturbance of the midnight silence. And then, as before, the voices come.

Help me! Help us!

Can this manifestation—for now I fear it can be nothing else—be heard in the Tower every night? Or is it just in this room? Or—and this chills my blood more than anything—is it intended for me alone?

There it is again! Pleading in tone, piteous . . . the voices of children, abandoned and maybe in dreadful danger . . .

Help us!

I gather all my courage and rise, cradling my swollen belly protectively in my hands. Beneath my fingers I can feel the babe moving sleepily. My heart is hammering so hard I fear he might take fright from it.

I creep on bare feet to the window and look out, alert to every faint sound. And then I hear, disembodied in the air, and with nothing in sight to account for them, those awful words once more. *Help us!*

But they are long beyond help now. I fear it is I and my child who are in deadly danger. At the realization, I start to tremble. Oh, my God! They could murder us both, immured within these walls and helpless as we are—just like those little princes were murdered. And our poor bones might lie here undiscovered like theirs for centuries, another of the secrets the Tower keeps hidden. Oh, sweet Jesus, save me and my child! Preserve us from the malice of our enemies. Let me live to behold my dear lord once more!

Sweating in panic, I pace up and down the room, hugging myself in distress and fear. I know I will not be able to sleep tonight. I am too frightened.

———

In the morning I am rational again, although still disturbed in my mind. I find myself needing to know what really happened to those poor princes. Despite being mere children, they were too close to the throne for comfort, and a deadly threat to their sovereign, just like me—and my unborn babe. If he lives, he may prove a similar threat to the Queen, and a focus for plots against her—as did Jane, and the princes. He might not need to lift a finger, for there are many who would prefer a man on the throne, and who regard a woman ruler as unnatural and against Nature. Of course, Elizabeth is no Richard III, but the birth of a male heir to her throne might provoke her beyond reason.

Trembling, I wonder if there are lessons to be learned from the princes' fate, lessons I would do well to heed. Yet how could one be sure exactly what happened to them? It is generally agreed that they were murdered by their wicked uncle Richard, but the means is often debated. And no bodies were ever found . . .

I wish I knew the truth about their disappearance. I know I am not being entirely rational, but I feel some strange affinity with those poor boys. I can identify with their peril because my own babe is under threat. I feel that, in some inexplicable way, their fate might have a bearing on his. But how could I, a prisoner in the Tower, find out the truth?

Suddenly, I remember that I may have the means right at hand. I hasten to my casket and take out the bundle of faded pages tied with old ribbon, which Harry and I found at Baynard's Castle, in another life. These are the pages written, I believe, by Katherine Plantagenet. I had forgotten them until now, but I recall that I never deciphered them fully. I see again the barely legible words *appreh . . . Raglan.* Apprehended? Who was apprehended? Katherine herself? Does this mean she was arrested at Raglan Castle, the old Herbert stronghold in Wales? Could it be that these writings are those of a young girl like myself, imprisoned long ago? Is this why I felt an affinity with her?

I struggle through the closely written pages, trying to read the cramped script. Yes, this is about the Princes in the Tower, but it is not the story everyone knows. This mysterious daughter of Richard III had another version of it entirely. She believed her father to be innocent.

Given what I heard in the night—or thought I heard—I am not sure I can agree with her. My belief is that the princes never left this place. Their unavenged bones still lie here somewhere. That is what all the world believes, and I have no reason to doubt it.

I struggle on, as the handwriting becomes increasingly spidery. There is more here than I ever read in history books. But at the end, frustratingly, the writing has faded away. It's the date 1487 on the first page that puzzles me. Everyone knows that Richard III was killed at the Battle of Bosworth in 1485, but what happened in 1487?

There is no end to the tale, no satisfying resolution. Nor is there any evidence that Katherine's belief in her father's innocence was justified. It seems to me she was deluding herself.

Did she ever find out the truth?

KATE

October 1485, Westminster Palace

William was most unhappy when Kate told him she was forbidden to reveal what the King had wanted, and he was even less enamored when, later that day, a page came saying that the King's mother, the Lady Margaret, wished to see her, and would she come at once—alone?

Lady Stanley—the Lady Margaret Beaufort, who was Countess of Richmond by her marriage to Henry's father—was now known as my lady the King's mother. For lack of a queen, that formidable matriarch was ruling the court—and no doubt the King too, Kate mused. She remembered the woman's cold eyes and haughty mien. The Lady Margaret was said to be very devout and learned, but Kate could only think of her as the woman who had plotted with Buckingham against her father. *Traitress,* she thought.

The Lady Margaret cut a far more regal figure than her son. She dressed like a nun in a severe black gown and pleated wimple; it was well known that she lived chastely (no doubt Lord Stanley had cause to be grateful for that, Kate thought irreverently). Her manner was quiet and dignified, and she spoke very softly. Only when she mentioned her son the King did she become animated.

She welcomed Kate coolly, then came to the point without bothering with the pleasantries.

"His Grace the King told me he spoke with you this morning, and that we can rely on your absolute discretion."

"Yes, my lady."

"My son means to give England peace and strong government. His crown has come as of right to him, and God Himself has endorsed it by giving him the victory at Bosworth. He rules most rightfully over his people—our Joshua, come to save us from tyranny."

Kate struggled to contain her anger. Was the Lady Margaret deliberately trying to provoke her?

"But how can he embark on his great task when there are those who might undermine his just title?" the insufferable woman was asking—rhetorically, of course. Dislike bristled from her; it was as if she was constrained to a disagreeable but necessary task. "Two years ago," she said, "the usurper, your father, told his friend the Duke of Buckingham—in confidence, of course—that he had no choice but to have the sons of King Edward put to death, if he was ever to feel secure on the throne. It finished the friendship. The duke could not countenance such an atrocity, and made an excuse to leave court. The usurper, unaware that there was a rift, continued to correspond with him, and in one of his letters he wrote something that Buckingham thought clearly indicated that the deed had been done. Indeed, Buckingham had no doubt of it, and he was horrified. It was then that he switched his allegiance to my son. He confided to him, and to me and our chief allies, what he knew; and we began to work for the overthrow of the tyrant."

Kate seethed. What she was hearing was bad enough, but the woman was baiting her and enjoying her discomposure, knowing she could say nothing in her father's defense that would not be construed as treason. Only with difficulty did she hold her peace while the Lady Margaret continued.

"Soon, rumors were circulating that the princes had been killed. We did not start these rumors, although we made use of them later. But we had no certain knowledge of how the boys had been murdered or how their bodies had been disposed of."

"May I ask, my lady, how you could be certain that they were dead? An ambiguous sentence in a letter could surely be taken two ways?"

The Lady Margaret eyed Kate distastefully. "You're a sharp one, aren't you? But you forget that the duke knew Richard very well: how his mind worked, and how ambition drove him."

"I knew him well too," Kate said in a quiet voice. "He was my father, and madam, I could never imagine him stooping to such a low and dreadful deed."

"Maybe you could not, but others could, all too easily!" the countess shrilled, abandoning her habitual calm for a moment. "Do you want me to rehearse the roll call of his crimes? What of the many rumors? They would not be stilled because they were believable—and they were true! My dear child, there are none so blind as those who will not see!"

"Forgive me, my lady," Kate murmured, trying to control her fury. "I can only speak from my own experience."

"Well, you were young and had evidently not yet learned to judge human nature. But I think you know more than you are prepared to say. What have you heard about the princes? If your father did not murder them, where are they?"

"I know nothing, my lady, beyond what I told the King," Kate insisted, wondering why she was being questioned again. Evidently the King had *not* believed her, and hoped his mother would get more out of her. But he was wrong there! Yes, she did know more than she had given them to believe, but of what she had learned from Pietro, Bishop Russell, and Bishop Stillington (although he had not said much), she intended to say nothing. Least said, soonest mended, she reasoned. No one should be called to account because of her.

"So you do not know anything about their murder?"

"I know nothing of a murder, my lady."

The Lady Margaret gave her a hard look.

"Are you being obstinate with me?" she demanded to know.

"No, my lady. I am as desirous as you are of having this matter brought to light."

"Well, we will have the truth soon, no doubt—and I can tell you what it will be. Now you may go. And if you recall anything that may have a bearing on this matter, you are to come and tell me at once."

INTERLUDE

August 1561, Hertford Castle

Queen Elizabeth glares at her council.

"No evidence of a conspiracy? Are you certain?" Her tone is disbelieving, her face above the delicate lace of her ruff thunderous and pale. She is extremely tense, and looks thin and gaunt.

"No, madam," Cecil says firmly. "The minister—if he ever existed—has gone to ground. Mrs. Leigh has vanished too. And Mr. Glynne, who helped me uncover this misconduct, is staying in Paris for now. He has nothing to add. We have questioned Mistress Saintlow again, but she knows no more than she told us to begin with. I am convinced, madam, that had there been any conspiracy, we would have found evidence of it by now. But there is none, and it is significant that Lady Katherine's support seems to have evaporated. As for the evidence of marriage, the deed of gift has been destroyed, along with the letters Hertford sent the Lady Katherine from France, in which he referred to her as his wife. My agent in Dover intercepted those, and hers to him, telling him she was with child."

"Is it certain that there were no marriage lines?" asks Lord Robert, lounging in his chair. Cecil and the other councillors regard him with dislike. It is no exaggeration to say that Dudley is the most hated and envied man at court. What a silly girl Katherine was, appealing to him of all people, the Secretary reflects.

"There never were any, according to Lady Katherine's testimony.

And no one appears to have been privy to this marriage but her maids and Lady Jane Seymour."

"I still think there was some greater drift in this." Elizabeth is obstinate in her opinion. "I am convinced there is more matter hid in this marriage than is uttered to the world."

"I can find none such, madam," Cecil declares decisively. "We should focus upon the immorality."

"Is Lord Hertford on his way home?" the Queen asks.

"He is, and he knows the reason for his summons," Cecil tells her. "Fearing he might choose not to obey it, I told him that Your Majesty does not mean to punish him, but that you require his presence merely in order to decide whether his marriage to the Lady Katherine is good and valid. I did not tell him that she is in the Tower."

"And what did he answer to that?" asks Sussex.

Cecil looks at Elizabeth.

"At first, he thought it would help matters if he stayed abroad until the scandal had died down. But—forgive me, madam—when one of my secret agents at the French court expressed the opinion that his marriage to the Lady Katherine would but facilitate your own to Lord Robert here, he changed his mind and took a more optimistic view of his situation."

"God's blood!" shouts Elizabeth, banging the table and making her councillors jump. "Is there no end to this lewd gossip? And you can wipe that smile off your face, Robin." Dudley has the grace to look chastened. "Well, enough of that," the Queen continues. "At least Lord Hertford is on his way home, and then we can get to the bottom of this matter."

KATE

October 1485, Westminster Palace

Kate pondered much on what the Tudor had said about the princes not being in the Tower now. It made sense to her. Her father had been a careful, cautious man. Once those conspiracies had come to light in the summer after the coronation, he might well have had the boys moved to a secret location whence there was no chance of their being rescued. He would have reasoned that, if at least one attempt had been made already, there would be others in the future.

So had the princes been at Sheriff Hutton all along? Had they been taken there when the King's Household in the North was set up under the governance of Lincoln? It had been a secure household of necessity, given the threat posed by Henry Tudor, and it had sheltered the heirs and bastards of York. Had the sons of Edward IV been of their number, secretly lodged there with their sisters?

Kate's brother John had been there too, but he was still in Calais, his future uncertain with their father dead, and he had not replied to her recent letters. Even if she had been able to reach him, she would never have dared to commit such a dangerous question to paper.

But it was highly doubtful that the princes were still at Sheriff Hutton. Henry Tudor would surely have checked, so desperate was he to find them. So if they had been there at the time Bosworth was fought, where were they now?

The answer, she was sure, lay with John de la Pole. Had he hastened to Sheriff Hutton after Bosworth and taken them into hiding with him? Were they the reason he had disappeared after the battle? Had he perhaps taken them abroad, to their aunt, Margaret, Duchess of Burgundy, whom Kate had never met, but of whom her father had always spoken with loving respect? Margaret had helped shelter Richard when, as a youth, he sought refuge with King Edward in Bruges after Edward had been driven from his kingdom by Warwick and Clarence. John had also spoken of Aunt Margaret with affection. Certainly she would willingly have offered a refuge both to the princes and to him.

The more Kate thought about this, the more it made sense, and with that came a welcome feeling of relief that at last she had an explanation as to why her father had never produced the princes alive. But it was still only speculation. She had to talk to John, or get a message to him, as soon as his whereabouts became known.

She wished she knew what had happened to him; not knowing was killing her. He might even be lying dead somewhere, his beloved body undiscovered. She caught her breath at that. *No! Don't think that way. He is an astute, resourceful man, and must be in hiding somewhere.* All at once she was seized with an unbearable longing to see him—not just to look once more upon the beauty of his face, and to touch him, but also to ask him that crucial question: Had he had the princes under his charge at Sheriff Hutton?

It was late when William returned that evening, and she was nearly asleep when he came in, doused the candle, and began to undress. She was grateful that her condition precluded his usual nightly attentions.

She turned over to face him. All discourse between them now was limited to necessities; there was no love lost on either side. Yet her curiosity was burning her.

"My lord, I have been wondering. Is there any news of my cousin Warwick?"

William started. He had thought her asleep, and was evidently unprepared for her to speak to him, let alone ask such a question.

"He's in the Tower of London, if you must know."

The news shook her. "What?" Another prince in the Tower? "Why?"

"By King Henry's order. Presumably he feels that Warwick is a threat, being so close in blood to the throne."

Yes. And he is also a threat because, simple lad that he is, he may blab about the princes being at Sheriff Hutton, and expose the truth: that they may well be alive, though Henry doesn't know where they are.

"That is terrible. That poor boy could not commit treason to save his life. He has not the wits for it—and he is so young."

"The King, for all his virtues, is not a sentimental man," William said stiffly. "He is a political realist, and knows well it is not Warwick himself he need fear, but those who might act on his behalf."

"But that poor, wretched boy . . ."

"It is a necessity, alas."

Kate shed a silent tear for her cousin, who had committed no crime save that of being born his father's son—and, perhaps, of knowing too much.

"Is there news of my brother coming home from Calais?" she asked, after William had risen from his prayers, used the piss pot, and climbed into bed.

"I heard he was deprived of the captaincy, but he's still in Calais, for all I know." How short a time young John had enjoyed his post in Calais, she reflected sadly.

"You should keep your nose out of great affairs," William reproved, "and don't go asking questions. It will be marked, surely."

"I do not intend to. But Warwick and John are my kinsmen, for whom I have much love. I ask only as their relation. And I was also going to ask if there are tidings of my lord of Lincoln."

"None, and good riddance I say. Now go to sleep."

She slept; but in the morning, when William—commanding her to stay in her room—had gone to seek out old acquaintances and reestablish himself in the pecking order at court, she got out her papers and wrote down every last detail of her theory that the princes had been taken, safe and well, to Sheriff Hutton. One day, she promised herself, her infant child would be able to hold his head up and say his grandfather's name with pride.

KATHERINE

September 1561, Tower of London

Ned is here, in the Tower. Sir Edward has informed me that he was arrested at Dover, brought here under guard, and imprisoned in the Lieutenant's Lodging. I do not know whether to laugh or cry, for while I am heartened to know that he is nearby, I am aware that there are now three of us in peril of our lives.

"May I see him?" I ask eagerly.

"I regret not, my lady. The Queen has expressly forbidden it. But my Lord Hertford sends you these, and asks after your health." He hands me a small posy of violets. Violets, for modesty, delicacy, and chastity. I feel choked. It is as if my good reputation has been given back to me.

"You are both to be questioned by the Privy Council, separately," Sir Edward tells me.

"But I have told you all I know," I protest.

"That remains to be seen, my lady," Sir Edward says, and makes to depart.

"Please tell my husband I am in good health," I call after him, and he pauses and nods.

Later, in the afternoon, I am visited by five lords of the council, among them the Bishop of London and the Marquess of Winchester, he who placed the crown on my sister's head in this very Tower.

"Lady Katherine," the marquess begins, "why did you not tell the lieutenant everything?"

"But I did," I declare.

"Let us go over what Lord Hertford has deposed." He reads Ned's own account of our wedding day, and I am shocked to hear that my lord has confessed all, even to the most intimate details, and find myself blushing hotly. Nevertheless, he has corroborated everything I myself told Sir Edward, even reciting the lines he composed for my wedding ring. Surely they must believe us now!

"Why did you not give all this information in your first interview?"

For shame, of course; how could they have expected me to say such things to a man not my husband? Even now I cannot bring myself to mention them. "I was in great agony of mind," I say, "for fear of the Queen Majesty's displeasure. I was distressed at my husband's absence, when I thought myself in a desperate case . . . being great with child . . ." I cannot speak anymore; I am quite broken down, and weeping uncontrollably. The lords sit in silence as a clerk writes down my words. The marquess nods to the rest.

"That is all," he says, to my astonishment. "We bid you good day, Lady Katherine."

KATE

October 1485, Westminster Palace

Kate had not gone out with the other peeresses to watch the coronation procession. She had no intention of witnessing the Tudor triumph, pretending to be a king. She had pleaded the sickness of her condition, and stayed in her chamber, resting on the bed, with Sir Thomas Malory's *Morte d'Arthur* for company.

William looked magnificent in his new purple velvet robe lined with ermine and guarded with three bands of gold lace and miniver, and a silken surcoat of the same hue, sashed in blue velvet. He had departed early, clutching his coronet, to take his place in the abbey. He was still angry with Kate for not telling him what the King and the Lady Margaret had discussed; it was clear he was terrified lest she had let slip something that might impact adversely on him. In the end he had given up, but her silence still rankled, she knew.

The palace seemed unusually still, although outside she could hear the bells of Westminster pealing joyfully and the crowds cheering. She said a prayer for the soul of her father, through whose death this day of celebration had come about. She thought too of John. Where was he now? Still in hiding? Was he even alive? If only she could see him again—just one glimpse was all she asked.

Hours passed. She awoke, realizing she had dozed off. The book lay splayed on the counterpane where it had fallen from her hand. She heard the abbey bells chiming four. They would be at the banquet in Westminster Hall now. Soft footfalls and women's laughter outside her door told her that the peeresses were returning.

She got up and splashed water on her face, then ventured out into the palace. Most of the galleries and chambers were deserted, apart from the guards on duty. They wore new uniforms, doublets of scarlet cloth with full sleeves and bases pleated from the waist, with black velvet bonnets, and carried halberds. William had told her that they were the King's newly instituted bodyguard, the Yeomen of the Guard, appointed to ensure his personal safety. They stood impassive at their posts, apparently unseeing as she passed by. As she entered a cloister, she thought she heard a footfall behind her, but when she waited to see who it was, no one appeared. A few minutes later she heard it again and paused a second time, but still the place seemed to be deserted.

She wondered if someone was following her—someone who did not want to be seen. It stood to reason that Henry Tudor might be having her movements watched, to discover whom she met and conversed with; possibly he believed she could lead him to someone who might know the truth about the princes, for there must be people at his court who knew more than they would ever now reveal. She resolved to be careful, just in case. And yet—there was no one to be seen. She must have imagined it.

She went out into the gardens by the river to get some air. And it was there that she espied someone she knew.

"Pietro!" she cried, and the man reading on a bench by St. Stephen's Chapel jumped in surprise.

"Madonna!" he exclaimed, but he did not look very pleased to see her.

She walked over to him. "We have come up to Westminster—my husband and I—for the coronation," she told him. "I did not look to find you still at court."

"Is that so surprising, Madonna?" Pietro looked a little offended. "A man has to seek his fortune where he must. This new King much liked the poems I wrote in praise of his victory and his virtues. He has asked me to stay on."

"I understand, Pietro," she said, although she could not help feeling a little taken aback at the speed with which the little Italian had turned his coat. Not so long ago he had been lauding her father's accession. But then she supposed that he was just one of many who'd had no real choice but to switch loyalties.

He was regarding her uncertainly. "Madonna, those things we spoke of secretly—you have not mentioned them to anyone?"

"I have never spoken of them," she assured him, not telling him she had written down all he had said. "Yet I still wonder about them, you know, those poor boys—"

"It is dangerous even to wonder, Madonna. Everyone now says they are dead," Pietro cut in, looking about him furtively.

"Well, they would. After all, the King is to marry Elizabeth of York."

"So they say. It is said that he wished to be crowned first, as King in his own right, before sending for her." No, Henry Tudor would not wish it thought that he owed his title to his wife! Kate knew a moment's pity for her cousin: imagine being married to that dark, suspicious prince, the Tudor!

"Elizabeth of York is at court now?"

"So I heard, Madonna. The Queen her mother has charge of her, but is not in favor. Do not ask me why—it is a mystery."

Indeed it was, unless the King was wary of a future mother-in-law notorious for her meddling. Or maybe Elizabeth Wydeville knew more than was good for her.

"Her son Dorset is returned from exile," Pietro said, his eyes darting here and there. "The King confirmed him in his titles." But it was unlikely, under the Tudor, that the Wydevilles would enjoy the power that was once theirs, Kate thought.

She took a deep breath. "Your mention of Sheriff Hutton brought to mind the Earl of Lincoln. Is there any news of him?"

"Not that I have heard, Madonna." Pietro was definitely looking anxious.

Kate felt another pang of anxiety for John. *Had* he fled abroad? Or was he near at hand? If only she could write to him. She did not mean to betray her marriage vows; she just wanted to ask him if the princes had been at Sheriff Hutton.

She wondered if she dared approach the Queen Dowager. But Elizabeth Wydeville was in disfavor. Was it because the Tudor suspected she was withholding information about her sons, the princes? Did she know or suspect that they were not dead? That would explain why she had consented to leave sanctuary with her daughters the previous year. But Kate feared that any contact with the Wydevilles might be noted; and even though they were her kin, they might not want to know her.

If anyone could help her on her quest, Kate thought, it was Bishop Russell. She asked Pietro if he was still in office as Lord Chancellor.

"No, he was dismissed by the King. He went back to his diocese. And Bishop Stillington is imprisoned at York, sorely crazed." *No doubt for laying that dubious evidence of a precontract,* Kate thought. The Tudor would not deal lightly with a man who had impugned his future Queen's legitimacy.

"Madonna, forgive me, I must go," Pietro said awkwardly. "I have work to do." He had been uncomfortable all through their talk. It was obvious he did not want to know her anymore, and her questions had certainly made him uneasy.

INTERLUDE

September 1561, Whitehall Palace

Midnight, and Sir William Cecil is closeted alone with the Queen. Elizabeth often likes to conduct private business at night, and is wont to summon her unsuspecting ministers without warning, not caring that she rouses them from their beds. But Cecil has not yet retired, and he is as alert as she. He knows they have something of great import to discuss.

The small paneled room is stuffy in the heat; only a tiny lattice stands open to the Thames. Somewhere outside, an owl hoots. There is no moon tonight.

Cecil, sweating, has just handed his mistress the depositions of Lord Hertford and Lady Katherine. She reads them, frowning.

"No discrepancies, I see. Do the other witness statements tally with these?"

"Yes, they do. The groom Barnaby testified that he saw the Lady Katherine and the Lady Jane arriving at Hertford House that morning. Jenkin, another groom, saw them too, from an upper window, as did the cook, when they walked by the kitchen door. I have discharged all these witnesses, and only Mistress Saintlow remains in the Tower. I assure you, I should not like to tangle with that lady again: she is trouble! But I verily believe she can tell us no more."

The Queen's eyes glitter in the candlelight. "Have her sent back home to Derbyshire to await our pleasure. I am not minded to dismiss her innocence so lightly, even if there is no proof against her." She pauses. "So, my Spirit—what now? Shall we have the marriage declared no marriage?"

"Not yet," Cecil says thoughtfully. "You see, madam, Lady Katherine is about to be delivered, and of course many are lost in childbed, mothers and infants both. Dame Nature might solve the problem for us."

Elizabeth rests her gimlet gaze on him. "I trust, William, that you are not intending to give Dame Nature any assistance."

"I, Your Majesty?" He is a little shocked. "I but leave her to take her course. And if the Lady Katherine and her child survive, we will think again about what is to be done with them. I bear in mind that she is your kinswoman."

"Would that she were not!" fumes the Queen.

KATE

October 1485, Westminster Palace

After Pietro had gone, Kate wandered along the paths between the fenced flower beds for a little while, but a stiff wind was building up, and she began to retrace her steps to the palace. William would be furious if he returned to their lodging and found her absent.

As she turned into the passage that ran beside the chapel, she glimpsed the tail of a black gown disappearing into the cloister. Was it the person she had imagined following her earlier? She sped along the passage, but when she got to the cloister it was empty. Warily, she walked on, past the guards in their red livery, up the spiral stairs, and so to her lodging, seeing nothing out of the way.

She lay down to rest, loosening the laces across her stomach, but her mind was agitated. Was she becoming too fanciful? Women in her condition did sometimes. She yearned for Mattie's sound common sense, but Mattie was far away in Raglan; she had been suffering too much morning sickness to accompany her on this journey, and Kate had been obliged to bring with her mousy little Gwenllian, one of her Welsh maids. She'd chosen her because the girl was unobtrusive and gentle, but today she was not here because Kate had given her permission to go out and watch the procession; by now she would no doubt be joining in the revelry that was going on in the streets. The din of it could be heard distantly.

Dusk fell. As Kate lit the candles she heard a scratching noise. What was that? It came again, from the keyhole. Someone was trying to open the door! Gingerly she pulled the key out, grateful that she had locked the door on her return earlier.

She was conscious of the sudden silence outside. And then she heard footsteps, stealthy and barely audible, retreating in the distance. Someone had definitely been trying to break into the room. As soon as they realized someone was within, they had retreated.

She sat on the bed, shaken, and tried to think about it rationally. She wished she had opened the door and challenged whoever it was, but the moment was gone now—and she'd been too fearful anyway.

What had they wanted? Had it been the person whose black gown she espied earlier? Had they come to search her room, or frighten her? She was chilled to her very marrow at the thought.

Had someone been spying on her as she spoke with Pietro this afternoon? Surely no one could have been near enough to hear what was said, although if they had been . . . She had seen not a soul nearby, but she recalled that Pietro kept looking about him. Had he glimpsed someone? Was that why he had made his hasty excuse and left?

If that person picking at the lock had gotten into the room, and she had not been here, what would they have found that was incriminating—or that could throw light on the mystery of the princes? There was nothing, surely . . . Ah, but there was: her papers! She flew to the table and lifted the lid of her casket—and there they were, undisturbed. She stood there, breathing heavily in relief.

What should she do with them? The lock-picker would be back, as surely as night followed day, so she must find somewhere safe to keep them. They must never fall into the wrong hands. She looked at the traveling chest. It had a secret compartment, but that was easily opened—even a child could work it out—and the King's spies would be skilled at such tricks. And they would search thoroughly too. There was nothing for it. She would have to keep the papers on her person.

She set to work at once, stitching two white kerchiefs into a small bag, through the top hem of which a long ribbon could be threaded. That she tied about her waist, under her gown, with the papers inside it. That her waistline was expanding daily made no matter: she and William would be away from here soon. *No one would ever suspect,* she thought as she surveyed herself in the mirror. The heavy folds of her skirt concealed the slight bulge of the bag completely.

The papers were safe now. And the Tudor's henchman could search her chamber as thoroughly as he wished.

KATHERINE

September 24, 1561, Tower of London

My labor began this morning as I lay abed. The midwife, a stout, no-nonsense body, had explained to me what the pains of travail would be like. I had also heard women's tales about the agonies and perils of childbirth, and for a while I was inclined to dismiss them, for these pains were easily bearable. Only as the morning wore on did they become fiercer, and then the midwife bade me lie down on the bed and pull, when I needed to, on a length of thick-woven material she had tied tautly between the bedposts. Then she sent Honor off to fetch Holland cloth, hot water, bread, cheese, and wine, and herself laid ready the cambric swaddling bands and rollers, the tiny shirt and coif I had embroidered, the taffeta coat with satin sleeves, the little bib and apron, the lace mittens. An old oak cradle, provided by Sir Edward, was placed beside my bed and made up with sheets and a miniature counterpane of crewelwork. Then the midwife closed the window, drew the curtains together, and hung a sheet over the faded tapestry.

"What are you doing?" I asked. "It's so hot in here—I need some air."

"The air of the City is noxious and bad for your babe," she told me, "and the child might be affrighted by the figures in the hanging. Best to be on the safe side!"

Stifling and perspiring, I have labored for what seems like hours, my pains growing stronger all the time, until I have to acknowledge that most of the gossips spoke truth. It is all I can do not to cry out. But then comes a change, an overwhelming urge to push downward—and when I do so, I find that I push the pain away.

"Nearly there!" the midwife pronounces, looking between my splayed legs. "I can see the head crowning." And suddenly here he is— my son. England has a Protestant male heir at last.

He is healthy, thanks be to God, and beautiful too. I cannot cease admiring him. When he tugs at my breast and blinks at me with his milky blue eyes, I am lost, my heart given over entirely. And it is a strange feeling, because I had thought I could never love anyone as much as I love Ned. Yet this is different, and I know now what women mean when they say they would lay down their lives for their children. It is a fierce love, a love that would protect at all costs, a love that is the complete negation of self for the tiny being who is utterly dependent on you for everything. And as I sit here in bed, my son in my arms, I vow he shall never suffer because of his parents' offense. I will make sure of that. And I assure us both that when all this trouble is far behind us, my little one will be a king one day.

Sir Edward Warner comes to see me. His face creases in a tender smile when he sees the swaddled babe lying contentedly beside me in his cradle.

"Allow me to offer you my congratulations, my lady," he says. "You have a fine boy there. I pray God give him long life and health. I have brought him a gift." His voice is gruff as he places a silver rattle, which must have cost him a goodly sum, on the counterpane.

"I thank you for your kindness, Sir Edward," I say, touched. "It is a very pretty toy; he will love it. You are most generous."

I perceive some emotion working in the lieutenant's rugged face.

"To have a healthy son like yours is a great blessing from God," he says. "My late wife bore me three boys, but they all died in infancy."

"I am sorry to hear that, sir," I tell him, genuinely moved. Now that I am a mother, I find I am inordinately sensitive about harm befalling little children. In fact, I can now hardly bear to think of the princes.

"I have married again this year," the lieutenant tells me. "My wife and I—well, we live in hope."

"I will pray for you both, that your hopes are fulfilled."

"That is kind, my lady. I am painfully aware that my duty to the Queen's Majesty requires me to be stricter than I would wish on occasion; but I want you to know that you have my goodwill, and that I will do all in my power to make your stay here as easy as possible."

"It gladdens me to know that," I smile.

"The midwife has asked me to engage a wet nurse and rockers," Sir Edward continues. "My lady, I am minded to ask Her Majesty if she will graciously agree to a suite of rooms being appointed in my lodging here for you, the child, and your attendants, and I also intend to request that you be provided with the comforts of your rank. There may be a charge for such privileges, but if there is anything you require brought to you, you have only to ask." I have heard that jailers and turnkeys supplement their fees by doing favors for prisoners, and that a man or woman can live well in prison, if they have the means.

"I thank you, good Sir Edward," I say. "But although I have some money of my own, I do not know how to get hold of it, shut up as I am here."

"That can safely be left to the Queen's Council," he tells me. "They will arrange everything. Would you like me to put forward these requests?"

"Yes, indeed!" I exclaim, eager to be out of this miserable chamber, which is no place for my child—my little prince, as I am already calling him secretly. A suite of rooms in the Lieutenant's Lodging! That is where Ned is held. We will be near each other.

"We will see what Her Majesty has to say," my good jailer is saying.

"Sir Edward!" I call him back as he prepares to leave. "Does my lord know of the birth of his son?"

"He does, my lady. I myself told him the good news, and he recorded it at once in his Bible, adding a prayer beseeching God to bless your child and to move the Queen's heart to pity."

"And did he show himself joyful at becoming a father?"

Sir Edward hesitates. "I am sure he felt it inwardly. But he seemed a little cast down, no doubt because he cannot see you or the child; and he observed that in human affairs, nothing is certain."

"A strange thing to say when a child is born."

"It is the circumstances, of course," he replies.

Why does Ned feel cast down? Inexplicably weepy, I lie fretting about it. Then I pick up my babe and hold him tight to my breast, marveling at his soft skin and downy head, his rosebud lips and milky blue eyes. How could anyone wish harm to such an enchanting, defenseless creature? The whole realm should be rejoicing in the birth of such a prince! It is the one blessing the Queen has not bestowed on her people.

But, insidiously, unwelcome thoughts fill my head. If I am to protect him, I must face the fact that there are those who would not see my son as merely an innocent, adorable baby, but as a deadly rival, young though he is. Thus did Richard III regard his nephews, though they were but children. And while I cannot believe the Queen could entertain one hostile thought against this little mite were she to meet him, we are both her prisoners in the Tower. What if they should take him away from me? What if I never see him again, and hear only rumors about his fate? It has happened before—and I am struck with terror lest it should happen again. I find myself brooding much upon the fate of the princes. I am desperate to know if they escaped, as Katherine Plantagenet believed. Could she still be alive? If she wrote with an adult hand in 1487, she would be very ancient now, so it is unlikely.

I drift off to sleep, and find myself dreaming about her, as I have not done in years. In my dream, I see the girl in the blue dress, the one whose portrait I saw hanging in the old wing in Baynard's Castle. I know it is her, the King's daughter. She is young and beautiful, a fine dark lady. She seems to be reaching out to me once more, mouthing words I cannot quite comprehend. She is pleading with me, as she did before . . .

I wake up suddenly. The dream was so real, more vivid than normal. It is night; the moon is up beyond my window. All is still.

And then, once more, that strange shifting of the air, and a distant cry—

Help me!

Help us!

I huddle, terrified, under the bedclothes. I wanted to believe I had dreamed what I'd heard before, but I am certainly not sleeping now. A dog barks. Has he heard the voices too? There they are again! *Help me! Help us!* The dog barks once more. Then silence.

I poke my head above the covers and sit up, looking about me fearfully. Everything seems normal. Had I really heard them? Or am I so weighed down with troubles that I am beginning to imagine things?

Eventually I drift into sleep, and in the morning I decide I could not have been dreaming.

"Sir Edward," I say, when the lieutenant comes to inquire after my health, and we have admired the baby, snug in his swaddling bands, "do you believe that the Princes in the Tower really were murdered here all those years ago?"

For a moment he looks uneasy, and I realize that it may still be unwise to speak of such things. For if the princes had survived, then the Tudors must be usurpers. Thinking of Queen Elizabeth, it is a heartening notion! But Sir Edward's qualms, if he has any, are fleeting.

"I have often wondered that myself," he confides. "In fact, I'm very interested in the subject, my lady—and have been for years. I know all the world thinks they were killed, but they never found them, you know. It's well known here that King Henry VII ordered several searches of the Tower, all of which revealed nothing. And without the bodies, there is no proof. Yet it is invariably said that Sir James Tyrell had them killed, on King Richard's orders."

Tyrell! That name again. I remember now. It was in Vergil's history that I read of him murdering the princes, seeking preferment as a reward. Yet I'm sure I've seen it somewhere else.

"Is it known how they were killed?" I ask.

"No one knows for certain, but many have guessed. Some say they were run through with a sword, some that they were suffocated or drowned in wine like the Duke of Clarence; others say they were poisoned, or walled up, or buried alive. The fact is, no one knows. I read that their bodies were chested and taken on a ship down the Thames, then thrown into the Black Deeps at the estuary. That would explain why they were never found here, in the Tower—but I have often wondered if it was a rumor put about to convince folk that they were dead."

I had read that tale too; it was in the popular chronicles.

"It's an intriguing mystery," I observe.

"I am moved to wonder, my lady, why you find it so," Sir Edward says. "It is a grim subject for a gentlewoman."

I wrestle with myself, wondering if I dare show him the account I keep secret. It can do no harm, surely; and he has told me he is interested in the matter. I realize we have become quite companionable; I know him to be a good man, despite the unpleasant calling of his office, and it is a relief to be speaking of matters other than the reason why I am here.

"It is because of some papers I have," I say, and, opening my casket, I take out the bundle. "I pray you, take them and read them."

The lieutenant sits down at the table and unties the ribbon. "What are these?" he asks. "Where did you get them?" I explain about finding them in the tower room at Baynard's Castle, and offer my theory as to who wrote them.

"Richard III had a daughter?" he asks in surprise.

"Yes, my first husband told me of her. She married one of his forebears. Her name was Katherine."

"Well, that is extraordinary." He peruses the yellowing pages. "These are very old."

"Oh, yes, Sir Edward. They are too old to pose any threat to the Queen—they are not evidence of any plot!"

He has to smile at my little jest. "I should like to read them. May I take them? My duties call me now."

"By all means."

"I will return them to you when I have finished, and then, perhaps, we may talk again."

"I should like that," I say. "Oh . . . Sir Edward, before you go—I must ask you something. Have you ever heard voices—children's voices, I think—calling in the night here?"

He stares at me, astonished. "Voices? I don't think so. What did they say?"

"'Help me. Help us.' I have heard them three times now."

He is at a loss. "Perchance it was some voices carrying on the wind. Or perchance you were dreaming, my lady." Poor man, he has not the imagination to think of any other explanation.

"Perchance," I agree.

KATE

November 1485, Westminster Palace

At last, there came a day when William begrudgingly agreed to take Kate with him into London.

"I miss it so much," she'd wheedled. "It was one of my great pleasures to go shopping in Cheapside." She dared not say she longed to see Crosby Hall just one more time—and in truth, she was not sure how she would feel when she did. It was hard to believe that they were all gone, her father, Anne, little Edward . . . her loved ones who had resided there with her not three years ago.

She had never until now so appreciated the freedom she'd had back then to wander around London with Mattie. Carefree days, gone forever. She would have loved to visit her grandmother, the Duchess Cecily, at Baynard's Castle; but William told her that the duchess had left London and gone to live out her days at her castle of Berkhamsted. She would be mourning the death of yet another son, of course.

William had hummed and huffed, but in the end he had relented and said that Kate might accompany him. He himself would escort her to Cheapside, and she could make her purchases while he consulted his lawyer in the Temple.

"But put on your cloak, wife, and pull down the hood. We don't want you being recognized," he fussed.

It was as they were approaching the palace stables, where her litter had been stored alongside their horses, that Kate saw John riding out. She was amazed to see him here. William had told her he was still in hiding, a hunted traitor, so how could he be at Westminster?

She looked up and her hood fell back. Her eyes met John's in a flash of astonishment, relief, and joy, before both looked quickly away. They could not acknowledge each other, of course. Kate was not only married, but the object of suspicion in high places, so she knew that any association between them was dangerous. When William turned around, her hood was in place again, and John was trotting off, two grooms riding behind him.

INTERLUDE

September 1561, Whitehall Palace

"A son?" Elizabeth cries in alarm.

"A bastard, no more," Cecil soothes. "Remember, they cannot bring either minister or witness to their marriage. We must either find that minister, or determine that the marriage is unlawful. That matter lies in your mercy, madam."

"It must be proved unlawful," the Queen insists, beside herself with agitation. "See to it!"

KATHERINE

October 1561, Tower of London

I could not believe it when the Queen's permission arrived for our babe to be honorably christened. Sir Edward had requested it, out of

charity, and his plea was granted without delay. And so I, fresh from
my childbed, and privately churched by the Tower chaplain, now find
myself standing in the chancel of the chapel royal of St. Peter ad Vincula, dressed in the best gown I have with me, and looking across the
font at Ned, standing there between two yeomen warders. We are
both under guard and not allowed to speak, but our eyes convey all
that cannot be said. Seeing my husband looking lovingly upon our tiny
son as Sir Edward takes him from the nurse, my heart is fit to burst
with bittersweet feelings.

For this day is one of pain and sadness as well as joy. I am sure that
Ned is aware, as I am, that a little way beneath our feet lie the sad remains of those we have loved: his father, my father, and my sister. I had
to steel myself to enter this place.

But I must try to be of good cheer: Ned has not yet been attainted,
we are both well treated, and our marriage has not been impugned. I
try to suppress my indignation against the Queen, who has graciously
permitted this ceremony, even though she has not allowed us a minister. Instead, Sir Edward Warner, as sponsor, sprinkles water from the
font over our child, baptizes him Edward, in the name of the Father,
the Son, and the Holy Ghost, and gives him his courtesy title Viscount
Beauchamp, which he has by right of being his father's heir.

That evening, when my young viscount is sleeping soundly, the lieutenant presents himself at my chamber door.

"Your papers, my lady." He hands them to me.

"You have read them, sir?"

"I have. It is an extraordinary tale. Shall we discuss it?"

"I should like to."

He sits down with me at the table and sends for wine, an unexpected privilege. I suspect he is growing fond of me—in a fatherly way.
He is too correct a man for it to be anything else. He has been a prisoner, like me; he understands how I am feeling, and has kept his word
to make my stay in the Tower as comfortable as possible. You might
say that we have become friends.

"Katherine wanted to believe that her father was innocent," I observe.

"I was left wondering if she ever found out," Sir Edward says. "After all, very few people could have known the truth, and they weren't telling."

"If there was a murder, it was kept so secret that we still don't know what really happened, even after all this time. Do you think Katherine was right to believe in her father's innocence?"

"The fact remains that Richard III never produced the princes alive to counteract the rumors, or explained their disappearance. Whatever happened to them, he *must* have known about it. They were his prisoners, held straitly in the innermost reaches of the Tower, and guarded by his faithful constable, Brackenbury."

"That name seems as familiar to me as that of Tyrell," I interrupt. "I have read of them in books, but I'm sure I have seen those names somewhere else. It will come to me soon."

"It might be credible that Richard had the boys removed from the Tower in the wake of the conspiracies," the lieutenant says. "If no one knew where they were, there could be no further attempts to rescue them. But I still think Richard himself made them disappear."

"Could Buckingham have been involved?"

"I think not, my lady. Bishop Russell said the princes were alive in September, but by then Buckingham was in Wales, miles away. How could he, or any agent of his, have breached the Tower's security without being discovered? If he had murdered the princes, the King would certainly have discovered it, and it's inconceivable he would not have made political capital out of that in the charges against Buckingham. Such knowledge would have been a powerful weapon in his hand."

"You speak sense, sir. But what of Henry VII? The thought did occur—"

"Hush!" the lieutenant hisses. "You must not speak so of the Queen's grandsire. It is clear he was as perplexed as everyone else. He'd had the Tower searched for the bodies, but none were found, so he could not say what had become of the princes. Why else would he have taken the threat posed by the pretender Perkin Warbeck so seriously? Warbeck pretended for years to be Richard, Duke of York, and convinced several of the monarchs of Europe before he was exposed as a fraud.

He had the King terrified. No, Henry VII did not kill the princes. Who else could have done it but Richard III?"

"Unless Katherine Plantagenet was right, and he had the princes moved." I so want that to have been the case.

"My lady, you are forgetting two vital things," Sir Edward says. "First, if the princes had been at Sheriff Hutton, what happened to them after Bosworth? Did they just disappear?"

"Maybe they escaped abroad."

"That would have been the wisest course, for they posed as much of a threat to King Henry as they had to King Richard. But there is no proof of their being alive after September of 1483."

"There is no proof of anything!" I lament. "It's all possibilities! It seems that every trail goes cold."

"After eighty years, what else can you expect? But there is another aspect you have not taken into account, my lady. Richard III was a twisted and ruthless man—a tyrant; there is no other word for it. He had his opponents beheaded without trial; he used scandalous and false precepts to stake his claim to the throne. These things are incontrovertible. We must ask ourselves if such a man was also capable of murdering his brother's children, whom he had dispossessed."

"But Katherine did not see him as a tyrant. She saw much that was good in him."

"She saw him as she wanted to see him."

"Yet he had been a loving and careful father all her life," I point out. "Surely that argues that there was some good in him? And maybe those things he did—maybe he did them because he felt he had no choice, because his enemies were plotting to destroy him."

"Reading between the lines in these papers, I think he exaggerated that threat; he lied about those weapons, don't forget. Yet I think that we should give him the benefit of the doubt for now, for there is, after all, no proof that the princes were murdered." Sir Edward's face creases in his endearing, craggy smile. "You have fired me up again about this mystery, my lady. For years it has nagged at me. It was the fact that no bodies were found; certainly something very secret—and possibly evil—took place here in the Tower, and I've often hoped there might still be a clue somewhere. This account by Richard's daughter is most illuminating, something I never dreamed I would see. And perchance there are other sources."

"Other sources?"

The lieutenant lowers his voice. "Much was suppressed, I'm sure. I believe there is far more to this mystery than we could ever suspect. There may also be histories I have not read. I am dining with a friend of mine, an alderman of the City of London, next week. With his help, I may be able to gain entry to Sir Richard Whittington's library at the Guildhall, and see what records are kept there. I will report back to you." He stands up. "But now I must go, for it grows late. I bid you good night, my lady. I have enjoyed our most enlivening talk. I would it had taken place in happier circumstances."

"I too, sir," I say with feeling. Yet it has offered me a welcome respite from my troubles and fears.

With my mind full of the princes, I am nervously anticipating hearing those voices again tonight; and hear them I do, as I lie wakeful in my bed, their thin cries plaintive, like a whisper on the breeze. I shudder. It could be anything, I tell myself. Why should it be the lost sons of King Edward? Or am I myself conjuring up voices that are not there?

KATE

November 1485, Westminster Palace

After they had returned from their outing to the City, William was much gratified to receive a summons to sup with the King and several other lords in the evening. The Tudor, it seemed, was making an effort to court popularity.

William began fretting about what to wear. His shirt was not fine enough, his best gown stained. Kate rubbed the stain and brushed the pile, then sat down to embroider the neck of the shirt. He nodded at her, more grateful than he would express, then left, saying he had to meet someone.

Kate unwrapped her few purchases, thinking joyfully of John. She was utterly relieved to know that he still lived and was safe. Maybe, God willing, he would try to contrive a meeting. She knew the dangers, but she was willing to risk much just to speak with him, and when they had known the rapture of being reunited, she could ask him about the princes.

Life was suddenly looking much brighter. Her heart lightened. If you waited long enough, good things happened, and prayers were answered.

Taking advantage of William's absence, she put on her cloak and sped down to the gardens to get some air, and to look out for John. The nights were drawing in much earlier now, and it was already dusk. She walked along by the river wall light of step, glad to feel the evening breeze on her face. There she came upon a boy kicking a ball along one of the paths. He was about seven or eight, a well-dressed, sturdily built child with a slightly lugubrious face.

"Hello," she said as he approached her.

"Good even, madam," he answered politely, and bowed. He had clearly been well drilled in courtesy, and his fine clothes proclaimed him of noble birth. "The Duke of Buckingham at your service," he said grandly.

The Duke of Buckingham? This must be the son of the traitor who had rebelled against her father. The last she had heard, this boy had been smuggled into hiding after his father's arrest.

She curtsied. "The Countess of Huntingdon, my lord."

"I have just been restored to my title," he told her with evident pride. "I was made a Knight of the Bath at the King's coronation."

"I am glad to hear it." She smiled. "You are in high favor, it seems!"

"It has not always been so," he told her, a shadow crossing his fresh young face. "You must have heard of my father, the old duke."

"I met him several times," she said. "He was hearty company."

"Aye, but he tried to overthrow the usurper Richard and lost his head for it. I had to go into hiding after that. My nurse shaved my head and dressed me as a girl; it was horrid. I hated it! But she got me away, and now I am restored to my rightful inheritance."

Kate wondered if this bright young lad might know something of his father's motives for rebelling against his king. There could be no harm in probing gently, surely. "Why did your father wish to over-throw Richard?" she asked.

"Because Richard had had the sons of King Edward put to death, of course." The answer came out almost unthinkingly.

"How did your father know that?"

The boy scratched his curly hair. "I don't know. But he hated the usurper because of it. After he was arrested, he craved an audience with him. He made out that he wanted to plead for his life, but really he meant to kill Richard with a hunting knife he had hidden in his bosom. But the usurper refused to see him. He died bravely, my father."

Kate suddenly realized they were not alone. Two dark figures were approaching along the path. When they emerged into the light of the flare set in a nearby wall bracket, she recognized the cold features of the Lady Margaret. With her was a man in clerical garb whom she did not know.

"My lady of Huntingdon, we meet again," the countess said, as Kate curtsied, never taking her eyes from that austere face. "I see you have made the acquaintance of my ward, the Duke of Buckingham. Come, my young lord, it grows late, and I'm sure you have detained the countess too long with your prattle." She put an arm about the boy's shoulder and made to lead him away.

"I was telling her about going into hiding, and how my father intended to kill the usurper."

"Indeed. I am sure my lady here found that most interesting," the Lady Margaret said, with a chilly smile at Kate.

"Yes, she did, and we talked about my father's rebellion!" the boy told her.

"Did you?" His guardian exchanged glances with her clerk. "Well, thank you, my lady, for keeping this young coxcomb entertained. His tongue does run away with him, I fear, usually on matters way beyond his understanding." The young duke made a face.

"Come," the Lady Margaret bade him, "it is time for prayers and bed. Good evening, Lady Huntingdon. If this young man should trouble you again, tell him to discuss something more edifying."

Kate knew she had been warned off. She was perturbed by the

Lady Margaret finding her talking of sensitive matters with young Buckingham. William would not like it at all, so she would not dare mention the encounter to him. She was not supposed to be out anyway, as it was. Yet she hadn't said anything remotely treasonous; she had but asked a couple of questions that anyone with any curiosity might have asked. It was the boy who had brought up the subject of his father and done most of the talking. Surely no one, even the King's menacing mother, could take issue with that?

William returned later that evening, ushering in, much to Kate's surprise, a stranger—clearly a lady of rank. She was a slender gentlewoman in middle life, her oddly familiar face pale, yet showing traces of great beauty. She was clad in a dark gown of soft wool bordered with fur, and one of the new long-lappeted hoods. She was regarding Kate intently and seemed tense and ill at ease.

"I have a visitor for you, Kate," William said quietly. "This lady is Mistress Katherine Haute. She is your mother."

Kate stared at the woman, utterly bewildered and confounded, with all sorts of emotions welling up inside her. The familiarity of that face—of course, she could see it now: it was so like her own.

"But how . . . ?" she stammered.

"My dear, I have made it my business to find out about you," the woman said. "When your father was alive, I knew you were well cared for. That gladdened my heart, for I was unable to play any part in your life. My duty was to my husband and our sons. My husband had forgiven me for—for what happened, and did not wish to be reminded of it; he insisted I put it behind me. It was not what I wanted, in fact it cost me dear, but you will know that a woman has no choice in such matters."

Kate nodded, glancing involuntarily at William. He was standing there watching them impassively. She wondered at him allowing this meeting.

She guessed that her mother had not had an easy life, and suspected it had been one long reparation for her sin. You could see that in Katherine Haute's face. Those lines had been etched there by suffering.

"I knew of your marriage," Katherine Haute went on. "We live up in Hertfordshire, but my husband and his family have links to the court, so we are kept well informed. And James did relent sufficiently to tell me that you had married my lord of Huntingdon. I was pleased for you: it is a good match." She smiled warily at William, who did not respond. "Then I heard of Richard's death at Bosworth. You must not think, my lady, that I did not love him. I never told him how I felt because I was aware that he did not feel the same way about me. He never knew." Her voice trailed off sadly. It was true. Kate remembered her father saying they had not loved each other.

"Please sit down," she invited. Katherine Haute gave her that nervous smile and took the stool by the fire.

"When I heard of your father's death, I was worried for you. I feared you would find life difficult without his protection. And when James said we would be coming up to London for the coronation, I resolved to see you, if I could. I reasoned your lord would be here to attend upon the King, and I hoped you would be with him. And so, as soon as we had settled into our lodgings—James has taken rooms in Fleet Street—I sent secret word to your lord at the palace, asking if he would arrange a meeting. And so he has, and may God bless him for it."

William reddened and muttered something gruffly about being pleased to oblige, and that he didn't see any harm in it.

"My dear," Katherine Haute said, "if I can do you any service within my little power, I am ready to do it. I know it is far too late, and that I can never be a proper mother to you, but I would at least be your friend, and have you know that, God willing, I will always be here for you." And she rose and held out her arms. With a cry of happiness, Kate went into them. It was like coming home.

They talked for hours, long after William had gone off to his supper with the King. They told each other more of their life stories, and laughed and cried in equal measure. And then Kate found herself confiding to this lovely lady who was, incredibly, her mother, all her doubts and fears about the disappearance of the princes. She knew instinctively that she could trust her.

"I have heard those evil rumors too," Katherine Haute said. "Of course, I never believed them. That was not the Dickon I knew." It was so good to hear that.

"I wanted, if I could, to speak with Queen Elizabeth, because she might know something," Kate said.

"I was supposed to be visiting her today," her mother told her. "That's what I told James, and indeed, I should see her before he comes to collect me. I've known her for years. She and James are cousins. I will ask her if she will receive you."

"She may not wish to see me. I am the daughter of her enemy, and Henry Tudor is hostile to me. He thinks I am withholding information about the princes—he may even imagine I am seeking it as a means of bringing him down! But all I want to know is the truth about my father. It could be difficult for the Queen, associating with me."

"Then, my lady, I will ask her myself what she knows, and come back to see you in the morning, at eleven o'clock. I can tell James she has invited me to dine with her."

"Would you? Oh that would be so kind," Kate breathed. "And please do not call me 'my lady'! I may be a countess, but I am your daughter, and I would like you to call me by the name we both bear."

Katherine Haute looked at her with brimming eyes. "Then you should call me Kat, for that is how I am usually known in the family."

"Nay," Kate said. "If I may, I will call you Mother."

KATHERINE

October 1561, Tower of London

"The furnishings ordered by the Queen have arrived from the Wardrobe," Sir Edward announces. At last! I can now leave the Bell Tower for a more commodious lodging.

"I thank you for your trouble, sir," I say, wondering why the lieutenant looks so uncomfortable. "The stuff will come in useful, I am sure."

"My lady, er—I am somewhat embarrassed by what the Queen has lent. Most of it is so old as to be unusable."

"I am sure Her Majesty is unaware of that, and it was not what she intended," I say hastily.

"My thoughts exactly, my lady," the lieutenant replies, as our eyes meet, conveying something else entirely. "I will have it all brought up, and you may choose anything you think suitable."

He escorts me to the rooms that have been prepared for me. They are paneled with oak and have latticed windows, and will do very well. But they face Tower Green and the chapel, and I know that every time I look out I will be reminded of my poor sister. Yet I will be far more comfortable here, and these lodgings are a more fitting residence for my son than the Bell Tower.

The furnishings sent by the Queen are indeed decrepit. The six tapestries might cover the walls and shield the drafts, but they must be hundreds of years old, and certainly look it. The pair of Turkish carpets might have been fine once, but they are threadbare and dirty. The oak armchair is rickety, its wood cracked, the stuffing spilling through rents in the rubbed cloth-of-gold padding on its seat and arms. An old purple velvet cushion lies upon it, a dark stain disfiguring its center.

"There is a bed too, in pieces," Sir Edward says. "It's not worth bringing it up here. It is too mean a thing, so I will have the one you used in the Bell Tower brought in." A disintegrating damask counterpane has been laid over Honor's pallet bed; it was probably made centuries ago. Sir Edward shakes his head. "A sorry jumble, my lady. As for the footstools, I forbear to show them to you."

"Why?" I ask.

"I recognize them as King Harry's, from the days I was at court. He would rest his ulcerated leg on them. The velvet is stained with pus, and is too far gone to clean. In truth, I am ashamed, my lady, that you should be so discommoded." Insulted, I think. These items were sent to slight me. They convey what Elizabeth thinks of me.

"I am very sorry about this, my lady," Sir Edward continues. "My wife and I will lend you some furnishings. And in compensation, I will have your maids and your pets sent for. They shall keep you company and make you and the babe merry."

And so it is that my old bed is brought in and reassembled, with new hangings of silk damask and a fine counterpane striped in red and gold silk; and Mrs. Ellen, Mrs. Coffin, my maids, and my two lapdogs, Arthur and Guinevere, are brought to the Tower, along with a more recent acquisition, my pet monkey, Jester. With them arrive four of my good gowns and French hoods, and several changes of body linen, which Honor lays away in the chest at the end of my bed. Effortlessly, after an emotional reunion—for she has been in this place before, in far more tragic circumstances—Mrs. Ellen takes charge, while I suckle and cuddle my child, with chaos all around me.

Arthur lies sleeping on the coverlet of the bed; Jester, perched on a stool, feeds daintily on a few morsels left over from the supper I could not face eating, and of which the dogs made short work. Guinevere gnaws a bone at my feet. And Sir Edward Warner regards them all with despair.

"My lady, they are wrecking the furnishings, and the servants are complaining about the messes they make. I beg of you to control them."

"I am trying, Sir Edward. Please do not take them away. They do cheer me, and I need it."

He sighs. "I would not deprive you of good cheer, my lady, but these three are a handful. And, having permitted them to be here, I will be accounted responsible for the damage."

"I will do my best," I promise. "I am so sorry. Arthur, Guinevere, Jester: you are very naughty animals!" Three pairs of soulful eyes look at me appealingly, and Jester tries again to climb into the cradle, but I tell him no, sharply, to demonstrate to the lieutenant that I mean to keep my word.

He sits down by the fire, shaking his head at them. "I came to tell you that I visited the Guildhall Library. I was not allowed to search for myself, but when I explained that I was looking for any records from the reign of Richard III, a clerk brought me the *Great Chronicle of London*. It contains testimony from those who were eyewitnesses to events. Alderman Smyth and I spent some hours going through it, and I do declare, he is now as interested as I am in the matter of the princes."

"And did you find anything that sheds light on our mystery?" I ask eagerly.

"Some things that were especially interesting," he tells me. "The chronicle, in referring to the murder of Henry VI, after his final defeat by Edward IV, states—I have it here; a moment please!" He draws from the pocket of his furred gown a folded paper covered with notes. "Ah, yes: 'The common fame went that the Duke of Gloucester was not altogether guiltless.' If that's true, Richard was seasoned in blood twelve years before the disappearance of his nephews. Alas, the affairs of kings are deadly games."

"As I am finding," I comment dryly. "I hope they are not deadly for me!"

"My lady, our sovereign lady may be strict, but she is just."

I forbear to answer that. "Did you discover anything more, Sir Edward?"

"I did. This chronicler clearly did not approve of Richard. He accused him of executing Hastings unlawfully without any process of law, and said it was this one act that convinced the citizens that the duke aimed for the throne. He wrote that Hastings was killed only for his truth and fidelity to Edward V. Later, he says that the princes were held 'more straitly' in the Tower."

"Katherine Plantagenet mentions their being behind bars. It probably means the same thing. Sir Edward, where do you think the princes were held?"

"In Caesar's Tower, most certainly. It is the innermost and strongest part of this fortress, and some of the upper windows have bars. It is the safest place to keep prisoners hidden from the eyes of the world." He shakes his head sadly, and turns back to his papers. "Under the heading 'Death of the Innocents,' the chronicler repeats all the rumors that were circulating after the princes' disappearance. People were saying they had been murdered between two feather beds, or given a venomous potion, and so forth—all speculation. But listen to this: 'Certain it was they were departed from this world, of which cruel deed Sir James Tyrell was reported to be the doer.'"

Tyrell again. "It's what Katherine Plantagenet heard. That name— trying to place it is vexing me sorely, because it might give us a clue . . ."

"Tyrell was merely 'reported' to be the doer. But the fact that he was actually named the murderer as early as 1484 might be significant.

And why Tyrell? He was not well known, so why should his name be tossed about?"

"I agree, sir, it is strange."

"It cannot but have done him harm. And Richard too, of course. The chronicler says the people grudged so sore against him because of the death of the innocents that they would rather have had the French to rule over them!"

"Now that is saying something!" I observe.

"There is another serious accusation against King Richard in this chronicle," Sir Edward continues, "that there was much whispering, even among his northern people who had loved him, that he poisoned his wife so that he could remarry."

"That's news to me. Do you think it could have been true?"

"It is impossible to say. By then, men would have believed anything of him."

"Yet he could have counteracted everything! Why did he not, unless he was guilty? Could he not see that these rumors were destroying him?"

"Well, my lady, he should have—he came to a bloody end because of them. Maybe he underestimated their power to bring him down. It's clear that most of his subjects hated him. After he was slain at Bosworth, the *Great Chronicle* says, his body was despoiled to the skin and he was trussed up like a hog or vile beast, thrown over his own herald's mount, and so carried naked into Leicester. And then he was indifferently buried in St. Mary's Church. Henry VII had his remains moved to the Grey Friars, which became known as the Tyrants' Sepulchre, because Cardinal Wolsey was buried there too."

"So much for gaining a crown," I reflect, thinking that, in the end, Richard III, like my sister Jane, had paid with his life for usurping the throne.

"Had it not been for his ambition, he might have grown old and respected by all, for he had the makings of a great prince."

"Unless the Wydevilles had done for him first."

"Yes, that was what he evidently feared. But I wonder. Was that just a pretext? Well, we may yet find out. When Alderman Smyth perceived that I was disappointed that there was no fresh light on the princes in the *Great Chronicle,* he told me in secrecy he had something in his house that might interest me. He said he dared not speak of it in public, because it might, even now, be dangerous to do so. Naturally, I asked him why, and he said it was one of the books that had been suppressed by Henry VII. Apparently it was Smyth's grandfather's. I know no more, for he would not divulge its title, and he has sworn me to secrecy anyway. I should not be telling you this, but I know I can rest assured you will not speak of it."

"I could not even if I would, shut in here!" I say with some spirit.

"Of course, of course," he answers, looking embarrassed. "Anyway, I am going to visit him tomorrow. Afterward, I have some stores to check, and some prisoners to question, but I will come to you as soon as I may. And, my lady, you should take heart. There are many that love and support you, as became clear in the City today." And with that unexpected revelation, which instantly revives my hopes, Sir Edward leaves me.

KATE

November 1485, Westminster Palace

It grew late, and still William had not returned from the King's supper. He would be enjoying himself, Kate thought, restored to the circles in which his rank and allegiance entitled him to move. She thought bitterly of how readily he had betrayed that other allegiance he had owed to her father, and yet it did not seem such a bitter betrayal now, for the events of this day had blotted out much of the misery and grief of the past months. Seeing John, and the spark of love flaring undimmed in his eyes, and then meeting the mother she had never known—no wonder she was finding it hard to sleep!

She felt an unaccustomed quivering in her belly, like a butterfly's wings, and supposed it was her excitement manifesting itself. But a few minutes later she felt it again, and knew it for what it really was: her child, making its existence felt for the first time. She had not come so far along during her first pregnancy. A sense of wonder filled her as she placed her hands on her stomach, rejoicing in the life within. Truly, God had been good to her this day.

She rose from the bed, put on her nightgown, and sank to her knees on the prayer stool below the latticed window; and there, in the moonlight, she gave thanks for this gift of new life, and the blessings and promises of love that had been vouchsafed her.

When she rose, she saw that a sealed letter had been pushed under the door. She snatched it up. There was no imprint on the wax, and no signature. The fine script she recognized instantly, though: it was John's. She broke the seal and devoured his words:

> *My heart, burn this when you have read it. I came to Westminster to make my submission to the King and swear to him not to maintain any felons, as he is pleased to call those men who have been in hiding with me. I have done this at my father's earnest entreaty. He would have his son at liberty to be a comfort to him in his old age.*
>
> *In return for my allegiance, the King did me the honor of permitting me to precede him in his coronation procession, and he has been gracious enough to appoint me to his council.*
>
> *Know that I still cherish my inordinate love for you, still feel that furiosity and frenzy of mind of which the poet wrote. I know I need not repeat all the words, you have them by heart, as I do; but saying them brings you so vividly to mind, my dearest lady, that I can almost imagine that you are here with me.*
>
> *Like the poet, I have no peace when I think of you. I burn for you eternally. The sweetest remembrance of all is of our one night together. It is not enough for a lifetime. Make shift to come to me tomorrow, I pray you. I will be by the fountain in New Palace Yard at nine o'clock in the morning. Let it look as if we are meeting by chance, and pray give me some hope that I may know the sweet joy of our loving again.*

Kate's heart beat fast as she read and reread the letter, then clutched it joyfully to her bosom. John had taken a tremendous risk in pushing it under her door, yet he would surely have known that William was otherwise occupied. Probably he had been at the King's supper himself.

He had been here at Westminster, probably for weeks. He had even played a part in the coronation! Secluded as William had kept her, she had not known of it.

She would go to him, of course she would. Neither William nor Henry Tudor, nor the whole company of Heaven, was going to stop her.

INTERLUDE

October 1561, Whitehall Palace

"Her Majesty is not pleased to hear that many of her subjects—and some of her courtiers to boot—are sympathetic to the Lady Katherine Grey," Mr. Secretary Cecil fumes. "Here are the reports—read them!" And he indicates a pile of papers on his desk. He and the Earl of Sussex have arrived early for the council meeting, and as yet are the only ones seated at the long table.

Sussex, a fair, florid man, leafs through the reports, grunting. "They remember Protector Somerset, 'the good duke,' as they called him. Hertford is his son, so it's only to be expected, I suppose."

"To them, he is a gallant hero, defying the Queen's unkindness and wrath to marry the lady he loves," Cecil sniffs.

"Some see the Lady Katherine as another like her sister, the Lady Jane," Sussex murmurs, reading on. "They view her as a brave Protestant heroine."

"They forget she has been plotting with the Spaniards," Cecil says dryly. "But what most people seem to be asking is why a man and his wife should be put asunder and imprisoned!"

"I see there's a lot of speculation that they will be attainted or even put to death; or that the Queen will have Parliament declare their child a bastard; many say the Lady Katherine should be named heir to the throne; and I see that you, my lord, are suspected by a few of being privy to her marriage." Sussex grins.

"Pure nonsense!" Cecil retorts.

"But tell me, are any of these other rumors true? Does the Queen still intend to have the child declared baseborn?"

"I believe so. Yet she is disturbed to find that there is a tide of opinion in the Lady Katherine's favor, and anxious lest she herself appear in an unsympathetic light, when in truth she is the person most injured by this pretended marriage. So she will do nothing just yet. In the meantime, Her Majesty is disposed to show some favor toward the couple, to placate public feeling."

KATHERINE

October 1561, Tower of London

Sir Edward Warner arrives at five o'clock, just as supper is being served. He orders an extra place set, then dismisses the servants, and himself serves the baked meats to us both and slices the pie.

"What I have to tell you is for your ears alone," he says.

"You saw the book, then, Sir Edward?" I ask eagerly.

"Yes, indeed," he answers, his angular face looking unusually animated. "It was a manuscript chronicle I had never heard of or seen before, from the abbey of Croyland, which was near Lincoln; and whoever wrote it had much to say about Richard III!"

Could this be the truth at last? I pray it will be. It's irrational, I know, but I cannot rid myself of the notion that the fate of the princes augurs well or ill for the safety of my child.

"The author described himself as a member of the King's Council, so he was at the center of affairs and clearly well informed," Sir Edward tells me. "He wrote his chronicle during a visit to the abbey, nine months after Bosworth. As it was written under Henry VII, it is only to be expected that the writer was hostile to Richard III. Yet it's plain he had no good opinion of him anyway."

"Then why was his book suppressed? Henry would surely have approved."

He frowns. "My lady, that exercised me and Alderman Smyth some-what. We perused the chronicle together closely; as I said, he has be-come interested in the matter, although he thinks it is still dangerous to speak openly of certain things. You see, the Queen Grace's title is inher-ited from Henry VII, and Henry married Elizabeth of York, who had been bastardized by Richard III. Henry must have had her legitimacy confirmed by Parliament. Yet I have never read anywhere that he did so."

"I don't understand."

"In the Croyland Chronicle there is the text of an Act of Parliament of 1484, entitled *Titulus Regius;* it confirms Richard III's right to the throne. In it are laid out the grounds of his claim, namely his brother's precontract with one Eleanor Butler; and it confirms the consequent bastardy of Edward IV's children by Elizabeth Wydeville."

"I still don't understand the significance," I say. "Surely that Act was repealed by Henry?"

Sir Edward lowers his voice. "I'm sure it was. But it was done dis-creetly. If you were Henry VII, and your queen's legitimacy had been impugned, would you want everyone to know about it? Henry must have known that his claim by blood was weak, and that there were many who would regard it as such until he strengthened it by marry-ing the Yorkist heiress. He could not afford to have his enemies pro-ducing evidence that she was baseborn, and denying his right to rule. So my belief is that he suppressed all copies of *Titulus Regius,* which is why the Croyland Chronicle had to go too."

This makes good sense. "But how did Alderman Smyth come to have it in his possession?"

"It was in a coffer of old books and papers left him by his grandfa-ther. His family came from Lincolnshire originally, and his great-uncle was a monk at Croyland, which was a mighty abbey in those days. There were two other old chronicles in the chest; Alderman Smyth showed them to me. They were hand-illuminated and very fine. His belief is that his uncle saved them from the King's men at the time of the Dissolution. They were burning lots of old chronicles then, and most of the monks' libraries were lost."

I am too excited to eat. "Pray tell me, good Sir Edward, what else is in this chronicle?"

He smiles. "Much that isn't flattering to Richard III. The author disapproved of him thoroughly, thought him dishonest and deceitful, and criticized him for extravagance and sensuality, and even for executing a man on a Sunday. He claims that he himself tried to be fair and unprejudiced, and wrote his history without hatred or favor—and I think he did. He says, for example, that Richard had a quick mind and high courage, and was vigilant in state affairs; and I noted he does not accuse him of murdering Henry VI; instead, he hints that Edward IV was responsible."

I sigh. "It is very confusing, having accounts that contradict each other. The *Great Chronicle* said Richard was there when Henry VI was murdered. How can one ever arrive at the truth?"

"Ah, my lady, there you have put your finger on the problem with history!" Sir Edward declares, wiping his fingers on his napkin, then offering me the plate of apples. "One has to weigh the sources well, and my belief is that this chronicler was closer to affairs than whoever wrote the *Great Chronicle*. He had inside knowledge of state matters."

I crunch into my apple; it's sweet but a bit shriveled, the best of the store having been eaten already.

"Again, I made some notes," the lieutenant says, and produces a sheaf of papers from the capacious pocket of his gown. "Croyland believed that Richard was plotting to take the throne from the time he learned of the death of his brother, King Edward. He states that after Richard, Duke of York, had been taken from the sanctuary to join his brother, Richard openly revealed his plans, and he and Buckingham did as they pleased."

This tallies with Katherine Plantagenet's account. And there's another connection somewhere, I'm sure of it.

"Richard then acted openly like a king," Sir Edward continues, "but the Croyland chronicler insists the precontract story was just a cover for his act of usurpation. He implies that many on the council thought it fraudulent too, but looked to their own safety, warned by the example of Hastings. And so, he writes, Richard occupied the kingdom."

"Is there anything about the princes?" I ask hopefully.

"Yes. He says the sons of King Edward remained in custody in the Tower; he mentions them being here under special guard during Richard's first progress through his realm, which he undertook after his coronation. They remained in the Tower while the coronation, the progress and the investiture of Richard's son as Prince of Wales were taking place."

I interrupt: "I know who this writer was! He was the Lord Chancellor, the Bishop of Lincoln, who told Katherine that the princes were alive at the time of the investiture in September."

"Of course! Croyland Abbey would have been in his diocese. Katherine wrote that he went back to Lincoln after Henry VII dismissed him."

"What else does he say?"

"He does not mention the princes again. It is very strange."

"But surely a man in his position must have known what became of them? He'd known about their whereabouts up till then."

"Well, my lady, if he knew, he wasn't telling."

"It would have been safe to tell in Henry VII's reign."

"Hardly, if the princes had not been murdered."

I gape at him. "You mean, you think Russell kept silent on the matter of the princes because he knew they had been sent into hiding?"

"It's possible. He knew the princes were in the Tower up to September, so it follows that he probably knew what happened to them after that. The King trusted him, so he must have been privy to many state secrets. In 1486, when he wrote his chronicle, it would have been perfectly acceptable to accuse Richard of their murder. Russell didn't scruple to accuse Richard of other crimes or castigate him for his vices, so if he knew or suspected that he had had the princes put to death, he would surely have said so. But all he says is that Richard suppressed his brother's progeny. 'Suppressed,' mark you, not murdered. Perhaps Katherine Plantagenet came close to the truth when she wondered if the princes were at Sheriff Hutton. But if so, what happened to them after Bosworth?"

"Surely, if they were there, King Henry would have found out about it?"

"Assuredly he would. Elizabeth of York knew much, I am sure, and maybe that was why she was kept in subjection by the King and his mother."

"Sir Edward, I still wonder . . . If Henry had discovered that the princes were at Sheriff Hutton, what would have been the logical, nay, the safest thing to do with them?"

The lieutenant looks hard at me. He says nothing.

"By vowing to marry their sister, he had effectively acknowledged them to be the legitimate heirs to York. But if they still lived, Edward V was the rightful King. And he would have been fifteen—old enough to rule. Sir Edward, no threat to Henry could have been deadlier."

"You forget, my lady, that Henry had the Tower searched for their bodies—three times. And he clearly viewed Perkin Warbeck as a serious threat; for years, Warbeck threatened his throne, and the measures Henry took against him are proof that he really did fear Warbeck was not an imposter. He *cannot* have known what had become of the princes. If he had, he would have dealt with Warbeck speedily and summarily."

"Yes, I suppose you are right, sir. It's just that I should like to think that the princes survived. That's what Katherine tried to prove; it mattered a lot to her."

"Is that why you pursue this quest for the truth?" Sir Edward asks gently.

"That's one reason, yes. And . . ." I find I cannot speak. I am suddenly close to tears, remembering that my son too is a threat to the throne. This matter goes very near to home. "I've always been interested in the princes," I say hastily.

Fortunately, Sir Edward has not noticed my distress. "These papers have revived my interest too, my lady. I had thought there was no more to be found out. But in keeping with my family motto, 'Go straight and fear not,' I must now press on until the end!" We laugh at that, and he even pats my hand, acknowledging that we are in this together. For once, we are not prisoner and jailer, but two friends united in solving a compelling mystery. Then the lieutenant turns back to his notes, peering at them in the dying candlelight.

"Going back to Bishop Russell," he says, "he mentions the rumors of the princes' murder, and writes that, within *weeks*, they had had their effect, and Richard was seen by his subjects as a wretched, bloody, and usurping boor. More crucially, Russell writes that many in Parliament were strongly critical of the legality of the Act *Titulus Regius,* but that even the stoutest were swayed by fear to approve and pass it. It seems that very few believed that tale about a precontract."

"I think Katherine convinced herself that her father believed it."

"We can only commend her for her loyalty." The lieutenant takes a page from his sheaf of papers. "The Bishop made this observation about Richard's forced loans: 'Why should we any longer dwell on things so distasteful and so pernicious that we ought not so much as to suggest them?' But then he writes—and this may be significant: 'So too with other things that are not written in this book, and of which I grieve to speak.'" He looks up. "What do you make of that, my lady?"

"Can he be referring to the princes?" I ask. "If so, it reads ominously."

"It might just be an oblique reference to the King's morals, of which the Bishop had a low opinion. Maybe he did not wish to be explicit on a subject like that."

"Was Richard III immoral? His daughter writes of his uprightness and good morals."

"She, I fear, saw the man she wished to see. Yet the Bishop viewed the death of Richard's son as a judgment on a man who had pursued his interests without the aid of God. That's pretty damning. He also condemned the King's pursuit of his niece Elizabeth as an incestuous passion, abominable before God. He says the Queen's illness grew worse because Richard shunned her bed, claiming it was by the advice of his physicians. Then he adds, 'Why enlarge?' It's obvious what he thinks of that excuse! In fact, he goes so far as to assert that the King hastened his wife's death by being unkind to her. Afterward, he says, Richard's councillors dissuaded him from marrying Elizabeth, warning him that if he did, the whole of the North would rise against him and impute to him the death of the Queen. But only reluctantly did he abandon the idea."

"That doesn't show Richard in a good light."

"No, but in Russell's account of the Battle of Bosworth, he writes that, in the fighting, and not in the act of flight, Richard was pierced with many mortal wounds, and fell in the field like a brave and most valiant prince. But if that sounds like praise, remember that immediately afterward the Bishop states that Providence gave a glorious victory to Henry Tudor. He was just being fair, as he had averred: it's well known that Richard died bravely. And that, my lady, is all. None of it is conclusive, and although it still appears that the princes were probably murdered, there is no proof, and there are still some things that don't make sense."

He shakes his head, looking vexed, then pauses. "You seem tired, my lady. You should rest. Again, I have enjoyed our discourse. I bid you good night."

When he has gone, I fall to pondering if this mystery of the princes will ever be solved. It may be that what happened to them might never be known. It is highly improbable that they still live, and since no one has heard from them in nigh eighty years, the likelihood must be that they did die at Richard III's hands.

Sir Edward visits me some days later to say that he has looked through the Tower records and is certain there is nothing of interest to us.

It is so frustrating. There must be some clue, somewhere! I read through Katherine's account again, checking to see if there is anything we have missed. But there is nothing. All we have are dark hints, rumors, and Bishop Russell's curious statement that the princes were suppressed. How can two boys just disappear, leaving no trace as to what became of them?

No sooner do I ask that question than I find myself looking out of my window at the grim walls of the Tower around me; and suddenly the answer seems very obvious.

KATE

November 1485, Westminster Palace

Kate crept down the spiral stair near her lodging. It was a bitterly cold morning and she had put on her warmest gown, with her fur-lined cloak over it, taking care to conceal her face. William had insisted upon that. She had told him she was going to see her mother, and prayed that God would forgive her the lie. She *was* going to see Kat Haute, but not for two hours and more, so it was only a white lie. She did not think there was any risk of Kat coming to seek her out earlier.

William had made difficulties, as she had thought he would. Couldn't her mother come here? he had asked, frowning. No, she'd told him, she had asked Kate to meet her in St. Stephen's Chapel. They wanted to give thanks together for being reunited, and then they would stay for the ten o'clock Mass. And may God forgive me, she'd prayed inwardly, hoping William would not insist on coming with them. But he didn't. He was going hunting with the King and other favored lords, and could talk of little else. At eight o'clock he'd set off to join the royal party.

She had looked anxiously about her as she left her room, taking care to shut the door behind her. There was no one about—or so it seemed. But as she descended the stairs, she heard a sound above her—muted, stealthy. Someone was coming down behind her. When she paused to listen, they paused too. Then there was silence. There had been a landing above her. Maybe whoever it was had turned off there, their business entirely innocent. This was a palace, she reminded herself firmly: people came and went all the time. She waited a little, but all stayed quiet, so she continued on her way.

The staircase spiraled down through a corner turret. At the bottom, she pushed open the heavy nailed door and forced herself to stroll past the guards and walk at a sedate pace toward the fountain.

John was waiting there, looking like a hero of legend: tall, vital, splendid, and illustrious—his beloved Chaucer's perfect gentle knight in person. And he was smiling jubilantly at her. Her heart leapt!

But as she reached the fountain, she saw the smile on John's face give way to an expression of horror. Without warning, strong arms grabbed her brutally from behind. She screamed, and instinctively reached out to John, but she was being pulled away, and she was appalled to see a man-at-arms rush forward and pinion him, holding a dagger to his throat.

"What in hell are you doing?" John roared. "Let her go! What is the meaning of this?"

Shrieking, and in terror for them both, Kate grabbed the stone rim
of the fountain, but her fingers were roughly pried away. "Don't struggle, my fine lady!" a harsh voice muttered as she was dragged back in
the direction of the stairs. She screamed and kicked, fighting against
her captor, but his grip was like a vice.

"Help me!" she shrieked, shocked at what was happening. It wasn't
real . . . It couldn't be . . .

"Stop at once!" John yelled. "Let her go, I said! She has done nothing to deserve this."

A man in black, his weapon drawn, lunged forward, threatening
John. "Yon lady is under suspicion of treason," he growled, "and if you
attempt to obstruct us in our duty, you too will be placed under arrest."

"Don't talk nonsense!" John spat. "She came here for a lovers'
tryst."

"One suspected traitor meeting another, more like!"

"No!" Kate howled, indignation and despair overwhelming her. She
saw that people had come running to hear what the commotion was,
but were being held back by the King's guard, who had materialized as
if from nowhere.

John's eyes blazed with fury. "Ignorant knave! Do you know who I
am? I have the King's favor. Do you think I am such a fool as to plot
against him?" he roared.

That, alas, was the last Kate heard, for her assailant had forced her
back through the turret door, and he and another burly man were half
pushing, half hauling her up the stairs, she struggling and screaming.
Still pinioned, she was manhandled into her room and flung down on
the bed before Gwenllian's horrified eyes, her fingers smarting where
they had been bent back.

"Give me the key," her captor demanded. Fumbling, Kate removed
it from her pocket and, shaking with shock, anger, and indignation,
handed it to him.

"How dare you treat me so roughly?" she gasped. "I am with
child. I mean none ill. My husband shall know of this."

"Rest assured, lady, he will," the man told her, with a nasty grin.
Then he locked her in.

KATHERINE

February 1562, Tower of London

Time drags. It is too cold to go out into the garden. I have been a prisoner in the Tower overlong, and yearn for my freedom. Little Edward is a delight, but a child should not be confined to these rooms. He should be taken for walks, see faces other than those that are familiar to him—and know his father.

I have not seen Ned since I was forced, near weeping, to leave him behind in the chapel on the day of the christening. Yet Sir Edward allows him to write to me regularly. Ned's letters are mainly declarations of love, which are the breath of life to me, yet sometimes they touch on the precariousness of our situation, with which he is naturally preoccupied. In the last one, he wrote:

> *Do not think I regret our marriage, yet by it I destroyed my credit with the Queen, and prejudiced your chance of being named her heir. Even so, sweet wife, I will never deny our union, not though it bring me the Queen's favor.*

And, of course, being me, and always thinking the worst, I had to wonder if he had seriously considered doing that. Now, though, I believe he wrote those words to reassure me of his devotion. And I have replied in kind, assuring him of my steadfastness.

The letters are a great comfort to me, although the lieutenant is kindness itself, and does his best for us both. I might wonder if he was a little in love with me, save for the fact that he speaks of his wife Audrey with tender affection. She spends most of her time at Polstead Hall, their home in Norfolk, yet sometimes she lodges here in the lieutenant's house, although I've never seen her. I wonder if she is a touch jealous of the attention her husband gives me—yet I'm sure she has no cause.

———

When the lieutenant visits me one freezing February evening, looking very pleased with himself, I expect him to tell me that my hopes of freedom have come to fruition, yet he has come on another matter entirely.

"I have something to show you, my lady," he says eagerly. "May I sit down and warm myself by the fire? It is bitter outside."

"By all means," I say, trying to stifle my disappointment, and he takes the stool opposite my chair.

"This," he says, producing a book, "contains an account of the murder of the Princes in the Tower."

"*Murder?*" I have been praying, against all reason, that those poor innocents escaped such a fate.

"Yes, my lady—it was murder, I fear. You may read it for yourself." He passes me the book, which is entitled *The Union of the Two Noble and Illustrious Families of Lancaster and York,* the author being Edward Hall.

"But I have read Hall's chronicle," I say. "We had a copy at Bradgate, and I'm sure there is nothing about the princes in that."

"It is true, there is nothing in the first edition, my lady, which must be the one you had. I have read that myself. But this is a much more recent edition, and in it you will find incorporated Sir Thomas More's history of Richard III."

"Sir Thomas More wrote about Richard III?"

"Aye, and it seems he had access to sources lost to us, for his account is the most detailed of them all. I was amazed to find this book on sale in Paul's Churchyard as I was passing by the cathedral yesterday—I had no idea they had brought out a later edition of Hall. You may keep it if you wish, and see what you make of it. I should be most interested to know your opinion."

"Have you formed one, Sir Edward?"

"I must say I find this convincing. But I will leave you to make up your own mind."

I take the book to bed with me, setting an extra candle on my bedside table in case I have need of it. I know I will not sleep until I have read to the end.

I know little of Sir Thomas More, save that he was a devout Papist who was Lord Chancellor of England, and that he was beheaded thirty years ago for refusing to take an oath acknowledging Henry VIII's marriage to Anne Boleyn. I've heard too that he was a great scholar, and indeed I am astonished by his breadth of knowledge—but there are many things in his book that startle me.

First, he repeats a lurid tale that Richard III was born after two years in his mother's womb, with teeth, long hair, a crooked back, and one shoulder higher than the other, although Sir Thomas does write scornfully that either men of hatred had reported the truth or nature had changed its course!

He accuses Richard of slaying Henry VI without commandment or knowledge of Edward IV—which is going further than any other account I have read, and indeed differs from some.

More did not believe that Richard was in danger from the Wydevilles; he suspected that he had had designs on the throne even before his brother's death. He wrote how the citizens of London donned armor after Richard's coup, fearing it was aimed at the young King himself. Katherine mentions that too. Like others, More says that Richard decided to eliminate Hastings because he was opposed to all his schemes.

I hold my breath as I read More's long account of the council meeting in the Tower at which Hastings was arrested, uncomfortably aware that Caesar's Tower, that forbidding white keep where these events took place, is just a stone's throw from where I lie. He says Hastings was allowed no time for any long confession before he was hustled to his death, which corroborates what Katherine witnessed. There are so many details in More's account—where did he discover them all?

He says that as soon as Richard had both the princes in his charge, he "opened his mind boldly" to the Duke of Buckingham. What to make of that? Did he tell Buckingham he meant to take the throne? Or did he, as Margaret Beaufort told Katherine, reveal a more sinister plan to him? I shall have to discuss all this with Sir Edward. He will understand it better than I.

More disapproved of Richard's attempts to declare Edward IV and the princes illegitimate. He states that the only fault of Rivers and

Grey lay in being good men, true to Edward V. And he describes Richard as a close and secret king from the first.

Here's an intriguing detail: More writes that when the deposed Edward V, then being in the Tower, was told that he should not reign, but that his uncle should have the crown, he was abashed and began to sigh, saying, "Alas, I would my uncle would let me have my life yet, though I lose my kingdom." More *must* have had access to secret information about what was going on in the Tower, otherwise how could he have known such a thing? Did he make it up, just to tell a good story? I think not. I have the strong impression that he was a man of staunch principle, and only wrote of what he believed—or knew—to be the truth.

He has much more to say about the princes. He tells how they were both shut up in the Tower, and all others removed from them, except for a ruffian called Black Will Slaughter, who was appointed to serve them and "keep them sure." It saddens me to read that young Edward, sick in his jaw, lingered on in heaviness and wretchedness, never even bothering to tie his hose. This all fits with what Brother Dominic and Bishop Russell and others wrote, but none of them gives these details.

Later, More says, the number of the princes' attendants was increased to four; one was Miles Forrest, "a fellow fleshed in murder," which sounds chillingly ominous, and as I read on, my flesh crawls even more. Immediately after learning about the conspiracies to free the princes, More says, King Richard devised to fulfill the thing he had long intended. For he believed that, his nephews living, men would not allow him the right to the realm. He decided therefore to be rid of them without delay.

I read how he summoned a man he trusted named John Green, and sent him to Robert Brackenbury, the Constable of the Tower, with a letter commanding Brackenbury to put the princes to death. But Brackenbury refused to commit such a dreadful deed, even though he should die for refusing.

The King, thinking his command was being carried out, now revealed to Buckingham that he had ordered the killing of the princes; and it was this that caused Buckingham to desert Richard. Buckingham then went home to Brecon and considered how best to remove this unnatural uncle—More calls him a "bloody butcher"—from his throne. I find it all believable. Why else would Buckingham, who had staunchly supported Richard, suddenly turn on him?

More's account is compulsive reading, and I cannot turn the pages fast enough. I hope I am about to find out what really happened to the princes. I read that when John Green returned to the King and told him of Brackenbury's refusal to carry out his order, Richard was angry. But then Green told him that his loyal servant, Sir James Tyrell, was so desperate to be promoted that he would agree to do anything to please his king. And so, writes More, Richard decided to entrust Tyrell with the murder of the princes, and dispatched him to Brackenbury. That fits with what Katherine wrote about Tyrell journeying to London to obtain wardrobe stuff for Prince Edward's investiture. At last I feel I am making sense of this mystery.

With Tyrell, More continues, rode a strong knave called John Dighton. When they got to the Tower, Tyrell, in the King's name, commanded Brackenbury to give up the keys for one night, the night he had appointed for the murder. I shiver again, for the scene of that dreadful deed is only yards away from this very room. I have no difficulty now in believing that those voices I have heard in the night are the shades of the princes, crying out to be rescued.

I can hardly bear to read on, but I must. Near to weeping, I learn that Tyrell removed Slaughter and the other attendants, then ordered Dighton and Forrest to kill the princes. At midnight, he positioned himself outside the door to the chamber where those poor boys lay sleeping, and waited there while his henchmen entered the room by stealth and pressed the feather pillows hard over the faces of the two innocents, who—More says—struggled in vain before finally giving up their souls to God. Then the murderers laid out the bodies naked on the bed, and called for Tyrell to inspect them.

Instinctively, I lean over and look upon my son sleeping peacefully in his cradle, and marvel that anyone could be so cruel to a defenseless child. I cannot bear to think of the princes' lives being cut off in the flower of their tender years—two little boys who not long before had been the hope of England. How bitter a thing it is to be cursed with royal blood! And I have suffered cruelly for it too—although never as cruelly as they did.

My eyes swim over the part where Tyrell makes the murderers bury the bodies in secret. It is very late when I lay down the book, long past midnight, and I feel wrung out, but slumber eludes me. I cannot forget the terrible things I have read. I toss and turn, overwrought, thinking of the fate of those wretched boys. I shudder to think what Katherine would have made of all this. Did she ever find out the truth? She could never have read More's account, written as it was many years later.

But was it the truth? If More knew all this, how come others did not? I try to convince myself that he had it all wrong, or was writing purely to illustrate a moral lesson, but the compelling detail in his account—and the man's patent integrity—argues otherwise.

I am willing myself to sleep when something comes to me. Tyrell . . . I knew I had seen that name somewhere. And Brackenbury too, in the same place. I have it now. It must be more than coincidence.

KATE

November 1485, Westminster Palace

Kate did not know how long she sat on her bed, dreading the confrontation that must take place when William returned from hunting. She was almost too frightened to move, but stayed there hunched over, her heart pounding, her head swimming, and her skin clammy and cold. Sick and faint, she could do no more than wring her hands and weep.

After a while she began to feel cramping pains in her stomach. Soon they were like dagger thrusts, and she was hugging herself and gasping with pain. Little Gwenllian was beside herself, knowing she must run for help, yet not daring to leave her mistress alone in such a state.

Then Kate felt a flood of warmth, and saw, to her horror, that bright red blood was seeping through her skirts onto the counterpane.

"My babe!" she cried, keening as the cramps grew fiercer. "Oh, help me, I think I am losing my baby!"

"What should I do?" begged Gwenllian, wide-eyed with helplessness.

"Fetch a guard, anyone! Please! Help me!"

The maid knocked timidly on the door. It opened, but to her dismay she found two halberdiers standing outside.

"Council's orders," said one, seeing her face. "What's all the fuss about?"

"My mistress's child is coming too early!" Gwenllian squealed. "We need help."

The man scratched his chin. "Best go find a physician," he said to his companion.

The other man looked doubtful. "We were told to stay at our post," he protested.

"But my lady is ill and in pain—she's *bleeding!*" Gwenllian wailed, as Kate began screaming behind her.

"Thank goodness I am here then," said a mellow voice, and Gwenllian exhaled with huge relief to see the welcome figure of Kat Haute—and burst into tears.

"I am come to see your mistress, as I promised," Kat said. "May I enter? What is going on?"

"Who are you?" the first guard asked.

"Her mother," Kat said firmly.

"Very well, go in. But she is not allowed to leave her room."

"As if she could!" Gwenllian wept. "She is losing her baby!"

Kat looked appalled. "What has she done to merit being shut up?" she asked.

"I'm not allowed to say, mistress."

"Very well." Her face was tense. "There are more urgent considerations right now. Please let me pass."

"Shouldn't one of us go in with her?" the second guard wondered.

"No, this is women's business!" Kat said firmly. "It would not be seemly."

"All right, mistress," the first guard agreed. "But mind—no seditious talk."

"I have no idea what you mean," she said haughtily, masking her dismay. She wondered anxiously if the authorities had learned of the inquiries Kate had been making about the princes. The girl had said she thought someone had been stalking her. Please God, let them not find out about her own meeting with Queen Elizabeth and Lord Dorset this morning! That had turned up some very interesting information, which she had come to impart to her daughter. But for now, of course, it would be better to say nothing.

With these thoughts whirling through her head, she hurried into the room. And there she saw Kate, writhing on her bed in a great pool of blood, and knew for a tragic certainty that this grandchild of Richard's, her lost lover, would never draw breath.

Later, when William returned, his face set grimly, it was all over and Kate lay sleeping, white and drained. Kat was sitting by the bed, watching over her.

"The child is lost," she said sadly. "I am very sorry."

He sat down and dropped his head in his hands. "Has God deserted me?" He sounded bitter, defeated. "This is not the only trouble heaped upon me. Everything I've built up in these past days—the King's trust and friendship, my standing at court, a good affinity here—all destroyed. By my wife!" He was in an agony of anger and disbelief. "Tell me, was it a son?"

Kat suppressed the remembrance of the tiny dead infant she had hurriedly shrouded in a white cloth. She had sent Gwenllian to the chapel with it, to find a priest who could tell her where it should be buried. Poor mite, its unbaptized soul, unfreed from original sin, would now be in limbo for all eternity, if you believed what the clergy said. But despite that, she believed that God was all-loving and merciful, and took every lost child to His breast. She would pray for her grandchild, whatever the Church decreed.

"Yes, it was a son," she said. William wept at that, slow, difficult tears that made his shoulders heave. "Straw upon straw has been laid upon me," he sobbed. Kat let him cry it out, not wishing to intrude on his grief. She guessed he would not welcome it.

"What is to happen now?" she asked some time later.

"I do not know." He sighed heavily. "I got back from hunting and found myself summoned before the King's Council, who demanded to know if I knew anything about my wife being in league with adherents of the late usurper. I told them I knew nothing of it and would not believe it. They said they had reason to suspect she was trying to gather information about the fate of the sons of King Edward, and that they doubted her motives. I told them that probably—misguidedly—she was merely seeking reassurance that her father, the usurper, had not had them murdered, for she could not bear to believe it. They were only half convinced, I am sure, but sufficiently to commit her to my custody, on pain of serious consequences if she meddles again. But we are to depart the court forthwith, and she is to remain in my charge at all times from henceforth. Great God, what has she been *doing*? They said she was arrested on her way to a meeting with the Earl of Lincoln. His loyalty is suspect, and no wonder, for he was Richard's heir, and the King is divining some conspiracy between them."

His voice rose, and Kate stirred in her sleep, as if she was having troubled dreams.

"I do not believe for a moment that she has had any thought of plotting against the King," Kat said. "She needs to know the truth about her father."

"But the danger? Did the foolish girl not realize what the consequences might be? Did she not think that I might be implicated?"

"I cannot answer for her. I only know how much it meant to her to prove that Richard was innocent of a dreadful crime."

"She must forget him!" William erupted. "It's bad enough for me, being married to the usurper's daughter. Now, I thank you for your care of her, but I would be alone."

"As you wish," Kat said, knowing better than to oppose him in this mood, and reluctantly departed.

The first thing Kate saw when she woke up was her husband's bleak face, staring resentfully at her. Then she remembered why she was here, shut up in this room and lying in this bed feeling so empty and ill.

She winced as she thought of the pain she had suffered. The cramps had ceased now, but if her body was recovering, her soul was still in torment.

She had been cruelly torn from John, and God knew what was happening to him now, for they had both been accused of treason. She had lost her child, and she knew she would grieve all her days for it. She was a prisoner in this lodging, with a dread fate no doubt hanging over her—what did they do to women who were condemned as traitors? Did they disembowel and quarter them as they did men, or did they commute the sentence to beheading if the victim was of noble birth? She recoiled, imagining the cold steel piercing her body, slicing, ripping . . . Finally—as if the rest was not enough—she had incurred her husband's wrath, which was plain to see. It was a terrible reversal after the burgeoning happiness she had felt—was it only hours earlier? How long had she slept? She had lost track of time. She lay there staring up at the tester, wanting to die.

"Are you awake?" William growled.

"Yes," she whispered.

"My son was born dead," he accused her. "It was through *your* folly."

She forced herself to speak. "Nay—it was through the brutality of those guards. And I suffered agonies. The pain was dreadful, and all for nothing." Tears filled her eyes. "I am so sorry, so very sorry. It was the shock. They were rough with me, and I was frightened. My lord, do you know what they have accused me of?"

"They suspect some dabbling in treason," he told her, his voice stern and aggrieved, and recounted his interrogation by the council.

"You spoke truth," she said. "I wanted only to clear my father's name."

"You're a bloody fool, Kate! The King is a suspicious man. He had you marked from the first, if only because you are the usurper's daughter. And what do you do? You seek out my lord of Lincoln, who was heir to the throne under your father, and is distrusted for obvious reasons. What did you do that for?" William's anger was rising.

"Sir, I was hoping the earl could tell me if my father had had the princes moved to Sheriff Hutton," Kate confessed. "He had charge of the household there."

William gaped at her. "What on earth made you think they were at Sheriff Hutton? They were slain in the Tower, I promise you, soon after the usurpation."

"And how do you know that?" she cried. "What if my father had them moved from the Tower and taken to a secret place?"

"It is common knowledge that they were murdered," he insisted.

"But there is no proof! Even Henry Tudor knows that." She should not have revealed this, she knew, but she had to make her point.

William looked taken aback. "Whatever the truth, you should not have meddled in the matter. It was madness!"

"What is to happen to me?" she whispered, dreading the answer.

William spoke tersely. "You are committed to my charge and we are commanded to leave for Raglan as soon as you are well enough to travel. Once there, I will be responsible for your conduct. I hope you realize that you have ruined me and put an end to all my hopes and prospects here at court!"

"I am very sorry," Kate said, and began weeping anew.

William ignored her distress. "There is another thing you must tell me. My lord of Lincoln told the King's officers that your meeting with him was but a lovers' tryst. How do you explain that, wife?"

Kate had to think quickly. "He is covering up for me, which is most chivalrous of him. I saw him at the stables and sent him a message asking him to meet with me," she lied. "He did not know the reason, I swear it."

"You did what? You deliberately embroiled a lord who was staunch in your father's cause in your nonsensical quest?"

"I was desperate to find out if the princes had been in his charge," she explained, wondering how much angrier William would be if he knew that Queen Elizabeth had been embroiled also. She wondered if Kat Haute had learned anything of interest from the Queen. Well, she was unlikely to find out now, she thought dejectedly. William would be watching her like a hawk.

"But why, not having any clue as to the reason you wished to see him, should the earl have told the council that it was a lovers' tryst?" William persisted, and Kate's resistance collapsed. John was safe—her husband would not dare challenge him, under a cloud as he was; as for herself, matters could not get very much worse than they already were.

"Because it was," she admitted. "He and I have loved each other secretly for a long time."

INTERLUDE

February 1562, Whitehall Palace

"Madam, I beg of you, if you will not marry, to name your successor," Cecil pleads, looking drawn with exhaustion. "The matter is now urgent."

"In a matter most unpleasing to me, your concern alone is welcome," Queen Elizabeth says doggedly. They have been wrangling for hours now, it is now two in the morning, and all Cecil wants to do is collapse into bed.

"The choice remains an unenviable one," his mistress sighs. "Mary, Queen of Scots, Katherine Grey, or Lady Lennox." Lady Lennox is the Queen's cousin, and aunt of the Queen of Scots.

"Your father King Henry excluded the Scottish line from the Act of Succession," Cecil reminds her. "And even if he had not, Queen Mary is a stranger, born out of this realm, and cannot inherit the crown."

"But Lady Lennox was born just south of the border; and she thinks she can, hence her impudence in boasting about her claim."

"It is not possible for her to succeed, under the terms of the Act," Cecil insists. "Will Your Majesty now proceed against her?"

"We will have her in the Tower for now, to teach her a lesson."

"That leaves the Lady Katherine and her son."

Elizabeth fumes. "She should not have a son!"

"In some quarters he is seen as a likely successor," Cecil says cautiously. He could add that there have also been calls for Elizabeth to be overthrown, so that this Protestant boy can be raised as a king, with his mother as nominal regent. But he remains silent. Those offenders—and they are a minority—will be dealt with efficiently and their sedition punished. There will be a few ears lopped in the weeks to come.

"Never!" the Queen snaps. "I'll not acknowledge a bastard as my successor. And I will never allow that false, vain girl to succeed me."

"Then, madam, with respect, who is there? You have rejected all other possibilities."

"I'll not have *her*. Her title to the crown is weak, as her right to the succession was invalidated by her father's attainder. As the lesser of two evils, I would prefer Mary, Queen of Scots. I believe the majority favor her."

Cecil sighs inwardly, exasperated. Tomorrow Her Majesty will no doubt change her mind again. This wrangling is not so much about lawful right as about personal animosity—and fear. Elizabeth, he knows, has never felt secure on her throne.

"What of the Lady Katherine?" he asks gently. "What happens now?"

"You say the minister can't be traced, so we will have the findings of the Privy Council laid before the Archbishop of Canterbury. He can examine the prisoners again at Lambeth Palace, and judge of their infamous intercourse and pretended wedlock. Mind ye, Cecil, they are to be taken there under guard, and they are not to speak to each other, or anyone else."

"I will convey Your Majesty's orders," Cecil says. At last they are getting somewhere.

KATHERINE

February 1562, Tower of London

When Sir Edward Warner presents himself in the morning, I am hollow-eyed from lack of sleep, but eager to talk about Thomas More's history. And I have something to tell him that is possibly of some import.

"You have read it already?" he asks in surprise.

"I could not put it down. Sir Edward, you believe this to be a true account, don't you?"

"Aye, my lady. Sir Thomas More had a reputation for honesty and was renowned throughout Christendom for his scholarship. He would not have written this book just to please his sovereign; as you well know, he lost his head for defying Henry VIII. He was an independent thinker who lived by his conscience, even though you and I, being of the new faith, would hold him to be largely in error. So I am inclined to believe much of what he writes."

"Much? Not all, then."

"Only because he himself says he divined upon conjectures in parts. But he makes it plain where he does that. The rest of it, which he recounts as fact, sounds credible. Why make the distinction if it was all a fiction? Why would More have made it up? What motive could he have had?"

"None that I can think of. But what I cannot fathom is how he got his information."

"It's obvious that he got a lot of it firsthand, although, probably for obvious reasons, he does not name his sources. He would have known a wide circle of people at court. And listen to this, which he writes at the beginning: 'I shall rehearse you the dolorous end of these babes, after what I have heard by such men and such means as methinks it must be true.' He says he got his information from 'them that knew much and had little cause to lie.'"

"It sounds as if he went to a great deal of trouble to find out the truth."

"He states he relied on a confession made by Sir James Tyrell," Sir Edward says. "Tyrell was executed by Henry VII."

"Because he murdered the princes?"

"No, my lady. It was for treason, because he had aided and abetted two malcontents, the brothers of the Earl of Lincoln. More says that when Tyrell was in the Tower, he confessed to the murder of the princes, as did Dighton, but neither could tell their interrogators where the bodies were because they both believed they had been reburied secretly."

"I doubt Henry VII was happy to hear that."

"I'm sure he was not. But at least he now knew that the princes were dead—too late, of course, to spare him years of anxiety over the pretender Warbeck, whom he had finally executed. It's interesting that More apparently spoke with John Dighton, who was still alive when he wrote his book; More clearly thought him a villain, and predicted he was likely to be hanged."

"It's odd that Henry didn't have Dighton executed too. After all, he also confessed to the murders."

"Aye, but maybe, as we have said before, Henry feared to draw public attention to the princes. Without any bodies, there was no proof that they were dead; and that very lack of proof might have been the spur for anyone else to set themselves up as a pretender. Henry had had his fill of pretenders by then."

"Sir Edward," I venture, "where do you think the princes might have been buried?"

"Well, More describes their first place of burial in detail. At the stair foot, deep under the ground, beneath a great heap of stones. Then they were supposedly dug up and reburied by Brackenbury's priest." He frowns. "But would a lone priest be able to shift all that rubble and dig down deep to where the bodies lay? It doesn't sound likely, unless Brackenbury aided him, but Brackenbury had made it clear he wanted no part in the murders. And involving anyone else would have been too risky. Even with two of them it would have been a mighty task. So I suspect this tale was put about to deflect attempts to find the bodies, and that they are still there, under a stairway in the Tower."

"That makes sense. But where?"

"My lady, there are several staircases in Caesar's Tower. If you will excuse me, I will go now and check for signs that any have been disturbed." And with that, Sir Edward hastens from the room, eager as a schoolboy dismissed from lessons.

It seems ages before he returns, his face downcast.

"Nothing!" he declares. "I checked the bottom of every stair, and there was no sign that any were ever dug up. Except perhaps for the one in the fore building that houses the entrance to Caesar's Tower. There was a cracked paving stone there, but that is only to be expected, with so many people coming and going."

He sits down heavily. "I think we must accept that we are at the end of our quest, and that Thomas More's history is the closest to the truth we are likely to get."

"If only we knew where he got all that information," I say. "I hate loose ends. But Sir Edward, before you go, I must tell you something that may be significant, or not—I don't know. Pray sit down. I have been puzzling for some time about where I had seen the name Tyrell— other than in books. And Brackenbury too seemed familiar. Last night, it came to me." I have his attention now.

"Before my father was granted Sheen Priory by King Edward, he owned a house in London, near the Tower. Bath Place, it was called, or the Minories, because it had been a convent of nuns—the Minoresses—before the monasteries were dissolved by King Henry. My father had the house for several years, by the favor of King Edward. Previously, it had been owned by the Bishop of Bath, who'd converted part of it into a mansion and renamed it Bath Place. But we always called it the Minories."

"Did you lodge there often, my lady?"

"Yes, Sir Edward, we stayed there many times when we came to London from Leicestershire. It is a goodly property, with many fine buildings around the great house, and the church still standing. It is of the church that I wish to speak. We used it as our chapel. Although all the Popish statues and ornaments had been removed, some of the old tombs remained. I used to be fascinated by the stone effigies of ladies in old-fashioned dress. They looked so beautiful and serene, with their alabaster faces and their hands joined in prayer. And I liked to read the inscriptions on the tombs, although I struggled with those because they were in Latin. But my sister Jane would translate them for me. Sir Edward, I remember now the names on two of those tombs: Mary Tyrell and Elizabeth Brackenbury. Is that not a coincidence? Or maybe it is more than that!"

Sir Edward considers. "It may well be. Certainly it bears investigating. My lady, forgive me for asking something that will distress you, but was this house—the Minories—confiscated at your father's death?"

"No. He had already conveyed it to his younger brother, my uncle, Lord John Grey, who still owns it today."

"I wonder if I might pay him a visit."

"I pray you, do not do so on my account," I ask fervently. "He did not want to know us after my father's execution. You will get short shrift from him if you mention my name."

"Then I shall ask if I may see the church, having heard it has some historic tombs." Sir Edward smiles, rising to his feet. "I will go this afternoon."

"Fare you well, sir," I say. "And pay no attention to my uncle's rude manner."

The bells of All Hallows' Church are striking six when the lieutenant returns. I rise hastily to greet him.

"Sir Edward! Did you gain entry to the Minories?"

"Indeed I did, my lady. I was lucky: his lordship was not there; he has gone to his house in Essex. But his steward willingly admitted me to the church, and left me alone to look around. He even brought me candles when it got dark."

"Did you see the tombs?" I ask.

"Aye, and I was surprised to see them in such good condition. Many were broken up after the Dissolution. You were right: Mary Tyrell and Elizabeth Brackenbury are there, and there are others too, as you may remember: the grandest tomb was that of Elizabeth Talbot, Duchess of Norfolk, who died in 1506."

"I remember that one. Her effigy shows her in widow's weeds."

"Indeed it does. And nearby is the tomb of a young girl, Anne Mowbray. According to the inscription, she was Duchess of York."

"Duchess of York? Yes, I remember that one too. But how could this Anne Mowbray have been Duchess of York? The only Duchess of York I know of was Cecily Neville."

"I cannot say. I have never heard of Anne Mowbray, and apart from Duchess Cecily's husband, Richard Plantagenet, the only other dukes of York I know of are the younger of the Princes in the Tower, and

King Henry VIII, who was given the title when he was a child. I will make some inquiries—someone must know. In the meantime, I wanted to ask if you recalled any of the other tombs. What of Joyce Lee, a widow, who died in 1507?"

"I remember her tomb, because it had a brass showing a lady in nun's attire."

"That is correct. My lady, it is possible—given the coincidence of the names—that you are right and there is a link between some, if not all, of these ladies, and that in some way they are connected with the fate of the princes."

"But how will we find that out?" I ask, perplexed.

"There is one chance," he tells me. "On my way out, I fell to talking with the steward about the tombs, saying how impressive they were; he said they were a fine collection, but not much prized these days. Then he told me that an old lady comes regularly to the church to pray, and often lingers by them. Lord John doesn't mind her coming, as she's harmless enough, and they've gotten used to her over the years. They think she was abbess at the Minories, many years ago. That would explain her interest. The steward said she could probably tell me more about the tombs. He said he'd look out for her and ask if she would meet with me. If she agrees, he'll send a boy 'round." Sir Edward fixes his gaze on me. "My lady, she may be of no help whatsoever. She may not even consent to see me. But it's worth asking."

"Indeed it is," I agree. Inwardly, though, I hold out little hope. Even if this woman had been abbess of the Minoresses' convent, she was hardly likely to have been there when Mary Tyrell, Elizabeth Brackenbury, and the rest were alive, or to have known anything about them. They died more than fifty years ago, their secrets—if they had any—no doubt buried in the grave with them. And the dead keep their secrets very well.

KATE

December 1485–March 1487, Raglan Castle

The journey back to Wales, in the depths of winter, had been a dreadful one. Since his outburst of jealous rage when he had learned of her love for John and lashed out at her, even as she lay in her bed, weak after her miscarriage, William had cut himself off from Kate. It was as well they had with them that comfortable litter he'd provided to take her to court, because she'd doubted he would have been so solicitous now. She had endured the endless, jolting miles huddled in her cloak and the cushions, with Gwenllian pressing close for warmth, for the weather was icy.

Begrudgingly, William had agreed to frequent stops at inns and monasteries along the way, for Kate was fatigued after her ordeal, and still bleeding a little, so needed to change her clouts. Whenever they stopped, or ate, or bedded down for the night, he treated her with indifferent courtesy. A proud man, he had not wanted to parade their estrangement to the world. But he would not share her bed, and slept with his men in their quarters.

At Westminster he had demanded to know how far the affair with John had gone. Had they ever lain together? She told him, quite truthfully, that she had never betrayed her marriage bed. He'd looked at her suspiciously, his face full of rage and pain, but he had not pressed her further. Instead, he had pronounced that the loss of her child, and the King's displeasure, were a judgment on her for her wicked, foolish behavior. And she must forget the Earl of Lincoln, because, by God, she would never set eyes on him again.

She had accepted her fate. She did not care what happened to her now, so long as John was safe. She'd prayed he had not fallen foul of the King as a result of her rashness. She'd wished there was some way of finding out if any measures had been taken against him, but that was impossible. William made sure he stayed with her, vigilant and unrelenting, throughout the days of her recovery at Westminster. The only visitor he'd allowed was Kat, who had to return to her house at Harpenden on the day after Kate's miscarriage, and came beforehand to see how she fared.

"Write to me, please, if your lord will permit," she had said, looking hopefully at William. "Remember, if I may do you any service, you have only to ask." She'd kissed Kate then, and Kate had clung to her, not wanting to let go of this mother whom she barely knew, and who—like everyone else she held dear—was being cruelly parted from her. That was how it seemed.

"Farewell!" she had cried. "Pray for me!"

"I will, never fear," promised Kat, and was gone.

Back inside the stout walls of Raglan, beyond which she had been told she must not go, she knew despair, keener than before. The Dowager Countess showed her a pained civility rather than her customary warmth, and young Elizabeth took her cue from that. All Kate's attempts to explain her actions met with studied evasion.

Only to Mattie, dear, comfortable Mattie, great with child now, could she unburden herself, and it was Mattie who saw her through those dark days of winter, wept with her for her lost babe, and listened to the outpouring of her fears for John. Without Mattie, she was certain, she would never have gotten through that awful time without going mad.

At table, William barely acknowledged her. In the evenings he made it clear that her presence was not welcome by the fire. When visitors called, she was made to keep to her chamber. Any purchases she required had to be made by Mattie, on her behalf, in the village or from the peddlers who came offering their wares and bringing news; and clearly there were to be no fine new gowns or jewels. Had it not been for the King commanding William to keep her in his custody, Kate was sure he would have consigned her to a nunnery.

Her marriage now seemed a life sentence. What had happened to the carefree, headstrong young girl she had once been? She was sixteen now, and felt old; and if life went on like this, she *would* be old, long before her time.

The slow, intolerable months passed. Thanks to Kat Haute's letters, doggedly scrutinized by William, and to Mattie, that inveterate gossip, she was able to keep abreast of news—weeks late—from the outside world, to which she listened with listless apathy. In the early spring, as the daffodils opened their faces to the strengthening sun, she learned from Kat that Henry Tudor had at last married Elizabeth of York. Poor Elizabeth, she thought—much joy she will get of him—and she wondered if the new Queen puzzled and fretted as much as she herself had over the fate of the princes, her brothers. But she, Kate, had put all that behind her now, of necessity.

She wondered if she would ever hear news of John; she desired the assurance of his health and prosperity more than anything else in the world. If she could be granted that boon, she would rest content.

And then her prayers were answered.

Mattie, nearing her time but as busy about her duties as ever, came hastening to Kate's chamber one bright day in May; she had been at the market.

"A letter's come for you," she announced. *"He* says you can have it." She would never, if she could help it, refer to her master by his rightful title.

It was from Kat. *The King has passed this way on progress to the North,* she wrote, *and I heard mention that the Earl of Lincoln was of the company and much in favor.*

"Thanks be to God!" Kate breathed with heartfelt relief. At least John had managed to convince Henry Tudor of his innocence.

"Well, I'm sure you're pleased to hear that, my lady!" Mattie smiled.

She was, oh, she was!

But after that, life went on as grimly as it had for months, and the only lightening of Kate's existence came when Mattie gave birth to a daughter in the balmy days of early summer; yet even that was a bittersweet thing, for, seeing her maid with the child at her breast, Kate could not but be reminded of the infant she had lost, who would have been of a similar age had he lived.

One night, William appeared in his nightgown at her chamber door, carrying a candle. His ferret face looked gaunt in its flickering light.

"My lord?" Kate rose up in the bed, alarmed.

"I would speak with you," he said coldly, looming over her. "I have received some news that will interest you. Your lover, the Earl of Lincoln, has married my niece, Margaret FitzAlan, Arundel's daughter. You had best forget him now, for he is lost to you for good."

He will never be lost to me, she thought fiercely, trying not to betray the engulfing emotion she felt. *Our hearts are one for always: we vowed it.*

"It is of no moment to me, this news," she said, and meant it, knowing this marriage could mean nothing to John.

"Then, since we are constrained to live together, you will not shrink from doing your duty, as my wife," William said, abruptly dousing the candle, stripping off his nightgown, and climbing into bed beside her, much to her dismay. "I am prepared to accept that you did not betray your marriage vows," he continued, "and for that reason I am willing to take you back and use you as my wife. I need an heir—and a man must live!"

He mounted her then, without further preamble, driving into her as if he meant to punish her for all the hurts she had done him. She bore it in silence, as best she could, not daring to betray by any slight gesture how unwelcome it was to her. She had long ago learned to detach herself from what he did to her in bed; after all, it was not as if this was a new thing. She had to force herself not to think of how joyous it had been with John. That way lay insanity.

When he had finished, William got up without a word, put on his robe, and went back to his own chamber. In the morning, if she had expected some improvement in his attitude toward her, she would have been disappointed, for he ignored her as before, and continued to do so. The only difference now was that he kept coming to her at night, demanding sex in his laconic, boorish way, and riding her as if he hated her.

Early in October, as the leaves were turning wondrous shades of red and gold, and autumn returned to the land, Mattie, her apple-cheeked babe on her hip, brought another letter from Kat with news of the birth of a prince to the Queen.

"He's to be called after King Arthur," Kate said. "An auspicious name. No doubt the Tudor wishes to invest his dynasty with some semblance of Arthur's greatness." Her tone was sarcastic.

In November, Kate realized that she was to bear another child. A grandson for my father at last, she thought, and resolved heartily to take up her pen again and commit to paper, for the benefit of this unborn innocent, her convictions about the murder of the princes. The knowledge of her pregnancy had reenergized her and given her new hope. At last she had something to live for.

"I am with child," she told William when next he came to her bed. He nodded slowly.

"That is good news," he said eventually. "I will not trouble you tonight, then." Or any other night, she realized thankfully—not while she was carrying his seed. He was too careful a husband to break that sanction. Yet he seemed hesitant, reluctant to go from her.

"You are well?" he asked, his manner awkward. Of course his concern was for his son—the son he now hoped was growing inside her.

"Yes, my lord, I am well. A little sick in the mornings, as before, but that is nothing."

"Good," he said, and paused again. "Well, wife, if there is anything you need for your comfort, let me know." Then he was gone. They were the first kind words he had spoken to her in a year; and she knew for a certainty that he would have extended the same consideration to his mare, had she been in foal.

Later that month a carter came to Raglan bringing strange tidings.

"It's certain that the Earl of Warwick has escaped from the Tower," he told the crowd that had gathered around him in the courtyard. "The word is everywhere. And it's said that more will be heard of Warwick afore long!"

"I do not believe it," Kate said to Mattie as they walked away. "Warwick would not know how to start a rebellion."

"But what if others are using him?" Mattie pondered. "It's been done before, as you well know, my lady."

"But would the people really prefer poor Warwick, a backward boy of eleven years, to Henry Tudor, a man of mature age and proven experience?"

"The people favor right over might!" Mattie declared stoutly.

"I wonder if they care, so long as there is peace, and taxes are not too burdensome," Kate retorted. She felt tired. This new pregnancy was sapping her strength, and she needed to lie down. She seemed to spend most of her time resting these days. And William was so anxious about this child surviving that he kept urging her to do so.

He was kinder with her now, a little less unbending. His mother too had relented toward her, and something of their old friendship had revived. And that brought Elizabeth running back, eager to be friendly. Time is a great healer, thought Kate, and this pregnancy had brought its own blessings. But the greatest blessing, she knew, would be to see John's face once more.

Christmas came and went, a much merrier occasion than it had been the previous year. Then there were the dead weeks of January, when the countryside lay covered with snow or frost and the peasants stayed huddled in their cottages, eking out the stores they had put by for the winter and biding their time until February arrived, and with it Plow Monday, when they would venture forth to work the fields again.

At the end of February another letter arrived from Harpenden. Kat sounded worried. She wrote that the King had deprived Elizabeth Wydeville of her lands, and the Dowager Queen had retired with only a small pension to the abbey of Bermondsey. Why? wondered Kate. What could Elizabeth Wydeville have done to deserve being stripped of her revenues? Only last autumn she had stood godmother to Prince Arthur. Was it a threat, a warning to keep her mouth shut?

But there was more disconcerting news as Kate read on. Kat had recently been at court with her husband.

The Lady Margaret rules all there. The King is no very indulgent husband to the Queen. His aversion to the House of York is such that it finds place not only in his politics but in his chamber and his bed. To the Queen, he is not at all uxorious. It is said she leads a miserable and

cheerless life, and certes she does not look a happy woman. She is be-
loved by the people because she is powerless and kept in subjection by
the Lady Margaret, whose influence she resents.

Did Elizabeth of York too know more than was good for her? Did
Henry Tudor keep her in this silken bondage because he knew—or
feared—that she possessed dangerous knowledge of the fate, or the
whereabouts, of her brothers?

The Dowager Countess, who had brought the letter, was standing
by, and Kate showed it to her. "It saddens me that Henry should treat
his Queen so distrustfully," Anne said. "It would not have been so had
he married our Maud, but then Maud would not have brought him a
crown."

"It seems strange that he treats both his wife and his mother-in-law
so unkindly," Kate said. "It is as if he does not trust them."

"He was ever a suspicious child," the countess said. "He grew up
under the shadow of civil war, a pawn in a game of kings. It is only
natural for him to wish to preempt any threat to his security. After all,
both the Queen and her mother are of the House of York, and both
meddled in high affairs in the last reign. As you know, your father, King
Richard, planned at one time to marry Elizabeth of York, and she, I
heard, was hot for it; but when he abandoned the plan, her love seemed
to turn to hate. No doubt she felt scorned. There was talk that she
began plotting with Lord Stanley on Henry's behalf. William told me."

Kate listened aghast: she had not known of this. No wonder Henry
Tudor kept his Queen in subjection; he must have known all about her
intrigues, and the fact that she had been hot for King Richard, as Anne
had put it.

Kate's babe had just quickened in her womb when another letter arrived from Kat, who informed her that the atmosphere at court was
tense because a young man had appeared in Ireland, calling himself
the Earl of Warwick and the rightful King of England:

But he cannot be the Earl of Warwick, because King Henry has just
had the true Earl of Warwick taken out of the Tower for a day and

paraded through the streets of London to prove to the people that the other is an imposter. James and I were up in London, and we went to see Warwick; I can tell you it was certainly him.

Two days later William rose to his feet at the dinner table and called for silence. The chatter of his household subsided about him as he spoke gravely.

"I have received a communication from the King's Council." He looked briefly at Kate, his eyes cold, before addressing the company. "I am commanded to place this castle in readiness against a possible invasion. Henceforth, all of you—knights, retainers, squires, even menials—must be on alert. The Earl of Lincoln has fled the realm and is reported to have sought refuge with his aunt, the Duchess Margaret, in Flanders. He is suspected of having nurtured and instructed the Irish pretender, whose real name is Lambert Simnel, in a traitorous conspiracy against the King. It stands to reason, of course," he went on. "Lincoln's house at Ewelme is near to Oxford, where the Simnel conspiracy was first plotted. There can be little doubt that he was the author of it. But notwithstanding the fact that the King has lately shown the real Earl of Warwick to the people, there are still ignorant fools who believe this Simnel really is him. Thus we must make ready, and be vigilant, in case the traitor Lincoln raises an army in Flanders and brings Simnel over from Ireland to press his false claim."

He sat down and glared at a white-faced Kate. "Now you can see what a fine gentleman you condescended to," he growled. "It is as well you have put all that folly behind you, for you may rest assured he will be dealt with as he deserves."

KATHERINE

May 1562, Tower of London

Sir Edward Warner has been summoned to court; he left after break-fast. The summons could be for a variety of reasons, but of course I am wondering if it concerns me and Ned. Ever since those painful examinations before Archbishop Parker, three months ago, when I briefly glimpsed my beloved again as we were conveyed in separate barges up the Thames, and then questioned at different times, going over the same ground as before, I have been fretting about the outcome. Surely there is now no question of us being accused of treason? If they had meant to do that, they would have done it long ago. And no one has actually used the word treason; they all focus on our marriage. They are obsessed with witnesses and the calling of banns and written proof. But supposing this investigation deems our marriage treasonable? What will happen to us then? And what of my poor child? Again, I cannot help thinking of the fate of the princes.

Thus turn my thoughts, so I am nearly in a frenzy by the time Sir Edward returns, and when I see his grave face, I feel I might faint with terror.

"Calm yourself, my lady," he says. "Sit down, I pray you. You are not in any danger, but the news is not what you will want to hear. I have had it from the Queen's Majesty herself."

I hold my breath, anguished with suspense. Sir Edward looks pityingly on me.

"I am commanded by her to tell you that the Archbishop of Canterbury has found that, in the absence of any documents or witnesses, your marriage to Lord Hertford cannot be proved, wherefore it has been declared no marriage, and your carnal copulation unlawful and worthy of punishment. I regret that it is my duty to inform you that his Grace of Canterbury has censured you and Lord Hertford for fornication, and that you have both been sentenced to be imprisoned here in the Tower at Her Majesty's pleasure." He falls silent, looking as if he would rather be anywhere else.

This is calamitous and unjust. I can barely believe it. "We *were* married!" I cry. "I am no fornicator, believe me. Before God, Sir Edward, we have been sharply handled; and the lack of proofs was our misfortune, not any fault in us. Why will they not believe us?"

"I am very sorry for you, my lady," the lieutenant says.

"They have intended this all along," I wail, with sudden clarity. "They have sought to discredit me. Oh, the very shame of it! How shall I hold my head up after this? And my little son, what is he now? What shall become of him?"

Sir Edward says nothing. He does not need to. The word "bastard" hangs mockingly in the air between us.

"Tell me, Lieutenant," I ask in bitterness, "is it now the fashion for those accused of fornication to be imprisoned in the Tower? Because if so, I wonder why half the world is not in here! And if that is all Ned and I are guilty of, then why cannot we be released?"

"In faith, I do not know, my lady. I understand your anger. You have suffered much."

"Maybe they fear that if we are freed, we will wed in another ceremony that none can dispute! Yes, that is why they are keeping us locked up! Have you seen my lord—what does he say?"

"He says he will appeal against the sentence. Now, madam, I pray you, rest a little. You are overwrought, and no wonder." Shaking his grizzly head, Sir Edward takes his leave. He clearly wants no part in this.

My life has become a nightmare. I am eaten up by the injustice of it all. I *am* married in the sight of God, and He knows the truth of it. I will *not* be labeled fornicator or anything else! And my child *is* lawfully begotten. When I get out of this place, I will fight this ruling in the courts, and defy the highest in the land to have the truth known, and neither Queen Elizabeth nor her entire Privy Council shall stop me!

Mrs. Ellen and the other women try to comfort me. The lieutenant performs many small kindnesses to cheer me. He even refrains from upbraiding my pets for making puddles on the floor or ripping the upholstery. But I am a raging tempest, either in a storm of weeping or a storm of fury. I snap at everyone, even my angry, bawling son. I could not feel more wretched.

I am lying abed one night and looking miserably at the moon beyond my window, wondering if I will hear those disembodied voices again, when the door opens and there is Ned, alone.

"I bribed my guards!" he whispers. They are the first words he has uttered to me in over a year. "I would comfort you, my dear wife, and lie with you!" And in two bounds he is at my bedside, gathering me in his arms and holding me as if he will never let me go. And I, for my part, am passionately kissing him back, clutching at him and running my fingers over his body, unable to believe he is really here.

"Oh, my sweet Ned!" I cry.

For an hour, a little hour, the world belongs to us, and nothing else exists. Oh, how we love each other, naked between the sheets, tumbling over and over, hands and lips touching, caressing, pleasing, and then our bodies locking in rapture.

"It has been so long, my love," Ned murmurs as we lie stretched out across the rumpled mattress afterward, my head on his belly, he stroking my hair.

"I do not know how I have borne it," I tell him.

The babe awakens and snuffles.

"How is my son?" Ned asks, rising up and leaning over to the cradle. "Hello, Edward! You are a fine young lord!" I watch them together for a moment, as Ned picks up the child, strokes his fine hair, and tries to make him smile. I am filled with happiness to see them thus, and will not spoil it by pointing out that Edward is no longer legally a young lord.

"Ned," I ask, "did the Queen give permission for us to be together?"

"No, but Sir Edward said he would allow it. He said there was no reason why we should not console one another."

My heart swells with gratitude. "He is a good man."

"He says we may meet whenever we please, so long as I pay the guards and take care to be discreet."

"He is a true friend, and has proved it in many ways, but this is the greatest blessing he has brought us," I say, and we fall to kissing again until a light tap on the door warns us that Ned must depart.

The lieutenant comes with news for me.

"My lady, I have just heard from the steward at the Minories. The old lady has returned; she has not been in good health, which was why he had not seen her. He told her about my interest in the tombs and the church, and she said she would gladly meet with me to tell me more about their history."

"That is encouraging news!" I exclaim. "I never thought to hear more of her."

"Well, you shall. I will invite her here, and you may meet her. My orders are to allow no one but your attendants to see you, but I know I can trust you, my lady—and I myself will be present to ensure you behave yourself!"

"Of course, Sir Edward!" I say warmly. "I will speak to her only of the tombs, I promise."

"Her name is Elizabeth Savage. The steward was right—she was the last abbess of the Minoresses' convent. Naturally, she does not like that to be known, so we will not mention it unless she does."

Can this old lady help us in our quest? She thinks she is coming to discuss some old tombs, not the disappearance of the princes. And she will surely be startled to meet me, probably one of the most notorious prisoners in the kingdom right now!

KATE

June 1487, Raglan Castle

News came regularly to the castle, by letter or word of mouth, and the news nowadays was momentous—but, for Kate, distressing. John was in Ireland with a Flemish army. Under his auspices, Lambert Simnel, despite being branded an imposter by the King, had been crowned as Edward VI in Dublin Cathedral late the previous month. Henry Tudor had mobilized his forces against an invasion.

Rumors and speculation were rampant everywhere, and the country, which had been in a ferment of uncertainty for weeks, now erupted in panic at the imminent prospect of invasion.

Even though Kate had been careful to express no word of support for John and the rebels, and had voiced her own fears about the conflict to come, William remained cold toward her, acting almost as if it were her fault that her sometime lover was in rebellion against the King. As if she could do anything to prevent it, she thought resentfully. She had not seen John in more than a year and a half, and there had been no communication at all between them. She wondered if he still cherished her memory, as she did his, or if his marriage had jolted him into reality and caused him to put his youthful passions behind him. She wondered too if he had spoken out in her defense after her arrest. The fact that he had stayed in favor with the Tudor argued that he had not. But she could not believe he had forsaken her. He would have reasoned that pragmatism was the safest course for them both.

Why was he backing the claims of Simnel so vigorously, and at such peril to himself? He must have heard that the Tudor had exhibited the real Warwick to the people—something her father should have done with the princes to quell the rumors that were destroying him. But perhaps her father had known what John's actions had now proved: that producing the princes alive wouldn't have made much difference anyway. Because people believe what they want to believe, she concluded. Even now, there were many, their number increasing, who held that the boy in Ireland really was Warwick.

It crossed Kate's mind that John had set up the whole charade as a pretext for claiming the throne himself. People would be more likely to rise up for Warwick, Clarence's heir, than for himself, whose claim came only through the female line. Even Henry Tudor had not accounted John a threat in the way he accounted Warwick.

Something Kat had written suggested to Kate that there was more to this matter than appeared on the surface.

It is said that the boy Simnel first claimed to be Richard, Duke of York, the younger of the Princes in the Tower, but the word is that Margaret of Burgundy refused to recognize him as York, so it was given out that he was Warwick.

But what if Simnel was in fact Richard, Duke of York? What if poor Edward V had died of the illness that was eating up his jaw, and his brother had survived in secrecy? It made sense that he had been taken to Sheriff Hutton and entrusted to John's guardianship—and that John, with his strong sense of honor, should have resolved to restore the true heir to the throne. Maybe pretending that York was Warwick was meant to dupe Henry Tudor into thinking he was dealing with a silly claim by an imposter. It was convoluted thinking, she knew, but there was so much that was mysterious about this affair of the pretender; and Kate had a strong hope that she might be nearing the end of her mission to clear her father's dishonored name. Her excitement conveyed itself to her child, which stirred within her, heavy now under her heart. The answer lay with John, she was sure. She had a strong feeling, in her bones, that Simnel was York in disguise.

KATHERINE

July 1562, Tower of London

I never thought I would ever come to regard the Tower as a bower of bliss, but that is what it became for a short time, even for us poor prisoners; and here I have enjoyed two of the happiest nights of my life, for Ned came again four nights later, and we consoled each other in the same loving ways, and were husband and wife in very truth. For that short space too we were a family, with our little boy to gladden us and take pride in. He thrives, sweet Edward, which is a joy and relief to us both.

In between those visits, we sent each other letters, expressing our pleasure to find each other still in health and unbowed after all the long months of anxiety and fear. *I long to be merry with you!* I wrote to Ned, signing myself *your most loving and faithful wife*, which I truly am, whatever the Archbishop may say.

"You could not know how I missed you too, darling, how I worried about you when I was in France," Ned told me as we lay entwined together that second night, all passion spent. His words ignited a painful memory. It was as if a cloud passed over the sun.

I could not help myself. I had to ask. "Those bracelets . . ."

"Bracelets? Those French ones the Queen asked me to commission? There were two for you. Did you get them?"

"The Queen commissioned them?"

"Yes, so that she and her ladies should be gay on the progress. That's what she wrote."

"Yes, I did get them. I just wanted to thank you." There was no need to question him. All had become clear. Elizabeth, to spite me, must have given her ladies to believe that Ned had sent them the bracelets as love tokens. So all was well between my love and me.

But last night Ned arrived to find my door locked and me weeping with frustration inside.

"Mayhap your guards have taken fright," he called softly, and verily I believed they had. But this morning Sir Edward presents himself, looking grave. There can be no more clandestine trysts. A new order has just come direct from the Queen, forbidding Ned and me to meet.

I miss Ned desperately. But at least our letters are not forbidden. *I long to be with you again, my sweet bedfellow,* I write. Ned responds in kind and sends me a book. *This is no small jewel to me,* I tell him. *I will read it at once, with my heart, as well as with my eyes.*

He writes of his fears that I will be constrained to forget him. Oh, no, no, my sweet lord, I breathe—that could never happen. I ask in reply:

Do you think I could ever forget all that is past between us? No, surely I cannot, but bear in memory far more than you think. And I have good cause to do so, when I call to mind what a husband I have in you, and my hard fate to have missed the having of so good a one.

Our brief idyll has ended, but soon I am dismayed to discover that there will be consequences. For I am with child again, and once more in terror lest I be found out. Some may think me a fool, but I had been so overjoyed to be reunited with my love that I let caution and reason fly into the wind.

When first I suspect my condition, I confide my fears to Ned, and he writes back, expressing defiant joy at the news. *This will be the true proof of our marriage,* he asserts.

I confess my state to my women—Mrs. Ellen, who deals with my linen, has already guessed—and then to Sir Edward. The poor man is utterly horrified.

"Great God in Heaven, we are all undone!" he declares, wringing his hands. "When this gets out, it will most grievously offend the Queen's Majesty, and with even more cause this time."

"I fear we will be punished heavily for it," I say, trembling and nauseous.

"Aye, and myself too."

I hang my head. This is not a fit reward for his kindness. Then an idea comes to me—an idea that might just work!

"Sir Edward, could this pregnancy not be kept a secret? Only my women and my husband know. I am straitly confined here, allowed to see no one, and once the babe is born, it can be sent out to nurse privily, and no one the wiser."

The lieutenant thinks about this, scratching his head in distress. "It is the only safe solution," he agrees, his ruddy cheeks pale. But we both know we are running a terrible risk.

After supper, Sir Edward appears again, ushering in an elderly lady wearing a plain gray woolen townswoman's gown with a white linen coif. Elizabeth Savage at last! Her face is pale and thin, the eyes light blue, the lips drawn down by fine lines, and her hands are clasped tightly before her.

She curtsies to me. She knows who I am. Her face is impassive, her eyes downcast, unreadable. It is easy to see that she was once a nun.

I take the chair by the fireside and invite her to be seated.

"Mistress Savage, the Lady Katherine is also interested in the tombs, so I thought we could discuss them together," the lieutenant explains.

Elizabeth Savage nods but says nothing. Maybe she was taught in her convent only to speak when necessary.

"My father once owned the Minories," I explain, "and I stayed there often when I was younger. There are some great ladies buried in the church. I remember seeing their tombs as a child, but cannot recall all their names."

A shadow crosses Mistress Savage's already wary face. *She knows something,* I think.

"They are particularly interesting monuments," Sir Edward puts in.

"Yet it is not just the tombs we wish to know about, but the women who were buried in them. We know you visit these tombs often. We wondered if you had any knowledge of those ladies."

"I know nothing, sir," the woman says, too quickly. I notice that her accent is refined, indicating gentle birth. She looks like a cornered deer.

"Please, mistress," I intervene. "This matter may concern a great wrong that was done many years ago to two kinsmen of mine. You will have heard of the Princes in the Tower . . ."

Mistress Savage sucks in her breath. Her involuntary response gives her away, and she knows it. "What is this about?" she asks. "Why are you asking me about that?"

"You know something about the matter, don't you?" the lieutenant says gently. "We had a suspicion you might." It is easy to see that he is experienced in the business of questioning people. "Come, there is nothing to fear, I assure you. This is no official inquiry. I, and my lady here, merely have an interest in finding out the truth. We have been investigating the matter privily for some time now. The fate of the princes is a mystery that has long intrigued us both." He leans forward. "You were the last abbess of the Minories. You visit those tombs often. I wonder why. I also believe that if anyone can tell us if there is a connection between them and the fate of the princes, it is you."

"I know nothing," says Elizabeth Savage again, flushing.

"Is that so?" Sir Edward asks. "Then why are you on the defensive? Why did you look so discomfited just now when the princes were mentioned? Madam, I know you can help us. And we would respect your confidence."

"We read Sir Thomas More's history," I add, "and I made the connection between the names Tyrell and Brackenbury and the tombs in the church. I recalled seeing the same names there when I was a child, and it seemed more than coincidental that they appeared in More's account."

"It is, my lady!" Elizabeth Savage blurts out. "But what I know I have kept to myself for many years now. It does a body no good to get tangled up in the affairs of the great. I reckon I managed pretty well when King Henry closed down the Minories, making sure the sisters left without any fuss and the surrender went smoothly. I got my pension, and since then I've kept quiet. If I were to tell you the secrets I have harbored all these years, I would need your absolute assurance that they would go no further than this room."

"I give you that assurance," I promise her.

"You have my word on that too," Sir Edward declares. "We have no cause to discuss this with anyone else."

Elizabeth Savage seems still to be struggling with herself, but then her resolve stiffens. "Very well," she says. "I will tell you what I know— and what no one else but me knows, the others having long since gone to their rest." And she tells us her extraordinary story.

"I was born at the turn of the century; my father was a courtier—we were gentry from Worcestershire. My cousin Nan served Queen Anne Boleyn, and later became Lady Berkeley. My father was a younger son with no inheritance to look forward to, and his minor court office paid little, so there was only a small dowry for me."

"I was a plain girl, and no one offered for me anyway, so it was decided that I should enter the Minoresses' convent at Aldgate. I was eighteen, and unhappy at the prospect, but in time I finally settled to the life, although that of a Poor Clare nun was no easy one. At the time of my profession, Alice FitzLewes was abbess; she died in 1524, when the community elected Dame Dorothy Cumberford. She ruled for five years until her death, and then I, by the grace of God, was chosen to be her successor. I was not quite thirty, and young for such a high office, but I had a good head for business, which is always a useful asset in a religious. I remained abbess until the friary was dissolved in 1539, and since then I have been living nearby in Hart Street. I do not go to the Minories now just to see the tombs. I like to maintain my links with the convent where I spent so many years, and the church where so many of my sisters lie buried. It is a miracle that it has escaped destruction. So many religious houses have gone."

She smiles wanly at us, and for the first time I see a sweetness in that sad, narrow face.

"I'm sorry, I am apt to wander in my mind," she says, "and I am not used to company. The tombs. Yes. It is of Abbess Dorothy Cumberford that I must speak. She had been here for many years before she was elected abbess; she was chosen for her age and holiness. She was an angel—and an inveterate gossip, like many nuns. But the tale she told me was no common gossip. Indeed, it was highly sensitive information, and she only imparted it when she knew she was dying—of a canker, bravely borne without complaint, I might add. She wanted to pass on the secrets of our house to someone she could trust. And so she confided them to me, as she had guessed I would be her successor; indeed, she had expressed her wishes in that behalf to the sisters.

"When Abbess Dorothy was a young nun, there were several ladies of noble or gentle birth living in the great house in the friary close. That was nothing unusual, because in those days widows and spinsters often retired from the world to live in convents as paying guests. But some of these particular ladies had good reason to want to hide from the world, for they knew more than was good for them about what had happened to those hapless princes. I think you know who they were." Again, that sweet smile crosses her face.

"Chief among them was Elizabeth, the Dowager Duchess of Norfolk. Her daughter, Anne Mowbray, was married to Richard, Duke of York, the younger of the princes, when they were just children, but died at the age of nine. She is buried in the choir next to her mother; she'd been laid first in St. Erasmus's Chapel in Westminster Abbey, but when King Henry VII pulled that down to build a tomb house for himself, her coffin was brought to the Minories and reburied. It was the duchess her mother who erected that monument to her beloved child.

"Naturally, the duchess had retained an affection for the little prince who had been her son-in-law; she'd been dismayed when his brother was deposed by the usurper, Richard of Gloucester, and horrified when later she heard dreadful rumors about the princes being murdered; and, having good connections, she made it her business to find out the truth about their fate."

"Did she ever discover what happened to them?" I wonder.

"She did, in the end," Elizabeth Savage reveals. "She heard Sir James Tyrell's name bruited about as the princes' murderer, and made so bold as to question him about what people were saying, but he would not talk to her." Just as he had refused to talk to Katherine Plantagenet.

"Then his sister Mary came to her. Sir James had told her of the duchess 'accosting' him, as he put it, but Mary had her own suspicions, and she unburdened herself to the duchess. She thought her brother had been involved in some way, and that he had protested his innocence a little too vehemently.

"Around that time the duchess and Mary Tyrell got to know Elizabeth Brackenbury, the daughter of Sir Robert, the Constable of the Tower. She too was troubled, and eventually disclosed that her father was stricken in his conscience because he had been obliged to hand over the keys of the Tower to Sir James Tyrell for one night—and when he'd returned the next day, the princes were gone, vanished into thin air, and Sir James and all his retainers with them. Mistress Brackenbury said her father had feared the worst, because earlier on King Richard had sent a letter in which he effectively commanded the constable to do away with those poor princes. Brackenbury refused to obey, saying he would not do it even if he should be put to death for it. How King Richard reacted he never found out, but the next thing he knew, Tyrell turned up with two ruffians, demanding the keys in the King's name."

"This is very like what Sir Thomas More wrote," I say, getting up and pouring some wine from a flagon that Sir Edward had thoughtfully placed ready on the table. I hand a cup to our guest.

"Thank you," she says humbly. "You are very kind, my lady. Yes, it is much as More wrote—although he didn't reveal it all—and soon you will know why. Now Elizabeth Brackenbury was very worried about her father. She told the duchess and Mary Tyrell how the King had rewarded him for his cooperation and his silence with grants, estates, and lucrative offices, but she said he regarded them as blood money and was uneasy about accepting them. He had been loyal to Richard up to the time he ordered him to slay the princes; now he was afraid of him, for Brackenbury knew too much, and Richard had proved just how ruthless he could be. So after that time, Elizabeth said, Brackenbury took care never to put a foot wrong. He obeyed the summons to fight for Richard at Bosworth, and was killed in the battle."

"Did Brackenbury ever uncover any proof that Tyrell did murder the princes?" Sir Edward asks.

"No. All trace of the boys had gone. Even their clothes had been removed." Elizabeth Savage shakes her head sadly and sips her wine. "After Henry Tudor became King, the duchess decided to retire to the Minoresses' convent as a boarder, and she invited Elizabeth Brackenbury and Mary Tyrell to join her."

"Why did she decide to go to the Minories?" I ask.

"Her kinswoman, Lady Talbot, was already living there, and there was space in the big house to accommodate several ladies quite comfortably. In due course the other two ladies joined her, and with them came Mary Tyrell's aunt, Anne Montgomery. Her husband had supported the usurper Richard, but she now wished to dissociate herself from that allegiance, and reckoned that retiring to the Minories was the safest way.

"Sir James Tyrell, as you probably know, had long been trusted by Richard, and he apparently would have done anything to gain preferment. It was he who had brought Richard's mother-in-law to him, so that he could lock her up and gain control of her lands. It was to Tyrell's charge that Richard committed the men arrested with Lord Hastings—you know about Hastings's fate, I presume?"

We nod.

"Tyrell was one of those who guarded his sovereign day and night, sleeping on a pallet outside his bedchamber. Richard trusted him, but he was a villain. Even his sister and his aunt feared him."

Yes, I know he was a villain. Look how he had treated poor Mattie, and how disrespectful he was to her mistress.

"Tyrell had long hoped for great rewards for his devoted service, but others stood in his way. By the time Richard asked Tyrell to go to the Tower, he was so desperate for advancement he would have agreed to anything. The rest you have read in Sir Thomas More's account. It is fact, not an officially approved version, as you have surely guessed."

"So Richard did have the princes murdered?" I ask. "How do you know that for certain?"

"I will tell you; just bear with me," Mistress Savage reproves gently. "After he had carried out the murders, Tyrell was rewarded with sufficient grants and offices to ensure that he could attain the high status that he had long sought at court. In fact, he became a wealthy man, richer than many barons. He was Master of the Horse, Chamberlain of the Exchequer, and Captain of Guisnes Castle near Calais, where he took up residence. He would write from there occasionally to his sister, bragging about the honors that had been bestowed on him; but she was more concerned with how they had been won, and showed herself cool toward him.

"After Bosworth, Tyrell came over from Calais and offered Henry VII his allegiance. The King confirmed him in his post, and he went back to Guisnes Castle, where he stayed for sixteen years. But then he made the foolish mistake of helping Edmund and Richard de la Pole, Richard III's nephews, who were plotting to overthrow King Henry, and that's how he ended up in the Tower." She sighs.

"Mary did her best for her brother. Out of her small income, she paid for him to have better food and a cleaner cell, and even bribed his guards to let her visit him twice. She found him a broken and defeated man. He had been warned there was a strong case against him, and that he could not look for mercy. He had been questioned about the murder of the princes, along with John Dighton, who had helped to suffocate them. He told Mary they had both confessed to that abominable crime, and confided to her the details of what had actually happened. She had no doubt that he was speaking the truth: he was a dying man, he told her, and wished to unburden his conscience before he faced God's judgment. And indeed, he was soon afterward condemned for a traitor, and died on the block."

Mistress Savage pauses for another sip of wine. I notice how abstemiously she drinks: another discipline learned in the religious life, no doubt. I wonder fleetingly if she regrets the passing of those days, or harbors resentment at being turned out of her convent, yet I am much more preoccupied at this moment with the murder of the princes. It was as I had greatly feared: they were done to death on Richard's orders. And when I think about it, I realize that he had really had no choice but to eliminate them. Alive, they would have been a constant threat to his crown, because clearly many did not believe the precontract tale. Yet the irony was that, dead, they were even more dangerous, for rumors of their murder effectively cost Richard his throne.

"Our quest is over," Sir Edward says sadly. "I had hoped it would have a different ending."

"There is one more question I must ask," I say. "How did Sir Thomas More know all this? Did he ever meet Mary Tyrell?"

"Yes, my lady, although I do not know if he spoke with her about this matter, and she was dead by the time he came to write his book. But there was another lady living in the house in the close; her name was Joyce Lee, and he was a friend of her family. They were grocers, I think. Joyce later became a member of our order; I remember hearing that she wore a hair shirt beneath her nun's habit. More sometimes visited her when he was a young lawyer living at Bucklersbury in London, and it was she who told him the story of the princes. She was close friends with the other ladies, and they had confided it to her. At Joyce's behest, More undertook never to publish his account. I don't believe he ever finished it. Alas, who could have foretold then that he would become a world-famous scholar and statesman, or that he would end on the block? After that, others got their hands on his work, and now it is in print, and all the world can read it. At least he has not named Joyce Lee as his source. She would have been grateful for that."

Mistress Savage stands up, her tale finished. "I must go now," she says. "My dog will be hungry. He's my companion, Old Rex, all I have in the world." She smiles uncertainly.

"I thank you for coming here today," I say. "We are very grateful for your help in solving this great mystery. You know you can rely on our discretion. We will not say a word about this to anyone."

"We shall have to think of another mystery to solve, now that we know the truth about this one," Sir Edward jests.

"You won't forget your promise, sir?" the former abbess asks. "I've spent my life keeping silent and I don't want this getting out. These are matters that bear some weight even today."

"No, I will not forget," the lieutenant assures her. "Yet I do not think there would be anything to fear." Indeed, there would not. For what Elizabeth Savage has just confided can only serve to confirm the Tudors' title to the throne.

"Then farewell," she says, and makes to follow Sir Edward out.

"One thing, mistress!" I cry. "Do you know where the princes were buried?"

There is no hesitation. "Meetly deep, under a stairfoot in the Tower, beneath a heap of stones," she says. "That's what Abbess Dorothy always said."

My eyes meet Sir Edward's. He shrugs. We both know it is unlikely that the hidden grave will ever be uncovered.

Lying in my bed later, I am conscious of a different atmosphere. It has nothing to do with my anxiety over my condition or what might happen to me if the Queen finds out I am with child. Nor is it connected in any way with Ned. It is something in the very air of the Tower, a strange peacefulness out of keeping with this grim fortress. Somewhere near here, I know for a certainty now, lie the bones of those two princes of York, cruelly done to death simply because they were of royal blood. Somehow I know I will hear their cries for help no longer. I have found out the truth about their end. They will trouble me no more. Against all my Protestant instincts, I say a prayer for the repose of their souls, as I was taught in the years when I was a Catholic. For that was the faith in which they lived and died.

When I fall asleep, gently, effortlessly, I find myself dreaming again of the girl in blue; she was Katherine Plantagenet, I cannot doubt it, and this time she is not reaching out to me. She is pensive and sad, but she is free of her torment, and at peace. The truth, however painful it might be, is infinitely better than the cruel anguish of uncertainty. I do not think I will dream of her again.

When I get up in the morning, I open my silver casket, take out her pendant, and put it around my neck, wondering if I will again experience those awful feelings of despair that almost made me faint when I first tried it on. But there is nothing—not even the faintest echo of those terrible sensations. I did not think there would be now. And I will wear the pendant in the future, old-fashioned as it is, in memory of that brave dark lady in blue.

For now, I lay it back in the casket with my other jewels. As I am replacing Katherine's papers, I notice again the date: *1487*. That still puzzles me. What happened in 1487?

KATE

June 1487, Raglan Castle

Lincoln had landed in the northwest, in Cumbria, with his mysterious protégé, a great army at their back! The news, brought by fast messenger, stirred William to vigorous activity, checking gates, posterns, locks, bolts, defenses, weapons, and stores, as if he were preparing for a siege. Every day he rode out, arraying men against the invasion, and when he returned he drilled them in the courtyards at Raglan, then sent them to join the royal forces at Kenilworth Castle, where the Tudor had set up his headquarters.

The women of the castle were not idle either. The Dowager Countess took command of the kitchens, requisitioning all the bread her servants could bake for the fighting men, then swooped down on the dairy, appropriating cheeses, and the brewhouse, where she demanded that great barrels be filled with ale. Kate, nearing her time, and Elizabeth helped, tearing up strips of material for bandages and winding them into neat rolls for the soldiers to take with them, and mixing salves for wounds in the still room.

Kate's heart had leapt when she heard that John had invaded. Every day, she kept thinking of him advancing farther south, marching to meet the Tudor's forces. She could not bear to think she was aiding his enemies. What if he really did have with him York, the rightful King? Even if he did not, he himself, come to that, had a better claim than the Tudor. He had the right of this, so God grant him the victory! It was her constant prayer.

William was too preoccupied with his defensive measures to concern himself with a wife in the last stages of pregnancy. That was women's business, and the women would look after her. He ordered Kate to rest, left her to her own devices, and busied himself with arming all the able-bodied men in his household.

"Guy is being sent with the rest to join the King," Mattie told Kate one morning, as she was brushing her mistress's hair. She looked worried, and Kate's heart went out to her.

"It is always the unfortunate lot of women to wait at home while men go to war," she said. "We must pray daily for his safety."

"He will need it, my lady," Mattie muttered, lowering her voice and glancing nervously at the door. "He is going to join my lord of Lincoln."

Kate gaped, and the child leapt beneath her heart. "Oh, Mattie!"

"Yes, he plans to ride some way with the others, then break away in the darkness when they camp overnight."

"It is a dangerous thing to do," Kate warned. "He could be hanged if he is caught. Please urge him to think seriously before he goes so far."

"I have," Mattie assured her, wringing her hands. "I've been at him for days, but he is adamant. The true line must be restored, he says, and the Tudor sent packing. He says he's not the only one that thinks that way, and he's right, for I hear there are others flocking to the earl's banner. But my lady, I do fear for him!"

There were tears in Kate's eyes as she reflected on the staunch hearts of these true friends.

"I wonder, my lady," Mattie said, dabbing her eyes too, "if you would like Guy to carry a letter to my lord of Lincoln."

"Oh, yes!" Kate cried. "Yes! I should like that very much. I will write a letter now, and you may take it to Guy with more hearty thanks from me."

"That I will, my lady. And I'd be grateful for your prayers for his safety."

"I will pray for us all, and especially for Guy—and for John. Let us hope that God defends the right," Kate said fervently.

To my right well beloved John de la Pole, Earl of Lincoln, Kate wrote as a preamble, thinking it looked rather stiff and formal, yet not knowing how else to begin; but then the words poured out of her.

It is long since I saw you, my own fair knight, and I recommend myself to you in my most faithful wise, and pray you to let me know of your welfare, which I pray God daily to increase. And if it shall please you to hear of me, I can never be in full good health of body nor of heart till I hear from you. I am with child and near my time, or I would have made haste to come to you myself. But in my absence, this good groom of mine has consented to bring this my letter.

I send you my prayers and good wishes for your great enterprise, and look soon to have joyful news of you. May God send the victory to the righteous. I will pray for that to the utmost of my power.

My lord, I did mean to ask you that last time, before I was cruelly prevented: were the sons of King Edward with you at Sheriff Hutton? I am in good hope that they were taken from the Tower and sent there in the wake of the conspiracies. I ask you this that I might know the truth about my father, King Richard. You know it would be the greatest comfort to me in this world to know that he did not put them to death. I have wondered too if the young gentleman you have with you is not what he says but some other of even greater importance. No doubt we shall all know the truth soon, God willing.

No more to you at this time, but the Holy Trinity have you in keeping. And I beseech you that this letter be not seen by any earthly creature save only yourself. And now farewell, mine own fair lord, and God give you good rest, and a great victory over our enemies.

Written at Raglan on St. Barnabas Day in the afternoon.

Your own Katherine Plantagenet.

When ye have read this, I pray you burn it or keep it secret to yourself, as my faithful trust is in you.

At dawn the next day, Kate stood by the mounting block holding the empty stirrup cup, watching William lead his company of soldiers out of the courtyard. Guy was with them, the letter in his bosom. When they had all gone from sight, she knew a moment of panic, for if it were to be intercepted by the King's men, this would undoubtedly be seen as treasonous; but it was too late to recall it. Yet when she envisaged John reading it, and its contents giving heart to him before he faced his enemies in battle, and the reply he might send when the world had righted itself, she knew for a certainty that she would not recall it even if she had the chance.

INTERLUDE

October 1562, Hampton Court Palace

"The Queen is dying," Robert Dudley groans, his head in his hands. "There is no hope."

The other councillors in the antechamber exchange glances. This display of grief is as much for Dudley himself as for Elizabeth, they convey, as once she is gone, good-bye, Lord Robert—and good riddance!

However, their minds are preoccupied with more weighty matters. They are all too conscious of the threat of civil war, should the Queen succumb to the smallpox without naming her heir.

"We must pray that Her Majesty recovers," Cecil says firmly. "And that we be not divided on the issue of her successor."

"My vote is for Lord Huntingdon," declares Pembroke, who has not forgiven Katherine's treatment of his son.

"His claim is weak." Mr. Secretary dismisses it with a wave of his hand.

"Then we are left with the Lady Katherine Grey," Winchester declares. Several voices, including those of the Duke of Norfolk and the Earl of Arundel, are heard saying aye. Pembroke snorts in derision.

"But she has been disgraced and discredited," Sussex reminds them. "She is hardly fit to succeed."

"She is a Protestant, and it's possible her marriage *was* lawful," Cecil opines. "But even if that could be proved, which of us would want Lord Hertford as King?"

There is a distinct lack of enthusiasm.

"It would be Philip of Spain all over again."

"The Seymours have always been too puffed up for their own good."

"But," says Cecil, "public opinion speaks in Lady Katherine's favor. There are many, I would remind you, who regard her marriage as valid, and think that she and Lord Hertford should be allowed to live as man and wife. They are popular with the people, and seen as sharply handled."

"What is your view, Lord Robert?" Winchester asks. "Lady Katherine is your sister-in-law."

"Was," Dudley says quickly. "I say we ask the Queen to release Lady Lennox from the Tower. Or choose Huntingdon. God's blood, if Her Majesty had an heir of her own body, we would not be in this pickle!"

"By you, my lord, you mean?" Norfolk smirks.

"Yes, if you will!" Dudley flares. "Or by anybody, come to that. But as she hasn't, we have to make a decision."

Arguments erupt. There are more calls for Katherine to succeed, while a few voices speak up for Mary, Queen of Scots. Cecil puts his hands over his ears, then holds up a warning finger.

"My lords, the Queen lies ill within! Have some respect. Now, a show of hands, by your leave. Who is for Lady Katherine?"

A majority respond. Cecil frowns. And at that moment, the German doctor attending the Queen emerges from her chamber.

"My lords! Come at once. She is better, praise Gott!"

KATE

June 1487, Raglan Castle

The news was good. There had been a great Yorkist victory at Bramham Moor, led by Lord Clifford, one of John's commanders. Then they heard that Lincoln, at the head of an army eight thousand strong, was advancing relentlessly: he was at York, at Sherwood Forest, at Nottingham. In the privacy of her chamber, Kate and Mattie rejoiced, but their fears would not be stilled, because it took days for news to get through to Raglan; who knew what had been happening in the meantime?

They had heard nothing from Guy, but then they had not expected to. He could not write. Kate prayed he had gotten through safely to the Yorkist army.

The King, it was reported, was marching toward Newark in Lincolnshire. The household at Raglan held its collective breath, as did the whole realm, because the inevitable confrontation, which might come any day now, would determine decisively which royal house would rule England. Sweating and ungainly with her precious burden in the heat of the summer, Kate prayed as she had never prayed before, for John's safety, and Guy's, and for a Yorkist victory. She wondered if John's wife, the Countess Margaret, was praying as fervently, wherever she was.

She prayed for William too, but only because it was her duty.

The news, when it came, was shocking. There had been a great, hard-fought battle at Stoke, a few miles southwest of Newark. The Tudor had finally vanquished his enemies. Four thousand, including the Earl of Lincoln, lay slain in the field.

How she kept her composure when William, returning triumphant, announced these tidings to his assembled household in the castle courtyard, she did not know. But she was not the descendant of a long line of great kings for nothing. Save for turning pale, which was not remarkable, given her condition, she gave nothing away; she even managed a cheer with the rest when her husband spoke of the Tudor's victory over the 'perfidious dark earl'—as William sneeringly called John. It was all over now, the long struggle between Lancaster and York; there was no one left to fight for the defeated dynasty.

Kate thought she too would die when she heard John was dead. It was unbelievable, incomprehensible, that her dear love was no more. Slain, dead in the field . . . that glorious young knight, in the flower of his youth and manhood, and just twenty-five years old. Never again would he hold her, kiss her, whisper love poems to her, or *love* her . . . She could not bear to hear that he had been buried in no sacred place, but where he fell, with a willow stave driven through his heart.

She took to her chamber, knowing her time was near. If she died in childbirth, she would be content. She did not want to live in a world without John.

But the world, in the person of Henry Tudor, was not done with her yet.

Mattie was distraught with anxiety for Guy, who had not returned. Knowing of the great slaughter at Stoke, she was near crazed in case he had been killed, and desperate to know how she could find out. There would be many with menfolk missing, praying they had gotten away. But short of traveling across the breadth of the kingdom to Lincolnshire, there was nothing she could do.

A week after the battle, two of the King's officers in their green and white livery presented themselves at the gatehouse at Raglan and demanded entry. Mattie espied them from a window, clattering into the courtyard, and saw William invite them into the great hall and shout for wine as he disappeared through the door. She thought little of their coming at the time, and went to sit with Kate, whose spirits were so low, and who lay on her bed listlessly, fully dressed, the great mound of her belly taut almost at term, and her long dark locks spread out around her haunted white face. Mattie feared for her: the child was draining her strength, and she seemed to have lost the will to live—and who could blame her? But if she did not rally, she might not have the strength she needed to face childbirth. And so Mattie, suppressing her own fears for Guy, was doing her very best to cheer Kate, talking to her about the coming child, preparing strengthening food and warming drinks for her, and putting fresh flowers daily into the little pewter vase on the window ledge.

She was sitting by the bed, showing Kate the new-fashioned gable hood she was making for her, when the door was suddenly flung open and William stood there, his face thunderous.

"What have you done?" he yelled at Kate. "What the hell do you think you have done?" Kate looked at him bewildered for a second, then awareness dawned, and she stared at him in horror, knowing that the forces of hell were about to be unleashed. Mattie started to shake.

"May we come in?" said a brisk voice, and William, red with fury, stood aside to allow the King's officers to enter.

"Are you the Lady Katherine, Countess of Huntingdon?" one of them, a young, dark-haired fellow, asked Kate.

"Yes," she replied in a hoarse voice.

"Did you write this?" He handed her a crumpled, blood-spotted piece of paper. Her face blanched as she gazed upon it. It was the letter she had written to John. She could not touch it: it was his lifeblood that had been spilled on the paper. Had he been carrying it in his bosom when he was killed?

She raised herself up on one elbow and faced her accusers calmly. "Yes," she said.

"What did you think you were doing?" William roared. "I swear to you, sirs, I had no knowledge of this."

"The King is aware of that, my lord," the second officer assured him. "It is clear from the letter. But, madam," he said, turning to Kate, "His Grace is mindful that you offered your support to the traitor Lincoln. That is treason. Do you admit that that was your intent?"

"Yes, I admit it," Kate said. "I was glad to do it." She did not care what they did to her now. The only truth in her life was her love for John, and she was not going to deny it. The memory of it was all she had left.

"Then, madam, the case is very serious for you. My orders are to arrest you and convey you to Kenilworth Castle, where the King is, for questioning, but I see you are great with child. In the circumstances, you must remain here as a prisoner until you are delivered. You may have your maid to attend you. My lord, will you ensure, on pain of the King's displeasure, that your wife is kept close in her chamber and that no one else is allowed access to her?"

"By God I will!" shouted William. "You have played me false, you strumpet, you traitress! It beggars belief what you have done."

Kate turned her face away. Mattie had her hands to her mouth, weeping in horror; she must be feeling terrible, for it was Mattie who had suggested that she send a letter to John. But she had not been responsible for its contents; as for Kate, she did not regret having sent it at all.

"Sirs!" she said, as the officers made to leave. "Can you tell me where that letter was found?"

"On the body of the traitor Lincoln," the dark-haired man said.

He *had* read her letter; he *had* died with her words of love in his heart. It was all she wanted to know. She smiled faintly. "Thank you, sir. I am content now." And she felt a welcoming sense of peace.

The officer looked at her curiously. William opened his mouth to castigate her again, but Mattie forestalled him. "Good sirs, do you know of the fate of my husband, Guy Freeman? He was a big, tall man with a red face and fair hair. You would recognize him because he has a large wen on his cheek."

The officers exchanged looks. "Wearing a tan leather jerkin and green hose?"

"Yes!" Mattie's voice was eager.

"Sorry, woman, but he's dead. He was found lying wounded in the ravine they're now calling the Bloody Gutter. He was another traitor, wearing Lincoln's badge. They hanged him."

Mattie screamed.

KATHERINE

August 1563, Tower of London

To write this is painful to me. My love is gone from me, forever, maybe, and it is as if a thousand distances lie between us.

I bore my child, little Thomas. *God gives us His great paternal blessings once again,* Ned wrote, delighted to learn he was the father of a second son.

I thought we had managed well, for none knew of my pregnancy until a servant blabbed of it. And then the word was out, and the Queen's wrath erupted; I heard later that she'd turned the color of a corpse when told the news. Poor Sir Edward, our kindly jailer, to whom I shall always be indebted, and who had gotten two of his warders to stand godfather at the second baptism, found himself that very day summarily dismissed from his post and clapped in one of his own dungeons.

Sir Edward's superior, Sir Robert Oxenbridge, the Constable of the Tower, took evident pleasure in telling me that Ned had been summoned immediately before the Court of Star Chamber at Westminster, charged with breaching his prison, deflowering a virgin of royal blood, and compounding that crime by defiling me a second time. They sentenced him to be fined—extortionately—and to remain in prison in the Tower during Her Majesty's pleasure.

The last sight I had of Ned was at Thomas's baptism. I remember him cradling our new son in his arms and uttering fervent thanks to God for my safe delivery, with toddling Edward clinging to his knee. By the good offices of Sir Edward Warner, I had my portrait painted for a locket, holding Edward in my arms, a miniature of my sweet lord about my neck. Ned admired it when we were in the chapel, and I snatched it off and covertly passed it to him as a keepsake before I watched him walk away under the stern guard of the constable. We had not been permitted even a farewell kiss.

That was six months ago, and since then I have pined here alone in my prison, cowed into subjection under the harsh rule of Sir Robert Oxen-bridge. Were it not for my precious babes, I think I would commit the great sin of killing myself.

And now, in the heat of summer, comes the plague. They are falling like flies in London, a frightened Mrs. Ellen reports. The word is that people are dying at a rate of a thousand a week. The stink from the City, when the wind is in the wrong direction, is all-pervading, contaminating everything, and making me fearful for my little ones. The court, I learn, has removed to Windsor, where the Queen has had a gallows put up and threatens to hang anyone from the capital venturing thither.

I am terrified for my sons. While they remain here with me in the Tower, they risk becoming infected. I contemplate asking if Mrs. Ellen can take them away to a safe place, just for now. But Sir Robert appears at my door.

"Lady Katherine," he says, "I am commanded by the Queen, out of compassion for the sake of your health, and that of your children, to send you all under guard into the country. Lord Hertford is to be sent away too, to a different place of residence, and you shall have separate custodians. The infant may stay with you, and young Master Edward must go with his father."

"No!" I cry in anguish. "No! I cannot live if I am parted from my child, or my sweet lord! I would rather die of plague."

The constable regards me disapprovingly. I know he thinks me a rash, foolish, even dangerous woman.

"Calm yourself, my lady. These measures are for your own safety, and that of your children and Lord Hertford. And my lord is content to obey. He has asked me to give you this as a farewell token. I permit it as a special favor."

It is a mourning ring, with a death's-head intaglio. He wore it for his father, I recall. And now, turning it over in trembling hands, I see there are words freshly engraved on it, as with a sharp knife. It reads: *While I live, yours.*

Part Four

Greedy Death

On the first day of July, in the year of grace 1487, Katherine, Countess of Huntingdon, daughter of Richard, sometime King of England, began her travail. Her infant, a son, was born dead, to the great grief of her husband, the earl. Soon afterward, the Lady Katherine herself gave up the ghost, and rendered her spirit to God most joyfully, uttering one last word, *John*. Upon hearing which, her lord was observed to groan woefully in grief. It was thought, by most of those kneeling by her bed, that she spoke of her brother, then far away in Calais.

After her death, a bundle of papers tied with ribbon was found among her effects by her maid, who hid it in an old muniment chest beneath the family documents. Only this maid, who took her secret with her to her grave, fifty years later, knew that her beloved mistress had died without ever finding out the truth about her father, King Richard. And that caused the maid to weep even more. For she alone was aware that death had prevented the countess from obtaining the answer to a question that she believed would have settled the matter once and for all. And she alone had borne witness to her heartbroken mistress writing a few final words about her arrest—which had been kept secret, and would never be made public, out of respect for her widower—and then laying down her pen forever. It is believed that the countess's papers were burned by Sir Owen Hopton in the reign of Elizabeth I.

The countess was laid to rest in the parish church of St. Cadoc in Raglan, without ceremony. The earl, her widower, stood stony-faced throughout the funeral. He was not a well man, although he did not yet know it, for his disease was a silent one, and he was gathered to his forefathers just four years later. He was interred in Tintern Abbey, having chosen not to be laid beside his lady, whose name would soon largely be forgotten, for no monument was ever built to her memory.

KATHERINE

Then began my Calvary. Years under house arrest in a succession of remote places in the depths of East Anglia: Pirgo Park, Ingatestone Hall, Gosfield Hall . . . Always a prisoner, an unwelcome guest. Never allowed to speak to anyone but my guardians, and made to behave at all times as if I were still in the Tower.

I wrote several times to Mr. Secretary, pleading to be reunited with my dear lord and my elder son, and begging him to intercede for me with the Queen's Majesty. I recall the groveling words I wrote, my abject plea for the obtaining of her most gracious pardon and favor toward me, which, with upstretched hands and down-bent knees, from the bottom of my heart most humbly I craved.

There was no reply.

I lost my appetite and grew thin. I wished myself dead and buried.

Just once was I permitted to write to Ned. It must have rent his heart to read my brave words, reminding him of the stolen hours we lay with joyful hearts as sweet bedfellows in the Tower, and assuring him we would do so again, I was certain of it.

I wrote again to the Queen and Mr. Secretary, appealing to them to relieve me from my continual agony. They ignored my pleas, and I was so crushed with disappointment that I took to my bed, coughing and feverish. I wept ceaselessly. I vomited and brought up foul phlegm, and my guardians trembled in case I had consumption. They feared I might die in their charge.

My cheeks grew pale, my cough more troublesome. My longing for my sweet lord and my son became a physical pain. I exchanged several secret letters with Ned, thanks to the ruses of my maids, receiving in return touching tokens of his devotion. But our separation was killing me.

My cough grew worse. I developed pains in my chest. Eating so little, I grew thinner. At night I began to sweat; by day, I was sunk in lassitude. And when, late in the year of Our Lord 1567, I was moved, still a prisoner, to this house, Cockfield Hall in Yoxford, Suffolk, I was in a very poor state indeed.

I am racked by another attack of coughing. In my mirror I see dull eyes, cheekbones high in a hectic face, hands near transparent, and a gown that is now much too big, hanging on bony shoulders.

I feel my strength ebbing. I am now spending more time in bed than in my chair. My appetite has gone completely. My jailer's wife, Lady Hopton, pays me anxious visits, asking after my health, while Sir Owen sends for the Queen's own physicians to tend me. He will not let it be said that I died for lack of care in his house.

I look at little Tom and feel anguish at the thought of him being left alone and motherless. Please God, I pray, do not let me die! I am but twenty-seven years old, and I need to live for my children, and for my love. I am convinced the very sight of Ned could make me well. And my little Edward . . . My arms ache for Edward.

I have beseeched them to let him visit me. He is six now, and it is four long years since I saw him. But they say it is not possible. Does my sweet lord know how ill I am? Will I ever look on his face again? Just once is all I ask. Just a glimpse of him to take to Heaven with me. For I fear that is where I am bound, very soon. I keep recollecting what my sister wrote to me from the Tower: *Trust not that the tenderness of your age shall lengthen your life, for, as soon as God will, go the young and the old.*

What did I ever do to deserve such trials? I but did what countless women do—I fell in love and married. Yet I am still being punished for that, and I know in my bones that the Queen will never release me now.

This morning, when I cough, there is blood on my kerchief. I stare at it, disbelieving; here is my executioner. I sit up shaking, my heart pounding. Not me, oh Lord, please, not me!

I sit there nervously on the edge of the bed, feeling like I am dying anyway, awaiting—and dreading—the next spasm. When it comes, there is another bright red streak: not as much as before, but still alarming. In a panic, I call Lady Hopton and she sends again for the physician.

———

"What is wrong with me?" I ask the doctor.

"It is phthisic," he says gravely. "A disorder of the lungs. I prescribe rest and pleasant pastimes. Take the air, read books, do a little embroidery, or play cards."

"My lady will take no pastime," Lady Hopton says. She has insisted on standing by through every consultation, like a jailer. What does she think I will do? Plot treason? I am a sick woman! All I want is to be well again. But I have no energy for anything. I can barely raise the pen to write this journal.

Dr. Symonds is brisk. "Then give her asses' milk and snails in shells to prolong life," he orders, and my lady nods. He has not reassured me. I dare not ply him with more questions, for fear of what he will answer, for he spoke of prolonging my life. I am not such a fool that I cannot understand the implications of those words.

January, in the year of grace 1568, comes in like a lamb. The parkland beyond my casement is still green, the bare trees unladen with snow. It is unseasonably mild.

I have been confined to my bed for three weeks, too weak to get out of it. I am resigned now, ready and prepared for the inevitable end, and aware of the need to make a good death, to satisfy the world that I was a worthy and devout woman.

I feel my strength ebbing. My women watch around the bed through the night hours as I ceaselessly recite psalms and prayers for the dying. I thank God I am going to Him with no malice in my heart. My last thoughts will be of my loved ones, Ned, Edward, and little Tom, who has crept beside me on the bed and snuggled into the crook of my arm, his face stained with tears. Young as he is, he is aware that something is badly wrong. Maybe someone has told him his mother is dying. He knows what death is.

Dawn breaks. I realize I have been praying all night.

"Madam, be of good comfort," says Lady Hopton. "Your strength is a marvel to us all. With God's help, you shall live and do well many years."

"No, no," I tell her, "there will be no more life for me in this world. But in the world to come, I hope to live forever. For here, there is nothing but care and misery, and there is life everlasting."

I summon up every vestige of energy to pray some more, to ease my passage. My maids enjoin me to sleep a little, but there is no point. Soon, I shall rest in that endless sleep from which there is no waking.

I start to feel myself slipping away.

"Lord, be merciful unto me," I murmur, "for now I begin to faint."

"She is cold," someone says, and I feel the women rubbing my hands and feet.

"My time has come," I murmur weakly. "It is not God's will that I should live any longer, and His will be done, not mine." I kiss Tom's sweet head, and someone carries him away. When next I see him it will be in Heaven.

I call for Sir Owen Hopton. I want him to be able to report to the Queen that I made an edifying end—and I have two final requests to make of him.

"Good madam, how are you?" he asks, gazing down with pity on me.

"I am going to God as fast as I can," I tell him. "I pray you all to bear witness that I die a good Christian. And I ask God and all the world forgiveness for my sins." I pause, breathless. "I beseech you, Sir Owen, to promise me this one thing: that you yourself, with your own mouth, will request the Queen's Majesty that she forgive her displeasure toward me. I confess I have greatly offended her, but I take God to witness that I never had the heart to think any evil against her. And I entreat her to be good to my children, whom I give wholly unto Her Majesty; for in my life they have had few friends, and they shall have fewer when I am dead, except Her Majesty be gracious to them."

Sir Owen bows his head. "I will do it," he promises.

"Another thing, sir," I whisper. "I desire Her Highness to be good unto my lord, for I know that my death will be heavy news to him; and I beg Her Grace will be so good as to send him his liberty to comfort his sorrowful heart."

Again my custodian nods, a touch reluctantly this time.

I make a final effort. There is one last thing I can do for my love.

"Sir Owen," I say, "I ask you to deliver from me certain tokens to my lord. Give me the casket wherein my wedding ring is."

I take out the ring I had for my betrothal. The diamond is as glittering and unfathomable as it was on that day, eight years ago, when Ned first put it on my finger. "Good Sir Owen, send this to my lord. This is the ring that I received of him when I gave myself to him, and pledged him my troth."

"Was this your wedding ring?" my custodian asks.

"No. This was the ring of my assurance to my lord. This is my wedding ring." And I lay in his palm the five-hooped band. "Deliver this also to him, and pray him, even as I have been unto him a true and faithful wife, to be a loving and natural father to my children. And here is the third ring you must give him." I bring forth the death's-head memento mori. "This shall be the last token unto my lord that ever I shall send him. It is the picture of myself."

As I hand him the ring, I catch sight of my fingers. The nails have turned an ominous purple. My hour is upon me.

I turn my eyes to the door.

"He is come," I say, and smile.

Afterward . . .

Lady Katherine Grey was first buried in Yoxford Church, with the Queen affording her a lavish funeral. She was mourned by many Protestants who had hoped to see her acknowledged Elizabeth's heir. Elizabeth expressed formal sorrow at her passing, but the Spanish ambassador observed, "It is not believed that she feels it, as she was afraid of her."

Ned outlived Katherine by fifty-five years. He did not remarry until 1596, his second bride being Frances Howard, daughter of Lord Howard of Effingham, the hero of the Armada. For years he fought to have his sons declared legitimate, but Queen Elizabeth remained obdurate. When she was dying in 1603, it was suggested that Katherine's son Edward be named her successor. "I will have no rascal's son to succeed me!" she retorted.

Edward and Thomas, who were brought up to honor their mother's memory, were finally declared legitimate the following year, by a statute of James I. In 1608, the priest who had married Katherine and Ned finally came out of hiding and testified to the legitimacy of their union. Edward, Viscount Beauchamp, died in 1612; his brother Thomas had passed away in 1600.

In 1611, Ned's grandson, William Seymour, made another misalliance with a lady of royal blood when he married Lady Arbella Stuart, the granddaughter of Margaret Douglas, Lady Lennox. Seymour escaped to France, but Arbella was imprisoned in the Tower and died there. Ned was still alive then. He heard the news of their elopement in the very room in Hertford House where he had married Katherine. He died in 1621, aged eighty-two.

Under Charles I, William Seymour was restored to favor and created Duke of Somerset. He died in 1660. It was he who, on his father's death, had Katherine's remains moved to Salisbury Cathedral, where she was laid to rest with her husband in a great "Golden Tomb" with effigies of herself and her "sweet lord Ned," with their two sons kneeling at either side.

The Latin epitaph on the tomb describes Katherine and Ned as "Incomparable consorts, who experienced the vicissitudes of fortune, and at last rest together here in the same concord in which they lived their lives."

AUTHOR'S NOTE

In telling this fictional version of the story of Lady Katherine Grey, I have adhered closely to the facts where they are known, although I have taken some dramatic license. For example, Katherine's stormy confrontation with Ned over his flirtation with Frances Mewtas was acted out in letters; here, I have shown it taking place face-to-face. Much here is quoted from contemporary documents, and the letters are genuine; although some passages in Katherine's letters have been used out of context, the sentiments relate accurately to the narrative. Archaic language has been modified to blend in with a modern text, although I have made use of many contemporary sources and idioms.

The long-accepted view of the Suffolks as harsh parents has recently been challenged, but there is no credible explaining away of Lady Jane Grey's own bitter testimony to that, as recorded firsthand by Roger Ascham, and at least one contemporary source records Jane being beaten and cursed when she resisted her betrothal to Guilford Dudley. New research undertaken by historian Nicola Tallis suggests that the traditional view of the Suffolks is correct. It is conceivable that a chastened Frances mellowed after Jane's execution, as portrayed in this novel, and that Katherine and Mary never suffered the rigor and expectations that their parents imposed on Jane. I would question the theory that there has been a deliberate attempt down the centuries to blacken Frances's character.

Hester Chapman put forward the theory that Katherine's head was so turned when she saw her sister made Queen that forever after her ambitions were focused on wearing a crown. Chapman believes that this is the only theory that makes sense of Katherine's behavior, but I think she was a self-obsessed girl who let her heart rule her head. Her instincts were emotional rather than logical, and because of that, she ended up out of her depth, in deep trouble.

Katherine *was* turned out of Pembroke's house immediately after Mary I was proclaimed Queen. I have done my best to make sense of her religious persuasions and her dealings with the Spanish ambassadors.

Confusion surrounds the date of Frances's second marriage, to Adrian Stokes, and the number of their children, yet an Inquisition Postmortem of 1600 dealing with Frances's estates gives the date as March 9, 1554, only weeks after Henry Grey's execution, and records their only issue as a daughter, Elizabeth, who was born in July 1555 at Knebworth and died there in February 1556. This Inquisition is listed in Vol. 34 of the *Calendar of State Papers: Domestic, Elizabeth I* (www .british-history.ac.uk). (I am indebted to Nicola Tallis for this reference.) Various historians have questioned Frances remarrying so soon after the death of her first husband, citing a report of the Spanish ambassador, Simon Renard, who, in April 1555, mentioned a proposal that she marry a descendant of the House of York, Edward Courtenay, Earl of Devon, although he added that the earl was unwilling. Courtenay's biographer, Horatia Durant, suggests that the marriage to Stokes, made over a year before, had been a well-kept secret, which is likely. William Camden, Elizabeth I's earliest biographer, wrote that Frances remarried "for her security." As Dulcie Ashdown says, Frances would have been aware that, as a widow, she was "a tempting match for an ambitious nobleman who saw in her a means to future power"; being in line for the throne, her position was potentially dangerous, so she may have regarded a speedy second marriage to a man with no pretensions as the safest option.

As the law stood, Katherine was Elizabeth I's heir, and many people supported her claim. I do not think she wanted to supplant Elizabeth, only to be acknowledged as her successor. To Elizabeth, though, she appeared a deadly rival whose very existence threatened her throne. If Elizabeth had had her way, Katherine would never have married. The Interludes in the book are there to show Elizabeth's point of view; without them, she comes across as a cruel persecutor.

Some sources state that Katherine was demoted from Lady of the Bedchamber (the highest rank) to Lady of the Privy Chamber, others that it was from Lady of the Privy Chamber to Lady of the Presence Chamber, and some even claim she was demoted upward from the privy chamber to the bedchamber! It seems that she was actually downgraded from the bedchamber to the presence chamber.

The course of Katherine's courtship by Edward Seymour, and his sister's role in it, was much as it is portrayed here, and the account of their wedding day—and 'night'—is based closely on their own depositions. Katherine's love for Edward was the overriding passion of her life, and she remained staunchly faithful through every trial, until her death.

Katherine was unsure for a time whether she was pregnant with her first child, and when she knew she was, she took pains to conceal it for as long as possible. During this period, she did come to fear that Ned had abandoned her, which was when she began to seriously consider remarrying Lord Herbert. His furious rejection of her is well documented.

It was Lord Robert Dudley who revealed Katherine's pregnancy to the Queen. There was no confrontation: Elizabeth ordered Katherine to be placed under arrest and taken to the Tower. Bess of Hardwick's role in the affair—as Lady Saintlow (or St. Loe)—is recounted in the depositions taken after Katherine's arrest.

It is possible that William Cecil did take a broader view of Katherine's marriage, and that he approved of her being named Elizabeth's heir. He himself said, "I have been noted a favorer of my Lady Katherine's title." However, as David Loades points out in *The Cecils* (The National Archives, 2007), Cecil did not declare for Katherine's succession when the Queen was thought to be dying of smallpox in 1562. Instead, he seems to have "favored an interim solution while further thought was taken"—which suggests he had doubts, although certainly he desired to see the matter of the succession settled. His inquiries persuaded him that Katherine's union with Hertford was no more than a love match—he called it 'that troublesome, fond matter'—and not part of a plot against Elizabeth, yet whatever his private feelings, he followed the Queen's lead in punishing the couple.

Katherine's prison in the upper chamber of the Bell Tower still exists. During the Second World War, Rudolf Hess was briefly imprisoned there, and a lavatory was installed for the convenience of another expected Nazi guest: Adolf Hitler. Katherine was later moved to rooms in the Lieutenant's Lodging, where her infant and her eight servants could be accommodated. The list of decayed furnishings sent by Queen Elizabeth still survives.

Sir Edward Warner did prove a sympathetic jailer. It was he who allowed Katherine and Edward Seymour to meet on two occasions, and when the Queen found out that Katherine's second pregnancy had been the result, she had Warner dismissed from his post and imprisoned.

In Tudor times, many people referred to the White Tower, the keep of the Tower of London, as Caesar's Tower, in the mistaken belief that Julius Caesar had built it.

It has long been thought that Katherine died of tuberculosis. The references to her suffering from heavy phlegm and being unable to eat may account for that. Recently, it has been suggested that her poor eating was symptomatic of anorexia, and that she literally starved herself to death. Certainly she was under immense stress for much of her life. The only telling symptom we have to go on is her nails turning purple just before she died. Commonly that indicates a lack of oxygen in the extremities, poor circulation, a respiratory or lung disorder, a cardiovascular problem and/or congestive heart failure. That might indicate tuberculosis, toward which malnutrition can be a major contributory factor. It is possible that Katherine caught it from Jane Seymour; she had been closely exposed to Jane for some time, as she would have needed to be to catch the disease, which is passed by droplet infection through sneezing or coughing. Sometimes the body's immune system fails to destroy those bacteria, and latent tuberculosis becomes active years later. This is more likely to happen if the immune system becomes weakened by other problems, such as being undernourished and underweight, as Katherine was, and influenza and other infections can play their part; her phlegm may have been a symptom of that kind of illness. Therefore I have adhered to the traditional theory in this book. The account of Katherine's death is closely based on fact.

Over the years, I have consulted numerous sources for the Tudor period, which inform my fiction, and the reader is referred to the bibliographies in my nonfiction books, *Children of England: The Heirs of Henry VIII* and *Elizabeth the Queen,* for those. For this novel, however, I am indebted particularly to the following works:

Ashdown, Dulcie M.: *Tudor Cousins: Rivals for the Throne* (Stroud, 2000)

Borman, Tracy: *Elizabeth's Women* (London, 2009)

Chapman, Hester W.: *Two Tudor Portraits* (Oxford, 1960)

Lisle, Leanda de: *The Sisters Who Would Be Queen* (London, 2008)

Lovell, Mary S.: *Bess of Hardwick* (London, 2005)

Plowden, Alison: *Lady Jane Grey: Nine Days Queen* (Stroud, 2003)

Somerset, Anne: *Ladies in Waiting* (London, 1984)

Stevenson, Joan: *The Greys of Bradgate* (Leicester, 1974)

While there are numerous sources for the life of Katherine Grey—although she never kept the journal mentioned in the story—we know very little about Katherine Plantagenet, who is mentioned in just four contemporary documents. The earliest reference to her is in her marriage covenant, dated February 29, 1484. In this, William Herbert covenanted with Richard III to take Dame Katherine Plantagenet to wife before Michaelmas (September 29), and to make her a jointure in lands of £200 per annum. The King undertook to bear the whole cost of the marriage and to settle lands and lordships valued at 1,000 marks (£666) yearly on them and the male heirs of their two bodies.

The couple was married by May 1484, when, at York, Richard III granted "William, Earl of Huntingdon and Katherine his wife" the proceeds of various manors in Devon, Cornwall, and Somerset.

In this period, couples could be married in childhood, and the Church permitted a girl to cohabit with her husband at the age of twelve. We do not know Katherine's date of birth, but I have placed it in 1470, on the premise that she married at fourteen, an age at which many girls were married in those days. She cannot have been much older, as Richard III was only eighteen in 1470.

The last reference to Katherine in contemporary sources occurs on

March 8, 1485, when a cash annuity of £152.10s.10d was granted by
Richard III to his kinsman, "William, Earl of Huntingdon and Katherine his wife, until they should have grants to themselves and the heirs
of their bodies of lordships etc. to the same value."

Aside from these sources, I have reconstructed Katherine's life
largely through external evidence, inference, and probability. Her
mother was possibly Katherine Haute, wife of James Haute, who was
the son of William Haute by Joan Wydeville, a cousin to the Queen.
Richard, Duke of Gloucester, made a grant of an annual payment of
100s. from his East Anglian estates to one Katherine Haute before, or
in, 1475. It is not known why he did so—unless it was for the support
of his child. It may be significant that his daughter shared the same
name as Katherine Haute, and that possibly she was named after St.
Catherine of Siena, one of Richard's favorite saints, and the patron
saint of young girls.

Some genealogies describe James Haute as being of Waltham,
Kent, but documents in the National Archives show that he held lands
in Hertfordshire and Bedfordshire, his chief seat being the manor of
Kinsbourne Hall (or Annable's) at Harpenden, which he bought from
William Annable soon after 1467. The site of his house lies to the east
of the surviving Tudor (with later additions) manor house, Annables
House, at Kinsbourne Green.

James Haute died before July 20, 1508, when his will was proved. A
court roll dating from the early sixteenth century refers to "silver and
stuffs, etc. at my house in my wife's custody," so Katherine Haute was
still alive then. Although Kinsbourne Hall remained in his family until
1555, James leased it to a Thomas Bray in 1506. There were two sons
of the marriage, his heir Edward Haute of London, who was his father's executor in 1512 and died in 1528, and Alan.

Richard Haute, James's brother, was an associate of Richard of
Gloucester. It seems that Richard's attitude toward the Wydeville affinity was complex!

John of Gloucester, or "of Pontefract," was Katherine's brother or
half brother. He was possibly conceived at Pontefract when Richard
was there in 1471, or during his visits in April or October 1473 or
March 1474 (John was still underage in 1485). Richard made a grant

in March 1474 to "my beloved gentlewoman" Alice Burgh of an annuity of £20 for life from issues from Middleham, "for certain special causes and considerations." Possibly she was John's mother. Later, Alice Burgh was granted another annuity of twenty marks from the revenues of Warwick, for acting as nurse to Edward, Earl of Warwick, Clarence's son. Richard continued the annuity when he became king. He clearly had a long association with Alice, who came from a Knaresborough family and had perhaps been in the service of his wife Anne. Her sister Isabel was wet nurse to Edward of Middleham.

There is no surviving great hall at Lincoln Castle. I have based my description of it partly on the one at Gainsborough Old Hall.

There is an unsubstantiated assertion on Wikipedia that Katherine was "almost certainly arrested" at Raglan Castle in June 1487 after Stoke Field. Although I have discovered no corroborative contemporary evidence, it was this that gave me my plotline involving her with John de la Pole. The love poems quoted are from the fifteenth century; the letters were composed by me, with a little help from the contemporary Paston Letters.

Shock can cause a woman to miscarry, according to German research published in *New Scientist* magazine in 2004. We do not know for certain that Katherine Plantagenet was ever pregnant, but we do know that she died young, for a list of peers present at the coronation of Elizabeth of York in November 1487 describes William Herbert as a widower. If Katherine lived to 1487, she would perhaps have been seventeen at the time of her death. The chances are that a young married woman dying at that age perished in childbirth; and as there were no recorded children of the marriage, I have assumed that she suffered miscarriages and a stillbirth. Maybe she was buried in St. Cadoc's Church at Raglan, which was endowed by her husband and father-in-law, and which dates from the fourteenth century. There is no record of her being buried at Tintern Abbey with her husband.

My theory as to the fate of the Princes in the Tower is set out in my book *The Princes in the Tower*, published in 1992. I have not read anything since that has moved me to revise my conclusions, although I like to keep an open mind on the matter. This, however, is a work of fiction, based on some of my research for that book, and not intended to be an authoritative source! Even so, I wanted to try to approach the mystery of the princes' disappearance from a different viewpoint, weighing the evidence accordingly and, I hope, with integrity.

There is no evidence whatsoever that either Katherine Grey or Katherine Plantagenet tried to find out the truth about the princes, although I imagine that the rumors implicating her father gave Katherine Plantagenet much pause for thought. In constructing the fictional investigations made by my two heroines, I had to give consideration to which sources of information would have been available to each of them. Therefore this novel does not contain a complete overview of the evidence, although even without that, I feel that the conclusion it reaches still carries some historical weight. This is how it might have happened . . .

The Minoresses' convent in Aldgate was surrendered to Henry VIII in 1539 during the Dissolution of the Monasteries. It was granted to the Bishop of Bath and Wells, who used part of it—Bath Place—as a town house and leased the rest.

Elizabeth Talbot, Duchess of Norfolk and mother-in-law of Richard, Duke of York, the younger of the Princes in the Tower, lived in a great house in the convent precincts and was buried in the church in 1506. With her lived Elizabeth, daughter of Sir Robert Brackenbury, Constable of the Tower (whose will of 1514 provided for her burial there), Mary Tyrell, Anne Montgomery, and Joyce Lee, a widow who took the veil and who was interred there in 1507. Sir Thomas More had dedicated a book to her in 1505; she was a family friend, and he must have visited her at the Minories. Several historians believe that he got much of his information from the ladies living with Joyce Lee.

Dame Elizabeth Savage was the last abbess of the Minories. At the Dissolution, she was granted a pension of £40 (£12,300 now); her nuns received just over £3. Elizabeth Savage would probably have known Alice FitzLewes, abbess from 1501 to 1524, or Dorothy Cumberford, abbess from 1526 to 1529. Alice FitzLewes must have known Joyce Lee; Dorothy Cumberford may well have met her.

My research uncovered some unexpected connections between the Grey family and the Minoresses' convent. Katherine's great-aunt, Mary

Reading, was buried in the church. Her father's sister, Elizabeth, Countess of Kildare, rented a house on the site after the Dissolution.

In 1548, Edward VI acquired Bath Place, or "the Minories," by exchange, and in 1553 he granted it to Katherine's father, Henry Grey, Duke of Suffolk, but it seems that Grey had been using it as a residence since 1548. Katherine Grey would therefore have known it well.

Soon after being formally granted the Minories in 1553, Suffolk received a further grant of the Carthusian priory (the Charterhouse) of Sheen, once the property of Protector Somerset. Suffolk preferred Sheen as a residence, so he conveyed the Minories to his younger brothers and half brother. They were involved in Wyatt's rebellion, but Lord John Grey was pardoned and retained Bath Place into Elizabeth's reign. The old convent buildings were destroyed by fire in 1797.

The Act of 1485 repealing *Titulus Regius* does not survive in the records of Parliament; a Year Book of Henry VII confirms that Richard III's Act of 1484 was "annulled and utterly destroyed, cancelled, and burnt, and put in perpetual oblivion."

Many may recognize that Kate's pendant is modeled on the famous Middleham Jewel. The bundle of papers tied up in a ribbon is, sadly, an invention.

ABOUT THE AUTHOR

ALISON WEIR is the *New York Times* bestselling author of the novels *A Dangerous Inheritance, Captive Queen, Innocent Traitor* and *The Lady Elizabeth,* and several historical biographies including *Mary Boleyn, The Lady in the Tower, Mistress of the Monarchy, Queen Isabella, Henry VIII, Eleanor of Aquitaine, The Life of Elizabeth I,* and *The Six Wives of Henry VIII.* She lives in Surrey, England, with her husband and two children.

www.alisonweir.org.uk
www.alisonweirtours.com

ABOUT THE TYPE

This book was set in Monotype Dante, a typeface designed by Giovanni Mardersteig (1892–1977). Conceived as a private type for the Officina Bodoni in Verona, Italy, Dante was originally cut only for hand composition by Charles Malin, the famous Parisian punch cutter, between 1946 and 1952. Its first use was in an edition of Boccaccio's *Trattatello in laude di Dante* that appeared in 1954. The Monotype Corporation's version of Dante followed in 1957. Though modeled on the Aldine type used for Pietro Cardinal Bembo's treatise *De Aetna* in 1495, Dante is a thoroughly modern interpretation of that venerable face.